# THE
# YEAR'S BEST
# FANTASY

# THE YEAR'S BEST FANTASY

First Annual Collection

Edited by

## Ellen Datlow
### and
## Terri Windling

ST. MARTIN'S PRESS

*New York*

THE YEAR'S BEST FANTASY: FIRST ANNUAL COLLECTION.
Copyright © 1988 by James Frenkel and Associates.
"Summation 1987: Fantasy" copyright © 1988 by Terri Windling—The Endicott Studio.
"Summation 1987: Horror" copyright © 1988 by Ellen Datlow.
"1987: Horror and Fantasy on the Screen" copyright © 1988 by Edward Bryant.

ISBN 0-312-01851-7 (hardcover)
ISBN 0-312-01852-5 (paperback)

First Edition
10 9 8 7 6 5 4 3 2 1

A Bluejay Books Production

# CONTENTS

# ACKNOWLEDGMENTS

I would like to thank the following for their encouragement, support and help: All the publishers and editors who allowed me to use them as sounding boards and who sent me material, Robert Frazier, Dean Koontz, Kevin Anderson, Gardner Dozois, Merilee Heifetz, Jim Frenkel, Tappan King, Steve Brown, J.N. Williamson, and, especially, for support beyond the call of professional and personal friendship, Ed Bryant.

Thanks also to Charles N. Brown, whose magazine *Locus* (Locus Publications, Inc., P.O. Box 13305, Oakland, CA 94661, $32.00 for a one-year first-class subscription, 12 issues) was used as a reference source throughout the Summation, and to Andrew Porter, whose magazine *Science Fiction Chronicle* (Algol Press, P.O. Box 2730, Brooklyn, NY 11202–0056, $27.00 for one year, 12 issues) was also used as a reference source throughout.

—E.D.

Many thanks are due to Jane Yolen, Ellen Kushner, Sheila Berry, Mark Arnold, Charles de Lint, Robin McKinley, Craig Gardner, Valerie Smith, the Minneapolis Fantasy Writers' Group, Greer Gilman, the Castignettis, and Stuart Moore for their help; and to Thomas Canty for the art.

Thanks are also due to *Locus Magazine, SF Chronicle, New Folk Magazine, Cricket, ALA Booklist, The School Library Journal*, and *Publishers Weekly*; to the patient staffs of the Boston Public Library, B. Dalton's Bookstore, and Books of Wonder NYC; and *especially* to Jim Frenkel.

—T.W.

# INTRODUCTION

# Summation 1987: Fantasy

To be asked to sum up the year in fantasy is a daunting assignment, as the realm of fantasy is as broad as the twilight lands in old British ballads. In American book publishing, with its obsessive love of categorization, we have a genre called Adult Fantasy (a phenomenon that began with the Ballantine Books's now classic Sign of the Unicorn line edited by Lin Carter), which is often lumped together with, or published side by side with, science fiction and/or horror. But fantasy extends far beyond this genre into mainstream publishing, literary publishing, small presses, young adult books, children's picture books, myth and folklore, romance—and is a strong tradition (indeed, often a *stronger* tradition) in the literature of other countries as well.

I won't pretend that I've read every fantastic work presented by every publisher here and abroad, or that this introduction can give you more than a brief overview of fantasy in the contemporary arts. But I hope my experiences in working with fantasy writers and artists across this country and England will help me to point the way to some material you might have overlooked, some new works you might enjoy.

Fantasy publishing is alive and well in the later half of the '80s, with new lines and more books planned daily. Indeed, the worry now is that there are too *many* books, and we may find that the market becomes saturated, or quality suffers. This is a far cry from the early days of the decade when fantasy was still a poor country cousin to profitable science fiction lines, and sales directors groaned when we tried to take up space in the science fiction lists for then unknown fantasy writers such as Robin McKinley or Sheri Tepper or Steven Brust. Fantasy now enjoys a prosperity that equals and sometimes surpasses science fiction, and many houses now publish these works under their own fantasy logo.

Baen Books has been the latest of science fiction publishers to separate their growing fantasy list from the science fiction list. The new Sign of the Dragon line, edited by Betsy Mitchell, is billed as "Fantasy with rivets"—solid entertainment in well-realized, logical worlds. It will be interesting to watch this line develop.

Del Rey/Ballantine continues to dominate the national bestseller lists with fantasy by writers such as Stephen R. Donaldson, Piers Anthony, Anne McCaffrey, and David Eddings—but below the bestseller level their fantasy list, sadly, no longer sparkles as it once did. Lester del Rey's own brand of fantasy adventure is still there, but there seems little in the list to balance this with innovation, to propel the line forward and keep it thriving. It is to be hoped that this respectable line, with its backlist of classic

Ballantine titles and the excellent Del Rey marketing and promotion which gets books into the hands of the broadest possible readership, will not be allowed to slump for long, or to focus exclusively on a few big name authors.

Bantam/Spectra, on the other hand, has been getting stronger in the fantasy area. They've always had a few excellent titles of the John Crowley ilk, but now the line seems to be becoming more consistent in terms of quality. Lou Aronica is a publisher who has expressed a commitment to building authors' careers from the first books up, rather than sitting back and waiting to lure famous name authors away from other houses with big money deals, and he deserves respect for it. Shawna McCarthy proved her editorial commitment to fantasy as well as science fiction when she brought fantasy into *Isaac Asimov's Science Fiction Magazine* during her editorial days there. And how can a line with writers like Crowley, R. A. MacAvoy, or Lisa Goldstein go wrong?

Arbor House is another publisher to look to for quality fantasy, although editor David G. Hartwell does not enjoy the commercial success a line like Spectra can produce. Still, his list is admirable for its literary quality, bringing good new writers like Terry Bisson and James P. Blaylock into hardcover editions.

Tor Books, under the editorial direction of Beth Meacham, has some of the best individual books in the field on its list and some of the field's best editors on its payroll, including consultants Betty Ballantine, James Frenkel, and David G. Hartwell. Yet it is to be hoped that the fantasy end of Tor's well-lauded science fiction line can be given a greater cohesion and an identity of its own—as Tor successfully did some years ago with their horror line—if Tor hopes to vie for Del Rey's position as the dominant force in the genre.

Ace Fantasy, which now includes the defunct Berkley Fantasy list, has begun a promising hardcover publishing program in addition to its paperback list under the direction of Susan Allison. The paperback line appears to be shifting its emphasis more and more toward light fantasy adventure and humorous fantasy of the Piers Anthony/Robert Asprin kind—which makes use of the particular strength of editor Ginjer Buchanan, who has a skill for discovering fantasy humorists such as Craig Shaw Gardner and Paula Volsky.

Warner's Questar line, particularly with the books acquired by editor Brian Thomsen, seems to be picking up Ace's old reputation as the scrappy, quirky, and innovative line where you never quite know what you're going to get next. I applaud Thomsen's enthusiasm and have enjoyed many of his choices.

DAW has been asserting itself in the fantasy field for the first time since its inception, edited by publisher Betsy Wollheim and by Sheila Gilbert, who is known for acquiring Joel Rosenberg, Robert Adams, and Dennis McKiernan in her previous job at New American Library—primarily adventure fantasy and the occasional romantic fantasy.

The NAL/Signet line has been inherited by John Silbersack who has always had an abiding love of good fantasy. It is too soon to tell what he will make of the list. I wish him success. John Douglas and the science fiction editors at Avon Books are still building their fantasy list with popular authors such as Piers Anthony—and interesting work from Terry Bisson and Esther Friesner saves the list from predictability.

Fantasy fiction of all sorts turns up regularly, though without the identifying label of fantasy, in the mainstream hardcover lists—though there have been no blockbusters this year of the *Winter's Tale* (by Mark Helprin) or *The Mists of Avalon* (by Marion Zimmer Bradley) type. I believe this is the reflection of a lack of experience with fantasy or lack of conviction on the part of the publishers and not due, judging by what I see coming across my desk, to a lack of good fantasy material. Harper & Row is particularly strong in fantasy right now, in the line edited by Antonia Markiet; and Susan Hirschman's Greenwillow list remains strong. Atheneum and Margaret MacElderry Books continue to do occasional good fantasy books by writers like Patricia A. McKillip— but the semiretirement of the excellent Jean Karl is sorely noticed.

Good fantasy short fiction appeared within the genre and without in 1987. Collections of short stories are still difficult to sell except to the library market; book buyers prefer novels. One way of getting around that has been the rise of "shared-world" anthologies, where several writers join together to write stories using a single setting and sharing characters, which readers seem more inclined to pick up than other collections. Some critics deplore this concept, feeling that it is ruining the short-fiction field—but I'm inclined to applaud anything that allows the short-fiction form to find a wider audience. The quality of the shared-world collections, like anything else, runs the gamut, including excellent anthologies as well as bad ones. Shared-world series that are continuing publication are the original *Thieves' World* series created by Robert Asprin and Lynn Abbey (Ace), the *Heroes in Hell* series (edited by Janst Morris/Baen), the *Liavek* series edited by Will Shetterly and Emma Bull (Ace), the *Magic in Ithkar* series edited by Andre Norton and Robert Adams (Tor), as well as the *Borderland* series for teenage readers edited by myself. The shared-world concept has spread into horror and science fiction as well; fantasy readers may also be interested in taking a look at the well done *Wild Card* series edited by George R.R. Martin (Bantam), which comes close to the line between fantasy and science fiction.

Other notable collections including fantasy in 1987 are: *Spaceships and Spells* edited by Jane Yolen (Harper & Row); *Tales of the Witch World* edited by Andre Norton (Tor); *Christmas Ghosts* edited by David G. Hartwell and Kathryn Cramer (Arbor House); *Other Edens* edited by Christopher Evans and Robert Holdstock (Unwin Hyman); *The Year's Best Fantasy Stories #13* edited by Arthur W. Saha (DAW); and *Fantastic Stories* edited by Martin H. Greenburg and Patrick L. Price (TSR).

Notable single author collections are: *The Unicorn Expedition and Other Fantastic Tales of India* by Satyajit Ray (Dutton); *Bella B's Fantasy and Other Stories*, magic realism and surrealism, by Raymond Jean, translated by Juliette Dickstein, and winner of the 1983 Prix Goncourt de la Nouvelle in its original French publication (Hermes House); *The Candles of Your Eyes,* Southern Gothic tales by James Purdy (Weidenfeld & Nicholson); *Star Game* by Lucia Nevai (University of Iowa Press); *A Goose on your Grave* by Joan Aiken (Gollancz, U.K.); *Elric at the End of Time* by Michael Moorcock (DAW)—and I'll cheat and add two 1986 collections (as there was no Fantasy roundup last year and you shouldn't miss these): *Collected Stories* by Richard Kennedy (Harper & Row), and *Hearts of Wood and Other Timeless Tales* by William Kotzwinkle (David R. Godine).

In the magazines, Ed Ferman of *Science Fiction and Fantasy Magazine* continued his usual fine job of publishing quality stories. Gardner Dozois, who has proved his fantasy expertise in the anthologies he edits with Jack Dann, picked up where Shawna McCarthy left off and continued to publish a wealth of good fantasy in *Isaac Asimov's Science Fiction Magazine*—more than one would expect with such a title. Tappan King has been steadily altering the tone at *The Twilight Zone Magazine* mixing fantasy tales in with the horror and featuring fantasy artists such as the superb Jeffrey Jones. Ellen Datlow has continued to feature some superlative fantasy in *OMNI*, and *Playboy* still runs the occasional piece. Robert and Nancy Garcia produce an informative and quirky magazine in Chicago called *American Fantasy*, which is well worth the notice of fantasy readers and seems to be getting good distribution; they too are featuring articles on fantasy artists, such as Thomas Canty. The British *Interzone* is never predictable, but well worth perusing. Fantasy stories can also be found in *Amazing, Whispers, Fantasy Books, Dragon*, in the occasional literary and university reviews and punk arts journals (if you keep your eyes open)—but not in the mainstream newstand magazines. *The New Yorker* and *Redbook* have been particularly disappointing lately, though they were once sources for the rare sterling tale.

Nineteen eighty-seven was a bumper year for good fantasy novels, and I don't envy this year's judges for the World Fantasy Awards (Mike Ashley, Scott Baker, R. S. Hadji, Maxim Jakubowski, and Donald A. Wollheim) their task in choosing just one. With the wealth of material published in and out of genre, plus my own editorial duties, I've not come close to reading *all* the fantasy novels of 1987, but I have read widely and received recommendations from a number of the field's writers. The following is an all-too-limited list of books to keep an eye open for—books by masters of the field through to promising, if not always flawless, books by talented newcomers.

If you have limited time and you can choose only a dozen fantasy novels to read this year (heaven forbid!), I would recommend:

*The Land of Dreams* by James P. Blaylock (Arbor House)
*Seventh Son* by Orson Scott Card (Tor)
*Dorothea Dreams* by Suzy McKee Charnas (Berkley, reprint paperback)
*Aegypt* by John Crowley (Bantam/Spectra)
*Bones of the Moon* by Jonathan Carroll (Arbor House)
*The Great Wheel* by Joyce Ballou Gregorian (Ace, last book of the "Tredana" trilogy)
*Swordspoint* by Ellen Kushner (Arbor House)
*The Grey Horse* by R. A. MacAvoy (Bantam/Spectra)
*The Trickster* by Margaret Mahy (Bantam, reprint paperback)
*The City in the Autumn Stars* by Michael Moorcock (Ace)
*On Stranger Tides* by Tim Powers (Ace)
*The Urth of The New Sun* by Gene Wolfe (Tor)

In addition, I would strongly recommend *The Sun, The Moon, and the Stars* by Steven Brust and *Jack the Giant-Killer: The Jack of Kinrowan* by Charles de Lint (the first two books of the adult Fairy Tales series, currently published by Ace) and *War for the Oaks* by Emma Bull (the first book of the Ace Fantasy Specials series, introducing first novelists)—but because my personal involvement with these titles is more pronounced than even the usual Ace fantasy titles, I'm not sure it would be fair of me to include them on the "Dozen Best" list. On the other hand, I'm not sure it's fair to the authors of these fine novels if they're not included. 'Nuff said.

Other works to look out for: "The Shadow on the Doorstep" by James P. Blaylock and "Trilobyte" by Edward Bryant (The Axolotl Press); *Rumors of Spring* by Richard Grant (Bantam/Spectra—strictly speaking, this is science fiction, but it reads like fantasy); *Caught in Crystal* by Patricia C. Wrede (Ace); *Teckla* by Steven Brust (Ace); *A Box of Nothing* by Peter Dickinson (Magnet, U.K.); *Guardians of the West* by David Eddings (Del Rey); *The Dream Catcher* by Monica Hughes (Atheneum); *Being Invisible* by Thomas Berger (Little, Brown); *A Sending of Dragons* by Jane Yolen (Delacorte); *Archer's Goon*, Diana Wynne Jones (Ace); *Reindeer Moon* by E. Marshall Thomas (Houghton, Mifflin), a finalist for the William Crawford Award; *The Hour of the Thin Ox* by Colin Greenland (Allen & Unwin, U.K.); *The Unlikely Ones* by Mary Brown (Baen); *The Witches of Wenshar* by Barbara Hambly (Del Rey); *The Wandering Fire* by Guy Gavriel Kay (Ace); *Undersea* by Paul Hazel (Bantam/Spectra); *Seaward* by Susan Cooper (Macmillan); *The Unconquered Country* by Geoff Ryman (Bantam/Spectra); *Children of the Northern Spring* by Persia Woolsey (Poseidon Press); *Fireshaper's Doom* by Tom Deitz (Avon); *The Leopard's Daughter* by Lee Killough (Questar); *To the Haunted Mountains* by Ru Emerson (Ace); *Soulstring* by Midori Snyder (Ace); *Darkspell* by Katherine Kerr (Doubleday); *A Rose Red City* by Dave Duncan (Del Rey); *Teot's War* by Heather Gladney (Ace); *The Hall of the Mountain King* and *The Lady of Han-Gilen* both by Judith Tarr (Tor); *A Night in Netherhels* by Craig Shaw Gardner (Ace).

My vote for best darn peculiar book of the year goes to K. W. Jeter's mad quasi-Victorian romp, *Infernal Devices* (St. Martin's Press); runners-up for the prize have to be Richard Bowes's wonderful urban fantasy, *Feral Cell* (Questar), and C. J. Koch's *The Doubleman*, which is about—I kid you not—a Steeleye Span-type band battling magic and touring Australia (Triad/Grafton, U.K.).

Among books whose publication must be considered major events in the field, whether for the popularity of their authors or the merits of the books themselves are the following new novels: *The Black Unicorn* by Terry Brooks (Del Rey); *The Mirror of Her Dreams—Mordant's Need* by Stephen R. Donaldson (Del Rey); *Guardian of the Empire* by Raymond Feist and Janny Wurtz (Bantam Spectra); *Heir Apparent* by Joel Rosenberg (NAL); *Lincoln's Dreams* by Connie Willis (Bantam/Spectra); *Sign of Chaos* by Roger Zelazny (Arbor House).

Celtic music is a realm of interest to many lovers of fantasy, as the old songs—particularly in the British and Scots folk music traditions—work with much of the same mythic and fairy-tale elements found in many fantasy stories. (For those who are not familiar with this material, the old 1970s recordings of the bands Steeleye Span, Fairport Convention, and Pentangle—widely available—provide a good introduction. Also look for Frankie Armstrong's album *Tam Lin*.)

Notable work released in the last year or so: *Legacy of the Scottish Harpers, Volume III* from modern bard and harpist Robin Williamson; June Tabor's *The Peel Sessions* taped ten years ago on the John Peel radio show; Scotland's Silly Wizards' *A Glint of Silver;* a reissue of Shirley and Dolly Collins' *Love, Death, and the Lady,* long unavailable;

Maddy Prior's *A Tapestry of Carols* with the Carnival Band; and The Oyster Band's new *Wild Blue Yonder*.

There are rumors of a Silly Sisters reunion between June Tabor and Maddy Prior. France's Malicorne has returned with *Les Cathedrales de l'Industrie*. A Finnish group called Pohjantah has emerged on the folk circuit decked out in "shaman robes and antlers"; their music has been reviewed as, "the stuff of long, dark, cold winter nights." Perhaps the strangest debut, however, has been Whiskey Trail's *Pooka*. Whiskey Trail consists of four Italian musicians playing Celtic music. "Their interest," promotional copy reads, "spaced more and more into the Celtic origins of Irish, Scottish and Breton's music, and in some themes (faery tales and mythology) pertaining to these cultures." The Canadian Celtic punk band Rare Air (formerly Na Cabarfeidh), who seemed to have stepped straight from the pages of *Borderland,* have a new album titled *Tribal Rites*. Minneapolis Celtic funk band Boiled in Lead, immortalized in Emma Bull's novel *War for the Oaks,* have released a second album, *Hotheads,* featuring their distinctive Celtic-jigs-on-Sax sound. American folksinger Greg Brown has released *Songs of Innocence and Experience,* setting poems of William Blake to music. *The Best of Steeleye Span* has been released on compact disc. An excellent film has been made of the 20th reunion of Fairport Convention in Croprody, England, chronicling the history of the band and providing a great deal of concert footage with Swarbrick, Thompson, Peg, et al. Directed by Paul Kovitz, *Fairport Convention: It All Comes 'Round Again* is available in this country on VHS cassette.

Other books of interest to readers of fantasy are: *Japanese Tales*, 200 medieval Japanese tales including many fairy tales, translated and edited by Royall Tyler (Pantheon); *The Black Cloth: A Collection of African Folktales* edited by Bernard Binliŋ Dadie, translated by Karen C. Hatch (University of Massachusetts Press); *The Broonie, Silkies, and Fairies—Traveller's Tales of the Otherworld* by Scots storyteller Duncan Williamson, illustrated by Alan B. Herriot (Harmony); *Don't Bet on the Prince: Contemporary Feminist Fairy Tales in North America and Europe* and *Victorian Fairy Tales* both edited by Jack Zipes (Methuen); *Penguin Folklore Library*, translated and edited by Inea Bushnag (Penguin), and *Wizardry and Wild Romance: A Study of Epic Fantasy* by Michael Moorcock (Gollancz.)

There were several notable fantastic picture books published this year. Two fine artists whose work puts them in the league of Golden Age fairy-tale illustrators such as Edmund Dulac, Arthur Rackham, or Kay Nielsen have new books out this year: Viennese illustrator Lisbeth Zwerger has a new edition of *The Nutcracker*, retold by Anthea Bell (Picture Book Studio); and Alan Lee, one of the best watercolorists in England, has teamed up with author Joan Aiken for *The Moon's Revenge* (Knopf). Chris Van Allsburg, the World Fantasy Award winning artist, has a wonderfully bizarre new book titled *The Z Was Zapped* (Houghton, Mifflin). Ruth Sanderson has produced a beautiful Burn-Jones influenced *Sleeping Beauty*, with the story retold by Jane Yolen (Knopf). Dennis Nolan, also known for his lovely Tor fantasy covers, wrote and illustrated *The Castle Builder*, a likely awards contender with it's fanciful and evocatively rendered story of a boy who journeys into his own sand castle. Martin Springett, known for his Ace fantasy covers, has illustrated Nicholas Stuart Gray's story "The Sorcerer's Apprentice" in a St. Martin's series that also contains three other artists known to paperback fantasy readers: Richard Salvucci (illustrating Nathaniel Hawthorne), Darrel Andersen (illustrating Ray Bradbury), and Dean Morrissey (illustrating Arthur Conan Doyle.)

In adult book illustration and design, Robert Gould and Thomas Canty continue to do distinctive and elegant work; Gould continues his work on Ace editions of Michael Moorcock books and Tor's Louise Cooper novels; Canty has designed and illustrated the adult Fairy Tales series from Ace's new hardcover line, and his cover for Bluejay/NAL's *The Copper Crown* was selected for the 1987 Society of Illustrators' Exhibit in New York City. James Christensen continues producing wonderfully surrealistic covers for Tor's surrealistic Sheri Tepper books. Don Maitz turned in a nicely humorous canvas for Ace's edition of Diana Wynne Jones's *Archer's Goon*. James Warhola and Dean Morrissey have also done work with a humorous touch: the former for Paula Volsky's *The Luck of Rhelian Kru* and the latter for John Morressey's *The Quest for Kedrigern* (Ace.) DAW's edition of Mercedes Lackey's *Arrows of the Queen* is interestingly designed by Jael Brown; as is Winslow Peel's painting for Berkley's *Dorothea Dreams*, by Suzy McKee Charnas. Yvonne Gilbert, Kinuko Kraft, and Leo and Diane Dillon have not been as active in the fantasy field this year, which is a loss.

Michael Whelan has a new collection of his artwork out, *Works of Wonder* (not to be confused with the earlier *Wonderworks*) from Del Rey. Alan Lee's *Castles* (with text by David Day) is now available in trade paperback from Bantam. Phil Hale has produced twelve controversial new paintings for Donald M. Grant's special edition of Stephen King's *The Dark Tower III: The Drawing of the Dark*. And Gervasio Gallardo, whom you may remember as the man who did all those adult fantasy Unicorn logo series covers for Ballantine some years ago (edited by Lin Carter), was commissioned for the cover to Richard Grant's *Rumors of Spring* from Bantam/Spectra.

In 1987, the World Fantasy Awards were held in Nashville, Tennessee, at the World Fantasy Convention, where Piers Anthony was the Guest of Honor, Kelly Freas the Artist Guest of Honor, Karl Edward Wagner and Ron and Val Lakey Lindahn the Special Guests, and Charles L. Grant the Toastmaster. The Awards were: Best Novel of 1986: *Perfume* by Patrick Suskind (Knopf). Runners up were (aphabetically): *Talking Man* by Terry Bisson (Arbor House); *The Pet* by Charles L. Grant (Tor); *It* by Stephen King (Viking); *Strangers* by Dean R. Koontz (Putnam); *The Trickster* by Margaret Mahy (Atheneum); *Soldier of the Mist* by Gene Wolfe (Tor). Best Novella: "Hatrack River" by Orson Scott Card (*IAsfm*). Runners up were: "The Hellbound Heart" by Clive Barker (*Night Visions III*); "Night Moves" by Tim Powers (Axolotl Press); "The Night Seasons" by J.N. Williamson (*Night Cry*); "Chance" by Connie Willis (*IAsfm*). Best Short Story: "Red Light" by David Schow (*The Twilight Zone*). Runners up: "The Brains of Rats" by Michael Blumlein (*Interzone*); "They're Coming For You" by Les Daniels (*Cutting Edge*); "The End of the Whole Mess" by Stephen King (*OMNI*); "Tight Little Stitches in a Dead Man's Back" by Joe R. Lansdale (*Nukes*); "The Rise and Fall of Father Alex" by Amyas Naegele (*F & SF*); "The Boy Who Plaited Manes" by Nancy Springer (*IAsfm*);

"Pain" by Whitley Streiber (*Cutting Edge*). Best Anthology or Collection: *Tales of the Quintana Roo* by the late James Tiptree, Jr. Runners up: *Cutting Edge* edited by Dennis Etchinson (Doubleday); *Dreams of Dark and Light* by Tanith Lee (Arkham House); *Night Visions III* edited by George R.R. Martin (Dark Harvest); *Liavek: Players of Luck* edited by Will Shetterly and Emma Bull (Ace); *Black Wine* edited by Douglas E. Winter (Dark Harvest); *Merlin's Booke* by Jane Yolen (ACE and Steeldragon Press). Best Artist: Robert Gould. Runners up: Stephen Gervais; J.K. Potter; Chris Van Allsburg.) Special Award, Professional: Jane Yolen, editor of *Favorite Tales from Around the World* (Pantheon). Runners up: Donald M. Grant (Donald M. Grant Publishers); David G. Hartwell (Arbor House and Tor); the editors of *Interzone* magazine; Jack Sullivan (Viking); *The Penguin Encyclopedia of Horror and the Supernatural* (Penguin); Terri Windling (Ace). Special Award, Nonprofessional: W. Paul Ganley (Weirdbook and Weirdbook Press). Runners up: Jeff Conner/Scream Press; Stephen Jones and David Sutton (*Fantasy Tales*); David B. Silva (*The Horror Show*.) Special Award: Andre Norton. Life Achievement Award: Jack Finney. Judges: John M. Ford, Paul Hazel, Tappan King, Michael McDowell, Melissa Ann Singer.

In England, the British Fantasy Society presented the following awards: Best Novel: *It* by Stephen King. Best Short Fiction: "The Olympic Runner" by Dennis Etchinson. Best Small Press: *Fantasy Tales* edited by Stephen Jones and David Sutton. Best Film: *Aliens*. Best Artist: J.K. Potter. Special Award: Charles L. Grant.

The I.A.F.A. Distinguished Scholar Award was presented to Brian Stableford.

The William Crawford Award for Best New Fantasy Writer went to Judith Tarr for her *The Hound and the Falcon* trilogy (Bluejay Books/Tor Books).

The 8th International Conference on the Fantastic in the Arts was held in Texas in March of 1987. Guests of Honor were Author—Stephen R. Donaldson. Scholar—Brian Stableford.

The Fourth Street Fantasy Convention was held in Minneapolis in June, 1987. Guests of Honor: authors—Patricia A. McKillip and Jane Yolen; artist—Robert Gould; editor—Terri Windling.

The Mythopoeic Conference was held in Milwaukee in July, 1987. Guests of Honor: Christopher Tolkien and John Bellairs.

—T.W.

# Summation 1987: Horror

In the past few years, murmurs of discontent have been heard at the annual World Fantasy Convention. Fantasy enthusiasts complain that the awards have been dominated by horror, horror enthusiasts have been clamoring for their own convention, and their own awards. In fact, fantasy and horror seem pretty equally represented at the convention itself and in the award-giving.

In any case, 1987 was the year the Horror Writers of America was incorporated. Initially discussed in 1986 by Robert McCammon and Melissa Mia Hall, the idea for a horror organization finally coalesced in 1987, with Dean R. Koontz and his wife Gerda largely responsible for its official formation and incorporation.

The officers in 1988 are Charles L. Grant, President; Thomas Monteleone, Vice President; Betsy Engstrom, Secretary; Maxine O'Callaghan, Treasurer. Membership costs $40.00, $45.00 outside the United States. To become an Active member you must possess certain publication credentials. Anyone can join as an Affiliate, though, and the biggest difference between the privileges of Active and Affiliate membership is that as an Active member you can vote for the final ballot and for officers. (For information contact Maxine O'Callaghan, Treasurer/Membership Committee, 25971 Serenata Drive, Mission Viejo, CA 92691).

Awards will be given for "superior achievement," rather than for the "Best" of the year, an attempt by the founders to avoid the sense of competitiveness engendered by most literary awards. The awards, named after Bram Stoker, the author of the classic *Dracula*, will be voted on by the full active membership, at this time over one hundred members. If any two nominees receive more than 30 percent of the votes, both will win. The first annual awards will be given in New York City on June 24th at a weekend convention. Whether or not this breaking off of horror writers into a new organization will make a difference to the character of the World Fantasy Convention and the World Fantasy Awards remains to be seen.

In a move initially announced when Eden Collinsworth left the company's helm June 1987, Arbor House as of January 1st was officially absorbed by William Morrow. The editorial department so far still exists but all other departments were dismissed. Under David G. Hartwell, Arbor House has published some important and critically well-received science fiction, horror, and fantasy, including the reprint anthology *Christmas Ghosts*, edited by Kathryn Cramer and David G. Hartwell and the excellent original anthology *The Architecture of Fear*, edited by Kathryn Cramer and Peter Pautz. Arbor House also published Robert Aickman's posthumous novel *The Model*.

Despite the uncertain status of Arbor House's editorial independence (at the end of 1987 it was announced that Howard Kaminsky would be taking over the publishing programs of the Hearst Corporation, a move that will most certainly herald more changes), Hartwell plans to continue publishing selected horror novels and anthologies. Jonathan Carroll's novel *Bones of The Moon* came out in January and *Anthony Shriek*, a novel by Jessica Amanda Salmonson, is scheduled for release in 1988.

Doubleday's hardcover science fiction publishing program, in close cooperation with the Bantam/Spectra program, has been revised, revamped, and renamed. It is now called Foundation Books, in honor of Isaac Asimov. Pat LoBrutto, Doubleday's science fiction and western editor, is editor of the revamped line. LoBrutto has been influential in the horror field by annually publishing the critically acclaimed original anthologies *Whispers* and *Shadows*. In 1986 he won the World Fantasy Award for Special Achievement (Professional). He reports to Lou Aronica, publisher of Bantam/Spectra. Virtually all Foundation titles will become Spectra paperbacks. The program was appropriately launched in May 1988 with Isaac Asimov's *Prelude to Foundation*.

Crown Publishers and Waldenbooks jointly announced a new mass-market line of genre books to be called Pageant. Editor-in-Chief is Arlene Friedman, formerly of Fawcett. Karen Haas is their acquiring editor for fantasy, science fiction, and horror. The first horror titles will be released in September.

Headline, the new British publisher, launched its paperback list in June with *Shadows* edited by Charles L. Grant, *The Power* by Ian Watson, *Watchers* by Dean Koontz, and *Who Made Stevie Crye* by Michael Bishop.

Bart Books, previously distributed through Critic's Choice Paperbacks, will now be distributed directly by the Kable News Company. They will start publishing books in June 1988 in various categories including horror and science fiction.

Lynx Books, published by Lou Wolfe, the former chief executive officer of Bantam, will begin publishing mass-market paperbacks in July 1988. Lynx will publish two horror titles a month in paperback. Lynx is reportedly well financed.

In other news, the semiprofessional review magazine, *Fantasy Review* folded. Published by the Meckler corporation, which bought it a year earlier, and edited by Robert A. Collins, the magazine was started as *Fantasy Newsletter* in 1978 by Paul C. Allen and taken over in 1981 by Collins and Florida Atlantic U. The magazine was informative and had some interesting regular columns as well as news and reviews. Under Robert Collins, the magazine sparked lively controversy, at least partly out of editorial insensitivity, and partly out of the troublemaking propensities of some of the contributors. It will be missed.

On the other hand, *Horrorstruck*, a semi-professional magazine covering exclusively the horror scene, was started in 1987. The first year's issues are quite promising, with articles about the process of writing and editing horror fiction, interviews with horror writers, market reports, and several review columns.

The other "semiprozine" specializing in horror and fantasy is *American Fantasy*. In addition to interviews, articles, and coverage of the media, this magazine contains some fiction.

(*Horrorstruck: The World of Dark Fantasy*, 155 Surrey Drive-E, Glen Ellyn, IL 60137, $15.00 for a one-year subscription; *American Fantasy*, P.O. Box 41714, Chicago, IL 60641, $16.00 for a one-year subscription, four issues. *Locus*, Locus Publications, Inc. P.O. Box 13305, Oakland, CA 94661, $32.00 for a one-year first-class subscription, 12 issues; *Science Fiction Chronicle*, P.O. Box 2730, Brooklyn, NY 11202-0056. $27.00 for one year, 12 issues).

The major loss to the horror field in 1987 was the suspension and subsequent killing of *Night Cry*, the sister publication of *Rod Serling's The Twilight Zone*. The digest-size magazine was edited by Alan Rodgers and was the only professional, exclusively horror fiction magazine being published. *Night Cry* had been developed as a spin off of *TZ* during the editorship of Ted Klein. The magazine was originally supposed to look like a paperback book, and Klein came up with the idea of having one artist illustrate an entire issue. Klein edited the first issue, in 1984, which was made up completely of *TZ* reprints. The second issue had three original stories. Rodgers became editor with the third issue, and he initiated a no-holds-barred policy as far as content. No taboos, no censorship. Some of *Night Cry*'s art, much of it by J. K. Potter, was as striking as its best stories.

While holding its own, the magazine was not making a large profit. With only newsstand distribution, it sold reasonably well compared to other digest-size magazines on the newsstand. But since most digests are essentially subscription supported this would have been the natural direction for Montcalm Publishers to take. They were either unwilling or unable to mount a subscription drive and, dissatisfied, put the magazine up for sale in spring 1987. Operations of *Night Cry* were suspended and the last issue came out in fall 1987. With the loss of *Night Cry,* the field is again without a single professional exclusively horror magazine.

Luckily, small-press horror magazines seem to be thriving, some of them excellent. The best small-press horror magazine being published right now is *The Horror Show.* It is consistently literate and interesting. The overall quality of the small-press magazines ranges from some high-quality fiction and decent design in *The Horror Show, Fantasy Tales, Eldritch Tales, Fantasy Macabre,* and other publications down to amateurish publications with unreadable layouts and type and barely literate stories. In general, however, the art in all these magazines is abysmal—obvious and heavy-handed—with some notable exceptions. *Deathrealm* ran some excellent illustrations by Jeffrey Osier for his own story; *The Horror Show* had some terrific covers by J. K. Potter. And the following artists did good interiors for several small presses: Jeannette Hopper, Allen Koszowski, John Borkowski, James Garrison, Denis Tiani, and Chris Pelletiere.

The year 1987 marks the first complete year with Tappan King at the helm of *The Twilight Zone.* Under his editorship the magazine has been redesigned with a more readable and slicker layout and seems to be playing down the media features somewhat. In general, the magazine is more upscale in look and content, and seems aimed at an older and more sophisticated audience. In 1987 King published some of the best horror stories of the year by genre writers as well as stories by Joyce Carol Oates and John Updike; there were theme issues and expanded coverage of the occult and the unexplained, perhaps modeled somewhat after *OMNI.* Fiction wordage increased by about 5–10,000 words per issue and in the course of the year King ran about six novelettes, unlike his predecessors, who ran only short stories.

Under Ted Klein, the first editor, the magazine was very much tied to the original concept of the *Twilight Zone* TV series as well as being somewhat Gothic in theme; then with Michael Blaine, the magazine became more New York literary establishment. Now King seems to be making the magazine more eclectic and to be trying to broaden the definition of the fantastic. Critically, the fantasy/horror community has responded favorably to the changes but the magazine has lost some of its traditional readers. Two of the strongest and best but also darkest stories he published last year, Lucius Shepard's "The Exercise of Faith" and Michael McDowell's "Halley's Passing," received considerable negative readership and management's response was to persuade King to ease off from the more overtly dark and violent stories—no matter how good they are. That means there is probably no longer a magazine market for these stories; although if the *Twilight Zone* can make up for the readers it's lost quickly enough to keep management happy, King will be able to occasionally sneak in some dark, ambitious work in the future.

Although other professional magazines occasionally publish horror—such as *The Magazine of Fantasy & Science Fiction, Isaac Asimov's Science Fiction Magazine, OMNI,*

*Interzone, Amazing,* and *Playboy*—they are hardly major markets for the genre. Currently the only thriving professional horror market is that of original and reprint anthologies and collections.

*Night Cry* published excellent stories and poems by A. R. Morlan, Lucius Shepard, Charles L. Grant, Paul Witcover, Lewis Shiner, and others. *Twilight Zone* published notable stories by Charles L. Grant, Michael McDowell, Ramsey Campbell, Lucius Shepard, David J. Schow, Marc Laidlaw, Jane Yolen, Richard Paul Russo, George Zebrowski, Barry Malzberg and Jack Dann, and others.

*The Magazine of Fantasy & Science Fiction* published some very good horror stories by Stephen Gallagher, Chet Williamson, Ian Watson, and Barbara Owens. The editor is Edward L. Ferman.

*Isaac Asimov's Science Fiction Magazine* had some strong horror by Charles de Lint, Steve Rasnic Tem, Nancy Kress, and Susan Palwick. The editor is Gardner Dozois.

*Whispers #23–24* had interesting stories by Julie Stevens, Barbara W. Durbin, and Brian Lumley but in general was disappointing. Long time editor-publisher is Stuart Schiff.

*The Horror Show* published top-notch stories by Lawrence C. Connolly, Joe R. Lansdale, Bentley Little, Poppy Z. Brite, Paul Olson, and Carol Reid. The publisher is David B. Silva.

*Eldritch Tales* published fine fiction and poems by Fred Croft, Steve Rasnic Tem, William Relling, Jr., and Sam Gafford. The publisher is Crispin Burnham.

*Fantasy Macabre* published good stories by Thomas Ligotti, Carol Reid, and Archie Roy. The editor is Jessica Amanda Salmonson.

*Grue Magazine* had good stories from Joe Lansdale and Thomas Ligotti. Peggy Nadramia is the editor.

There were strong stories by George R. R. Martin, George Alec Effinger, Michael Bishop, Susan Casper, Sue Marra, Thomas Ligotti, Rudy Kremberg, and Joe Lansdale in *OMNI, Playboy, Amazing, Ouroboros, The Crypt of Cthulhu, Haunts, Nightmares,* and *Opus.*

(Most small press horror magazines are only available through subscription. Following are some of the best (issues do not always come out on a regular schedule): *Whispers,* 770 Highland Avenue, Binghamton, NY 13905, $13.95 for two double issues; *The Horror Show,* 14848 Misty Springs Lane, Oak Run, CA. 96069, $14.00 a year for four issues and premium; *Grue Magazine,* P.O. Box 370, Times Square Station, New York, NY 10108, $11.00 for a one-year subscription of three issues—check or money order payable to Peggy Nadramia; *Fantasy Tales,* 130 Park View, Wembley, Middlesex, HA9 6JU, England, $11.00 for three-issue subscription; *Ouroboros,* 3912 24th Avenue, Rock Island, IL 61201, $13.00 for a four-issue subscription; *Eldritch Tales,* 1051 Wellington Road, Lawrence, KS 66044, $20.00 for a four-issue subscription; *Fantasy Macabre,* R. H. Fawcett, 61 Teecomwas Drive, Uncasville, CT 06382, $9.00 for a three-issue subscription.)

*Weird Tales,* the granddaddy of horror magazines, has been revived for the fifth time, and although the first new issue has a cover date of spring 1988, it was made available Halloween weekend at the 1987 World Fantasy Convention in Nashville. It is being produced by a triumvirate consisting of George Scithers, John Gregory Betancourt, and Darrell Schweitzer. The title, owned by Robert Weinberg, is being licensed to the publishers.

As mentioned above, the strongest market for dark fantasy and horror short fiction today is the anthology market. There were several major original anthologies published in 1987. *Whispers VI*, edited by Stuart Schiff, is one of the longest-running horror anthologies. It's generally made up of original stories and some of the best reprints from Schiff's *Whispers* magazine. As usual, there were some top-notch original stories this year, particularly by William F. Nolan, Steve Rasnic Tem, Lucius Shepard, and Charles L. Grant. The next *Whispers* will be published as an original paperback by Bantam/Spectra in 1988. The plan is to eventually go back to hardcover once an audience for the anthology is built up. Another reliable source of good original horror stories is Charles L. Grant's ongoing *Shadows* anthology series. *Shadows 10* is an important showcase for newer horror writers of the low-keyed style Grant's own writing exemplifies. There are excellent stories by Lisa Tuttle, T. M. Wright (who rarely writes short stories), Thomas Sullivan, Melissa Mia Hall, Mona A. Clee, and Ken Wisman. From now on *Shadows* will be published by the Foundation imprint of Doubleday/ Bantam in an expanded size every other year.

*Dark Harvest* publisher Paul Mikol has been putting out beautifully packaged triple-author collections for the last few years under the series title *Night Visions*. *Night Visions IV*, published in 1987, included original stories and novelettes by Robert McCammon, Dean Koontz, and Edward Bryant. While the stories are all high quality, and the overall production and design is excellent, the copyediting and proofreading continue to be very poor. This is inexcusable considering the obvious care taken with every other aspect of these books.

Another original anthology of note was *Masques II* (Maclay), edited by J. N. Williamson. The most ambitious story in the volume was Douglas E. Winter's controversial "Splatter." It also contained notable stories by John Robert Bensink, Richard Matheson, G. Wayne Miller, and Steve Rasnic Tem (and a minor one by Stephen King).

Theme anthologies abounded in 1987. One of the best of the original theme anthologies was *The Architecture of Fear* (Arbor House), edited by Kathryn Cramer and Peter Pautz. There's not a clinker in the bunch and some of the stories are very good, indeed. All the stories were originals, except for a Robert Aickman reprint. Another good original anthology was *Doom City* (Tor), edited by Charles L. Grant, based in the imaginary town of Greystone Bay, conceived of by Grant. Unlike most shared-world anthlogies, and to the book's credit, the stories are only tenuously related and stand very much on their own. The standouts are those by Nancy Holder, Kathryn Ptacek, and Bob Booth.

The best of the reprint theme anthologies were *The Dark Descent* (Tor), David G. Hartwell's massive and ambitious attempt to trace the evolution of horror fiction from the psychological investigations of Edgar Allan Poe, William Faulkner, and Thomas M. Disch through the supernatural allegories of J. Sheridan Le Fanu, Nathaniel Hawthorne, Ray Bradbury, and Harlan Ellison to the disturbing stories of Edith Wharton, Robert Aickman, and Gene Wolfe; *Vampires* (Doubleday) edited by Alan Ryan and covering stories of vampires from Clark Ashton Smith and August Derleth to Richard Matheson, Suzy McKee Charnas, and Steve Rasnic Tem. This volume was a good overview of this subgenre; *Christmas Ghosts*, edited by Kathryn Cramer and David G. Hartwell; *Daphne Du Maurier's Classics of the Macabre* (Doubleday), featuring the stories "Don't Look Now" and "The Birds," effectively illustrated by Michael Foreman; *Devils and Demons* (Doubleday), edited by Marvin Kaye. Also of note were *Dracula's Brood* (Inner Traditions International), edited by Richard Dalby and featuring "rare" vampire stories; *Demons!* (Berkley) edited by Jack Dann and Gardner Dozois; *Vamps* (DAW), edited by Martin H. Greenberg and Charles G. Waugh; *Nightmares in Dixie*, thirteen horror tales from the American South (August House) edited by Frank McSherry, Charles G. Waugh, and Martin H. Greenberg; *Casting the Runes and Other Ghost Stories of M. R. James* (Oxford University Press) edited by Michael Cox; *House Shudders* (DAW), edited by Rosalind M. Greenberg, Martin H. Greenberg, and Charles G. Waugh, and *The Year's Best Horror Stories* edited by Karl Edward Wagner.

This is only a sampling of the available anthologies of horror fiction. There seems to be a never-ending production (particularly by university presses) of "classic" horror anthologies, probably because most of these "classics" are no longer covered by copyright law. For example, there were at least three collections of M. R. James's ghost stories published in 1987 and at least three anthologies of "classic" vampire stories. There's such a glut of them, it's hard to believe they sell.

Two other theme anthologies published in 1987 deserve special note, only in part because of the high quality of the stories. The first is *In the Field of Fire* (Tor), edited by Jeanne van Buren Dann and Jack Dann, a combination of science-fiction, fantasy, and horror stories concerning the Vietnam war. More than half the stories were original to this volume and several could be considered horror stories (supernatural or psychological). The second, *Other Edens* (Unwin Hyman) edited by Christopher Evans and Robert Holdstock, serves as a showcase for British speculative fiction (except for Lisa Tuttle, an honorary Briton). Its science fiction borders on fantasy, its fantasy borders on horror, its horror on mainstream. Among the best "horror" stories in this anthology were those by Lisa Tuttle, M. John Harrison, Garry Kilworth, and Robert Holdstock. So far, it's only been published in England.

What is most interesting about the two volumes is that both continue the movement of the overlapping of genres in the field of the fantastic. Many of the best collections in 1987 are by authors whose work seems to point this out. Lucius Shepard's *The Jaguar Hunter* (Arkham House), George R. R. Martin's *Portraits of his Children* (Dark Harvest), *The Essential Ellison*, a collection of Harlan Ellison's work (Nemo Press), Roald Dahl's *Two Fables* (Farrar, Straus & Giroux), *The Stories of Muriel Spark* (Bodley Head), *The Best of Pamela Sargent* (Academy Chicago), Leigh Kennedy's *Faces* (Atlantic Monthly Press), Josephine Saxton's *Little Tours of Hell* (Pandora), Ramsey Campbell's *Dark Feasts*, and Ian Watson's *Evil Water and Other Stories* (Gollancz)—all these collections contain various types of speculative or fantastic fiction.

Other good collections were *Scars* (Scream/Press) by Richard Christian Matheson; *Scared Stiff* (Scream/Press) by Ramsey Campbell; *Polyphemus* (Arkham House) by Michael Shea; *Why Not You and I* (Dark Harvest) by Karl Edward Wagner; *A Goose on Your Grave* (Gollancz) by Joan Aiken; *Other Engagements* (Dream House) by John Maclay, all of which include some material never before published; *The Valley So Low* (Doubleday) by Manley Wade Wellman; *Dark Feasts* (Robinson Publishing) by Ramsey Campbell;

*Midnight Pleasures* (Doubleday) by Robert Bloch; *Expiration Dates* (Regions Press) by Jeannette Hopper (all four original); *Cthulhu: The Mythos and Kindred Horrors* (Baen) by Robert Howard; and *Deep Things out of Darkness* (Tales After Dark) by Roger Johnson.

The year 1988 looks even better for the anthology market with major collections due from Dennis Etchison (Scream/Press), John Farris (Tor), the trade edition of Richard Christian Matheson's *Scars* (Tor), *Night Visions V* (Dark Harvest) with stories by Stephen King, Dan Simmons and George R.R. Martin. There are high expectations for the original anthologies *Tropical Chill* (Avon) edited by Timothy Robert Sullivan; *Women of Darkness* (Tor) edited by Kathryn Ptacek; *Silver Scream* (Tor) edited by David J. Schow; a zombie anthology called *The Book of the Dead* (Bantam) edited by John Skipp and Craig Spector; *Prime Evil* (NAL) edited by Douglas E. Winter, which will be "defining what horror fiction will be at the end of the millennium" (curiously enough, it will be without female practitioners, if this anthology is any sample); *Ripper*, edited by Susan Casper and Gardner Dozois.

Two very special projects scheduled to appear in 1988 are from Lord John Press, a fine and expensive small-press publisher. An unpublished novella by Stephen King, *Dolan's Cadillac,* will be available as a limited signed edition of 1000 copies. Also, in celebration of the press's tenth anniversary, there will be an anthology of short stories, essays, poetry, photographs, and a play—these from Ray Bradbury, Whitley Strieber, Raymond Carver, James Crumley, Jack Dann, Barry Malzberg, Ramsey Campbell, Dennis Etchison, and John Updike, among others. The volume is edited by Dennis Etchison and is available in limited and trade editions. (For information write: 19073 Los Alamos Street, Northridge, CA 91326)

Other anthologies scheduled to appear in 1988 are *The Collected Stories of Richard Matheson* (Scream/Press); *Books of Blood IV–VI* (Scream/Press) illustrated by Harry O. Morris in three separate volumes; *Charles Beaumont's Selected Stories* (Dark Harvest) including five previously unpublished stories; The *Haunting of Hill House* by Shirley Jackson (Hill House); *John the Balladeer* (Baen), Manley Wade Wellman's Silver John stories; *Red Jack* edited by Robert Adams (DAW); *Masters of Darkness II* edited by Dennis Echison (Tor); *Best of Masques* edited by J. N. Williamson (Berkley); and *Tales from the Darkside* edited by Charles L. Grant (Berkley).

As in science fiction, there is a booming business in small-press short-story collections and anthologies of horror fiction. Books are published in limited editions that quickly go out of print and become instant collector's items. Often, at that point a trade publisher will pick up the book for reprint.

There were some excellent chapbooks published in 1987. Perhaps only in the fields of fantasy and horror does this form retain the tradition that once was common to a broader spectrum of literature. Chapbooks are labors of love, usually with miniscule press runs and limited circulation. The Axolotl Press (John Phelan, publisher) published *Fat Face* by Michael Shea, in an edition of some 1300 copies. Footsteps Press, (Bill Munster, publisher) brought out two chapbooks: *Splatter* by Douglas E. Winter and *Medusa* by Ramsey Campbell.

Since *Locus* only considers supernatural horror in its tallies of novel releases, it's difficult to know exactly how much horror was published in 1987. But there were at least ninety-six supernatural novels according to *Locus*. And judging from the various horror programs and mainstream publishers who only occasionally publish horror, there was probably double that number of horror novels. I only read a handful of the horror novels published in 1987, but I particularly liked *Shadow Stalker* (Berkley) by Jorge Saralegui, a multilayered psychological thriller along the lines of Thomas Harris's brilliant *Red Dragon*. Stephen King's *Misery* (Viking) is the tightest, most consistently riveting and frightening novel King has written for some time. It too is psychological rather than supernatural horror. Clive Barker's first novel, *The Damnation Game* (Putnam) pointed out both his flaws and strengths as a writer—not quite under control, yet his energy knocks the socks off the reader. It's a powerful, entertaining shocker. *Live Girls* (Pocket Books) by Ray Garton has a great premise—vampire/hookers in Times Square—and is a good read; Joe R. Lansdale's *The Nightrunner* (Dark Harvest) is so violent and raw that it might offend some readers, but the power of Lansdale's story-telling makes the experience worth it. Dean R. Koontz's *Watchers* (Putnam) is a science fiction/horror thriller that features two escapees from a genetic engineering experiment. A terrifically satisfying read.

Other novels that received a good deal of attention include *The Cleanup* (Bantam) by John Skipp and Craig Spector; *The Eyes of the Dragon* (Viking) by Stephen King; *The Tommyknockers* (Putnam) by Stephen King; *Weaveworld* (Poseideon) by Clive Barker (more fantasy than horror); *Ghosts of Night and Morning* (Charter) by Marvin Kaye; *The Hunting Season* (Macmillan) by John Coyne; *Rapture* (Atheneum) by Thomas Tessier; *Dark Seeker* (Tor) by K.W. Jeter; *The Harvest Bride* (Tor) by Tony Richards; *Saga of the Swamp Thing* (Warner graphic novel) by Alan Moore; *Ronin* (Warner graphic novel) by Frank Miller; *The Magic Cottage* (NAL) by James Herbert; *The Drawing of the Three* (Donald M. Grant) by Stephen King; *Swan Song* (Pocket) by Robert McCammon; *Down on the Farm* (St. Martin's Press) by John Stchur; *Slob* (NAL) by Rex Miller; *A Flame in Byzantium* (Tor) by Chelsea Quinn Yarbro; and for fans of Gahan Wilson, *Eddy Deco's Last Caper: An Illustrated Mystery* (Times Books) written and illustrated in Wilson's most grotesque, best style.

It seems that almost every major publisher has at least some horror on its list. The most visible horror programs are those of Berkley, Tor, and NAL, who are regularly publishing horror novels or anthologies each month, Tor's being the most ambitious program, with three titles per month. Bantam has upcoming novels and a zombie anthology from the "splatter punks" John Skipp and Craig Spector and has John Saul on its list. Foundation, the new SF/fantasy Doubleday/Bantam line is touting Raymond Feist's epic horror novel *Fairie Tale* and plans to continue publishing the two major horror anthologies *Shadows* and *Whispers*. In addition, they've signed a multibook contract with Al Sarrantonio. Avon is reprinting Whitley Strieber's early horror novels and publishes Steve Rasnic Tem, a talented poet and short-story writer who is just breaking out as a novelist. Pocket Books published Ray Garton's notable *Live Girls* with considerable energy, and has published Clive Barker's *Books of Blood IV–VI* in paperback. St. Martin's plans to continue the *Masques* series, and publishes horror novels regularly.

As David Hartwell points out in *The Dark Descent*, horror has only recently evolved from being primarily a short-story genre to a novel genre. Until fairly recently, horror novels were marketed (successfully) simply as "fiction" or "literature" (*Frankenstein, Dracula, Rosemary's Baby, The Exorcist*). Now, with publishers creating "horror lines," the genre is suddenly being treated as a category, much the same as science fiction. More and more bookstores have horror sections. Tor and other publishers are deliberately making the covers on their books identifiable as horror, which will bring in the predisposed reader but is as likely to turn off the general reader. In the long run, a horror genre ghetto, much like that of science fiction, with predetermined ceilings on sales of most genre titles, might result. It would be extremely unfortunate if the boom we're seeing is sowing the seeds of disaster for the future of the horror novel.

There were some useful nonfiction/reference books concerning horror in 1987. Charles N. Brown and William G. Contento's *Science Fiction, Fantasy and Horror: 1986* (Locus Press) is the companion volume to last year's *Science Fiction in Print: 1985*. A useful volume for novice writers is *How to Write Tales of Horror, Fantasy and Science Fiction*, edited by J. N. Williamson (Writers' Digest Books). Some of the more interesting critical books were *The Monster in the Mirror: Gender and the Sentimental/Gothic Myth in Frankenstein* by Mary K. Patterson-Thornburg (UMI Research Press); *Spector or Delusion? The supernatural in Gothic Fiction* by Margaret L. Carter (UMI Research Press); *Aliens in the Home: The Child in Horror* fiction by Sabine Bussing (Greenwood); *Mary Shelley: A Biography* by Muriel Spark (Dutton/William Abrahams); *The Delights of Terror: An Aesthetics of the Tale of Terror* by Terry Heller (University of Illinois Press); *Dark Romance: Sexuality in the Horror Film* by David J. Hogan (McFarland & Co.); and *Werewolves in Western Culture* by Charlotte Ottin (Syracuse University Press). And of course, there was the usual rash of books on Stephen King: *The Stephen King Phenomenon* by Michael R. Collings (Starmont); *Under Cover of Darkness* edited by Don Herron with an introduction by Dennis Etchison (Underwood–Miller); and *Bare Bones: Talking of Terror with Stephen King* edited by Chuck Miller and Tim Underwood (Underwood–Miller).

—E. D.

# 1987: Horror and Fantasy on the Screen

This was a year during which the nation's movie screens saw a respectable number of horror and fantasy films, but few of those even came close to blockbuster status. Three major disappointments included Alan Parker's *Angel Heart*, John Schlesinger's *The Believers*, and John Carpenter's *Prince of Darkness*. The first was the most successful, possibly because it was based on William Hjortsberg's literate (and literary) novel that combined horror and hard-boiled detective plots, *Falling Angel*. Stars Mickey Rourke and Lisa Bonet generated lots of sexual sparks and chicken blood, and Robert DeNiro adequately did his bit as the devil, but the film never really progressed beyond being a terrific exercise in cinematic style. *The Believers* thrust Martin Sheen into a brew of urban voodoo, but finally foundered in a silly plot. *Prince of Darkness*, unfortunately, was just silly all around.

The year got off to a lavish, if overstuffed, start with the big-screen version of *Little Shop of Horrors*. It had its moments (musical and otherwise), one of the better being Bill Murray's cameo. Unfortunately the downbeat ending got scrapped, but at least Levi Stubbs (of the Four Tops) got a good job providing the voice for the carnivorous plant. Then there was Eddie Murphy starring in *The Golden Child*, a disappointing outing that suggested a much paler version of *Big Trouble in Little China*.

There was the usual plethora of sequels. *Nightmare on Elm Street III* was adequate, not coming terribly close to matching Wes Craven's initial entry in the series, but it beat out *Elm Street II* by a country mile. It was buoyed by repeating many of Craven's splendidly nightmarish images from the original. If it worked once . . . Unfortunately the same cannot be said for *House II: The Second Story*, which did not match the amusing qualities of its predecessor. Silly stuff. Ditto *Creepshow II*; The Stephen King/George Romero collaboration was a paler version of the first *Creepshow*. *Prom Night II: Hello Mary Lou* had little to do with its namesake original, which was just as well for *Prom Night I*. PN II had its moments, but they were all too few. *Teen Wolf Too* was a yawner.

The one really cheery spot in this gray portrait of entropic sequelitis was Sam Raimi's successor to his own cult classic, *The Evil Dead*. Actually *Evil Dead II* seemed less a sequel than it did a larger-budget remake of its ancestor. What it mainly had going for it was a crude and vital energy coupled with a manic humor, along with a perhaps too-generous special effects budget for ooze and belch. A sort of Coyote and Roadrunner cartoon with live actors beset by icky dead things, *Evil Dead II* was indulgent and excessive, but always amusing. There were a few scares here, but mainly a lot of studied gross-outs and very deliberate, gut-level laughs. Writer-director Raimi is apparently someone who has a healthy appreciation for the valid use of humor to heighten horrific effect.

Someone else with a talented but askew sense of humor is director Stuart Gordon. He followed up the brilliantly warped *Re-animator* with *From Beyond*, another Lovecraftian homage from Empire Pictures. The special effects hydraulics were great, but the comedic elements were not quite so whacko as in the film's predecessor.

Two pictures spotlighted younger performers. *The Gate* concerned kids who unluckily open an occult portal in the backyard, a shaft that plunges all the way down to you-know-where. The plot didn't always make sense. *The Monster Squad* was cuter, but likewise essentially dumb. There was a certain nostalgic value to a movie that united Dracula, the Frankenstein monster, the mummy, the wolfman, and the gill man, but the plot (and continuity) were again something less than adequate.

Good old-fashioned, straightforward monster movies were also represented. Arnold Schwarzenegger was back as a tough mercenary obliged to fight a nasty alien trophy hunter in *Predator*. The effects were terrific; the story limped. In *The Blue Monkey*, Steve Railsback got to fight a mutant bug-critter in the basement of a modest appearing Toronto hospital that somehow housed the world's largest and most spiffy laser lab. The charm of this one was that *The Blue Monkey* did a pretty fair job of re-creating the basic stereotypes of the classic '50s monster movie. It was all pleasantly familiar.

New Line Cinema's headline fall release was also their most expensive to date—about $7 million in production cost. Kyle MacLachlan starred in *The Hidden*, a cops-and-robbers chase picture about the hunt for an alien creature that hops from possession of one Earthling body to another, all the while indulging a passion for fast cars and loud music. *The Hidden* had some humor, good production values, a halfway complicated plot, and some male-bonding pathos. It came very close.

Probably the biggest monster flick of the year was Adrian Lynn's *Fatal Attraction*. While this wasn't technically a film of the fantastic, it still hewed to the tried-and-true formula of any number of outright shock pictures. Michael Douglas and Glenn Close had juicy roles, but the script was unconscionably manipulative. Rarely have topical paranoias been so crassly mined.

The picture that *should* have shared some of *Fatal Attraction*'s audience—but didn't—was the spottily released *The Stepfather*. Directed by Joseph Rubin from a script by Donald Westlake, the film starred Terry O'Quinn as a family man who simply bought the American Dream at too high a cost. Whenever his wife and kids would disappoint his rigorous expectations, he'd just massacre them and move on to the next family. It's a very taut, extremely effective suspense thriller.

Too bad one couldn't say the same for Ken Russell's *Gothic*: great idea, depicting the macabre events of that stormy night when Mary Shelley got the idea for *Frankenstein*, but bad literary history and a hideously overblown approach to storytelling.

For especially effective social commentary in terms of horror structures, one could productively opt for *Robocop*. This summer hit, directed by Paul Verhoeven, was a disturbing and effective movie that laid a foundation of police/violence/adventure conventions, and then built a terrifically effective satire attacking the genuine terror of an extrapolated corporate America. All this was conducted with a savagely dark humor that apparently misled quite a few viewers.

*Nightflyers*, based on the novella by George R. R. Martin, was a splendid failure. Nominally science fiction, this low budget epic was produced and filmed to look like the darkest of space Gothics. The amazement was that the picture looked as though it had cost ten times what it did. The disappointment was that the continuity suggested scenes arbitrarily chopped or dropped. What was left was reminiscent of, say, *The Keep* or *The Hunger*—something beautiful to behold, but short on such things as character relationships. This was another one that came close.

One of the odd and interesting trends in the field in 1987 was the proliferation of bargain basement (or *sub*-bargain basement) exploitation flicks such as *Blood Diner*, *I Was a Teenage Zombie*, *Return to Horror High*, *The Class of Nukem High*, and *Surf Nazis Must Die*. These are fantasy/horror/science fiction movies that are made for seven bucks and a few food stamps, star (mostly) nobody you ever heard of, and have absolutely nothing to lose. Because of that last item, they're a brash, crude, energetic breed of guerrilla filmmaking that's rarely completely successful, but they are usually interesting and often entertaining. To track down this prey, however, the wily filmgoer will have to frequent midnight movies and attend double features in disreputable neighborhoods.

As ever, there was a herd of middle-of-the-road low-budget pictures. *Trick or Treat* took as its premise that the far-right fundamentalist critics are literally right in their condemnation of heavy metal as a tool of the devil. The rest of the film didn't measure up to that amusing conceit. *My Demon Lover* was a lackluster attempt at combining romantic comedy with demonic possession. *Witchboard* took a slick, low-cost fling at combining Ouija boards and possession and came close to making it work.

I'm not even going to belabor the clutch of pictures about mannequins coming to life, heroines returning from the dead, dates with angels, characters exchanging minds, and other botched attempts at frothy fantasies. Almost without exception, they came across as derivative versions of old *Twilight Zone* scripts.

One of the most eagerly awaited horror films in 1987 was Clive Barker's debut as a director, *Hellraiser*. New World gave it a healthy promo budget, and the movie made money for all concerned. Based on Barker's script from his own novella, *The Hellbound Heart, Hellraiser* had lots of style, a modicum of disgusting scenes, and a healthy dollop of depravity and corruption. The movie was very similar to Barker's prose: When it worked, it functioned wonderfully well, but occasionally it staggered. There is reason to suspect that some of the film's problems were due to, or at least aggravated by, company interference—dubbing a number of the supporting roles into American English from the British, for example. But it did prove that New World's confidence and money were not misplaced in giving Barker a shot at direction. His theater background clearly stood him in good stead. Barker's next film project should be anticipated with well-founded glee.

The initial signs looked good for the summer's *Lost Boys*, a film about punk teenage vampires on the prowl in a modern California city. The music and flash turned out to be there. The plot wasn't, though there was a lot to be said for Kiefer Sutherland in the role of the leader of the band. Sutherland's eyes can look even meaner than those of Donald, his daddy. The entertainment aspect held up for most of the picture—but the ending seemed to be written into a corner. It never escaped.

So what was the best horror picture of 1987, or at least the most interesting? My nominee, humbly submitted, is a low-budget vampire drama called *Near Dark*. Cowritten by Eric Red (who also wrote yesteryear's impressive *The Hitcher*) and directed on location in such exotic locales as Oklahoma by Kathryn Bigelow, *Near Dark* is a sort of *Bonnie and Clyde* with bloodsucking. That doesn't do the movie justice. More properly, *Near Dark* is about a Civil War-era vampire who has assembled a makeshift nuclear family in contemporary America. They're all vampires, too, and they're frozen at various ages: the woman who is his companion, a teenage girl and a male teenage hood, an even younger boy named Homer who chafes at being forever prepubescent. The son of a small-town Oklahoma veterinarian gets involved with the vampire family and soon starts to learn an accelerated course in life, death, and undeath.

Some of *Near Dark* is extraordinarily fine in its execution (a bar scene and a shootout at a motel come to mind). Its only real weaknesses are a few shaky spots in the plot and a shorting of information about some of the vampire characters. By and large, *Near Dark* functions very effectively as melodrama about solid characters with consistent, understandable motives. Its characters have lives. That puts it ahead of most other horror films right there. Filmmakers should never discount wit and intelligence. *Near Dark* has those, as well as real style.

Made for probably a quarter of what *Lost Boys* cost, *Near Dark*'s plot shares a number of parallels with the former. On virtually every count, *Near Dark* comes out ahead. Catch it on video.

There weren't too many outright fantasies released last year. There was *Harry and the Hendersons*, true, but about the only successful aspect of this gentle family comedy about an American family adopting a Sasquatch was John Lithgow's performance as the father.

If you blinked, you missed *Wild Thing*, made from a script by John Sayles. *Wild Thing* was a *Tarzan/Greystoke*—like film about an urban foundling, his hippie parents murdered by drug traffickers, who is reared by a bag lady and the other denizens of the inner (and under) city. Naturally the sound track includes The Troggs.

A major fantasy for 1987 was the big-budget version of John Updike's *The Witches of Eastwick*. Cher, Susan Sarandon, and Michelle Pfeiffer were all, of course, a splendid ensemble of women raising the devil. As the latter, Jack Nicholson was terrific. The lavish look of the film belied the conventionality of the basic story.

*The* hit fantasy of the year was *The Princess Bride*. Directed by Rob Reiner from a script by William Goldman based on his novel, the picture had a considerable amount of straight-faced swordplay and derring-do, along with fairy-tale romance, humor, giant rats, and a pair of terrific cameos by Billy Crystal and Carol Kane. This was a confection that didn't sit comfortably with *all* viewers, but it satisfied quite a few people's craving for sheer entertainment. Audiences didn't feel they had to wash and sterilize their brains after watching.

There wasn't much of note on television. Fox Television syndicated *Werewolf*, a sort of *Fugitive* with paws. Super low-budget (one almost expects to see the ghost of Broderick Crawford from *Highway Patrol*), *Werewolf* entertains.

After much advance skepticism, *Beauty and the Beast* became the darling of the critics as well as CBS's most successful fall debut show. Storyedited by George R. R. Martin, the series depicts the purest, sweetest romance on television, as Ron Perlman's beast-man Vincent sighs and growls his way through dramatic plots with beauteous Linda Hamilton. Demographics have indicated that *Beauty and the Beast*'s audience is split about evenly between men and women. But all the mail comes from females. One of the show's staffers says, "We're deluged with letters from women who want to have Vincent's kittens." It isn't Cocteau, but what the heck.

And no, I'm not going to round out this report with a review of *The Garbage Pail Kids Movie*.

—Edward Bryant

# OBITUARIES

The following people involved in fantasy and horror died in 1987: **Donald A. Wandrei,** 79, who was a member of the Lovecraft circle, writer of early Weird Tales and cofounder with August Derleth of Arkham House, the small press book publisher. **Terry Carr,** 50, one of the finest editors of fantasy and science fiction for the last three decades, and the only free-lance editor to win the Hugo Award for Best Editor in Science Fiction. He edited numerous anthologies of new stories and reprints; his Universe series was a proving ground for many brilliant and innovative new writers. He edited two series of Ace Science Fiction Specials, landmark novels, some of which were fantasy. He was also a writer, although his strong, vivid fiction was always taking a back seat to his editing and his activity in fandom. **Randall Garrett,** 60, was a major writer of fantasy and science fiction, as well as one of the most beloved characters in the field. **Joseph Campbell,** 83, was best known as a writer on myth, and his book, *The Hero of a Thousand Faces,* is considered a seminal critical work. **James Tiptree, Jr.,** 71, was primarily known for her science fiction. Her real name was Alice Sheldon, and she won many major awards for her finely crafted and popular stories. **Danny Kaye,** 74, the actor, was perhaps best known for his portrayal of the title character in *The Secret Life of Walter Mitty.* **Bil Baird,** 82, was a pioneer puppeteer whom Jim Henson, the creator of the Muppets, felt was a major influence in teaching Henson and many of his puppet makers much of what they knew of the craft. **Rouben Mamoulian,** 90, directed, among many films, the classic *Dr. Jekyll and Mr. Hyde* (1932) that starred Fredric March. **Hugh Wheeler,** 75, playwright, novelist, and screenwriter, was perhaps best known for the book of the musical play, *Sweeney Todd.* **Mervyn Le Roy,** 86, produced *The Wizard of Oz,* and directed many other films in a long Hollywood career. **C. L. Moore,** 76, was one of the best known fantasy and science fiction writers of the '40s and '50s, and a screen and television writer on several popular series and a number of films. **Cecil Madden,** 84, was a radio and TV producer. In 1936 he invited Algernon Blackwood to appear on the first TV program, *Picture Page* in Great Britain. He also produced *Nightmare,* a series of weird stories for BBC radio. **Lee Wright,** 82, started the Inner Sanctum mystery imprint at Simon & Shuster in the early 1940s. It was the premier suspense, mystery, and horror line of its era. In 1956 she moved to Random House and later was the editor of *Rosemary's Baby* by Ira Levin. **Bernhardt J. Hurwood,** 60, wrote *My Savage Muse,* an Imaginary Autobiography of Edgar Allen Poe, *Vampires, Werewolves and Ghouls,* and *Passport to the Supernatural.* **Carlos Clarens,** 56, film historian and author of *An Illustrated History of the Horror Film* (Putnam, 1967). His work also appeared in such magazines as *Film Quarterly* and *Films in Review.* **Arch Oboler,** 79, was known to radio audiences for his *Lights Out* radio dramas of the 1930s and '40s, stories, "not for the squeamish." He also wrote, produced, and directed the first feature-length commercial 3-D motion picture, *Bwana Devil,* which opened to universal pans. In 1951 he made the film *Five,* one of the first films to deal with survivors of an atomic war and *The Twonky,* in 1953, based on Henry Kuttner's short story.

**Will Sampson,** 53, was the six-foot-seven-inch actor who played the silent Indian in the film *One Flew over the Cuckoo's Nest* and most recently portrayed a demon-battling Indian in *Poltergeist II: The Other Side.* **Madge Kennedy,** 96, had parts in many TV series including The Twilight Zone and *Alfred Hitchcock Presents.* **Judge Robert H. Gollmar,** 84, presided over the 1957 trial of Ed Gein, the murderer upon whom the *Texas Chainsaw Massacre* is based and the situation upon which Robert Bloch based his novel *Psycho,* which later become the movie directed by Alfred Hitchcock. **Jack Rabin** was a pioneer special effects technician and matte artist. His films included *The Night of the Hunter,* based on Davis Grubb's novel, and *The Black Book,* and with his partner Irving Block, *Invaders From Mars.* **King Donovon,** 69, was a character actor who appeared in *The Beast From 20,000 Fathoms, The Magnetic Monster,* and *The Invasion of the Body Snatchers.* **George Franju,** 75, was the French film director of the horror classic *Les Yeux Sans Visage (Eyes Without a Face).*

—E.D.

# URSULA K. LE GUIN

## Buffalo Gals, Won't You Come Out Tonight

Ursula Le Guin, the award-winning author of such science fiction novels as *The Left Hand of Darkness* and *The Dispossessed,* is also a master fantasist, having influenced a generation of new fantasy writers with her now classic "Earthsea" trilogy, published as young adult fiction: *A Wizard of Earthsea, The Tombs of Atuan*, and *The Farthest Shore*. Le Guin is also the author of many fantasy stories—from imaginary-land fantasy to stories that could be described as "magic realism" or surrealism—in the collections *The Wind's Twelve Quarters, Orsinian Tales*, and *The Compass Rose*, in numerous anthologies, and in magazines as varied as *The Magazine of Fantasy and Science Fiction* and *The New Yorker*. "Buffalo Gals, Won't You Come Out Tonight?" is an evocative adult fable using magical imagery drawn from America's own rich folkloric traditions, rather than relying on the European and British traditions so prevalent in modern fantasy writing.

—T.W.

# BUFFALO GALS, WON'T YOU COME OUT TONIGHT

## Ursula K. Le Guin

### 1

"You fell out of the sky," coyote said.

Still curled up tight, lying on her side, her back pressed against the overhanging rock, the child watched the coyote with one eye. Over the other eye she kept her hand cupped, its back on the dirt.

"There was a burned place in the sky, up there alongside the rimrock, and then you fell out of it," the coyote repeated, patiently, as if the news was getting a bit stale. "Are you hurt?"

She was all right. She was in the plane with Mr. Michaels, and the motor was so loud she couldn't understand what he said even when he shouted, and the way the wind rocked the wings was making her feel sick, but it was all right. They were flying to Canyonville. In the plane.

She looked. The coyote was still sitting there. It yawned. It was a big one, in good condition, its coat silvery and thick. The dark tear line back from its long yellow eye was as clearly marked as a tabby cat's.

She sat up slowly, still holding her right hand pressed to her right eye.

"Did you lose an eye?" the coyote asked, interested.

"I don't know," the child said. She caught her breath and shivered. "I'm cold."

"I'll help you look for it," the coyote said. "Come on! If you move around, you won't have to shiver. The sun's up."

Cold, lonely brightness lay across the falling land, a hundred miles of sagebrush. The coyote was trotting busily around, nosing under clumps of rabbitbrush and cheatgrass, pawing at a rock. "Aren't you going to look?" it said, suddenly sitting down on its haunches and abandoning the search. "I knew a trick once where I could throw my eyes way up into a tree and see everything from up there, and then whistle, and they'd come back into my head. But that goddamn bluejay stole them, and when I whistled, nothing came. I had to stick lumps of pine pitch into my head so I could

2

see anything. You could try that. But you've got one eye that's O.K.; what do you need two for? Are you coming, or are you dying there?"

The child crouched, shivering.

"Well, come if you want to," said the coyote, yawned again, snapped at a flea, stood up, turned, and trotted away among the sparse clumps of rabbitbrush and sage, along the long slope that stretched on down and down into the plain streaked across by long shadows of sagebrush. The slender gray-yellow animal was hard to keep in sight, vanishing as the child watched.

She struggled to her feet and—without a word, though she kept saying in her mind, "Wait, please wait"—she hobbled after the coyote. She could not see it. She kept her hand pressed over the right eye socket. Seeing with one eye, there was no depth; it was like a huge, flat picture. The coyote suddenly sat in the middle of the picture, looking back at her, its mouth open, its eyes narrowed, grinning. Her legs began to steady, and her head did not pound so hard, though the deep black ache was always there. She had nearly caught up to the coyote, when it trotted off again. This time she spoke. "Please wait!" she said.

"O.K.," said the coyote, but it trotted right on. She followed, walking downhill into the flat picture that at each step was deep.

Each step was different underfoot; each sage bush was different, and all the same. Following the coyote, she came out from the shadow of the rimrock cliffs, and the sun at eye level dazzled her left eye. Its bright warmth soaked into her muscles and bones at once. The air, which all night had been so hard to breathe, came sweet and easy.

The sage bushes were pulling in their shadows, and the sun was hot on the child's back when she followed the coyote along the rim of a gully. After a while the coyote slanted down the undercut slope, and the child scrambled after, through scrub willows to the thin creek in its wide sand bed. Both drank.

The coyote crossed the creek, not with a careless charge and splashing like a dog, but single foot and quiet like a cat; always it carried its tail low. The child hesitated, knowing that wet shoes make blistered feet, and then waded across in as few steps as possible. Her right arm ached with the effort of holding her hand up over her eye. "I need a bandage," she said to the coyote. It cocked its head and said nothing. It stretched out its forelegs and lay watching the water, resting but alert. The child sat down nearby on the hot sand and tried to move her right hand. It was glued to the skin around her eye by dried blood. At the little tearing-away pain, she whimpered; though it was a small pain, it frightened her. The coyote came over close and poked its long snout into her face. Its strong, sharp smell was in her nostrils. It began to lick the awful, aching blindness, cleaning and cleaning with its curled, precise, strong, wet tongue, until the child was able to cry a little with relief, being comforted. Her head was bent close to the gray-yellow ribs, and she saw the hard nipples, the whitish belly fur. She put her arm around the she-coyote, stroking the harsh coat over back and ribs.

"O.K.," the coyote said, "let's go!" And set off without a backward glance. The child scrambled to her feet and followed. "Where are we going?" she said, and the coyote, trotting on down along the creek, answered, "On down along the creek. . . ."

There must have been a time while she was asleep that she walked because she felt like she was waking up, but she was walking along only in a different place. They were still following the creek, though the gully had flattened out to nothing much, and there was still sagebrush range as far as the eye could see. The eye—the good one—felt rested. The other one still ached, but not so sharply, and there was no use thinking about it. But where was the coyote?

She stopped. The pit of cold into which the plane had fallen reopened, and she fell. She stood falling, a thin whimper making itself in her throat.

"Over here!"

The child turned.

She saw a coyote gnawing at the half-dried-up carcass of a crow, black feathers sticking to the black lips and narrow jaw.

She saw a tawny-skinned woman kneeling by a campfire, sprinkling something into a conical pot. She heard the water boiling in the pot, though it was propped between rocks, off the fire. The woman's hair was yellow and gray, bound back with a string. Her feet were bare. The upturned soles looked as dark and hard as shoe soles, but the arch of the foot was high, and the toes made two neat curving rows. She wore blue jeans and an old white shirt. She looked over at the girl. "Come on, eat crow!" she said.

The child slowly came toward the woman and the fire, and squatted down. She had stopped falling and felt very light and empty; and her tongue was like a piece of wood stuck in her mouth.

Coyote was now blowing into the pot or basket or whatever it was. She reached into it with two fingers, and pulled her hand away, shaking it and shouting, "Ow! Shit! Why don't I ever have any spoons?" She broke off a dead twig of sagebrush, dipped it into the pot, and licked it. "Oh boy," she said. "Come on!"

The child moved a little closer, broke off a twig, dipped. Lumpy pinkish mush clung to the twig. She licked. The taste was rich and delicate.

"What is it?" she asked after a long time of dipping and licking.

"Food. Dried salmon mush," Coyote said. "It's cooling down." She stuck two fingers into the mush again, this time getting a good load, which she ate very neatly. The child, when she tried, got mush all over her chin. It was like chopsticks: it took practice. She practiced. They ate turn and turn until nothing was left in the pot but three rocks. The child did not ask why there were rocks in the mush pot. They licked the rocks clean. Coyote licked out the inside of the pot-basket, rinsed it once in the creek, and put it onto her head. It fit nicely, making a conical hat. She pulled off her blue jeans. "Piss on the fire!" she cried, and did so, standing straddling it. "Ah, steam between the legs!" she said. The child, embarrassed, thought she was supposed to do the same thing, but did not want to, and did not. Bareassed, Coyote danced around the dampened fire, kicking her long, thin legs out and singing:

> *Buffalo gals, won't you come out tonight*
> *Come out tonight, come out tonight,*
> *Buffalo gals, won't you come out tonight,*
> *And dance by the light of the moon?*

She pulled her jeans back on. The child was burying the remains of the fire in creek sand, heaping it over, seriously, wanting to do right. Coyote watched her.

"Is that you?" she said. "A Buffalo Gal? What happened to the rest of you?"

"The rest of me?" The child looked at herself, alarmed.

"All your people."

"Oh. Well, Mom took Bobbie—he's my little brother—away with Uncle Norm. He isn't really my uncle or anything. So Mr. Michaels was going there anyway, so he was going to fly me over to my real father, in Canyonville. Linda—my stepmother, you know—she said it was O.K. for the summer anyhow if I was there, and then we could see. But the plane."

In the silence the girl's face became dark red, then grayish white. Coyote watched, fascinated. "Oh," the girl said, "oh—oh—Mr. Michaels—he must be—Did the—"

"Come on!" said Coyote, and set off walking.

The child cried, "I ought to go back—"

"What for?" said Coyote. She stopped to look round at the child, then went on faster. "Come on, Gal!" She said it as a name; maybe it was the child's name, Myra, as spoken by Coyote. The child, confused and despairing, protested again, but followed her. "Where are we going? Where *are* we?"

"This is my country," Coyote answered with dignity, making a long, slow gesture all round the vast horizon. "I made it. Every goddamn sage brush."

And they went on. Coyote's gait was easy, even a little shambling, but she covered the ground; the child struggled not to drop behind. Shadows were beginning to pull themselves out again from under the rocks and shrubs. Leaving the creek, Coyote and the child went up a long, low, uneven slope that ended away off against the sky in rimrock. Dark trees stood one here, another way other there; what people called a juniper forest, a desert forest, one with a lot more between the trees than trees. Each juniper they passed smelled sharply—cat-pee smell the kids at school called it—but the child liked it; it seemed to go into her mind and wake her up. She picked off a juniper berry and held it in her mouth, but after a while spat it out again. The aching was coming back in huge black waves, and she kept stumbling. She found that she was sitting down on the ground. When she tried to get up, her legs shook and would not go under her. She felt foolish and frightened, and began to cry.

"We're home!" Coyote called from way on up the hill.

The child looked with her one weeping eye, and saw sagebrush, juniper, cheatgrass, rimrock. She heard a coyote yip far off in the dry twilight.

She saw a little town up under the rimrock: board houses, shacks, all unpainted. She heard Coyote call again, "Come on, pup! Come on, Gal, we're home!"

She could not get up, so she tried to go on all fours, the long way up the slope to the houses under the rimrock. Long before she got there, several people came to meet her. They were all children, she thought at first, and then began to understand that most of them were grown-people, but all were very short; they were broad-bodied, fat, with fine, delicate hands and feet. Their eyes were bright. Some of the women helped her stand up and walk, coaxing her, "It isn't much farther, you're doing fine." In the late dusk, lights shone yellow-bright through doorways and through unchinked cracks between boards. Woodsmoke hung sweet in the quiet air. The short people talked and laughed all the time, softly. "Where's she going to stay?"—"Put her in with Robin, they're all asleep already!"—"Oh, she can stay with us."

The child asked hoarsely, "Where's Coyote?"

"Out hunting," the short people said.

A deeper voice spoke: "Somebody new has come into town?"

"Yes, a new person," one of the short men answered.

Among these people the deep-voiced man bulked impressive; he was broad and tall, with powerful hands, a big head, a short neck. They made way for him respectfully. He moved very quietly, respectful of them also. His eyes when he stared down at the child were amazing. When he blinked, it was like the passing of a hand before a candle flame.

"It's only an owlet," he said. "What have you let happen to your eye, new person?"

"I was—We were flying—"

"You're too young to fly," the big man said in his deep, soft voice. "Who brought you here?"

"Coyote."

And one of the short people confirmed: "She came here with Coyote, Young Owl."

"Then maybe she should stay in Coyote's house tonight," the big man said.

"It's all bones and lonely in there," said a short woman with fat cheeks and a striped shirt. "She can come with us."

That seemed to decide it. The fat-cheeked woman patted the child's arm and took her past several shacks and shanties to a low, windowless house. The doorway was so low even the child had to duck down to enter. There were a lot of people inside, some already there and some crowding in after the fat-cheeked woman. Several babies were fast asleep in cradleboxes in the corner. There was a good fire, and a good smell, like toasted sesame seeds. The child was given food and ate a little, but her head swam, and the blackness in her right eye kept coming across her left eye, so she could not see at all for a while. Nobody asked her name or told her what to call them. She heard the children call the fat-cheeked woman Chipmunk. She got up courage finally to say, "Is there somewhere I can go to sleep, Mrs. Chipmunk?"

"Sure, come on," one of the daughters said, "in here," and took the child into a back room, not completely partitioned off from the crowded front room, but dark and uncrowded. Big shelves with mattresses and blankets lined the walls. "Crawl in!" said Chipmunk's daughter, patting the child's arm in the comforting way they had. The child climbed onto a shelf, under a blanket. She laid down her head. She thought, "I didn't brush my teeth."


2


She woke; she slept again. In Chipmunk's sleeping room it was always stuffy, warm, and half dark, day and night. People came in and slept and got up and left, night and day. She dozed and slept, got down to drink from the bucket and dipper in the front room, and went back to sleep and doze.

She was sitting up on the shelf, her feet dangling, not feeling bad anymore, but dreamy, weak. She felt in her jeans pocket. In the left front one was a pocket comb and a bubble gum wrapper; in the right front, two dollar bills and a quarter and a dime.

Chipmunk and another woman—a very pretty, dark-eyed, plump one —came in. "So you woke up for your dance!" Chipmunk greeted her, laughing, and sat down by her with an arm around her.

"Jay's giving you a dance," the dark woman said. "He's going to make you all right. Let's get you all ready!"

There was a spring up under the rimrock, which flattened out into a pool with slimy, reedy shores. A flock of noisy children splashing in it ran off and left the child and the two women to bathe. The water was warm on the surface, cold down on the feet and legs. All naked, the two soft-voiced, laughing women, their round bellies and breasts, broad hips and buttocks gleaming warm in the late-afternoon light, sluiced the child down, washed and stroked her limbs and hands and hair, cleaned around the cheekbone and eyebrow of her right eye with infinite softness, admired her, sudsed her, rinsed her, splashed her out of the water, dried her off, dried each other off, got dressed, dressed her, braided her hair, braided each other's hair, tied feathers on the braid-ends, admired her and each other again, and brought her back down into the little straggling town and to a kind of playing field or dirt parking lot in among the houses. There were no streets, just paths and dirt; no lawns and gardens, just sagebrush and dirt. Quite a few people were gathering or wandering around the open place, looking dressed up, wearing colorful shirts, bright dresses, strings of beads, earrings. "Hey there, Chipmunk, Whitefoot!" they greeted the women.

A man in new jeans, with a bright blue velveteen vest over a clean, faded blue work shirt, came forward to meet them, very handsome, tense, and important. "All right, Gal!" he said in a harsh, loud voice, which startled among all these soft-speaking people. "We're going to get that eye fixed right up tonight! You just sit down here and don't worry about a thing." He took her wrist, gently despite his bossy, brassy manner, and led her to a woven mat that lay on the dirt near the middle of the open place. There, feeling very foolish, she had to sit down, and was told to stay still. She soon got over feeling that everybody was looking at her, since nobody paid her more attention than a checking glance or, from Chipmunk or Whitefoot and their families, a reassuring wink. Every now and then, Jay rushed over to her and said something like, "Going to be as good as new!" and went off again to organize people, waving his long blue arms and shouting.

Coming up the hill to the open place, a lean, loose, tawny figure—and the child started to jump up, remembered she was to sit still, and sat still, calling out softly, "Coyote! Coyote!"

Coyote came lounging by. She grinned. She stood looking down at the child. "Don't let that Bluejay fuck you up, Gal," she said, and lounged on.

The child's gaze followed her, yearning.

People were sitting down now over on one side of the open place, making an uneven half circle that kept getting added to at the ends until there was nearly a circle of people sitting on the dirt around the child, ten or fifteen paces from her. All the people wore the kind of clothes the child was used to—jeans and jeans jackets, shirts, vests, cotton dresses—but they were all barefoot; and she thought they were more beautiful than the people she knew, each in a different way, as if each one had invented beauty. Yet some of them were also very strange: thin black shining people with whispery voices, a long-legged woman with eyes like jewels. The big man called Young Owl was there, sleepy-looking and dignified, like Judge McCown who owned a sixty-thousand acre ranch. And beside him was a woman the child thought might be his sister, for like him she had a hook nose and big, strong hands; but she was lean and dark, and there was a crazy look in her fierce eyes. Yellow eyes, but round, not long and slanted like Coyote's. There was Coyote sitting yawning, scratching her armpit, bored. Now somebody was entering the circle: a man, wearing only a kind of kilt and a cloak painted or beaded with diamond shapes, dancing to the rhythm of the rattle he carried and shook with a buzzing fast beat. His limbs and body were thick yet supple, his movements smooth and pouring. The child kept her gaze on him as he danced past her, around her, past again. The rattle in his hand shook almost too fast to see; in the other hand was something thin and sharp. People were singing around the circle now, a few notes repeated in time to the rattle, soft and tuneless. It was exciting and boring, strange and familiar. The Rattler wove his dancing closer and closer to her, darting at her. The first time, she flinched away, frightened by the lunging movement and by his flat, cold face with narrow eyes, but after that she sat still, knowing her part. The dancing went on, the singing went on, till they carried her past boredom into a floating that could go on forever.

Jay had come strutting into the circle and was standing beside her. He couldn't sing, but he called out, "Hey! Hey! Hey! Hey!" in his big, harsh voice, and everybody answered from all round, and the echo came down from the rimrock on the second beat. Jay was holding up a stick with a ball on it in one hand, and something like a marble in the other. The stick was a pipe: he got smoke into his mouth from it and blew it in four directions and up and down and then over the marble, a puff each time. Then the rattle stopped suddenly, and everything was silent for several breaths. Jay squatted down and looked intently into the child's face, his head cocked to one side. He reached forward, muttering something in time to the rattle and the singing that had started up again louder than before; he touched the child's right eye in the black center of the pain. She flinched and endured. His touch was not gentle. She saw the marble, a dull yellow ball like beeswax, in his hand; then she shut her seeing eye and set her teeth.

"There!" Jay shouted. "Open up. Come on! Let's see!"

Her jaw clenched like a vise, she opened both eyes. The lid of the right one stuck and dragged with such a searing white pain that she nearly threw up as she sat there in the middle of everybody watching.

"Hey, can you see? How's it work? It looks great!" Jay was shaking her arm, railing at her. "How's it feel? Is it working?"

What she saw was confused, hazy, yellowish. She began to discover, as everybody came crowding around peering at her—smiling, stroking and patting her arms and shoulders—that if she shut the hurting eye and looked with the other, everything was clear and flat; if she used them both, things were blurry and yellowish, but deep.

There, right close, was Coyote's long nose and narrow eyes and grin. "What is it, Jay?" she was asking, peering at the new eye. "One of mine you stole that time?"

"It's pine pitch," Jay shouted furiously. "You think I'd use some stupid secondhand coyote eye? I'm a doctor!"

"Ooooh, ooooh, a doctor," Coyote said. "Boy, that is one ugly eye. Why didn't you ask Rabbit for a rabbit dropping? That eye looks like shit." She put her lean face yet closer, till the child thought she was going to kiss her; instead, the thin, firm tongue once more licked accurately across the pain, cooling, clearing. When the child opened both eyes again, the world looked pretty good.

"It works fine," she said.

"Hey!" Jay yelled. "She says it works fine! It works fine; she says so! I told you! What'd I tell you?" He went off waving his arms and yelling. Coyote had disappeared. Everybody was wandering off.

The child stood up, stiff from long sitting. It was nearly dark; only the long west held a great depth of pale radiance. Eastward, the plains ran down into night.

Lights were on in some of the shanties. Off at the edge of town, somebody was playing a creaky fiddle, a lonesome chirping tune.

A person came beside her and spoke quietly: "Where will you stay?"

"I don't know," the child said. She was feeling extremely hungry. "Can I stay with Coyote?"

"She isn't home much," the soft-voiced woman said. "You were staying with Chipmunk, weren't you? Or there's Rabbit, or Jackrabbit; they have families. . . ."

"Do you have a family?" the girl asked, looking at the delicate, soft-eyed woman.

"Two fawns," the woman answered, smiling. "But I just came into town for the dance."

"I'd really like to stay with Coyote," the child said after a pause, timid but obstinate.

"O.K., that's fine. Her house is over here." Doe walked along beside the child to a ramshackle cabin on the high edge of town. No light shone from inside. A lot of junk was scattered around the front. There was no step up to the half-open door. Over a battered pine board, nailed up crooked, said: "Bide-A-Wee."

"Hey, Coyote? Visitors," Doe said. Nothing happened.

Doe pushed the door farther open and peered in. "She's out hunting, I guess. I better be getting back to the fawns. You going to be O.K.? Anybody else here will give you something to eat—you know. . . . O.K.?"

"Yeah. I'm fine. Thank you," the child said.

She watched Doe walk away through the clear twilight, a severely elegant walk, small steps, like a woman in high heels, quick, precise, very light.

Inside Bide-A-Wee it was too dark to see anything, and so cluttered that she fell over something at every step. She could not figure out where or how to light a fire. There was something that felt like a bed, but when she lay down on it, it felt more like a dirty-clothes pile, and smelled like one. Things bit her legs, arms, neck, and back. She was terribly hungry. By smell, she found her way to what had to be a dead fish hanging from the ceiling in one corner. By feel, she broke off a greasy flake and tasted it. It was smoked, dried salmon. She ate one succulent piece after another until she was satisfied, and licked her fingers clean. Near the open door, starlight shone on water in a pot of some kind; the child smelled it cautiously, tasted it cautiously, and drank just enough to quench her thirst, for it tasted of mud and was warm and stale. Then she went back to the bed of dirty clothes and fleas, and lay down. She could have gone to Chipmunk's house, or other friendly households; she thought of that as she lay forlorn in Coyote's dirty bed. But she did not go. She slapped at fleas until she fell asleep.

Along in the deep night, somebody said, "Move over, pup," and was warm beside her.

Breakfast, eaten sitting in the sun in the doorway, was dried-salmon-powder mush. Coyote hunted, morning and evenings, but what they ate was not fresh game but salmon, and dried stuff, and any berries in season. The child did not ask about this. It made sense to her. She was going to ask Coyote why she slept at night and waked in the day like humans, instead of the other way round like coyotes, but when she framed the question in her mind, she saw at once that night is when you sleep and day when you're awake; that made sense, too. But one question she did ask, one hot day when they were lying around slapping fleas.

"I don't understand why you all look like people," she said.

"We are people."

"I mean, people like me, humans."

"Resemblance is in the eye," Coyote said. "How is that lousy eye, by the way?"

"It's fine. But—like you wear clothes—and live in houses—with fires and stuff—"

"That's what *you* think. . . . If that loudmouth Jay hadn't horned in, I could have done a really good job."

The child was quite used to Coyote's disinclination to stick to any one

subject, and to her boasting. Coyote was like a lot of kids she knew, in
some respects. Not in others.

"You mean what I'm seeing isn't true? Isn't real—like TV or something?"

"No," Coyote said. "Hey, that's a tick on your collar." She reached
over, flicked the tick off, picked it up on one finger, bit it, and spat out
the bits.

"Yecch!" the child said. "So?"

"So, to me, you're basically grayish yellow and run on four legs. To that
lot"—she waved disdainfully at the warren of little houses next down the
hill—"you hop around twitching your nose all the time. To Hawk, you're
an egg, or maybe getting pinfeathers. See? It just depends on how you look
at things. There are only two kinds of people."

"Humans and animals?"

"No. The kind of people who say, 'There are two kinds of people,'
and the kind of people who don't." Coyote cracked up, pounding her
thighs and yelling with delight at her joke. The child didn't get it, and
waited.

"O.K.," Coyote said. "There's the first people, and then the others.
Those're the two kinds."

"The first people are—?"

"Us, the animals . . . and things. All the old ones. You know. And you
pups, kids, fledglings. All first people."

"And the—others?"

"Them," Coyote said. "You know. The others. The new people. The
ones who came." Her fine, hard face had gone serious, rather formidable.
She glanced directly, as she seldom did, at the child, a brief gold sharpness.
"We are here," she said. "We are always here. We are always here. Where
we are is here. But it's their country now. They're running it. . . . Shit,
even I did better!"

The child pondered and offered a word she had used to hear a good deal:
"They're illegal immigrants."

"Illegal!" Coyote said, mocking, sneering. "Illegal is a sick bird. What
the fuck's illegal mean? You want a code of justice from a coyote? Grow
up kid!"

"I don't want to."

"You don't want to grow up?"

"I'll be the other kind if I do."

"Yeah. So," Coyote said, and shrugged. "That's life." She got up and
went around the house, and the child heard her pissing in the backyard.

A lot of things were hard to take about Coyote as a mother. When her
boyfriends came to visit, the child learned to go stay with Chipmunk or
the Rabbits for the night, because Coyote and her friend wouldn't even wait
to get on the bed, but would start doing that right on the floor or even

out in the yard. A couple of times, Coyote came back late from hunting with a friend, and the child had to lie up against the wall in the same bed and hear and feel them doing that right next to her. It was something like fighting and something like dancing, with a beat to it, and she didn't mind too much except that it made it hard to stay asleep. Once she woke up and one of Coyote's friends was stroking her stomach in a creepy way. She didn't know what to do, but Coyote woke up and realized what he was doing, bit him hard, and kicked him out of bed. He spent the night on the floor, and apologized next morning—"Aw, hell, Ki, I forgot the kid was there; I thought it was you—"

Coyote, unappeased, yelled, "You think I don't got any standards? You think I'd let some coyote rape a kid in my *bed*?" She kicked him out of the house, and grumbled about him all day. But a while later he spent the night again, and he and Coyote did that three or four times.

Another thing that was embarrassing was the way Coyote peed anywhere, taking her pants down in public. But most people here didn't seem to care. The thing that worried the child most, maybe, was when Coyote did number two anywhere and then turned around and talked to it. That seemed so awful. As if Coyote were—the way she often seemed, but really wasn't—crazy.

The child gathered up all the old dry turds from around the house one day while Coyote was having a nap, and buried them in a sandy place near where she and Bobcat and some of the other people generally went and did and buried their number twos.

Coyote woke up, came lounging out of Bide-A-Wee, rubbing her hands through her thick, fair, grayish hair and yawning, looked all round once with those narrow eyes, and said, "Hey! Where are they?" Then she shouted, "Where are you? Where are you?"

And a faint chorus came from over in the draw: "Mommy! We're here!"

Coyote trotted over, squatted down, raked out every turd, and talked with them for a long time. When she came back, she said nothing, but the child, red-faced and heart pounding, said, "I'm sorry I did that."

"It's just easier when they're all around close by," Coyote said, washing her hands (despite the filth of her house, she kept herself quite clean, in her own fashion).

"I kept stepping on them," the child said, trying to justify her deed.

"Poor little shits," said Coyote, practicing dance steps.

"Coyote," the child said timidly. "Did you ever have any children? I mean real pups?"

"Did I? Did I have children? Litters! That one that tried feeling you up, you know? That was my son. Pick of the litter. . . . Listen, Gal. Have daughters. When you have anything, have daughters. At least they clear out."

3

The child thought of herself as Gal, but also sometimes as Myra. So far as she knew, she was the only person in town who had two names. She had to think about that, and about what Coyote had said about the two kinds of people; she had to think about where she belonged. Some persons in town made it clear that as far as they were concerned, she didn't and never would belong there. Hawk's furious stare burned through her; the Skunk children made audible remarks about what she smelled like. And though Whitefoot and Chipmunk and their families were kind, it was the generosity of big families, where one more or less simply doesn't count. If one of them, or Cottontail, or Jackrabbit, had come upon her in the desert lying lost and half blind, would they have stayed with her, like Coyote? That was Coyote's craziness, what they called her craziness. She wasn't afraid. She went between the two kinds of people; she crossed over. Buck and Doe and their beautiful children were really afraid, because they lived so constantly in danger. The Rattler wasn't afraid, because he was so dangerous. And yet maybe he was afraid of her, for he never spoke, and never came close to her. None of them treated her the way Coyote did. Even among the children, her only constant playmate was one younger than herself, a preposterous and fearless little boy called Horned Toad Child. They dug and built together, out among the sagebrush, and played at hunting and gathering and keeping house and holding dances, all the great games. A pale, squatty child with fringed eyebrows, he was a self-contained but loyal friend; and he knew a good deal for his age.

"There isn't anybody else like me here," she said as they sat by the pool in the morning sunlight.

"There isn't anybody much like me anywhere," said Horned Toad Child.

"Well, you know what I mean."

"Yeah. . . . There used to be people like you around, I guess."

"What were they called?"

"Oh—people. Like everybody. . . ."

"But where do *my* people live? They have towns. I used to live in one. I don't know where they are, is all. I ought to find out. I don't know where my mother is now, but daddy's in Canyonville. I was going there when. . . ."

"Ask Horse," said Horned Toad Child sagaciously. He had moved away from the water, which he did not like and never drank, and was plaiting rushes.

"I don't know Horse."

"He hangs around the butte down there a lot of the time. He's waiting till his uncle gets old and he can kick him out and be the big honcho. The old man and the women don't want him around till then. Horses are weird. Anyway, he's the one to ask. He gets around a lot. And his people came here with the new people; that's what they say, anyhow."

Illegal immigrants, the girl thought. She took Horned Toad's advice, and one long day when Coyote was gone on one of her unannounced and unexplained trips, she took a pouchful of dried salmon and salmonberries and went off alone to the flat-topped butte miles away in the southwest.

There was a beautiful spring at the foot of the butte, and a trail to it with a lot of footprints on it. She waited there under willows by the clear pool, and after a while Horse came running, splendid, with copper-red skin and long, strong legs, deep chest, dark eyes, his black hair whipping his back as he ran. He stopped, not at all winded, and gave a snort as he looked at her. "Who are you?"

Nobody in town asked that—ever. She saw it was true: Horse had come here with her people, people who had to ask each other who they were.

"I live with Coyote," she said cautiously.

"Oh sure, I heard about you," Horse said. He knelt to drink from the pool. Long, deep drafts, his hands plunged in the cool water. When he had drunk, he wiped his mouth, sat back on his heels, and announced, "I'm going to be king."

"King of the horses?"

"Right! Pretty soon now. I could lick the old man already, but I can wait. Let him have his day," said Horse, vainglorious, magnanimous. The child gazed at him, in love already, forever.

"I can comb your hair, if you like," she said.

"Great!" said Horse, and sat still while she stood behind him, tugging her pocket comb through his coarse, black, shining, yard-long hair. It took a long time to get it smooth. She tied it in a massive ponytail with willow bark when she was done. Horse bent over the pool to admire himself. "That's great," he said. "That's really beautiful!"

"Do you ever go   where the other people are?" she asked in a low voice.

He did not reply for long enough that she thought he wasn't going to; then he said, "You mean the metal places, the glass places? The holes? I go around them. There are all the walls now. There didn't used to be so many. Grandmother said there didn't use to be any walls. Do you know Grandmother?" he asked naively, looking at her with his great, dark eyes.

"Your grandmother?"

"Well, yes—Grandmother—you know. Who makes the web. Well, anyhow. I know there're some of my people, horses, there. I've seen them across the walls. They act really crazy. You know, we brought the new people here. They couldn't have got here without us: they have only two legs, and they have those metal shells. I can tell you that whole story. The king has to know the stories."

"I like stories a lot."

"It takes three nights to tell it. What do you want to know about them?"

"I was thinking that maybe I ought to go there. Where they are."

"It's dangerous. Really dangerous. You can't go through—they'd catch you."

"I'd just like to know the way."

"I know the way," Horse said, sounding for the first time entirely adult and reliable; she knew he did know the way. "It's a long run for a colt." He looked at her again. "I've got a cousin with different-color eyes," he said, looking from her right to her left eye. "One brown and one blue. But she's an Appaloosa."

"Bluejay made the yellow one," the child explained. "I lost my own one. In the . . . when. . . . You don't think I could get to those places?"

"Why do you want to?"

"I sort of feel like I have to."

Horse nodded. He got up. She stood still.

"I could take you, I guess," he said.

"Would you? When?"

"Oh, now, I guess. Once I'm king I won't be able to leave, you know. Have to protect the women. And I sure wouldn't let my people get anywhere near those places!" A shudder ran right down his magnificent body, yet he said, with a toss of his head, "They couldn't catch *me*, of course, but the others can't run like I do. . . ."

"How long would it take us?"

Horse thought for a while. "Well, the nearest place like that is over the red rocks. If we left now, we'd be back here around tomorrow noon. It's just a little hole."

She did not know what he meant by "a hole," but did not ask.

"You want to go?" Horse said, flipping back his ponytail.

"O.K.," the girl said, feeling the ground go out from under her.

"Can you run?"

She shook her head. "I walked here, though."

Horse laughed, a large, cheerful laugh. "Come on," he said, and knelt and held his hands back-turned like stirrups for her to mount to his shoulders. "What do they call you?" he teased, rising easily, setting right off at a jog trot. "Gnat? Fly? Flea?"

"Tick, because I stick!" the child cried, gripping the willow bark tie of the black mane, laughing with delight at being suddenly eight feet tall and traveling across the desert without even trying, like the tumbleweed, as fast as the wind.

Moon, a night past full, rose to light the plains for them. Horse jogged easily on and on. Somewhere deep in the night, they stopped at a Pygmy Owl camp, ate a little, and rested. Most of the owls were out hunting, but an old lady entertained them at her campfire, telling them tales about the ghost of a cricket, about the great invisible people, tales that the child heard interwoven with her own dreams as she dozed and half woke and dozed again. Then Horse put her up on his shoulders, and on they went at a tireless, slow lope. Moon went down behind them, and before them the sky paled into rose and gold. The soft night wind was gone; the air was sharp, cold, still. On it, in it, there was a faint, sour smell of burning. The child felt Horse's gait change, grow tighter, uneasy.

"Hey, Prince!"

A small, slightly scolding voice: the child knew it, and placed it as soon as she saw the person sitting by a juniper tree, neatly dressed, wearing an old black cap.

"Hey, Chickadee!" Horse said, coming round and stopping. The child had observed, back in Coyote's town, that everybody treated Chickadee with respect. She didn't see why. Chickadee seemed an ordinary person, busy and talkative like most of the small birds, nothing so endearing as Quail or so impressive as Hawk or Great Owl.

"You're going on that way?" Chickadee asked Horse.

"The little one wants to see if her people are living there," Horse said, surprising the child. Was that what she wanted?

Chickadee looked disapproving, as she often did. She whistled a few notes thoughtfully, another of her habits, and then got up. "I'll come along."

"That's great," Horse said thankfully.

"I'll scout," Chickadee said, and off she went, surprisingly fast, ahead of them, while Horse took up his steady, long lope.

The sour smell was stronger in the air.

Chickadee halted, way ahead of them on a slight rise, and stood still. Horse dropped to a walk, and then stopped. "There," she said in a low voice.

The child stared. In the strange light and slight mist before sunrise, she could not see clearly, and when she strained and peered, she felt as if her left eye were not seeing at all. "What is it?" she whispered.

"One of the holes. Across the wall—see?"

It did seem there was a line, a straight, jerky line drawn across the sagebrush plain, and on the far side of it—nothing? Was it mist? Something moved there—

"It's cattle!" she said.

Horse stood silent, uneasy. Chickadee was coming back toward them.

"It's a ranch," the child said. "That's a fence. There're a lot of Herefords." The words tasted like iron, like salt in her mouth. The things she named wavered in her sight and faded, leaving nothing—a hole in the world, a burned place like a cigarette burn. "Go closer!" she urged Horse. "I want to see."

And as if he owed her obedience, he went forward, tense but unquestioning.

Chickadee came up to them. "Nobody around," she said in her small, dry voice, "but there's one of those fast turtle things coming."

Horse nodded but kept going forward.

Gripping his broad shoulders, the child stared into the blank, and as if Chickadee's words had focused her eyes, she saw again: the scattered white-faces, a few of them looking up with bluish, rolling eyes—the fences—over the rise a chimneyed house roof and a high barn—and then in the distance, something moving fast, too fast, burning across the ground straight at them at terrible speed. "Run!" she yelled to Horse. "Run away! Run!" As if released from bonds, he wheeled and ran, flat out, in great reaching strides, away from sunrise, the fiery burning chariot, the smell of acid, iron, death. And Chickadee flew before them like a cinder on the air of dawn.

4

"Horse?" Coyote said. "That prick? Cat food!"

Coyote had been there when the child got home to Bide-A-Wee, but she clearly hadn't been worrying about where Gal was, and maybe hadn't even noticed she was gone. She was in a vile mood, and took it all wrong when the child tried to tell her about where she had been.

"If you're going to do damn fool things, next time do 'em with me; at least I'm an expert," she said, morose, and slouched out the door. The child saw her squatting down, poking an old white turd with a stick, trying to get it to answer some questions she kept asking it. The turd lay obstinately silent. Later in the day the child saw two coyote men, a young one and a mangy-looking older one, loitering around near the spring, looking over at Bide-A-Wee. She decided it would be a good night to spend somewhere else.

The thought of the crowded rooms of Chipmunk's house was not attractive. It was going to be a warm night again tonight, and moonlit. Maybe she would sleep outside. If she could feel sure some people wouldn't come around, like the Rattler. . . . She was standing indecisively halfway through town when a dry voice said, "Hey, Gal."

"Hey, Chickadee."

The trim, black-capped woman was standing on her doorstep shaking out a rug. She kept her house neat, trim like herself. Having come back across the desert with her, the child now knew, though she still could not have said, why Chickadee was a respected person.

"I thought maybe I'd sleep out tonight," the child said, tentative.

"Unhealthy," said Chickadee. "What are nests for?"

"Mom's kind of busy," the child said.

"Tsk!" went Chickadee, and snapped the rug with disapproving vigor. "What about her little friend? At least they're decent people."

"Horny-toad? His parents are so shy. . . ."

"Well. Come in and have something to eat, anyhow," said Chickadee.

The child helped her cook dinner. She knew now why there were rocks in the mush pot.

"Chickadee," she said, "I still don't understand; can I ask you? Mom said it depends who's seeing it, but still; I mean, if I see you wearing clothes and everything like humans, then how come you cook this way, in baskets, you know, and there aren't any—any of the things like they have—there where we were with Horse this morning?"

"I don't know," Chickadee said. Her voice indoors was quite soft and pleasant. "I guess we do things the way they always were done, when your people and my people lived together, you know. And together with everything else here. The rocks, you know. The plants and everything." She looked at the basket of willow bark, fern root, and pitch, at the blackened rocks that were heating in the fire. "You see how it all goes together. . . ."

"But you have fire—That's different—"

"Ah!" said Chickadee, impatient, "you people! Do you think you invented the sun?"

She took up the wooden tongs, plopped the heated rocks into the water-filled basket with a terrific hiss and steam and loud bubblings. The child sprinkled in the pounded seeds and stirred.

Chickadee brought out a basket of fine blackberries. They sat on the newly shaken-out rug and ate. The child's two-finger scoop technique with mush was now highly refined.

"Maybe I didn't cause the world," Chickadee said, "but I'm a better cook than Coyote."

The child nodded, stuffing.

"I don't know why I made Horse go there," she said after she had stuffed. "I got just as scared as he did when I saw it. But now I feel again like I have to go back there. But I want to stay here. With my friends, with Coyote. I don't understand."

"When we lived together, it was all one place," Chickadee said in her slow, soft home-voice. "But now the others, the new people, they live apart. And their places are so heavy. They weigh down on our place, they press on it, draw it, suck it, eat it, eat holes in it, crowd it out. . . . Maybe after a while longer, there'll be only one place again, their place. And none of us here. I knew Bison, out over the mountains. I knew Antelope right here. I knew Grizzly and Graywolf, up west there. Gone. All gone. And the salmon you eat at Coyote's house, those are the dream salmon, those are the true food; but in the rivers, how many salmon now? The rivers that were red with them in spring? Who dances, now, when the First Salmon offers himself? Who dances by the river? Oh, you should ask Coyote about all this. She knows more than I do! But she forgets. . . . She's hopeless, worse than Raven; she has to piss on every post; she's a terrible housekeeper. . . ." Chickadee's voice had sharpened. She whistled a note or two, and said no more.

After a while the child asked very softly, "Who is Grandmother?"

"Grandmother," Chickadee said. She looked at the child and ate several blackberries thoughtfully. She stroked the rug they sat on.

"If I built the fire on the rug, it would burn a hole in it," she said. "Right? So we build the fire on sand, on dirt. . . . Things are woven together. So we call the weaver the Grandmother." She whistled four notes, looking up the smoke hole. "After all," she added, "maybe all this place —the other places, too—maybe they're all only one side of the weaving. I don't know. I can look with one one eye at a time; how can I tell how deep it goes?"

Lying that night rolled up in a blanket in Chickadee's backyard, the child heard the wind soughing and storming in the cottonwoods down in the draw, and then slept deeply, weary from the long night before. Just at sunrise she woke. The eastern mountains were a cloudy dark red as if the level light shone through them as through a hand held before the fire. In the tobacco patch—the only farming anybody in this town did was to raise a little wild tobacco—Lizard and Beetle were singing some kind of growing song or blessing song, soft and desultory, *huh*-huh-huh-huh, *huh*-huh-huh-huh, and as she lay warm-curled on the ground, the song made her feel rooted in the ground, cradled on it and in it, so where her fingers ended and the dirt began, she did not know, as if she were dead—but she was wholly alive; she was the earth's life. She got up dancing, left the blanket folded neatly on Chickadee's nest and already empty bed, and danced up the hill to Bide-A-Wee. At the half-open door, she sang:

> *Danced with a gal with a hole in her stocking*
> *And her knees kept a knocking and her toes kept a rocking.*
> *Danced with a gal with a hole in her stocking.*
> *Danced by the light of the moon!*

Coyote emerged, tousled and lurching, and eyed her narrowly. "Sheeeoot," she said. She sucked her teeth and then went to splash water all over her head from the gourd by the door. She shook her head, and the water drops flew. "Let's get out of here," she said. "I have had it. I don't know what got into me. If I'm pregnant again, at my age, oh shit. Let's get out of town. I need a change of air."

In the fuggy dark of the house, the child could see at least two coyote men sprawled snoring away on the bed and floor.

Coyote walked over to the old white turd and kicked it. "Why didn't you stop me?" she shouted.

"I *told* you," the turd muttered sulkily.

"Dumb shit," Coyote said. "Come on, Gal. Let's go. Where to?" She didn't wait for an answer. "I know. Come on!"

And she set off through town at that lazy-looking, rangy walk that was so hard to keep up with. But the child was full of pep, and came dancing, so that Coyote began dancing, too, skipping and pirouetting and fooling around all the way down the long slope to the level plains. There she slanted their way off northeastward. Horse Butte was at their backs, getting smaller in the distance.

Along near noon the child said, "I didn't bring anything to eat."

"Something will turn up," Coyote said. "Sure to." And pretty soon she turned aside, going straight to a tiny gray shack hidden by a couple of half-dead junipers and a stand of rabbitbrush. The place smelled terrible. A sign on the door said: Fox. Private. No Trespassing!—but Coyote pushed it open, and trotted right back out with half a small smoked salmon. "Nobody home but us chickens," she said, grinning sweetly.

"Isn't that stealing?" the child asked, worried.

"Yes," Coyote answered, trotting on.

They ate the fox-scented salmon by a dried-up creek, slept a while, and went on.

Before long the child smelled the sour burning smell, and stopped. It was as if a huge, heavy hand had begun pushing her chest, pushing her away, and yet at the same time as if she had stepped into a strong current that drew her forward, helpless.

"Hey, getting close!" Coyote said, and stopped to piss by a juniper stump.

"Close to what?"

"Their town. See?" She pointed to a pair of sage-spotted hills. Between them was an area of grayish blank.

"I don't want to go there."

"We won't go all the way in. No way! We'll just get a little closer and look. It's fun," Coyote said, putting her head on one side, coaxing. "They do all these weird things in the air."

The child hung back.

Coyote became businesslike, responsible. "We're going to be very careful," she announced. "And look out for big dogs, O.K.? Little dogs I can handle. Make a good lunch. Big dogs, it goes the other way. Right? Let's go, then."

Seemingly as casual and lounging as ever, but with a tense alertness in the carriage of her head and the yellow glance of her eyes, Coyote led off again, not looking back; and the child followed.

All around them the pressures increased. It was as if the air itself were pressing on them, as if time were going too fast, too hard, not flowing but pounding, pounding, pounding, faster and harder till it buzzed like Rattler's rattle. "Hurry, you have to hurry!" everything said. "There isn't time!"

everything said. Things rushed past screaming and shuddering. Things turned, flashed, roared, stank, vanished. There was a boy—he came into focus all at once, but not on the ground: he was going along a couple of inches above the ground, moving very fast, bending his legs from side to side in a kind of frenzied, swaying dance, and was gone. Twenty children sat in rows in the air, all singing shrilly, and then the walls closed over them. A basket, no, a pot, no, a can, a garbage can, full of salmon smelling wonderful, no, full of stinking deer hides and rotten cabbage stalks—keep out of it. Coyote! Where was she?

"Mom!" the child called. "Mother!"—standing a moment at the end of an ordinary small-town street near the gas station, and the next moment in a terror of blanknesses, invisible walls, terrible smells and pressures and the overwhelming rush of Time straightforward rolling her helpless as a twig in the race above a waterfall. She clung, held on trying not to fall— "Mother!"

Coyote was over by the big basket of salmon, approaching it, wary but out in the open, in the full sunlight, in the full current. And a boy and a man borne by the same current were coming down the long, sage-spotted hill behind the gas station, each with a gun, red hats—hunters; it was killing season. "Hey, will you look at that damn coyote in broad daylight big as my wife's ass," the man said, and cocked, aimed, shot—all as Myra screamed and ran against the enormous drowning torrent. Coyote fled past her yelling, "Get out of here!" She turned and was borne away.

Far out of sight of that place, in a little draw among low hills, they sat and breathed air in searing gasps until, after a long time, it came easy again.

"Mom, that was *stupid*," the child said furiously.

"Sure was," Coyote said. "But did you see all that food!"

"I'm not hungry," the child said sullenly. "Not till we get all the way away from here."

"But they're your folks," Coyote said. "All yours. Your kith and kin and cousins and kind. Bang! Pow! There's Coyote! Bang! There's my wife's ass! Pow! There's anything—BOOOOM! Blow it away, man! BOOOOOOM!"

"I want to go home," the child said.

"Not yet," said Coyote. "I got to take a shit." She did so, then turned to the fresh turd, leaning over it. "It says I have to stay," she reported, smiling.

"It didn't say anything! I was listening!"

"You know who to understand? You hear everything, Miss Big Ears? Hears all—See all with her crummy, gummy eye—"

"You have pine-pitch eyes, too! You told me so!"

"That's a story," Coyote snarled. "You don't even know a story when you hear one! Look, do what you like; it's a free country. I'm hanging around here tonight. I like the action." She sat down and began patting her hands on the dirt in a soft four-four rhythm and singing under her breath, one of the endless, tuneless songs that kept time from running too fast, that wove the roots of trees and bushes and ferns and grass in the web that held the stream in the streambed and the rock in the rock's place and the earth together. And the child lay listening.

"I love you," she said.

Coyote went on singing.

Sun went down the last slope of the west and left a pale green clarity over the desert hills.

Coyote had stopped singing. She sniffed. "Hey," she said. "Dinner." She got up and moseyed along the little draw. "Yeah," she called back softly. "Come on!"

Stiffly, for the fear-crystals had not yet melted out of her joints, the child got up and went to Coyote. Off to one side along the hill was one of the lines, a fence. She didn't look at it. It was O.K. They were outside it.

"Look at that!"

A smoked salmon, a whole chinook, lay on a little cedar-bark mat.

"An offering! Well, I'll be darned!" Coyote was so impressed she didn't even swear. "I haven't seen one of these for years! I thought they'd forgotten!"

"Offering to whom?"

"Me! Who else? Boy, *look* at that!"

The child looked dubiously at the salmon.

"It smells funny."

"How funny?"

"Like burned."

"It's smoked, stupid! Come on."

"I'm not hungry."

"O.K. It's not your salmon anyhow. It's mine. My offering, for me. Hey, you people! You people over there! Coyote thanks you! Keep it up like this, and maybe I'll do some good things for you, too!"

"Don't, don't yell, Mom! They're not that far away—"

"They're all my people," said Coyote with a great gesture, and then sat down cross-legged, broke off a big piece of salmon, and ate.

Evening Star burned like a deep, bright pool of water in the clear sky. Down over the twin hills was a dim suffusion of light, like a fog. The child looked away from it, back at the star.

"Oh," Coyote said. "Oh shit."

"What's wrong?"

"That wasn't so smart, eating that," Coyote said, and then held herself and began to shiver, to scream, to choke—her eyes rolled up; her long arms and legs flew out jerking and dancing; foam spurted out between her teeth. Her body arched tremendously backward, and the child, trying to hold her, was thrown violently off by the spasms of her limbs. The child scrambled back and held the body as it spasmed again, twitched, quivered, went still.

By moonrise, Coyote was cold. Till then there had been so much warmth under the tawny coat that the child kept thinking maybe she was alive, maybe if she just kept holding her, keeping her warm, Coyote would recover, she would be all right. The child held her close, not looking at the black lips drawn back from the teeth, the white balls of the eyes. But when the cold came through the fur as the presence of death, the child let the slight, stiff corpse lie down on the dirt.

She went nearby and dug a hole in the stony sand of the draw, a shallow pit. Coyote's people did not bury their dead; she knew that. But her people did. She carried the small corpse to the pit, laid it down, and covered it with her blue and white bandanna. It was not large enough; the four stiff paws stuck out. The child heaped the body over with sand and rocks and a scurf of sagebrush and tumbleweed held down with more rocks. She also heaped dirt and rocks over the poisoned salmon carcass. Then she stood up and walked away without looking back.

At the top of the hill, she stood and looked across the draw toward the misty glow of the lights of the town lying in the pass between the twin hills.

"I hope you all die in pain," she said aloud. She turned away and walked down into the desert.

5

It was Chickadee who met her, on the second evening, north of Horse Butte.

"I didn't cry," the child said.

"None of us do," said Chickadee. "Come with me this way now. Come into Grandmother's house."

It was underground, but very large, dark and large, and the Grandmother was there at the center, at her loom. She was making a rug or blanket of the hills and the black rain and the white rain, weaving in the lightning. As they spoke, she wove.

"Hello, Chickadee. Hello, New Person."

"Grandmother," Chickadee greeted her.

The child said, "I'm not one of them."

Grandmother's eyes were small and dim. She smiled and wove. The shuttle thrummed through the warp.

"Old Person, then," said Grandmother. "You'd better go back there now, Granddaughter. That's where you live."

"I lived with Coyote. She's dead. They killed her."

"Oh, don't worry about Coyote!" Grandmother said with a little huff of laughter. "She gets killed all the time."

The child stood still. She saw the endless weaving.

"Then I—Could I go back home—to her house—?"

"I don't think it would work," Grandmother said. "Do you, Chickadee?"

Chickadee shook her head once, silent.

"It would be dark there now, and empty, and fleas. . . . You got outside your people's time, into our place, but I think that Coyote was taking you back, see. Her way. If you go back now, you can still live with them. Isn't your father there?"

The child nodded.

"They've been looking for you."

"They have?"

"Oh yes. Ever since you fell out of the sky. The man was dead, but you weren't there—they kept looking."

"Serves him right. Served them all right," the child said. She put her hands up over her face and began to cry terribly, without tears.

"Go on, little one, Granddaughter," Spider said. "Don't be afraid. You can live well there. I'll be there, too, you know. In your dreams, in your ideas, in dark corners in the basement. Don't kill me, or I'll make it rain. . . ."

"I'll come around," Chickadee said. "Make gardens for me."

The child held her breath and clenched her hands until her sobs stopped and let her speak.

"Will I ever see Coyote?"

"I don't know," the Grandmother replied.

The child accepted this. She said, after another silence, "Can I keep my eye?"

"Yes. You can keep your eye."

"Thank you, Grandmother," the child said. She turned away then and started up the night slope toward the next day. Ahead of her in the air of dawn for a long way, a little bird flew, black-capped, light-winged.

# T. M. WRIGHT

## A World Without Toys

T. M. (Terry) Wright writes: "I'm forty years old (born, in fact, eleven days before Stephen King; if you check, you'll find that a good number of horror writers were born in '47 and '48). My thirteenth novel (fourteenth book—my first book was *The Intelligent Man's Guide to Flying Saucers*, A. S. Barnes, 1968), *The Island*, is a March 1987 hardcover from Tor. Tor has also published under my own name: *A Manhattan Ghost Story* (1986), and *The People of the Dark* (1985) among others. I've also written under the pseudonym F. W. Armstrong: *The Changing* (Tor, 1985) and *The Devouring* (Tor, 1987). I live in Ithaca, New York with my wife, Chris, daughter, Erika, and son, Dorian. I like to build miniature houses out of old manuscripts."

"A World without Toys," was published in *Shadows 10*, edited by Charles L. Grant (Doubleday). Its horror is of a quietly thoughtful nature, and perhaps more abidingly disturbing than stories more overtly violent in nature.

—E.D.

# A WORLD WITHOUT TOYS

## T. M. Wright

When the County Department of Public Works tore up part of St. Paul Street so workers could lay new pipe, they found a small green clapboard house 20 feet below street level. Only the front of the house and its rusted tin roof were visible from the street; there was a chimney, half of it gone, and small sections of the roof's cap were missing, exposing portions of the framing beneath.

Subsequently, two people from the Historical Society were summoned. They peered down at the house and exclaimed that it was, indeed, of great and consuming interest, if only a way could be found to get down to it. A way was found. Workers widened the big hole, a ladder was carefully lowered in, and the two people from the Historical Society climbed down with hard hats firmly in place and encountered the front door of the house.

One of these people, a man in his late 40s who was wiry and bright and always wore colorful bow ties, said, "Should we knock?" and chuckled.

The woman with him, also in her late 40s, her name was Blanche, said through tight, thin lips, "This is hardly a joking matter, Alex. This house could be of extreme historical importance. And you know, of course, that there may be people in it."

Alex gave her a feigned look of alarm. "People? You mean *dead* people?"

"Yes," she told him grimly, "dead people." And she stepped forward in the few feet between the ladder and the oak front door and tried the brass knob. She stepped back.

"What's the matter?" Alex asked.

"It's locked," she said. "The door is locked. It was something I hadn't expected."

From above, a workman called, "You people OK?"

Alex said, "What do you mean it's locked?"

"I mean it won't open. I need a key."

"Maybe the people who live here stepped out for a few minutes." He smiled. "Maybe we can leave them a note and tell them when we'll be back."

She gave him a hard look. "Alex," she proclaimed, "if there *are* people

27

here, in this house, then I would say that in all likelihood it is their maus*oleum*. So my guess is that they'd be even less responsive to your so-called humor than I am. If that's possible."

Alex continued smiling. "Well put," he said.

Again the workman, 20 feet up at street level, called down, "Are you people OK?"

Blanche called back. "We have a problem. The house is locked."

"Locked," the workman said, parroting her.

"Maybe we can get in through a window," Alex suggested.

There were three windows in the front of the house—two, with lace curtains drawn to either side of the door, and one very tall and narrow window six or seven feet above it, in what apparently was the attic. Blanche and Alex could not get to either lower window easily because there was water pooled around the house; since the house rested on what appeared to be a natural limestone hump, they had no idea how deep the water could be. ("You got some troughs down there," a workman had told them, "that you could step in and never come out of. It ain't no place for no one to go walking alone.")

Alex got back on the ladder and climbed it so he could peer into the attic window.

Blanche called to him, "Do you see anything?"

He called back, "Yes. I do."

Blanche waited a few moments for him to continue. When he didn't, she called, "*What* do you see, Alex?"

He answered, "I see . . . toys."

"Toys?"

"Yes. A rocking horse. Some blocks. Wooden blocks with the alphabet on them. A train set. And a doll—no, two dolls. Raggedy Ann, I think . . . Blanche, I think it's a Raggedy Ann and a Raggedy Andy." He smiled. "*I* had a Raggedy Andy."

*And I had a Raggedy Ann*, Blanche thought, but she said nothing and within a few seconds had chased the thought away. "That's about it," Alex called. "Toys," he murmured, and when Blanche looked up at him through the gloom below the street, she saw a tiny, quivering smile on his face. "Come down from there," she told him. Reluctantly, he came down.

She said, "It's remarkably well preserved," paused, continued. "And it has no business being here, but it *is* here, of course, so it's something we'll have to deal with." She studied the house a moment. "I think it is possibly pre-Victorian, and, well preserved though it is, it lacks character, of course, so it is clearly the house of a laborer of the day—"

A workman called down, "You two gotta come up outa there now."

Blanche called back, "I'm sorry, we can't do that. We have hardly begun our investigation—"

olored sky. And
animals, out of
ece their worlds
hurled at them

the street and
he sides of the
house was not

him a small
d.

, Blanche,"

do that?"
ght. It had
nt."

sorry."

, and ad-

in order
d no real
ded, had
as much
a dirty
gerous.

eyond

at."
e.
s

hard."

changed, that it had grown even
come down the ladder. "We *must*
that, of course."

then you're gonna go swimmin.'"

e looked briefly into the attic. Alex,
inche?"

This is a very strange place. I'm not
ortable." She paused. She realized that
ig about. "There's light in that room,"
said "room" because that's the way it
no child had ever used. It was too much
ig.

"I was speaking . . . metaphorically." She
assment. She added, "You understand that,

ied.

, in fact, that this house makes me extremely

said.

tone very serious and very instructive, "Alex, I
d going on 12." It was very similar to what she'd
ore: "Alex I believe you are 43 years old going on
you are 42 years old going on 14." She kept him
hat was very reassuring to her.

It was not a gentle rain, not comforting or restful,
nat soothes and heals. It was a torrent, as if an ocean
e things that got caught in it—hoboes, night workers,
were marked by it and their lives made shorter because

stumbling to her window by it and she watched in awe
d at her that there were things beyond her control, after
imething she would have admitted aloud, although she
here were many things that she understood. Things about
id grown into and become a part of—a world made up of
inches and decision-making and exhaustion. A world she'd
i for centuries. A world that pinched. A world without toys.
or a very long time at her window. She watched the storm

reach a peak, then watched it groan back to practically
if it were relieved or sated, almost instantly to nothing at
morning and there were shiny black streets and a peach-
there were people, too. They moved tentatively, like small
their houses. And they nodded at each other and began to p
together from the debris left behind by what the earth had
the night before.

When, late that morning, Blanche arrived at the hole in
looked down, she saw that sunlight was bouncing gaily off t
hole all the way to the bottom. She saw, as well, that the
there.

She looked at a workman standing beside her. She gave
incredulous, quivering smile. "The house isn't there," she sai

"I know it isn't," he said.

Alex came up alongside her then. "The storm washed it awa
he told her.

She shook her head slowly. She said, "How could the storm

The workman said, "Hell, lady, there was a lot of rain last ni
to go somewhere." He nodded at the hole. "That's where it we

Alex repeated, "And it washed the house away, Blanche. I'm

"Sorry?"

"It was probably of great historical importance," he explained
justed his bright bow tie.

She said nothing. She looked stunned, Alex thought. He said,
to comfort her, "Chances are, Blanche, that it broke up." He ha
idea why such a statement would comfort her. He might have deci
he examined it, that it would have comforted her because there w
work to do elsewhere. And besides, working below the street was
business, and smelly, too, and was without a doubt extremely dan

"Broke up?" she said.

He nodded. "Yes. Broke up. Into pieces."

"And?"

"And so . . . and so. . . ." He smiled. "It got swept away and is
us and we can get on to other things."

She shook her head. "Alex, we have to go and find it."

He shook his head. "We can't do that. We're not equipped to do

She looked from his face to the hole in the street, then back to
She said, "As you pointed out, Alex, as you pointed out, that h
of great *historical* importance. And besides. . . ." She stopped. S
confused.

"Besides?" Alex coaxed.

"Besides," she said, "there were toys in it."

The workman said, "Toys?"

"Yes," she said. "In the house."

"Toys?" the workman said again, as if it were a word he just then had encountered.

Alex explained, "There was a rocking horse, yes. And a train set. And some blocks."

"With the alphabet on them," Blanche cut in, smiling a broad, childlike smile that Alex had never seen on her before. "And a Raggedy Ann and Raggedy Andy."

The workman shrugged. "Well they ain't there no more, and that's about as true as yesterday."

It was a week of storms, all of them as angry and as destructive as the first, all of them interrupted, during the day, by sunlight and still, clear air. It was a week that sat on Blanche like a bullfrog, a week that she moved about in leadenly from place to place, from responsibility to responsibility, as if her world were some grim amusement park where the carousel horses didn't move and the fun house consisted only of darkness and the prize for knocking over milk bottles on the midway was a trip back in time to do it all over again.

To grow up all over again.

To be here. And be precisely who she was.

"Did you ever wonder," Alex asked her at the end of that week, "how it got there?"

"It?"

"The house below the street."

"No," she told him. "I never wondered. It was there, that was all we needed to know. It was all anybody needed to know."

Alex smiled. They were in a big gray brick Victorian on Mount Hope Avenue, and they were trying to decide if it qualified for landmark status. "Or *why* it was there, Blanche? Did you ever wonder *why* it was there?"

"No," she answered at once, as if the question frightened her.

"You don't need to know very much, do you, Blanche?"

"Sorry?" she said, though she knew what he meant.

He explained, "You don't need to look around the edges of things. You don't need to see around corners. You've got your eyes glued only on the road ahead."

"No," she told him. "No," she repeated thoughtfully, as if to herself. "I *do* want to see around corners. I want that very much. But I don't know how."

Alex adjusted his bright bow tie. Adjusting it was a nervous habit, and he often adjusted it when it didn't need adjusting. He was nervous because he wanted to tell her something that had pounced on him just then but that he didn't have the nerve to tell her. He wanted to tell her that he cared for her.

"It's possible," he said, "that the house under the street wasn't there at all."

He didn't know *why* he cared for her—now; perhaps it was a fault within himself that had caused it, some growth had taken over a lobe of his brain and had made him stupid. He'd worked with Blanche for five years, and in that time she had said only one kind thing to him: "I'm sorry about your hamster, Alex; *I* had a hamster once."

"Yes," she said now, in the gray brick Victorian on Mount Hope Avenue, "I know. It's possible that the house under the street wasn't there at all."

This surprised him. "But it *was* there," he said. "I was only . . . joking. It was only a joke."

"The room we looked at could have been anything," she said. "It could have been a concoction. It could have been a dream, Alex."

He looked at her and saw that she was smiling oddly, as if at the memory of something that warmed her slowly from the inside, like pudding. "But it *was* there, Blanche," he insisted.

"And now it's gone," she said. "And that's what matters. It matters that it was there, under the street, and now it's gone, and we can . . . get on to other things." It sounded to Alex like a plea. She looked away, as if embarrassed.

*I care for you*, he said, but it was to himself, in his head, in preparation for saying it aloud, and he didn't say it aloud because it didn't make any sense to him.

That night Blanche threw her cool sheets off her cold legs, put on her terry-cloth robe and her blue slippers and padded to the window that overlooked her street. *The rain has stopped*, she told herself.

She smiled. Light from a streetlamp below bounced off her face, then off the window, and she saw her reflection. It was, she realized, the first time in a very long time that she'd seen her own smile.

Suddenly she wished she had a cat. Something to talk to. She didn't know for sure what she'd say to it, but she knew that she would make sounds at it and that it would respond in its way. Maybe she'd tell it what she'd been afraid to tell herself all these years, that there really was a world made up of Raggedy Anns and Raggedy Andys, toy trains and wooden blocks. A world that didn't pinch. A world that was buried as deep within her as the house and its wonderful attic room were buried beneath the street.

"And all I have to do is find it." She turned from the window. She hesitated. Her smile broadened. She slipped out of her terry-cloth robe and her slippers. She dressed. And she walked out of her apartment and into the night.

\*     \*     \*

The following morning, toward noon, a workman at the hole in the street, where the house had been, handed Alex a hard hat and told him, "The hole wasn't closed up, mister, 'cuz we wasn't finished working in it." He paused very briefly then continued, "You know it's gonna rain?"

"Yes," said Alex.

"An' you know," the workman pressed on, "that if you get caught down there and it's rainin' real hard, then you'll drown for sure. There are troughs you could walk into and never come out of—"

"I know that."

The workman shrugged. "You got your lamp?"

Alex held up the battery powered lantern that the foreman of the work crew had given him.

"Good," said the workman. "There ain't no lights."

"I know," said Alex, and a moment later he was climbing down into the hole in the street on the same ladder Blanche had used eight hours before.

He could hear the other rescue workers. He could hear bits of conversation, grumbled curses, and he thought as he listened that those men could be anywhere in the maze of tunnels under the street, that he could head in their direction and get to where he'd thought they were and find that they were somewhere else entirely.

But he knew this, also, as he listened to them: He knew that they were not going to find Blanche. He knew that *he* was going to find her.

He could see their lights, then, and he realized that they were moving in his direction. He stayed still. He said nothing. He did not call out to them, as he'd been told to do. For a few moments he watched their lights—dulled by reflection from half a dozen wet stone walls—then he turned and walked in the other direction, through ankle-deep water; as he walked, the dull orange light of his lantern showed him only the angles of dark walls intersecting other dark walls.

He walked this way—slowly, through the water—for ten minutes. Then he saw the house.

And at that same moment, he heard from far behind him, "I found her. God, I found her!"

He smiled. *No*, he thought. *No, you haven't found her.*

"Bring a light," shouted the same voice. "Mine ain't much good no more. Bring a light."

The house was listing in the tunnel, like a ship beginning to sink, the left side in one of the troughs he'd been warned about, so his lamp could not show him much of it—only the lower right-hand window, some of the right-hand wall, green clapboards trailing off into the darkness, the softly glistening front edge of the rusted tin roof. And all of the attic window, too, which he could see very well because it was illuminated from within.

He heard then, from far behind him, "It's her. God, it's her!"

And another voice answered, "How are we going to get to her?"

*No,* Alex called to them in his head, smiling. *No, you're mistaken. That's not her at all. No. She's here.*

He set his light down on a ledge near where the tunnel wall intersected the floor.

He moved forward through the ankle-deep water toward the little house under the street. He longed to peer into the attic window, but he couldn't; even though the house was listing, the window was still too far above him. He stepped up to the door, saw the soft reflection of his lamplight on the brass knob, reached out, grasped the knob hard.

He heard from far behind him, "She's rolled over. I can see her face!"

"Can you get to her?" shouted another voice.

"I don't know," answered the first voice. "I don't know. Get me a line."

Alex turned the knob. "Blanche?" he whispered. The door was locked. He heard from behind him, and above—at street level, he guessed—"Come on outa there!"

He shook his head. *No,* he thought. He stepped back from the door and peered up through the gloom below the street and into the attic. He saw the attic ceiling; he saw a shadow on it. He saw the shadow move.

And he watched as a small face, the face of a child, appeared at the attic window.

He heard from behind him, and above, "It's raining! Get outa there!"

He smiled at the face of the child in the window. The face smiled back. "Blanche," he whispered. The child's lips mouthed his name: "Alex."

From behind him, he heard again, "It's raining, dammit! Get outa there!"

"We can't! We ain't got her. We ain't got her yet!"

"She'll have to wait. Get outa there. Now!"

Alex stepped up to the front door of the house under the street. He grasped the knob. Turned it. The door opened.

Above, at street level, it rained. It was not a gentle rain, not comforting or restful, not the kind of rain that soothes and heals. It was a torrent, as if an ocean were draining.

And Alex stepped into the house.

# JOE HALDEMAN

## DX

Joe Haldeman, who was drafted and sent to Vietnam, used the experience for this poem and several books, including *The Forever War*, which won both the Hugo and Nebula awards. His latest novel is *Tool of the Trade*. He is currently a visiting professor in the writing department of the Massachusetts Institute of Technology, and he and his wife, Gay, live together in Gainesville, Florida, and in Cambridge, Massachusetts.

Appropriate to *DX*, Haldeman wrote in the April 1986 issue of *Isaac Asimov's Science Fiction Magazine*: "The march of technology may affect the gruesome details of war, what device kills you and how well and how fast it works, but the fictionally important parts don't change. Pain, confusion, fear, heroism, cowardice; all are the same from Homer to Hemingway, from dumb rocks to smart bombs." The following poem originally appeared in *In the Field of Fire*.

—E.D.

# DX

## Joe Haldeman

So every night
You build a little house

You dig a hole
and cover it with
logs

Cover with logs
with sandbags
A house you          against the
sleep beside         shrapnel weather
and hope not
to enter

Some nights you wake
to noise and light
and metal singing

Roll out of the bag
and into the house
        with all the scorpions
        centipedes    roaches
but no bullets flying inside it

Most nights
you just sleep

deep sleep
and dreamless
mostly
from labor

This night was just sleep.

*In the morning*
*you unbuild the house*

        *hours of work*
        *again*
        *for nothing*

    *Kick the logs away*
    *pour out the sandbags*
    *into the hole*

*Roll up the sandbags*
*for the next night's bit*
*of rural urban renewal*

*Eat some cold bad food*         *Check the tape on*
*Clean your weapon*            *the grenades;*
*Drink instant coffee*          *check the pins.*
*from a can*    *Most carefully*   *Inspect ammo clips*
    *repack the demolition*   *(Clean the top*
    *bag: blasting caps*      *rounds with*
    *TNT*   *plastic*   *time fuse*    *illegal*
    *det cord——*         *gasoline.)*

    *ten kilograms of fragile*
    *most instant*
    *death*

*Then shoulder the heavy rucksack*
*Secure your weapons and tools*
*and follow the other primates*
*into the jungle*            *watching the trees*

    *walk silently*
    *as possible*
    *through the green*
           *watching the ground*

*Don't get too close*
*to the man in front of you*

    *This is good advice:*
    *don't let the enemy*
    *have two targets.*

   *Remember that: don't get too close to any man.*

Only a fool, or an officer,
doesn't grab the ground                              high-pitched
at the first shot                                              rattle
                                                                     of M-16s

                    even if it's rather distant
                                              louder
                                              Russian rifles
                                              answer

           even if it's
           a couple of klicks away                   manly chug
                                                                of heavy
    God knows which way they're shooting   machine
                                                                guns


                                  grenade's
                                  flat
                                  bang

Like fools, or officers,
we get up off the ground and move

                                         All that metal
                                         flying through
                                              the air—
                                         and do we move away
                                              from it?


                                    no


We make haste                         like fools or officers
in the wrong direction             we head for the
                                                action


making lots of noise now
who cares now

            but careful not to bunch up

            Remember: don't get too close to any man.



It's over before we get there.
The enemy, not fools
(perhaps lacking officers)
went in the proper direction.

As we approach
the abandoned enemy camp
a bit of impolite and
(perhaps to you)                        "You wanna get some
incomprehensible                        X-Rays down here?
dialogue greets us:                     Charlie left
                                        a motherfuckin'
                                        DX pile
                                        behind."

          TERMS:

X-Rays are engineers,
demolition men,                         Charlie is the enemy.
us.

                    "DX" means destroy;
                    A DX pile is a collection
                    of explosives that are no longer
                    trustworthy. When you leave
                    the camp finally, you
                    put a long fuse on the DX pile, and
                                              blow it up.

(Both "motherfucker" and "DX"
are technical terms that can serve as
polite euphemisms:
                    "Private,                    "Private,
                    you wanna        instead     kill
                    DX that          of          that
                    motherfucker?"               man.")
We'd been lucky.
No shooting.
Just a pile of
explosive
leftovers
to dispose of.

               And we'd done it before.

               It was quite a pile,        artillery shells
               though,                      mortar rounds
               taller than a man            satchel charges
                                            rifle grenades
                    enough to kill   all

*everybody*        *festooned with*
*with some left over*    *chains of*
                      *fifty-caliber*
                         *ammunition*


                      *The major wouldn't*
                      *let us*
                      *evacuate his troops*
              *then put a long fuse on the pile*

*We had to stand there*
*nervous*                         *no*
*and guard it*

                *They'd been working hard*
                *first they get lunch and a nap*
                *then we can move them out*
                *and we can blow it.*


                         *(we liked his "we")*

*We didn't know*
*it was wired for sound*


        *it was booby-trapped*


        *Remember: don't get too close to any man:*


*Don't know that Farmer*
*has an actual farm waiting*      *and*       *Don't know that*
*back in Alabama*                              *Crowder*
                                              *has new grandbabies*
                                              *and is headed*
                                              *for retirement*
    *and*     *don't know that Doc*           *when he gets home*
              *was a basketball champ*
              *in his black high school*
              *and really did want*
              *to be a doctor*


*Because they all are*
*one   short   beep*
*of a radio detonator*

*away*
*from*

    *a sound*
    *so loud*     *grey smoke*
    *you don't*
    *hear it*     *blood*
    *really*

    *It just hits you like a car.*

            *everywhere blood*
*Doc*             *and screaming*
*both his long legs*
*blown off*         *Sergeant Crowder*
*dies quickly*       *separated from one*
              *foot*
           *is unconscious*
           *or stoic*

*Farmer had his belly spilled*
*but lived long enough to shout*
   *"Professor?*
   *Where'd they get you?"*      *and*     *since I didn't have*
           *enough breath*
       *for a complete catalog*

       *(foot   shins   knees*
       *thigh   groin   genitals*
       *arm   ear   scalp*
       *and   disposition)*

    *I settled for "the balls."*
*Oh my God*
*Farmer said*
*then he died*

    *Two days later*
    *I woke up in a dirty hospital*
    *(sewed up like Frankenstein's charge)*
    *woke up in time*
    *to see Crowder leave*
    *with a sheet   over his eyes*
*and so it was over*

*in a way*

> *the whole squad DX*
> *but me*

*there is nothing for it*
*there is nothing you can take for it*
*they are names on a wall now*
*they are compost in Arlington*
*and somehow   I am not*

*but give me this*

*There are three other universes, like this:*

*In one,   Farmer curses the rain*
*wrestles his tractor through the mud*
*curses the bank that owns it*
*and sometimes remembers*
*that he alone survived*

> *In another   Crowder tells grown grandchildren*
> *for the hundredth time*
> *over a late-night whiskey*
> *his one war story*
> *that beats the others all to hell*

*In the third   Doc stands over a bloody patient*
*steady hand   healing knife*
*and sometimes he recalls*
*blood years past   and sometimes*
*remembers   to be glad to be alive;*

*in these worlds*
*I am dead*

*and at peace.*

# JONATHAN CARROLL

## Friend's Best Man

Though it was originally published in the literary mainstream, I have been convinced that the work of Jonathan Carroll would find a wide audience among readers of adult fantasy fiction since acquiring reprint rights to *The Land of Laughs*, a remarkable fantasy *tour de force*, for the Ace Fantasy line some years ago—so it is with great pleasure that I watch his work now appearing in places like *The Magazine of Fantasy and Science Fiction*, from which the following story, "Friend's Best Man," is drawn. Carroll makes his home in Vienna, and his latest work is the novel *The Bones of the Moon*.

—T.W.

# FRIEND'S BEST MAN

## Jonathan Carroll

### 1

It was in all of the papers. Two even carried the same headline: "FRIEND'S BEST MAN!" But I didn't see any of that until long afterward; until I was home from the hospital awhile and the shock had begun to wear off.

After it happened, scores of eyewitnesses suddenly appeared. But I don't remember seeing anyone around that day: just Friend and me and a very long freight train.

Friend is a seven-year-old Jack Russell Terrier. He looks like a mutt: stubby legs, indiscriminate brown and white coloring; a very plain dog's face topped with intelligent, sweet eyes. But truth be told, Jack Russells are rare and I ended up spending a wad for him. Although I've never had much money to play with until recently, one of my quirks has always been to buy the best whenever I could afford it.

When it came time to buy a dog, I went out searching for a real *dog*. Not one of those froufrou breeds that constantly need to be clipped and combed. Nor did I want one of those chic things that came from Estonia or somewhere strange that looked more like an alligator than a dog. I went to animal shelters and kennels and finally found Friend through an ad in a dog magazine. The only thing I didn't like about him on first sight was his name: Friend. It was too full of kitsch and didn't belong to a dog that looked like it would be very comfortable smoking a corncob pipe. Even as a puppy he was built low to the ground and looked fuzzily solid. He was a "Bill," a "Ned." "Jack" would have suited him, too, if he hadn't already had that as a breed name. But the woman who sold him to me said he had that name for a very specific reason: whenever he barked (which was rarely), it came out sounding like the word *friend*. I was skeptical, but she was right; while his brothers and sisters yapped and yelped, this guy stood solidly there and said, "Friend! Friend! Friend!" time after time while his tail wagged back and forth. It was a strange thing to hear, but I liked him even more for it. As a result, he stayed "Friend."

I have always marveled at how well dogs and people get along. They move so comfortably into your life, choose a chair to sleep on, figure out

44

your moods, and have no trouble bending themselves to a curve that should be completely strange and inappropriate. From the first, they fall asleep so easily in a foreign land.

Before I go on, I must say that Friend never struck me as being anything more special or rare than a very good dog. He was excited when I came home from work, and liked to rest his head on my lap when I watched television. But he was not Jim the Wonder Dog: he didn't know how to count, or drive a car, or other marvels you sometimes read about in an article about dogs that appear to have "special" powers. Friend liked scrambled eggs, too, and would go jogging with me so long as it wasn't raining out and I wasn't going too far. By all accounts, I had gotten exactly what I wanted: a dog-dog who staked a small claim on part of my heart with his loyalty and joy. One who never asked much in return except a couple of pats often and a corner of the bed to sleep on when the weather turned cold.

The day it happened was sunny and clear. I put on my gym suit and shoes and did a few stretching exercises. Friend watched all of this from his chair, but when I got ready to go out, he hopped down and accompanied me to the door. I opened it, and he took a look at the weather.

"Do you want to go along?" If he didn't, his usual procedure was to collapse on the floor and not move again until I returned. But this time he wagged his tail and went outside with me. I was glad for his company.

We started down the hill toward the park. Friend liked to run alongside, about two feet away. When he was a puppy, I'd tripped over him a couple of times because he had the habit of running in and out of my path, fully expecting me to keep tabs on where he was at all times. But I'm one of those joggers who watches everything but his feet when I go. As a result, we'd had a few magnificent collisions and mad yelps that left him wary of my sense of navigation.

We crossed Ober Road and ran through Harold Park toward the railroad tracks. Once we got there, we'd go about a mile and a half along them until we reached the station, then circle slowly back toward home.

Friend knew the route so well that he could afford to make stops along the way, both to relieve himself and to investigate any new interesting sights or smells that had appeared since our last trip there.

Once in a while a train came along, but you could hear it from far off and there was lots of time to move off to the side and give it wide berth. I liked it when trains came through; liked hearing them lumber up behind you and pass while you picked up pace to see how long you could keep up with the engine. A couple of the engineers knew us and tooted their shrill whistles as they passed. I liked that, and I think Friend did, too, because he always stopped and barked a couple of times just to let them know who was boss.

That morning we were about halfway to the station when I heard one coming. As always, I looked to see where Friend was. A couple of feet away, he ran jauntily along, his tongue a pink sliver out the side of his mouth.

As the train's giant clatter approached, I watched a car cross the tracks a couple of hundred feet in front of us. How dumb of the driver to do that when he knew a train was so close! What was the hurry? By the time that thought passed, the train felt close over my left shoulder. I looked to my right to check on Friend again, but he wasn't there. I whipped my head this way and that, but he was nowhere around. In a complete panic, I spun around and saw him in the middle of the tracks sniffing at something, all of his attention concentrated there.

"Friend! Come here!"

He wagged his tail but didn't lift his head. I ran for him and called again and again.

"Friend! Goddamn it, Friend!"

The tone of my voice finally got through to him because when the train was only fifteen feet away, already putting on its brakes, he looked up.

I ran as fast as I could and felt stones fly out from beneath my sneakers. "Friend, get out!"

He didn't know the words, but the tone told him he was in for a hell of a smack. He did the worst possible thing: tucked his head down into his small shoulders and waited for me to come get him.

The train was there. In the instant before I jumped, I knew I had one choice, but I'd already made it before I ever moved. Lunging for my Friend, I bent down and tried to grab him up and roll out of the way all at once. And I almost succeeded. I almost succeeded—except for my leg, which stuck straight behind me as I jumped and was sliced cleanly off by the huge wheels.

2

I met Jasenka in the hospital. Jasenka Ciric. No one could say ya-ZEN-ka very well, so people had been calling her "Jazz" all her life.

She was seven years old and had spent most of her life connected to one or another ominous machine that helped her fight a long, losing battle against her undependable body. Her skin was the color of a white candle in a dark room, lips the violet of foreign money. Her many illnesses made her serious, while her youth kept her buoyant and hopeful.

Because she'd spent so much time in bed in hospital rooms surrounded by unfamiliar faces, white walls, and few pictures on the walls, she had only two hobbies: reading and watching television. When she watched TV, her face contracted and then set into complete solemnity and concentration: a member of the family reading someone's will for the first time. But when she read, no matter what the book, that face was expressionless and empty of anything.

I met her because she'd read about Friend and me in the newspapers. One of the nurses came to my room a week after it happened, and asked if I'd be willing to have a visit with Jazz Ciric (CHEER-itch). When she explained the girl and her situation to me, I envisioned an ill angel along the lines of Shirley Temple or at least Darla in "The Little Rascals." Instead, Jasenka Ciric had a peculiar, interesting face where everything was pointy and too close together. Her thick hair curled like the stuffing in old furniture and was just about the same color.

The nurse introduced us and then went off on her rounds. Jazz sat in the chair next to my bed and sized me up. I was still in great pain, but had earlier decided to be a little less selfpitying. This visit was to be my first move in that direction.

"What's your favorite book?"

"I don't know. I guess *The Great Gatsby*. What's yours?"

She shrugged and tsk'd her tongue once, as if the answer were self-evident.

*"Ladies with Their Nightgowns on Fire."*

"That's a book? Who wrote it?"

"Egan Moore."

I smiled. *My* name is Egan Moore. "What's the story?"

She looked at me very carefully and proceeded to spin out one of those endlessly rambling tales only a kid could love.

"Then the monsters jumped out of the trees and took them all back to the evil castle where Scaldor the Evil King . . ."

What I liked about it was the way she acted out the story as she went on. Scaldor had a nasty squint; which Jazz demonstrated to perfection. When someone got crept up on, her fingers curled into a witch's grip and tiptoed like little devils across the air separating us.

". . . And they they got home *just* in time for their favorite TV show." She sat back, tired but obviously satisfied with her performance.

"Sounds like a terrific story. I wish I *had* written it."

"It is. Can I ask you a question now?"

"Ask away."

"Who's taking care of Friend now?"

"My next-door neighbor."

"Have you seen him since the accident?"

"No."

"Are you mad at him for making you lose your leg?"

I thought for a minute, deciding whether to talk to her as a child or as an adult. A quick scan of her face said she demanded adult standing; had no time to fool around.

"No, I'm not mad at him. I guess I'm mad at somebody, but I don't know who. I don't know if it was anyone's fault. I'm sure not mad at Friend."

She came to visit me every day after that. Usually sometime in the morning when both of us were fresh from sleep and chipper. I was all right mornings, but not most afternoons. For some reason, the enormity of what had happened to me and how it would affect the rest of my life came in the door with my lunch tray and stayed long after visiting hours were over. I thought about things like the bird that stands around on one leg all day. Or the joke about the one-legged man in an ass-kicking contest. I thought about the fact that words like *kick* would no longer be part of my body's vocabulary. I knew they made remarkable prosthetic legs—Science on the March!—but that was little comfort. I wanted back what was mine: not something that would make me, at best, "as good as new," as the therapist said every time we talked about it.

Jazz and I became good friends. She made my days in the hospital happier and my perspective wider. I have known only two mortally ill people in my life, my mother and Jasenka. Both of them looked at the world through the same urgent yet grateful eyes. When there is not much time left, it seems the eyes' capacity to see broadens tenfold. The things they see are more often than not details that were previously ignored but are, suddenly, an important part of what makes the scene complete. On her visits to my room, Jazz's observations about people we knew in common, or the way the light came through the window in different-sized blades . . . were both mature and compelling. Dying, she had fast developed a poet's, a cynic's, an artist's eye for the world around her, small as it was.

On the first day I was allowed outside, my next-door neighbor Kathleen surprised me by bringing Friend to the hospital to say hello. Dogs weren't normally allowed on the grounds, but an exception had been made because of the circumstances.

I was glad to see the old boy, and it was a surprisingly long time before I remembered he was the reason for my being there. He kept trying to climb into my lap, and I would have liked that if his scrambling to get there hadn't hurt my leg so much. As it was, I threw his ball for him a few thousand times while I chatted with Kathleen. Half an hour later, I asked the nurse if it would be possible for Jazz to come down and meet my friends.

It was arranged and, bundled to her ears in blankets, Ms. Ciric was introduced to His Nibs, Friend Moore. They shook hands gravely (Friend's one and only trick—he loved to "Shake!"), and he allowed her to stroke his head while the four of us sat there and enjoyed the mild afternoon sun.

I had been encouraged by the doctor to take a small walk on my crutches

so, half an hour later while Jazz kept Friend by her side, I tried out my
new aluminum crutches with Kathleen alongside just in case.

It was the wrong time to do it. In happier days, I had passed many
pleasant hours fantasizing what it would be like to live with Kathleen. I
think she liked me, too, despite the fact that we were relatively new neighbors. Before the accident we had been spending more and more time together, and that was just fine with me. I'd been trying to figure out how
to move in closer to her heart. But now, when I dared look up from the
treacherous ground in front of me, I saw that her face was full of all the
wrong kind of concern and compassion. More than any other time before
or after, I was aware of my loss.

The day was ruined, but I tried hard to hide that from Kathleen. I said
I was tired and cold, and would she mind if we went back to Jazz and
Friend. From a distance, the two of them were so still and serious: they
looked like one of those early photographs of people living in the American
West.

"What've you two guys been doing?"

Kathleen looked quickly at me to see if she'd done anything to deserve
this not-so-subtle dismissal. I avoided her eyes.

Twenty minutes later I was back in bed, feeling nasty, impotent, lost.
The phone next to me rang. It was Jazz.

"Egan, Friend's going to help you now. He told me that today when
you were walking with Kathleen. He said I could tell you."

"Really? What's he going to do?" I smiled, thinking she was about to
launch into another of her wacky stories over the phone. I liked hearing her
voice, liked her being in the room with me then.

"He's going to do a lot! He said he'd been thinking about the best thing
he could do for you, but now he knows. I can't tell you because it's going
to be a big surprise."

"What does his voice sound like, Jazz?"

"Kind of like Paul McCartney."

Every couple of days, Kathleen and Friend came by to visit. Most of
the time it was just the three of us, but once in a while Jazz felt well
enough to come down and join us. When that happened, we'd all sit
together for a while, then I would take my stroll around the grounds with
Kathleen.

Jazz didn't say anything more about Friend talking to her, but the Paul
McCartney part sent Kathleen into howls of laughter when I told her the
story.

Kathleen turned out to be a genuinely nice woman who did whatever
she could to make life happier for both Jazz and me. Of course that niceness
and consideration made me fall completely in love with her, which only

complicated and made matters worse. Life had begun to show it had an extremely cynical sense of humor.

"I have to tell you something."
"What?"
"I love you."
Eyes widened in fear. "No you don't."
"Oh, but I do, Egan." she said to me. *To me.* "When you come home, can we live together?"
I looked across the lawn. Jazz and Friend were way over there. Jazz raised her arm slowly and waved it back and forth: her sign that everything was all right.

The night before I left the hospital for home, I want to Jazz's room for a last visit. Some innard had once again betrayed her, and she looked terribly tired and pale. I sat by her bed and held her cool hand. Although I tried to dissuade her, she insisted on telling me a long new installment about Sloothack, the Fire Pig. Like Jazz's family, Sloothack was from Yugoslavia; way, way up in the mountains where sheep walked on their two hind legs and secret agents from all countries hid out between assignments. Jazz was crazy about secret agents.
I'd heard a lot of Slooth stories, but this last one was a dilly. It involved a Nazi tank, the lakes of Plitvice, Uncle Vuk from Belgrade, and a leather window.
When she was through, she looked even paler than before. So pale that I was a little worried about her.
"Are you O.K., Jazz?"
"Yes. Will you come and see me every week, Egan, like you promised?"
"Absolutely. All three of us will come if you'd like."
"That's O.K.—maybe just you and Friend in the beginning. Kathleen can stay at home if she's tired."
I smiled and nodded. She was jealous of the new "woman in my life." She knew Kathleen and I had decided to try and live together. Maybe I had the guts to drop my self-pity and fight to make things work the right way. I was certainly scared, but just as eager and excited about the chances and possibilities.
"Can I call you when I need you, Jazz?" I said it because I knew she'd like hearing she was needed even when lying in bed, weak as a mouse.
"Yes, you can call me, but I'll have to call you, too, to tell you what Friend says."
"Yeah, but how will you know what he says? He'll be over at my house."
She scowled and rolled her eyes. I was being dumb again. "How many times do I have to tell you, Egan? I get *messages.*"

"That's right. What was the last one?"

"Friend said he was going to fix you and Kathleen up."

"Friend did that? I thought I did."

"Yes, you did some, but he did the rest. He said you needed some help."
She said it with such conviction.

What surprised me most about what followed was how quick and easy
it was to get used to an entirely different life. Kathleen wasn't an angel,
but she gave me all the kindness and space I needed. It made me feel both
loved and free, which is a pretty remarkable combination. In return, I tried
to give her what she said she liked most about me: humor, respect, and a
way of seeing life that—according to her—was both ironic and forgiving.

Actually, I was living two entirely new lives: one as a partner, the other
as one of the disabled. It was an emotional, often overwhelming time, and
I don't know if I'd ever want to repeat it, although much of it was as close
to the sublime as I'll ever get.

Kathleen went to work in the morning, leaving Friend and me to our
own devices. That usually meant a slow walk down to the corner store for
a newspaper and then an hour or two outdoors in the sun on the patio. The
rest of the day was spent puttering and thinking and learning to readjust
to a world that had been knocked slightly off-center for me in many different
ways.

I also talked frequently with Jasenka and went to visit her once a week,
always with Friend along for the ride. If the weather was bad and Jazz
couldn't come outside, I'd park Friend with Nurse Dornhelm at the reception
desk and pick him up on my way out.

One afternoon I entered her room and saw a mammoth new machine
clicking eerily and importantly away by the side of her bed. The tubes and
wires that connected her to it were all either silvery or a vague pink.

But what really clubbed my heart were the new pajamas she was wearing:
*Star Wars* pajamas with two-inch-high robots and creatures printed at all
angles and in all colors everywhere. She had been talking about those pajamas
for a long time; from before I left the hospital. I knew her parents had
promised them to her for her next birthday if she was good. I could only
surmise she had them now because of the new machine; because there might
not be another birthday.

"Hey Jazz, you got the new jams!"

She was sitting up very straight and smiling, happy as hell, a pink tube
in her nose, a silver one in her arm.

The machine percolated and hummed, its green and black dials registering
levels and drawing graphs that said everything but explained nothing.

"You know who gave them to me, Egan? Friend! Friend sent them to
me from the store. They came in a box in my favorite color—red. He got

my pajamas and he sent them to me in a red box. Aren't they beautiful? Look at R2D2. Right here." She pointed to a spot above her belly button.

We talked for a while about the pajamas, Friend's generosity, the new *Star Wars* figure I'd brought for her collection. She didn't bring up the subject of Kathleen, and neither did I. Although she approved of Kathleen in a brusque, sort of sisterly way, Jazz had no time for "her" now because our time together was so much less than before. Besides, Jazz and I had a separate world of our own we shared that consisted of hospital gossip, Friend gossip, and Jasenka Ciric stories, the latest of which, "A Pet Mountain," I had to hear once again from start to finish.

" 'And then Friend gave Jazz the pajamas and they all hopped into bed and watched television all night.' "

"Friend really gave you them, Jazz? What a great guy."

"He is! And you know what, Egan? He told me he's going to fix it up so you win that contest."

"What contest?"

"You know—the one from the magazines? The one you told me about last time? Million Dollar FlyAway?"

"I'm going to win a million bucks? That'd be nice."

She shook her head, eyes closed, and moved the pink tube to one side.

"No, not the million dollars. You'll win the hundred thousand dollars. Fourth Prize."

A few minutes later (after we'd decided how I'd spend my winnings), Mr. and Mrs. Ciric came in. The scared look on both of their faces when they saw the new machine told me it was time to go.

Out in the hall, Mrs. Ciric stopped me and gently pulled me aside. She looked at my crutches and touched my hand.

"The doctors say this new machine will do wonderful things, but my husband, Zdravko, he doesn't believe them."

Having spent so much time with Jazz, I felt comfortable with Mrs. Ciric and hugely admired her for having the strength to face this constant sadness every day of her life.

"Well, I don't know if it's that machine or just those new pajamas, but I think she looks really fine today, Mrs. Ciric. There's certainly a lot more color in her cheeks."

Looking straight at me, she began to cry. "I bought those for her for her birthday, you know? Now, I don't like to think about her birthday, Egan. I wanted her to have them now." She tried to smile. Then, unembarrassedly, wiped her hand across her nose. "Mothers are very stupid, eh? I saw Friend downstairs. I said to him, 'Shake hands!' and he did right away. Jasenka, you know, loves him very much. She says he calls her up on the telephone sometimes."

She turned and went back into the room. As I walked away, I pictured her and her husband standing over that complicated bed, watching their daughter with helpless eyes, trying to figure out what any of them had done to deserve this.

A few weeks passed. I went back to work. The new machine did help Jazz. Kathleen finished moving the rest of her stuff into my apartment.

One of the television networks calls and asked if I'd be willing to go on a show and talk about how I'd saved Friend. I thought it over and decided against it: there had been enough hoopla in the newspapers already, and something deep inside told me capitalizing on this wasn't the right thing to do. Kathleen agreed and gave me a nice hug to seal it. I consulted Friend while he lay across my lap one evening, but he didn't even lift his head.

Life wouldn't ever really return to the normal I had once known, but it *did* take its foot off the gas a little, slowing to cruising speed. Things weren't going by in such a blur anymore, and that was good.

The last glimmer of craziness came in the form of a large registered letter from *The Truth*, that god-awful newspaper that sports headlines like "I GAVE BIRTH TO A TRUCK" and is sold in supermarket checkout lines everywhere.

An editor offered me two thousand dollars for the exclusive rights to my story. But, according to him, it wasn't "quite vivid enough." so *The Truth* wanted to spice things up a little by saying Friend was either from outer space or The Lost Continent of Atlantis, et cetera, et cetera . . .

I wrote a very nice letter back saying I was all for it, but my dog had sworn me to secrecy about certain crucial matters of state, so I wasn't at liberty to . . .

"Egan?"

"Jazz? Hi, pal! How are you?"

"Not very good, but I had to call you up and tell you what Friend just told me."

Unconsciously, I looked around for the dog. He was on the other side of the room, looking straight at me. It made me feel a little funny.

"He's there with you, isn't he?"

"Yeah, Jazz, he's right here."

"I know. He said to tell you there's a man outside who's watching your house. Be very careful because he's a secret agent!"

"Now, Jazz—" I took a deep breath and stopped short of giving her a lecture over the phone about lying. It was fine to tell Sloothack stories. It was all right to say Friend talked to her sometimes. "Watch out for the creep at your door" stuff wasn't all right.

"Uh-oh, someone's coming, Egan. I have to go. Be careful!"

I hung up after she did. Standing there looking at the receiver, I wondered what I should do. Against my better judgment, I hobbled to the window and looked out. Naturally no one was there.

Then the doorbell rang. It scared me so much, I dropped one of my crutches.

"One second!" Bending to pick it up, I felt my heart drumming in my chest. There are moments in life when, for the smallest reason, you're filled with such dread or shock that there's little room left inside for anything else. What's most annoying is the smallness of the reason: the phone ringing you out of the trance of a good book, a person coming up behind and tapping you lightly on the left shoulder . . .

My hand was so fluttery, I couldn't even pick up the damned crutch for a long few seconds. The doorbell rang again.

"I'm coming! Wait!"

"Mr. Moore?" A postman stood there with a clipboard in his hand.

"Yes?"

"Registered letter. Sign here." He looked at my leg as I shifted my weight to take the clipboard.

"I read about you in the papers. Where's the dog?"

I signed and handed back the clipboard. "Somewhere around. Can I have the letter?"

"Yeah, sure, there you go. That must be some dog for you to do a thing like that."

His tone ticked me off, and he wouldn't stop looking at my leg. Some secret agent! I didn't even look at the letter. I just wanted him gone, the door closed, and my heart to calm down.

"Did you get a reward or something?"

"For what?"

"For saving your dog! You know, from the ASPCA or something."

"No, but I'll tell you something. He's going to take me to Mars with him the next time he goes!"

I looked right at him and smiled as insanely as I knew how. He took a step backward and beat it out of there lickety-split.

After I read the letter, I called Kathleen at work and told her I'd won ten thousand dollars in a contest.

There was silence on the other end. I could hear typewriters clacking in the background.

"Jazz told you that before."

"Yeah, but she said I'd win a *hundred* thousand, not ten. Not ten!" Too loud, too scared. I closed my eyes and waited, hoped for Kathleen to break the silence.

"What are you going to do?"

"I don't know. Um, Friend just came into the room."

He padded across the floor and sat down under the telephone table without looking at me.

"Kathleen, how come my dog is suddenly making me nervous?"

"I—"

"And how come there's this money?"

That evening both of us went to the hospital to visit Jazz. We left Friend at home, asleep in his favorite chair.

There were more tubes this time. The same machine as before, only a great many more tubes sprouting out from different parts of it, sneaking under the covers to her body.

She looked very ill. So much so that the first thing that came to mind when I saw her was: she's going to die. Cruel and true and obvious: she was going to die.

The left side of her mouth crawled up a notch in a tiny smile when she saw us. It was the tiredest, most resigned smile I had ever seen.

Kathleen stood in the doorway while I crossed to the bed. Jazz's eyes went from me to Kathleen to me again, watching to see what we would do.

I propped the crutches against the wall and maneuvered down into the chair next to the bed.

"Hiya, kid."

The smile again and a finger wiggle from one of the hands lying crossed on the small hill of her chest.

"You won, didn't you?" The voice was thick and coated with phlegm.

I'd planned to be funny but firm when we spoke, but my plans were no match for her broken energy. Death was in charge here; she was its deputy, so she held all the cards.

"Can I talk to you alone, Egan?"

It was said so quietly that I was sure Kathleen couldn't have heard, but I winced anyway.

"Kat, would you mind if we were alone for a bit?"

She nodded, her face a mix of pity and confusion. She left, closing the door silently behind her.

"Kathleen sees another man sometimes, Egan. His name is Vitamin D. Sometimes she says she's going to work, but she goes over to his house instead." She watched me while she spoke, her eyes vacant, her voice untenanted by any kind of expression. Then she reached over and took my hand as gently as you pick up a pin that's fallen to the floor. "Just ask her. Friend told me before. He said you should know."

Our drive home was silent. The wind had picked up, and everything would whip back and forth for a while and then stop dead.

It was my night to make the dinner, so I went straight to the kitchen as soon as we got back to the apartment. Kathleen turned on the television in the living room. I heard her say something to Friend that sounded like a greeting.

I poured water into a pot for spaghetti and thought about the ten thousand dollars. I put butter and minced garlic into a frying pan and thought about Vitamin D, whoever *that* was.

"Oh damn! Friend, take that off! Friend! No!"

"What's the matter?"

"Nothing. Friend just jumped up on the couch with his bone. He made a spot. I'll get it."

She came into the kitchen shaking her head. "That beast! I keep telling him not to do that. It's the only time he ever growls at me." She was smiling and shaking her head.

"He's used to my old couch. It didn't matter much on that one."

She made a big fuss at the sink getting a rag, the cleaner, turning on the tap. "Well, this is a new couch and a new day!"

"Kat, stop for a moment, will you? I want to ask you something. Do you know a guy named Vitamin D?"

"A *guy* named 'Vitamin D'? No, but I know the guy who started it. Victor Dixon. He's the lead guitarist." She turned off the tap and squeezed the rag into the sink. "How do you know about Vitamin D? You never listen to rock."

"Who's Victor Dixon?"

"An old boyfriend of mine, who started that group. They've just begun to make it. They've begun showing their first video on MTV now. Did you see it?"

The water came to a boil. I wanted to drop the spaghetti in, but I couldn't right then. Too . . . scared?

"What went on with. . . . What went on between you two?"

She crossed her arms and sighed. Her eyes were twinkling. "Jealous, huh? That's good! Well, I knew him in college. After that he disappeared for a few years, then he turned up one day and we hung around together for a couple of months. He was more friend than boyfriend, even though a lot of people thought we had a big thing going. Why're you asking? How'd we get onto this?"

"Jazz told me—"

Friend started barking crazily in the other room. "Friend! Friend! Friend!" It sounded like he'd gone totally nuts. Kathleen and I looked at each other and moved.

On television, a man beat a white baby seal over the head with a wooden truncheon. The seal screamed while its head spewed dark blood onto the snow.

Friend stood next to the set and barked.

"Friend, stop!"

He kept on.

On television, a man pried open a wooden crate with a crowbar. Inside were ten dead parrots clumped together in a colorful, orderly row. Over the barking, I made out something about the illegal importation of rare birds into the United States.

"Friend, shut up!"

"Oh, Egan, look!"

A dog was strapped to an operating table. Its stomach was cut wide open, and its mouth was twisted up over its teeth.

All we needed then—a special on educational television about cruelty to animals.

It had been an impossible, weird day. The kind when the best thing you can do is throw up your hands, go directly to bed after dinner, and hope it ends at that.

But the air was full of something wrong and deep, and we ended up having everything out over dinner.

Victor Dixon was still around. No, she hadn't *touched* him since we'd been together. Yes, he called her at work sometimes. Yes, they'd gone out to lunch once or twice. *No*, nothing had happened. Didn't I believe her? How could I even think that?

I said I wanted very much to believe her, but why hadn't she told me about him before?

Because it only made things more confused . . .

Our voices got louder, and dinner, a nice dinner, got colder.

Friend stayed with us until about Round Three, then slunk out of the room, head and tail low. I felt like telling him to stay, hadn't he started this war in the first place?

"So what is *your* definition of trust, Egan? As far as you can throw me?"

"Oh, come on, Kathleen. How would you feel if you were in my place? Turn the situation around."

"I'd feel fine, thank you. Because I'd *believe* what you told me."

"Gee, you're quite a girl."

That did it. She got up and left, mad as hell.

While I waited and worried, Jasenka called twice within an hour.

The first time she said only that Kathleen was at Vitamin D's house, and gave me his telephone number.

I called. A very sleepy man with a Southern accent answered. I asked for her.

"Hey, bud, do you know what *time* it is? Kat isn't here. I haven't seen her in days. Jesus, do you know what time it is? Hey, how'd you get this number in the first place? It's unlisted! Did Kat give it to you? Man, *she's* going to get it when I see her. She promised she wouldn't give it out to anyone."

"Look, this is really important. I'd really appreciate it if you'd let me talk to her. I'm her brother, and we've got some very serious family problems."

"Oh no, I'm really sorry. But she isn't here, honest to God. Hold it a sec—I do have this other number where you might be able to reach her."

He gave me my number.

The second call from Jasenka lasted longer. Her voice was a child's whisper in a parent's ear. The words slowed and died at the end of every sentence.

"Egan? It's me again. Listen, you have to listen to me. The animals are rising. It's happening much sooner than I thought. They're going to kill everyone. They've had enough. Only their friends will be saved. Every animal in the world will do it. They'll kill everyone.

"Get a map as soon as you hang up. There's an island in Greece called Formori. F-O-R-M-O-R-I. You must go there immediately tomorrow. Everything will be starting in three days."

"Jazz—"

"No, be quiet! Formori is the place where they'll let some people live. People who are the animals' friends. Friend says you can go there and live, they'll let you. But not Kathleen. She wouldn't let him have his bone. Please, please go, Egan. Good-bye. I love you!"

It was the last time I ever talked to her. By the time I reached the hospital twenty minutes later, a sad-faced nurse told me she had just died.

Now it's almost three-thirty in the morning. I've looked at my world almanac and there it was: F-O-R-M-O-R-I.

I let Friend out three hours ago, and he hasn't returned. Neither has Kathleen.

The moon is still extraordinarily bright. While standing in the open doorway a few minutes ago, I saw what must have been thousands and thousands and thousands of birds flying in strict, unchanging patterns over its calm, lit face.

I must decide soon.

# GWYNETH JONES

## The Snow Apples

Gwyneth Jones is a name that may not yet be familiar to most American fantasy readers; and I am grateful to have had the opportunity to hear Jones speak eloquently on the subject of fantasy at the '86 British Fantasy Covention in Birmingham, or her work might have remained unknown to me as well. Her novels *Escape Plans* and *Divine Endurance* were, until recently, available only in British editions. The latter book is now an Arbor House edition in the United States.

Jones lives on the South Coast of England and writes for *The Women's Review*. "The Snow Apples" is a lovely original fairy tale published in the U.K. anthology *Tales from the Forbidden Planet*.

—T.W.

# THE SNOW APPLES

## Gwyneth Jones

Once upon a time there was a country where the mountains were so high that navigators of the coastland far away took the gleaming of their icy peaks for constellations in the night sky, and it was said that it would take no less than a lifetime to scale their heights. The people who lived in the lowland cities and towns did not often look up to where the cloud-piercing giants could be glimpsed, far away. But they often told each other stories about the mountains, and had vague hopes and great expectations about what might come out of them—some day.

Now in this country there was a king who had three wives—consecutively, in deference to important foreign interests. The first wife he believed he loved, but she had to be put aside because she produced no children. The second wife divorced him, owing to some trouble over the marriage settlement. The third wife did not interest the king at all, but she had a son. The naming day was a serious occasion. The king made sure that no doubtful elements were present: neither fairies of any kind, nor shaven-headed monks. But in private, to appease the conservative party in the country, he had arranged a discreet consultation with an astrologer.

The king, the queen and the baby sat in a small audience room. The soothsayer was ushered in, and the king saw at once that he did not look happy. He stayed close to the door, glancing around him uneasily.

"Sire," he said. "I am afraid I have an unpleasant duty to perform."

The king assumed the air of indulgent scepticism he had been keeping in reserve for such an eventuality, and vaguely waved his hand. The wave might have been indicating the presence of some large persons in uniform and dark glasses: this king was enlightened, but not foolishly so. The astrologer shuddered, but he spoke.

"While I was in the process of making, as you commanded, Sire, those calculations which impress our ignorant people—I found myself overtaken by a . . . a stronger influence."

"A what?"

"I mean, Sire, I had been acting on your commands. Suddenly I found that someone else had taken over from you. As a result of that intervention I now find myself compelled to pronounce a curse."

The queen, who thought all this was nonsense, gave a startled exclamation. The king looked calmer than ever. "Go on," he said.

The soothsayer's eyes seemed to have gone blank, but perhaps that was the result of extreme fear. He began to speak again, in a high strange voice:

*"King, your heir is doomed to suffer, or your kingdom to perish. A time of choice is coming, a moment of decision. Your son must lose his only love, or your lands must be destroyed."*

There was a short silence. Then the king said: "Thank you, you may go. You will be rewarded at the proper rate."

The man gave a sad smile and went out of the door, followed by two of the persons in uniform. The queen breathed a sigh of relief.

"Well, that wasn't too bad."

"Not too bad!" exclaimed the king. He snapped his fingers to dismiss the other guards and began to pace up and down, his face suddenly haggard.

"I don't understand," said the queen. "It was only a piece of impertinence. Very likely the boy *will* love some girl on his own account, without asking us. That is the way of this modern world. And he will have to 'give her up'. It happened to you, didn't it? It is nothing to make a fuss about."

But the king was afraid. He knew what power is. And he had just felt it in this room.

"You don't understand about curses," he told her. "How they sneak about and find you out. Have you never heard of a king called Oedipus?"

The queen had had a foreign education. She thought of the bare mountain, and began to feel frightened. But the king said: "There's only one thing to do. We must keep love out of his life. He is never to hear of it, he is never to say the word. He is never to feel its heat. I shall remake the world for him, and in his world there will be no such thing as—love."

The queen was shocked, but the king soon made her see that a life without love could be perfectly comfortable.

"I don't think we need worry about ordinary pleasant social manners," he explained. "You can be as nice to him as you like, as long as it all remains as meaningless as the smile one smiles when introduced to a stranger. He can have as many toys as you like. It is only when he starts to single out one of those toys as special that we must watch out. The same with nursemaids. Frequent changes, and constant impersonal attention should do the trick. Look at it this way, my dear. 'True Love' has always been something to cry about. We'll keep him laughing. In the end, I think he'll thank us for this. But of course if it works, he'll never be able to understand what we've done."

The scheme worked perfectly. The young prince was indeed a very pleasant child. For although he was constantly indulged, it was all done as a matter of course, unemotionally. The feeling of power that a spoiled child can express so unpleasantly was missing. He grew up among pleasant, friendly and obliging people, none of whom appeared to care whether he lived or died.

When he was old enough, to the queen's surprise, the king sent him abroad to finish his education.

"But, my dear," she protested, "suppose he falls in love?"

The king smiled calmly. "He won't. He's safe. He is in far more danger if he stays here."

The king had a feeling that 'arranged marriage' might not be a good thing for the prince to see. He would observe youths who had been his companions surrendering themselves for life to alien family ties—submitting to tradition, quite frequently against their will. This curious behaviour was bound to raise awkward questions. It suggested some kind of passionate excess: love of family, love of duty; of religion. The prince must not know about such things. His wife, when she came, would be presented as another toy for his collection. Meanwhile, let the loveless youth roam among the 'free' young people who would swear to him that to take a lover was purely a matter of selfish pleasure.

So the young prince went abroad. He enjoyed himself thoroughly, and his special education was never in any danger. But then an unfortunate thing happened. The king, of course, had made sure the 'curse' was never spoken of in his own country. But somehow somebody had heard of it. The prince found himself mentioned, as an interesting example, in an anthropological quarterly in the University library.

He was most unpleasantly surprised. He flew home at once, and the next day bounced into his father's office, blazing with passionate indignation.

"There's a curse on me!" he cried. "And you believe it or you wouldn't have kept it secret. *I'm* under a curse! I want to know what it is!"

The king picked up a pen and smiled suavely.

"I'm afraid I can't tell you."

"You've got to tell me."

"I'm afraid I just can't."

The prince collapsed on a chair. "Is that one of the conditions?"

The king seemed amused. "Well, it is one of your conditions, you might say."

The prince stared in angry bewilderment, and left, scowling.

The king began to laugh. He had never felt more sure of his son, and his son's training.

But the prince, who did not care about anything very much, had one deep interest in life. He went straight to a girl he had known in the days before he went abroad. She was engaged now, and alarmed at being seen with another man, even the prince. But she had the remains of very bitter feelings, so she did as he asked. The prince guessed there was no point in going to any respectable practitioner of the old Arts: his father would have got at them. He was looking for a back-street magician.

Five days later, when the moon was waning, the prince found himself standing outside a nasty little hovel in a back alley down by the stinking river. He was having second thoughts. From the way the old crone had cackled, he guessed his former girlfriend had arranged some kind of practical joke: he couldn't think why.

"You can come in now," croaked the voice of the seer, and the prince stooped and entered.

The atmosphere, which had been fetid before, was now thick with the fumes of some herb she had put on the fire. Where was the old woman? He made out her figure in the shadows. Then a flame shot up, and he was able to see her face. It had changed. The grimy network of wrinkles had disappeared. The eyes that looked out of the smoothed mask were strangely clear and bright. Perhaps the girl had paid this old hag to do some petty evil, but something different had happened. She was now in the power of a force greater than herself. No king's son could mistake that look. It was horrible.

The old woman's mouth moved stiffly. A voice came out.

"Prince, among the peaks of the far white mountains there grows a little fruit tree that bears apples of snow. Set an axe to the roots of that tree, and you will find out how you have been cursed . . ."

There was no more. The natural stink of the place began to overcome the smoke again. The prince felt disgusted. He flung down another handful of money and left. He shivered involuntarily as he stepped out of the alley . . . someone walking over his grave. Religion was a reasonable business, but he had always hated these old murky regions of traditional belief. He had never known why.

But as he walked away, back towards the modern city, he raised his head and looked to the east. He could see nothing but the city and its glow in the sky, but he knew that somewhere over there lay the white mountains of his quest. And suddenly, as sharp as that shiver of dread, he was overtaken by a great longing to be on his way. He smiled a promise to the east, and then turned for home.

He made his preparations in secret and left as if for a short holiday in the hills; without taking any special equipment or supplies. He was surprised, when he came to the villages in the foothills, to find how far he had left civilisation behind. He couldn't buy anything like proper mountain gear or food concentrates. Instead he bought quantities of thick felt clothes; and four little silent men with round dark faces and short thick limbs. They would carry the tins of butter and canvas tents and other old-fashioned provisions. He never talked to these little men, only to the go-between.

He kept his identity a secret of course. Perhaps it would have made a difference, perhaps not. On the ninth day of the expedition he woke up to find they had left him.

He had to give up and head back after them, carrying what he could. But without those four stolid bundles of garments how oppressive this other silence seemed: an icy oblivion of white light and blue shadow stretching limitless in every direction. "At least I should be able to tell up from down," the prince told himself firmly, "and that's all I need."

He tried to maintain the proper stolid state of mind, as he pecked his way onward, across an endless slope of white crisp snow. But the implacable silence, and the fear of what might happen next time he put his foot down, were too much for him. Shadows began to shift, taking on improbable shapes and colours. Voices called to him. He had no idea which way was up, or down. He panicked and began to run, fell down breathless and began to go to sleep. "No, no," he told himself, "mustn't go to sleep. Find the little fruit tree—"

And suddenly he saw it. It must have been there all the time, just ahead of him. The snow face was split, and in the V was greenery and sunlight —a magic valley full of fruit trees; and one of them bore snow-white apples. The prince gave a great yell of triumph and began to leap across the snow, laughing and shouting. Until he began to fall into a great blue-mouthed crevasse that opened beneath his feet. There was no magic valley.

The creature who lived in the cave at the bottom of the crevasse was stronger than she looked, and fearless. When she heard the crump of something falling she went out, examined it, and dragged it in. She put it on her bed and wrapped it in fleeces. She thought it was dead so she slept on the floor that night: because the dead ought to be treated with respect.

In the morning she found it had its eyes open.

"Are you dead?" she asked it.

"No—" answered the prince weakly.

"Then I won't kill you, either."

The prince looked at the fragile little white hand lying on his arm, and laughed feebly. Then he lost consciousness again.

He found out later that he should not have laughed. She was supposed to kill anybody who somehow found this cave and looked on her: and she had been trained rigorously in ways of killing that did not depend on height and weight. She was a priestess. Her name was Ari-gan, which means 'white child'. She was slight and wiry, with strange colourless hair and skin. Her eyes, which were a very pale blue, had a curious wavering, unfocussed stare. Probably that was because she had never looked at a human being before, not even her own face in a mirror. Her eyes had been bound from birth to the day she was brought here, sleeping, and abandoned. The prince was

worried about her being a priestess. He could see there would be trouble
if a man was found with her. But apparently the people who came twice a
year to bring her supplies never approached the cave.

"I know when they have come, by the weather and by a dream I have.
Then I go out and find the food and leave a sign, so they know I am still
here. That is all."

He tried to get Ari-gan to explain the purpose of her ritual isolation,
but she was rather vague about it. "Not to be touched," she said. "Not to
see the face, not to touch the hand. So that I will be empty. Ready."

"Ready for what?" asked the prince. But Ari-gan couldn't or wouldn't
tell. She had known no other life, she was happy. In time she would die.
And would another white child be brought here then? Not necessarily. The
white child was only born sometimes; quite often not for generations.

"What about me?" asked the prince. "You have seen my face now——"

Ari-gan looked at him thoughtfully. "I was told to kill people. At first,
I thought I did wrong to leave you alive. But now I know you. You are
like me, not like them. I feel it. So I think it is all right."

The prince understood. He was so different from her own primitive
mountain community, that she considered him outside the ban. She probably
thinks I'm as holy as herself, he thought wryly. But naturally he didn't
argue.

By the time the prince had recovered from his fall the short summer was
over, and the full fury of the autumn storms was on the ice peaks. He had
no hope of getting away. In the spring people from below would come again
with Ari-gan's supplies. He must find some way of reaching them without
letting them know he had been with their priestess. Until that time he was
trapped. When he realised this he had already been alone with the white
child for many days, sharing her food and tended by her. The winter ahead
did not seem terribly long.

They talked, they exchanged smiles and pleasant silence. The prince got
to know the white child's face as well as he knew his own. And he felt a
strange sensation creeping towards him. One night he sat up straight in
the bed of fleeces, in the darkness, and shouted 'Father!' so loud he woke
himself up. When he put his hands on his cheeks he found tears there.
What was it that had taken hold of him? He didn't know its name.

Ari-gan woke to find him rocking to and fro on the bed, sobbing loudly.
She began to cry too, and jumped up beside him.

"I feel it, I feel it too. Oh, what is happening?"

Neither of them could understand. They clung close to each other for
comfort, hoping that the thing would go away.

Some while after this, in the depth of winter, Ari-gan and the prince
had forgotten all about their nightmares. They had become lovers. They
never thought of what this might mean for the priestess if it was discovered:

they were living in the present. They lay together wrapped in warmth. The prince had told her nothing about his quest, but now, while the wind was howling outside in the desolation, something made him speak to her of the magic valley he had seen: the greenness and the sunlight and the little apple trees . . .

"How could there be apples here?" asked Ari-gan idly.

The prince said, "This is an apple. I will bite it." He put his hand round the curve of her small white breast; delicately round, and white as snow.

Ari-gan laughed. But the prince suddenly jumped up. He had remembered the words of the seer. He saw, all at once, how his presence here would destroy Ari-gan. That was the price that had been asked . . .

"No—!" he shouted. "I won't do it. I cannot!"

Ari-gan was too bewildered to stop him. He packed up some food and left the cave there and then. It was the act of a madman. She ran after him. But the snow was falling fast, the wind was strong and deadly. She had no chance at all, and neither had he. When she realised that, she went back to the cave and stood looking at their bed. A great shudder ran through all her white sapling body, as if some woodman had set his axe to her roots; and she stumbled and fell.

In the spring they came for Ari-gan. She was expecting this. She detected the drug in her food, and had prepared herself when sleep overcame her. It was her time. The purpose she had not even told the prince about would be fulfilled now. They painted the proper symbols over her bound eyes and they dressed her in the ancient robes. They led her to the holy place, and put fire before her. Acrid smoke rose, and the tension in the little dark room grew as the wise women and holy men of the mountain people waited for the god to speak. This was something older far than the state religion. It was something that might happen once in five hundred years. Generation on generation might live and die after this before another white one was born, and made into a perfect vessel: the mouthpiece of the god.

They waited. Suddenly the girl's face was twisted into a horrible grimace. She screamed and fell down from the high seat, her body writhing in pain.

The holy people jumped up and ran to the body. In a moment, the oldest of the women pronounced:

"There was no room. The child was not empty. She has betrayed us. The god cannot speak."

There was a murmur of horror. At once they began to think how to hide this disaster. In the end, they just put the spoiled priestess in a hole and shut the lid, poking in food and water so no one could say they had killed her. The mountain people went about their business, trying to ignore the whole incident. But everyone was waiting for the catastrophe.

Meanwhile, the shrivelled, frozen body of a young man was brought down from the mountain by a foreign climbing expedition. They had found him wandering, babbling about fruit trees, up in the snow fields. Everyone told him he was lucky to be alive. The king was very angry: and also anxious, in case his son had been risking his life for any particular reason. But this didn't seem to be the case. The young man appeared as unemotional and casual as ever.

Eventually he went abroad again, and continued his education. If he had had any real friends they would have noticed a change in him. He was very silent now. He was waiting for the curse to find him. He did not doubt its reality for a moment. But the price for evading it had seemed to him too high.

It came quite soon. He had not been looking at newspapers, so the first he knew of what had happened was a telex from his father. As he opened the envelope at the porter's desk, the headline on a newspaper lying on the counter seemed to leap out in front of his eyes. The telex message said: DOOMED TO PERISH. WHAT HAVE YOU DONE? COME HOME AT ONCE. FATHER.

Tears. It seemed as if the whole world was in mourning. The salt rain had fallen for ten days before the panic set in, before people realised that all the country was drowning in the same uncanny downpour. It was twenty days now, and scarcely a green thing remained standing. The roads were rivers of mud. The rivers were inland seas stinking with corpses of all kinds. Tears. The windless air was solid with falling water as the prince waded across the runways to the streaming bullock cart that waited for him. Motorised transport was almost at a standstill, and there would be no more flights in or out of this doomed land. They were all condemned to drown in a sea of tears. Here was his father, his hard face doubly ravaged by grief and fear, screaming at him crazily, "What have you done? What have you done?" and then, as they led the old man back to his bed, muttering bitterly, "Where did I fail?"

The prince had work to do. He had to direct the relief that had been organised for his unhappy people, and he had to try, hopelessly, to find a way to stop the rain. He worked hard. He did not know that he had changed. He did not notice how surprised the people he worked with were, to find what kind of prince they had—he was too busy.

Stories had begun to come to the capital of a place where it wasn't raining. It was said that there was a holy village, in a remote area, where they had an old Oracle temple, that had been famous a long time ago. This village was protected. Moreover, the people in it knew all about the reason for the rain.

"I'll go," said the prince.

The ordinary people got the idea their prince was going to consult the Oracle. "You must stop that," said the prince to his aides. "I don't want any of that kind of talk."

Still, they set off. The journey was comfortless and hopeless. There was nothing to see but the cruel, salt water falling, and through that veil the desperate antics of a dying people. Then one evening there was a breath of wind, through the murk of salt and decay, that seemed to hold the scent of growing things. The next morning they found their chain-shod jeeps rattling over hard ground. And then they drove out of the rain.

The silence was appalling at first, the air was incredibly dry.

"What did the people in the last village say about this place?"

"They said it was accursed, Sir. It does seem odd, doesn't it."

"Perhaps life itself becomes a curse when everybody else is dying. I wonder where the locals are."

The dry streets were empty. The prince and his party searched for and found the old, crooked, little beehive building that was the famous Oracle temple. There were sounds from inside.

"They must all be in there," said the prince and squelched to the door, still sticky and weighed down with salt rain. He did not notice how the others stayed back. The ritual said the suppliant must go alone.

He stepped into the dark. A long, muttering sigh passed around him. He could feel there were lots of people crouching in here; probably the whole population of the village.

"Who comes?" whispered an ancient voice.

"The king," said the prince. For the time being, that was the truth.

"We knew you must come."

The prince suddenly realised he was alone, with these hungry muttering shadows and the acrid smell of holiness that he hated.

"I think you are making a mistake. I only came to find out—"

"Yes, the king must come. He is the only substitute, this everybody knows."

The prince backed away. These people wanted to change him from being the one who asks, into the one things are asked of. The thick holy smell was terrifying. At his back was an oblong of sunlight, and his friends . . .

The people all around him, he could see them now, were short and dark with stolid, silent faces. The ancient woman who spoke for them fixed her claw of a hand on his arm.

"We guard the Oracle," she said. "We know when the voice will be coming, because a child is born who seems not of our race. All our women, while they are childbearers, carry the binding cloths with them. You have perhaps seen the cloths, they are wound around the arm. This is so that whenever, wherever a white child is born, the midwife and the mother will bind its eyes at birth. The child is not to be touched with bare hands, not to see any face. She is prepared carefully. When she is of age she is put away in a secret place. She never sees those who bring her food. To see or touch her then is destruction. Then the time comes—"

The dry voice faltered. The woman covered her face and sobbed.

"Her time came, her time came but she was not ready. Where did we fail? For her mind is broken and the god is angry. The god must speak but cannot speak because the vessel was not empty . . . Oh Ari-gan, Ari-gan, why did you betray us?"

Then the prince understood.

They showed him Ari-gan in the hole. The starved filthy creature looked up at him with mindless eyes, and the noise of her crying was terrible.

"She doesn't die," whispered the old priestess. "She doesn't eat and she doesn't drink but she doesn't die. And cries like that, always. No tears."

The prince was seeing through a stinging mist. He tried to control his voice.

"What must I do?"

But he knew.

They painted the proper symbols over his bound eyes; they wrapped the robes around him, set him on the seat with fire before him. The bitter smoke rose up. The prince found that every nightmare, every secret fear of his life, had just been some shadow cast by this moment. He was opened up, and something walked into him. If Ari-gan had been untouched, she would have been able to welcome this *Something* like an invited guest. Not so the prince. The submission, the denial of self, nearly killed him. He thought he would go mad, and the god remain dumb after all. But Ari-gan had recognised the prince as one of her own kind; and she was right, in a way. His heart for so many years had been quite empty. There was room, even now.

The prince's face became a smooth mask. The lips moved stiffly. A voice that was not the prince's voice flowed out, filling the room. And outside, in the village, it began to rain.

What did the god say? No one is telling. The prince's party did not even stay to find out. They carried Ari-gan, washed and tended, on a stretcher back to the jeeps. All the while, a pure rain of sweet water fell. It continued through their journey, until the salt was washed away. Then it ceased.

Later, the old king was heard testily accusing his wife of some ancient crime. "You ought to have told me," he complained. "What do I know about babies? I always said these curses are devious things. But *you* ought to have known surely—that the only love a nine-day-old baby has is himself . . . is himself . . ."

But just now the prince sat by Ari-gan's stretcher in the back of the jolting jeep, holding her hand. She was too weak to talk, but her eyes were speaking: not mad and empty anymore. He had the feeling he had left some small possession behind at the Oracle hut. But he was sure it wasn't anything very valuable.

# SUSAN PALWICK

## Ever After

Susan Palwick is a graduate of Princeton University's Creative Writing Program and of Clarion West Writer's Workshop. Her fiction and poetry have appeared in *Isaac Asimov's Science Fiction Magazine* and in *Amazing*. Her poem "The Neighbor's Wife," which won the Rhysling Award for Best Short Poem of 1985, will be reprinted in *Nebula Awards 22*. She lives in Manhattan, where she works part-time at an executive search firm and serves on the editorial board of *The Little Magazine*.

Professionals in the field are frequently asked where fantasy ends and horror begins. In all fairy tales the words "and they lived happily ever after" mean just that. But in the real world we all know that can never be. If life goes on, then people and circumstances change. In Palwick's horrific fractured fairy tale, the heroine has unfortunately bought the promise without hearing the catch.

—E.D.


"Traditional" fairy tales have never existed in a single rigid form. Each age, each society adapts the tale to fit the audience. *Cinderella* can be followed from fragments by anonymous storytellers, to the somewhat grisly tales of Cat Cinderella, to the more moral version Charles Perrault penned for the French court of Louis the Sun King, to the watered-down and sanitized Disney version with which most people today are familiar. Susan Palwick follows in an ancient fantasy tradition in taking the threads of the fairy tale and weaving them into a pattern of her own.

—T.W.

# EVER AFTER

## Susan Palwick

"Velvet," she says, pushing back her sleep-tousled hair. "I want green velvet this time, with lace around the neck and wrists. Cream lace—not white—and sea-green velvet. Can you do that?"

"Of course." She's getting vain, this one; vain and a little bossy. The wonder has worn off. All for the best. Soon now, very soon, I'll have to tell her the truth.

She bends, here in the dark kitchen, to peer at the back of her mother's prized copper kettle. It's just after dusk, and by the light of the lantern I'm holding a vague reflection flickers and dances on the metal. She scowls. "Can't you get me a real mirror? That ought to be simple enough."

I remember when the light I brought filled her with awe. Wasting good fuel, just to see yourself by! "No mirrors. I clothe you only in seeming, not in fact. You know that."

"Ah." She waves a hand, airily. She's proud of her hands: delicate and pale and long-fingered, a noblewoman's hands; all the years before I came she protected them against the harsh work of her mother's kitchen. "Yes, the prince. I have to marry a prince, so I can have his jewels for my own. Will it be this time, do you think?"

"There will be no princes at this dance, Caitlin. You are practicing for princes."

"Hah! And when I'm good enough at last, will you let me wear glass slippers?"

"Nonsense. You might break them during a gavotte, and cut yourself." She knew the story before I found her; they always do. It enters their blood as soon as they can follow speech, and lodges in their hearts like the promise of spring. All poor mothers tell their daughters this story, as they sit together in dark kitchens, scrubbing pots and trying to save their hands for the day when the tale becomes real. I often wonder if that first young woman was one of ours, but the facts don't matter. Like all good stories, this one is true.

"Princess Caitlin," she says dreamily. "That will be very fine. Oh, how they will envy me! It's begun already, in just the little time since you've

72

made me beautiful. Ugly old Lady Alison—did you see her giving me the evil eye, at the last ball? Just because my skin is smooth and hers wrinkled, and I a newcomer?"

"Yes," I tell her. I am wary of Lady Alison, who looks too hard and says too little. Lady Alison is dangerous.

"Jealousy," Caitlin says complacently. "I'd be jealous, if I looked like she does."

"You are very lovely," I say, and it is true. With her blue eyes and raven hair, and those hands, she could have caught the eye of many princes on her own. Except of course, that without me they never would have seen her.

Laughing, she sits to let me plait her hair. "So serious! You never smile at me. Do magic folk never smile? Aren't you proud of me?"

"Very proud," I say, parting the thick cascade and beginning to braid it. She smells like smoke and the thin, sour stew which simmers on the hearth, but at the dance tonight she will be scented with all the flowers of summer.

"Will you smile and laugh when I have my jewels and land? I shall give you riches, then."

So soon, I think, and my breath catches. So soon she offers me gifts, and forgets the woman who bore her, who now lies snoring in the other room. All for the best; and yet I am visited by something very like pity. "No wife has riches but from her lord, Caitlin. Not in this kingdom."

"I shall have riches of my own, when I am married," she says grandly; and then, her face clouding as if she regrets having forgotten, "My mother will be rich too, then. She'll like you, when we're rich. Godmother, why doesn't she like you now?"

"Because I am stealing you away from her. She has never been invited to a ball. And because I am beautiful, and she isn't any more."

What I have said is true enough, as always; and, as always, I find myself wondering if there is more than that. No matter. If Caitlin's mother suspects, she says nothing. I am the only chance she and her daughter have to approach nobility, and for the sake of that dream she has tolerated my presence, and Caitlin's odd new moods, and the schedule which keeps the girl away from work to keep her fresh for dances.

Caitlin bends her head, and the shining braids slip through my fingers like water. "She'll come to the castle whenever she wants to, when I'm married to a prince. We'll make her beautiful too, then. I'll buy her clothing and paint for her face."

"There are years of toil on her, Caitlin. Lady Alison is your mother's age, and all her riches can't make her lovely again."

"Oh, but Lady Alison's mean. That makes you ugly." Caitlin dismisses her enemy with the ignorance of youth. Lady Alison is no meaner than anyone, but she has borne illnesses and childlessness and the unfaithfulness of her rich lord. Her young nephew will fall in love with Caitlin tonight —a match Lord Gregory suggested, I suspect, precisely because Alison will oppose it.

Caitlin's hair is done, piled in coiled, lustrous plaits. "Do you have the invitation? Where did I put it?"

"On the table, next to the onions."

She nods, crosses the room, snatches up the thick piece of paper and fans herself with it. I remember her first invitation, only six dances ago, her eagerness and innocence and purity, the wide eyes and wonder. *I? I have been invited to the ball?* She refused to let go of the invitation then; afraid it might vanish as suddenly as it had come, she carried it with her for hours. They are always at their most beautiful that first time, when they believe most fully in the story and are most awe-stricken at having been chosen to play the heroine. No glamour we give them can ever match that first glow.

"Clothe me," Caitlin commands now, standing with her eyes closed in the middle of the kitchen, and I put the glamour on her and her grubby kitchen-gown is transformed by desire and shadow into sea-green velvet and cream lace. She smiles. She opens her eyes, which gleam with joy and the giddiness of transformation. She has taken easily to that rush; she craves it. Already she has forsaken dreams of love for dreams of power.

"I'm hungry," she says. "I want to eat before the dance. What was that soup you gave me last night? You must have put wine in it, because it made me drunk. I want more of that."

"No food before you dance," I tell her. "You don't want to look fat, do you?"

No chance of that, for this girl who has starved in a meager kitchen all her life; but at the thought of dancing she forgets her hunger and takes a few light steps in anticipation of the music. "Let me stay longer this time—please. Just an hour or two. I never get tired any more."

"Midnight," I tell her flatly. It won't do to change that part of the story until she knows everything.

So we go to the dance, in a battered carriage made resplendent not by any glamour of mine but by Caitlin's belief in her own beauty. This, too, she has learned easily; already the spells are more hers than mine, although she doesn't yet realize it.

At the gates, Caitlin hands the invitation to the footman. She has grown to relish this moment, the thrill of bending him to her will with a piece of paper, of forcing him to admit someone he suspects—quite rightly— doesn't belong here. It is very important that she learn to play this game. Later she will learn to win her own invitations, to cajole the powerful into admitting her where, without their permission, she cannot go at all.

Only tonight it is less simple. The footman glances at the envelope, frowns, says, "I'm sorry, but I can't admit you."

"Can't admit us?" Caitlin summons the proper frosty indignation, and so I let her keep talking. She needs to learn this, too. "Can't admit us, with a handwritten note from Lord Gregory?"

"Just so, mistress. Lady Alison has instructed—"

"Lady Alison didn't issue the invitation."

The footman coughs, shuffles his feet. "Just so. I have the very strictest instructions—"

"What does Lord Gregory instruct?"

"Lord Gregory has not—"

"Lord Gregory wrote the invitation. Lord Gregory wants us here. If Lord Gregory learned we were denied it would go badly for you, footman."

He looks up at us; he looks miserable. "Just so," he says, sounding wretched.

"I shall speak to her for you," I tell him, and Caitlin smiles at me and we are through the gates, passing ornate gardens and high, neat hedges. I lean back in my seat, shaking. Lady Alison is very dangerous, but she has made a blunder. The servant could not possibly refuse her husband's invitation; all she has done is to warn us. "Be very careful tonight," I say to Caitlin. "Avoid her."

"I'd like to scratch her eyes out! How dare she, that jealous old—"

"Avoid her, Caitlin! I'll deal with her. I don't want to see you anywhere near her."

She subsides. Already we can hear music from the great hall, and her eyes brighten as she taps time to the beat.

The people at the dance are the ones who are always at dances; by now, all of them know her. She excites the men and unnerves the women, and where she passes she leaves a trail of uncomfortable silence, followed by hushed whispers. I strain to hear what they are saying, but catch only the usual comments about her youth, her beauty, her low birth.

"Is she someone's illegitimate child, do you think?"

"A concubine, surely."

"She'll never enter a convent, not that one."

"Scheming husband-hunter, and may she find one soon. I don't want her taking mine."

The usual. I catch sight of Lady Alison sitting across the wide room. She studies us with narrowed eyes. One arthritic hand, covered with jeweled rings, taps purposefully on her knee. She sees me watching her and meets my gaze without flinching. She crosses herself.

I look away, wishing we hadn't come here. What does she intend to do? I wonder how much she has learned simply by observation, and how much Gregory let slip. I scan the room again and spot him, in a corner, nursing a chalice of wine. He is watching Caitlin as intently as his wife did, but with a different expression.

And someone else is watching Caitlin, among the many people who glance at her and then warily away: Randolph, Gregory's young nephew, who is tall and well-formed and pleasant of face. Caitlin looks to me for confirmation and I nod. She smiles at Randolph—that artful smile there has never been need to teach—and he extends a hand to invite her to dance.

I watch them for a moment, studying how she looks up at him, the angle of her head, the flutter of her lashes. She started with the smile, and I gave her the rest. She has learned her skills well.

"So," someone says behind me, "she's growing accustomed to these late nights."

I turn. Lady Alison stands there, unlovely and shrunken, having crossed the room with improbable speed. "Almost as used to them as you," she says.

I bow my head, carefully acquiescent. "Or you yourself. Those who would dance in these halls must learn to do without sleep."

"Some sleep during the day." Her mouth twitches. "I am Randolph's aunt, mistress. While he stays within these walls his care lies in my keeping, even as the care of the girl lies in yours. I will safeguard him however I must."

I laugh, the throaty chuckle which thrills Gregory, but my amusement is as much an act as Caitlin's flirtatiousness. "Against dancing with pretty young women?"

"Against being alone with those who would entrap him with his own ignorance. He knows much too little of the world; he places more faith in fairy tales than in history, and neither I nor the Church have been able to persuade him to believe in evil. I pray you, by our Lord in heaven and his holy saints, leave this house."

"So you requested at the gates." Her piety nauseates me, as she no doubt intended, and I keep my voice steady only with some effort. "The Lord of this castle is Lord Gregory, Lady Alison, by whose invitation we are here and in whose hospitality we will remain."

She grimaces. "I have some small power of my own, although it does not extend to choosing my guests. Pray chaperone your charge."

"No need. They are only dancing." I glance at Caitlin and Randolph, who gaze at each other as raptly as if no one else were in the room. Randolph's face is silly and soft; Caitlin's, when I catch a glimpse of it, is soft and ardent. I frown, suddenly uneasy; that look is a bit too sudden and far too unguarded, and may be more than artifice.

Lady Alison snorts. "Both will want more than dancing presently, I warrant, although they will want different things. Chaperone her—or I will do it for you, less kindly."

With that she turns and vanishes into the crowd. I turn back to the young couple, thinking that a chaperone would indeed be wise tonight; but the players have struck up a minuet, and Caitlin and Randolph glide gracefully through steps as intricate and measured as any court intrigue. The dance itself will keep them safe, for a little while.

Instead I make my way to Gregory, slowly, drifting around knots of people as if I am only surveying the crowd. Alison has positioned herself to watch Caitlin and Randolph, who dip and twirl through the steps of the dance; I hope she won't notice me talking to her husband.

"She is very beautiful," says Gregory softly when I reach his side. "Even lovelier than you, my dear. What a charming couple they make. I would give much to be Randolph, for a few measures of this dance."

He thinks he can make me jealous. Were this any other ball I might pretend he had succeeded, but I have no time for games tonight. "Gregory, Alison tried to have us barred at the gate. And she just threatened me."

He smiles. "That was foolish of her. Also futile."

"Granted," I say, although I suspect Lady Alison has resources of which neither of us are aware. Most wives of the nobility do: faithful servants, devoted priests, networks of spies in kitchens and corridors.

Gregory reaches out to touch my cheek; I draw away from him, uneasy. Everyone here suspects I am his mistress, but there is little sense in giving them public proof. He laughs gently. "You need not be afraid of her. She loves the boy and wishes only to keep him cloistered in a chapel, with his head buried in scripture. I tell her that is no sport for a young man and certainly no education for a titled lord, who must learn how to resist the blandishments of far more experienced women. So he and our little Caitlin will be merry, and take their lessons from each other, with no one the worse for it. See how they dance together!"

They dance as I have taught Caitlin she should dance with princes: lingering over the steps, fingertips touching, lips parted and eyes bright. Alison watches them, looking worried, and I cannot help but feel the same way. Caitlin is too obvious, too oblivious; she has grown innocent again, in a mere hour. I remember what Alison said about history, and fairy tales; if Caitlin and Randolph both believe themselves in that same old story, things will go harshly for all of us.

"Let them be happy together," Gregory says softly. "They have need of happiness, both of them—Randolph with his father surely dying, and the complexities of power about to bewilder him, and Caitlin soon to learn her true nature. You cannot keep it from her much longer, Juliana. She has changed too much. Let them be happy, for this one night; and let their elders, for once, abandon care and profit from their example."

He reaches for my hand again, drawing me closer to him, refusing to let go. His eyes are as bright as Randolph's; he has had rather too much wine.

"Profit from recklessness?" I ask, wrenching my fingers from his fist. Alison has looked away from her nephew and watches us now, expressionless. I hear murmurs around us; a young courtier in purple satin and green hose raises an eyebrow.

"This is my castle," Gregory says. "My halls and land, my musicians, my servants and clerics and nobles; my wife. No one can hurt you here, Juliana."

"No one save you, my lord. Kindly retain your good sense—"

"My invitation." His voice holds little kindness now. "My invitation allowed you entrance, as it has many other times; I provide you with splendor, and fine nourishment, and a training ground for the girl, and I am glad to do so. I am no slave of Alison's priests, Juliana; I know full well that you are not evil."

"Kindly be more quiet and discreet, my lord!" The courtier is carefully ignoring us now, evidently fascinated with a bunch of grapes. Caitlin and Randolph, transfixed by each other, sway in the last steps of the minuet.

Gregory continues in the same tone, "Of late you have paid far more attention to Caitlin than to me. Even noblemen are human, and can be hurt. Let the young have their pleasures tonight, and let me have mine."

I lower my own voice, since he refuses to lower his. "What, in the middle of the ballroom? That would be a fine entertainment for your guests! I will come to you tomorrow—"

"Tonight," he says, into the sudden silence of the dance's end. "Come to me tonight, in the usual chamber—"

"It is a poor lord who leaves his guests untended," I tell him sharply, "and a poor teacher who abandons her student. You will excuse me."

He reaches for me again, but I slip past his hands and go to find Caitlin, wending my way around gaudily-dressed lords and ladies and squires, catching snippets of gossip and conversation.

"Did you see them dancing—"

"So the venison disagreed with me, but thank goodness it was only a trifling ailment—"

"Penelope's violet silk! I said, my dear, I simply must have the pattern and wherever did you find that seamstress—"

"Gregory's brother in failing health, and the young heir staying here? No uncle can be trusted that far. The boy had best have a quick dagger and watch his back, is what I say."

That comment hurries my steps. Gregory's brother is an obscure duke, but he is a duke nonetheless, and Gregory is next in the line of succession after Randolph. If Randolph is in danger, and Caitlin with him—

I have been a fool. We should not have come here, and we must leave. I scan the colorful crowd more anxiously than ever for Caitlin, but my fears are groundless; she has found me first, and rushes towards me, radiant. "Oh, godmother—"

"Caitlin! My dear, listen: you must stay by me—"

But she hasn't heard me. "Godmother, he's so sweet and kind, so sad with his father ill and yet trying to be merry—did you see how he danced? Why does it have to be a prince I love? I don't care if he's not a prince, truly I don't, and just five days ago I scorned that other gawky fellow for not having a title, but he wasn't nearly as nice—"

"Caitlin!" Yes, we most assuredly must leave. I lower my voice and take her by the elbow. "Listen to me: many men are nice. If you want a nice man you may marry a blacksmith. I am not training you to be a mere duchess."

She grows haughty now. "Duchess sounds quite well enough to me. Lord Gregory is no king."

Were we in private I would slap her for that. "No, he isn't, but he is a grown man and come into his limited power, and so he is still more useful to us than Randolph. Caitlin, we must leave now—"

"No! We can't leave; it's nowhere near midnight. I don't want to leave. You can't make me."

"I can strip you of your finery right here."

"Randolph wouldn't care."

"Everyone else would, and he is outnumbered."

"Randolph picks his own companions—"

"Randolph," I say, losing all patience, "still picks his pimples. He is a fine young man, Caitlin, but he is young nonetheless. My dear, many more things are happening here tonight than your little romance. I am your magic godmother, and on some subjects you must trust me. We are leaving."

"I won't leave," she says, raising her chin. "I'll stay here until after midnight. I don't care if you turn me into a toad; Randolph will save me, and make me a duchess."

"Princesses are safer," I tell her grimly, not at all sure it's even true. On the far side of the room I see the courtier in the green hose talking intently to Lady Alison, and a chill cuts through me. Well, he cannot have heard much which isn't general rumor, and soon we will be in the carriage, and away from all this.

"Caitlin!" Randolph hurries up to us, as welcoming and guileless as some friendly dog. "Why did you leave me? I didn't know where you'd gone. Will you dance with me again? Here, some wine if you don't mind sharing, I thought you'd be thirsty—"

She takes the goblet and sips, laughing. "Of course I'll dance with you."

I frown at Caitlin and clear my throat. "I regret that she cannot, my lord—"

"This is my godmother Juliana," Caitlin cuts in, taking another sip of wine and giving Randolph a dazzling smile, "who worries overmuch about propriety and thinks people will gossip if I dance with you too often."

"And so they shall," he says, bowing and kissing my hand, "because everyone gossips about beauty." He straightens and smiles down at me, still holding my hand. His cheeks are flushed and his fingers very warm; I can feel the faint, steady throb of his pulse against my skin. What could Caitlin do but melt, in such heat?

"Randolph!" Two voices, one cry; Alison and Gregory approach us from opposite directions, the sea of guests parting before them.

Alison, breathless, reaches us a moment before her husband does. "Randolph, my love—the players are going to give us another slow tune, at my request. You'll dance with your crippled old aunt, won't you?"

He bows; he can hardly refuse her. Gregory, standing next to Caitlin, says smoothly, "And I will have the honor of dancing with the young lady, with her kind godmother's assent."

It isn't a petition. I briefly consider feigning illness, but such a ruse would shake Caitlin's faith in my power and give Gregory the excuse to protest that I must stay here, spend the night and be made comfortable in his household's care.

Instead I station myself next to a pillar to watch the dancers. Alison's lips move as Randolph guides her carefully around the floor. I see her press a small pouch into his hand; he smiles indulgently and puts it in a pocket.

She is warning him away from Caitlin, then. This dance is maddeningly slow, and far too long; I crane my neck to find Caitlin and Gregory, only to realize that they are about to sweep past me. "Yes, I prefer roses to all other blooms," Caitlin says lightly. (That too is artifice; she preferred forget-me-nots until I taught her otherwise.)

So at least one of these conversations is insignificant, and Caitlin safe. Alison and Randolph, meanwhile, glare at each other; she is trying to give him something on a chain, and he is refusing it. They pass me, but say nothing; Caitlin and Gregory go by again a moment later. "Left left right, left left right," he tells her, before they are past my hearing, "it is a pleasing pattern and very fashionable; you must try it."

A new court dance, no doubt. This old one ends at last and I dart for Caitlin, only to be halted by a group of rowdy acrobats who have just burst into the hall. "Your pleasure!" they cry, doing flips and twists in front of me as the crowd laughs and gathers to watch them. "Your entertainment, your dancing hearts!" I try to go around them, but find myself blocked by a motley-clad clown juggling pewter goblets. "Hey! We'll make you merry, at the generous lord's invitation we'll woo you, we'll win you—"

You'll distract us, I think—but from what? I manage to circle the juggler, but there is no sign of Caitlin or Randolph. Gregory seems likewise to have disappeared.

Alison is all too evident, however. "Where are they? What have you done with them?" She stands in front of me, her hands clenched on the fine silk of her skirt. "I turned away from Randolph for a mere moment to answer a servant's question, and when I looked back he was gone—"

"My lady, I was standing on the side. You no doubt saw me. I am honestly eager to honor your wishes and be gone, and I dislike this confusion as much as you do."

"I know you," she says, trembling, her voice very low. "I know you for what you are. I told Randolph but he would not believe me, and Gregory fairly revels in dissolution. I would unmask you in this hall and send town criers to spread the truth about you, save that my good lord would be set upon by decent Christian folk were it known he had trafficked with such a creature."

And your household destroyed and all your riches plundered, I think; yes, the poor welcome such pretexts. You do well to maintain silence, Alison, since it buys your own safety.

But I dare not admit to what she knows. "I am but a woman as yourself, my lady, and I share your concern for Randolph and the girl—"

"Nonsense. They are both charming young people who dance superbly." Gregory has reappeared, affable and urbane; he seems more relaxed than he has all evening, and I trust him less.

So does Alison, by the look of her. "And where have you hidden our two paragons of sprightliness, my lord?"

"I? I have not hidden them anywhere. Doubtless they have stolen away and found some quiet corner to themselves. The young will do such things. Alison, my sweet, you look fatigued—"

"And the old, when they get a chance. No: I am not going to retire conveniently and leave you alone with this creature. I value your soul far more than that."

"Although not my body," Gregory says, raising an eyebrow. "Well, then, shall we dance, all three? With linked hands in a circle, like children? Shall we sit and discuss the crops, or have a hand of cards? What would you, my lovelies?"

Alison takes his hand. "Let us go find our nephew."

He sighs heavily and rolls his eyes, but he allows himself to be led away. I am glad to be rid of them; now I can search on my own and make a hasty exit. The conversation with Alison worries me. She is too cautious to destroy us here, but she may well try to have us followed into the countryside.

So I make my way through corridors, through courtyards, peering into corners and behind pillars, climbing winding staircases and descending them, until I am lost and can no longer hear the music from the great hall. I meet other furtive lovers, dim shapes embracing in shadows, but none are Randolph and Caitlin. When I have exhausted every passageway I can find I remember Caitlin and Gregory's discussion of roses and hurry outside, through a doorway I have never seen before, but the moonlit gardens yield nothing. The sky tells me that it is midnight: Caitlin will be rejoicing at having eluded me.

Wherever she is. These halls and grounds are too vast; I could wander all night and still not find her by dawn. Gregory knows where she is: I am convinced he does, convinced he arranged the couple's disappearance. He may have done so to force me into keeping the tryst with him. That would be very like him; he would be thrilled by my seeking him out while his guests gossip and dance in the great hall. Gregory delights in private indiscretions at public events.

So I will play his game this once, although it angers me, and lie with him, and be artful and cajoling. I go back inside and follow hallways I know to Gregory's chambers, glancing behind me to be sure I am not seen.

The small chapel where Lady Alison takes her devotions lies along the same path, and as I pass it I hear moans of pain. I stop, listening, wary of a trap—but the noise comes again, and the agony sounds genuine: a thin, childish whimpering clearly made by a woman.

*Caitlin?* I remember Alison's threats, and my vision blackens for a moment. I slip into the room, hiding in shadows, tensed to leap. If Alison led the girl here—

Alison is indeed here, but Caitlin is not with her. Doubled over in front of the altar, Gregory's wife gasps for breath and clutches her side; her face is sweaty, gray, the pupils dilated. She sees me and recoils, making her habitual sign of the cross; her hand is trembling, but her voice remains steady. "So. Didn't you find them, either?"

"My lady Alison, what—"

"He called it a quick poison," she says, her face contorting with pain, "but I am stronger than he thinks, or the potion weaker. I was tired—my leg . . . we came here; it was close. I asked him to pray with me, and he repented very prettily. 'I will bring some wine,' he said, 'and we will both drink to my salvation.' Two cups he brought, and I took the one he gave me . . . I thought him saved, and relief dulled my wits. 'Mulled wine,' he said, 'I ground the spices for you myself,' and so he did, no doubt. Pray none other taste them."

So much speech has visibly drained her; shaken, I help her into a chair. What motive could Gregory have for killing his wife? Her powers of observation were an asset to him, though he rarely heeded them, and he couldn't have felt constrained by his marriage vows; he never honored them while she was alive.

"It is well I believe in the justice of God," she says. "No one will punish him here in the world. They will pretend I ate bad meat, or had an attack of bile."

"Be silent and save your strength," I tell her, but she talks anyway, crying now, fumbling to wipe her face through spasms.

"He tired of me because I am old. He grew tired of a wife who said her prayers, and loved other people's children although she could have none of her own. No doubt he will install you by his side now, since you are made of darkness and steal the daughters of simple folk."

Gregory knows far better than to make me his formal consort, whatever Alison thinks. "We choose daughters only when one of us has been killed, Lady Alison. We wish no more than anyone does—to continue, and to be safe."

"I will continue in heaven," she says, and then cries out, a thin keening which whistles between her teeth. She no longer sounds human.

I kneel beside her, uncertain she will be able to understand my words. This does not look like a quick-acting potion, whatever Gregory said; it will possibly take her hours to die, and she will likely be mad before then. "I cannot save you, my lady, but I can make your end swift and painless."

"I need no mercy from such as you!"

"You must take mercy where you can get it. Who else will help you?"

She moans and then subsides, trembling. "I have not been shriven. He could have allowed me that."

"But he did not. Perhaps you will be called a saint someday, and this declared your martyrdom; for now, the only last rites you will be offered are mine."

She crosses herself again, but this time it is clearly an effort for her to lift her hand. "A true death?"

"A true death," I say gently. "We do not perpetuate pain."

Her lips draw back from her teeth. "Be merciful, then; and when you go to your assignation, tell Gregory he harms himself far worse than he has harmed me."

It is quick and painless, as I promised, but I am shaking when I finish, and the thought of seeing Gregory fills me with dread. I will have to pretend not to know that he has murdered his wife; I will have to be charming, and seductive, and disguise my concern for my own safety and Caitlin's so I can trick her whereabouts out of him.

I knock on his door and hear the soft "Enter." Even here I need an invitation, to enter this chamber where Gregory will be sprawled on the bed, peeling an apple or trimming his fingernails, his clothing already unfastened.

Tonight the room is unlit. I see someone sitting next to the window, silhouetted in moonlight; only as my eyes adjust to the dimness do I realize that Gregory has not kept our appointment. A priest waits in his place, surrounded by crucifixes and bottles of holy water and plaster statues of saints. On the bed where I have lain so often is something long and sharp which I force myself not to look at too closely.

"Hello," he says, as the door thuds shut behind me. I should have turned and run, but it is too late now; I have frozen at the sight of the priest, as they say animals do in unexpected light. In the hallway I hear heavy footsteps—the corridor is guarded, then.

The priest holds an open Bible; he glances down at it, and then, with a grimace of distaste, sideways at the bed. "No, lady, it won't come to that. You needn't look so frightened."

I say nothing. I tell myself I must think clearly, and be very quick, but I cannot think at all. We are warned about these small rooms, these implements. All the warnings I have heard have done me no good.

"There's the window," he explains. "You could get out that way if you had to. That is how I shall tell them you escaped, when they question me." He gestures at his cheek, and I see a thin, cruel scar running from forehead to jaw. "When I was still a child, my father took me poaching for boar on our lord's estate. It was my first hunt. It taught me not to corner frightened beasts, especially when they have young. Sit down, lady. Don't be afraid."

I sit, cautiously and without hope, and he closes the book with a soft sound of sighing parchment. "You are afraid, of course; well you should be. Lord Gregory has trapped you, for reasons he says involve piety but doubtless have more to do with politics; Lady Alison has been weaving her own schemes to destroy you, and the Church has declared you incapable of redemption. You have been quite unanimously consigned to the stake. Which is—" he smiles "—why I am here. Do you believe in God, my dear? Do your kind believe in miracles?"

When I don't answer he smiles again and goes on easily, as if we were chatting downstairs at the dance, "You should. It is a kind of miracle that has brought you to me. I have prayed for this since I was very young, and now I am old and my prayer has been answered. I was scarcely more than a boy when I entered the religious life, and for many years I was miserable, but now I see that this is why it happened."

He laughs, quite kindly. His kindness terrifies me. I fear he is mad. "I came from a poor family," he says. "I was the youngest son, and so, naturally, I became a priest. The Church cannot get sons the normal way, so it takes other people's and leaves the best young men to breed more souls. You and I are not, you see, so very different."

He leans back in his chair. "There were ten other children in my family. Four died. The littlest and weakest was my youngest sister, who was visited one day by a very beautiful woman who made her lovely, and took her to parties, and then took her away. I never got to say good-bye to my sister —her name was Sofia—and I never got to tell her that, although I knew what she had become, I still loved her. I thought she would be coming back, you see."

He leans forward earnestly, and his chair makes a scraping sound. "I have always prayed for a way to reach her. The Church tells me to destroy you, but I do not believe God wants you destroyed—because He has sent you to me, who thinks of you only with pity and gratitude and love. I am glad my little sister was made beautiful. If you know her, Sofia with green eyes and yellow hair, tell her Thomas loves her, eh? Tell her I am doubtless a heretic, for forgiving her what she is. Tell her I think of her every day when I take the Holy Communion. Will you do that for me?"

I stare at him, wondering if the watchers in the hallway can distinguish words through the thick wooden door.

He sighs. "So suspicious! Yes, of course you will. You will deliver my message, and I'll say you confounded me by magic and escaped through the window. Eh?"

"They'll kill you," I tell him. The calmness of my voice shocks me. I am angry now: not at Lord Gregory who betrayed me, not at Lady Alison, who was likewise betrayed and died believing me about to lie with her husband, but with this meandering holy man who prattles of miracles and ignores his own safety. "The ones set to guard the door. They'll say you must have been possessed by demons, to let me escape."

He nods and pats his book. "We will quite probably both be killed. Lady Alison means to set watchers on the roads."

So he doesn't know. "Lady Alison is dead. Gregory poisoned her."

He pales and bows his head for a moment. "Ah. It is certainly political, then, and no one is safe tonight. I have bought you only a very little time; you had best use it. Now go: gather your charge and flee, and God be with you both. I shall chant exorcisms and hold them off, eh? Go on: use the window."

I use the window. I dislike changing shape and do so only in moments of extreme danger; it requires too much energy, and the consequent hunger can make one reckless.

I have made myself an owl, not the normal choice but a good one; I need acute vision, and a form which won't arouse suspicion in alert watchers. From this height I can see the entire estate: the castle, the surrounding land, gardens and pathways and fountains—and something else I never knew about, and could not have recognized from the ground.

The high hedges lining the road to the castle form, in one section, the side of a maze, one of those ornate topiary follies which pass in and out of botanical fashion. In the center of it is a small rose garden with a white fountain; on the edge of the fountain sit two foreshortened figures, very close to one another. Just outside the center enclosure, in a cul-de-sac which anyone exiting the maze must pass, another figure stands hidden.

*Left left right*. Gregory wasn't explaining a new dance at all: he was telling Caitlin how to reach the rose garden, the secret place where she and Randolph hid while Alison and I searched so frantically. Doubtless he went with his wife to keep her from the spot; with Alison's bad leg, and the maze this far from the castle, it wouldn't have been difficult.

I land a few feet behind him and return to myself again. Hunger and hatred enhance my strength, already greater than his. He isn't expecting an approach from behind; I knock him flat, his weapons and charms scattering in darkness, and have his arms pinned behind his back before he can cry out. "I am not dead," I say very quietly into his ear, "but your wife is, and soon you will be."

He whimpers and struggles, but I give his arm an extra twist and he subsides, panting. "Why, Gregory? What was all of this for? So you could spy on them murmuring poetry to one another? Surely not that. Tell me!"

"So I can be a duke."

"By your wife's death?"

"By the boy's."

"How?" I answer sharply, thinking of Randolph and Caitlin sharing the same goblet. "How did you mean to kill him? More poison?"

"She will kill him," he says softly, "because she is aroused, and does not yet know her own appetites or how to control them. Is it not so, my lady?"

My own hunger is a red throbbing behind my eyes. "No, my lord. Caitlin is no murder weapon: she does not yet know what she is or where her hungers come from. She can no more feed on her own than a kitten can, who depends on the mother cat to bring food and teach it how to eat."

"You shall teach her with my puling nephew, I warrant."

"No, my lord Gregory. I shall not. I shall not teach her with you either, more's the pity; we mangle as we learn, just as kittens do—and as kittens do, she will practice on little animals as long as they will sustain her. I should like to see you mangled, my lord."

Instead I break his neck, cleanly, as I broke Alison's. Afterwards, the body still warm, I feed fully; it would be more satisfying were he still alive, but he shall have no more pleasure. Feeding me aroused him as coupling seldom did; he begged to do it more often, and now I am glad I refused. As terrible as he was, he would have been worse as one of us.

When I am finished I lick my fingers clean, wipe my face as best I can, and drag the body back into the cul-de-sac, where it will not be immediately visible. Shaking, I hide the most obvious and dangerous of Gregory's weapons and step into the rose garden.

Caitlin, glowing in moonlight, sits on the edge of the fountain, as I saw her from the air. Randolph is handing her a white rose, which he has evidently just picked: there is blood on his hands where the thorns have scratched him. She takes the rose from him and bends to kiss his fingers, the tip of her tongue flicking towards the wounds.

"Caitlin!" She turns, startled, and lets go of Randolph's hands. "Caitlin, we must leave now."

"No," she says, her eyes very bright. "No. It is already after midnight, and you see—nothing horrid has happened."

"We must leave," I tell her firmly. "Come along."

"But I can come back?" she says, laughing, and then to Randolph, "I'll come back. Soon, I promise you. The next dance, or before that even. Godmother, promise I can come back—"

"Come along, Caitlin! Randolph, we bid you goodnight—"

"May I see you out of the maze, my ladies?"

I think of the watchers on the road, the watchers who may have been set on the maze by now. I wish I could warn him, teach him of the world in an instant. Disguise yourself, Randolph; leave this place as quickly as you can, and steal down swift and secret roads to your father's bedside.

But I cannot yet speak freely in front of Caitlin, and we have time only to save ourselves. Perhaps the maze will protect him, for a little while. "Thank you, my lord, but we know the way. Pray you stay here and think kindly of us; my magic is aided by good wishes."

"Then you shall have them in abundance, whatever my aunt says."

Caitlin comes at last, dragging and prattling. On my own I would escape with shape-changing, but Caitlin doesn't have those skills yet, and were I to tell her of our danger now she would panic and become unmanageable. So I lead her, right right left, right right left, through interminable turns.

But we meet no one else in the maze, and when at last we step into open air there are no priests waiting in ambush. Music still sounds faintly from the castle; the host and hostess have not yet been missed, and the good father must still be muttering incantations in his chamber.

And so we reach the carriage safely; I deposit Caitlin inside and instruct the driver to take us to one of the spots I have prepared for such emergencies. We should be there well before sun-up. I can only hope Lady Alison's watchers have grown tired or afraid, and left off their vigil; there is no way to be sure. I listen for hoofbeats on the road behind us and hear nothing. Perhaps, this time, we have been lucky.

Caitlin doesn't know what I saw, there in the rose garden. She babbles about it in the carriage. "We went into the garden, in the moonlight—he kissed me and held my hands, because he said they were cold. His were so warm! He told me I was beautiful; he said he loved me. And he picked roses for me, and he bled where the thorns had pricked him. He bled for me, godmother—oh, this is the one! This is my prince. How could I not love him?"

I remain silent. She doesn't yet know what she loves. At length she says, "Why aren't we home yet? It's taking so long. I'm hungry. I never had any dinner."

"We aren't going home," I tell her, lighting my lantern and pulling down the shades which cover the carriage's windows. "We have been discovered, Caitlin. It is quite possible we are being followed. I am taking you somewhere safe. There will be food there."

"Discovered?" She laughs. "What have they discovered? That I am poor?

That I love Randolph? What could they do to me? He will protect me; he said so. He will marry me."

This is the moment I must tell her. For all the times I have done this, it never hurts any less. "Caitlin, listen to me. You shall never marry Randolph, or anyone else. It was never meant that you should. I am sorry you have to hear this now. I had wanted you to learn some gentler way." She stares at me, bewildered, and, sadly, I smile at her—that expression she has teased me about, asked me for, wondered why I withhold; and when she sees it she understands. The pale eyes go wide, the beautiful hands go to her throat; she backs away from me, crossing herself as if in imitation of Lady Alison.

"Anyway," she tells me, trembling. "I exorcise thee, demon. In vain dost thou boast of this deed—"

I think of kind Thomas, chanting valiantly in an empty stone chamber as men at arms wait outside the door. "Keep your charms, Caitlin. They'll do you no good. Don't you understand, child? Why do you think everyone has begun to look at you so oddly; why do you think I wouldn't give you a mirror? What do you think was in the soup I gave you?"

The hands go to her mouth now, to the small sharp teeth. She cries out, understanding everything at once—her odd lassitude after the first few balls, the blood I took from her to cure it, her changing hours and changing thirsts—and, as always, this moment of birth rends whatever I have left of a heart. Because for a moment the young creature sitting in front of me is not the apprentice hunter I have made her, but the innocent young girl who stood holding that first invitation to the ball, her heart in her eyes. *I? I have been invited?* I force myself not to turn away as Caitlin cries out, "You tricked me! The story wasn't true!"

She tears at her face with shapely nails, and ribbons of flesh follow her fingers. "You can't weep anymore," I tell her. I would weep for her, if I could. "You can't bleed, either. You're past that. Don't disfigure yourself."

"The story was a lie! None of it was true, ever—"

I make my voice as cold as iron. "The story was perfectly true, Caitlin. You were simply never told all of it before."

"It wasn't supposed to end like this!" All the tears she can't shed are in her voice. "In the story the girl falls in love and marries the prince and— everyone knows that! You lied to me! This isn't the right ending!"

"It's the only ending! The only one there is—Caitlin, surely you see that. Living women have no more protection than we do here. They feed off their men, as we do, and they require permission to enter houses and go to dances, as we do, and they depend on spells of seeming. There is only one difference: you will never, ever look like Lady Alison. You will never look like your mother. You have escaped that."

She stares at me and shrinks against the side of the carriage, holding her hands in front of her—her precious hands which Randolph held, kissed, warmed with his own life. "I love him," she says defiantly. "I love him and he loves me. That part of it is true—"

"You loved his bleeding hands, Caitlin. If I hadn't interrupted, you would have fed from them, and known then, and hated him for it. And he would have hated you, for allowing him to speak of love when all along you had been precisely what his aunt warned him against."

Her mouth quivers. She hates me for having seen, and for telling her the truth. She doesn't understand our danger; she doesn't know how the woman she has scorned all these weeks died, or how close she came to dying herself.

Gregory was a clever man; the plot was a clean one. To sacrifice Randolph to Caitlin, and kill Caitlin as she tried to escape the maze; Gregory would have mourned his nephew in the proper public manner, and been declared a hero for murdering one fiend in person as the other was destroyed in the castle. Any gossip about his own soul would have been effectively stilled; perhaps he had been seduced, but surely he was pure again, to summon the righteousness to kill the beasts?

Oh yes, clever. Alison would have known the truth, and would never have accepted a title won by Randolph's murder. Alison could have ruined the entire plan, but it is easy enough to silence wives.

"Can I pray?" Caitlin demands of me, as we rattle towards daybreak. "If I can't shed tears or blood, if I can't love, can I still pray?"

"We can pray," I tell her gently, thinking again of Thomas who spared me, of those tenuous bonds between the living and the dead. "We must pray, foremost, that someone hear us. Caitlin, it's the same. The same story, with that one difference."

She trembles, huddling against the side of the carriage, her eyes closed. When at last she speaks, her voice is stunned. "I'll never see my mother again."

"I am your mother now." What are mothers and daughters, if not women who share blood?

She whimpers in her throat then, and I stroke her hair. At last she says, "I'll never grow old."

"You will grow as old as the hills," I tell her, putting my arm around her as one comforts a child who has woken from a nightmare, "but you will never be ugly. You will always be as beautiful as you are now, as beautiful as I am. Your hair and nails will grow and I will trim them for you, to keep them lovely, and you will go to every dance, and wear different gowns to all of them."

She blinks and plucks aimlessly at the poor fabric of her dress, once again a kitchen smock. "I'll never be ugly?"

"Never," I say. "You'll never change." We cannot cry or bleed or age; there are so many things we cannot do. But for her, now, it is a comfort.

She hugs herself, shivering, and I sit beside her and hold her, rocking her towards the certain sleep which will come with dawn. It would be better if Randolph were here, with his human warmth, but at least she doesn't have to be alone. I remember my own shock and despair, although they happened longer ago than anyone who is not one of us can remember; I too tried to pray, and afterwards was thankful that my own godmother had stayed with me.

After a while Caitlin's breathing evens, and I am grateful that she hasn't said, as so many of them do, *Now I will never die.*

We shelter our young, as the mortal mothers shelter theirs—those human women who of necessity are as predatory as we, and as dependent on the invitation to feed—and so there are some truths I have not told her. She will learn them soon enough.

She is more beautiful than Lady Alison or her mother, but no less vulnerable. Her very beauty contains the certainty of her destruction. There is no law protecting women in this kingdom, where wives can be poisoned in their own halls and their murderers never punished. Still less are there laws protecting us.

I have told her she will not grow ugly, but I have not said what a curse beauty can be, how time after time she will be forced to flee the rumors of her perpetual loveliness and all that it implies. Men will arrive to feed her and kiss her and bring her roses; but for all the centuries of gentle princes swearing love, there will inevitably be someone—jealous wife or jaded lord, peasant or priest—who has heard the whispers and believed, and who will come to her resting place, in the light hours when she cannot move, bearing a hammer and a wooden stake.

# WILLIAM F. NOLAN

## My Name Is Dolly

William F. Nolan created the *Logan's Run* film, the book, and the television series. His most recent book in the genre is *Things Beyond Midnight,* published in 1984 by Scream/Press. He has written forty-seven books and seven hundred stories and articles and is currently writing two movies-of-the-week for television.

"My Name is Dolly," asks the unanswerable geographical question concerning the boundaries of sanity and madness. The most truly frightening aspect of the story is perhaps the inability of the reader to discern when the line is crossed.

—E.D.

# MY NAME IS DOLLY

## William F. Nolan

MONDAY—Today I met the witch—which is a good place to start this diary. (I had to look up how to spell it. First I spelled it dairy but that's a place you get milk and from this you're going to get blood—I hope—so it is plenty different.)

Let me tell you about Meg. She's maybe a thousand years old I guess. (A witch can live forever, right?) She's all gnarly like the bark of an oak tree, her skin I mean, and she has real big eyes. Like looking into deep dark caves and you don't know what's down there. Her nose is hooked and she has sharp teeth like a cat's are. When she smiles some of them are missing. Her hair is all wild and clumpy and she smells bad. Guess she hasn't had a shower for a real long time. Wears a long black dress with holes in it. By rats most likely. She lives in this old deserted cobwebby boathouse they don't use anymore on the lake—and it's full of fat gray rats. Meg doesn't seem to mind.

My name is Dolly. Short for Dorothy like in the Oz books. Only nobody ever calls me Dorothy. I'm still a kid and not very tall and I've got red hair and freckles. (I really *hate* freckles! When I was real little I tried to rub them off but you can't. They stick just like tattoos do.)

Reason I went out to the lake to see old Meg is because of how much I hate my father. Well, he's not really my father, since I'm adopted and I don't know my real father. Maybe he's a nice man and not like Mister Brubaker who adopted me. Mrs. Brubaker died of the flu last winter which is when Mister Brubaker began to molest me. (I looked up the word molest and it's the right one for what he keeps trying to do with me.) When I won't let him he gets really mad and slaps me and I run out of the house until he's all calmed down again. Then he'll get special nice and offer me cookies with chocolate chunks in them which are my very favorite kind. He wants me to like him so he can molest me later.

Last week I heard about the witch who lives by the lake. A friend at school told me. Some of the kids used to go down there to throw rocks at her until she put a spell on Lucy Akins and Lucy ran away and no one's seen her since. Probably she's dead. The kids leave old Meg alone now.

I thought maybe Meg could put a spell on Mister Brubaker for five dollars. (I saved up that much.) Which is why I went to see her. She said she couldn't because she can't put spells on people unless she can see them up close and look in their eyes like she did to Lucy Akins.

The lake was black and smelly with big gas bubbles breaking in it and the boathouse was cold and damp and the rats scared me but old Meg was the only way I knew to get even with Mister Brubaker. She kept my five dollars and told me she was going into town soon and would look around for something to use against Mister Brubaker. I promised to come see her on Friday after school.

We'll have his blood, she said.

FRIDAY NIGHT—I went to see old Meg again and she gave me the doll to take home. A real big one, as tall as I am with freckles and red hair just like mine. And in a pretty pink dress with little black slippers with red bows on them. The doll's eyes open and close and she has a big metal key in her back where you wind her up. When you do she opens her big dark eyes and says hello, my name is Dolly. Same as mine. I asked Meg where she found Dolly and she said at Mister Carter's toy store. But I've been in there lots of times and I've never seen a doll like this for five dollars. Take her home, Meg told me, and she'll be your friend. I was real excited and ran off pulling Dolly behind me. She has a box with wheels on it you put her inside and pull along the sidewalk.

She's too big to carry.

MONDAY—Mister Brubaker doesn't like Dolly. He says she's damn strange. That's his words, damn strange. But she's my new friend so I don't care what he says about her. He wouldn't let me take her to school.

SATURDAY—I took some of Mister Brubaker's hair to old Meg today. She asked me to cut some off while he was asleep at night and it was really hard to do without waking him up but I got some and gave it to her. She wanted me to bring Dolly and I did and Meg said that Dolly was going to be her agent. That's the word. Agent. (I try to get all the words right.)

Dolly had opened her deep dark eyes and seen Mister Brubaker and old Meg said that was all she needed. She wrapped two of Mister Brubaker's hairs around the big metal key in Dolly's back and told me not to wind her up again until Sunday afternoon when Mister Brubaker was home watching his sports. He always does that on Sunday.

So I said okay.

SUNDAY NIGHT—This afternoon, like always, Mister Brubaker was watching a sports game on the television when I set Dolly right in front of him and did just what old Meg told me to do. I wound her up with the big key and then took the key out of her back and put it in her right hand. It was long and sharp and Dolly opened her eyes and said hello, my name is Dolly and stuck the metal key in Mister Brubaker's chest. There was a lot of blood. (I told you there would be.)

Mister Brubaker picked Dolly up and threw the front of her into the fire. I mean, that's how she landed, just the front of her at the edge of the fire. (It's winter now, and real cold in the house without a fire.) After he did that he fell down and didn't get up. He was dead so I called Doctor Thompson.

The police came with him and rescued Dolly out of the fire when I told them what happened. Her nice red hair was mostly burnt away and the whole left side of her face was burnt real bad and the paint had all peeled back and blistered. And one of her arms had burnt clear off and her pink dress was all char-colored and with big fire holes in it. The policeman who rescued her said that a toy doll couldn't kill anybody and that I must have stuck the key into Mister Brubaker's chest and blamed it on Dolly. They took me away to a home for bad children.

I didn't tell anybody about old Meg.

TUESDAY—It is a long time later and my hair is real pretty now and my face is almost healed. The lady who runs this house says there will always be big scars on the left side of my face but I was lucky not to lose my eye on that side. It is hard to eat and play with the other kids with just one arm but that's okay because I can still hear Mister Brubaker screaming and see all the blood coming out of his chest and that's nice.

I wish I could tell old Meg thank you. I forgot to—and you should always thank people for doing nice things for you.

# JOAN AIKEN

## The Moon's Revenge

Joan Aiken, the prominent British writer of novels and stories, has published many different kinds of work from adult mystery novels to children's picture books during her long and celebrated career. Fanatasy readers tend to know her work best through young adult books such as *The Wolves of Willoughby Chase,* and the classic Battersea series.

"The Moon's Revenge " comes from a picture book of the same title originally published by Jonathan Cape in the United Kingdom and then by Alfred A. Knopf in the United States, exquisitely illustrated by Alan Lee.

A second story by Aiken, "The Old Poet," published in the collection *A Goose on Your Grave,* is also one of the best fantasy stories of the year and readers are strongly urged to take the time to seek out this evocative tale.

—T.W.

# THE MOON'S REVENGE

## Joan Aiken

Once there was a boy called Seppy, and he was the seventh son of a seventh son. This was long ago, in the days when women wore shawls and men wore hoods and long pointed shoes, and the cure for an earache was to put a hot roasted onion in your ear.

Seppy's father was a coach maker. He made carts and carriages for all the farmers and gentry nearby. At the age of seven, Seppy had learned how to cut a panel for a carriage door and shave a spoke for a cartwheel. But what he *really* wanted was to play the fiddle. He had made himself a little one from odds and ends of wood in the yard. Sep's grandfather, people said, had been the best fiddler in the country. He had played so beautifully that two kings, King Henry and King Richard, had stopped fighting a great battle to listen, and the tears ran like rain down their faces until he finished playing and went on his way; then they picked up their swords and finished the battle.

"If it had been me," thought Sep, "I'd not have stopped playing. I'd have made those kings listen till they promised never to fight another battle."

Sep's father said he must learn the coach maker's trade.

"Put the fiddle away," he said. "That's for Sunday's and holidays. You've got to earn your living."

There was an empty, ruined house in the little seaport where Sep lived. Nobody would stay in the house, because you could hear voices talking inside, even when it was empty. People said they must be the voices of devils.

"They might just as well be angels," thought Sep, and he climbed out of his bedroom window one frosty midnight and slipped along the dark cobbled street and stood, with his heart going pitapat, outside the broken door, listening.

He put his ear to a crack. Yes! He could hear voices, talking in quiet tones. What were they talking about? Afterward Sep could never remember.

But with his heart thumping even louder he tapped, and called in a whisper through the hole.

"Hey! You in there! If you please! How can I learn to be the best fiddler in the country?"

He laid his ear to the crack. A cold breeze blew out of it so sharply that Sep jumped back in fright.

"Throw your shoe at the moon," whispered a voice. "Each night for seven nights, thrown your shoe at the moon."

"B-b-b-but *how?*" stammered Sep. "What shoe?"

Nobody answered. He could hear the voices talking again, to each other, not to him.

Sep tiptoed back to bed, scratching his head. He had only one pair of shoes, hogskin clogs in which he clattered about the coach yard. But when his feet were smaller he had worn other shoes, some passed on by his elder brothers. His mother, who never wasted anything, kept all these little old pairs in a bag inside the grandfather clock.

So the next day, when his mother was out feeding the ducks and geese who swam in the river by the coach yard, Sep went quietly and found the bag. He took a pair of tiny, soft kidskin shoes that he had worn when he was one year old. And on a night when the moon was nearly full, he went down to the beach. He laid one of the shoes on the sea wall, looked at the cold, shiny sea and the black, wrinkled waves; then, with all his energy, he hurled the other little white shoe up—straight up—into the face of the white, watching moon.

What happened to the shoe? Sep couldn't see. It certainly didn't fall down onto the sand or into the sea; he was sure of that. He left the other shoe lying on the sea wall and went home to bed.

The next night he went to the beach again, and this time he threw up the small rabbitskin boot he had worn when he was two. Right into the face of the blazing moon. As before, he heard no sound of it falling back to the ground. And, leaving the other boot on the sea wall, he went home to bed.

On the third night, he threw up a red crocodile-skin slipper that a lord's wife had given his mother. Sep had worn them when he was three, and they were his favorite shoes, but he soon outgrew them. Straight into the face of the shining moon he threw the red shoe, and he left its mate lying on the sea wall.

On the fourth night he threw up a doeskin boot that a traveling musician had given his mother in exchange for a plate of stew. Sep had loved those boots, which were very light and comfortable; he had worn them when he was four. Into the face of the moon he tossed the boot. And he left the other boot on the sea wall.

On the fifth night he flung up a shiny calfskin shoe with a pewter buckle that all his brothers had worn in turn before him. And he left the other buckled shoe on the sea wall.

On the sixth night he threw up a sheepskin slipper that one of his six uncles had made for him when he was ill with measles at the age of six. And he left the other slipper on the sea wall.

On the seventh night he threw up one of his two hogskin clogs that he wore every day.

"One's no use without the other," thought Sep. He left the other clog on the sea wall. Now there were seven shoes in a row.

"People will think that a seven-foot monster has gone in swimmming," thought Sep.

He looked up at the moon and blinked in fright. For the moon was blazing down at him with a face of fury. Its whiteness was all dirtied over with marks where he had thrown his shoes. And he could feel its anger scorching him, like the breath of an ice-dragon.

Sep turned and ran home as fast as he could on his bare feet, leaving the row of seven shoes on the wall casting long shadows in the moon's blaze of rage. But as he ran a thick white sea fog slid in over the beach; the shoes, the shadows, and the moon all vanished from view.

"I hope the moon isn't coming after me," thought Sep. He felt a prickle between his shoulders at the thought of the moon rolling after him, like a great wheel, through the fog.

Back home, he scurried up to his little attic bedroom, and jumped into bed, and hid under the covers. He soon fell asleep, but in the middle of the night he woke again, for now his room was full of moon, absolutely brimful of moon, like a goldfish bowl full of water.

Sep gasped with fright. But then he remembered that he was the seventh son of a seventh son, and he sat up boldly in bed.

"You must give me a wish," he told the moon. "It's the rule. They said so."

The moon's reply came in a freezing trickle of notes, like a peal of ice-bells, which made Sep's ears tingle all the way down to his stomach.

"Yes! I have to give you a wish, you impertinent boy! But you have marked my face forever with your dirty shoes, and for that I shall punish you. You must go barefoot for seven years. And until the day when you put those shoes back in the clock, your sister will not speak. And you and all your family will be in great danger—but I shan't tell you what it's going to be. You can just wait and see!"

With that, the moon sucked itself backward out of Sep's room, like a cloud through a keyhole, leaving the boy cold and scared and puzzled.

"Sister! I haven't got a sister," he thought. "What did the moon mean? And what can the danger be? I wish I knew. But at least I can get those shoes that I left on the sea wall, and put them back in the clock. Perhaps that will help."

The next morning, before sunrise, Sep ran down to the beach. From a long way off he could see the seven shoes on the wall, throwing long shadows as the sun slipped up out of the silver water. But just before Sep got there, a huge wave came rolling—green and black and blue, curved like a claw, rolling from far over the sea's rim—snatched up the seven shoes in its foaming lip, and carried them away, back over the rim of the sea.

"Bother it!" said Sep, greatly annoyed and disappointed, and he walked home slowly, feeling the path cold and gritty under his bare feet.

Back at home, he found hot water and wine and towels and milk, for a new baby had just been born to Sep's mother, a little girl called Octavia, with gray eyes and silvery pale hair. Everybody was so pleased, Sep didn't get much of a scolding for losing his shoes.

"But," said his father, "you'll go barefoot till you make yourself another pair."

Which was what Sep could *not* do: no shoes he made would stay on his feet more than half an hour. They cracked or split, the soles fell off, the laces broke, the canvas tore, the leather crumbled to powder. Sep's feet grew hard as horn and, except in the snowy winter, he did not mind this result of the moon's anger. The really unfair punishment had fallen on his little sister Octavia. When Sep looked at her he felt sadness like a skin of ice around his heart, for, though pretty as a peach and good as gold, she never learned to speak or sing, she never cried, she never made a single sound. She was dumb.

The years began to roll past, ticked away by the grandfather clock. Each evening Sep slipped away to the loft of one of his uncles, who was a sailmaker, and there he played his fiddle where no one could hear him—no one except the gulls and swallows who flew around the roof, and the mice who lived under the floorboards. As Sep taught himself to play better and better, they all stopped their flying and chewing, their pecking and scratching and munching, in order to listen, and remained stone-still all the time he played.

And little Octavia loved his playing best of all. As soon as she could crawl and scramble and walk, she followed Sep everywhere and sat for hours sucking her thumb while he played his tunes.

When there was a holiday, Sep carried her into the fields, or the woods, or up on the moors, or for miles along the rocky beach, and played his music where nobody listened but the rabbits, or the wild deer, or the seals splashing in the foam. And everywhere he went the moon followed, watching him with its cold eye.

When Octavia was a year old, beginning to walk, Sep's mother looked in the clock for the bag of shoes.

"That's queer," she said. "I could have sworn I left the bag in here—"

Sep was about to speak when his father said, "No, Meg, don't you remember? You gave the shoes to the clock mender—that time when the clock stopped and he set it going again?"

And to Sep's utter atonishment she answered, "Oh, yes, so I did, I gave them to the old man. And the clock has kept perfect time ever since."

Ticktock, ticktock, the clock went on keeping perfect time. Sep made

Octavia shoes from sail canvas, with stitched rope soles. And she still followed him wherever he went.

One autumn day when she was three, Sep carried her on his shoulders along the shore. A great ship had been wrecked in a gale, far out to sea, and pieces of gilded wood, fine silks and velvets, colored wax candles, glass jars, and ivory boxes came floating and tossing ashore.

Sep was looking for a piece of wood. His little fiddle was no longer big enough, and he wanted a piece of rare maple, or royal pine, or seasoned sycamore—woods which were not to be found in his father's yard—so that he could make himself a new fiddle.

While he hunted along the water's edge, little Ocatvia skipped along at the foot of the cliff, picking up here a pebble or a shell, there a brooch or a pin that the waves had flung ashore.

Sep was tugging at the brass handle of a chest all wrapped in green weed when she ran up and jerked at his arm, beckoning him to come and pointing with her other hand.

What was she pointing at? Sep stared, and stared again. The thing at the cliff foot that he had at first taken for a gray rock was in fact a huge shoe—covered with barnacles and half-filled with pebbles—but *whose* shoe could it possibly be? Large as a fishing smack, it lay sunk in the sand. Little Octavia was dying to climb on it, but Sep would not let her. Suppose the shoe's owner came looking for it?

"Come away!" he said. "Come away, Octavia!"

The wind blew chilly, and a sea mist was rising. Sep felt a queer pitapat of the heart, as he had once before when he listened outside the empty house. He took his fiddle from his knapsack and played a tune—a frisking, laughing tune, to keep bad luck away. As he played, the mist grew thicker, and Sep was almost sure that he could see the ghost of a king in his robes at the water's edge. And was there not, also, the ghost of a ship, far out to sea, waiting for its master? The king nodded at Sep as if he were listening hard to the music—and liking it, too—then pointed his finger at the great gray shoe. As he pointed there came a rumbling—a louder rumbling—then a tremendous roaring crash—and half the cliff fell down, burying the shoe under a mountain of rock. If Sep and Octavia had been beside the shoe, they would have been buried as well.

A smaller rock, bouncing down the beach, split open the chest which Sep had been trying to drag free. Inside the chest was a canvas bag, waxed, and tied with cords. Inside that was another bag. Inside that was a leather case. And inside *that* was a beautiful violin, which had been so carefully packed that not one drop of sea water had touched it.

Sep carefully lifted out the violin, holding it as if it were made of gold.

Then he turned to where the ghost had stood by the water's edge—but nobody was there, not even a footprint.

"Did you see him?" Sep asked Octavia. But she shook her head.

Sep walked home with the new violin under his arm and Octavia riding on his back.

That evening he set the old violin on a plank, with a lighted candle stuck beside it, and let it float away, out to sea.

Ticktock, ticktock, the grandfather clock went on keeping perfect time until little Octavia was nearly seven, could sew and spin, could make butter and cakes and bread. She was good and pretty and cheerful, but still she never said a word.

Sep went on practicing his music as often and as long as he could.

"Perhaps someday," he thought, "The music will teach Octavia how to speak." For in the meantime the music had saved them from some tight corners and helped them in several difficulties: when the smith's mastiff turned savage and ran at Octavia, when Sep's mother's blackberry jam would have boiled all over the kitchen if Sep's music hadn't calmed it down, and—worst of all—when the grandfather clock suddenly stopped ticking. Quick as a flash Sep, who happened to be beside it, snatched up his fiddle and played a rattling-quick tune, and the clock hummed, hawed, cleared its throat, and was off again, ticking as hard as ever.

One Sunday evening after church, all the village people were down on the slipway, chatting as they always did.

"A magpie has sat on the steeple for three days," someone said. 'That means trouble."

"And there was a big red ring round the moon last night."

"And the bush in the churchyard has three black roses on it."

"Something dreadful must be going to happen," they all agreed.

"It's getting very dark," said Sep's father. "Look at that big black cloud."

The moon had risen, large, pale, and scowling, but a solid black cloud began to spread wider and wider across the sky, until it swallowed the moon in a pool of inky dark. For a moment a thin layer of light lay between black cloud and black sea; then something odd and bulky crossed the line of light.

"What was *that*?" said one of Sep's uncles. "Looked like a horned whale—"

"Maybe it was a boat," said somebody else.

"Daft kind of a boat—with horns!"

"There it goes again."

"It's coming closer!"

Now everybody could see something—some great Thing—coming in out of the sea, toward the land.

It moved so fast that it seemed to double in size as it came along.

"Oh! Oh! It's a dreadful beast!" screamed little Octavia. "Hide me, hide me, brother Seppy! It's coming this way. It's going to eat us all!"

The crowed scattered, screaming and terrified. For the monster churning toward them through inky waves had two great horns on its forehead and a jawful of teeth as long as doorposts; it had spines or prickles or plates of shell on its back and sides; and it had seven great feet at the end of seven great legs, which stomped and splashed through the water. As the creature came closer the townspeople caught a whiff of its smell, a damp, rotting, sickly, weedy breath, like water that flowers have been in for far too long. When it reached the end of the harbor bar, the beast stood still on its seven legs and let out a loud, threatening cry, like a sea lion that has swallowed a copper trumpet.

"It's hungry. We're all done for," gasped Sep's aunt Lucy. "That beast will swallow the lot of us, like a spoonful of peas."

"Please, brother Sep," squeaked little Octavia, "play it a tune on your fiddle. Pray, pray, play it a tune. You stopped the charging bull and the mad dog—perhaps you can stop this beast!"

All in the midst of his fright and horror, Sep suddenly noticed something. "Octavia! You spoke! You said words!"

"Oh, never mind that, brother Sep! Fetch your fiddle!"

Still carrying Octavia, Sep hurried through the crowd to his uncle's sail loft, where he kept his fiddle hidden. A stair led up from the harbor front to an outside door. Sep stood on this stair and played his fiddle.

At first no one heard him. The crowd were yelling in terror, and the monster was booming most balefully. Then one or two people noticed Sep and began to jeer.

"What does the fool think he's doing?"

"Clodpole!"

"Loony!"

"Coward! You think it can't reach you up there?"

But as Sep calmly went on playing, the monster stopped its wailing and began to listen. Or so it seemed. The seven jerking, stamping legs stood still. The horned head slowly turned in the direction of Sep's music. Then the head began to nod up and down in time with the tune Sep was playing—which was a very lively tune, a sailors' hornpipe.

Then the monsters began to dance.

Stomp, stomp went its legs again, but now they kicked high and gaily out of the water. The monster jigged and joggled, nodding its head, flapping all its prickles and plates. As the great scaly feet came up splashing out of the waves, it could be seen that they wore shoes. On one foot was a huge clog. On another, a laced boot. On another, a red slipper. On another, a black shoe with a buckle.

"If those are my shoes," thought Sep, astonished, playing away for dear life, "if those are my shoes, they have certainly grown."

"Don't stop playing, brother Sep!" squeaked little Octavia, jumping up and down in time to the tune. "The monster simply loves your music!"

"Don't stop, don't stop!" shouted all the people on the harbor front. "Don't stop for a single minute."

"Everybody play, who can!" shouted Sep, sawing away with his bow.

Anyone in the village who had a musical instrument ran home for it. They brought fiddles, drums, flutes, krummhorns, and tabors. They played and played. And the ones who had no instruments to play danced and sang. Sailors on ships far out to sea heard the sound and wondered what was going on. If Sep stopped playing for a moment, the monster noticed, through all the noise, that the sound of his fiddle was missing, and it began to cry.

"Don't stop, Sep!" everybody shouted. "You must keep on playing!"

It was like a frantic party that went on all night.

"How long *can* I go on?" Sep wondered. His arms ached so badly that he wondered if they were going to fall off. Morning would soon be here; the sky was growing pale.

"Don't stop, don't stop!" Octavia cried anxiously. Then she said, "Look, Seppy! The monster is shrinking!"

Sep saw that this was true. Now the monster was no bigger than a house. Now it was as small as a fishing boat. Now it was the size of a cart. Now not even as large as a cow. Now, shrinking all the time, it made a tremendous effort and sprang up onto the end of the pier. Then, with an expiring squeak, it vanished altogether, whirling into the air like a blown feather, just as the sun rose.

The townspeople were so tired that they flopped onto the cobbles where they stood, and fell asleep. But Sep, with little Octavia, ran down to the end of the pier, where they found seven odd shoes: a red slipper, a doeskin boot, a white kidskin shoe, a sheepskin slipper, a buckled shoe, a rabbitskin boot, and a hogskin clog.

Octavia helped Sep carry them home. "It's lucky we found them," she said, skipping along by him with her arms full of shoes. "We can put them in the bag in the clock, and all *my* children will be able to wear them when they are little."

"But there's only one of each pair," said Sep.

"No, there isn't! The others have been in that bag inside the clock ever since I can remember. I've played with them lots of times, pretending a seven-footed monster was wearing them."

Sure enough, Octavia pulled the bag out of the clock and put back the shoes. But she kept out the hogskin clogs and put them on. They fitted her feet exactly.

When the people on the quay woke up, they had forgotten all about the monster. Puzzled, scratching their heads, the wandered off homeward.

From that day, little Octavia could speak as well as anybody, and she did it twice as fast, to make up for lost time.

Sep went on working in his father's coach yard, but now, as well, he began to play his fiddle at weddings and feasts and parties. By and by he became famous all over the country—so famous that he was invited to play at all six weddings of King Henry VIII. And each time he played, the tears ran down King Henry's cheeks, and he said, "Oh, Sep, boy! I couldn't have played better myself."

For the king was a musician too.

Often, often, when Sep was walking homeward on a dark night, after playing his music at a wedding or a party, he would look up at the silvery face of the moon, with its black, dirty marks, and think: "Did I really put those marks there? Did I really do that dreadful thing to the poor moon? Or was it all a dream? I wish the moon would tell me!"

But the moon, scowling down at Sep, never spoke to him again.

# EDWARD BRYANT

## Author's Notes

Ed Bryant writes: "The older I get and the more dark fantasy I create, the more I seem to write from experience. Weird. I haven't quite got it figured out yet. I don't know if it worries my friends, but it certainly gives *me* pause. There's just something about zombies and vampires and all the other midnight baggage that seems to resonate with the ways I perceive real people functioning in the real world these days.

I never deliberately tried to create a subsidiary career in dark fantasy, but that's what I seem to be attempting after spending a decade and a half writing stuff generally assigned to the science fiction pigeonhole. It may have something to do with my perception that dark fantasy— horror, splatterpunk, whatever label you wish to append—is presently the area of imaginative fiction where most of the artistic excitement is."

Ed neglects to mention that he's won Nebula awards for two of his science fiction stories, "Stone," and "GiAnts." His dark fiction is deeply disturbing, occasionally causing readers to confuse his own identity with the personas of his characters, proving how effective he is at writing about the dark side of human nature.

—E.D.

# AUTHOR'S NOTES

## Edward Bryant

### (NOTE 1)

Try this at a party, sometime.

I have and it works.

Pick somebody out of the crowd. It doesn't matter if they're a man or a woman. All that matters is that they're human. Back them into a corner. Not by the chip-and-dip table. Find a place that's quieter, less congested. If you can, try the bedroom where all the coats are stacked on the bed.

Make them tell you if they've ever killed anyone.

Don't let them weasel with their war stories and auto crashes and fatal sins of omission. Find out if they ever put the serrated blade of the bread knife between someone's ribs and then sawed back and forth, or if they know what it's like to gently wiggle the barrel of the pistol into someone's mouth and squeeze the trigger. Ask if they know what human blood *really* smells like. How much of it spills out of the punctured human body. What it tastes like when it isn't yours.

I'm never surprised at how many answer me honestly.

I'm never surprised at how many *know*.

### (NOTE 2)

I suppose what you're really asking is, "So where *do* you get your ideas?"

I'm not talking about stupid conversations at parties or bars, for god's sake. I never talk to you there. I never want to. I'm talking about a more intimate time, when we're even closer than during sex. I can see you, you know. It doesn't matter how dark it is or how alone in the house you think you are. I can hear you.

You lean back with the sick fascination on your face and feel the questions ooze out with the fluids. You ask: is that sorry son of a bitch just exorcizing his own fear? Or is he trying to avoid the admission that he'd *do* it if he just could?

106

It's a sucker's quiz. You'd never ask it of a genuine artist. And I wouldn't answer, even if you did.

Ask the Marquis. If you could find him. De Sade was a clever magpie, plucking up lambent fragments of truth to piece into his fabricated stories. He was probably the most accomplished magpie, coming close to knowing the truth and the language of blood. But his more gifted literary progeny depend less on vivid imaginations, more on direct experience.

It's a funny thing. For the longest time as a kid, I didn't understand the difference between fiction and journalism. Everything was equally real to me. Even after one of my teachers explained the distinction, I still wondered: in fiction, didn't the storyteller have to live the story? What good were tales that were made up?

## (NOTE 3)

If there's one thing I can't do, it's work for someone else. Writing is bad enough, since I have to deal with editors and my agent. But I'm not really working for them. They are working for me.

Before I started writing, I had lots of jobs. None of them lasted. The trouble with working is that bosses want to screw you over. They do it endlessly, finding an infinite number of new and terrible injustices to shovel on your head.

There's never any recourse.

It just isn't fair.

When I lived in Seattle, the summer before my wife died, I met a guy who had worked at the Hanford Nuclear Reservation. He'd had some sort of low-level job handling chemicals in a laboratory. There had been an accident and the man had breathed in something like fifty micrograms of plutonium oxide dust—not even enough, he told me over boilermakers, to see in a dot, if it had collected on my thumbnail.

To help my friend, the laboratory had scrubbed him, cleansing his skin as much as they could. Then they drowned him. Three times. The procedure was called a lung lavage. The doctors filled his lungs with water, drew the water out, repeated the process, did it again. Nothing got all the dust out. It was encapsulated in his cells. In his blood.

The message was there forever.

When I met him, the ex-nuclear worker was living off what his wife could make waiting tables at Ivar's Acres of Clams. He couldn't get Workman's Comp because the government said there were no accidents like the one he'd suffered. Nuclear plants were safer than Teddy Kennedy's car at Chappaquidick. Actuarial tables would be compiled from the accidents and subsequent deaths of people like my friend. I thought about his predicament a long while.

Seattle was a rough period. I was fired from my own job at Boeing. I think I knew then that Joyce's death was in the future, but not that far away. I think my bosses knew too.

I remember the sixth of August that year. We decided to have a backyard party. Before any of the guests arrived, I got roaring drunk. I remember I wanted to hit Joyce. I wanted to beat her to death.

Then I called up the guy who'd had the lab accident to ask if he'd like to come over and light up our lives.

All I reached was his wife. He'd died that morning.

The message was clear.

## (NOTE 4)

When I was a child, I ran into a lot of psychotic kids. At least that was my assumption. I had no friends. The other children were irrational monsters who hated me because I achieved more than they.

Apparently I threatened them.

It wasn't my fault I could do things better than they.

Since I had a lot of time on my hands, I learned to function quite well on my own.

When I was nine, my father took me to work with him one day. Nothing strange about that, except that he was an assistant M.E.—medical examiner—for the city of Baltimore. That was not long before we moved west.

I still remember the sight of the autopsy rooms, but what I recall most are the temperature and the smell. It was cold—an absolute chill that seemed forboding in spite of our having come in from a sweltering August afternoon. And the smell. It was the first time I'd filled my nose with the fumes of formaldehyde.

My father told me that workers in a room like this were only good for about twelve years. Then the formaldehyde got to their brains. He introduced me to some of his colleagues and I speculated how long each had worked here. It was harder to tell just from their faces or how they spoke than I expected.

I looked for a slackness in their features.

Some sign that their minds had started to strip away the upper layers of intelligence.

That the beast was peeking out.

I returned frequently that summer. School was on vacation and my mother was visiting her dying sister in Cleveland. Everyone let me have the run of the place. I saw things I knew would help me out in school when the teacher asked me to write about what I'd done on my summer vacation.

Everything went smoothly until one afternoon when I walked in on one of my father's friends who had been working alone in one of the smaller rooms. Years later, I decided he must have been chopping off bits he wasn't supposed to.

And playing with them.

How was I supposed to know? It looked educational. He asked me not to tell anyone of what I'd seen. I agreed, not because I was intimidated, but because I wanted to know something more.

Many years later, at the University of Wisconsin, I briefly joined a fraternity. It seemed like a good idea at the time. Of course I learned that my new "brothers" were no better than the boys who had made my life hellish when I was a child.

But at any rate, there were elements of the initiation ritual that reminded me of those halcyon August days in Baltimore.

### (NOTE 5)

Have I ever met a witch?

Certainly I've met women—and a few eccentric men—who believed they had supernatural powers.

You can always tell.

They speak and act and even move with a sense of *power*, an attitude of knowing they control the what and whom around them.

They look at you so smugly and read your mind.

Some claim they are simply terribly accomplished at interpreting body language and nuance of expression. Perhaps that is only protective camouflage.

What is inarguable is that they use their power to influence and control human beings.

From time to time, I've felt their power. Always I have been able to resist it. Always.

Whether you believe such talent is paranormal or simply acquired and exercised through completely rational means doesn't matter. The point is that such people have sacrificed their humanity. They should not be allowed to exist.

I rarely think of the *Bible* anymore, but the phrase about not "suffering a witch to live" haunts me.

Doesn't *your* skin crawl at the thought of another's mind violating your own? Another's unwanted touch fouling your life?

My judgment may seem harsh at first, but I think you can see my point in making it.

## (NOTE 6)

They are so damnably naive.

For many writers, it seems, the act of creating fictions, the actual sequence of putting words down on paper, is their catharsis. Writing is too sacred to be a mere confessional. I must create something, and my writing is what I build.

I build it in the hope it will withstand the attacks of those who would tear down everything they are too ignorant or too stupid to understand.

I have sat at writing classes, laughing inside, listening to the failed creators enter endless, futile debates about whether writing is a causative act or only a reflection of reality.

Fools. They finally claim it is the chicken or the egg.

I can solve that idiocy.

The chicken came first.

Think about the egg.

Think about the sharpness of the chicken's beak.

It is very sharp.

Sharp and oh, so unforgiving.

When Joyce died of birth complications along with my son, I suspected what had really happened.

I could never prove what the doctors had done.

Now I live alone.

I write my little stories, knowing how we writers are all obliged to write from experience. We are to suck the lifeblood from the lives around us in the manner of vampires. The justification is that our creations will be richer, fuller to the point of bursting. Brutal honesty is the key.

There are no experiences too dreadful to cannibalize.

## (NOTE 7)

Since moving to Denver, I've spent endless nights travelling the length of Colfax Avenue.

Colfax is the longest continuous thoroughfare in any American city. I have ample opportunity from dusk to dawn to observe the hookers and pimps, the dealers and junkies, the homeless and the wanderers. All too frequently, I must pull over to allow the ambulances or the police to pass. Their flashers splash light like blood.

Every once in a while, I take out the sharpened screwdriver from the glove compartment. Touching it to my cheek makes for a cold caress. Then I go on and observe all the people, attempting to guess who are the victims and who are the killers.

It exorcises the pain.
It soothes my mind.
It's what I do.

*Author's Note to "Author's Notes"*: Most people who read my mini-collection in *Night Visions 4* heeded the listings on the table of contents and assumed I had contributed only six stories. Not so. The seventh was there all along, sneakily hiding in the form of a series of "author's notes," a were-fiction if you will. I wanted to depict the sort of persona many readers of my acquaintance seem to assume *must* belong to the typical horror writer. Or maybe, as one reviewer suggested, I've too blurred the line between author and creation. I don't know about you, but that scares hell out of me. I haven't ritually sacrificed a small, cute animal in just ages.

# JOHN ROBERT BENSINK

## Lake George in High August

John Robert Bensink has published fiction and nonfiction in *New York* magazine, *Playboy, Money* and the *New York News*, and is working on a short-story collection called *New York Weird.*

This story deals with ordinary people and a single brief event. Seldom does fiction illustrate so succinctly how such an event can galvanize individuals and permanently alter their seemingly ordered lives.

—E.D.

# LAKE GEORGE IN HIGH AUGUST

## John Robert Bensink

It's only a lousy week, but at least they're getting out of the city. Felder displays the house to wife and son: They're awed; better than he described it. For six springs now, Felder has been saying, *We're getting out of the city this summer*. That means: June, July, August. This year's reality: Finally, a week they can't really afford. But okay: So they eat macaroni and cheese and hot dogs for a week, and Felder will try not to think of the cash advance on their MasterCard that's paying for most of this bargain rent of twelve hundred dollars.

The house is cabinlike, musty even though it's hot out, hitting past ninety, full of rustic furniture he tells the kid Indians made. Almost right on the water.

What they want to do immediately is be in the lake, baptize their arrival, their entire week together, their good luck at finding such a good place so late in the season. The rental car isn't even unloaded—and it can wait.

Felder's wife has her bathing suit in her shoulder bag. She changes quickly in the bathroom. The kid grows a pout. His wife the magician makes it vanish by producing, out of her bag, his little orange trunks— *voilà!* His smile lasts longer than it takes him to strip and shimmy the things up over his skinny legs. Backwards, but who cares—all communicated with a half glance between husband and wife that also says: This is the moment, let's not risk it by getting hung up on technicalities, the kid's about to burst, let's get down to the lake, get in—get *on* with this vacation!

They do, racing out of the house, running along the path to the water, the kid, in the middle, not quite figuring out why the trunks are pulling at his crotch—and not giving a damn—Felder's wife up ahead, leading the way, a natural in bare feet, not picking her way to avoid pebbles but prancing along gracefully, never looking down and never hitting a pebble.

Felder follows, holding back a bit not so much because he's not caught up like they are but because he's appreciative, wants this vantage on them:

113

Wife and child running along the overgrown path, laughing, shots of sun hitting them. He has had so little time to be as overcome as he should be with his good fortune in the last few years: This wife who loves him so much that he *does* manage to make the time to wonder what she sees in him, this son whose worship is total, who for Daddy can stop agonized crying at the gentle command *Let's have a smile*, that smile coming up like an abrupt sunrise. He has been so caught up in his job, in surviving in New York, in worrying about how he—*they*—will continue to survive and in trying not to worry about how expensive everything is . . . and in bitching about how expensive everything is. He wants this moment: This is happy. He wants to freeze-frame them right on the path. Just for a moment. And let him have a movable point of view. So he's allowed to walk up close to wife and son and take intimate looks. He's allowed to touch them. . . .

*She does not say goodbye—but how was she to know?*

Felder's wife hits the wooden dock running. She dives, her long-legged slim body arching out over the water. Her city-white limbs stand out against her black tank suit.

Not too far away (but too far to help) is a man in a row boat. Fishing, casting, standing up in the boat, looking toward their shore. Felder's wife slips into the water. The kid stands at the end of the dock. Felder comes up next to him.

They stare at the water. Nothing happens. Almost black water. Lake George in high August: You can swim, but still there are currents that survived a thousand winters, bone-chillers that swirl up from the middle, from the bottom, cramping swimmers, freezing them.

*That's what the medical examiner will say.* . . .

Felder's wife is not seen again.

And she hit her head on a rock, and a leg got entangled, in some old bedsprings somebody threw down there—were they from the very house they rented?

*The medical examiner will say at least two of these three things: A wicked Lake George current caught her; she struck her head on a rock; her leg became entangled . . .*

*And the husband and son* drowned *trying to save her.* . . .

She doesn't come up, she's not going to come up. Felder does not, cannot, forget: He can't swim. He always thought that, in this situation (but it would never really come up, couldn't), if a loved one's life hung in the balance between his inability and his desire, he would strip and dive and save that life. Everything he could never learn would come to him. *Later,* he'd realize a miracle had occurred—like those mothers who lift automobiles off their trapped children, shocked that they mustered the superhuman strength for a few moments.

Felder cannot swim. Never could, never would. And Felder will die trying to save his wife. Felder strips to his underwear fast, shucking his clothes into the water. He dives in.

Well, a dive for him. Mouthful of water. Spit out. Head under, find the wife, she's a great swimmer—he likes that part: Why do drownings occur so often to people who are great swimmers?—it's just that she hit her head or a current got her or her foot was caught in something. And he cannot manage the simplest thing: Opening his eyes under water. He could never do that. He must, now. How else to find her down there on the bottom? He forces himself. And laughs inside. All is black.

Felder comes up—not because he wants to or wills himself to, simply because he does. He thinks he can feel water in his lungs. And there's the kid, twenty feet away on the dock, stripping down like Daddy, pulling those orange trunks down over those bony legs, gonna dive in and help Daddy save Mommy. His foot gets caught on the trunks when they're almost off and he goes tumbling into the water. He can swim a little. But not enough. Felder could laugh or weep: Wife and son in water, him, a guy who can't swim in the shower, trying to save them.

*But this is better*: Another awful summer tragedy. The fisherman in the boat: He'll let people know the sequence of events. He'll have rowed over, trying to help: there will probably be a newspaper story quote full of resignation from him: *Knew it was too late before I even got there.* . . .

This is better. Felder is on the bottom, the light in his head shrinking to nothing, stray thoughts not quite coming into focus before blipping off somewhere.

This is better. He does not have to make calls to parents and in-laws; his sister, her brothers; their friends, some funeral director. This is poignant, a real tragedy, a tragedy without qualification, something that will resonate profoundly with people who knew them well for years to come. They'll never consider summer vacation without thinking of the awful thing that happened to the Felders. No one who knows them will ever vacation at Lake George.

All he'd said was, *Next summer, we get the hell out of the city for the whole three months, I don't care if I have to quit!* And the three of them cackled like maniacs about to get away with murder and Felder turned away from the back seat and the unbridled glee on his son's face and saw the back of the U-Haul rushing up so fast it looked like it was going backwards.

This is better: The mother who was a great swimmer but who somehow got into trouble; the father who could not swim at all but who refused to let his wife drown; the four-year-old who fell in—he was the one who got his foot caught in the bedsprings, that's what happened—trying to help his parents.

This is much, much better than standing on I-87 with the state troopers, nothing wrong with him but a forehead gash.

This is better: This way Felder gets to die too.

Felder hugs the bottom, swallowing hard, cold black water running fast.

# STEVEN BRUST

# Csucskári

Steven Brust is one of the most talented of the new generation of fantasy writers, combining a flair for penning tales of rousing adventure with a fine regard for the elements of literary style; Brust is a young author who is always pushing himself to learn more about the art of storytelling, and it is a pleasure to watch his work evolve from book to book. He is the author of the Vlad Taltos fantasy/science fiction series; *To Reign in Hell* (a witty fantasy set in Heaven); and the splendid *Brokedown Palace*. He makes his home in Minneapolis and is a founding member of the Minneapolis Fantasy Writers' Group that has also produced Patricia C. Wrede, Emma Bull, Kara Dalkey, Pamela Dean, and Will Shetterly. With other talented writers such as Caroline Stevermer, John M. Ford, and Joel Rosenberg also making their homes in the Twin Cities, Minneapolis is fast becoming the Fantasy Capital of this country . . . it must be something in the water.

"Csucskári" is a retold folktale drawing on the author's Hungarian heritage. It is a part of a larger work, the novel *The Sun, The Moon, and The Stars*, the first book of the Fairy Tales Series of adult novels by different authors who are reworking classic fairy tales. Though used in the book as a mirror held up against the struggles of a group of artists in a contemporary city, the folktale easily stands on its own as a witty and magical story typical both of Steven Brust's style and the style of Hungarian storytelling.

Pronunciation note: The title of the story is pronounced, more or less, *chuch´ car-y*.

—T.W.

# CSUCSKÁRI

## Steven Brust

Once upon a time there were three Gypsies playing in a thicket near a road. One of them would gather up dust from the road, the second would build it into a mound, and the third would squash it flat. Then they would all roll on the ground, laughing in the fashion of Gypsies, their hands clasped together in front of their bellies.

Who knows how they came to be there? Perhaps their poor father, having no way to feed them, left them there. Perhaps they wandered off from their camp and became lost. It could even be that they were created there, out of the very dust with which they played. I don't know, but I know they were there, because I saw them myself, as I had pulled off the road to rest my horses and have a drink of *pálinka*.

In fact, I was going to offer them a drink, when a man dressed in a yellow gown came along the road and stopped before them. They looked at him, and he looked at them, and pretty soon up comes another man, dressed in a white gown, and stops next to the first and he looks at the Gypsies too. And pretty soon a third man comes along, and he has a black gown, and he stops by the first two. A fourth man comes along then, and he's dressed in green.

Well, just then the first one, who had the yellow gown, says to the second, "Brother, our master the King has commanded us to spread the word to all living souls, whomever or wherever we may find them, even if they are only three Gypsy boys living in the thicket by the side of the road."

The second man (he had the white gown, you remember) nodded and turned to the third man. "Well, brother, we should begin then with these three Gypsy boys, who are playing in the dust."

The third man, who was dressed in black, turned to the fourth man, and he said, "Our three hundred and sixty-two comrades will be along soon. We can get the jump on them if you will tell these three Gypsy boys of our quest, and then we can go on the next."

The fourth man (he was in green, if you recall) nodded and addressed the Gypsies, saying, "As you know, we do not now have a sun, a moon, or any stars." (I forgot to mention that this happened long ago, before we had the sun, the moon, or the stars.)

"Well, our master, who is King of all his Kingdom, will give half of this Kingdom and his daughter's hand in marriage to anyone who can fix the sun, the moon, and the stars in the heavens."

Well, two of the Gypsies started laughing, and the four men started to leave, but the youngest of the Gypsies stood up and he said, "Go no further. My name is Csucskári the Gypsy, and these are my brothers who are called Holló and Bagoly, and you may tell the King that between us we will do as he wishes." (You might say that Csucskári should have said *among* us, but he was young and a Gypsy, so don't judge him too harshly.) He went on, then, and said, "But, to do this, the King must bring us three things. First, he must bring us the tallest tree in the world, for we will need to climb very high to fix the sun, the moon, and the stars. Next, he must bring us a rope that will go all around the world, so we can stop the world to put the sun, the moon, and the stars in place. Third, he must bring us an iron skillet and two eggs so we can eat breakfast."

Well, the four counselors (for that's what they were) hurried off, and soon came back with the iron skillet and the eggs, and the three Gypsy boys sat down to breakfast. While they were eating, one of his brothers said, "Come now, Csucskári, you have earned us a meal for nothing, it is true, but surely you are having a joke with the foolish counselors, aren't you?"

Csucskári said, "No, Holló." (The one who had spoken was Holló.) "All we need are those things I have asked for and I will do as I have promised." Then he told them that he was a *taltos*, and, in fact, he hadn't eaten any breakfast, but had left the eggs for his brothers, for a *taltos* can't eat, as we all know. "You, my dear brothers, must agree to let me lead in all matters concerning this business, and I promise you that we will all become rich, and I will marry the King's daughter."

Well, his brothers agreed, and they settled down to wait for the King's counselors to return.

The next day there came a man who wore a gown of blue. He stopped at the thicket and said, "Is one of you Csucskári the Gypsy?"

Well, Csucskári stood up and bowed in the manner of Gypsies, with his back leg bent and his hands curled to his sides, and he said, "I am Csucskári the Gypsy."

"Well," says the counselor, "my three hundred and sixty-five companions and I told the king what you said, and he seemed pleased enough, but we have thought and thought and we don't know how to find the tallest tree in the world, or a rope long enough to go around the world."

"Well," said Csucskári, "if three hundred and sixty-six of you couldn't find these things, I daresay I'd be at a loss to better your work."

The counselor's face fell at these words, and he seemed so unhappy that Csucskári said, "Come now, there is certainly something we can do. If we cannot find the tallest tree in the world, we will use Mount Szaniszlo, for surely its branches are in the sky and its roots deep in the ground. And as for the rope, well, if the River Tündér doesn't go all around the world, at least it must come close, for I've never met anyone who has seen the end of it. So you take us to the king and we'll sign a contract with him, and then we'll be off to set the sun, the moon, and the stars up in the heavens where they belong."

That was enough for the counselor, so he led the Gypsies back down the road and over seven seas and six mountains and five rivers and four deserts and through three valleys and two villages until they came to the kingdom, where they were led into a palace that was so big a barn would have been lost in it.

The counselor led them through seven halls and up six stairs and through five libraries and four kitchens and three pantries and two dining rooms until they were before the king.

"Good day, Sire Your Majesty My Liege Lord, I am Csucskári the Gypsy, and these are my brothers Holló and Bagoly, and we are here to place the sun, the moon, and the stars in heaven."

"That's good," said the king. And he called for pen and paper. But before they came, Csucskári held his little finger up in the air, and with it he wrote out a contract in glowing gold letters, so the contract burned where the king and his three hundred and sixty-six counselors could see it. The contract said that if Csucskári and his brothers should succeed in putting the moon and the sun and the stars in the heavens, they would have half the kingdom to share and Csucskári would marry the king's daughter, and Csucskári signed it before their eyes.

When the pen and paper arrived, the letters burned themselves into the paper where they appeared as gold ink, and the king signed it with pen, below where Csucskári had signed it.

Then Csucskári borrowed seven swords from seven of the king's hussars, and on the seven hilts of the seven swords made his brothers swear to follow him without question in everything that came after. This done, they took their leave of the king and set out on their mission.

Csucskári and his brothers left the palace and started walking. They came to a high cliff, and Csucskári led them along a path to the bottom. After a while Holló said, "Well, Csucskári; where are you taking us?"

"I don't know," said Csucskári.

"What?" said Bagoly. "You don't know where you are taking us?"

"That is true, my dear brothers," says Csucskári, "I don't know where I am taking you. That is why you must trust me."

They came to a river and Csucskári led them over it on the rocks so they wouldn't fall in.

"But," says Holló, "are you looking for something?"

Csucskári says, "Yes, I am looking for something."

"Well then," says Bagoly, "what is it you're looking for?"

"I don't know," says Csucskári. "That is why you must trust me."

They came to a pasture, and Csucskári led them around the herd so the bull wouldn't see them.

"But, when you find it, will you do something?" asks Holló.

"Yes, then I'll do something," says Csucskári.

"But what will you do?" asks Bagoly.

"I don't know," was the answer. "That is why you must trust me."

Then Holló said, "How can we trust you when you don't know where you're taking us, or what you are looking for, or what you will do when you find it?"

"You can trust me because I have led you down a cliff, and over a river, and past a bull, and you have come to no harm. I suppose that is worth something."

Well, his brothers saw the wisdom of this and agreed readily enough, and soon they came to the edge of a big, black, wild forest.

Then Holló said, "Do we enter this forest, brother, or must we go around?"

Csucskári considered this, and said, "I must look around carefully, to see where we should go." And he looked around, and soon he saw the glint of gold high up in an oak. (You must not ask me how there could be a glint with no sun or moon or stars to make it. I don't know, but I know there was the glint because I saw it.)

Well, quick as thought, Csucskári was up the tree. Sure enough, one of the leaves was made of gold, and there was writing on it in red ink. Csucskári came back down the tree and showed the leaf to his brothers.

"Well, Csucskári, what does it say?" asked Holló.

"It says, 'If you wish to place the sun, the moon, and stars in the sky, you should first beware of the great boar who is coming to rip you to pieces.' "

"What?" cried Bagoly. "A great boar is coming to rip us to pieces? We are lost!"

"Well," says Csucskári, "I guess it is time to decide what to do."

Csucskári leapt to the tree, for a sudden fire seemed to come over him. He pulled a branch from the tree. He breathed on it and it became a spear with a glowing iron tip. Then he called, "Come on, you boar, let us play a game, one with the other, and see who is the stronger."

Well, you know how it is when a *taltos* yells, so you can bet the forest rang like the bells of Ujoltar. The old boar came up out of the forest, and it was the biggest, blackest, meanest boar Csucskári had ever seen. But it saw the spear in Csucskári's hand, and it didn't charge. It said, "So, Csucskári, you wish to place the sun, the moon, and stars up in the sky, do you? Well, I see you have a spear, and no doubt will get the better of me if we fight, so I may as well tell you what I know."

So the boar told him where to find a stream in the forest, and that if he followed the stream he would come to a cave, and inside the cave would be a sow with nine piglets. "Now Csucskári," says the boar, "you must cut open the sow, and inside her you will find a box, and inside the box are twelve wasps, which are the sun, the moon, and stars. But be a good fellow Csucskári, and when you're done, sew her belly back up, for she needs to be able to feed her nine piglets doesn't she?"

"Well," says Csucskári, "if I say I'll sew the sow, what will you tell me about dangers I'll run into on the way?" (You see, Csucskári sensed the boar wasn't telling him everything.)

"You are clever, Csucskári. Very well. You should know that there is a troll guarding the mouth to the cave, and even you, with your glowing spear, had better have a care for that troll, or he will eat you up."

Csucskári called out, "Ho! Holló and Bagoly, be sure to wait for me here until I get back." Then he turns to the boar and says, "Since you tried to trick me, you can carry me to the cave yourself, and you'll see how I deal with the troll."

The boar wasn't too happy to hear this, but he saw that it was either that or face Csucskári's spear, so he agreed, and Csucskári mounted upon his back and the boar carried him into the forest.

Csucskári hung onto the boar for all he was worth, and at last they came to a stream. The boar plunged into the stream up to his neck, but Csucskári hung on until they were on the other side. There, just as the boar had said, there was a path. They followed the path around twists and turns and over and under hills, until they were outside a cave. Here the boar stopped, and Csucskári got off its back.

"Very well, friend boar," he says. "You have brought me safely to the cave. Now you may leave if you wish, or you can stay and see how I deal with this monster."

He'd no sooner spoken than up pops an enormous troll. He was almost twice as tall as Csucskári, and had teeth the size of fingers, and his skin was hard as granite.

The troll says, "Well Csucskári, so you want to put the sun, the moon and stars up in the heavens, eh? When you were smaller than the hundredth part of a grain in your mother's womb, I knew I'd have to kill you, so you may as well put down that spear right now."

So Csucskári says, "I can see that it will be no easy matter to fight you, especially since I have with me only a spear that couldn't even pierce your skin, and since I'm tired after a long day's trials. How about if we take a rest now, so after a good sleep we can wake up refreshed and have a real test to see which one of us is the better."

The troll says, "Ho, are you trying to trick me? Well, Csucskári, it's no use, because trolls can't sleep any more than *taltos* can."

"What?" cried Csucskári. "Can't sleep? You have never slept in your life?"

"Well," says the troll, "it is true that when I was a little troll, my mother used to tell stories that would put me to sleep, but my old mother is long gone now."

"Ah," says Csucskári, "I'll tell you a story then." And, before the troll could say another word, Csucskári began telling the story of the Yak Who Visited the Monastery. Soon the troll sat down to listen. From time to time, Csucskári would stop his tale, in the manner of the orchard-workers of the North, and he would say, "Bones?" And, time after time, the troll would answer him, saying, "Tiles," meaning he was still awake.

But at last, once when Csucskári said, "Bones?" there came no answer, and Csucskári knew that the troll had fallen asleep. Then, quick as the wind, Csucskári slipped past him and into the cave.

Csucskári followed the cave, which was long and dark. It went up and down, and twisted from side to side so that he was afraid he would become lost. But suddenly he knew what he could do, and he made a light spring up around him. It came none too soon, either, because he had been about to fall into a pit.

With the light around him, he soon comes to a place where the sow is nursing her nine piglets. Before you could say, *palacsinták*, he takes out his jackknife and slits open her belly. Inside, he finds a box. He holds it up to his ear, and he hears the twelve wasps buzzing around inside. He puts the box into his pocket, then he starts to leave.

The sow says, "Come, Csucskári, didn't my husband the boar ask you to sew me back up, so I may feed my nine piglets?"

"Well, yes he did," says Csucskári. "Since you have reminded me of it, I will do so." Csucskári found a spider's web, and from it he made a length of thread, and with a bee's stinger he made a needle. With these he quickly sewed up the wound in the sow's belly.

When he had finished, the sow said, "You have been faithful and sewed up my belly, so I will tell you something."

Csucskári said, "What is it you will tell me then?"

The sow says, "You should know that there is a dragon with twelve heads, a dragon with ten heads, and a dragon with eight heads, and you will have to fight them all if you wish to set the sun, the moon, and the stars up in the sky."

"Well, mother," says Csucskári, "it is good of you to tell me this. How will I find these dragons?" You see, he was determined to meet them head on.

The sow said, "You must continue through the cave not going back the way you came, and you will soon be on a path, and then you will see a cottage where lives the dragon with twelve heads. No more can I tell you."

"Then thank you, and may you live a long time and have many children."

With these words, Csucskári set off through the cave, still surrounded by his own light, until he emerged at last onto a path. He took the path, and soon saw a small cottage, and as he approached it his light went out.

Csucskári stood outside the house and looked at it for a long time (he was waiting for the dragon, you know). He went closer and closer, but didn't see any dragon. Finally, he goes inside. He sees a woman there. She says, "Ah, you are Csucskári!"

"Well, yes I am," says Csucskári.

The woman says, "When you were smaller than a hundredth part of a grain in your mother's womb, I knew my husband would kill you."

"Oh, you don't need to worry about that," says Csucskári. "Is your husband a dragon?"

"A dragon!" cries the woman. "Why, he is a dragon with twelve heads!"

"That's all right then," says Csucskári. (He wasn't frightened.) "Only tell me, is there a sign of his coming?"

"Yes there is," said the woman. "When he is twelve miles away, he grips his mace, which weighs twelve hundred pounds, and hurls it with such force that it makes the cornerstones crack."

Csucskári went outside, and saw that the mace had already arrived and made the cornerstones crack. He picked up the mace and started walking. Then he threw it with such force that it traveled more than twelve miles back the way it had come.

Soon he came to a field, and in the field was a ditch, and over the ditch was a bridge. He went down into the ditch and picked up a big rock and broke it over his knee. Then he broke it again and again until it looked like a sword, and this he sharpened with his teeth. Then he thrust the sword through the cracks of the bridge.

Well, pretty soon along comes the dragon on his horse. First thing you know, the horse trips over the sword and the dragon falls down on the bridge.

"What is this?" cries the dragon to his horse. "May your blood be lapped up by dogs! Haven't you done twelve good miles this day without as much as a false step? I guess it's Csucskári who is playing a nasty trick on us. If I knew for sure, I'd make him pay with his head."

When Csucskári heard these words, he was so mad that his anger melted the rock he was standing on, and he jumped up onto the bridge.

"Ho, my twelve-headed friend!" he cries. "You want my head? I'd like to know what you wish to do with it, since you have twelve of your own, and not a brain in any of them. A poor reward, I'd call it, for all the trouble I'm taking to fix the sun and the moon in the sky so that we may live in light instead of darkness."

Says the dragon with twelve heads, "Never mind about that now. You'd better tell me how you want to fight me. Is it to be the sword, or shall we measure each other's strength in a fist fight?"

Now, Csucskári is still pretty mad about what the dragon had said, so he says, "It is neither by the sword nor in a fist fight that we are going to settle this. My father was neither a cattle driver nor a cowherd, so why should I bother about your challenge?"

Then he stepped up and, with two strokes, cut off all twelve of the dragon's heads. Then he went on his way again, off down the road.

Csucskári was tired after the battle with the dragon with twelve heads, so he set off down the road looking for a place to rest. Soon, he comes to a house. He goes inside and says, "Hello, woman," to the woman who is there.

"Well, good day to you, Csucskári," she says (she recognizes him).

"How is it you know me, woman?" asked Csucskári.

The woman said, "When you were smaller than the hundredth part of a grain in your mother's womb, I knew that my husband, the dragon with ten heads, would fight you because you killed his brother."

"Ah," said Csucskári. "So this is the home of the dragon with ten heads? Well, I had hoped for a bit of rest after fighting his brother, but I can see I have more work to do. So you tell me then, what is the sign of his coming?"

"When he gets within ten miles of his house, he grips his mace, which weighs a thousand pounds, and hurls it at this castle with such force that the weathercock on the top of the roof will make an about-face."

So Csucskári stepped out of the house, and, just as he did, it all happened as the woman had predicted. As quick as you please, Csucskári went and hid in a nearby ditch spanned by a bridge, just as before. Again, he thrust his sword through the boards. When the dragon came riding up the bridge, his horse suddenly tripped over the sword.

"Ho!" cried the dragon. "May your blood be lapped up by dogs. What's that? Haven't you done ten good miles this day without as much as a false step? I know this is all Csucskári's doing. To be sure I'll make him pay for it. He killed my brother, the dragon with twelve heads, and I'll take his life for it."

When Csucskári heard this kind of talk, all thoughts of rest were gone and he leapt up onto the bridge. "Come on, comrade, let's see whether your fighting is as good as your words."

At that they rushed at one another. All the clock round they were dealing each other blows with the flats of their swords, and they made such a tumult that all of the grain was swept out of the fields and into bins, yet they continued.

Another day went by, and they tried each other with the points of their swords, but neither could gain the advantage; each was the equal of the other, yet they kicked up such a fuss that all the hay was struck down and baled and put into the barns.

On the third day, Csucskári at last brought the fight to a close by dealing a blow with his sword, cutting off all ten of the dragon's heads at one mighty sweep.

Then he set off down the road, looking for a place to rest.

Soon Csucskári came to a house and went inside. He said, "Good day, woman." (There was a woman in the house.)

She said, "Hey, Csucskári, what business have you here? You've killed the two brothers of my husband."

"What?" cries Csucskári. "Your husband must be the dragon with eight heads."

"None other," says the woman. "Now he's going to finish with you whether by fire or by water or by the point of his sword."

"Well, well," says Csucskári. "I call this a fine thank you, after I've gone to all this trouble to put the sun and the moon up in the sky. But tell me, pray, what is the sign of his coming?"

"There is no sign. There he comes."

And, indeed, the ground was trembling from the weight of the dragon. Now Csucskári was so tired from his other fights (you remember, he fought the two other dragons) that all he could think of to do was to hide. He winked at the woman in the manner of the gypsies, then hid himself under the bed.

"Heigh-ho, wife," says the dragon. "I smell a stranger there in my house."

"There is no smell and there is no stranger you smell. It must be your comings and goings that take you far from your home which fill your nostrils with strange smells." (You see, she concealed from him that Csucskári was there.)

"Look here, woman, tell me the truth at once, or I'll kill you outright. What is the strange smell I smell in my house?"

"Since I cannot keep it from you, I'd better tell you. Csucskári is in there."

"I could have guessed that it was Csucskári. And what of your false words to me? Have you grown so fond of him? Step forth at once, Csucskári. Tell me by what death you choose to die."

Well, Csucskári comes out from under the bed and dusts himself off just as if there was nothing the matter. "You'd better ask what death you'd choose for yourself," he says.

"Not so fast, fellow," says the dragon. "Do you think that because you've killed my two brothers you can do away with me as well? Come on. Let us measure each other's strength by the points of our swords." (You know, he took it for granted that he would finish with Csucskári.)

"Well, that's all right with me, but let's go outside first, so we'll have more room."

And so they went outside to fight, though Csucskári was so tired he could barely walk.

Csucskári and the dragon measured their swords, and all the clock round they fought. Each was as strong as the other, each was as fast as the other, each was as skilled as the other.

But Csucskári became more and more tired, until he was almost at the end of his tether. Just as he was about to fall, the dragon called to him, "Listen, Csucskári. It seems to me that a valiant fighter like you is now at the very point of death. I know that you are a great champion, so let us agree upon taking a day's rest and after it we may start all over again in some other way."

Well, Csucskári thanked the dragon for his courtesy, and when the day was past they went at each other again. But even the rest of one day wasn't enough for Csucskári to fully recover his strength, so at last he was ready to fall again. But at just the last moment the dragon said, "Listen, comrade, there's nothing doing. In strength you're my equal and I am yours. So from now on we'll turn into flames; you'll be the green flame and I shall be the red flame."

"That's a good plan," says Csucskári, and straightaway turned into a green flame. As he changed, he felt a new strength come into his body, so he knew he could keep going a while longer.

So for another day the two flames tried to smother each other or push each other into the river (there was a river nearby). Finally the red flame burned so strongly that it nearly destroyed Csucskári. Just as he was about to fail, he lifted his eyes to heaven and saw, right above him, that there was an eagle, who was croaking away with a mournful sound.

Csucskári called to the eagle, saying, "Right you are to bemoan the ruin of the hero who is striving to fix the sun and the moon and the stars in the sky so that there may be light for all."

The eagle looked down and said, "Yes, Csucskári. When you were smaller than the hundredth part of a grain in your mother's womb, I knew that I would look down and watch you be destroyed by the dragon with eight heads."

"Never mind about that," says Csucskári, "but if you wish to live in light instead of darkness, go get as much water as you can carry in your mouth and on your wings, and let it run over the red flame."

"Well," says the eagle, "I wouldn't mind living in light instead of darkness, but I'd like to know what you'll give me if I do this for you."

And Csucskári says, "I'll give you all of the dragon's eight heads, and the flesh and hide of a whole cattle herd which he owns, and above it there will be light." But look! The red flame is still growing stronger than the green flame.

The eagle flew off, and, quick as an eagle, brought water in his mouth and on his wings and let it run over the red flame so that it began to die at once. Then Csucskári gripped his sword and at one mighty sweep cut off the eight heads of the dragon.

Then Csucskári gave the eagle the heads of the dragon and its herd of cattle, and at last lay down on the ground and rested.

While Csucskári slept, the wife of the dragon with twelve heads went to see the wife of the dragon with ten heads. They talked in the way of wives for a while, then they said, "What should we do about this Csucskári, who has killed our husbands?" They thought about tying him up and throwing him in the river, but they were afraid he would burst his bonds and escape. They thought about throwing him into fire, but they were afraid he would put the fire out with water he had saved in his mouth from being thrown into the river.

At last they decided to see the wife of the dragon with eight heads, so they set off to her house. When they got there, they talked for a while in the way of wives, then said, "What should we do about this Csucskári, who has killed our husbands?" The wife of the dragon with eight heads said, "We should go at once to see our old father-in-law, who will know how to deal with this rascal."

So they marched off to do that. Meanwhile, Csucskári wakes up, and goes walking down the road. When the wives got to their old father-in-law, they paid their respects and passed the time with him as good daughters will, then they said, "What should we do about this Csucskári, who has killed our husbands?"

The old dragon asked his eldest daughter-in-law, "Well, my dear daughter, what curse would you put upon Csucskári who has killed your husband, the dragon with twelve heads?"

"Well, dear father," she says, "only this: I would bring hunger upon him and then make him eat a loaf of bread of which a single bite would make him burst into twelve pieces."

"Right you are, my eldest daughter-in-law. Well, what about you, my second daughter-in-law? What curse would you put upon Csucskári who killed your husband, the dragon with ten heads?"

"Only this: Within a mile from the place hunger comes upon him, I would make him thirst so much he would almost perish from it. Then I would make him pass a well so that when he drinks of it, its water would make him burst into ten pieces."

"Right you are, my second daughter-in-law. So what about you, my youngest daughter-in-law? What pains would you put upon Csucskári who killed your husband, the dragon with eight heads?"

"I would make him pass a pear tree laden with the biggest and finest pears so that when he'd take a bite into a pear it would make him burst into eight pieces."

Oh, there is something I forgot to mention. When Csucskári woke up and started walking down the road, he saw the three wives of the three dragons, and so he followed them. So now while this was going on, he slipped into the house and found the old tom-cat and shook its insides out and slipped into its skin. Then he jumped into the lap of the youngest daughter-in-law.

The youngest daughter-in-law said to the wife of the old dragon, "Well, dear mother, what curse would you put upon Csucskári who killed your three sons?"

"As for me," said the hag, "I'm going to sit on the shovel blade and ride after him and burn his buttocks."

Hearing this, Csucskári defecated on the lap of the youngest daughter-in-law and took off.

The old dragon said, "We may as well go to hell now. All of us. Csucskári has overheard us talking. There is nothing we could do against him."

Csucskári walked back until he came to the house of the dragon with eight heads. He went inside and found a bushel of pears. Then he walked until he came to the house of the dragon with ten heads. He went inside and found a bottle of wine. Then he walked until he came to the house of the dragon with twelve heads. He went inside and found a loaf of bread.

He carried these until he came to the cave where the sow lay with her nine piglets. He walked through the cave until he was near the sleeping troll and the boar. Then he walked through the forest until he came to his brothers, who were waiting for him next to a brook.

"Well, how are you, brothers?" he asked.

"Since you are asking us, brother," they said, "we are hungry."

"You say you are hungry," said Csucskári, and he brings out the loaf of bread, the bushel of pears, and the bottle of wine. The two brothers eat their fill, but Csucskári being a *taltos* doesn't touch anything, neither food nor drink.

When they had finished eating, Csucskári took out his sword. "See here, brothers. This sword has slain the dragon with twelve heads, the dragon with ten heads, and the dragon with eight heads. Now you must swear upon its hilt that you will let me be first in everything we do from now on, or otherwise you will perish by a horrible death. But I have the sun, the moon, and the stars in this little box in my pocket. Hereafter I shall win myself a royal palace, and until then our lives are still at stake."

So Bagoly and Holló swear an oath on the hilt of the sword that they will allow Csucskári to be first in all they do, and after that they set out upon the road.

All that day Csucskári led his brothers on and on, not stopping for anything. Nor would he answer when they asked where Csucskári was leading them. At last when they stopped and rested Bagoly said, "Come now, brother, can't you tell us where we're going, and why we haven't yet put the sun, the moon, and the stars up into the heavens?"

"We are waiting for the wives of the three dragons, who will try to kill us. Until they do, and I have defeated them, it isn't safe for us to stop for more than a few minutes. If they find us resting, we've had it."

So after a moment they stood up again, and walked on and on until the eldest brother, Holló, says, "Oh, brother, the most horrible hunger has come upon me, and I think I will die upon this spot if I do not eat."

So Csucskári says, "Do not worry, brother. I see a loaf of bread yonder there. It won't take us long to get there and then we can have our fill of it. Just keep your courage up till we come to that bread. But remember, you must let me go first."

Well, pretty soon they reach the loaf. Csucskári takes it in one hand, and instead of breaking it to feed them, he pierces it with his spear (you remember; he had the spear for fighting the boar). Well, as soon as he pierced it the spear broke into twelve pieces, but red blood came forth from the bread, and that was the end of the wife of the dragon with twelve heads.

They had been traveling some little time after that when Bagoly said, "Csucskári, I hate to burden you with my troubles after all you've been through, but the most terrible thirst has come upon me, that I fear I shall die from it."

"Do not worry, brother. I see a well over there. We are going to have a drink from it, but I must go first."

When they reached the well, Csucskári pulled out his sword and struck the well with it. Well, the sword breaks into ten pieces, but a great crack appears in the wall of the well, and red blood flows forth from it. And that was the end of the wife of the dragon with ten heads.

They walked on until they came to a pear tree. Then Holló says, "Look, Csucskári. I see a pear tree yonder there. How I wish I could pick a pear or two for myself."

"Do not worry, my dear brother. In less than a minute you can pick a pear or two for yourself, but I must go there first."

Then he goes up to the tree and takes a pear down, and with his pocket knife he cuts the pear in two. And, lo! red blood flows forth from the pear, the knife breaks into eight pieces, and the tree cracks and falls. And that was the end of the wife of the dragon with eight heads.

They walked on a little more, until suddenly Csucskári looks behind him and sees the hag riding up on a shovel hot enough to burn her buttocks.

Bagoly turns to Csucskári and says, "Come, Csucskári, what now? How will you defeat her?"

And Csucskári shakes his head and says, "She is too much for me. I can't."

The old hag is still riding toward them, and look! Csucskári is standing, frightened. But then, suddenly, he sees a cottage not too far away.

"Come brothers," he says. "We must try to find shelter in that cottage. Perhaps it will be safe."

So they run for the cottage. Just in the nick of time, they make it to the cottage and shut the door in the hag's face. Meanwhile, she begins circling the cottage, waiting for them to come out.

The cottage was a blacksmith's shop, and the blacksmith was there. Csucskári said, "Sir blacksmith, we are being chased by an old hag. If you can save us, we'll give you anything we have."

"Well, I can save you," says the blacksmith, "but in return, you must swear to serve me for the rest of your lives."

So, having no choice, Csucskári and his brothers swear to serve the blacksmith for the rest of their lives.

The old hag with the iron nose (I forgot to mention, she had an iron nose) rode up on her shovel. She came to the door and called out, "Hey, my friend, didn't Csucskári and his two brothers come here?"

The blacksmith winks at Csucskári then calls out past the door, "So he did, mother."

"Then you must give them to me at once. He has killed my three sons. Three champions they were, and you would not find their equal, not in seven countries."

The blacksmith winks at Csucskári again, then says, "Oh, mother, you'd better forget about it. It's not so simple at all with a fellow like Csucskári. If I were to give him to you through the window, he might run away; if I were to give him to you through the door, he might knock you off your feet and get away. Why, there's no way of getting him to you unless I cut a hole in my wall and push him straight into your mouth."

"Well, then," says the hag. "That is what you shall do."

"Oh, but mother, will you repair my wall?"

"If you cut a hole in it and push Csucskári through, then I will repair your wall after I have eaten him."

"Very good then, mother. I will cut a hole in this wall and push him through. You must stand there and catch him in your mouth. Then you can bite him into pieces."

Well, as quick as lightning, the smith takes a pot big enough to hold sixty quarts and starts to boil some lead in it. When the lead was melted, Csucskári took hold of the pot while the blacksmith cut a hole in the wall. When the hole was cut, the blacksmith called out, "Hey, mother! You'd better put your mouth close up to the hole so that not even an inch of Csucskári may slip past it, or he might get away."

"Well," says the hag, "I'm ready. Push Csucskári through the hole."

As soon as she says this, Csucskári pours all sixty quarts of lead through the hole. Then they go rushing outside, and the hag with the iron nose lay dead as a doornail.

"Thank you," says Csucskári. "We owe you our lives."

"Well," says the blacksmith, "and you shall repay me, too. Don't you remember that you have promised to serve me for the rest of your life? And don't think to fool me, either, for this is what I can do." And with that, he took a manikin and tied it into three hundred and sixty-six knots.

Time passed, and the brothers began to become anxious. Hadn't they gotten the box with the sun, the moon, and the stars in it? Weren't they ready to finish their task? But how could they escape from this blacksmith who could tie a manikin into three hundred and sixty-six knots?

The blacksmith had a wife. Soon Csucskári fell in love with her. So every day when he left the breakfast table he would bow to her in the manner of the gypsies. And every evening when he finished his work, he would wink at her in the manner of the gypsies. And every night before retiring to bed, he would blow her a kiss in the manner of the gypsies.

Well, soon she falls in love with him, too, and he wastes no time in asking her the secret of her husband's strength. How is it that he could move easily through hoops of steel, reaching up right to his knee, and by what trick could he tie up a man into three hundred and sixty-six knots? Well, his wife doesn't know, but she promises to find out.

At noon the blacksmith came home for his meal, and his wife said, "Oh dear and wonderful husband, I have been living with you for some thirty years now, but I have never asked you wherein lies that magnificent strength of yours."

At that the blacksmith fetched her such a blow in the face that she passed out for twenty-four hours. Next time she saw Csucskári, she said, "Oh, I tried to find out, but he struck me so hard I slept for twenty-four hours."

Csucskári said, "Never mind about that. If you ask him again, he'll tell you."

So the next day, she asked her husband again, "My dear husband, do tell me, pray, wherein lies your magnificent strength."

"Listen, wife. As you are so keen to find out, though heaven only knows whether I shall not be sorry for it, I am willing to tell you. Look at that chain mail I always wear for a shirt. Without it, I possess no more strength than any other human being."

"Oh dear husband, if I had known it before, I would have had it gilded for you."

When the day turned to night and the smith went to sleep in his bed, his wife took off his shirt and gave it to Csucskári. At once Csucskári slipped into the shirt. Then he goes to his sleeping brother and ties him into three hundred and sixty-six knots to test the magic power of the shirt. Then he unties his brother.

Midnight came. The blacksmith wakes from sleep. At once Csucskári goes up to him. "Listen, brother smith. I am not going to serve you any longer."

Says the smith, "And why not, may I ask? Didn't you make a pledge that all three of you were to serve me as long as you live?"

"Indeed, we did, but that was some time ago."

"Just listen, brother. I know that all this is my wife's doing. I dare say, you have enough guts to oppose me, with tying up your brother, though you could not have done it without having taken my strength from me. But here you shall remain."

At this Csucskári seized the smith and tied him into three hundred and sixty-six knots.

"Oh, comrade, didn't I spare your life and your brother's lives? Surely I may trust your kind heart and you will untie me before you leave this place."

Csucskári untied the smith and with his brothers took leave of him.

The brothers set off wandering, and after a while Csucskári says, "My dear brothers, after all the trouble I went through, let me take a little rest so that I may sleep for a while."

Now since Csucskári was a *taltos*, he didn't need any sleep. It was just that he wanted to test his brothers, to see if they were loyal to him.

Said Holló, "Indeed, you deserve as much rest as you want. You sleep, and we'll keep watch."

Said Bagoly, "My dear brother Csucskári, you can make yourself comfortable when we have completed our mission and are at the king's palace. There you can take off your clothes and take a bath. That's where you should rest."

But Csucskári did not take heed of his words. There and then he lay down and soon was snoring away in sleep. Then Holló drew forth a razor and began to sharpen it. Bagoly said, "What are you doing, brother? Didn't you have a shave just last week? Surely you don't need another one now."

"I am going to cut Csucskári's throat, so that I may marry the king's daughter and get half his kingdom. Be quiet now, and I will share it with you, that way you'll get a quarter of the kingdom for yourself."

"And could you cut your brother's throat in cold blood knowing that it was Csucskári who did all the fighting and endured the many hardships? What else did we but follow him about, and surely that did not amount to much." And he called to the sleeper, "Wake up, my dear brother Csucskári! Our eldest brother is going to cut your throat."

Csucskári opened his eyes and said, "I knew it, my dear brother. I was not sleeping. It was only to test the true feelings of your hearts for me. But now you must disown our eldest brother and pledge yourself to have nothing to do with him, whatever state you may rise to in this world. He may not even hope to be taken on as a herdboy for your turkeys."

After that they took leave of Holló, and Csucskári and Bagoly came to the king's palace. There Csucskári said to the king, "Good day to you, sire. Your majesty, I have brought the sun and the moon and the stars for you but on the condition that you give your daughter in marriage and half of your kingdom to my brother and not to me because I am a *taltos*."

"That's all right by me," said the king.

Then they did justice to their agreement. Csucskári and Bagoly climbed to the top of Mount Szaniszlo. There Csucskári gave to Bagoly the shirt from the blacksmith, and Bagoly put it on so he could hold onto the River Tundar and make the earth stand still. Then Csucskári released the twelve wasps and the sun and the moon and the stars were fixed in the sky. And so there was light.

Throughout seven countries the drums went rolling and all the dukes and counts and great lords came together to celebrate the wedding. For seven years and seven winks the wedding feast went on.

And if they are not dead, they are still alive to this day.

# RAMSEY CAMPBELL

## The Other Side

Ramsey Campbell was born in 1946 in Liverpool. He worked as a tax officer and in libraries for eleven years before becoming a full-time writer in 1973. He is the author of eight novels, six collections of short stories and the editor of five anthologies. He has won more awards for horror fiction than any other writer.

A master of the subtle shock, Campbell forces the reader to become involved in the lives of characters who may be unlikeable, but whose inner torment is undeniably mirrored in the lives of people we all know. This compelling quality in his work sets him apart from other writers, and readers familiar with Campbell's work will inevitably find themselves looking with dread for clues to the particular terror that propels each new story.

—E.D.

# THE OTHER SIDE

## Ramsey Campbell

When Bowring saw where the fire engines were heading, he thought at first it was the school. "They've done it, the young swine," he groaned, craning out of his high window, clutching the cold, dewy sill. Then flames burst from an upper window of the abandoned tenement a mile away across the river, reddening the low clouds. That would be one less place for them to take their drugs and do whatever else they got up to when they thought nobody was watching. "Bow-wow's watching, and don't you forget it," he muttered with a grin that let the night air twinge his teeth, and then he realized how he could.

A taste of mothballs caught at the back of his throat as he took the binoculars from the wardrobe where they hung among his suits. The lenses pulled the streets across the river toward him, cut-out terraces bunched together closely as layers of wallpaper. The tenement reared up, a coaly silhouette flaring red, from the steep bank below them. Figures were converging to watch, but he could see nobody fleeing. He let the binoculars stray upward; to the flames, which seemed calming as a fireside, too silent and distant to trouble him. Then his face stiffened. Above the flames and the jets of water red as blood, a figure was peering down.

Bowring twisted the focusing screw in a vain attempt to get rid of the blur of heat, to clear his mind of what he thought he was seeing. The figure must be trapped, crying for help and jumping as the floor beneath its feet grew hotter, yet it appeared to be prancing with delight, waving its hand gleefully, grinning like a clown. To believe that was to lose control, he told himself fiercely. A jet of water fought back the flames below the window he was staring at, and he saw that the window was empty.

Perhaps it had always been. If anyone had been crying for help, the firemen must have responded by now. Among the spectators he saw half a dozen of his pupils sharing cigarettes. He felt in control again at once. He'd be having words with them tomorrow.

In the morning he drove ten miles to the bridge, ten miles back along the far bank. The school was surrounded by disorder, wallpaper flapping beyond broken windows, houses barricaded with cardboard against casual missiles, cars stranded without wheels and rusting in streets where nothing moved except flocks of litter. Ash from last night's fire settled on his car like an essence of the grubby streets. In the midst of the chaos, the long, low, ruddy school still looked as it must have a hundred years ago. That felt like a promise of order to him.

He was writing a problem in calculus on the blackboard when those of his class who'd come to school today piled into the classroom, jostling and swearing, accompanied by smells of tobacco and cheap perfume. He swung round, gown whirling, and the noise dwindled sullenly. Two minutes' slamming of folding seats, and then they were sitting at their desks, which were too small for some of them. Bowring hooked his thumbs in the shoulders of his gown. "Which of you were at the fire last night?" he said in a voice that barely reached the back of the room.

Twenty-three faces stared dully at him, twenty-three heads of the monster he had to struggle with every working day. There was nothing to distinguish those he'd seen last night across the river, not a spark of truth. "I know several of you were," he said, letting his gaze linger on the six. "I suggest you tell your friends after class that I may have my eye on you even when you think nobody's watching."

They started, challenging him to identify them, and waited until dark to answer him with a scrawl of white paint across the ruined tenement. FUCK OFF, BOW WOW, the message said. The binoculars shook until he controlled himself. He was damned if he'd let them reach him in his home, his refuge from all they represented. Tomorrow he'd deal with them, on his patch of their territory. He moved the binoculars to see what he'd glimpsed as they veered.

A figure was standing by the tenement, under one of the few surviving streetlamps. The mercury-vapor glare made its face look white as a clown's, though at first he couldn't see the face; the long hands that appeared to be gloved whitely were covering it while the shoulders heaved as if miming rage. Then the figure flung its hands away from its face and began to prance wildly, waving its fists above its spiky hair. It was then that Bowring knew it was the figure he'd seen above the flames.

It must be some lunatic, someone unable to cope with life over there. Suddenly the mercury-vapor stage was bare, and Bowring resisted scanning the dark: whatever the figure was up to had nothing to do with him. He was inclined to ignore the graffiti too, except that next morning, when he turned from the blackboard several of his class began to titter.

He felt his face stiffen, grow pale with rage. That provoked more titters, the nervous kind he'd been told you heard at horror films. "Very well," he murmured, "since you're all aware what I want to hear, we'll have complete silence until the culprit speaks up."

"But sir, I don't know—" Clint began, pulling at his earlobe where he'd been forbidden to wear a ring in school, and Bowring rounded on him. "Complete silence," Bowring hissed in a voice he could barely hear himself.

He strolled up and down the aisles, sat at his desk when he wanted to outstare them. Their resentment felt like an imminent storm. Just let one of them protest to his face! Bowring wouldn't lay a finger on them—they wouldn't lose him his pension that way—but he'd have them barred from his class. He was tempted to keep them all in after school, except that he'd had enough of the lot of them.

"Wait until you're told to go," he said when the final bell shrilled. He felt unwilling to relinquish his control of them, to let them spill out of his room in search of mischief, sex, drugs, violence, their everyday lives; for moments that seemed disconcertingly prolonged, he felt as if he couldn't let go. "Perhaps on Monday we can get on with some work, if you haven't forgotten what that's like. Now you may go," he said softly, daring them to give tongue to the resentment he saw in all their eyes.

They didn't, not then. He drove across the bridge to be greeted by the scent of pine, of the trees that April sunlight was gilding. Hours later he lay in his reclining chair, lulled by a gin and tonic, by Debussy on the radio. Halfway through the third movement of the quartet, the phone rang. "Yes?" Bowring demanded.

"Mr. Bowring?"

"Yes?"

"Mr. Bowring the teacher?"

"This is he."

"It's he," the voice said aside, and there was a chorus of sniggers. At once Bowring knew what the voice would say, and so it did: "Fuck off, Bow-wow, you—"

He slammed the phone down before he could hear more, and caught sight of himself in the mirror, white-faced, teeth bared, eyes bulging. "It's all right," he murmured to his mother in the photograph on the mantelpiece below the mirror. But it wasn't: now they'd found him, they could disarray his home life any time they felt like it; he no longer had a refuge. Who had it been on the phone? One of the boys with men's voices, Darren or Gary or Lee. He was trying to decide which when it rang again.

No, they wouldn't get through to him. Over the years he'd seen colleagues on the teaching staff break down, but that wouldn't happen to him. The phone range five times in the next hour before they gave up. Since his mother's death he'd only kept the phone in case the school needed to contact him.

Sunlight woke him in the morning, streaming from behind his house and glaring back from the river. The sight of figures at the charred tenement took him and his binoculars to the window. But they weren't any of his pupils, they were a demolition crew. Soon the tenement puffed like a fungus, hesitated, then collapsed. Only a rumble like distant thunder and a microscopic clink of bricks reached him. The crowd of bystanders dispersed, and even the demolition crew drove away before the dust had finished settling. Bowring alone saw the figure that pranced out of the ruins.

At first he thought its face was white with dust. It sidled about in front of the jagged foundations, pumping its hips and pretending to stick an invisible needle in its arm, and then Bowring saw that the face wasn't covered with dust; it was made up like a clown's. That and the mime looked doubly incongruous because of the plain suit the man was wearing. Perhaps all this was some kind of street theater, some anarchist nonsense of the kind that tried to make the world a stage for its slogans, yet Bowring had a sudden disconcerting impression that the mime was meant just for him. He blocked the idea from his mind—it felt like a total loss of control— and turned his back on the window.

His morning routine calmed him, his clothes laid out on the sofa as his mother used to do. His breakfast egg waiting on the molded ledge in the door of the refrigerator, where he'd moved it last night from the egg box farther in. That evening he attended a debate at the Conservative club on law and order, and on Sunday he drove into the countryside to watch patterns of birds in the sky. By Sunday evening he hadn't given the far side of the river more than a casual glance for over twenty-four hours.

When he glimpsed movement, insect-like under the mercury lamp, he sat down to listen to Elgar. But he resented feeling as if he couldn't look; he'd enjoyed the view across the river ever since he'd moved across, enjoyed knowing it was separate from him. He took as much time as he could over carrying his binoculars to the window.

The clown was capering under the lamp, waving his fists exultantly above his head. His glee made Bowring nervous about discovering its cause. Nervousness swung the binoculars wide, and he saw Darren lying among the fallen bricks, clutching his head and writhing. At once the clown scampered off into the dark.

In the false perspective of the lenses Darren looked unreal, and Bowring felt a hint of guilty triumph. No doubt the boy had been taunting the clown—maybe now he'd had a bit of sense knocked into him. He watched the boy crawl out of the debris and stagger homewards, and was almost certain that it had been Darren's voice on the phone. He was even more convinced on Monday morning, by the way that all Darren's cronies sitting round the empty desk stared accusingly at him.

They needn't try to blame him for Darren's injury, however just it seemed. "If anyone has anything to say about any of your absent colleagues," he murmured, "I'm all ears." Of course they wouldn't speak to him face to face, he realized, not now that they had his number. His face stiffened so much he could barely conduct the lesson, which they seemed even less eager to comprehend than usual. No doubt they were anticipating unemployment and the freedom to do mischief all day, every day. Their apathy made him feel he was drowning, fighting his way to a surface which perhaps no longer existed. When he drove home across the bridge, their sullen sunless sky came with him.

As soon as he was home he reached out to take the phone off the hook, until he grabbed his wrist with his other hand. This time he'd be ready for them if they called. Halfway through his dinner of unfrozen cod, they did. He saw them before he heard them, three of them slithering down the steep slope to a phone box, miraculously intact, that stood near a riverside terrace that had escaped demolition. He dragged them toward him with the binoculars as they piled into the box.

They were three of his girls: Debbie, who he'd seen holding hands with Darren—he didn't like to wonder what they got up to when nobody could see them—and Vanessa and Germaine. He watched Debbie as she dialed, and couldn't help starting as his phone rang. Then he grinned across the river at her. Let her do her worst to reach him.

He watched the girls grimace in the small lit box, shouting threats or insults or obscenities at the phone in Debbie's hand as if that would make him respond. "Shout all you like, you're not in my classroom now," he whispered, and then, without quite knowing why, he swung the binoculars away from them to survey the dark. As his vision swept along the top of the slope he saw movement, larger than he was expecting. A chunk of rubble half as high as a man was poised on the edge above the telephone box. Behind it, grinning stiffly, he saw the glimmering face of the clown.

Bowring snatched up the receiver without thinking. "Look out! Get out!" he cried, so shrilly that his face stiffened with embarrassment. He heard Debbie sputter a shocked insult as the binoculars fastened shakily on the lit box, and then she dropped the receiver as Vanessa and Germaine, who must have seen the danger, fought to be first out of the trap. The box shook with their struggles, and Bowring yelled at them to be orderly, as if his voice might reach them through the dangling receiver. Then Vanessa wrenched herself free, and the others followed, almost falling headlong, as the rubble smashed one side of the box, filling the interior with knives of glass.

Maybe that would give them something to think about, but all the same, it was vandalism. Shouldn't Bowring call the police? Some instinct prevented him, perhaps his sense of wanting to preserve a distance between himself and what he'd seen. After all, the girls might have seen the culprit too, might even have recognized him.

But on Tuesday they were pretending that nothing had happened. Debbie's blank face challenged him to accuse her, to admit he'd been watching.

Her whole stance challenged him, her long legs crossed, her linen skirt ending high on her bare thighs. How dare she sit like that in front of a man of his age! She'd come to grief acting like that, but not from him. The day's problems squealed on the blackboard, the chalk snapped.

He drove home, his face stiff with resentment. He wished he hadn't picked up the phone, wished he'd left them at the mercy of the madman who, for all Bowring knew, had gone mad as a result of their kind of misbehavior. As he swung the car onto the drive below his flat, a raw sunset throbbed in the gap where the tenement had been.

The sun went down. Lamps pricked the dark across the river. Tonight he wouldn't look, he told himself, but he couldn't put the other side out of his mind. He ate lamb chops to the strains of one of Rossini's pre-adolescent sonatas. Would there ever be prodigies like him again? Children now were nothing like they used to be. Bowring carried the radio to his chair beside the fire, and couldn't help glancing across the river. Someone was loitering in front of the gap where the tenement had been.

He sat down, stood up furiously, grabbed the binoculars. It was Debbie, waiting under the mercury lamp. She wore a pale blue skirt now, and stockings. Her lipstick glinted. She reminded Bowring of a streetwalker in some film, that image of a woman standing under a lamp surrounded by darkness.

No doubt she was waiting for Darren. Women waiting under lamps often came to no good, especially if they were up to none. Bowring probed the dark with his binoculars, until his flattened gaze came to rest on a fragment of the tenement, a zigzag of wall as high as a man. Had something pale just dodged behind it?

Debbie was still under the lamp, hugging herself against the cold, glancing nervously over her shoulder, but not at the fragment of wall. Bowring turned the lenses back to the wall, and came face to face with the clown, who seemed to be grinning straight at him from his hiding-place. The sight froze Bowring, who could only cling shakily to the binoculars and watch as the white face dodged back and forth, popping out from opposite edges of a wall. Perhaps only a few seconds passed, but it seemed long as a nightmare before the clown leapt on the girl.

Bowring saw her thrown flat on the scorched ground, saw the clown stuff her mouth with a wad of litter, the grinning white face pressing into hers. When the clown pinned her wrists with one hand and began to tear at her clothes with the other, Bowring grabbed the phone. He called the police station near the school and waited feverishly while the clown shied Debbie's clothes into the dark. "Rape. Taking place now, where the tenement was demolished," he gasped as soon as he heard a voice.

"Were are you calling from, sir?"

"That doesn't matter. You're wasting time. Unless you catch this person in the act you may not be able to identify him. He's made up like a clown."

"What is your name, please, sir?"

"What the devil has my name to do with it? Just go to the crime, can't you? There, you see," Bowring cried, his voice out of control, "you're too late."

Somehow Debbie had struggled free and was limping naked toward the nearest houses. Bowring saw her look back in terror, then flee painfully across the rubble. But the clown wasn't following, he was merely waving the baggy crotch of his trousers at her. "I need your name before we're able to respond," the voice said brusquely in Bowring's ear, and Bowring dropped the receiver in his haste to break the connection. When he looked across the river again, both Debbie and the clown had gone.

Eventually he saw police cars cruising back and forth past the ruined tenement, policemen tramping from house to house. Bowring had switched off his light in order to watch and for fear that the police might notice him, try to involve him, make an issue of his having refused to name himself.

He watched for hours as front door after front door opened to the police. He was growing more nervous, presumably in anticipation of the sight of the clown, prancing through a doorway or being dragged out by the police.

Rain came sweeping along the river, drenching the far bank. The last houses closed behind the police. A police car probed the area around the ruined tenement with its headlights, and then there was only rain and darkness and the few drowning streetlamps. Yet he felt as if he couldn't stop watching. His vision swam jerkily toward the charred gap, and the clown pranced out from behind the jagged wall.

How could the police have overlooked him? But there he was, capering beside the ruin. As Bowring leaned forward, clutching the binoculars, the clown reached behind the wall and produced an object which he brandished gleefully. He dropped it back into hiding just as Bowring saw that it was an axe. Then the clown minced into the lamplight.

For a moment, Bowring thought that the clown's face was injured— distorted, certainly—until he realized that the rain was washing the makeup off. Why should that make him even more nervous? He couldn't see the face now, for the clown was putting his fists to his eyes. He seemed to be peering through his improvised binoculars straight at Bowring—and then, with a shock that stiffened his face, Bowring was sure that he was. The next moment the clown turned his bare face up to the rain that streamed through the icy light.

Makeup began to whiten his lapels like droppings on a statue. The undisguised face gleamed in the rain. Bowring stared at the face that was appearing, then he muttered a denial to himself as he struggled to lower the binoculars, to let go his shivering grip on them, look away. Then the face across the river grinned straight at him, and his convulsion heaved him away from the window with a violence that meant to refute what he'd seen.

It couldn't be true. If it was, anything could be. He was hardly aware of lurching downstairs and into the sharp rain, binoculars thumping his chest. He fumbled his way into the car and sent it slewing toward the road, wipers scything at the rain. As trees crowded into the headlights, the piny smell made him swim.

The struts of the bridge whirred by, dripping. Dark streets, broken lamps, decrepit streaming houses closed round him. He drove faster through the desertion, though he felt as if he'd given in to a loss of control; surely there would be nothing to see—perhaps there never had been. But when the car skidded across the mud beside the demolished tenement, the clown was waiting bare-faced for him.

Bowring wrenched the car to a slithering halt and leapt out into the mud in front of the figure beneath the lamp. It was a mirror, he thought desperately: he was dreaming of a mirror. He felt the rain soak his clothes, slash his cheeks, trickle inside his collar. "What do you mean by this?" he yelled at the lamplit figure, and before he could think of what he was demanding, "Who do you think you are?"

The figure lifted its hands toward its face, still whitewashed by the mercury lamp, then spread its hands toward Bowring. That was more than Bowring could bear, both the silence of the miming and what the gesture meant to say. His mind emptied as he lurched past the lamplight to the fragment of tenement wall.

When the figure didn't move to stop him, he thought the axe wouldn't be there. But it was. He snatched it up and turned on the other, who stepped toward him, out of the lamplight. Bowring lifted the axe defensively. Then he saw that the figure was gesturing toward itself, miming an invitation. Bowring's control broke, and he swung the axe toward the unbearable sight of the grinning face.

At the last moment, the figure jerked its head aside. The axe cut deep into its neck. There was no blood, only a bulging of what looked like new pale flesh from the wound. The figure staggered, then mimed the axe toward itself again. None of this could be happening, Bowring told himself wildly; it was too outrageous, it meant that anything could happen, it was the beginning of total chaos. His incredulity let him hack with the axe, again and again, his binoculars bruising his ribs. He hardly felt the blows he was dealing, and when he'd finished there was still no blood, only an enormous sprawl of torn cloth and chopped pink flesh whitened by the lamplight, restless with rain. Somehow the head had survived his onslaught, which had grown desperately haphazard. As Bowring stared appalled at it, the grinning face looked straight at him, and winked. Screaming under his breath, Bowring hacked it in half, then went on chopping, chopping, chopping.

When at last exhaustion stopped him he made to fling the axe into the ruins. Then he clutched it and reeled back to his car, losing his balance in the mud, almost falling into the midst of his butchery. He drove back to the bridge, his eyes bulging at the liquid dark, at the roads overflowing their banks, the fleets of derelict houses sailing by. As he crossed the bridge, he flung the axe into the river.

He twisted the key and groped blindly into his house, felt his way upstairs, peeled off his soaked clothes, lowered himself shakily into a hot bath. He felt exhausted, empty, but was unable to sleep. He couldn't really have crossed the river, he told himself over and over; he couldn't have done what he remembered doing, the memory that filled his mind, brighter than the streetlamp by the ruin.

He stumbled naked to the window. Something pale lay beside the street-lamp, but he couldn't make it out; the rain had washed the lenses clean of the coating that would have let him see more in the dark. He sat there shivering until dawn, nodding occasionally, jerking awake with a cry. When the sunlight reached the other side, the binoculars showed him that the ground beside the lamp was bare.

He dragged on crumpled clothes, tried to eat breakfast but spat out the mouthful, fled to his car. He never set out so early, but today he wanted to be in his classroom as soon as he could, where he still had control. Rainbows winked at him from trees as he drove, and then the houses gaped at him. As yet the streets were almost deserted, and so he couldn't resist driving by the tenement before making for the school. He parked at the top of the slope, craned his neck as he stood shivering on the pavement, and then, more and more shakily and reluctantly, he picked his way down the slope. He'd seen movement in the ruin.

They must be young animals, he told himself as he slithered down. Rats, perhaps, or something else newborn—nothing else could be so pink or move so oddly. He slid down to the low jagged gappy well. As he caught hold of the topmost bricks, which shifted under his hands, all the pink shapes amid the rubble raised their faces, his face, to him.

Some of the lumps of flesh had recognizeable limbs, or at least portions of them. Some had none, no features at all except one or more of the grimacing faces, but all of them came swarming toward him as best they could. Bowring reeled, choked, flailed his hands, tried to grab at reality, wherever it was. He fell across the wall, twisting, face up. At once a hand with his face sprouting from its wrist scuttled up his body and closed its fingers, his fingers, about his throat.

Bowring cowered into himself, desperate to hide from the sensation of misshapen crawling all over his body, his faces swarming over him, onto his limbs, between his legs. There was no refuge. A convulsion shuddered through him, jerked his head up wildly. "My face," he shrieked in a choked whisper, and sank his teeth into the wrist of the hand that was choking him.

It had no bones to speak of. Apart from its bloodlessness, it tasted like raw meat. He shoved it into his mouth, stuffed the fingers in and then the head. As it went in it seemed to shrink, grow shapeless, though he felt his teeth close on its eyes. "*My* face," he spluttered, and reached for handfuls of the rest. But while he'd been occupied with chewing, the swarming had left his body. He was lying alone on the charred rubble.

They were still out there somewhere, he knew. He had to get them back inside himself, he mustn't leave them at large on this side of the river. This side was nothing to do with him. He swayed to his feet and saw the school. A grin stiffened his mouth. Of course, that was where they must be, under the faces of his pupils, but not for long. The children couldn't really be as unlike him as they seemed; nothing could be that alien—that was how they'd almost fooled him. He made his way toward the school, grinning, and as he thought of pulling off those masks to find his face, he began to dance.

# DAVID J. SCHOW

## Pamela's Get

David J. Schow was the winner of the 1987 World Fantasy Award for his short story "Red Light." His most recent projects include his first novel, *The Kill Riff*, published by Tor in May: *Silver Scream*, an anthology of cinema horror stories which he edited and was published by Dark Harvest in March; and a collection of his short fiction (due in late 1988), called *Seeing Red*, including "Coming to a Theater Near You," winner of the *Twilight Zone Magazine* Dimension Award for best short story of 1985. He is also the author of the non-fiction book *The Outer Limits: The Official Companion* (Ace, 1986).

"Pamela's Get," originally published in *Twilight Zone Magazine*, is a story of contemporary society and the perils of close relationships. Its horror lies in the inexplicable workings of the life and death of friendship.

—E.D.

# PAMELA'S GET

## David J. Schow

"This is a scam, young lady. Or some sort of unpolished joke I lack the crust to understand."

That *young lady* had been aimed and fired like a bullet: *Me Caesar—you bimbo*. Jaime's lip tried to curl, but when powwowing with Pavel Drake it was always a more prudent strategy to maintain a corporate attitude, an unfeeling stonewall posture. Beneath the black slate circle of the cocktail table her fist locked tight, an evil flower, slowly feeding. She was going to have to tread very cautiously to get what she wanted from this man—this cruel and condescending being whom she had kept distant from any part of her life he might corrupt. Until tonight. Now she had a painful lot to do, and maybe not much time left to do it in.

That Obscure Object of Desire was a membership-only Beverly Hills venue waitressed by foldout-class women two steps down from the game show and soap opera stratum of failure. Some still managed a local television commercial or two; all were leftovers, staling, what a Hollywood Hopeful looks like on the wane. The cheap thrill was to witness these budding stars as they shanghaied themselves into topless duty after hawking carpets and spas on the tube, still desperately pretty, willing to risk nearly anything for one more shot at popcorn fame. Every customer was therefore a potential backer for a career breakthrough, so each got a generous smile . . . and the only thing tainting the biological purity of such mutual parasitism was the bitterness calcifying each smile. Those smiles told you stories of how hope could sabotage lives.

Industry people—that is, movie, TV, and music video rollers, high and low—pointedly shunned the Object; some kinds of failures might prove disastrously communicable. The mainstay clientele consisted of businessmen who could appreciate such failure, in the way a conqueror might savor the captured vintages of a newly ransacked village. The Object offered the opportunity to taste the blood of one killed right beside you, and enjoy that taste because it meant you were still alive. Fat billfolds were entreated and a Hellfire Club mentality encouraged.

It was not a place a man would invite a woman for whom he held the

147

slightest degree of good regard. It was a useful arena for tacit humiliation, or the nastier subtleties of revenge.

Jaime watched Pamela Drake's father reread the single typed page she had given him. "Maybe you should order a drink," he said, releasing a huge sigh, his eyes still relentlessly scanning. Seeking faults, footholds for assault.

A thinly misted glass of ice water stood untouched before her on its cocktail napkin. Drake's purely professional scotch and soda was half dead. At his beckoning a splay-breasted cooch hostess jiggled over to swap empties for fulls. Jaime did not want anything from the Object getting inside of her, but her throat was arid and she knew the way Drake's brain worked. A libation might signal some rough truce. Just this once. That was all she needed.

"White wine," she said. "Dry." Stay generic. One glass. Give a little that you might gain everything. If she had been out boozing with Pamela, outrageous new drinks in funny colors would have been the ground rule.

Fifty-six, without a thread of gray, was Pavel Drake of Drake Polyvinyl Products Inc. *He dyes his hair*, she thought, suddenly shocked. Any vanity implied a crumb of human feeling somewhere in the convolutions of this man's mean, small mind. In this place of hopelessness, where women were literally Objectified, it was a spark of hope.

Jaime needed hope. Because if the man sitting across from her did not affix his signature to that piece of paper, she was going to die.

Tears had rinsed the mascara down Jaime's face hours before. There was no denying that the person in the box had been her best friend—the kind you are permitted one per lifetime, with luck; the kind you win if the timing is just so and the clockwork of the universe smiles on you in its random way. Jaime had watched the box slide into the ground at half past ten in the morning, signing off the eight years of that friendship, leaving her to hold nothing but death and thoughts of death.

She refused to believe the way she had just *stood* there, dumbly, Wayfarer shades hiding the ravaged state of her eyes, her black stiletto heels sinking slowly into the cemetery turf as Pamela was subjected to ritual and clumsy eulogizing. She had died intestate so there had been no cremation; whatever she had insisted upon in private did not count here. Case closed. The box's showroom finish was kissed by grave dirt and the strangers in attendance (relatives lacking better diversions this weekend) would soon depart to make merry on Pavel Drake's tab, their pocket obligation dispatched. If there was a casting house where one rented extras for funerals—natty folks with gerbil eyes and tight, insurance broker smiles—then Drake had scribbled them a hefty check. It was all very businesslike. Jaime's eyes kept looking for the camera crews.

Thank God for Jason.

He ignored the cattle and stepped across the line to wrap Jaime up in a genuine hug. She linked arms with him and hung on. They were the only two attendees on the far side of the grave, away from the tent and folding chairs.

People expect their parents to die some dim date in the future. No one is surprised when Grandpa stops drooling long enough to bite the big one. Jaime knew she herself would experience what the medics called an "event" if she drank or tooted or drove too fast, or kept getting horizontal with those faceless and monied Brentwood body-builders. They had great asses, charm and cash to burn, and hard chromium eyes that flattened and rejected her once the contour of flesh beneath clothing was no longer sufficient mystery to hold them. When you saw yourself crying in the mirrors, when your own eyes reflected back the pain inside, then you expected bad news if only subconsciously. But buddies just did not keel over from unannounced pulmonary embolisms, not after a 20/20 checkup. Especially not buddies like Pamela, who seemed put on the earth to babysit you through one crisis after another. They were not supposed to die at twenty-eight, sitting on a sofa, eyes open, holding cold coffee in a mug that read MY OTHER COFFEE CUP IS A MERCEDES. No.

The tears just would not stanch, and Jaime hated her own loss of control. There could never be enough tears for Pamela. Mickey was nowhere in sight; he hadn't bothered to show up. This angered Jaime, and she saw that Jason was flat pissed. His eyes glinted as they scanned the group and came back to her, minus Mickey. Then they settled into a dull expression of hurt and loss.

Jaime knew then just what had been lost, to all of them.

She could call up a picture-postcard-perfect image of the foursome right now: Pamela, cross-legged on a leather hassock in her living room, sipping white Bordeaux and waving her hands. Jason would be on the floor, unconsciously assuming a Sears Catalogue model pose so perfect it was funny. He'd refill glasses and sit with one forearm hooked around Pamela's thigh in a comfy way that looked possessive yet not restrictive. He hated being what he called the "whore of fashion," and so was shaggier than GQ might dictate. He was sexier than an incubus anyway. While Pamela animatedly held forth, he'd roll his eyes in that here-we-go-again expression that made him look like a befuddled cocker spaniel.

And then came Mickey, less polished, not as brash, but still a contender. His position would be directly across from Pamela's, and he would lean into her commentary as though inviting charades. Unerringly, he would call from the air the very words her gesticulations begged, causing her to take a big gulp of wine and nod yes, *yes!*

Last, watching all, submerged in the cushions of Pamela's thronelike Prince recliner, eyes bemused and just visible above the silvery rim of the wine goblet, would be her. Jaime. Thinking.

A perverse, I-told-you-so feeling welled up within her. More than once, she had dutifully dunned Pamela about neatening her affairs on paper. Both had acknowledged that day in the misty future when one would precede the other into death, leaving one to clean up and carry on. Neither of them had counted on their coffee conversation lopping over into nerve-numbing reality so bloody soon.

Now it was just one more thing to prompt the tears.

"I want to be cremated when I buy it," Pamela had said. "I hate the idea of people standing around, sniffling, going *oh woe!* while I do nothing but suck formaldehyde, you know what I mean? Yuck." Her eyes, deep green, lambent as the glass of a champagne bottle, scanned Jaime's neat rooms. Her lips busied themselves, worrying, as she contemplated just what she *did* want at her funeral, instead.

Pamela was a slender woman, given to jeans and Reeboks and the first tee or sweat off a chairback or doorknob that could pass the Pamela Drake patented Nasal Cleanliness Test. She'd settled down on the floor, nursing one of Jaime's new Napas mugs, heavy porcelain and full of hot cinnamon coffee. Her fingertips, nails bitten rigorously to the quick, traced patterns in the burgundy carpeting.

Jaime had gone to the bedroom to shuck her working duds. Pamela raised her voice. "Don't you ever get the feeling those uniforms are gonna smother you?" She rose and wandered into the hallway. The bedroom door was demurely half-shut.

"Nope," came Jaime's voice from beyond. "Did it ever occur to you that if you had been born ten years earlier, you would have been sucked into the hippie mythos and would now be a screaming, headband-wearing anachronism?"

"Ho, ho, ho."

"I'm serious, girl. Put together *1984* and designer denim and you get uniforms that would do Orwell proud."

Pamela booted the door open, grinning like a gremlin. Jaime, naked to the waist, yelped and jumped for cover, then gave it up as hopeless.

"Hey, whoa, it's only me!" Pamela's hands were up. "I come to learn, not to grope. I want to glimpse corporate American with its uniform off."

"Do you *mind*?" Pamela was always jumping frantically ahead, and Jaime resented straining to keep pace. When the decorum had been passed out, Jaime had gotten both her and Pamela's shares.

Pamela blew out breath in a huff. "Geez, okay, already!" She lifted her arms and stripped off her Ducks Deluxe t-shirt, tossing it the floor and seizing Jaime's bare arm to drag her to the dressing mirror. She posed them side-by-side, adopting an exaggerated buddy stance with one hip cocked. "There. Check this out. The gene pool doesn't have a prayer."

Jaime covered her eyes and laughed, helpless now.

She admired the casual street-poet disdain with which Pamela wore clothes, or discarded them. She liked Pamela's body as well. It was lower-slung, larger breasted, not padded. She had scrappy, healthy honey-blond hair in contrast to Jaime's overstyled brunette, which got trimmed shorter every year in an endless process of distillation. Where Pamela had none, Jaime had fingernails—sculpted, medium-length, glossy, perfect. Pamela had wide tiger-paw feet that Jaime at first thought were snubbed and odd-looking, then came to love for their musculature and power. Pamela squinted, going on tiptoe to hold her right breast level with Jaime's left. "I think your tits are more proportionate than mine," she said with an absolutely straight face. "I'm gonna be in trouble when I turn fifty."

The contact was unexpectedly electric; a thrill zipped through Jaime's skin and her nipple condensed to a nub.

She had never wanted to have sex with Pamela. *Call me Victorian.* Many times she had wanted to hold Pamela while she slept, to warm her when the emotionally calloused men she attracted called "time" and began sniffing elsewhere. But she was pretty sure this did not mean she wanted to jump Pamela's bones.

Well. Maybe once.

Women had invented the thing the magazines now called "male bonding," she thought. Her love and friendship with Pamela expressed itself in a million tiny gestures and touches—tactile reassurance for the constitutionally handicapped. A superstitious shielding against urban hostilities, built like a flawless pearl, layer upon layer accumulating day by day. Pamela was her Hyde half, different, damned near opposite, but essential. At times she could be infuriating. Jaime had recorded so much about her—things that were annoying, even insignificant, but which resonated later and now made her want to weep to mourn their permanent loss. The queer tic Pamela developed, for example, when something pierced her armor and punctured her feelings—a rapidfire batting of one eyelid plus a startled, quick sniffing noise, as though she was recoiling from an actual blow. Her maddening use of non-words. *Excape. Idear. Irregardlessly.* Her approach to laundry, which up until recently had been to dump in half a box of detergent and set the machine on HOT.

HOT could deal with anything. Other traits were less quaint.

"You didn't ask me how my folio went down at Penn Publishing," Pamela would say. "I took it in two days ago."

"Oh. I was wondering about that," Jaime would begin, dreading what came next. "How'd it go?"

"You're so tied up in what *you're* doing, you don't care."

"Don't give me that, of course I care," Jaime was confrontational, and often not as gentle as she might be in such engagements. She had to stay in character. "So how'd—"

"You're just asking me *now* because I brought it up!" Pamela would get petulant and stick out her lip (*See, you* don't *really care*).

"No. Seriously. How'd it go (*Goddamnit!*)?"

"I don't want to talk about it." Which meant, of course, *I win*. And just when Jaime would be ready to scream and tear hair, Pamela would humanize. "I guess I'm really a bitch, huh?"

(*Go on, tell me I'm a bitch, that's what you want.*)

Ready to shriek . . .

At times like that, Jaime hated her best friend, knowing all along she still loved her twice as strongly. It was a problem now and then, as it is any time you get to know another human being intimately. But she did need Pamela to know she would always be there for her . . . even if Pamela pissed her off beyond rational endurance.

The carpeting, the Napas mugs, the wardrobe were all courtesy of Jaime's rise in retail from assistant buyer to buyer for Sanger Harris. Now, instead of lording over the paperwork for Glassware, Linens, and Bath Shoppe, she got to make the purchasing trips to New York and points past. Such work necessitated a wardrobe that Pamela would have considered an insurmountable feat of program planning, and a methodical approach to documents totally at odds with her pile-file habit.

"1984 has come and gone," Pamela said, jumping ahead to pour Jaime coffee while her friend made a pit stop in the bathroom. "In 1980, I figured we'd all be dead by then anyhow. Now I guess it's 1990."

Jaime emerged in slacks and an oversized, shapeless epaulette shirt from Banana Republic. On anyone else it would have been all wrinkles. "You'd better *not* just die on me! Without telling me, warning me first."

"I won't. I promise. But did you hear what I said about cremation? What do you think?"

"I want to sell my body to science—if I don't die old and decrepit, that is. Let 'em recycle me. Why trash corneas like these? I mean have you ever *seen* corneas this classy?"

Pamela giggled. "Not a bad idea." She pondered it, but only for an instant. Then she was off and running toward whatever came next. She never wasted too much time on a single topic; it was another lineament of her character that her anal-retentive corporate daddy hated most. Finally, she said, "Have you got a will, Jaime?"

Her response was too offhand. "Sure." She had never mentioned it to anyone. More forgotten paper.

Pamela seemed to go far away fast. "I didn't know."

"Hey . . . I left everything to you, kiddo." It was the only reponse Jaime could think of to lighten the tone.

Pamela's voice remained tiny. "Oh. Good."

That, for Jaime, summed up Pamela's lifelong hate affair with documents.

It had been inspired, doubtless, by her father's obsession with same. No insurance. No will. No messages. Nothing.

Nobody dies this young.

When Jason caught Pavel Drake staring at them over the flower-bedecked casket, he put a protective arm around Jaime. His nearness was comforting, even if the day was too muggy, and her glove-tight formal getup too close.

"He's probably checking out my legs," she said.

"It's sweltering out here," Jason said, breaking eye contact with the far side of the fresh grave. "But I'll be goddamned if I'm going to stand around with those mouth breathers under her dad's little circus tent."

"I was thinking the same thing. Have I ever told you what dear Daddy did at Pamela's birthday party?"

"You'll have to . . . some other time." They leaned into each other. It would be so easy to simply split the funeral and go home with Jason. If they no longer had Pamela . . . well, who did they have?

It was Maurois, as Jaime recollected, who wrote, "In literature, as in love, we are astonished at what is chosen by others." Approval of your best friend's lovemates (or books) was nice, but usually inappropriate if not embarrassing. In the case of Jason Parrish, the test was irrelevant. He was the sort of guy whose food looked better than yours because *he* had ordered it.

Pamela and Jason had met in Chicago at a horror film titled *Piece by Piece.* Charming. The screening had been downtown at Facett's Multimedia, and Jason had come to review it for the *Trib.* They were the only two who lasted through to the end credits. They wound up warming a booth at some sleepy suburban coffee shop while predawn snow drifted down to bury the city.

Career-wise, Pamela had lit off on another of her flank attacks, and half a year had passed. Jaime knew she would soon be magnetized back to her home ground. The care packages and correspondence were voluminous enough to fill a Knudsen dairy crate. When Pamela returned, live and in person, Jaime had filed the crateful of memories in the rear of her clothes closet.

Near the end of the Chicago phase had come one postcard Jaime never forgot. In it, Pamela had specified the qualities she preferred in her closest friends, and its implication was that the arrival of Jason on the scene had completed her personal equation for happiness. During one of their thousands of long-distance calls (the bills for which overrode the gross national product of Paraguay), Jaime had gotten the lowdown on Jason in salacious detail.

Pamela had gone on at length about how considerate he was in the sack, and Jaime thought ruefully of little acorns and mighty oaks.

Jason got fired from the *Tribune,* but he had savings, and Pamela gladly filled the gaps. Then the film magazine she was designing collapsed, and she flew back to Jaime. Two months later, her connections in graphics yielded up a post at the *Herald Examiner*, and Jason was booked west on United.

Jaime's attraction to Jason was crude, at first, and entirely the fault of Pamela's giddy enthusiasm. She had seeded in Jaime the sort of interest that could not really be helped. Or stopped. It had taken a few months, but the inevitable finally happened.

Jaime felt the sparks jump across her nerve endings.

Pamela had gotten roped into an all-night session of paste-up, purely a la carte, at good pay. Jason had been loafing around her apartment; it was his day off. And Jaime had dropped by with a bottle of gray Reisling. No excuse was needed.

It was not merely the unspoken commonality between them. In the end, Jaime had moved first, casually touching him when their automatic dialogue ran thin. Their embrace quickly waxed to critical mass. They were blameless. They finished folded together on Pamela's fake Persian rug, naked, purring, and spent.

To Jaime's certain knowledge, Pamela had never guessed. Today, only the vibrations of unease lingered. She found it difficult, even with him right beside her, to recall the specifics of how they furiously plundered each other in a pile of still-warm clothing, except that she had passed into light unconsciousness following her third orgasm. Pamela had been right about his magic tongue.

"I'm sorry," she said to the casket. "I wish you were here so I could tell you I'm sorry, so you could get mad, so we could make up. It only happened that once. I guess I messed up. But you promised you wouldn't die on me. Does this make us even?"

It was too damned easy to forget how much you could love someone, until they died and it became impossible.

The unconcerned mourners filed away and Pavel Drake beckoned the cemetery attendant, who released the catches on the aluminum rack supporting the casket. Canvas straps slowly unreeled, clicking metronomically, and the box containing Pamela settled into the dark hole.

It was almost as if Jason's infidelity was unthinkable to Pamela. Or just not relevant. With Mickey, she'd tried to matchmake.

"You want to fuck Mickey, doncha?" Pamela had opined at lunch one day. It was during the hiatus before Jason had come to Los Angeles and he and Pamela had spent a whole weekend in bed before emerging into the daylight to say hello. She could get spiteful or sharp when she wasn't getting laid regularly.

"Say what?" Jaime returned with a pained expression.

"Oh, Mickey's attracted, you bet. I saw him gobbling you up with his eyeballs."

"Jump his bones, maybe, but sleep with him, never. I'd get athlete's sheet." They both laughed. Tension defused.

Mickey was the one who never forgot Pamela. He picked the most appropriate oddball Christmas gifts for her, and beat everyone to the punch-line by phoning her at midnight sharp on each of her birthdays. Mickey Banks and Pamela were a pair that quickly discovered they were better friends than lovers. The thing that endeared Mickey was his knack for bestowing just the right words to vocalize feelings, on those rare days Pamela found herself inarticulate over some transient grief. He never overlooked dates important to her. He was constitutionally incapable of it. Maybe that was why he had ducked the burial. There was no more Pamela to remember . . . except for the one inside their heads.

Mickey had saved Jaime from Pavel Drake at Pamela's twenty-fifth birthday party.

After four flutes of Perrier Jouet, Pamela had begun to pout and sink into her "quarter of a century" bad-rap. Her smile had turned tipsy, brittle, and forced. The whole awkward bash had come at the insistence of Pamela's father, who Jaime had heard was a big plastics baron. She had retreated to the wet bar to grab a sparkling mineral water, and somewhere behind her Jason proposed a jokey toast to lighten the mood. Ah, the things we suffer for our friends . . .

"We've achieved eye contact several times, dear, but I don't believe we've been formally inflicted on each other." Jaime turned around and shook a hand. "Pavel Drake. I'm Pamela's father. The one who's getting stuck with the bill for this rodeo."

They traded chat; Jaime thought of empty calories. She had only heard penny dreadfuls about Pamela's father, from Pamela. By the time she got a peek at his engraved business card and had mentioned her own job in retail, she saw the wattage in his eyes bump up and realized that the brown stuff eroding the ice in his glass was not tea.

He nodded too much as he talked, working his lips probably because they were getting numb. "Good advancement in retail," he said. "Upward mobility. I admire that. It's always been Pamela's big problem—no ambition. She daydreams, you see. Twenty-five and nowhere, and she wonders why she's not happy, and with her great imagination she can't figure out why." He sniffed imperiously and glanced at Jaime's bosom before meeting her eyes again. "Oh, my daughter has a terrific imagination, Miss Ralston. But it's unproductive; she can't turn a penny profit with it. Twenty-five now. And I'm beginning to fear she's never going to amount to anything."

Already Jaime's body was begging to flee, but for Pamela's sake she made a game try: "I wouldn't say that, Mr. Drake. She's knocking out a nice little berth for herself with the graphics and designs and layouts. She's

the point where he had not even noticed Jaime talking to herself—to Pamela—graveside. "I have to go home," he said after a deep breath. "I have something to do."

It's hitting him, she thought. He was going to burst into tears if she didn't stop hanging onto him, if she did not leave him alone right now. And the more she thought about Mickey's truancy, the madder she got. She could do this by herself. "Well . . . fine. We'll link up later, yes?"

"Yeah. We'll all get together later."

He escorted her to her car and kissed her. It was like cold, damp fog on her lips. Like nothing.

Terrific—some moron was trying to pummel the front door right out of its rickety frame.

Mick's brain thumped right along. A caber had crash-landed on his skull. He shot to wakefulness muggy with sweat, his throat arid, his mouth clogged with a thick, dog-turd tang that had reached up and nailed his sinuses shut. He had come up from sleep too fast; his eyes had the bends. This was definitely the most cacklingly awful biorhythmic phase of his entire life. He *arrghed* to the corners of his studio apartment. The mambo beat between his head and the door just kept right on rocking.

The doorknob began rattling. Foot-shadows interrupted the clean crack of daylight separating the bottom of the door from its threshold.

"Coming!" he croaked, at his faceless tormentor. He rubbed his face and his palm came away glistening with perspiration and oil. Falling asleep fully dressed had made him look like his own unmade bed. His hair was . . . awful. His stereo stylus, long since finished with side one of *Goodbye Yellow Brick Road*, skritched out a soft cadence. Mick had once bragged—to somebody or other—about his totally manual, belt-driven, smooth-as-lucite turntable with its twelve-pound professional deejay platter. Now a forty-dollar needle was grinding itself to diamond dust because he had passed out, and not even in the middle of a decent album. Whatever had inspired him to unsleeve the Elton John oldie was forgotten now, irrelevant.

Pound, thump, pound, skritch-skritch. It was not a sterling afternoon.

He yawned cavernously, smoothed back his hair and struggled to look intelligent as he unbolted and opened up.

"*Christ*, Mickey, I've been beating on this goddamned thing for five minutes! Why aren't you answering your phone?"

The adrenaline jolt helped wake him up. The woman on his stoop was simply lovely. His brain raced to catalogue her assets, and did not resist the list as it rolled up. Though cogent, he was still woozy and fantasy-inclined.

The gray suit-dress was strictly conservative chic. Short, peppy dark brown hair. Large-lensed glasses in spidery frames, more young exec stuff.

The eyes, the color of amber and brandied chocolate. She was sinfully tall, cut with confidence and regal bearing. Strong chin, small mouth, laugh lines. His eyes gave her the once-over. Twice.

"What the hell is *wrong* with you? Do I have a tarantula on my head?" She rolled her eyes and began to push past him. "Let me in—it's broiling out here."

. . . a charming stranger indeed, Mick's romanticist brain concluded. But his body instinctively shifted to block intrusion into his home by a stranger, charming or less, and when they collided she dropped her shoulder bag.

"I'm sorry?" he said, bending to retrieve. They nearly bonked heads. "I mean, I beg your pardon? You're not a Jehovah's Witness or something . . . I hope?"

She yanked the bag free of him without thanks, and gaped as though he had just asked her to suck his toes.

He shrugged. "So what is it? Census bureau? Meter reader? Avon Lady? What can I do for you, um . . .?" His eyebrows went up, urging her to reveal her identity. It was a good place to begin.

She stopped dead for only an instant, then shook her head with the fatefulness of a woman who must endure a thick-headed little brother. "You picked a hell of a day to screw around with stupid jokes, love. It hasn't even been six hours. You going to tell me you forgot to set your alarm?" Her anger was growing. Past the frank glare in her eyes, Mick could see the redness of some recent hurt.

He coughed out a commiserative laugh which she did not share. "Uh . . . what are you talking about, Miss?"

"*Mickey!* What's the secret word, today? Too much blow on our Fruit Loops this morning? Why are you being such an asshole?"

She tried to enter; he rebuffed her again.

"I'd really rather not let anyone in," he said. "My place is kind of a mess."

She looked upset, disoriented. "Your place is always a hog wallow, Mickey . . ."

That was another thing, Mick thought, his pique kicking up from preheat to simmer. Where did this (admittedly gorgeous) nonentity get off calling him that? *Mick* was clipped, sharp, rock and roll, he liked it. *Mickey* preceded *mouse*, and he could live without either.

He overrode her, firming up. "Lady. I do *not* know what you're talking about. Honest. I do *not* know who you are. And I don't know if I'm as eager to talk to you as I was fifteen seconds ago."

He saw the change wash over her expression, and its speed caught him unprepared. He could sense the gooseflesh scaring up on her back, the snap chill of a suppressed shudder, so out of place in the midday heat. Her mouth unhinged, drifting open. She seemed to dwindle horribly, like a person trying to shrink against an unyielding wall.

"Oh . . . no," she whispered. Not to him.

He fought to lighten up, be boyish on short notice, to bring her back to where she had been seconds before, because her irritation was better to experience than her abrupt fear. He could hate himself later. "Hey, no, I—"

At the sound of his voice she began to edge back along the narrow breezeway, as though she could see him transmogrifying into a drooling werewolf.

He shook his head and got pain. The woman on his stoop was crazy; next case. His concern was easily overwhelmed by the idea that this was more than a joke . . . it was an assault entrapment, or apartment filmflam, or other setup. Los Angeles was packed to the spires with predators that could look like this woman.

"Fine," he said, shutting the door. The bolt sprang to automatically.

He heard a muffled *no*, almost a cry of pain, and the futile thump of a small fist against the door. He ignored it, making for the bathroom and many aspirins. He was in no mood; he just wanted to lie down and go away for a while. His bones and muscles ached, empty of vitality. He felt like a train wreck.

After a while the woman, whoever she was, however she had gotten his name, gave up and went away for good.

Jaime tried to swallow hot tears and her throat knotted shut. Strangers gawked at her wet face from their own cars.

It was Mickey, Mickey Banks, he of the corduroy jacket and cowboy boots and athlete's sheet, who had just slammed his door in her face. His rejection, his wariness, his utter nonrecognition of her was frightening. It made her stomach cramp helplessly. His eyes held the same lost expression as Jason's had, at Pamela's gravesite. Jaime's hand tried to quiver; she gripped the wheel tighter.

Jason's machine had answered five times when Jaime ran out of payphone change. When she pulled up at his address, she saw exactly what she would see again on that evening's metro news.

The manner in which Jason Parrish had killed himself after Pamela Drake's funeral was reeled off in a hydrophobic torrent of babble by a TV newshound broadcasting from inside a fluttering yellow LAPD cordon. Jaime watched the slow zoom up to the wide open main door, and the equally predictable closeup of a body-bagged shape on a stretcher en route to the ambulance. It lolled.

Tomorrow, the *Herald Examiner* would bid adieu to one of its own, with an even bigger wallow in the grisly Known Facts.

Jason Arthur Parrish, 31, was found dangling from his dining room archway, his neck pulled long, face a deep indigo from cyanosis, eyes bloated and dry. His tongue had swollen to the size of a black hockey puck. The nylon cord that had strangled him had stretched as his corpse sagged, but the give did not matter. His feet still cleared the floor by ten inches.

There was a note, displayed prominently on an antique writing desk Pamela had helped him pick out at Poor Ruth's. The nylon cord had come from a camping trip to the Sierra Nevada range that life in retail had prevented Jaime from joining.

Mercifully, the only photo to be included in the paper would be a staff glossy three years old. The note would not be reproduced. Jaime already knew it was about nothing but Pamela.

Jason was gone. Mickey was gone. While Jaime had endured a nasal recitation of the Twenty-third Psalm by a hired minister with a game leg, Pavel Drake's hired movers had lain siege to Pamela's apartment. They received time-and-a-half for Sunday work, plus a fat tip for speed. By the time Pamela had filled the boxlike hole she would never leave, another box—a U-Haul storage locker much like a tomb itself—had been efficiently loaded with her possessions. The slickness of the arrangement would have offended Pamela, who would resent being so easily erased.

There was only one piece of Pamela left, and Jaime fled to it.

The anarchic untidiness of Jaime's clothes closet was a source of queer pride. With her promotion had come total whirlpool chaos in this one niche of her otherwise ordered living space; here was a guilty pleasure she could hold in common with Pamela. In the back of the closet (perhaps sucked back there as food by the forgotten and now-sentient blobs of polyester waiting in the darkness) was the Knudsen crate. In it were the letters, the snapshots, the physical residue of Pamela's passage through her life. It was more than enough to get drunk on.

The crate was the only piece of Pamela that Pavel Drake had not absorbed. There had to be a reason Jaime was permitted this one piece, and she found it, forgotten, buried in the back of the crate. Jaime thought of a Chinese box puzzle.

It was a fireproof Smythe document box, a steel rectangle in outdated industrial maroon, with a lock. Pamela had provided no key. Dimly, Jaime remembered being handed the box and being asked in a casual way to stash it.

Pamela's irresponsibility with minutiae was legendary. Jaime maintained a rolodex; Pamela had been known to write phone numbers in ink on the back of her hand. She only threw out the receipts she would later need. Jaime balanced her checkbook; Pamela's utilities usually avoided termination by scant hours. Clearly, more complex items like insurance—or wills, say—were scheduled for the turn of the century, because twenty-eight-year-olds should not have to worry about dying until later.

The incidents with Mickey, with Jason, had flooded Jaime with a sense of lost control, urgently accelerating. If her best friend Pamela had anything to say to her after death, now was the time to hear it.

Breaking the Smythe box's lock with the blade of a butcher knife was distasteful, akin to violation. A rape. Jaime wondered whether Pavel Drake's movers had broken into Jaime's apartment, similarly, to plunder.

The lid squeaked when she bent it back. Even if she had recalled the box earlier, she never would have considered peeking. Pamela had banked successfully on her trust. Jaime felt a pang of resentment at being so predictable.

Boxes within boxes. Suddenly this did not look so random, so unplanned, so Pamela.

The tear tracks were dry on her face. She lifted out long pages, legal-sized, stapled to sky-blue stock backings, folded into oblongs and tucked into a vinyl folder. Her heart thudded and her breath pulled short. From Pamela of all people, could this be something for the record in black on white?

A handwritten note had been placed on top, but had fallen to one side and gotten creased thanks to the box's rough ride. Jaime immediately recognized the distinctive paraph of her best friend's script:

Dear Jaime,
    Please trust me when I say what your going to see here is real. I'm sorry you have to find out this way, but if your reading this than I'm probabbly dead. You know how I work, your my best friend. So maybe youll understand without bad explanations. Your the puzzle solver. I love you.

                                                                          Pamela

It was Pamela, sure as hell. The horrific spelling and grammar were ironclad verification. New tears made a bid for escape but Jaime swallowed them down. The note had been rendered with a soft-tipped art pen, in purple, Pamela's favorite color. She favored such pens for all kinds of jotting, and had thrown a fit when the manufacturer terminated them a couple of years back. The violet ink had already begun to fade.

You could not buy these pens anymore at any price. Like Pamela, they were part of the past now.

Jaime unsnapped the folder and counted three separate documents, each headed with the legend AGREEMENT in Gothic. The text nosedove straight away into legalese so dense that Jaime's eyes rejected such unpalatably large glops. These were contracts. Her recognition of them scared her a bit—it was like Pamela sneaking into the paperwork she hustled daily at Sanger Harris.

The top one was drawn between PAMELA LYNN DRAKE and JAIME ANYA

RALSTON. On the last page she saw Pamela's signature, again in florid purple ink.

In the adjacent blank, written with the same pen, Jaime found her own signature.

The contracts seemed to jump from her lap, to fan themselves across the floor. Her throat dried up and began to pulse achingly. She had never seen these papers before.

Nervously, she gathered them, checking the other two, fearing what she would see.

The second bore the name JASON ARTHUR PARRISH. Jason had been at the funeral, holding Jaime because there was no longer a Pamela to hold. The third contract was in the name of MICHAEL MARQUIS BANKS.

Known to his intimates as Mickey.

Her eyes hurt from scrutinizing the contracts. She squeezed them shut; tried to force more tears to come . . . and got nothing.

She sat rereading Pamela's postcard, the specific one from Chicago she had remembered earlier. It had waited for her in the crate. Her eyes drifted over it dryly. Here was Pamela's description of their cozy little foursome in the days before madness and funerals.

From the bedamned contracts to the postcard and back again she went . . . and her heart began to thud hard and fast. The love had been drained out, but there was still enough muscle remaining to give her whole body a sound jump at a sudden shock of inspiration.

The trendy pressure to have babies before thirty-five was nothing compared to the deadline with which she was now squared off. She raced back to her closet. An old Smith-Corona manual typewriter had been lost in there for at least as long as the Knudsen crate, and now she needed it as badly as air to breathe.

When she found it, she phoned Pavel Drake.

The silence on the line was adjudicatory, punctuated by the measured respiration of a self-important man, weighing trifles. Drake had delivered a terse reminder that any imposition less than twenty-four hours after his only child's funeral deserved nothing from him past an angry hang-up. Jaime had known he would not disconnect for two reasons.

Once she had rejected him. By making contact now she was offering him another shot, an opportunity to salve his bruised ego. He was the type of mercenary business mind who would never forget any slight, no matter how trivial. Now he might make her crawl, or wait, or beg his help. Now he might do something so small as make her run the telephonic gauntlet to be granted the privilege of speaking with him.

More importantly, she mentioned the Smythe box—the single item that had eluded the neat dragnet of Pamela's life arranged by Drake's legal chickenhawks.

Beats of silence on the telephone can be exquisitely cruel. Drake wanted this acid quiet to slowly tear Jaime's heart out. He could not know that an hour ago she had run out of tears, and now her heart functioned only as a pump.

He instructed Jaime to ask for his table at That Obscure Object of Desire in half an hour. He called her *Miz Ralston* and made sure that he sounded properly put upon.

Before she flew out the door, she tried one last time to call Mickey. Or Mick. His line was already out of service.

Charlene the waitress faded, butt switching saucily to let Pavel Drake know she was still on call. Jaime took a tentative sip of her white wine, watching as the frost of condensation filled in her lip prints and restored uniformity to the surface of the glass. Drake had just made his snide remark about scams and polish and *crust* . . . whatever the hell that meant.

"You want me to sign this," he said. His voice was low, disbelieving, calculatedly ugly.

"You have Pamela's power of attorney," Jaime said. "She can't sign it."

He caught her off guard by evidencing interest in her explanation. It was a trick of executive strategy—the lull before the kicker—but Jaime knew it. She had seen the momentary glint in his eyes. "Now . . . you're trying to say that Pamela . . . made up her friends? Imaginary friends, like little kids have?"

"She *conceptualized* her ideal friends. Then she created pacts, promises of duties including every trait from loyalty to good housekeeping, and inscribed them with pseudonyms. See? They're even notarized. I don't have to remind you how imaginative she was."

No, that was the thing Drake had disliked most about his daughter. It had prevented her from becoming like him and following his corporate footprint trail. That would have been an alternative version of Pamela . . . and what had become of that possibility, Jaime now realized with abrupt horror. It was spelled out in one of the clauses on the contract headed JAIME ANYA RALSTON, because there is a fragment of every daughter that wants to please Daddy. Even if Daddy is a philistine, even if the daughter is intractably rebellious.

"Pamela is dead. That hurts me more than I can say, Mr. Drake. I'm sure it hurts you, too, and people tend to lash out when they're in pain."

Again she spotted what might have been a ghostly wisp of human feeling, trapped in the darkness of his eyes, quickly engulfed. "Yes," he said, lifting his drink, then replacing it unsipped as though thinking better of the action. His stiff silence, just now, was a license for her to continue.

"If the contracts are bona fide, then my whole life history came out of Pamela's head. It's a great system—with one flaw. There is no provision for the contractor's death. She didn't factor it in; how many people under thirty bother with wills? But now that she's gone, the obligations of the contractees are discharged. Jason is dead. Mickey is gone . . . or changed, I don't know. Either way he's not Mickey anymore. I was on the scene before either of them. Maybe that's how I lasted long enough to talk to you now."

Drake looked the page in his hand up and down one more time. It did not seem to surprise him.

"That's a new contract," said Jaime. "It supersedes Pamela's, and grants me an existence independent of hers. It's simply worded to assure you I'm trying to gain nothing through trickery. It's a simple business proposition, Mr. Drake. You sign, and I hand over Pamela's filebox, plus all her letters to me. A whole aspect of her you didn't see and never owned. No strings. All I get out of it is my own life, and I never bother you again."

He shifted his glass on the black tabletop like a chess piece. He could press a legal claim to the contents of the Smythe box, but the only thing in it had been the contracts. He rested the page Jaime had typed on the table. It took up nearly half the dry area. "You realize I'm under no obligation to indulge this sort of . . . behavior."

She leaned forward in entreaty. "Okay, so I'm as crazy as a firefly in a meth bottle. What's wrong with humoring me if you get something you want?"

Drake laughed. It was a harsh sound, like a cough. "I win either way. With a story like you've just told me, if you bother me again I can have you detained. If I endorse this fantasy fiction you've laid before me, you'll leave me alone. And if I don't—according to you—you'll vanish anyway, like the other two." He could taste the blood. "I think you've prepared for everything in this tactless scenario *except* for your bluff being called."

He produced a pen from a breast pocket and held it before her, like a magician preparing to prestidigitate. Jamie's heart went *bang*.

"I'll sign. But you must do something for me in return." He slid a brass-colored metal object across the slate tabletop. "Let's find out just how deeply you believe your own story, Ms. Ralston."

It was a hotel key embossed with a room number.

"Everyone gets what they want," he said.

The room seemed to plunge vertiginously. In one hideously elongated instant she flashed back to the crude scene at Pamela's birthday party, and realized that in some quarters the war never stopped, ever. The urge toward vengeance had swelled in both of them, poisonously heavy, dense as a tumor. That was how Pamela's letters had become her trump card. Let Drake win them and find out what his daughter *really* thought of him.

His angle of attack was clear. Here was a chance to slap her down, hard and humiliatingly, to neutralize her through collusion. His ejaculate could scorch away the tough fiber of her determination, which, in a way, he had been responsible for creating by founding Pamela's tortuous childhood—the upbringing that made her crave her imaginary allies just strongly enough.

Jaime saw the hotel key as chance to spit in Pavel Drake's face for Pamela, for herself. Payback time for all the grief and rotten karma. All the gesture would cost her was her existence.

*I love you, Pamela*, she thought bitterly, as her mind raced toward the hard truth of her situation. The end it reached was not pleasant to acknowledge.

*I love you and I want to do right by you. But I'm also terrified. I want to live very much. Would you call this a betrayal? Or common survival sense? If you would forgive me this, why didn't I tell you about Jason that once? and if you won't forgive me . . . is there anything I could ever do that . . .*

Her soul was crippled, and odious, and it did what it had to. "Sign," she said, taking the key, already thinking that the true pain would be brief.

"In due time." His smile was like a pleat in his face. "Excuse me for just a moment." He was all the smooth mercenary now. He had a fast colloquy with Charlene, and pointed toward Jaime. Then he disappeared into the neon murk near the restrooms. There was probably a meeting to cancel.

In Jamie's bag was Pamela's contract. She'd read it a thousand times today, and soon she might burn this mortgage on her life. Tucked into a fold of the document was the postcard, from which she hoped to draw strength. She examined both while Drake was gone. When she saw her signature side by side with Pamela's on the contract's final page, a solitary tear leaked from her eye. Just one. It burned coming out, a generous, salty reaffirmation of her own being. It struck the page and skidded through the middle of her name. The faded purple ink blotted and ran.

You could not buy these pens anymore, she remembered. They stopped making them. Pamela had gotten livid.

Charlene checked in at the bar and glided back to Drake's table just as a raucous stripper's hymn began to bump and grind out of the Object's migraine-sized PA system. She smiled at what she saw. Pavel Drake's latest Bambi had fled back to the forest, forgetting her purse and leaving behind a hotel key, an untouched drink, and a scatter of papers. With schooled motions Charlene swept up the bag and stuffed the papers into it. It was time for her to make a discreet trip to the Ladies. The postcard was the last item in. It featured a timed-exposure of Chicago's Lake Shore Drive at night. It would get chucked into the Object's dumpster along with the other junk just as soon as the wallet was vacuumed of cash and plastic.

Charlene cut loose a snort of disgust that caused her bare tits to bob. That girl, that amateur, had been young enough to be Drake's *daughter*, for christsake.

\*      \*      \*

Dear Jamie. . . .

Phone not in yet but plenty of time to write as I got here just in time for the blizards. In re our "what do I want from my friends" disc earlier I gave it some thot and here it is, gameshow style: (1) I'd want a person who'd *always* be my friend and *never* forget me and *always* remember the right dates and places, which I'm lousy at. (2) A handsome-ass lover who loved me enough to die for me (oh romantic notion) . . . or at least say so. (3) A buddy whose more organized than me, but who thinks like me—someone I could COUNT ON no matter what to take care of the odds and ends I allways forget & am too sloppy to finish, or something.

Somebody to be there for me, somebody JUST LIKE YOU, doo-dah, doo-dah.

Its freezing here. Windy City, big dealski. Outta space, stay tuned for next card. Miss you terribly and love you lots. STAY WARM and XOXOXOXOX

Love,
Pamela

# ELIZABETH S. HELFMAN

## Voices in the Wind

Elizabeth S. Helfman is a lifelong journalist who has turned her hand to fiction in this lovely and simply rendered folktale written for Jane Yolen's young adult collection *Spaceships and Spells*.

"Voices in the Wind" echoes the theme of Richard Peck's "Shadows," reminding us of what fragile things dreams are, and how quickly magic half-glimpsed from the corner of one's eye can vanish as one turns one's head . . .

—T.W.

# VOICES IN THE WIND

## Elizabeth S. Helfman

At the window of his cottage by the sea sat old Tom Anthony. His eyes were in a dream, and he held his head a little to one side, listening, it seemed, to something far away but very pleasant to his hearing. His wife, Sarah, set down a bowl of sauerkraut on the table in the center of the room. She felt suddenly very lonely. There sat Tom, as he had every afternoon and evening, ever since he had been too old to go out fishing. It was worse for her than when he used to be away all day. Then she had expected no companionship. Only occasionally he would come home with a lost look in his eyes and a fantastic tale of the wind and the sea on his lips. She would forgive him, and laugh. And he laughed with her.

He was so different now, content to merely sit and listen to nothing. It was strange, too, that he no longer sought out old Jonah, who lived across the fence at the south. So often, before, they would tell and re-tell long tales of the sea and hazardous fishing.

"Tom, your supper is ready."

She had called him just like this for so many days. He came, as she had known he would, slowly, with a look of childlike apology. "I ought to be more talkative, I suppose, Sarah. I'm sorry."

They sat at the table in silence, and the food stood waiting. Time hesitated for a moment, then went on again. Sarah was a little afraid.

"Tom, why do you sit at the window every day, so long, staring out and looking lost, as if you were listening to something? You seem so far away, you might as well be miles out at sea."

Tom looked at her apologetically. "I'm sorry, Sarah, and I'd tell you but you'd think me crazy."

"I'll think you worse than crazy if you go on this way, Tom. Tell me!"

Tom leaned his elbows on the table so suddenly that the candle flame trembled. The shadows in the corner of the room drew back. "All right, Sarah, I'll tell you."

Sarah bent forward eagerly. "Yes, Tom."

"It's the wind, Sarah, and the sea."

"Tom, haven't you heard enough of the wind and the sea all your life without spending hour after hour listening to them now?"

"It's different now, Sarah. I never knew until some weeks ago that the wind has words to say when it runs about outside the house and cries and moans around the corners. If you listen long enough you can hear what the sea, too, is saying as it comes tumbling in, one wave after another."

Sarah's face was blank. But Tom kept on.

"It tells secrets to the old pines, Sarah."

"You *are* crazy, Tom Anthony."

"Why shouldn't the wind say something, Sarah, when it goes crying about, always restless, as if it were searching for something?"

He *is* crazy, thought Sarah. The thought went through her head over and over again, dully, like a headache.

"I said you'd call me crazy, Sarah."

What should she do with him now? she wondered.

"Come with me to the window and listen," he begged.

"Tom, it's witches, or—or something. Oh, Tom! *Are* you crazy?"

He was silent; then he sighed a little and finished eating. The same thought went through Sarah's head over and over again—what should she do?

Of course Sarah did nothing about it. Somehow thinking that Tom was a little crazy did not make things much different from what they were before. Only now he pleaded with her every evening to come with him to the window and listen. He wanted so much for her to believe.

At last one evening she went to the window with him and sat there a long time, her hand in his, listening.

"Do you hear them, Sarah?"

"Yes, I hear them, not being deaf. But no words, Tom, no words."

He was disappointed, but he was not less confident. "Listen again," he said.

She listened. "No words, Tom."

Nevertheless, after that she went to the window with him every evening, to sit there quietly and listen, even if there were no words to hear. She felt closer to Tom that way, and she was sure he felt closer to her. On evenings when there was no wind she could feel the loneliness in them both.

Sarah had almost forgotten that she thought Tom crazy. And yet, when she took time to think about it, she supposed he must be a little simple minded. For she could not hear words in the wind's moaning, nor a message in the sea's murmurs.

"Can't you hear them, Sarah? Can't you?" Tom would ask.

On an evening in July there was a wild wind wandering about the house, and the sea roared loud on the shore. Tom left his supper before he was half finished to go to the window and listen. Sarah washed the dishes, dried them, and followed. They sat there a long time, Tom with an expression of ecstasy on his face, Sarah passive and rather tired. The wind and the sea roared, echoed each other, roared again. Suddenly an expression of wonder and a kind of terror came to Sarah's face.

"Tom!"

She seized his arm.

"Tom, I thought I heard—"

Tom was not disturbed, not surprised. A triumphant smile spread over his face.

"Of course you heard them, Sarah."

She was silent again, listening. What was it the wind said? She couldn't be sure. Oh, it was all nonsense. And yet . . .

"Tom, am I crazy, too?"

He laughed. "It doesn't matter—if we *both* are—does it?"

She could hear only a word now and then, but there was no denying it. After a while she grew weary of sitting there and went to bed, a little afraid but very happy. Tom followed much later, softly whistling a strange tune she had never heard before.

Sarah had to listen many times, hour after hour, while the wind went around the house, before she was sure of the words it used. She was almost as eager to listen as Tom, though she always washed the dishes and put them away before she went to the window.

One night, when they were listening together, the words of the wind came clearer than ever before. They made a chant like this:

> "*The wind is wild with wandering,*
> *Wild with moaning through the trees,*
> *Wild with whispering in the pines,*
> *Wild with crying to the sea. . . .*
> *The wind is wild with wandering,*
> *Over the troubled sea again,*
> *Whistling around the house again.*
> *I am the wind,*
> *The wandering wind.*"

Sarah smiled somewhat foolishly and murmured, " 'The wind is wild with wandering.' Who could have known . . . ?"

Tom was listening to still other words, for a gentle rain was falling. And he heard the rain say:

> "*I come with murmurs,*
> *Murmurs,*
> *Out of the clouds that know the thunder,*

*Out of the sea that roars and tumbles,*
*Down to the earth that waits and wonders—*
*I am the murmuring rain."*

"The rain sings, too, Sarah," Tom said.

The rain kept on murmuring. The wind in its wandering blew open the door, put out the candle, and left Tom and Sarah in sudden darkness. He took her hand in his and they stood there in that darkness, silent and unafraid.

There was a day in late July when an unexpected rain came out of a sky that had been still and blue an hour before. Tom and Sarah were at the window, listening to what the angry rain might say, when there was a knock at the door. Sarah was afraid, why she did not know.

"I won't go, Tom. I won't."

He crossed to the door and opened it. On the doorstep stood a teenage boy, wet all over, with little rivulets running from the ends of his long, blond hair.

Tom recognized him—Oliver Trowbridge, from the nearby summer resort. He had taken Oliver sailing many times and let him dangle a line over the edge of the boat until he caught a fish or two.

Oliver ambled in, past Tom, to the fireplace, where Tom had built a roaring fire against the dampness. "Whew!" he said. "I thought you'd never get to the door. I got soaked in all this rain, and I thought you'd let me dry off for a minute or two."

Suddenly Sarah hated Oliver Trowbridge. He had come just when she had been listening to catch a few words the rain said. Now he stood there by the fire as if it were his own, babbling things she had no patience with. But she said only, "You're welcome here. Would you like something to eat?" And she brought out a dish of her sauerkraut.

"Oh," said Oliver. "Thanks." After a slow start he ate it eagerly.

Sarah saw that Tom was at the window looking out, no longer listening to Oliver. And yet she knew he was not content to have him there.

"What's the matter with the old man?" Oliver gulped his last mouthful. "Is he deaf?"

"No, he's not deaf. He's listening to things you'd be glad to hear, if you could."

"Oh, of course. Yes, of course," Oliver drawled. Then he smiled and crossed to the window, where he stood beside Tom. He put one hand on Tom's shoulder and received no answer. He touched Tom's shoulder, again with no success. Feeling playful, he pulled Tom's ear, very gently.

Tom turned to him angrily. "What do you want with me?"

Oliver answered, "I want to know what it is you're listening to."

"You won't believe, but if you want to know—I listen to what the wind says, what the sea mumbles, what the rain murmurs when it comes out of the clouds."

Oliver laughed long and loud. "Well, let me listen with you, old man."

Tom turned back to the window. Oliver stood beside him, minute after minute. Then he said, "All I hear is a little bit of rain falling, a little bit of ocean coming in, the way it always does, and the wind blowing around. No words."

"I wouldn't expect *you* to hear them."

"Does your wife hear them?"

Sarah nodded emphatically. "Of course."

Oliver broke again into shrill laughter, then stopped as suddenly as he had begun. "Well, I'll be going. The rain's about over. But first, let me tell you this—if you really think you hear any words in the sound of wind, and rain, and sea, you are absolutely crazy. Absolutely."

Tom turned to the window again, as if he wished he had not heard. Sarah smiled to herself, as if she knew things Oliver could never dream of. And he mistook her smile.

"Oh, I suppose you've been fooling all this time," he said. "You *were* clever. For a while I thought you really meant it. Time to go. Good-bye, everybody!" And he was gone.

"What a fool!" said Sarah. Tom nodded in agreement. "Of course *he* couldn't hear the voices, not even wanting to believe."

"Of course not."

They went to listen again and heard the wind murmuring, *I am the wind, the wind that murmurs in the pines.*

They were troubled, though. Tom felt for the first time that it would be pleasant to hear someone besides Sarah and himself swear to the truth of the words in the wind's voice. And so he sought out old Jonah the next day. He found him sitting in a corner of his kitchen, looking out to the sea and dreaming.

Jonah woke from dreaming to astonishment when he saw Tom. "Well, Tom! Where have you been all this time? I thought likely you'd fallen into the sea and drowned, or something even better!" He laughed heartily, as if this were the greatest joke in the world.

Tom shook his head. "No, I've simply been at home, listening to things."

"Well, Tom," said Jonah cheerfully, "I guess that's about all there is to do now that we can't go fishing anymore."

Tom was thoughtful. "I suppose no one around here knows more about the sea than you do, Jonah."

Jonah laughed again, finding this an even greater joke. "You're right, Tom, I reckon no one could know more about the sea than old Jonah."

"Well, have you ever heard the wind at sea telling you things?"

"Of course, and you have, too, Tom. It used to tell me when I'd better make for home instead of being caught in a storm and when it would be safe to steer north."

"But, Jonah, did the wind ever *speak* to you? Did you ever hear words in its voice?"

"Of course not, and neither did you, Tom."

"Not until a few weeks ago. But now both Sarah and I listen at the window when the wind is blowing, and it chants strange words."

Old Jonah laughed comfortably. "What a queer thing to dream about."

"It's not a dream, Jonah. We've listened hour after hour and we hear what the wind says, the sea, and the rain."

"Sarah hears this, too?"

"Both of us."

"No one knows more about the sea and the wind than I do, and I never heard any words. You're getting old, Tom, getting old. And so is Sarah. Perhaps you've both become a little simple. That makes me sad. You used to be one of the best fishermen on the coast."

That night there was again a wind, and Tom and Sarah went to listen to its song. But they remembered Oliver with his scornful laughter, and the careless disbelief of old Jonah. Tom heard some of the words the wind said, but Sarah's thoughts were so busy that she heard none of them.

The night after that there was also a wind. Tom and Sarah were troubled as they sat at supper.

"He was a fool, that Oliver person," grumbled Tom. "And old Jonah, he's a good enough old man, but he can't have listened to the wind for very long."

Sarah nodded. "Oliver was crazy. And old Jonah pretty near it, I guess."

"And yet," said Tom, suddenly thoughtful, "are they crazy or are we? Have we been wrong all the time?"

Sarah, too, grew thoughtful. "I don't know, Tom."

"Why, we've been right, haven't we, Sarah?"

"I suppose so, Tom."

Sarah remembered that she was, above all, a sensible woman. And yet —surely she had heard what the wind said.

"Aren't you *sure*, Sarah?"

"Yes, Tom, of course."

There was silence for a moment.

"Sarah, you don't sound so sure."

"Well, Tom, perhaps I'm not, after all."

"Do you think we *are* a little crazy?"

"Oh, Tom, I don't know." And she didn't. Perhaps they were right, perhaps wrong; likelier wrong, and yet she'd rather be right. Why did Tom keep asking such questions?

"Look, Sarah, the way to be sure is to go to the window now and listen. Come with me."

She went willingly with him, and they stood a long time listening. At first she thought she heard a word or two in the wind's voice. Then she thought, and in a minute was sure, that she was hearing nothing but inarticulate sounds.

"I don't hear the wind saying anything, Tom."

The look on his face told her that he, too, had heard nothing.

"Oh, just a minute, Sarah. Perhaps . . ."

Again they listened, while the inarticulate wind wandered about outside.

"Perhaps what, Tom?"

There was a silence in which even the wind made no sound.

"I don't know, Sarah."

"Tom," Sarah said. "It was a beautiful dream we had together."

The cry of the wind had ceased, and the sound of the sea as it murmured seemed very far away.

# JANE YOLEN

## Once Upon a Time, She Said

Dr. Jane Yolen is one of the undisputed masters of modern fantasy. With her deft touch for both retelling and creating brand new fairy tales for children and adults, she has been called the Hans Christian Andersen of our time. Yolen is the author of over one hundred adult, young adult, nonfiction and picture books, as well as poetry; readers new to her work should in particular seek out the picture books *The Girl Who Cried Flowers* (illustrated by David Palladini), *Dreamweaver* (illustrated by Michael Hague), and *Neptune Rising* (illustrated by David Wiesner); *Touch Magic*, collected essays on faerie and fantasy in children's literature; *Tales of Wonder*, a collection of adult and children's fantasy stories; her first adult fantasy/science fiction novel, *Cards of Grief*; and Steeldragon Press's beautifully produced edition of Yolen's Arthurian tales, *Merlin's Booke* (illustrated by Thomas Canty).

In addition to her prolific output, Yolen edits collections of stories and folklore; has discovered and aided many talented new writers and artists; speaks at libraries and schools across the country; and is currently the president of the Science Fiction Writers of America. Yolen lives in rural Massachusetts with her husband and youngest son; her daughter attends college in Florida and her older son is in a Minneapolis rock band with fantasy writers Steven Brust and Emma Bull.

"Once Upon a Time, She Said" comes from *The National Storytelling Journal*.

—T. W.

# ONCE UPON A TIME, SHE SAID

## Jane Yolen

*"Once upon a time," she said,*
*and the world began anew:*
*a vee of geese flew by,*
*plums roasting in their breasts;*
*a vacant-eyed princess*
*sat upon a hillock of glass;*
*a hut strolled through a tangled wood,*
*the nails on its chickenfeet,*
*blackened and hard as coal;*
*a horse's head proclaimed advice*
*from the impost of an arch;*
*one maiden spoke in toads,*
*another in pearls,*
*and a third with the nightingale's voice.*
*If you ask me,*
*I would have to say*
*all the world's magic*
*comes directly from the mouth.*

# CAROL EMSHWILLER

## The Circular Library of Stones

Carol Emshwiller has published fiction in magazines as diverse as *OMNI, Twilight Zone*, and *Triquarterly*, as well as contributing to Harlan Ellison's *Dangerous Visions* anthologies. This story, "The Circular Library of Stones," comes from the pages of *OMNI* magazine. The story is a moving piece of "Magic Realism," challenging the very notion of fantasy, of what is real and what is not. Through her evocative, poetic prose, Emshwiller transforms an ordinary life into the grandeur of myth. The story does what all good fantasy should do: Enable us to perceive the real world all the more clearly.

Emshwiller is a teacher at New York University.

—T.W.

# THE CIRCULAR LIBRARY OF STONES

## Carol Emshwiller

They said all this wasn't true. That there had been no city on this site since even before the time of the Indians . . . that there had been no bridge across the (now dried up) river and no barriers against the mud. "If you have been searching for a library here," they said, "or for old coins, you've been wasting your time."

For lack of space I had put some of the small, white stones in plant baskets and hung them from the ceiling by the window. I don't argue with people about what nonexistent city could have existed at this site. I just collect the stones. (Two have X's scratched on them, only one of which I scratched myself.) And I continue digging. The earth, though full of stones of all sizes, is soft and easy to deal with. Often it is damp and fragrant. And I disturb very little in the way of trees or plants of any real size here. Also most of the stones, even the larger ones, are of a size that I can manage fairly well by myself. Besides, mainly it's the stones that I want to reveal. I don't want to move them from place to place, except some of the most important small ones, which I take home with me after a day's digging. Often I have found battered aluminum pots and pans around the site. Once I found an old boot and once, a pair of broken glasses; but these, of course, are of no significance whatsoever, being clearly of the present.

Gaining access to their books! If I could find the library and learn to read their writing! If I could find, there, stories beyond my wildest dreams. A love story, for instance, where the love is of a totally different kind . . . a kind of ardor we have never even thought of, more long lasting than our simple attachments, more world-shaking than our simple sexualities. Or a literature that is two things at once, which we can only do in drawings where a body might be, at one and the same time, a face in which the breasts also equal eyes; or two naked ladies sitting side by side, arms raised, that also form a skull, their black hair the eye sockets.

For quite some time now I have had sore legs, so digging is an exercise I can do better than any other, and though at night my back pains me, the pains usually go away quite soon. By morning I hardly feel them. So the digging, in itself, pleases me. There is the pleasure of work. A day well spent. Go home tired and silent. But mostly, of course, it is the slow revelation of the stones that I care about. Sometimes they cluster in groups so that I think that here must have been where a fireplace was, or perhaps a throne. Sometimes they form a long row that I think might have been a wall or a bench. And I have found a mirror. Two feet underground, and so scratched that one can see oneself only in little fish-shaped flashes—a bit of an eye, a bit of lip, but for even that much of it to have been preserved all this time is a miracle. I feel certain that if they had a library, it's logical they would also have had mirrors. Or if they had mirrors, it certainly follows they could have had a library.

I keep the mirror with me in my breast pocket. (I wear a man's old fishing vest.) When people ask me what I'm doing out here, I show the mirror to them along with a few smooth stones.

At night I write. I shut my eyes and let my left hand move as it wishes. Usually it makes only scratchings, but other times words come out. Once I wrote several pages of nothing but *no, no, no, no, no,* and after that, *on, on, on,* and *on,* but more and more often there are larger words now, and more and more often they are making some kind of sense. Yesterday, for instance, I found myself writing: *Let us do let us us do and do and let us not be but do and you do too.* And then, and for the first time, a whole phrase came out clear and simple: *Cool all that summer and at night returned to the library.*

Certainly I would suppose the library, being built of stone, to be always cool in summer, always warm in winter. The phrase is surely, then, true and of the time. It is interesting that the library itself is referred to in this, the first real phrase I've written so far. That is significant. What I have been hoping to do is to reproduce some of the writings from the library, or reasonable facsimiles. Perhaps this is the beginning of one of their books.

The circle is sacred to all peoples except for us. We are the only ones that don't care if a thing is square or a circle or oblong or triangular. The shape has no meaning to us. A circle could be oval for all we care. I'm thinking about this because I think I have come across a giant circle. About a foot down I found what looked like a path of stones, and I dug along it all day thinking I was going in a straight line; but when I turned around to look back on what I had accomplished, I saw that although I had dug only a few yards, clearly I was curving. Though I had thought to finish for the day, I turned and vigorously revealed another yard of the stones, yet knowing full well it would be perhaps a month before I could uncover a really significant portion of the circle. I was thinking that probably here, at last, was where the very walls of the library had been and that, if true, this would be a great revelation of stones (even though done by an old woman . . . a useless old woman, so everyone thinks). I felt happy . . .

happy and tired after that, and though I came home very late and my back hurt even more than usual, I sat down, dirty as I was, at my little table. I shut my eyes and let my left hand write: *Let us oh let us do and do and dance and do the dance of the library in the cool in the sanctuary of the library.*

It rained that night and all the next day, and I knew it had filled up all my pits and paths with mud. I would have to do much of my digging over again, and yet I wasn't terribly unhappy about it. Such things come in every life. It's to be expected. (And doing is digging. Digging is doing. Do, not be. That's my philosophy and it seems to be theirs, too.) And my latest discovery was momentous, to say the least. Who would have thought it: a great white, stone, circular library to be danced in!

Mostly on rainy days like these I do as the other old women do. I knit or make pot holders. I make soup and muffins. While I was there doing old-woman things and looking out the window, I thought, *How nice if I found even only another stone with, perhaps, an O on it. People who search as I do must be happy with small and seemingly insignificant discoveries. People who search as I do must understand, also, that the lack of something is never insignificant; so even if there was nothing to be found, I was never disappointed, because that, too, was significant*—as, for instance, a library and only one stone with an X on it. *Besides, the less discovered, the more open the possibilities.* I always console myself with that thought.

That night I let my left hand write. It took a long time to get from scratches to X's; to *no, no, no*; but finally it wrote: *Let us then stone on stone on stone a library that befits a library each door face the sun one at dawn and one at dusk. Many queens saw it.* (Perhaps they were all queens in those days. Or perhaps when they reached my age they became queens. I would like to think so.)

This was on my mind when I went to sleep and I dreamed a row of dancing women, all my age and all wearing crowns of smooth white pebbles. They were calling to me to wake up . . . to wake up, that is, into my dream, and I did, and I was still in my boots and fishing vest and my old gray pants. I didn't, in other words, dream myself to be one of them, as some sort of queen or other. I was my dirt-stained self, holding out my grimy hands. And it seemed that they gave me my mirror—the one I had already found, and even in my dream it wasn't shiny and new but just as scratched as when I found it. They showed me that I must place the mirror exactly where I found it in the first place so that I could find it—as I did find it—near the former riverbed and on a slight rise. This I did in my dream as the old women beat stones together with a loud *clack, clack.* And of course it's true; that's where I *did* find the mirror. It all fits together perfectly!

(All those old women lacked grace, but perhaps it's not required.)

My daughters. . . . I suppose they tell me the truth about myself, though no need to. Why do they do it? Why feel free to say such things? Do I talk too much? Do I go on and on about it or about anything? Why, I've almost stopped talking altogether, wanting, now, other kinds of meanings. My argument is one Xed stone or a particularly smooth one or several in a row. I let them speak their ambiguities for themselves.

I showed my daughters my moonstone. I wanted to convince them. I said it came from the library.

"What library?"

"You know. Out by the dried-up stream."

"You've always had that moonstone. Grandma gave it to you."

"Well," I said, "I found it lying in the mud there." (I knew I was just making everything worse.)

"You must have dropped it yourself. What were you doing wearing that out there, anyway? You ought to be more careful."

I suppose I should have been. I know it will be theirs someday.

Later they told me about a place (I've seen it) where there's a doctor's office in the basement and art rooms, pot-holder rooms, television rooms, railings along all the halls. Everybody has a cane. I've seen that. I told my daughters no.

Just as crossroads, fire, seashells, oak trees, and circles have special meanings, stones have meanings, too. Some, upright and lumpy on the hillsides, are named after women. All the best houses are of stone, therefore the library also. Molloy sucked them (I have too, sometimes), found them refreshing. Stone doors into the mountain balance on a single point and open at the slightest caress. The sound stone makes as door is not unlike the rustling of pebbles on beaches. It is fitting that stones should be open to question, as my stones are. I liked letting them speak their ambiguities. When I was not out at my dig, I remembered stones. I dreamed them. I imagined I heard their *clack, clack.*

I warned my daughters that if I should be found awkwardly banging stones together on some moonlit night, it would be neither out of senility nor sentimentality, but a scientific test.

But then I found a stone of a different kind and color: reddish and lumpy. Essentially nine lumps: two in front, two in back, plus one head, two arms, and two leg posts. I recognized it instantly. Fecund *and* wise. Big breasted *and* a scholar. Fat *and* elegant. I wanted to bring this librarian to her true place in the scheme of things. Restore her to her glory. Clearly, she not only had babies and nursed them, but she read all the books.

After this find, I dug in a frenzy. I knew I should be more careful of myself at my age: follow some rules of rest and recreation, but I believe in *do*, not *be*. Do! Though why should I so desperately want more . . . more, that is, than the mother of the library? (My daughters will call her a lumpy, pink stone.) Am I never satisfied?

Never! (My left hand has written: *Stone on stone on stone on stone on stone*, almost as though I were building the library out of the words.)

And then as I dug frantically, my eyes were blinded by the setting sun. Everything sparkled, and I thought I actually saw the library: all white with a great, clear river before it and a landing where the books (stone books) were brought in on little ships with big sails. The glistening of the waves hurt my eyes, but I could see, even so, the librarians dancing on the beach in front of the sacred circle of the library. And they were all old. Old as I am or even older—wrinkled, hobbling women—I could see that their backs were hurting them too, but they kept on with the dancing, just as I kept on with my digging. And I heard the soft, sweet, fluty music of the library and felt the cool of it, for I, too, stood close to the western doorway. And we could see each other. I'm sure of it. I saw eyes meet mine, and not just once or twice.

I stepped forward, then, to dance with them, but I fell—it seemed a long, slow fall—and as I fell, the sun was no longer in my eyes and I saw then my rocky ground and my dried-up streambed.

After I got up, I felt extraordinarily lucid. As though I had drunk from the ice-cold river. Clearheaded and happy—happier than I'd been in a long time (though I've not been unhappy digging here. On the contrary). I didn't want to go home and rest—I felt so powerful—but I forced myself. I had hardly eaten all day, and most important, if I tried to dig in the dark I might miss something. I might toss away a stone like my important librarian and not see what it really was.

When I got home that night I found that someone had been at my stones. They were all, all gone. I was so happy about my little librarian that I didn't notice it at first. It wasn't until I went to put her on my night table (I wanted her to be close to me as I slept) that I noticed there were no other stones there, not a single one. I knew right away what had happened. My daughters had decided that I'm being crowded out by stones. They think —because *they* would feel that way—that it must be uncomfortable to live like this. But I was brought up on stones, don't they remember that? I had geodes. I had chunks of amber. I had a cairngorm set in silver. Still have it somewhere, unless they took that off for safekeeping. They think I will lose it out there. Well, perhaps I already have, but if I did, it's been worth it many times over. And now even my hanging baskets of stones, gone, and stones from every surface, every shelf, all gone. Thank goodness I carry my most important ones with me in my vest pockets.

All these old stones. Mother wouldn't have appreciated them either. The work, yes, the care I've taken, the effort—she did appreciate effort and would have praised me for that, but she had no understanding of science and its slow, laborious unfolding. The care, the cataloging, she would have praised, but perhaps not when all this work involves merely stones. Back in those days she didn't even like my geodes (especially those that had not been opened yet). It can't be hoped that she would have liked my little naked librarian. Also, Mother disapproved of nakedness of any sort. I, on the other hand, want to stress the importance of childbearing librarians and so the importance of the bodies of the librarians, and so all the glory of their old-lady sexuality. (And I have seen it at the local library . . . the woman in charge sitting with her breasts against the table.)

Coming in like that, then, and no stones, my little librarian in hand, I couldn't possibly sleep. I was both too happy and too upset. I sat down instead to draw my new find. If I am, someday in the future, to be judged for this work by someone who really knows what it's all about; I don't want to make any mistakes that will spoil the scientific accuracy of the study. I labeled all the parts: these slits, eyes; that slit, the opening to the womb. (The look on her face was intelligent and self-sufficient.)

I hid the drawings under my socks. (Who knows what my daughters will think worth nothing?) I put the librarian in the top breast pocket of the vest, where tomorrow she will rest over my heart. Then I checked all the other pockets with my most important stones (all there, thank goodness) and went to bed. It was nearly morning.

Even so, the next day I woke still extraordinarily clearheaded. I fairly jogged out to my site. Worked hard all day but found nothing, saw nothing. Once or twice I did think I heard the sound of flutes and perhaps some drumming, but I knew that was just my imagination plus the beat of my own heart in my ears. I always hear that on hot days when I lean over too much or get up too fast.

When I got home I sensed, again, a change. (Why do they always come in the daytime when I'm not here? Why are they afraid to face me?) I couldn't see the changes this time, but I knew they'd been there and I knew things were gone. I checked my closet first, and yes, those few dresses I have that I hardly ever wear weren't there. Also the suitcase that I keep at the back on the closet floor. A pair of walking shoes were gone, and my best dressy shoes. Also a white sweater my daughters gave me but that I never wear, except to please them once in a while to make them think I like it. Then, in the drawers, I found half my underwear gone and my jewelry, such as I have. (Probably my cairngorm. I didn't see it there.)

They have already packed me up and taken my things off somewhere, and I think I know where. From the looks of what they thought I'd need there—dresses, jewelry, stockings—I knew what it would be like: Dress for dinner, sit on porches, play cards, watch TV, sing, entertainment every Saturday night. Did they think I was so senile I wouldn't notice what was going on? I knew it wouldn't be long before they'd come for me, and I wondered exactly when that would be. Perhaps very early in the morning, before I was up and out at my dig. Well, I would just have to go back out there right away. The thing was, I wasn't ready yet. Now I would have to make something happen before I really understood anything. Before I went out, though, I thought I would sit down, have a cup of tea, and let my left hand write a bit. I thought it might have something to tell me.

*Why not why not lie down and in the sanctuary of the library why not come cool all night and see the shores of the sky.*

(My daughters have never been interested in libraries nor in anything they can't put their finger on nor anything they can't understand the first time they see it.)

*Take a white string long and measure and dig in the center of the library a place to lie down with quilts and pillows.*

Nothing much else to do that I could think of right then. I didn't wait. I did as they said, got white cord and quilt and pillow. I didn't bring a flashlight. The night was clear, stars out but no moon. I could see well enough to find the center of the library. I dug a shallow grave just my size and lay down there, facing up, looking at the constellation Swan. I kept my eyes on that. It took effort, but everything worth doing takes effort. Effort is what makes it all worthwhile, so I held my eyes open and on the Swan, her wings stretched out, flying out there so high I knew I couldn't even conceive of the distance. I forced myself not to sleep. Pretty soon the Swan seemed to move and wobble and then began to swoop about the sky. My God, I'd never seen anything so strange and wonderful as that swooping Swan of stars. And then I heard—faintly at first—that *clack, clack, clack* of stones that meant all the librarians were there around me. I didn't see them, but I knew they were there. I was afraid to turn my eyes away from the Swan. Nor did I want to by then. I liked watching it loop and tumble and glide. And then it whizzed by directly over my head so close I felt the rush of air. And after that, there was the fat red Venus, life-size, sitting right beside me. "Sanctuary," she said, but she didn't need to say it. I knew that. "Stay," she said, and all of a sudden I knew it was death, death now and had been death all along. But I thought, *I could be working in the sanctuary of the vegetable garden at the old ladies' home. Or I might even be sitting on the porch, but I'd be alive if only for a little longer . . . not much, but a little bit.* "No," I said. But she kept nodding, and now I couldn't have turned away even if I wanted to, and the *clack, clack* of stones was loud and painful and right over my head.

"Why not later?"

"It's now or never."

# SOFT MONKEY

## Harlan Ellison

At twenty-five minutes past midnight on 51st Street, the wind-chill factor was so sharp it could carve you a new asshole.

Annie lay huddled in the tiny space formed by the wedge of locked revolving door that was open to the street when the document copying service had closed for the night. She had pulled the shopping cart from the Food Emporium at First Avenue near 57th into the mouth of the revolving door, had carefully tipped it onto its side, making certain her goods were jammed tightly in the cart, making certain nothing spilled into her sleeping space. She had pulled out half a dozen cardboard flats—broken-down sections of big Kotex cartons from the Food Emporium, the half dozen she had not sold to the junkman that afternoon—and she had fronted the shopping cart with two of them, making it appear the doorway was blocked by the management. She had wedged the others around the edges of the space, cutting the wind, and placed the two rotting sofa pillows behind and under her.

She had settled down, bundled in her three topcoats, the thick woolen merchant marine stocking cap rolled down to cover her ears, almost to the bridge of her broken nose. It wasn't bad in the doorway, quite cozy, really. The wind shrieked past and occasionally touched her, but mostly was deflected. She lay huddled in the tiny space, pulled out the filthy remnants of a stuffed baby doll, cradled it under her chin, and closed her eyes.

She slipped into a wary sleep, half in reverie and yet alert to the sounds of the street. She tried to dream of the child again. Alan. In the waking dream she held him as she held the baby doll, close under her chin, her eyes closed, feeling the warmth of his body. That was important: his body was warm, his little brown hand against her cheek, his warm, warm breath drifting up with the dear smell of baby.

*Was that just today or some other day?* Annie swayed in reverie, kissing the broken face of the baby doll. It was nice in the doorway; it was warm.

The normal street sounds lulled her for another moment, and then were shattered as two cars careened around the corner off Park Avenue, racing toward Madison. Even asleep. Annie sensed when the street wasn't right. It was a sixth sense she had learned to trust after the first time she had been mugged for her shoes and the small change in her snap-purse. Now she came fully awake as the sounds of trouble rushed toward her doorway. She hid the baby doll inside her coat.

The stretch limo sideswiped the Caddy as they came abreast of the closed repro center. The Brougham ran up over the curb and hit the light stanchion full in the grille. The door on the passenger side fell open and a man scrabbled across the front seat, dropped to all four on the sidewalk, and tried to crawl away. The stretch limo, angled in toward the curb, slammed to a stop in front of the Brougham, and three doors opened before the tires stopped rolling.

They grabbed him as he tried to stand, and forced him back to his knees. One of the limo's occupants wore a fine navy blue cashmere overcoat; he pulled it open and reached to his hip. His hand came out holding a revolver. With a smooth stroke he laid it across the kneeling man's forehead, opening him to the bone.

Annie saw it all. With poisonous clarity, back in the V of the revolving door, cuddled in darkness, she saw it all. Saw a second man kick out and break the kneeling victim's nose. The sound of it cut against the night's sudden silence. Saw the third man look toward the stretch limo as a black glass window slid down and a hand emerged from the back seat. The electric hum of opening. Saw the third man go to the stretch and take from the extended hand a metal can. A siren screamed down Park Avenue, and kept going. Saw him return to the group and heard him say, "Hold the motherfucker. Pull his head back!" Saw the other two wrench the victim's head back, gleaming white and pumping red from the broken nose, clear in the sulfurous light from the stanchion overhead. The man's shoes scraped and scraped the sidewalk. Saw the third man reach into an outer coat pocket and pull out a pint of scotch. Saw him unscrew the cap and begin to pour booze into the face of the victim. "Hold his mouth open!" Saw the man in the cashmere topcoat spike his thumb and index fingers into the hinges of the victim's jaws, forcing his mouth open. The sound of gagging, the glow of spittle. Saw the scotch spilling down the man's front. Saw the third man toss the pint bottle into the gutter where it shattered; and saw him thumb press the center of the plastic cap of the metal can; and saw him make the cringing, crying, wailing victim drink the Drano. Annie saw and heard it all.

The cashmere topcoat forced the victim's mouth closed, massaged his throat, made him swallow the Drano. The dying took a lot longer than expected. And it was a lot noisier.

The victim's mouth was glowing a strange blue in the calcium light from overhead. He tried spitting, and a gobbet hit the navy blue cashmere sleeve. Had the natty dresser from the stretch limo been a dunky slob uncaring of what *GQ* commanded, what happened next would not have gone down.

Cashmere cursed, swiped at the slimed sleeve, let go of the victim; the man with the glowing blue mouth and the gut being boiled away wrenched free of the other two, and threw himself forward. Straight toward the locked revolving door blocked by Annie's shopping cart and cardboard flats.

He came at her in fumbling, hurtling steps, arms wide and eyes rolling, throwing spittle like a racehorse; Annie realized he'd fall across the cart and smash her flat in another two steps.

She stood up, backing to the side of the V. She stood up: into the tunnel of light from the Caddy's headlights.

"The nigger saw it all!" yelled the cashmere.

"Fuckin' bag lady!" yelled the one with the can of Drano.

"He's still moving!" yelled the third man, reaching inside his topcoat and coming out of his armpit with a blued steel thing that seemed to extrude to a length more aptly suited to Paul Bunyan's armpit.

Foaming at the mouth, hands clawing at his throat, the driver of the Brougham came at Annie as if he were spring-loaded.

He hit the shopping cart with his thighs just as the man with the long armpit squeezed off his first shot. The sound of the .45 magnum tore a chunk out of 51st Street, blew through the running man like a crowd roar, took off his face and spattered bone and blood across the panes of the revolving door. It sparkled in the tunnel of light from the Caddy's headlights.

And somehow he kept coming. He hit the cart, rose as if trying to get a first down against a solid defense line, and came apart as the shooter hit him with a second round.

There wasn't enough solid matter to stop the bullet and it exploded through the revolving door, shattering it open as the body crashed through and hit Annie.

She was thrown backward, through the broken glass, and onto the floor of the document copying center. And through it all, Annie heard a fourth voice, clearly a fourth voice, screaming from the stretch limo, "Get the old lady! Get her, she saw everything!"

Men in topcoats rushed through the tunnel of light.

Annie rolled over, and her hand touched something soft. It was the ruined baby doll. It had been knocked loose from her bundled clothing. *Are you cold, Alan?*

She scooped up the doll and crawled away, into the shadows of the reproduction center. Behind her, crashing through the frame of the revolving door, she heard men coming. And the sound of a burglar alarm. Soon police would be here.

All she could think about was that they would throw away her goods. They would waste her good cardboard, they would take back her shopping cart, they would toss her pillows and the hankies and the green cardigan into some trashcan; and she would be empty on the street again. As she had been when they made her move out of the room at 101st and First Avenue. After they took Alan from her . . .

A blast of sound, as the shot shattered a glass-framed citation on the wall near her. They had fanned out inside the office space, letting the headlight illumination shine through. Clutching the baby doll, she hustled down a hallway toward the rear of the copy center. Doors on both sides, all of them closed and locked. Annie could hear them coming.

A pair of metal doors stood open on the right. It was dark in there. She slipped inside, and in an instant her eyes had grown acclimated. There were computers here, big crackle-gray-finish machines that lined three walls. Nowhere to hide.

She rushed around the room, looking for a closet, a cubbyhole, anything. Then she stumbled over something and sprawled across the cold floor. Her face hung over into emptiness, and the very faintest of cool breezes struck her cheeks. The floor was composed of large removable squares. One of them had been lifted and replaced, but not flush. It had not been locked down; an edge had been left ajar; she had kicked it open.

She reached down. There was a crawlspace under the floor.

Pulling the metal-rimmed vinyl plate, she slid into the empty square. Lying face-up, she pulled the square over the aperture, and nudged it gently till it dropped onto its tracks. It sat flush. She could see nothing where, a moment before, there had been the faintest scintilla of filtered light from the hallway. Annie lay very quietly, emptying her mind as she did when she slept in the doorways; making herself invisible. A mound of rags. A pile of refuse. Gone. Only the warmth of the baby doll in that empty place with her.

She heard the men crashing down the corridor, trying doors. *I wrapped you in blankets, Alan. You must be warm.* They came into the computer room. The room was empty, they could see that.

"She *has* to be here, dammit!"

"There's gotta be a way out we didn't see."

"Maybe she locked herself in one of those rooms. Should we try? Break 'em open?"

"Don't be a bigger asshole than usual. Can't you hear that alarm? We gotta get out of here!"

"He'll break our balls."

"Like hell. Would he do anything else than we've done? He's sittin' on the street in front of what's left of Beaddie. You think he's happy about it?"

There was a new sound to match the alarm. The honking of a horn from the street. It went on and on, hysterically.

"We'll find her."

Then the sound of footsteps. Then running.

Annie lay empty and silent, holding the doll.

It was warm, as warm as she had been all November. She slept there through the night.

The next day, in the last Automat in New York with the wonderful little windows through which one could get food by insertion of a token, Annie learned of the two deaths.

Not the death of the man in the revolving door; the deaths of two black women. Beaddie, who had vomited up most of his internal organs, boiled like Chesapeake Bay lobsters, was all over the front of the *Post* that Annie now wore as insulation against the biting November wind. The two women had been found in midtown alleys, their faces blown off by heavy caliber ordnance. Annie had known one of them; her name had been Sooky and Annie got the word from a good Thunderbird worshipper who stopped by her table and gave her the skinny as she carefully ate her fish cakes and tea.

She knew who they had been seeking. And she knew why they had killed Sooky and the other street person: to white men who ride in stretch limos, all old nigger bag ladies look the same. She took a slow bite of fish cake and stared out at 42nd Street, watching the world swirl past; what was she going to do about this?

They would kill and kill till there was no safe place left to sleep in midtown. She knew it. This was mob business, the *Post* inside her coats said so. And it wouldn't make any difference trying to warn the women. Where would they go? Where would they *want* to go? Not even she, knowing what it was all about . . . not even she would leave the area: this was where she roamed, this was her territorial imperative. And they would find her soon enough.

She nodded to the croaker who had given her the word, and after he'd hobbled away to get a cup of coffee from the spigot on the wall, she hurriedly finished her fish cake and slipped out of the Automat as easily as she had the document copying center this morning.

Being careful to keep out of sight, she returned to 51st Street. The area had been roped off, with sawhorses and green tape that said *Police Investigation—Keep Off.* But there were crowds. The streets were jammed, not only with office workers coming and going, but with loiterers who were fascinated by the scene. It took very little to gather a crowd in New York. The falling of a cornice could produce a *minyan.*

Annie could not believe her luck. She realized the police were unaware of a witness: when the men had charged the doorway, they had thrown aside her cart and goods, had spilled them back onto the sidewalk to gain entrance; and the cops had thought it was all refuse, as one with the huge brown plastic bags of trash at the curb. Her cart and the good sofa pillows, the cardboard flats and her sweaters . . . all of it was in the area. Some in trash cans, some amid the piles of bagged rubbish, some just lying in the gutter.

That meant she didn't need to worry about being sought from two directions. One way was bad enough.

And all the aluminum cans she had salvaged to sell, they were still in the big Bloomingdale's bag right against the wall of the building. There would be money for dinner.

She was edging out of the doorway to collect her goods when she saw the one in navy blue cashmere who had held Beaddie while they fed him Drano. He was standing three stores away, on Annie's side, watching the police lines, watching the copy center, watching the crowd. Watching for her. Picking at an ingrown hair on his chin.

She stepped back into the doorway. Behind her a voice said, "C'mon, lady, get the hell outta here, this's a place uhbizness." Then she felt a sharp poke in her spine.

She looked behind her, terrified. The owner of the haberdashery, a man wearing a bizarrely cut gray pinstripe worsted with lapels that matched his ears, and a passion flame silk hankie spilling out of his breast pocket like a crimson afflatus, was jabbing her in the back with a wooden coat hanger. "Move it on, get moving," he said, in a tone that would have gotten his face slapped had he used it on a customer.

Annie said nothing. She *never* spoke to anyone on the street. Silence on the street. *We'll go, Alan; we're okay by ourselves. Don't cry, my baby.*

She stepped out of the doorway, trying to edge away. She heard a sharp, piercing whistle. The man in the cashmere topcoat had seen her; he was whistling and signaling up 51st Street to someone. As Annie hurried away, looking over her shoulder, she saw a dark blue Oldsmobile that had been double-parked pull forward. The cashmere topcoat was shoving through the pedestrians, coming for her like the number 5 uptown Lexington express.

Annie moved quickly, without thinking about it. Being poked in the back, and someone speaking directly to her . . . that was frightening: it meant coming out to respond to another human being. But moving down her streets, moving quickly, and being part of the flow, that was comfortable. She knew how to do that. It was just the way she was.

Instinctively, Annie made herself larger, more expansive, her raggedy arms away from her body, the dirty overcoats billowing, her gait more erratic: opening the way for her flight. Fastidious shoppers and suited businessmen shied away, gave a start as the dirty old black bag lady bore down on them, turned sidewise praying she would not brush a recently Martinized shoulder. The Red Sea parted miraculously permitting flight, then closed over instantly to impede navy blue cashmere. But the Olds came on quickly.

Annie turned left onto Madison, heading downtown. There was construction around 48th. There were good alleys on 46th. She knew a basement entrance just three doors off Madison on 47th. But the Olds came on quickly.

Behind her, the light changed. The Olds tried to rush the intersection, but this was Madison. Crowds were already crossing. The Olds stopped, the driver's window rolled down and a face peered out. Eyes tracked Annie's progress.

Then it began to rain.

Like black mushrooms sprouting instantly from concrete, Totes blossomed on the sidewalk. The speed of the flowing river of pedestrians increased; and in an instant Annie was gone. Cashmere rounded the corner, looked at the Olds, a frantic arm motioned to the left, and the man pulled up his collar and elbowed his way through the crowd, rushing down Madison.

Low places in the sidewalk had already filled with water. His wing-tip cordovans were quickly soaked.

He saw her turn into the alley behind the novelty sales shop (*Nothing over $1.10!!!*); he *saw* her; turned right and ducked in fast; *saw* her, even through the rain and the crowd and half a block between them; *saw* it!

So where was she?

The alley was empty.

It was a short space, all brick, only deep enough for a big Dempsey Dumpster and a couple of dozen trash cans; the usual mounds of rubbish in the corners; no fire escape ladders low enough for an old bag lady to grab; no loading docks, no doorways that looked even remotely accessible, everything cemented over or faced with sheet steel; no basement entrances with concrete steps leading down; no manholes in the middle of the passage; no open windows or even broken windows at jumping height; no stacks of crates to hide behind.

The alley was empty.

*Saw* her come in here. *Knew* she had come in here, and couldn't get out. He'd been watching closely as he ran to the mouth of the alley. She was in here somewhere. Not too hard figuring out where. He took out the .38 Police Positive he liked to carry because he lived with the delusion that if he had to dump it, if it were used in the commission of a sort of kind of felony he couldn't get snowed on, and if it were traced, it would trace back to the cop in Teaneck, New Jersey from whom it had been lifted as he lay drunk in the back room of a Polish social club three years earlier.

He swore he would take his time with her, this filthy old porch monkey. His navy blue cashmere already smelled like soaked dog. And the rain was not about to let up; it now came sheeting down, traveling in a curtain through the alley.

He moved deeper into the darkness, kicking the piles of trash, making sure the refuse bins were full. She was in here somewhere. Not too hard figuring out where.

Warm. Annie felt warm. With the ruined baby doll under her chin, and her eyes closed, it was almost like the apartment at 101st and First Avenue, when the Human Resources lady came and tried to tell her strange things about Alan. Annie had not understood what the woman meant when she kept repeating *soft monkey, soft monkey*, a thing some scientist knew. It had made no sense to Annie, and she had continued rocking the baby.

Annie remained very still where she had hidden. Basking in the warmth. *It is nice, Alan? Are we toasty; yes, we are. Will we be very still and the lady from the City will go away? Yes, we will.* She heard the crash of a garbage can being kicked over. *No one will find us. Shh, my baby.*

There was a pile of wooden slats that had been leaned against a wall. As he approached, the gun leveled, he realized they obscured a doorway. She was back in there, he knew it. Had to be. Not too hard figuring that out. It was the only place she could have hidden.

He moved in quickly, slammed the boards aside, and threw down on the dark opening. It was empty. Steel-plate door, locked.

Rain ran down his face, plastering his hair to his forehead. He could smell his coat, and his shoes, oh god, don't ask. He turned and looked. All that remained was the huge dumpster.

He approached it carefully, and noticed: the lid was still dry near the back side closest to the wall. The lid had been open just a short time ago. Someone had just lowered it.

He pocketed the gun, dragged two crates from the heap thrown down beside the Dempsey, and crawled up onto them. Now he stood above the dumpster, balancing on the crates with his knees at the level of the lid. With both hands bracing him, he leaned over to get his fingertips under the heavy lid. He flung the lid open, yanked out the gun, and leaned over. The dumpster was nearly full. Rain had turned the muck and garbage into a swimming porridge. He leaned over precariously to see what floated there in the murk. He leaned in to see. *Fuckin' porch monk—*

As a pair of redolent, dripping arms came up out of the muck, grasped his navy blue cashmere lapels, and dragged him headfirst into the metal bin. He went down, into the slime, the gun going off, the shot spanging off the raised metal lid. The coat filled with garbage and water.

Annie felt him struggling beneath her. She held him down, her feet on his neck and back, pressing him face-first deeper into the goo that filled the bin. She could hear him breathing garbage and fetid water. He thrashed, a big man, struggling to get out from under. She slipped, and braced herself against the side of the dumpster, regained her footing, and drove him deeper. A hand clawed out of the refuse, dripping lettuce and black slime. The hand was empty. The gun lay at the bottom of the bin. The thrashing intensified, his feet hitting the metal side of the container. Annie rose up and dropped her feet heavily on the back of his neck. He went flat beneath her, trying to swim up, unable to find purchase.

He grabbed her foot as an explosion of breath from down below forced a bubble of air to break on the surface. Annie stomped as hard as she could. Something snapped beneath her shoe, but she heard nothing.

It went on for a long time, for a time longer than Annie could think about. The rain filled the bin to overflowing. Movement under her feet lessened, then there was hysterical movement for an instant, then it was calm. She stood there for an even longer time, trembling and trying to remember other, warmer times.

Finally, she closed herself off, buttoned up tightly, climbed out dripping and went away from there, thinking of Alan, thinking of a time after this was done. After that long time standing there, no movement, no movement at all in the bog beneath her waist. She did not close the lid.

When she emerged from the alley, after hiding in the shadows and watching, the Oldsmobile was nowhere in sight. The foot traffic parted for her. The smell, the dripping filth, the frightened face, the ruined thing she held close to her.

She stumbled out onto the sidewalk, lost for a moment, then turned the right way and shuffled off.

The rain continued its march across the city.

No one tried to stop her as she gathered together her goods on 51st Street. The police thought she was a scavenger, the gawkers tried to avoid being brushed by her, the owner of the document copying center was relieved to see the filth cleaned up. Annie rescued everything she could, and hobbled away, hoping to be able to sell her aluminum for a place to dry out. It was not true that she was dirty; she had always been fastidious, even in the streets. A certain level of dishevelment was acceptable, but this was unclean.

And the blasted baby doll needed to be dried and brushed clean. There was a woman on East 60th, near Second Avenue; a vegetarian who spoke with an accent; a white lady who sometimes let Annie sleep in the basement. She would ask her for a favor.

It was not a very big favor, but the white woman was not home; and that night Annie slept in the construction of the new Zeckendorf Towers, where S. Klein-On-The-Square used to be, down on 14th and Broadway.

The men from the stretch limo didn't find her again for almost a week.

\*      \*      \*

She was salvaging newspapers from a wire basket on Madison near 44th when he grabbed her from behind. It was the one who had poured the liquor into Beaddie, and then made him drink the Drano. He threw an arm around her, pulled her around to face him, and she reacted instantly, the way she did when the kids tried to take her snap-purse.

She butted him full in the face with the top of her head, and drove him backward with both filthy hands. He stumbled into the street, and a cab swerved at the last instant to avoid running him down. He stood in the street, shaking his head, as Annie careened down 44th, looking for a place to hide. She was sorry she had left her cart again. This time, she knew, her goods weren't going to be there.

It was the day before Thanksgiving.

Four more black women had been found dead in midtown doorways.

Annie ran, the only way she knew how, into stores that had exits on other streets. Somewhere behind her, though she could not figure it out properly, there was trouble coming for her and the baby. It was so cold in the apartment. It was always so cold. The landlord cut off the heat, he always did it in early November, till the snow came. And she sat with the child, rocking him, trying to comfort him, trying to keep him warm. And when they came from Human Resources, from the City, to evict her, they found her still holding the child. When they took it away from her, so still and blue, Annie ran from them, into the streets; and she ran, she knew how to run, to keep running so she could live out here where they couldn't reach her and Alan. But she knew there was trouble behind her.

Now she came to an open place. She knew this. It was a new building they had put up, a new skyscraper, where there used to be shops that had good throwaway things in the cans and sometimes on the loading docks. It said Citicorp Mall and she ran inside. It was the day before Thanksgiving and there were many decorations. Annie rushed through into the central atrium, and looked around. There were escalators, and she dashed for one, climbing to a second storey, and then a third. She kept moving. They would arrest her or throw her out if she slowed down.

At the railing, looking over, she saw the man in the court below. He didn't see her. He was standing, looking around.

Stories of mothers who lift wrecked cars off their children are legion.

When the police arrived, eyewitnesses swore it had been a stout, old black woman who had lifted the heavy potted tree in its terracotta urn, who had manhandled it up onto the railing and slid it along till she was standing above the poor dead man, and who had dropped it three storeys to crush his skull. They swore it was true, but beyond a vague description of old, and black, and dissolute looking, they could not be of assistance. Annie was gone.

\*       \*       \*

On the front page of the *Post* she wore as lining in her right shoe, was a photo of four men who had been arraigned for the senseless murders of more than a dozen bag ladies over a period of several months. Annie did not read the article.

It was close to Christmas, and the weather had turned bitter, too bitter to believe. She lay propped in the doorway alcove of the Post Office on 43rd and Lexington. Her rug was drawn around her, the stocking cap pulled down to the bridge of her nose, the goods in the string bags around and under her. Snow was just beginning to come down.

A man in a Burberry and an elegant woman in a mink approached from 42nd Street, on their way to dinner. They were staying at the New York Helmsley. They were from Connecticut, in for three days to catch the shows and to celebrate their eleventh wedding anniversary.

As they came abreast of her, the man stopped and stared down into the doorway. "Oh, Christ, that's awful," he said to his wife. "On a night like this, Christ, that's just awful."

"Dennis, *please!*" the woman said.

"I can't just pass her by," he said. He pulled off a kid glove and reached into his pocket for his money clip.

"Dennis, they don't like to be bothered," the woman said, trying to pull him away. "They're very self-sufficient. Don't you remember that piece in the *Times?*"

"It's damned near Christmas, Lori," he said, taking a twenty dollar bill from the folded sheaf held by its clip. "It'll get her a bed for the night, at least. They can't make it out here by themselves. God knows, it's little enough to do." He pulled free of his wife's grasp and walked to the alcove.

He looked down at the woman swathed in the rug, and he could not see her face. Small puffs of breath were all that told him she was alive. "Ma'am," he said, leaning forward. "Ma'am, please take this." He held out the twenty.

Annie did not move. She never spoke on the street.

"Ma'am, please, let me do this. Go somewhere warm for the night, won't you . . . please?"

He stood for another minute, seeking to rouse her, at least for a *go away* that would free him, but the old woman did not move. Finally, he placed the twenty on what he presumed to be her lap, there in that shapeless mass, and allowed himself to be dragged away by his wife.

Three hours later, having completed a lovely dinner, and having decided it would be romantic to walk back to the Helmsley through the six inches of snow that had fallen, they passed the Post Office and saw the old woman had not moved. Nor had she taken the twenty dollars.

He could not bring himself to look beneath the wrappings to see if she had frozen to death, and he had no intention of taking back the money. They walked on.

In her warm place, Annie held Alan close up under her chin, stroking him and feeling his tiny black fingers warm at her throat and cheeks. *It's all right, baby, it's all right. We're safe. Shhh, my baby. No one can hurt you.*

# MICHAEL SHEA

## Fat Face

Michael Shea was born in Los Angeles in 1946, and after graduating from the University of California, moved to the San Francisco Bay Area where he has held a variety of jobs, including instructor of languages, construction laborer, and night clerk in a Mission District flophouse. His second novel *Nifft the Lean* won the World Fantasy Award in 1983. His most recent book is *Polyphemus*, a collection of his short stories published by Arkham House. Forthcoming are two novels, *Momma Durtt* and *The Plunderers*.

"Fat Face" is a story of the Cthulhu mythos, and, like the body of Shea's work, takes a harshly realistic view of life. This tale is not for the faint of heart.

—E.D.

# FAT FACE

## Michael Shea

"They were infamous, nightmare sculptures, even when telling of age-old, by-gone things; for Shoggoths and their work ought not to be seen by human beings, nor portrayed by any beings . . ."

—*At the Mountain of Madness*
by Howard Phillips Lovecraft

When Patti started working from the lobby of the Parnassus Motel again, it was clear she was liked from the way the other girls teased her, and unobtrusively took it easy on her for the first few weeks, while she got to feel steadier. She was deeply relieved to be back.

She had been doing four nights a week at The Encounter, a massage parlor. Her man was part owner, and he insisted that this schedule was to her advantage, because it was "strictly a hand-job operation," and the physical demands on her were lighter than with street work. Patti would certainly have agreed that the work was lighter—if it hadn't been for the robberies and killings. The last of these had been the cause of her breakdown, and though she never admitted this to her man, he had no doubt sensed the truth, for he had let her go back to the Parnassus, and told her she could pay him half rate for the next few weeks, till she was feeling steady again.

In her first weeks at the massage parlor, she had known with all but certainty of two clients—not hers—who had taken one-way drives from The Encounter up into the Hollywood Hills. These incidents wore, still, a thin, merciful veil of doubt. It was the third one which passed too nearly for her to face away from it.

From the moment of his coming in, unwillingly she felt spring up in her the conviction that the customer was a perfect victim; physically soft, small, fatly walleted, more than half drunk, out-of-state. She learned his name when her man studied his wallet thoroughly on the pretext of checking his credit cards, and the man's permitting of this liberty revealed how fuddled he was. She walked ahead swinging her bottom, and he stumbled after, down the hall to a massage room, and she could almost feel in her own head the ugly calculations clicking in her man's.

The massage room was tiny. It had a not-infrequently-puked-on carpet, and a table. As she stood there, pounding firmly on him under the towel, trying to concentrate on her rhythm, exclusively, a gross, black cockroach ran boldly across the carpet. Afterwards, she was willing to believe she had hallucinated, so strange was the thing she remembered. The bug, half as big as her hand, had stopped at mid-floor and *stared* at her, and she in that instant had seen clearly and looked deep into the inhuman little black-bead eyes, and known that the man she was just then firing off into the towel was going to die later that night. There would be a grim, half-slurred conversation in some gully under the stars, there would be perhaps a long signing of travelers cheques payable to the fictitious name on a certain set of false I.D. cards, and then the top of the plump man's head would be blown off.

Patti was a lazy girl who lazily wanted things to be nice, but was very good at adjusting to things that were not nice at all, if somebody strong really insisted on them. This, however, struck her with a terror that made her legs feel rubbery under her. Her man met her in the hall and sent her home before the mark had finished dressing inside. The body was found in three days and given scarcely two paragraphs in the paper. Patti was already half sick with alcohol and insomnia by the time she read them, and that night she took some pills which she was lucky enough to have pumped out of her an hour or so later.

But if her life-patterns offered any one best antidote for her cold, crippling fear, it was working out of the Parnassus. Some of her sweet-bitter apprentice years had been spent here or near it, and the lobby's fat, shabby, red furniture still showed a girl to advantage, to the busy streets beyond the plate-glass windows.

The big, dowdy hotel stood in the porno heartland of Hollywood. It was a district of neon, and snarled traffic on narrow, overparked streets engineered back in the thirties. It offered a girl a host of strolling and lounging places good for pick-ups, and in fact most of the girls who spent time at the Parnassus spent as much or more of each night at other places too.

But Patti liked to work with minimum cruising. Too much walking put her in mind of the more painful recollections from her amateur years—the alley beatings, the cheats who humped and dumped and drove off fast, the quick, sticky douches with a shook-up soda taken between trash bins in back of a market . . . All the deskmen at the Parnassus were fairly unextortionate. They levied an income-related tax, demanded only that a reasonable protocol govern use of the lobby, and made a small number of rooms available for the hookers' use. Patti worked the nearest bus stops from time to time, or went to the Dunk-O-Rama to sit over coffee and borrow many napkins and much sugar from single, male customers, but primarily she worked the Parnassus, catching the eyes of the drivers who slowed to turn at the intersection, and strolling out when she noticed one starting to circle and trying to catch her eye. She usually took her tricks to the Bridgeport, or the Azteca Arms, which were more specifically devoted to this phase of the trade than the Parnassus was.

This virtual exemption of her home base from the ultimate sexual trafficking suited Patti to the ground. It aided a certain sunny sentimentalism with which she was apt to regard the "little community" that she and her colleagues were, after all, long-term members of. Because of these views, and also, perhaps, because she came from a rural hamlet, her friends called her Hometown.

And though they could always get her to laugh at her own notions, it still comforted her—for instance—to greet the man at the drug store with cordial remarks on the traffic or the smog. The man, bald and thin moustached, never did more than grin at her with timid greed and scorn. The douches, deodorizers and fragrances she bought from him so steadily had prejudiced him, and guaranteed his misreading of her folksy genialities.

Or she would josh the various pimply employees at the Dunk-O-Rama in a similar spirit, saying things like "They sure got you working, don't they?" or, of the tax, "The old Governor's got to have his bite, don't he?" When asked how she wanted her coffee, she always answered with neighborly amplitude: "Well, let's see—I guess I'm in the mood for cream today." These things, coming from a vamp-eyed brunette in her twenties, wearing a halter top, short-shorts and Grecian sandals, disposed the adolescent counterhops more to sullen leers than to answering warmth. Yet she remained persistent in her fantasies. She even greeted Arnold, the smudged, moronic vendor at the corner newsstand, by name—this in spite of an all-too-lively and gurgling responsiveness on his part.

Now, in her recuperation, Patti took an added comfort from this vein of sentiment. This gave her sisterhood much to rally her about in their generally affectionate recognition that she was much shaken and needed some feedback and some steadying.

A particular source of hilarity for them was Patti's revival of interest in Fat Face, whom she always insisted was their friendliest "neighbor" in their "local community."

An old ten-story office building stood on the corner across the street from the Parnassus. As is not uncommon in L.A., the simple, box-shaped structure bore ornate cement frieze work on its facade, and all along the pseudo-architraves capping the pseudo-pillars of the building's sides. Such friezes always have exotic clichés as their theme—they are an echo of DeMille's Hollywood. The one across from the Parnassus had a Mesopotamian theme—ziggurat-shaped finials crowning the pseudo-pillars, and murals of wrenched profiles, curly-bearded figures with bulging calves.

A different observer from Patti would have judged the building *schlock*, but effective for all that, striking the viewer with a subtle sense of alien portent. Patti seldom looked higher than its fourth floor, where the usually open window of Fat Face's office was.

His appeared to be the only lively businesses maintained in that building. He ran two, and their mere combination could still set people cackling in the lobby of the Parnassus; a hydrotherapy clinic, and a pet refuge.

The building's dusty directory listed other offices. But the only people seen entering were unmistakably Fat Face's—all halting or ungainly, most toiling along on some shiny prosthetic or other.

Fat Face himself was often at his window—a dear, ruddy, bald countenance beaming, as often as not, avuncularly down on the hookers in the lobby across the street. His bubble baldness was the object of much lewd humor among the girls and the pimps. Fat Face was much waved-at in sarcasm, whereat he always smiled a crinkly smile that seemed to understand and not to mind. Patti, when she sometimes waved, did so with pretty sincerity.

But she had to laugh at him too. He seemed destined to be comic. His patients were generally a waddling pachydermous lot, shabbily and baggily dressed. They often compounded the impact of their grotesqueness by arriving in number for what must have been group sessions. And, as if more were needed, they often arrived with stray dogs and cats in tow. That the animals were not their own was made ludicrously plain by the beasts' struggles with leash or carrying cage. The doctor obviously recruited his patients to the support of his stray clinic, exploiting their dependency with a charitable unscrupulousness. For it seemed that the clinic had to be an altruistic work. It supported several collection vans, and leafleted widely— even bought cheap radio spots. The bulletins implored telephone notification of strays wherever observed. Patti had fondly pocketed one of the leaflets:

> *Help us Help!*
> *Let our aid reach these*
> *unfortunate creatures.*
> *Nourished, spayed, medicated,*
> *they may have a better*
> *chance for health and life!*

This generosity of feeling in Fat Face did not prevent his being talked of over in the lobby of the Parnassus, where great goiter-rubbing, water-splashing orgies were raucously hypothesized, with Fat Face flourishing whips and baby oil, while cries of "rub my blubber!" filled the air. At such times Patti was impelled to leave the lobby, because it felt like betrayal to be laughing so hard at the goodly man.

Indeed, in her convalescent mellowness, much augmented by Valium, she had started to fantasize going up to his office, pulling the blinds, and ravishing him at his desk. She imagined him lonely and horny. Perhaps he had nursed his wife through a long illness and she had at last expired gently . . . He would be so grateful!

This fancy took on such a quality of yearning that it alarmed Patti. Although she was a good and well-adapted hooker, she was, outside her trade's rituals of exchange, very shy in her dealing with people. She was not forward in these emotional matters, and she felt her longing to *be* forward as an impulse in some way alien to her, put upon her. Nonetheless, the sweet promptings retained a fascination, and she was kept swinging between these poles of feelings, to the point where she felt she had to talk about them. Late one afternoon she dragged Sheri, her best friend, out of the lobby and into a bar a couple of blocks away. Sheri would keep confidence, but on first hearing the matter, she was as facetious as Patti had forseen.

"Jesus, Patti," she said. "If the rest of him's as fat as his face it'd be like humping a hill!"

"So you pile only superstars? I mean, so what if he's fat? Try and think how *nice* it would be for him!"

"I bet he'd blush till his whole head looked like an eggplant. Then, if there was just a slit in the top, like Melanie was saying—" Sheri had to break off and hold herself as she laughed. She had already done some drinking earlier in the afternoon. Patti called for another double and exerted herself to catch up, and meanwhile she harped on her theme to Sheri and tried to get her serious attention:

"I mean I've been working out of the Parnassus—what? Maybe three years now? No, four! Four years. I'm part of these peoples' community—the druggist, Arnold, Fat Face—and yet we never do anything to show it. There's no getting together. We're just faces. I mean like Fat Face—I couldn't even *call* him that!"

"So let's go look in the directory of his building!"

Patti was about to answer when, behind the bar, she saw a big roach scamper across a rubber mat and disappear under the baseboard. She remembered the plump body in the towel, and remembered—as a thing actually seen—the slug-fragmented skull.

Sheri quickly noted the chill in her friend. She ordered more drinks and set to work on the idea of a jolly expedition, that very hour, over to Fat Face's office. And when Patti's stomach had thawed out again, she took up the project with grateful humor, and eagerly joined her friend's hilarity, trading bawdy suppositions of the outcome.

They lingered over yet a further round of drinks and at length barged, laughing, out into the late-afternoon streets. The gold-drenched sidewalks swarmed, the pavements were jammed with rumbling motors. Jaunty and loud, the girls sauntered back to their intersection, and crossed over to the old building. Its heavy oak-and-glass doors were pneumatically stiff, and cost them a stagger to force open. But when they swung shut, it was swiftly, with a deep click, and they sealed out the street sound with amazing, abrupt completeness. The glass was dirty and it put a sulphurous glaze on the already surreal copper of the declining sun's light outside. Suddenly it might be Mars or Jupiter out beyond those doors, and they themselves stood within a great dim stillness that might have matched the feeling of a real Meso-potamian ruin, out on some starlit desert. The images were alien to Patti's thought—startling intrusions in a mental voice not precisely her own. Sheri gave a comic shiver but otherwise made no acknowledgment of similar feelings. She merrily cursed the old elevators with a hand-written out-of-order sign affixed to their switchplate by yellowed Scotch tape, and then gigglingly led the way up the green-carpeted stairs, up which a rubber corridor mat ran that gave Patti murky imaginings of scuffed, supple, reptilian skin. She struggled up the stairs after her skylarking friend, gaping with amazement at the spirit of gaity which had so utterly deserted her own thoughts at the instant of those doors' closing.

At the first two landings they peeked down the halls at similar vistas: green-carpeted corridors of frosted-glass doors with rich brass knobs. Bulbs burned miserly few, and in those corridors Patti sensed, with piercing vividness, the feeling of *kept* silence. It was not a void silence, but a full one, made by presences not stirring.

Patti's dread was so fierce and gratuitous, she wondered if it was a freak of pills and booze. She desperately wanted to stop her friend and retreat with her, but she couldn't find the breath or the words to broach her crazy panic. Sheri leapt triumphantly onto the fourth-floor landing and bowed Patti into the corridor.

Every door they passed bore the clinic's rubric and referred the passer to the room at the end of the hall, and every step Patti took toward that door sharpened the kick of panic in her stomach. They'd gotten scarcely half-way down the hallway when she reached her limit, and knew that no imaginable compulsion could make her go nearer to that room. Sheri tugged at her, and rallied her, but finally abandoned her and tiptoed hilariously up to the door, trying to do a parody of Patti's sudden fear.

She didn't knock, to Patti's relief. She took out her notepad, and mirthfully scrawled a moderately long message. She folded the note, tucked it under the door, and ran back to Patti.

When they reached the last flight of stairs, Patti dared speech. She scolded Sheri about the note.

"Did you think I was trying to steal him?" Sheri taunted, "giving him my address?" She alluded to a time, at a crowded party, when Patti had given Sheri a note to pass to a potential john, and Sheri had tampered with it and brought the trick to her own apartment. Patti was shocked at the possibility of such a trick, before discarding the idea as exceeding even Sheri's quirkishness.

"Did you hear any music up there?" Patti asked as they stepped out on the street. Coming into the noise outside was a blessed relief—breaking out into the air and the color, as if surfacing from the long, crushing stillness of a deep drowning. But even in this sweet rush she could call up clearly a weird, piping tune—scarcely a tune really, more an eerie melodic ramble—which had come into her mind as they hurried down the slick, rubbered flight of stairs. What bothered her as much as the strange feeling of the music was the way in which she had received it. It seemed to her that she had not *heard* it, but rather *remembered* it—suddenly and vividly—though she hadn't the trace of an idea now where she might have heard it before. Sheri's answer confirmed her thought:

"Music? Baby, there wasn't a sound up there! Wasn't it kind of spooky?" Her mood stayed giddy and Patti gladly fell in with it. They went to another bar they liked and drank for an hour or so—slowly, keeping a gloss on things, feeling humorous and excited like schoolgirls on a trip together. At length they decided to go to the Parnassus, find somebody with a car and scare up a cruising party.

As they crossed to the hotel Sheri surprised Patti by throwing a look at the old office building and giving a shrug that may have been half shudder. "Jesus. It was like being under the ocean or something in there, wasn't it, Patti?"

This echo of her own dread made Patti look again at her friend. Then Arnold, the vendor, stepped out from the newsstand and blocked their way.

The uncharacteristic aggressiveness gave Patti a nasty twinge. Arnold was unlovely. There was a babyish fatness and redness about every part of him. His scanty red hair alternately suggested infancy or feeble age, and his one eyeless socket, with its weepy red folds of baggy lid, made his whole face look as if screwed to cry. Over all his red, ambling softness there was a bright blackish glaze of inveterate filth. And, moronic though his manner was most of the time, Patti now felt a cunning about him, something sly and corrupt. The cretinous, wet-mouthed face he now thrust close to the girls seemed, somehow, to be that of a grease-painted con man, not an imbecile. As if it were a sour fog that surrounded the newsman, fear entered Patti's nostrils, and dampened the skin of her arms. Arnold raised his hand. Pinched between his smudgy thumb and knuckle were an envelope and a fifty-dollar bill.

"A man said to read this, Patti!" Arnold's childish intonation now struck Patti as an affectation, like his dirtiness, part of a chosen disguise.

"He said the money was to pay you to read it. It's a trick! He gave me twenty dollars!" Arnold giggled. The sense of cold-blooded deception in the man made Patti's voice shake when she questioned him about the man who'd given him the commission. He remembered nothing, an arm and a voice in a dark car that pulled up and sped off.

"Well, how is she supposed to read it?" Sheri prodded. "Should she be by a window? Should she wear anything special?"

But Arnold had no more to tell them, and Patti willingly gave up on him to escape the revulsion he so unexpectedly roused in her.

They went into the lobby with the letter, but such was its strangeness— so engrossingly lurid were the fleeting images that came clear for them— that they ended taking it back to the bar, getting a booth, and working over it with the aid of whisky and lively surroundings.

The document was in the form of an unsigned letter, which covered two pages in a lucid, cursive script of bizarre elegance, and which ran thus:

*Dear Girls*

*How does a Shoggoth Lord go wooing? You do not even guess enough to ask! Then let it be asked and answered for you. As it is written: "The Shoggoth Lord stumbleth unto his belusted, lo, he cometh heavily unto her, upon alien feet. From the sunless sea, from under the mountains of ice, cometh the mighty Shoggoth Lord unto her." Dear, dear girls! Where is this place the Shoggothoi come from? In your tender, sensual ignorance you might well lack the power to be astonished by the prodigious gulfs of Space and Time this question probes. But let it once more be asked and answered for you. Thus has the answer been written:*

*"Shun the gulf beneath the peaks, The caverned ocean black as night, Where star-spawned gods made their retreat From the slowly freezing world of light.*

*"For even star-spawn may grow weak, While what has been its slave gains strength; Even star-spawn's will may break, While slaves feed on their lords at length."*

*Sweet harlots! Darling, heedless trollops! You cannot imagine the Shoggoth Lord's mastery of shapes! His race has bred smaller since modern man last met with it. Oh, but the Shoggoth lords are limber now! Supremest polomorphs — though what they are beneath all else, is Horror itself. But how is it they press their loving suit? What do they murmur to her they hotly crave? You must know that the Shoggoth craves her fat with panic — full of the psychic juices of despair. Therefore he taunts her with their ineluctable union; therefore he pipes and flutes to her his bold, seductive lyric, while he vows with a burning glare in his myriad eyes that she'll be his. Thus he sings:*

*"Your veil shall be the wash of blood That dims and drowns your dying eyes. You'll have for bridesmaids Pain and Dread,*

*For vows, you'll jabber blasphemies.*
*My scalding flesh will be your gown,*
*And Agony your bridal song.*
*You shall both be my bread*
*And, senses reeling, watch me fed.*

*"O maids, prepare her swiftly!*
*Speedily her loins unlace!*
*Her tender paps annoint,*
*And bare unto my seething face!"*

*Thus, dear girls, he ballads and rondelays his belusted, thus he waltzes her spirit through dark, empty halls of expectation, of always-harkening Horror, until the dance has reached that last, closed room of consummation!*

As many times as the girls flung these pages onto the table, they picked them up again after short hesitation. Both Sheri and Patti were very marginal readers, but the flashes of coherent imagery in the letter kept them coming back to the murky parts, trying to pick the lock of their meaning. They held menace even in their very calligraphy, whose baroque, barbed elegance seemed sardonic and alien. The mere sonority of some of the obscure passages evoked vivid images, a sense of murky submersion in benthic pressures of fearful expectation, while unseen giants abided in the dark nearby.

It put Patti in a goose-fleshy melancholy, but of real fear it raised little, even though it meant that some out-to-lunch hurt freak had quite possibly singled her and Sheri out. The letter held as much creepy entertainment for her as it did threat. The ones really into letter writing were much less likely to be real doers. Besides that, it was a very easy fifty dollars.

She was the more surprised, then, at Sheri's sudden, jagged confession of paranoia. She had been biting back panic for some time, it appeared, and Patti was sure that even as she spoke she was holding back more than she told. She was afraid to go home alone.

"All this bullshit," she pointed at the letter, "It's spooked me, Patti. I can't explain it. I've got the bleep scared out of me, girl. Come on, we can sleep in the same bed, just like slumber parties in school, Patti. I just don't want to face walking into my living room tonight and turning on the light."

"Sure you can sleep over! But no kicking, right?"

"Oh that was only because I had that dream!" Sheri shrilled. She was so happy and relieved it was pitiful, and Patti found herself developing an answering chill that made her glad of the company.

They got some sloe gin and some vodka and some bags of ice and bottles of Seven-Up. They got several bags of chips and puffs and cookies and candybars, and repaired with their purchases to Patti's place.

She had a small cottage in a four-cottage court, with very old people living in the other three units. The girls shoved the bed into the corner so they could prop pillows against all the walls to lean back on. They turned on the radio, and the TV, and got out the phone book, and started making joke calls to people with funny names while eating, drinking, smoking, watching, listening and bantering with each other.

Their consciousness outlasted their provisions, but not by long. Soon, back to back, they slept; bathed and laved by the gently burbling soundwash, and the ash-grey light of pulsing images.

They woke to a day that was sunny, windy and smogless. They rose at high, glorious noon, and walked to a coffee shop for breakfast. The breeze was combing buttery light into the waxen fronds of the palms, while the Hollywood Hills seemed most opulently brocaded—under the sky's flawless blue—with the silver-green of sagebrush and sumach.

As they ravened breakfast, they plotted borrowing a car and taking a drive. Then Sheri's man walked in. She waved him over brightly but Patti was sure she was as disappointed as herself. Rudy took a chair long enough to inform Sheri how lucky she was he'd run into her, since he'd been trying to find her. He had something important for her that afternoon. Contemptuously he snatched up the bill and paid for both girls. Sheri left in tow, and gave Patti a rueful wave from the door.

Patti's appetite left her. She dawdled over coffee, and stepped at last, unwillingly, out into the day's polychrome splendor. Its very clarity took on a sinister quality of remorselessness. Behold, the whole world and all its children moved under the glaring sun's brutal, endless revelation. Nothing could hide. Not in this world . . . though of course there were other worlds, where beings lie hidden immemorially . . .

She shivered as if something had crawled across her. The thoughts had passed through her, but were not hers. She sat on a bus stop bench and tightly crossed her arms as if to get a literal hold on herself. The strange thoughts, by their feeling, she knew instinctively to be echoes raised somehow by what they had read last night. Away with them, then! The creep had had more than his money's worth of reading from her already, and now she would forget those unclean pages. As for her depression, it was a freakish sadness caused by the spoiling of her holiday with Sheri, and it was silly to give in to it.

Thus she rallied herself, and got to her feet. She walked a few blocks without aim, somewhat stiff and resolute. At length the sunlight and her natural health of body had healed her mood, and she fell into a pleasant, veering ramble down miles of Hollywood residential streets, relishing the cheap cuteness of the houses, and the lushness of their long-planted trees and gardens.

Almost she left the entire city. A happy, rushing sense of her freedom grew upon her and she suddenly pointed out to herself that she had nearly four hundred dollars in her purse. She came within an ace of swaggering into a Greyhound station with two quickly packed suitcases, and buying a ticket either to San Diego or Santa Barbara, whichever had the earliest departure time. With brave suddenness to simplify her life and remove it, at a stroke, from the evil that had seemed to haunt it recently . . .

It was her laziness that, in the end, made her veer away from the decision—her dislike of its necessary but inherently tedious details; the bus ride, looking for an apartment, looking for a job. As an alternative to such dull preliminaries, the endless interest and familiarity of Hollywood took on renewed allure.

She would stay then. The knowledge didn't dull her sense of freedom. Her feet felt confident, at home upon these shady, root-buckled sidewalks. She strode happily, looking on her life with new detachment and ease. Such paranoias she'd been having! They seemed now as fogs that her newly freshened spirit could scatter at a breath.

She had turned onto a still, green block that was venerably overhung by great old pepper trees, and she'd walked well into it before she realized that the freeway had cut it off at the far end. An arrow indicated a narrow egress to the right, however, so she kept walking. Several houses ahead, a very large man in overalls appeared, dragging a huge German shepherd across the lawn.

Patti saw a new, brown van parked by the curb, and recognized it and the man at once. The vehicle was one of two belonging to Fat Face's stray refuge, and the man was one of his two full-time collectors.

He had the struggling brute by the neck with a noosed stick. He stopped and looked at Patti with some intensity as she approached. The vine-drowned cottage whose lawn he stood on was dark, tight-shut, and seemed deserted—as did the entire block—and it struck Patti that the man might have spotted the dog by chance, and might now be thinking it hers. She smiled and shook her head as she came up.

"He's not mine! I don't even *live* around here!"

Something in the way her words echoed down the stillness of the street gave Patti a pang. She was sure they had made the collector's eyes narrow. He was tall, round and smooth, with a face of his employer's type, though not as jovial. He was severely club-footed and bloat-legged on the left, as well as being inordinately bellied, all things to which the coveralls lent a merciful vagueness. The green baseball cap he wore somehow completed the look of ill balance and slow wit that the man wore.

But as she got nearer, already wanting to turn and run the other way, she received a shocking impression of strength in the uncouth figure. The man had paused in a half turn and was partly crouched—not a position of firm leverage. The dog—whose paws and muzzle showed some Bernard—

weighed at least 170, and it resisted violently—yet scarcely stirred the heavy arms. Patti edged to one side of the walk, pretending a wariness of the dog which its helplessness made droll, and moved to pass. The collector's hand, as if absently, pressed down on the noose. The beast's head seemed to swell, its struggles grew more galvanic and constricted by extreme distress. And while thus smoothly he began throttling the beast, the collector cast a glance up and down the block, and stepped into Patti's path, effortlessly dragging the animal with him.

They stood face to face, very near. The ugly mathematics of peril swiftly clicked in her brain; the mass, the force, the time—all were sufficient. The next couple of moments could finish her. With a jerk he could kill the dog, drop it, seize her and thrust her into the van. Indeed, the dog was at the very point of death. The collector began to smile nastily and his breath came—foul and oddly cold—gusting against her face. Then something began to happen to his eyes. They were rolling up, like a man's when he's coming—but they didn't roll white—they were rolling up a jet black—two glossy obsidian globes eclipsing from below the watery blue ones. Her lungs began to gather air to scream. A taxicab swung onto the street.

The collector's grip eased on the half-unconscious dog. He stood blinking furiously, and it seemed he could not unwind his bulky body from the menacing tension it had taken on. He stood, still frozen on the very threshold of assault, and the cold foulness still gusted from him with the labor of his breathing. In another instant Patti's reflexes fired and she was released with a leap from the curb out into the street, but there was time enough before for her to have the thought she *knew* that stench the blinking gargoyle breathed.

And then she was in the cab. The driver sullenly informed her then of her luck in catching him on his special shortcut to a freeway on-ramp. She looked at him as if he'd spoken in a foreign tongue. More gently he asked her destination, and without thought she answered, "The Greyhound station."

Flight. With sweet, simple motion to cancel Hollywood, and its walking ghosts of murder, and its lurking plunderers of the body, and its nasty, nameless scribblers of letters whose pleasure it was to defile the mind with nightmares. But of course, she must pack. She re-routed the driver to her apartment.

This involved a doubling back which took them across the street of her encounter. The van was still parked by the curb, but neither collector nor dog were in sight. Oddly, the van seemed to be moving slightly, rocking as if with interior movement of fitful vigor. Her look was brief, from a half block distance, but in the shady stillness the subtle tremoring made a vivid impression.

Then she bethought herself of Fat Face. She could report the collector to him! That just and genial face instantly quelled all the horror attaching to the collector's uglier one. What, after all, had happened? A creepy, disabled type with some eye infection had been dangerously tempted to rape her, and she had lucked out. That last fact was grounds for celebration, while all that was strong and avuncular in the good doctor's expression promised that she would be vigorously protected from further danger at the same hands. She even smiled to imagine the interview; her pretty embarrassment, the intimate topic, her warmly expressed girlish gratitude. It could become the tender seduction of her fantasy.

So she rerouted the driver again—not without first giving him a ten dollar tip in advance—to the boulevard. There she walked a while, savoring the sunlight, and lunched opulently, and went to two different double bills, one right after the other.

But her mood could have been better. She kept remembering the collector. It was not his grotesqueness that nagged at her so much as a fugitive familiarity in the whole aura of him. His chill, malignant presence was like a gust out of some *place* obscurely known to her. What dream of her own, now lost to her, had shown her that world of dread and wonder and colossal age which now she caught—and knew—the scent of, in this man? The thought was easy to shake off as a freak of mood, but it was insistent in its return, like a fly that kept landing on her, and after the movies, feeling groggy and cold in the dusk, she called Sheri.

Her friend had just got home, exhausted from a multiple trick, and wearing a few bruises from a talk with Rudy afterwards.

"Why don't I come over, Sheri? Hey?"

"No, Patti. I'm wrung out, girl. You feel OK?"

"Sure. So get to sleep, then."

"Naw, hey now—you come over if you want to, Patti, I'm just gonna be dead to the world, is all."

"Whaddya mean? If you're tired you're tired and I'll catch you later. So long." She could hear, but not change the anger and disappointment in her own voice. It told her, when she'd hung up but remained staring at the phone, how close to the territory of Fear she stood. Full night had surrounded her glass booth. Against the fresh, purple dark, all the street's scribbly neon squirmed and swam, like sea-things of blue and rose and gold, bannering and twisting cryptically over the drowned pavements.

And, almost as though she expected a watery death, Patti could not, for a moment, step from the booth out onto those pavements. Their lethal, cold strangeness lay, if not undersea, then surely in an alien, poisonous atmosphere that would scorch her lungs. For a ridiculous moment, her body defied her will.

Then she set her sights on a bar half a block distant. She plunged from the booth and grimly made for that haven.

Some three hours later, no longer cold, Patti was walking to Sheri's. It was a weeknight and the stillness of the residential streets was not unpleasant. The tree-crowded streetlamps shed a light that was lovely with its whisky gloss. The street names on their little banners of blue metal had a comic flavor to her tongue and she called out each as it came into view.

Sheri, after all, had said to come over. The petty cruelty of waking her seemed, to Patti, under the genial excuse of the alcohol, merely prankish. So she sauntered through sleeping Hollywood, knowing the nightwalker's exhilaration of being awake in a dormant world.

Sheri lived in a stucco cottage that was a bit tackier than Patti's, though larger, each cottage possessing a little driveway and a garage in back. And though there was a light on in the living room, it was up the driveway that Patti went, deciding, with sudden impishness, to spook her friend. She crept around the rear corner, and stole up to the screened window of Sheri's bedroom, meaning to make noises through a crack if one had been left open.

The window was in fact fully raised, though a blind was drawn within. Even as Patti leaned close, she heard movement inside the darkened room. In the next instant a gust of breeze came up and pushed back the blind within.

Sheri *was* on her back in the bed and somebody was on top of her, so that all Patti could see of her was her arms and her face, which stared round-eyed at the ceiling as she was rocked again and again on the bed. Patti viewed that surging, grappling labor for two instants, no more, and retreated, almost staggering, in a primitive reflex of shame more deep-lying in her than any of the sophistications of her adult professional life.

Shame and a weird, childish glee. She hurried out to the sidewalk. Her head rang, and she felt giggly and frightened to a degree that managed to astonish her even through her liquor. What was with her? She'd been paid to watch far grosser things than a simple coupling. On the other hand, there had been a foul smell in the bedroom, and there had been a nagging hint of music too, she thought, a faint, unpleasant, twisty tune coming from somewhere indefinite . . .

Those vague feelings quickly yielded to the humorous side of the accident. She walked to the nearest main street and found a bar. In it, she killed half an hour with two further doubles and then, reckoning enough time had passed, walked back to Sheri's.

The living room light was still on. Patti rang the bell and heard it inside, a rattly probe of noise that raised no stir of response. All at once she felt a light rush of suspicion, like some long-legged insect scuttling daintily up her spine. She felt that, as once before in the last few days, the silence she was hearing concealed a presence, not an absence. But why should this make her begin, ever so slightly, to sweat? It could be Sheri playing possum. Trying by abruptness to throw off her fear she seized the knob. The door opened and she rushed in, calling:

"Ready or not, one, two, three."

Before she was fully in the room, her knees buckled under her, for a fiendish stench filled it. It was a carrion smell, a fierce, damp rankness which bit and pierced the nose. It was so palpable an assault it seemed to crawl all over her—to wriggle through her scalp and stain her flesh as if with brimstone and graveslime.

Clinging still to the doorknob she looked woozily about the room, whose sloppy normality, coming to her as it did through that surreal fetor, struck her almost eerily. Here was the litter of wrappers, magazines and dishes—thickest around the couch—so familiar to her. The TV, on low, was crowned with ashtrays and beer cans, while on the couch which it faced a freshly opened bag of Fritos lay.

But it was from the bedroom door, partly ajar, that the nearly visible miasma welled most thickly, as from its source. And it would be in the bedroom that Sheri would lie. She would be lying dead in its darkness. For, past experience and description though it was, the stench proclaimed that meaning grim and clear: death. Patti turned behind her to take a last clean breath, and stumbled towards the bedroom.

Every girl ran the risk of rough trade. It was an ugly and lonely way to die. With the dark, instinctive knowledge of their sisterhood, Patti knew that it was only laying out and covering up that her friend needed of her now. She shoved inward on the bedroom door, throwing a broken rhomb of light upon the bed.

It and the room were empty—empty save the near physical mass of the stench. It was upon the bed that the reek fumed and writhed most nastily. The blankets and sheets were drenched with some vile fluid, and pressed into sodden seams and folds. The coupling she had glimpsed and snickered at—what unspeakable species of intercourse had it been? And Sheri's face staring up from under the shadowed form's lascivious rocking—had there been more to read in her expression than the slack-faced shock of sex? Then Patti moaned:

"Oh, Jesus God!"

Sheri was in the room. She lay on the floor, mostly under the bed, only her head and shoulders protruding, her face to the ceiling. There was no misreading its now frozen look. It was a face wherein the recognition of Absolute Pain and Fear had dawned, even as death arrived. Dead she surely was. Living muscles did not achieve utter fixity. Tears jumped up in Patti's eyes. She staggered into the living room, fell on the couch and wept. "Oh, Jesus God," she said again; softly, now.

She went to the kitchenette and got a dish towel, tied it around her nose and mouth, and returned to the bedroom. Sheri would not, at least, lie half thrust from sight like a broken toy. Her much-used body would have a shred of that dignity which her life had never granted it. She bent, and hooked her hands under those dear, bare shoulders. She pulled and, with her pull's excess force, fell backwards to the floor; for that which she fell hugging to her breasts needed no such force to move its lightness. It was not Sheri, but a dreadful upper fragment of her, that Patti hugged: Sheri's head and shoulders, one of her arms . . . gone were her fat, funny feet they used to laugh at, for she ended now in a charred stump of ribbage. As a little girl might clutch some unspeakable doll, Patti lay embracing tightly that which made her scream, and scream again.

Valium. Compazene. Mellaril. Stellazine. Gorgeous, technicolored tabs and capsules. Bright-hued pillars holding up the Temple of Rest. Long afternoons of Tuinal and TV; night sweats and quiet, groggy mornings. Patti was in County for more than a week.

She had found all there was to be found of her friend. Dismemberment by acid is a new wrinkle, and Sheri got some press, but in a world of trashbag murders and mass graves uncovered in quiet back yards, even a death like Sheri's could hope for only so much coverage. Patti's bafflement made her call the detectives assigned to the case at least once a day. With gruff tact they heard through her futile rummagings among the things she knew of Sheri's life and background, but soon knew she was helpless to come up with anything material.

She desperately wanted a period of unsleeping rest, but always a vague dread marred her drug buoyed ease. For she could be waked, even from the glassiest daze, by a sudden sense that the number of people surrounding her was dwindling—that they were, everywhere, stealing off, or vanishing, and that the hospital, and even the city, was growing empty around her.

She put it down to the hospital itself—its constant shifts of bodies, its wheelings in and out on silent gurneys. She obtained a generous scrip for Valium and had herself discharged, hungry for the closer comfort of her friends. A helpful doctor was leaving the building as she did, and gave her a ride. With freakish embarrassment about her trade and her world, Patti had him drop her at a coffee shop some blocks from the Parnassus. When he had driven off, she started walking. The dusk was just fading. It was Saturday night, but it was also the middle of a three-day weekend (as she had learned with surprise from the doctor) and the traffic on both pavement and asphalt was remarkably light.

Somehow it had a small-town-on-Sunday feel, and alarm woke in her and struggled in its heavy Valium shackles, for this was as if the confirmation of her frightened hallucinations. Her fear mounted as she walked. She pictured the Parnassus with an empty lobby, and imagined that she saw the traffic beginning everywhere to turn off the street she walked on, so that in a few moments it could stretch deserted for a mile either way.

But then she saw the many lively figures through the beloved plate-glass windows. She half ran ahead, and as she waited with happy excitement for

the light, she saw Fat Face up in his window. He spotted her just when
she did him, and beamed and winked. Patti waved and smiled and heaved
a deep sigh of relief that nearly brought tears. This was true medicine, not
pills, but friendly faces in your home community! Warm feelings and simple
neighborliness! She ran forward at the "walk" signal.

There was a snag before she reached the lobby, for Arnold from his
wooden cave threw at her as she passed a leer of wet intensity that scared
her even as she recognized that some kind of frightened greeting was intended
by the grimace. There was such . . . *speculation* in his look. But then she
had pushed through the glass doors, and was in the warm ebullience of
shouts and hugs and jokes and droll nudges.

It was sweet to bathe in that bright, raucous communion. She had called
the desk man that she was coming out, and for a couple of hours various
friends whom the word had reached strolled in to greet her. She luxuriated
in her pitied celebrity, received little gifts and gave back emotional kisses
of thanks.

It ought to have lasted longer, but the night was an odd one. Not much
was happening in town, and everybody seemed to have action lined up in
Oxnard or Encino or some other bizarre place. A few stayed to work the
home grounds, but they caught a subdued air from the place's emptiness
at a still-young hour. Patti took a couple more Valiums and tried to seem
like she was peacefully resting in a lobby chair. To fight her stirrings of
unease, she took up the paperback that was among the gifts given her—
she hadn't even noticed by whom. It had a horrible face on the cover and
was entitled *At the Mountains of Madness*.

If she had not felt the need for some potent distraction, some weighty
ballast for her listing spirit, she would never have pieced out the ciceronian
rhythms of the narrative's style. But when, with frightened tenacity, she
had waded several pages into the tale, the riverine prose, suddenly limpid,
snatched her and bore her upon its flowing clarity. The Valium seemed to
perfect her uncanny concentration, and where her vocabulary failed her, she
made smooth leaps of inference and always landed square on the necessary
meaning.

And so for hours in the slowly emptying lobby that looked out upon the
slowly emptying intersection, she wound through the icy territories of the
impossible, and down into the gelid, nethermost cellars of all World and
Time, where stupendous aeons lay in pictured shards, and massive, sentient
forms still stirred, and fed, and mocked the light.

Strangely, she began to find underlinings about two-thirds of the way
through. All the marked passages involved references to *Shoggoths*. It was a
word whose mere sound made Patti's flesh stir. She reached the flyleaf and
inner covers for explanatory inscriptions, but found nothing.

When she laid the book down in the small hours, she sat amid a near-total desertion which she scarcely noticed. Something tugged powerfully at memory, something which memory dreaded to admit. She realized that in reading the tale, she had taken on an obscure, terrible weight. She felt as if impregnated by an injection of tainted knowledge whose grim fruit, an almost physical mass of cryptic threat, lay aripening in her now.

She took a third floor room in the Parnassus for the night, for the simplest effort, like calling a cab, lay under a pall of futility and sourceless menace. She lay back, and her exhausted mind plunged instantly through the rotten flooring of consciousness, straight down into the abyss of dreams.

She dreamed of a city like Hollywood, but the city's walls and pavements were half alive, and they could feel premonitions of something that was drawing near them. All the walls and streets of the city waited in a cold-sweat fear under a blackly overcast sky. She herself, she grasped, was the heart and mind of the city. She lay in its midst, and its vast, cold fear was hers. She lay and somehow she knew the things that were drawing near her giant body. She knew their provenance in huge, blind voids where stood walls older than the present face of Earth; she knew their long, cunning toil to reach her own cringing frontiers. Giant worms they were, or jellyfish, or merely giant clots of boiling substance. They entered her deserted streets, gliding convergingly. She lay like carrion that lives and knows the maggots assault on it. She lay in her central citadel, herself the morsel they sped towards, piping their lust from foul, corrosive jaws.

She woke late Sunday afternoon, drained and dead of heart. She sat in bed watching a big, green fly patiently hammer itself against the pane where the gold light flooded in. Endlessly it fought the impossible, battering with its frail, bejewelled head. With swift fury and pain, Patti jumped out of bed and snatched up her blouse. She ran to the window and with her linen bludgeon, killed the fly.

Across the street, in a window just one story higher than her own, sat Fat Face. She stood looking back for a moment, embarrassed by her little savagery, but warmed by the way the doctor's smile was filled with gentle understanding, as if he read the anguish the act was born of. She suddenly realized she was wearing only her bra.

His smile grew a shade merrier at her little jolt of awareness, and she knew he understood this too, that this was inadvertance, and not a hooker's come-on.

And so, with a swift excitement, she turned it into coquetry, and applied her blouse daintily to her breasts. She would make her fantasy real and by tenderness would heal the horror that had dogged her life. She pointed to herself with a smile, and then to Fat Face with inquiry. How he beamed then! Did she even see his eyes and lips water? He nodded energetically. With thumb and forefinger she signaled a short interval. As she left the window she noted the arrival, down the side walk, of a gaggle of hydro-therapy patients, several with leashed strays in tow.

This bothered her, and she washed more slowly than she had meant to. Their arrival not only potentially inconvenienced her interview—it also put her in mind of the collector, and the memory laid a chill on her sexual enthusiasm. She came down slowly to the lobby. It was empty. The streets lay in a Sunday desolation such as only rarely befell this part of the city. Suddenly, all she wanted was a party. To hell with kinky charities. And as she stood at the window, a car full of her friends pulled up to the curb, and waved her to join them.

Almost she went—but then noted that Sheri's sister was in the car. She shuddered at any so near a reminder, and waved them off with a smile. Then she stepped out onto the sidewalk. No. Those patients with their strays had made the building too creepy for her.

She turned towards her favorite bar. Arnold darted from his booth and made a grab for her arm.

She was edgy and quick, and jumped away. He seemed to fear leaving the booth's proximity, and came no nearer, but pleaded with her from where he stood:

"Please, Patti! Come here and listen."

Like a thunderbolt, the elusive memory of last night now struck Patti. "Shoggoth" was eerie, and that whole story familiar, because they were precisely what that letter had been all about! She was stunned that she could so utterly put from her mind that lurid document. It had spooked Sheri badly the night before she died. It had come from Arnold—and so had that book! That was the meaning of his look. The red, moronic face glared at her urgently.

"Please, Patti. I've had knowledge. Come here—"

He darted forward to catch her arm and she sprang back, again the quicker, with a yelp. Arnold, thus drawn from the screening of his booth, froze fearfully. Patti looked up, and thrilled to find Fat Face looking down—not in amity, but in wrath upon Arnold. The newsman gaped, and mumbled apologetically, as if to the sidewalk: "No. I said nothing. I only *hinted* . . ." Joyfully, Patti sprang across the street and in moments was flying up these stairs she had climbed once before with such reluctance.

The oppression she had first found in these muted corridors was not gone from them—the quality of dread in some manner belonged to them—but she outran it. She moved too quickly in her sunny fantasy to be overtaken by that heaviness. She ran down the fourth floor hall and, at the door where Sheri had knelt giggling and she had balked, she seized the knob and knocked simultaneously with pushing her way in, so impetuous was her rush towards benign sanity. There Fat Face sat at a big desk by the window she'd always known him through. He was even grosser-legged and more bloat-bellied than his patients. It gave her a funny shock that did not change her amorous designs.

He wore a commodious doctor's smock and slacks. His shoes were bulky, black and orthopedically braced. Such a body less enkindled by spirit might have repelled. His, surmounted by the kindly beacon of his smile, seemed only grandfatherly, afflicted—dear. From somewhere there came, echoing as in a large, enclosed space, a noise of agitated water and of animals—strangely conjoined. But Fat Face was speaking:

"My dear," he said, not yet rising, "you make an old, old fellow very, very happy!" His voice was a marvel which sent half lustful gooseflesh down her spine. It was an uncanny voice, reedy and wavering and shot with flute-like notes of silver purity, sinfully melodious. That voice knew seductions, quite possibly, that Patti had never dreamed of. She was speechless, and spread her arms in tender selfpreservation.

He leapt to his feet, and the surging pep with which his great bulk moved sent a new thrill down the lightning rod of her nerves. On pachy-dermous legs he leapt spry as a cat to a door behind his desk, and bowed her through. The noise of animals and churning water gusted fresher from the doorway. Perplexed, she entered.

The room contained only a huge bowl-shaped hydrotherapy tub. Its walls were blank cement, save one, which was a bank of shuttered windows through which the drenched clamor was pouring. She finally conquered disbelief and realized a fact she had been struggling with all along: those dozens of canine garglings and cat shrieks were sounds of agony and distress. Not hospital sounds. Torture chamber sounds. The door boomed shut with a strikingly ponderous sound followed by a sharp click. Fat Face, energet-ically unbuttoning his smock, said, "Go ahead and peek out, sweet, heedless trollop! Oh yes, oh yes, oh yes—soon we'll *all* dine on lovely flesh—men and women, not paltry vermin!"

Patti gaped at the lurid musicality of his speech, struggling to receive its meaning. The doctor was shucking his trousers. It appeared that he wore a complex rubber suit, heavily strapped and buckled, under his clothes. Dazed, Patti opened a shutter and looked out. She saw a huge indoor pool, as the sounds had suggested, but not of the same shape and brightly chlor-inated blue she expected. It was a huge, slime-black grotto that opened below her, bordered by rude, sea-bearded rocks of cyclopean size. The sooty, viscous broth of its waters boiled with bulging elephantine shapes . . .

From those shapes, when she had grasped them, she tore her eyes with desperate speed; long instants too late for her sanity. Nightmare ought not to be so simply *there* before her, so dizzyingly adjacent to Reality. That the shapes should be such seething plasms, such cunning, titan maggots as she had dreamed of, this was just half the horror. The other half was the human head that decorated each of those boiling multimorphs, a comic excrescence from the nightmare mass—this and the rain of panicked beasts that fell from cage work above the pool and became in their frenzies both the toys and the food of the pulpy abominations.

She turned slack-mouthed to Fat Face. He stood by the great empty tub working at the big system of buckles on his chest. "Do you understand, my dear? Please try! Your horror will improve your tang. *Your veil shall be the wash of blood that dims and drowns your dying eyes* . . . You see, we find it easier to hold most of the shape with suits like these. We could mimic the entire body, but far more effort and concentration would be required."

He gave a last pull and the row of buckles split crisply open. Ropy, purple gelatin gushed from his suit front into the tub. Patti ran to the door, which had no knob. As she tore her nails against it and screamed, she remembered the fly at the window, and heard Fat Face continue behind her:

"So, we just imitate the head, and we never dissolve it, not to risk resuming it faultily and waking suspicions. Please struggle!"

She looked back and saw huge palps, like dreadful comic phalluses spring from the tub of slime that now boiled with movement. She screamed.

"Oh, yes!" fluted the Fat Face that now bobbed on the purple simmer. Patti's arms smoked where the palps took them. She was plucked from the floor as lightly as a struggling roach might be. "Oh, yes, dear girl—*you'll have for bridesmaids Pain and Dread, for vows you'll jabber blasphemies* . . ." As he brought her to hang above the cauldron of his acid body, she saw his eyes roll jet black. He lowered her feet into himself. A last time before shock took her, Patti threw the feeble tool of her voice against the massive walls. She kicked as her feet sank into the scorching gelatin, kicked till her shoes dissolved, till her feet and ankles spread nebulae of liquefying flesh within the Shoggoth Lord's greedy substance. Then her kicking slowed, and she sank more deeply in . . .

# CHARLES DE LINT

## Uncle Dobbin's Parrot Fair

Charles de Lint is one of the leading writers in what is sometimes called the "Magic Realism" school of fantasy—fantasy tales set in the real world, rather than in an imaginary Nevernever Land. De Lint specializes in bringing ancient Celtic legendry (as well as Indian, Romany, and other traditions) into modern urban settings. His novels thus far are *Moonheart, Mulengro, Yarrow,* and *Jack the Giant-Killer: The Jack of Kinrowan,* as well as the imaginary-world fantasies *Riddle of the Wren* and *Harp of the Grey Rose.* He has published short fiction in *Liavek, Swords and Sorceresses,* and other anthologies and magazines, and has published a novella in the young adult "urban fantasy" anthology *Borderland.*

De Lint is also a prolific reviewer of horror and fantasy fiction, runs a small fantasy publishing operation called Triskell Press, has been a judge for the World Fantasy Awards, and is a professional Celtic folk musician. Born in the Netherlands, de Lint now makes his home in Ottawa, Ontario, with his wife, a fine artist.

"Uncle Dobbin's Parrot Fair" is a story typical of de Lint's best work, and shows one of the more interesting new directions the fantasy field has been heading in with its mix of contemporary pop culture and classic fairy tale elements.

—T.W.

# UNCLE DOBBIN'S PARROT FAIR

## Charles de Lint

### 1

She would see them in the twilight when the wind was right, roly-poly shapes propelled by ocean breezes, turning end-over-end along the beach or down the alley behind her house like errant beach balls granted a moment's freedom. Sometimes they would get caught up against a building or stuck on a curb and then spindly little arms and legs would unfold from their fat bodies until they could push themselves free and go rolling with the wind again. Like flotsam in a river, like tumbleweeds, only brightly colored in primary reds and yellows and blues.

They seemed very solid until the wind died down. Then she would watch them come apart like morning mist before the sun, the bright colors turning to ragged ribbons that tattered smoke-like until they were completely gone.

Those were special nights, the evenings that the Balloon Men came.

In the late sixties in Haight Ashbury, she talked about them once. Incense lay thick in the air—two cones of jasmine burning on a battered windowsill. There was an old iron bed in the room, up on the third floor of a house that no one lived in except for runaways and street people. The mattress had rust-colored stains on it. The incense covered the room's musty smell. She'd lived in a form of self-imposed poverty back then, but it was all a part of the Summer of Love.

"I know what you mean, man," Greg Langman told her. "I've seen them."

He was wearing a dirty white T-shirt with a simple peace symbol on it and scuffed plastic thongs. Sticking up from the waist of his bell-bottomed jeans at a forty-five degree angle was a descant recorder. His long blond hair was tied back with a rubber band. His features were thin—an ascetic-looking face, thin and drawn-out from too much time on the streets with too little to eat, or from too much dope.

"They're like . . . ." His hands moved as he spoke, trying to convey what he didn't feel words alone could say—a whole other language, she often thought, watching the long slender fingers weave through the air between them. ". . . they're just too much."

"You've really seen them?" she asked.

"Oh, yeah. Except not on the streets. They're floating high up in the air, y'know, like fat little kites."

It was such a relief to know that they were real.

" 'Course," Greg added, "I gotta do a lot of dope to clue in on 'em, man."

Ellen Brady laid her book aside. Leaning back, she flicked off the light behind her and stared out into the night. The memory had come back to her, so clear, so sharp, she could almost smell the incense, see Greg's hands move between them, little colored after-image traces following each movement until he had more arms than Kali.

She wondered what had ever happened to the Balloon Men.

Long light-brown hair hung like a cape to her waist. Her parents were Irish—Munster O'Healys on her mother's side, and Bradys from Derry on her father's. There was a touch of Spanish blood in her mother's side of the family, which gave her skin its warm dark cast. The Bradys were pure Irish and it was from them that she got her big-boned frame. And something else. Her eyes were a clear grey—twilight eyes, her father had liked to tease her, eyes that could see beyond the here and now into somewhere else.

She hadn't needed drugs to see the Balloon Men.

Shifting in her wicker chair, she looked up and down the beach, but it was late and the wind wasn't coming in from the ocean. The book on her lap was a comforting weight and had, considering her present state of mind, an even more appropriate title. *How to Make the Wind Blow.* If only it *was* a tutor, she thought, instead of just a collection of odd stories.

The author's name was Christy Riddell, a reed-thin Scot with a head full of sudden fancies. His hair was like an unruly hedgerow nest and he was half a head shorter than she, but she could recall dancing with him in a garden one night and she hadn't had a more suitable partner since. She'd met him while living in a house out east that was as odd as any flight of his imagination. Long rambling halls connected a bewildering series of rooms, each more fascinating than the next. And the libraries. She'd lived in its libraries.

"When the wind is right," began the title story, the first story in the book, "the wise man isn't half so trusted as the fool."

Ellen could remember when it was still a story that was told without the benefit of pen and paper. A story that changed each time the words traveled from mouth to ear.

There was a gnome—or a gnomish sort of a man—named Long, who lived under the pier at the end of Main Street. He had skin as brown as dirt, eyes as blue as a clear summer sky. He was thin, with a fat tummy and a long crooked nose, and he wore raggedy clothes that he'd found discarded on the beach and worn until they were threadbare. Sometimes he bundled his tangled hair up under a bright yellow cap. Other times he wove it into many braids festooned with colored beads and the discarded tabs from beer cans that he'd polished on his sleeve until they were bright and shiny.

Though he'd seem more odd than magical to anyone who happened to spy him out wandering the streets or along the beach, he did have two enchantments.

One was a pig that could see the wind and follow it anywhere. She was pink and fastidiously cleanly, big enough to ride to market—which Long sometimes did—and she could talk. Not pig-talk, or even pig-Latin, but plain English that anyone could understand if they took the time to listen. Her name changed from telling to telling, but by the time Long's story appeared in the book either she or Christy had settled on Brigwin.

Long's other enchantment was a piece of plain string with four complicated elf-knots tied in it—one to call up a wind from each of the four quarters. North and south. East and west. When he untied a knot, that wind would rise up and he'd ride Brigwin in its wake, sifting through the debris and pickings left behind for treasures or charms, though what Long considered a treasure, another might throw out, and what he might consider a charm, another might see as only an old button or a bit of tangled wool. He had a good business trading his findings to woodwives and witches and the like that he met at the market when midnight was past and gone, ordinary folk were in bed, and the beach towns belonged to those who hid by day, but walked the streets by night.

Ellen carried a piece of string in her pocket, with four complicated knots tied into it, but no matter how often she undid one, she still had to wait for her winds like anyone else. She knew that strings to catch and call up the wind were only real in stories, but she liked thinking that maybe, just once, a bit of magic could tiptoe out of a tale and step into the real world. Until that happened, she had to be content with what writers like Christy put to paper.

He called them mythistories, those odd little tales of his. They were the ghosts of fancies that he would track down from time to time and trap on paper. Oddities. Some charming, some grotesque. All of them enchanting. Foolishness, he liked to say, offered from one fool to others.

Ellen smiled. Oh, yes. But when the wind is right. . . .

She'd never talked to Christy about the Balloon Men, but she didn't doubt that he knew them.

Leaning over the rail of the balcony, two stories above the walkway that ran the length of the beach, Christy's book held tight in one hand, she wished very hard to see those roly-poly figures one more time. The ocean beat its rhythm against the sand. A light breeze caught at her hair and twisted it into her face.

When the wind is right.

Something fluttered inside her, like wings unfolding, readying for flight. Rising from her chair, she set the book down on a wicker arm and went inside. Down the stairs and out the front door. She could feel a thrumming between her ears that had to be excitement moving blood more quickly through her veins, though it could be an echo of a half-lost memory—a singing of small deep voices, rising up from diaphragms nestled in fat little bellies.

Perhaps the wind *was* right, she thought as she stepped out onto the walkway. A quarter moon peeked at her from above the oil rigs far out from the shore. She put her hand in the pocket of her cotton pants and wound the knotted string she found there around one finger. It was late, late for the Balloon Men to be rolling, but she didn't doubt that there was something waiting to greet her out on the street. Perhaps only memories. Perhaps a fancy that Christy hadn't trapped on a page yet.

There was only one way to find out.

2

Peregrin Laurie was sharp-faced like a weasel—a narrow-shouldered thin whip of a teenager in jeans and a torn T-shirt. He sat in a doorway, knees up by his chin, a mane of spiked multi-colored hair standing straight up from his head in a two-inch Mohawk swath that ran down to the nape of his neck like a lizard's crest fringes. Wrapping his arms around bruised ribs, he held back tears as each breath he took made his chest burn.

Goddamn beach bums. The bastards had just about killed him and he had no one to blame but himself. Scuffing through a parking lot, he should have taken off when the car pulled up. But no. He had to be the poseur and hold his ground, giving them a long cool look as they came piling drunkenly out of the car. By the time he realized just how many of them there were and what they had planned for him, it was too late to run. He'd had to stand there then, heart hammering in his chest, and hope bravado'd see him through, because there was no way he could handle them all.

They didn't stop to chat. They just laid into him. He got a few licks in, but he knew it was hopeless. By the time he hit the pavement, all he could do was curl up into a tight ball and take their drunken kicks, cursing them with each fiery gasp of air he dragged into his lungs.

The booger waited until he was down and hurting before making its appearance. It came out from under the pier that ran by the parking lot, black and greasy, with hot eyes and a mouthful of barracuda teeth. If it hadn't hurt so much just to breathe, he would have laughed at the way his attackers backed away from the creature, eyes bulging as they rushed to their car. They took off, tires squealing, but not before the booger took a chunk of metal out of the rear fender with one swipe of a paw.

It came back to look at him—black nightmare head snuffling at him as he lifted his head and wiped the blood from his face, then moving away as he reached out a hand towards it. It smelled like a sewer and looked worse, a squat creature that had to have been scraped out of some monstrous nose, with eyes like hot coals in a smear of a face and a slick wet look to its skin. A booger, plain and simple. Only it was alive, clawed and toothed. Following him around ever since he'd run away. . . .

His parents were both burnouts from the sixties. They lived in West Hollywood and got more embarrassing the older he became. Take his name. Laurie was bad enough, but Peregrin . . . Lifted straight out of that *Lord of the Rings* book. An okay read, sure, but you don't use it to name your kid. Maybe he should just be thankful he didn't get stuck with Frodo or Bilbo. By the time he was old enough to start thinking for himself, he'd picked out his own name and wouldn't answer to anything but Reece. He'd gotten it out of some book, too, but at least it sounded cool. You needed all the cool you could get with parents like his.

His old man still had hair down to his ass. He wore wire-framed glasses and listened to shit on the stereo that sounded as burned-out as he looked. The old lady wasn't much better. Putting on weight like a whale, hair a frizzy brown, as long as the old man's, but usually hanging in a braid. Coming home late some nights, the whole house'd have the sweet smell of weed mixed with incense and they'd give him these goofy looks and talk about getting in touch with the cosmos and other spacey shit. When anybody came down on him for the way he looked, or for dropping out of school, all they said was let him do his own thing. His own thing. Jesus. Give me a break. With that kind of crap to look forward to at home, who wouldn't take off first chance they got? Though wouldn't you know it, no sooner did he get free of them than the booger latched onto him, following him around, skulking in the shadows.

At first, Reece never got much of a look at the thing—just glimpses out of the corner of his eyes—and that was more than enough. But sleeping on the beaches and in parks, some nights he'd wake with that sewer smell in his nostrils and catch something slipping out of sight, a dark wet shadow moving close to the ground. After a few weeks, it started to get bolder, sitting on its haunches a half-dozen yards from wherever he was bedding down, the hot coal eyes fixed on him.

Reece didn't know what it was or what it wanted. Was it looking out for him, or saving him up for its supper? Sometimes he thought, what with all the drugs his parents had done back in the sixties—good times for them, shit for him because he'd been born and that was when his troubles had started—he was sure that all those chemicals had fucked up his genes. Twisted something in his head so that he imagined he had this two-foot-high, walking, grunting booger following him around.

Like the old man'd say. Bummer.

Sucker sure seemed real, though.

Reece held his hurt to himself, ignoring Ellen as she approached. When she stopped in front of him, he gave her a scowl.

"Are you okay?" she asked, leaning closer to look at him.

He gave her a withering glance. The long hair and jeans, flowered blouse. Just what he needed. Another sixties burn-out.

"Why don't you just fuck off and die?" he said.

But Ellen looked past the tough pose to see the blood on his shirt, the bruising on his face that the shadows half-hid, the hurt he was trying so hard to pretend wasn't there.

"Where do you live?" she asked.

"What's it to you?"

Ignoring his scowl, she bent down and started to help him to his feet.

"Aw, shit—" Reece began, but it was easier on his ribs to stand up than to fight her.

"Let's get you cleaned up," she said.

"Florence fucking Nightingale," he muttered, but she merely led him back the way she'd come.

From under the pier a wet shadow stirred at their departure. Reece's booger drew back lips that had the rubbery texture of an octopus's skin. Row on row of pointed teeth reflected back the light from the streetlights. Hate-hot eyes glimmered red. On silent leathery paws, the creature followed the slow-moving pair, grunting softly to itself, claws clicking on the pavement.

3

Bramley Dapple was the wizard in "A Week of Saturdays," the third story in Christy Riddell's *How to Make the Wind Blow*. He was a small wizened old man, spry as a kitten, thin as a reed, with features lined and brown as a dried fig. He wore a pair of wire-rimmed spectacles without prescription lenses that he polished incessantly, and he loved to talk.

"It doesn't matter what they believe," he was saying to his guest, "so much as what *you* believe."

He paused as the brown-skinned goblin who looked after his house came in with a tray of biscuits and tea. His name was Goon, a tallish creature at three-foot-four who wore the garb of an organ-grinder's monkey: striped black and yellow trousers, a red jacket with yellow trim, small black slippers, and a little green and yellow cap that pushed down an unruly mop of thin, dark, curly hair. Gangly limbs with a protruding tummy, puffed cheeks, a wide nose, and tiny black eyes added to his monkey-like appearance.

The wizard's guest observed Goon's entrance with a startled look which pleased Bramley to no end.

"There," he said. "Goon proves my point."

"I beg your pardon?"

"We live in a consensual reality where things exist because we want them to exist. I believe in Goon, Goon believes in Goon, and you, presented with his undeniable presence, teatray in hand, believe in Goon as well. Yet, if you were to listen to the world at large, Goon is nothing more than a figment of some fevered writer's imagination—a literary construct, an artistic representation of something that can't possibly exist in the world as we know it."

Goon gave Bramley a sour look, but the wizard's guest leaned forward, hand outstretched, and brushed the goblin's shoulder with a feather-light touch. Slowly she leaned back into the big armchair, cushions so comfortable they seemed to embrace her as she settled against them.

"So . . . *anything* we can imagine can exist?" she asked finally.

Goon turned his sour look on her now.

She was a student at the university where the wizard taught; senior, majoring in fine arts, and she had the look of an artist about her. There were old paint stains on her jeans and under her fingernails. Her hair was a thick brown tangle, more unruly than Goon's curls. She had a smudge of a nose and thin puckering lips, workman's boots that stood by the door with a history of scuffs and stains written into their leather, thick woolen socks with a hole in the left heel, and one shirttail that had escaped the waist of her jeans. But her eyes were a pale, pale blue, clear and alert, for all the casualness of her attire.

Her name was Jilly Coppercorn.

Bramley shook his head. "It's not imagining. It's *knowing* that it exists —without one smidgen of doubt."

"Yes, but someone had to think him up for him to . . ." She hesitated as Goon's scowl deepened. "That is . . ."

Bramley continued to shake his head. "There *is* some semblance of order to things," he admitted, "for if the world was simply everyone's different conceptual universe mixed up together, we'd have nothing but chaos. It all relies on will, you see—to observe the changes, at any rate. Or the differences. The anomalies. Like Goon—oh, do stop scowling," he added to the goblin.

"The world as we have it," he went on to Jilly, "is here mostly because of habit. We've all agreed that certain things exist—we're taught as impressionable infants that this is a table and this is what it looks like, that's a tree out the window there, a dog looks and sounds just so. At the same time we're informed that Goon and his like don't exist, so we don't—or can't see them."

"They're not made up?" Jilly asked.

This was too much for Goon. He set the tray down and gave her leg a pinch. Jilly jumped away from him, trying to back deeper into the chair as the goblin grinned, revealing two rows of decidedly nasty-looking teeth.

"Rather impolite," Bramley said, "but I suppose you do get the point?"

Jilly nodded quickly. Still grinning, Goon set about pouring their teas.

"So," Jilly asked, "how can someone . . . how can *I* see things as they really are?"

"Well, it's not that simple," the wizard told her. "First you have to know what it is that you're looking for—before you can find it, you see."

Ellen closed the book and leaned back in her own chair, thinking about that, about Balloon Men, about the young man lying in her bed. To know what you were looking for. Was that why when she went out hoping to find Balloon Men, she'd come home with Reece?

She got up and went to the bedroom door to look in at him. After much protesting, he'd finally let her clean his hurts and put him to bed. Claiming to be not the least bit hungry, he'd polished off a whole tin of soup and the better part of the loaf of sourdough bread that she had bought just that afternoon. Then, of course, he wasn't tired at all and promptly fell asleep the moment his head touched the pillow.

She shook her head, looking at him now. His rainbow Mohawk made it look as though she'd brought some hybrid creature into her home—part rooster, part boy, it lay in her bed snoring softly, hardly real. But definitely not a Balloon Man, she thought, looking at his thin torso under the sheets.

About to turn away, something at the window caught her eye. Frozen in place, she saw a dog-like face peering back at her from the other side of the pane—which was patently impossible since the bedroom was on the second floor and there was nothing to stand on outside that window. But impossible or not, that dog-like face with its coal-red eyes and a fierce grin of glimmering teeth was there all the same.

She stared at it, feeling sick as the moments ticked by. Hunger burned in those eyes. Anger. Unbridled hate. She couldn't move, not until it finally disappeared—sliding from sight, physically escaping rather than vanishing the way a hallucination should.

She leaned weakly against the doorjamb, a faint buzzing in her head. Not until she'd caught her breath did she go to the window, but of course there was nothing there. Consensual reality, Christy's wizard had called it. Things that exist because we want them to exist. But she knew that not even in a nightmare would she consider giving life to that monstrous head she'd seen staring back in at her from the night beyond her window.

Her gaze went to the sleeping boy in her bed. All that anger burning up inside him. Had she caught a glimpse of something that *he'd* given life to?

Ellen, she told herself as she backed out of the room, you're making entirely too much out of nothing. Except something had certainly seemed to be there. There was absolutely no question in her mind that *something* had been out there.

In the living room she looked down at Christy's book. Bramley Dapple's words skittered through her mind, chased by a feeling of . . . of strangeness that she couldn't shake. The wind, the night, finding Reece in that doorway. And now that thing in the window.

She went and poured herself a brandy before making her bed on the sofa, studiously avoiding looking at the windows. She knew she was being silly—she had to have imagined it—but there was a feeling in the air tonight, a sense of being on the edge of something vast and grey. One false step, and she'd plunge down into it. A void. A nightmare.

It took a second brandy before she fell asleep.

Outside, Reece's booger snuffled around the walls of the house, crawling up the side of the building from time to time to peer into this or that window. Something kept it from entering—some disturbance in the air that was like a wind, but not a wind at the same time. When it finally retreated, it was with the knowledge in what passed for its mind that time itself was the key. Hours and minutes would unlock whatever kept it presently at bay.

Barracuda teeth gleamed as the creature grinned. It could wait. Not long, but it could wait.

4

Ellen woke the next morning, stiff from a night spent on the sofa, and wondered what in God's name had possessed her to bring Reece home. Though on reflection, she realized, the whole night had proceeded with a certain surreal quality of which Reece had only been a small part. Rereading Christy's book. That horrific face at the window. And the Balloon Men— she hadn't thought of them in years.

Swinging her feet to the floor, she went out onto her balcony. There was a light fog hazing the air. Surfers were riding the waves close by the pier —only a handful of them now, but in an hour or so their numbers would have multiplied beyond count. Raking machines were cleaning the beach, their dull roar vying with the pounding of the tide. Men with metal detectors were patiently sifting through the debris the machines left behind before the trucks came to haul it away. Near the tide's edge a man was jogging backwards across the sand, sharply silhouetted against the ocean.

Nothing out of the ordinary. But returning inside she couldn't shake the feeling that there was someone in her head, something flying dark-winged across her inner terrain like a crow. When she went to wash up, she found its crow eyes staring back at her from the mirror. Wild eyes.

Shivering, she finished up quickly. By the time Reece woke she was sitting outside on the balcony in a sweatshirt and shorts, nursing a mug of coffee. The odd feeling of being possessed had mostly gone away and the night just past took on the fading quality of half-remembered dreams.

She looked up at his appearance, smiling at the way a night's sleep had rearranged the lizard crest fringes of his Mohawk. Some of it was pressed flat against his skull. Elsewhere, multicolored tufts stood up at bizarre angles. His mouth was a sullen slash in a field of short beard stubble, but his eyes still had a sleepy look to them, softening his features.

"You do this a lot?" he asked, slouching into the other wicker chair on the balcony.

"What? Drink coffee in the morning?"

"Pick up strays."

"You looked like you needed help."

Reece nodded. "Right. We're all brothers and sisters on starship earth. I kinda figured you for a bleeding heart."

His harsh tone soured Ellen's humor. She felt the something that had watched her from the bathroom mirror flutter inside her and her thoughts returned to the previous night. Christy's wizard talking. *Things exist because we want them to exist.*

"After you fell asleep," she said, "I thought I saw something peering in through the bedroom window . . ."

Her voice trailed off when she realized that she didn't quite know where she was going with that line of thought. But Reece sat up from his slouch, suddenly alert.

"What kind of something?" he asked.

Ellen tried to laugh it off. "A monster," she said with a smile. "Red-eyed and all teeth." She shrugged. "I was just having one of those nights."

"You *saw* it?" Reece demanded sharply enough to make Ellen sit up straighter as well.

"Well, I thought I saw something, but it was patently impossible so . . ." Again her voice trailed off. Reece had sunk back into his chair and was staring off towards the ocean. "What . . . what was it?" Ellen asked.

"I call it booger," he replied. "I don't know what the hell it is, but it's been following me ever since I took off from my parents' place. . . ."

The stories in Christy's book weren't all charming. There was one near the end called "Raw Eggs" about a man who had a *Ghostbusters*-like creature living in his fridge that fed on raw eggs. It pierced the shells with a needle-fine tooth, then sucked out the contents, leaving rows of empty eggshells behind. When the man got tired of replacing his eggs, the creature crawled out of the fridge one night, driven forth by hunger, and fed on the eyes of the man's family.

The man had always had a fear of going blind. He died at the end of the story, and the creature moved on to another household, more hungry than ever. . . .

Reece laid aside Christy Riddell's book and went looking for Ellen. He found her sitting on the beach, a big, loose T-shirt covering her bikini, her bare legs tucked under her. She was staring out to sea, past the waves breaking on the shore, past the swimmers, body-surfers, and kids riding their surfboards, past the oil rigs, to the horizon hidden in a haze in the far-off distance. He got a lot of weird stares as he scuffed his way across the sand to finally sit down beside her.

"They're just stories in that book, right?" he said finally.

"You tell me."

"Look. The booger, it's—Christ, I don't know what it is. But it can't be real."

Ellen shrugged. "I was up getting some milk at John's earlier," she said, "and I overheard a couple of kids talking about some friends of theirs. Seems they were having some fun in the parking lot last night with a punker when something came at them from under the pier and tore off part of their bumper."

"Yeah, but—"

Ellen turned from the distant view to look at him. Her eyes held endless vistas in them and she felt the flutter of wings in her mind.

"I want to know how you did it," she said. "How you brought it to life."

"Look, lady. I don't—"

"It doesn't have to be a horror," she said fiercely. "It can be something good, too." She thought of the gnome that lived under the pier in Christy's story and her own Balloon Men. "I want to be able to see them again."

Their gazes locked. Reece saw a darkness behind Ellen's clear grey eyes, some wildness that reminded him of his booger in its intensity.

"I'd tell you if I knew," he said finally.

Ellen continued to study him, then slowly turned to look back across the waves. "Will it come to you tonight?" she asked.

"I don't kn—" Reece began, but Ellen turned to him again. At the look in her eyes, he nodded. "Yeah," he said then. "I guess it will."

"I want to be there when it does," she said.

Because if it was real, then it could all be real. If she could see the booger, if she could understand what animated it, if she could learn to really *see* and, as Christy's wizard had taught Jilly Coppercorn, *know* what she was looking for herself, then she could bring her own touch of wonder into the world. Her own magic.

She gripped Reece's arm. "Promise me you won't take off until I've had a chance to see it."

She had to be weirded-out, Reece thought. She didn't have the same kind of screws loose that his parents did, but she was gone all the same. Only, that book she'd had him read . . . it made a weird kind of sense. If you were going to accept that kind of shit as being possible, it might just work the way that book said it did. Weird, yeah. But when he thought of the booger itself . . .

"Promise me," she said.

He disengaged her fingers from his arm. "Sure," he said. "I got nowhere to go anyway."

5

They ate at The Green Pepper that night, a Mexican restaurant on Main Street. Reece studied his companion across the table, re-evaluating his earlier impressions of her. Her hair was up in a loose bun now and she wore a silky cream-colored blouse above a slim dark skirt. Mentally she was definitely a bit weird, but not a burn-out like his parents. She looked like the kind of customer who shopped in the trendy galleries and boutiques on Melrose Avenue where his old lady worked, back home in West Hollywood. Half the people in the restaurant were probably wondering what the hell she was doing sitting here with a scuzz like him.

Ellen looked up and caught his gaze. A smile touched her lips. "The cook must be in a good mood," she said.

"What do you mean?"

"Well, I've heard that the worse mood he's in, the hotter he makes his sauces."

Reece tried to give her back a smile, but his heart wasn't in it. He wanted a beer, but they wouldn't serve him here because he was underage. He found himself wishing Ellen wasn't so much older than him, that he didn't look like such a freak sitting here with her. For the first time since he'd done his hair, he was embarrassed about the way he looked. He wanted to enjoy just sitting here with her instead of knowing that everyone was looking at him like he was some kind of geek.

"You okay?" Ellen asked.

"Yeah. Sure. Great food."

He pushed the remainder of his rice around on the plate with his fork. Yeah, he had no problems. Just no place to go, no place to fit in. Body aching from last night's beating. Woman sitting there across from him, looking tasty, but she was too old for him and there was something in her eyes that scared him a little. Not to mention a nightmare booger dogging his footsteps. Sure. Things were just rocking, mama.

He stole another glance at her, but she was looking away, out to the darkening street, wine glass raised to her mouth.

"That book your friend wrote," he said.

Her gaze shifted to his face and she put her glass down.

"It doesn't have anything like my booger in it," Reece continued. "I mean it's got some ugly stuff, but nothing just like the booger."

"No," Ellen replied. "But it's got to work the same way. We can see it because we believe it's there."

"So was it always there and we're just aware of it now? Or does it exist *because* we believe in it? Is it something that came out of us—out of me?"

"Like Uncle Dobbin's birds, you mean?"

Reece nodded, unaware of the flutter of dark wings that Ellen felt stir inside her.

"I don't know," she said softly.

"Uncle Dobbin's Parrot Fair" was the last story in Christy Riddell's book, the title coming from the name of the pet shop that Timothy James Dobbin owned in Santa Ana. It was a gathering place for every kind of bird, tame as well as wild. There were finches in cages and parrots with the run of the shop, not to mention everything from sparrows to crows and gulls crowding around outside.

In the story, T.J. Dobbin was a retired sailor with an interest in nineteenth century poets, an old bearded tar with grizzled red hair and beetling brows who wore baggy blue cotton trousers and a white T-shirt as he worked in his store, cleaning the bird cages, feeding the parakeets, teaching the parrots words. Everybody called him Uncle Dobbin.

He had a sixteen-year-old assistant named Nori Wert who helped out on weekends. She had short blonde hair and a deep tan that she started working on as soon as school was out. To set it off she invariably wore white shorts and a tank top. The only thing she liked better than the beach was the birds in Uncle Dobbin's shop, and that was because she knew their secret.

She didn't find out about them right away. It took a year or so of coming in and hanging around the shop and then another three weekends of working there before she finally approached Uncle Dobbin with what had been bothering her.

"I've been wondering," she said as she sat down on the edge of his cluttered desk at the back of the store. She fingered the world globe beside the blotter and gave it a desultory spin.

Uncle Dobbin raised his brow questioningly and continued to fill his pipe.

"It's the birds," she said. "We never sell any—at least not since I've started working here. People come in and they look around, but no one asks the price of anything, no one ever buys anything. I guess you could do most of your business during the week, but then why did you hire me?"

Uncle Dobbin looked down into the bowl of his pipe to make sure the tobacco was tamped properly. "Because you like birds," he said before he lit a match. Smoke wreathed up towards the ceiling. A bright green parrot gave a squawk from where it was roosting nearby and turned its back on them.

"But you don't sell any of them, do you?" Being curious, she'd poked through his file cabinet to look at invoices and sales receipts to find that all he ever bought was birdfood and cages and the like, and he never sold a thing. At least no sales were recorded.

"Can't sell them."

"Why not?"

"They're not mine to sell."

Nori sighed. "Then whose are they?"

"Better you should ask *what* are they."

"Okay," Nori said, giving him an odd look. "I'll bite. What are they?"

"Magic."

Nori studied him for a moment and he returned her gaze steadily, giving no indication that he was teasing her. He puffed on his pipe, a serious look in his eyes, then took the pipe stem from his mouth. Setting the pipe carefully on the desk so that it wouldn't tip over, he leaned forward in his chair.

"People have magic," he said, "but most of them don't want it, or don't believe in it, or did once, but then forgot. So I take that magic and make it into birds until they want it back, or someone else can use it."

"Magic."

"That's right."

"Not birds."

Uncle Dobbin nodded.

"That's crazy," Nori said.

"Is it?"

He got up stiffly from his chair and stood in front of her with his hands outstretched towards her chest. Nori shrank back from him, figuring he'd flaked out and was going to cop a quick feel now, but his hands paused just a few inches from her breasts. She felt a sudden pain inside—like a stitch in her side from running too hard, only it was deep in her chest.

Right in her lungs. She looked down, eyes widening as a beak appeared poking out of her chest, followed by a parrot's head, its body and wings.

It was like one of the holograms at the Haunted House in Disneyland, for she could see right through it, then it grew solid once it was fully emerged. The pain stopped as the bird fluttered free, but she felt an empty aching inside. Uncle Dobbin caught the bird, and soothed it with a practiced touch, before letting it fly free. Numbly, Nori watched it wing across the store and settle down near the front window where it began to preen its feathers. The sense of loss inside grew stronger.

"That . . . it was in me . . . I . . . ."

Uncle Dobbin made his way back to his chair and sat down, picking up his pipe once more.

"Magic," he said before he lit it.

"My . . . my magic . . . ?"

Uncle Dobbin nodded. "But not anymore. You didn't believe."

"But I didn't know!" she wailed.

"You got to earn it back now," Uncle Dobbin told her. "The side cages need cleaning."

Nori pressed her hands against her chest, then wrapped her arms around herself in a tight hug as though that would somehow ease the empty feeling inside her.

"E-earn it?" she said in a small voice, her gaze going from his face to the parrot that had come out of her chest and was now sitting by the front window. "By . . . by working here?"

Uncle Dobbin shook his head. "You already work here and I pay you for that, don't I?"

"But then how . . . ?"

"You've got to earn its trust. You've got to learn to believe in it again."

Ellen shook her head softly. Learn to believe, she thought. I've always believed. But maybe never hard enough. She glanced at her companion, then out to the street. It was almost completely dark now.

"Let's go walk on the beach," she said.

Reece nodded, following her outside after she'd paid the bill. The lemony smell of eucalyptus trees was strong in the air for a moment, then the stronger scent of the ocean winds stole it away.

6

They had the beach to themselves, though the pier was busy with strollers and people fishing. At the beach end of the long wooden structure, kids were hanging out, fooling around with bikes and skateboards. The soft boom of the tide drowned out the music of their ghetto blasters. The wind was cool with a salt tang as it came in from over the waves. In the distance, the oil rigs were lit up like Christmas trees.

Ellen took off her shoes. Carrying them in her tote bag, she walked in the wet sand by the water's edge. A raised lip of the beach hid the shorefront houses from their view as they walked south to the rocky spit that marked the beginning of the Naval Weapons Station.

"It's nice out here," Reece said finally. They hadn't spoken since leaving the restaurant.

Ellen nodded. "A lot different from L.A."

"Two different worlds."

Ellen gave him a considering glance. Ever since this afternoon, the sullen tone had left his voice. She listened now as he spoke of his parents and how he couldn't find a place for himself either in their world, or that of his peers.

"You're pretty down on the sixties," she said when he was done.

Reece shrugged. He was barefoot now, too, the waves coming up to lick the bottom of his jeans where the two of them stood at the water's edge.

"They had some good ideas—people like my parents," he said, "but the way they want things to go . . . that only works if everyone agrees to live that way."

"That doesn't invalidate the things they believe in."

"No. But what we've got to deal with is the real world and you've got to take what you need if you want to survive in it."

Ellen sighed. "I suppose."

She looked back across the beach, but they were still alone. No one else out for a late walk across the sand. No booger. No Balloon Men. But something fluttered inside her, dark-winged. A longing as plain as what she heard in Reece's voice, though she was looking for magic and he was just looking for a way to fit in.

Hefting her tote bag, she tossed it onto the sand, out of the waves' reach. Reece gave her a curious look, then averted his gaze as she stepped out of her skirt.

"It's okay," she said, amused at his sudden sense of propriety. "I'm wearing my bathing suit."

By the time he turned back, her blouse and skirt had joined her tote bag on the beach and she was shaking loose her hair.

"Coming in?" she asked.

Reece simply stood and watched the sway of her hips as she headed for the water. Her bathing suit was white. In the poor light it was as though she wasn't wearing anything—the bathing suit looking like untanned skin. She dove cleanly into a wave, head bobbing up pale in the dark water when she surfaced.

"C'mon!" she called to him. "The water's fine, once you get in."

Reece hesitated. He'd wanted to go in this afternoon, but hadn't had the nerve to bare his white skinny limbs in front of a beachful of serious tanners. Well, there was no one to see him now, he thought as he stripped down to his underwear.

The water hit him like a cold fist when he dove in after her and he came up gasping with shock. His body tingled, every pore stung alert. Ellen drifted further out, riding the waves easily. As he waded out to join her, a swell rose up and tumbled him back to shore in a spill of floundering limbs that scraped him against the sand.

"Either go under or over them," Ellen advised him as he started back out.

He wasn't much of a swimmer, but the water wasn't too deep except when a big wave came. He went under the next one and came up spluttering, but pleased with himself for not getting thrown up against the beach again.

"I love swimming at night," Ellen said as they drifted together.

Reece nodded. The water was surprisingly warm, too, once you were in it. You could lose all sense of time out here, just floating with the swells.

"You do this a lot?" he asked.

Ellen shook her head. "It's not that good an idea to do this alone. If the undertow got you, it'd pull you right out and no one would know."

Reece laid his head back in the water and looked up at the sky. Though they were less than an hour by the freeway out of downtown L.A., the sky seemed completely different here. It didn't seem to have that glow from God knows how many millions of lights. The stars seemed closer here, or maybe it was that the sky seemed deeper.

He glanced over at Ellen. Their reason for being out here was forgotten. He wished he had the nerve to just sort of sidle up to her and put his arms around her, hold her close. She'd feel all slippery, but she'd feel good.

He paddled a little bit towards her, riding a swell up and then down again. The wave turned him slightly away from her. When he glanced back, he saw her staring wide-eyed at the shore. His gaze followed hers and then that cold he'd felt when he first entered the water returned in a numbing rush.

The booger was here.

It came snuffling over a rise in the beach, a squat dark shadow in the sand, greasy and slick as it beelined for their clothing. When it reached Ellen's tote bag, it buried its face in her skirt and blouse, then proceeded to rip them to shreds. Ellen's fingers caught his arm in a frightened grip. A wave came up, lifting his feet from the bottom. He kicked out frantically, afraid he was going to drown with her holding on to him like that, but the wave tossed them both in towards the shore.

The booger looked up, baring its barracuda teeth. The red coals of its eyes burned right into them both, pinning them there on the wet sand where the wave had left them. Leaving the ruin of Ellen's belongings in torn shreds, it moved slowly towards them.

"Re-Reece," Ellen said. She was pressed close to him, shivering.

Reece didn't have the time to appreciate the contact of her skin against his. He wanted to say, this is what you were looking for, lady, but things weren't so cut and dried now. Ellen wasn't some nameless cipher anymore—just a part of a crowd that he could sneer at—and she wasn't just something he had the hots for either. She was a person, just like him. An individual. Someone he could actually relate to.

"Can—can't you stop it?" Ellen cried.

The booger was getting close now. Its sewer reek was strong enough to drown out the salty tang of the ocean. It was like something had died there on the beach and was now getting up and coming for them.

Stop it? Reece thought. Maybe the thing had been created out of his frustrated anger, the way Ellen's friend made out it could happen in that book of his, but Reece knew as sure as shit that he didn't control the booger.

Another wave came down upon them and Reece pushed at the sand so that it pulled them partway out from the shore on its way back out. Getting to his knees in the rimey water, he stood in front of Ellen so that he was between her and the booger. Could the sucker swim?

The booger hesitated at the water's edge. It lifted its paws fastidiously from the wet sand like a cat crossing a damp lawn and relief went through Reece. When another wave came in, the booger backstepped quickly out of its reach.

Ellen was leaning against him, face near his as she peered over his shoulder.

"It can't handle the water," Reece said. He turned his face to hers when she didn't say anything. Her clear eyes were open wide, gaze fixed on the booger. "Ellen . . . ?" he began.

"I can't believe that it's really there," she said finally in a small voice.

"But you're the one—you said . . ." He drew a little away from her so that he could see her better.

"I know what I said," Ellen replied. She hugged herself, trembling at the stir of dark wings inside her. "It's just . . . I *wanted* to believe, but . . . wanting to and having it be real . . ." There was a pressure in the center of her chest now, like something inside pushing to get out. "I . . ."

The pain lanced sharp and sudden. She heard Reece gasp. Looking down, she saw what he had seen, a bird's head poking gossamer from between her breasts. It was a dark smudge against the white of her swimsuit, not one of Uncle Dobbin's parrots, but a crow's head, with eyes like the pair she'd seen looking back at her from the mirror. Her own magic, leaving her because she didn't believe. Because she couldn't believe, but—

It didn't make sense. She'd always believed. And now, with Reece's booger standing there on the shore, how could she help *but* believe?

The booger howled then, as though to underscore her thoughts. She looked to the shore and saw it stepping into the waves, crying out at the pain of the salt water on its flesh, but determined to get at them. To get at her. Reece's magic, given life. While her own magic . . . She pressed at the half-formed crow coming from her chest, trying to force it back in.

"I believe, I believe," she muttered through clenched teeth. But just like Uncle Dobbin's assistant in Christy's story, she could feel that swelling ache of loss rise up in her. She turned despairing eyes to Reece.

She didn't need a light to see the horror in his eyes—horror at the booger's approach, at the crow's head sticking out of her chest. But he didn't draw away from her. Instead, he reached out and caught hold of her shoulders.

"Stop fighting it!" he cried.

"But—"

He shot a glance shoreward. They were bracing themselves against the waves, but a large swell had just caught the booger and sent it howling back to shore in a tumble of limbs.

"It was your needing proof," he said. "Your needing to see the booger, to know that it's real—that's what's making you lose it. Stop trying so hard."

"I . . ."

But she knew he was right. She pulled free of him and looked towards the shore where the booger was struggling to its feet. The creature made rattling sounds deep in its throat as it started out for them again. It was hard, hard to do, but she let her hands fall free. The pain in her chest was a fire, the aching loss building to a crescendo. But she closed herself to it, closed her eyes, willed herself to stand relaxed.

Instead of fighting, she remembered. Balloon Men spinning down the beach. Christy's gnome, riding his pig along the pier. Bramley Dapple's advice. Goon pinching Jilly Coppercorn's leg. The thing that fed on eggs and eyeballs and, yes, Reece's booger too. Uncle Dobbin and his parrots and Nori Wert watching her magic fly free. And always the Balloon Men, tumbling end-over-end, across the beach, or down the alleyway behind her house . . .

And the pain eased. The ache loosened, faded.

"Jesus," she heard Reece say softly.

She opened her eyes and looked to where he was looking. The booger had turned from the sea and was fleeing as a crowd of Balloon Men came bouncing down the shore, great round roly-poly shapes, turning end-over-end, laughing and giggling, a chorus of small deep voices. There was salt in her eyes and it wasn't from the ocean's brine. Her tears ran down her cheeks and she felt herself grinning like a fool.

The Balloon Men chased Reece's booger up one end of the beach and then back the other way until the creature finally made a stand. Howling it waited for them to come, but before the first bouncing round shape reached it, the booger began to fade away.

Ellen turned to Reece and knew he had tears in his own eyes, but the good feeling was too strong for him to do anything but grin right back at her. The booger had died with the last of his anger. She reached out a hand to him and he took it in one of his own. Joined so, they made their way to the shore where they were surrounded by riotous Balloon Men until the bouncing shapes finally faded and then there were just the two of them standing there.

Ellen's heart beat fast. When Reece let go her hand, she touched her chest and felt a stir of dark wings inside her, only they were settling in now, no longer striving to fly free. The wind came in from the ocean still, but it wasn't the same wind that the Balloon Men rode.

"I guess it's not all bullshit," Reece said softly.

Ellen glanced at him.

He smiled as he explained. "Helping each other—getting along instead of fighting. Feels kind of good, you know?"

Ellen nodded. Her hand fell from her chest as the dark wings finally stilled.

"Your friend's story didn't say anything about crows," Reece said.

"Maybe we've all got different birds inside—different magics." She looked out across the waves to where the oil rigs lit the horizon.

"There's a flock of wild parrots up around Santa Ana," Reece said.

"I've heard there's one up around San Pedro, too."

"Do you think . . . ?" Reece began, but he let his words trail off. The waves came in and wet their feet.

"I don't know," Ellen said. She looked over at her shredded clothes. "Come on. Let's get back to my place and warm up."

Reece laid his jacket over her shoulders. He put on his T-shirt and jeans, then helped her gather up what was left of her belongings.

"I didn't mean for this to happen," he said, bundling up the torn blouse and skirt. He looked up to where she was standing over him. "But I couldn't control the booger."

"Maybe we're not supposed to."

"But something like the booger . . ."

She gave his Mohawk a friendly ruffle. "I think it just means that we've got be careful about what kind of vibes we put out."

Reece grimaced at her use of the word, but he nodded.

"It's either that," Ellen added, "or we let the magic fly free."

The same feathery stirring of wings that she felt moved in Reece. They both knew that that was something neither of them was likely to give up.

\*     \*     \*

In Uncle Dobbin's Parrot Fair, Nori Wert turned away from the pair of cages that she'd been making ready.

"I guess we won't be needing these," she said.

Uncle Dobbin looked up from a slim collection of Victorian poetry and nodded. "You're learning fast," he said. He stuck the stem of his pipe in his mouth and fished about in his pocket for a match. "Maybe there's hope for you yet."

Nori felt her own magic stir inside her, back where it should be, but she didn't say anything to him in case she had to go away, now that the lesson was learned. She was too happy here. Next to catching some rays, there wasn't anywhere she'd rather be.

*For the Lowentrouts of Seal Beach*

# GEORGE R. R. MARTIN

## The Pear-shaped Man

George R. R. Martin was born in Bayonne, New Jersey and has been a chess tournament director, VISTA volunteer, sports writer, and college teacher. Currently, he's a producer on the popular television series *Beauty and the Beast*. The author of the horror novels *Fevre Dream* and *The Armageddon Rag*, he has won three Hugo Awards, two Nebula Awards, and the coveted Balrog Award. His most recent novella, "The Skin Trade," has just come out in *Night Visions V*.

"The Pear-shaped Man," originally published in *OMNI*, is a fine example of Martin's horror fiction. Written in a clear, lucid style, it never stays its hand from the execution of its descending journey. And it undoubtedly marks the first time cheese curls have ever been used as a symbol of horror.

—E.D.

# THE PEAR-SHAPED MAN

## George R. R. Martin

The Pear-shaped Man lives beneath the stairs. His shoulders are narrow and stooped, but his buttocks are impressively large. Or perhaps it is only the clothing he wears; no one has ever admitted to seeing him nude, and no one has ever admitted to wanting to. His trousers are brown polyester double knits, with wide cuffs and a shiny seat; they are always baggy, and they have big, deep, droopy pockets so stuffed with oddments and bric-a-brac that they bulge against his sides. He wears his pants very high, hiked up above the swell of his stomach, and cinches them in place around his chest with a narrow brown leather belt. He wears them so high that his drooping socks show clearly, and often an inch or two of pasty white skin as well.

His shirts are always short-sleeved, most often white or pale blue, and his breast pocket is always full of Bic pens, the cheap throwaway kind that write with blue ink. He has lost the caps or tossed them out, because his shirts are all stained and splotched around the breast pockets. His head is a second pear set atop the first; he has a double chin and wide, full, fleshy cheeks, and the top of his head seems to come almost to a point. His nose is broad and flat, with large, greasy pores; his eyes are small and pale, set close together. His hair is thin, dark, limp, flaky with dandruff; it never looks washed, and there are those who say that he cuts it himself with a bowl and a dull knife. He has a smell, too, the Pear-shaped Man; it is a sweet smell, a sour smell, a rich smell, compounded of old butter and rancid meat and vegetables rotting in the garbage bin. His voice, when he speaks, is high and thin and squeaky; it would be a funny little voice, coming from such a large, ugly man, but there is something unnerving about it, and something even more chilling about his tight, small smile. He never shows any teeth when he smiles, but his lips are broad and wet.

Of course you know him. Everyone knows a Pear-shaped Man.

Jessie met hers on her first day in the neighborhood, while she and Angela were moving into the vacant apartment on the first floor. Angela and her boyfriend, Donald the student shrink, had lugged the couch inside and

245

accidentally knocked away the brick that had been holding open the door to the building. Meanwhile Jessie had gotten the recliner out of the U-Haul all by herself and thumped it up the steps, only to find the door locked when she backed into it, the recliner in her arms. She was hot and sore and irritable and ready to scream with frustration.

And then the Pear-shaped Man emerged from his basement apartment under the steps, climbed onto the sidewalk at the foot of the stoop, and looked up at her with those small, pale, watery eyes of his. He made no move to help her with her chair. He did not say hello or offer to let her into the building. He only blinked and smiled a tight, wet smile that showed none of his teeth and said in a voice as squeaky and grating as nails on a blackboard, "Ahhhh. *There* she is." Then he turned and walked away. When he walked he swayed slightly from side to side.

Jessie let go of the recliner; it bumped down two steps and turned over. She suddenly felt cold, despite the sweltering July heat. She watched the Pear-shaped Man depart. That was her first sight of him. She went inside and told Donald and Angela about him, but they were not much impressed. "Into every girl's life a Pear-shaped Man must fall," Angela said, with the cynicism of the veteran city girl. "I bet I met him on a blind date once."

Donald, who didn't live with them but spent so many nights with Angela that sometimes it seemed as though he did, had a more immediate concern. "Where do you want this recliner?" he wanted to know.

Later they had a few beers, and Rick and Molly and the Heathersons came over to help them warm the apartment, and Rick offered to pose for her (wink wink, nudge nudge) when Molly wasn't there to hear, and Donald drank too much and went to sleep on the sofa, and the Heathersons had a fight that ended with Geoff storming out and Lureen crying; it was a night like any other night, in other words, and Jessie forgot all about the Pear-shaped Man. But not for long.

The next morning Angela roused Donald, and the two of them went off, Angie to the big downtown firm where she was a legal secretary, Don to study shrinking. Jessie was a freelance commercial illustrator. She did her work at home, which as far as Angela and Donald and her mother and the rest of Western civilization were concerned meant that she didn't work at all. "Would you mind doing the shopping?" Angie asked her just before she left. They had pretty well devastated their refrigerator in the two weeks before the move, so as not to have a lot of food to lug across town. "Seeing as how you'll be home all day? I mean, we really need some food."

So Jessie was pushing a full cart of groceries down a crowded aisle in Santino's Market, on the corner, when she saw the Pear-shaped Man the second time. He was at the register, counting out change into Santino's hand. Jessie felt like making a U-turn and busying herself until he'd gone. But that would be silly. She'd gotten everything she needed, and she was a grown woman, after all, and he was standing at the only open register. Resolute, she got in line behind him.

Santino dumped the Pear-shaped Man's coins into the old register and bagged up his purchase: a big plastic bottle of Coke and a one-pound bag of Cheez Doodles. As he took the bag, the Pear-shaped Man saw her and smiled that little wet smile of his. "Cheez Doodles are the best," he said. "Would you like some?"

"No, thank you," Jessie said politely. The Pear-shaped Man put the brown paper sack inside a shapeless leather bag of the sort that schoolboys use to carry their books, gathered it up, and waddled out of the store. Santino, a big grizzled man with thinning salt-and-pepper hair, began to ring up Jessie's groceries. "He's something, ain't he?" he asked her.

"Who is he?" she asked.

Santino shrugged. "Hell, I dunno. Everybody just calls him the Pear-shaped Man. He's been around here forever. Comes in every morning, buys a bottle of Coke and a big bag of Cheez Doodles. Once we run out of Cheez Doodles, so I tell him he oughta try them Cheetos or maybe even potato chips, y'know, for a change? He wasn't having none of it, though."

Jessie was bemused. "He must buy something besides Coke and Cheez Doodles."

"Wanna bet, lady?"

"Then he must shop somewhere else."

"Besides me, the nearest supermarket is nine blocks away. Charlie down at the candy store tells me the Pear-shaped Man comes in every afternoon at four-thirty and has himself a chocolate ice-cream soda, but far as we can tell, that's all he eats." He rang for a total. "That's seventy-nine eighty-two, lady. You new around here?"

"I live just above the Pear-shaped Man," Jessie confessed.

"Congratulations," Santino said.

Later that morning, after she lined the shelves and put away the groceries, set up her studio in the spare bedroom, made a few desultory dabs on the cover she was supposed to be painting for Pirouette Publishing, ate lunch and washed the dishes, hooked up the stereo and listened to some Carly Simon, and rearranged half of the living room furniture, Jessie finally admitted a certain restlessness and decided this would be a good time to go around the building and introduce herself to her new neighbors. Not many people bothered with that in the city, she knew, but she was still a small-town kid at heart, and it made her feel safer to know the people around her. She decided to start with the Pear-shaped Man down in the basement and got as far as descending the stairs to his door. Then a funny feeling came over her. There was no name on the doorbell, she noticed. Suddenly she regretted her impulse. She retreated back upstairs to meet the rest of the building.

The other tenants all knew him; most of them had spoken to him, at least once or twice, trying to be friendly. Old Sadie Winbright, who had lived across the hall in the other first-floor apartment for twelve years, said he was very quiet. Billy Peabody, who shared the big second-floor apartment with his crippled mother, thought the Pear-shaped Man was creepy, especially that little smile of his. Pete Pumetti worked the late shift, and told her how those basement lights were always on, no matter what hour of the night Pete came swaggering home, even though it was hard to tell on account of the way the Pear-shaped Man had boarded up his windows. Jess and Ginny Harris didn't like their twins playing around the stairs that led down to his apartment and had forbidden them to talk to him. Jeffries the barber, whose small two-chair shop was down the block from Santino's, knew him and had no great desire for his patronage. All of them, every one, called him the Pear-shaped Man. That was who he was. "But who is he?" Jessie asked. None of them knew. "What does he do for a living?" she asked.

"I think he's on welfare," Old Sadie Winbright said. "The poor dear, he must be feebleminded."

"Damned if I know," said Pete Pumetti. "He sure as hell don't work. I bet he's a queer."

"Sometimes I think he might be a drug pusher," said Jeffries the barber, whose familiarity with drugs was limited to witch hazel.

"I betcha he writes them pornographic books down there," Billy Peabody surmised.

"He doesn't do anything for a living," said Ginny Harris. "Jess and I have talked about it. He's a shopping-bag man, he has to be."

That night, over dinner, Jessie told Angela about the Pear-shaped Man and the other tenants and their comments. "He's probably an attorney," Angie said. "Why do you care so much, anyway?"

Jessie couldn't answer that. "I don't know. He gives me goose bumps. I don't like the idea of some maniac living right underneath us."

Angela shrugged. "That's the way it goes in the big, glamorous city. Did the guy from the phone company come?"

"Maybe next week," said Jessie. "That's the way it goes in the big, glamorous city."

Jessie soon learned that there was no avoiding the Pear-shaped Man. When she visited the laundromat around the block, there he was, washing a big load of striped boxer shorts and ink-stained short-sleeved shirts, snacking on Coke and Cheez Doodles from the vending machines. She tried to ignore him, but whenever she turned around, there he was, smiling wetly, his eyes fixed on her, or perhaps on the underthings she was loading into the dryer.

When she went down to the corner candy store one afternoon to buy a paper, there he was, slurping his ice cream soda, his buttocks overflowing the stool on which he was perched. "It's homemade," he squeaked at her. She frowned, paid for her newspaper, and left.

One evening when Angela was seeing Donald, Jessie picked up an old paperback and went out on the stoop to read and maybe socialize and enjoy the cool breeze that was blowing up the street. She got lost in the story, until she caught a whiff of something unpleasant, and when she looked up from the page, there he was, standing not three feet away, staring at her. "What do you want?" she snapped, closing the book.

"Would you like to come down and see my house?" the Pear-shaped Man asked in that high, whiny voice.

"No," she said, retreating to her own apartment. But when she looked out a half hour later, he was still standing in the same exact spot, clutching his brown bag and staring at her windows while dusk fell around him. He made her feel very uneasy. She wished that Angela would come home, but she knew that wouldn't happen for hours. In fact, Angie might very well decide to spend the night at Don's place.

Jessie shut the windows despite the heat, checked the locks on her door, and then went back to her studio to work. Painting would take her mind off the Pear-shaped Man. Besides, the cover was due at Pirouette by the end of the week.

She spent the rest of the evening finishing off the background and doing some of the fine detail on the heroine's gown. The hero didn't look quite right to her when she was done, so she worked on him, too. He was the usual dark-haired, virile, strong-jawed type, but Jessie decided to individualize him a bit, an effort that kept her pleasantly occupied until she heard Angie's key in the lock.

She put away her paints and washed up and decided to have some tea before calling it a night. Angela was standing in the living room, with her hands behind her back, looking more than a little tipsy, giggling. "What's so funny?" Jessie asked.

Angela giggled again. "You've been holding out on me," she said. "You got yourself a new beau and you didn't tell."

"What are you talking about?"

"He was standing on the stoop when I got home," Angie said, grinning. She came across the room. "He said to give you these." Her hand emerged from behind her back. It was full of fat, orange worms, little flaking twists of corn and cheese that curled between her fingers and left powdery stains on the palm of her hand. "For you," Angie repeated, laughing. "For you."

That night Jessie had a long, terrible dream, but when the daylight came she could remember only a small part of it. She was standing at the door to the Pear-shaped Man's apartment under the stairs; she was standing there in darkness, waiting, waiting for something to happen, something awful, the worst thing she could imagine. Slowly, oh so slowly, the door began to open. Light fell upon her face, and Jessie woke, trembling.

He might be dangerous, Jessie decided the next morning over Rice Krispies and tea. Maybe he had a criminal record. Maybe he was some kind of mental patient. She ought to check up on him. But she needed to know his name first. She couldn't just call up the police and say, "Do you have anything on the Pear-shaped Man?"

After Angela had gone to work, Jessie pulled a chair over by the front window and sat down to wait and watch. The mail usually arrived about eleven. She saw the postman ascend the stairs, heard him putting the mail in the big hall mailbox. But the Pear-shaped Man got his mail separately, she knew. He had his own box, right under his doorbell, and if she remembered right it wasn't the kind that locked, either. As soon as the postman had departed, she was on her feet, moving quickly down the stairs. There was no sign of the Pear-shaped Man. The door to his apartment was down under the stoop, and farther back she could see overflowing garbage cans, smell their rich, sickly sweet odor. The upper half of the door was a window, boarded up. It was dark under the stoop. Jessie barked her knuckles on the brick as she fumbled for his mailbox. Her hand brushed the loose metal lid. She got it open, pulled out two thin envelopes. She had to squint and move toward the sunlight to read the name. They were both addressed to Occupant.

She was stuffing them back into the box when the door opened. The Pear-shaped Man was framed by bright light from within his apartment. He smiled at her, so close she could count the pores on his nose, see the sheen of the saliva on his lower lip. He said nothing.

"I," she said, startled, "I, I . . . I got some of your mail by mistake. Must be a new man on the route. I, I was just bringing it back."

The Pear-shaped Man reached up and into his mailbox. For a second his hand brushed Jessie's. His skin was soft and damp and seemed much colder than it ought to be, and the touch gave her goose bumps all up and down her arm. He took the two letters from her and looked at them briefly and then stuffed them into his pants pocket. "It's just garbage," squeaked the Pear-shaped Man. "They shouldn't be allowed to send you garbage. They ought to be stopped. Would you like to see my things? I have things inside to look at."

"I," said Jessie, "uh, no. No, I can't. Excuse me." She turned quickly, moved out from under the stairs, back into the sunlight, and hurried back inside the building. All the way, she could feel his eyes on her.

\*   \*   \*

She spent the rest of that day working, and the next as well, never glancing outside, for fear that he would be standing there. By Thursday the painting was finished. She decided to take it in to Pirouette herself and have dinner downtown, maybe do a little shopping. A day away from the apartment and the Pear-shaped Man would do her good, soothe her nerves. She was being overimaginative. He hadn't actually done anything, after all. It was just that he was so damned *creepy*.

Adrian, the art director at Pirouette, was glad to see her, as always. "That's my Jessie," he said after he'd given her a hug. "I wish all my artists were like you. Never miss a deadline, never turn in anything but the best work, a real pro. Come on back to my office, we'll look at this one and talk about some new assignments and gossip a bit." He told his secretary to hold his calls and escorted her back through the maze of tiny little cubicles where the editors lived. Adrian himself had a huge corner office with two big windows, a sign of his status in Pirouette Publishing. He gestured Jessie to a chair, poured her a cup of herb tea, then took her portfolio and removed the cover painting and held it up at arm's length.

The silence went on far too long.

Adrian dragged out a chair, propped up the painting, and retreated several feet to consider it from a distance. He stroked his beard and cocked his head this way and that. Watching him, Jessie felt a thin prickle of alarm. Normally, Adrian was given to exuberant outbursts of approval. She didn't like this quiet. "What's wrong?" she said, setting down her teacup. "Don't you like it?"

"Oh," Adrian said. He put out a hand, palm open and level, waggled it this way and that. "It's well executed, no doubt. Your technique is very professional. Fine detail."

"I researched all the clothing," she said in exasperation. "It's all authentic for the period; you know it is."

"Yes, no doubt. And the heroine is gorgeous, as always. I wouldn't mind ripping her bodice myself. You do amazing things with mammaries, Jessie."

She stood up. "Then what is it?" she said. "I've been doing covers for you for three years now, Adrian. There's never been any problem."

"Well," he said. He shook his head, smiled. "Nothing, really. Maybe you've been doing too many of these. I know how it can go. They're so much alike, it gets boring, painting all those hot embraces one after another; so pretty soon you feel an urge to experiment, to try something a little bit different." He shook a finger at her. "It won't do, though. Our readers just want the same old shit with the same old covers. I understand, but it won't do."

"There's nothing experimental about this painting." Jessie said, exasperated. "It's the same thing I've done for you a hundred times before. *What* won't do?"

Adrian looked honestly surprised. "Why, the man, of course," he said. "I thought you'd done it deliberately." He gestured. "I mean, look at him. He's almost *unattractive*."

"What?" Jessie moved over to the painting. "He's the same virile jerk I've painted over and over again."

Adrian frowned. "Really now," he said. "Look." He started pointing things out. "There, around his collar, is that or is that not just the faintest hint of a double chin? And look at that lower lip! Beautifully executed, yes, but it looks, well, gross. Like it was wet or something. Pirouette heroes rape, they plunder, they seduce, they threaten, but they do not drool, darling. And perhaps it's just a trick of perspective, but I could swear"— he paused, leaned close, shook his head—"no, it's not perspective, the top of his head is definitely narrower than the bottom. A pinhead! We can't have pinheads on Pirouette books, Jessie. Too much fullness in the cheeks, too. He looks as though he might be storing nuts for the winter." Adrian shook his head. "It won't do, love. Look, no big problem. The rest of the painting is fine. Just take it home and fix him up. How about it?"

Jessie was staring at her painting in horror, as if she were seeing it for the first time. Everything Adrian had said, everything he had pointed out, was true. It was all very subtle, to be sure; at first glance the man looked almost like your normal Pirouette hero, but there was something just the tiniest bit off about him, and when you looked closer, it was blatant and unmistakable. Somehow the Pear-shaped Man had crept into her painting. "I," she began, "I, yes, you're right, I'll do it over. I don't know what happened. There's this man who lives in my building, a creepy-looking guy, everybody calls him the Pear-shaped Man. He's been getting on my nerves. I swear, it wasn't intentional. I guess I've been thinking about him so much it just crept into my work subconsciously."

"I understand," Adrian said. "Well, no problem, just set it right. We do have deadline problems, though."

"I'll fix it this weekend, have it back to you by Monday," Jessie promised.

"Wonderful," said Adrian. "Let's talk about those other assignments then." He poured her more Red Zinger, and they sat down to talk. By the time Jessie left his office, she was feeling much better.

Afterward she enjoyed a drink in her favorite bar, met a few friends, and had a nice dinner at an excellent new Japanese restaurant. It was dark by the time she got home. There was no sign of the Pear-shaped Man. She kept her portfolio under her arm as she fished for her keys and unlocked the door to the building.

When she stepped inside, Jessie heard a faint noise and felt something crunch underfoot. A nest of orange worms clustered against the faded blue of the hallway carpet, crushed and broken by her foot.

*　　*　　*

She dreamed of him again. It was the same shapeless, terrible dream. She was down in the dark beneath the stoop, near the trash bins crawling with all kinds of things, waiting at his door. She was frightened, too frightened to knock or open the door yet helpless to leave. Finally the door crept open of its own accord. There he stood, smiling, smiling. "Would you like to stay?" he said, and the last words echoed, *to stay to stay to stay to stay*, and he reached out for her, and his fingers were as soft and pulpy as earthworms when he touched her on the cheek.

The next morning Jessie arrived at the offices of Citywide Realty just as they opened their doors. The receptionist told her that Edward Selby was out showing some condos; she couldn't say when he'd be in. "That's all right," Jessie said. "I'll wait." She settled down to leaf through some magazines, studying pictures of houses she couldn't afford.

Selby arrived just before eleven. He looked momentarily surprised to see her, before his professional smile switched on automatically. "Jessie," he said, "how nice. Something I can do for you?"

"Let's talk," she said, tossing down the magazines.

They went to Selby's desk. He was still only an associate with the rental firm, so he shared the office with another agent, but she was out, and they had the room to themselves. Selby settled himself into his chair and leaned back. He was a pleasant-looking man, with curly brown hair and white teeth, his eyes careful behind silver aviator frames. "Is there a problem?" he asked.

Jessie leaned forward. "The Pear-shaped Man," she said.

Selby arched one eyebrow. "I see. A harmless eccentric."

"Are you sure of that?"

He shrugged. "He hasn't murdered anybody yet, at least that I know of."

"How much do you know about him? For starters, what's his name?"

"Good question," Selby said, smiling. "Here at Citywide Realty we just think of him as the Pear-shaped Man. I don't think I've ever gotten a name out of him."

"What the hell do you mean?" Jessie demanded. "Are you telling me his checks have THE PEAR-SHAPED MAN printed on them?"

Selby cleared his throat. "Well, no. Actually, he doesn't use checks. I come by on the first of every month to collect, and knock on his door, and he pays me in cash. One-dollar bills, in fact. I stand there, and he counts out the money into my hand, dollar by dollar. I'll confess, Jessie, that I've never been inside the apartment, and I don't especially care to. Kind of a funny smell, you know? But he's a good tenant, as far as we're concerned. Always has his rent paid on time. Never bitches about rent hikes. And he certainly doesn't bounce checks on us." He showed a lot of teeth, a broad smile to let her know he was joking.

Jessie was not amused. "He must have given a name when he first rented the apartment."

"I wouldn't know about that," Selby said. "I've only handled that building for six years. He's been down in the basement a lot longer than that."

"Why don't you check his lease?"

Selby frowned. "Well, I could dig it up, I suppose. But really, is his name any of your business? What's the problem here, anyway? Exactly what has the Pear-shaped Man *done?*"

Jessie sat back and crossed her arms. "He looks at me."

"Well," Selby said, carefully, "I, uh, well, you're an attractive woman, Jessie. I seem to recall asking you out myself."

"That's different," she said. "You're normal. It's the way he looks at me."

"Undressing you with his eyes?" Selby suggested.

Jessie was nonplussed. "No," she said. "That isn't it. It's not sexual, not in the normal way, anyhow. I don't know how to explain it. He keeps asking me down to his apartment. He's always hanging around."

"Well, that's where he lives."

"He bothers me. He's crept into my paintings."

This time both of Selby's eyebrows went up. "Into your paintings?" he said. There was a funny hitch in his voice.

Jessie was getting more and more discomfited; this wasn't coming out right at all. "Okay, it doesn't sound like much, but he's *creepy*, I tell you. His lips are always wet. The way he smiles. His eyes. His squeaky little voice. And that smell. Jesus Christ, you collect his rent, you ought to know."

The realtor spread his hands helplessly. "It's not against the law to have body odor. It's not even a violation of his lease."

"Last night he snuck into the building and left a pile of Cheez Doodles right where I'd step in them."

"Cheez Doodles?" Selby said. His voice took on a sarcastic edge. "God, not *Cheez Doodles*! How fucking heinous! Have you informed the police?"

"It's not funny. What was he doing inside the building anyway?"

"He lives there."

"He lives in the basement. He has his own door, he doesn't need to come into our hallway. Nobody but the six regular tenants ought to have keys to that door."

"Nobody does, as far as I know," Selby said. He pulled out a notepad. "Well, that's something, anyway. I'll tell you what, I'll have the lock changed on the outer door. The Pear-shaped Man won't get a key. Will that make you happy?"

"A little," said Jessie, slightly mollified.

"I can't promise that he won't get in," Selby cautioned. "You know how it is. If I had a nickel for every time some tenant has taped over a lock or propped open a door with a doorstop because it was more convenient, well . . ."

"Don't worry, I'll see that nothing like that happens. What about his name? Will you check the lease for me?"

Selby sighed. "This is really an invasion of privacy. But I'll do it. A personal favor. You owe me one." He got up and went across the room to a black metal filing cabinet, pulled open a drawer, rummaged around, and came out with a legal-sized folder. He was flipping through it as he returned to his desk.

"Well?" Jessie asked, impatiently.

"Hmmmm," Selby said. "Here's your lease. And here's the others." He went back to the beginning and checked the papers one by one. "Winbright, Peabody, Pumetti, Harris, Jeffries." He closed the file, looked up at her, and shrugged. "No lease. Well, it's a crummy little apartment, and he's been there forever. Either we've misfiled his lease or he never had one. It's not unknown. A month-to-month basis . . ."

"Oh, great," Jessie said. "Are you going to do anything about it?"

"I'll change that lock," Selby said. "Beyond that, I don't know what you expect of me. I'm not going to evict the man for offering you Cheez Doodles."

The Pear-shaped Man was standing on the stoop when Jessie got home, his battered bag tucked up under one arm. He smiled when he saw her approach. *Let him touch me*, she thought; *just let him touch me when I walk by, and I'll have him booked for assault so fast it'll make his little pointy head swim.* But the Pear-shaped Man made no effort to grab her. "I have things to show you downstairs," he said as Jessie ascended the stairs. She had to pass within a foot of him; the smell was overwhelming today, a rich odor like yeast and decaying vegetables. "Would you like to look at my things?" he called after her. Jessie unlocked the door and slammed it behind her.

*I'm not going to think about him*, she told herself inside, over a cup of tea. She had work to do. She'd promised Adrian the cover by Monday, after all. She went into her studio, drew back the curtains, and set to work, determined to eradicate every hint of the Pear-shaped Man from the cover. She painted away the double chin, firmed up the jaw, redid those tight wet lips, darkened the hair, made it blacker and bushier and more wind tossed so the head didn't seem to come to such a point. She gave him sharp, high, pronounced cheekbones—cheekbones like the blade of a knife—made the face almost gaunt. She even changed the color of his eyes. Why had she given him those weak, pale eyes? She made the eyes green, a crisp, clean, commanding green, full of vitality.

It was almost midnight by the time she was done, and Jessie was exhausted, but when she stepped back to survey her handiwork, she was delighted. The man was a real Pirouette hero now: a rakehell, a rogue, a hell-raiser whose robust exterior concealed a brooding, melancholy, poetic soul. There was nothing the least bit pear-shaped about him. Adrian would have puppies.

It was a good kind of tiredness. Jessie went to sleep feeling altogether satisfied. Maybe Selby was right; she was too imaginative, she'd really let the Pear-shaped Man get to her. But work, good hard old-fashioned work, was the perfect antidote for these shapeless fears of hers. Tonight, she was sure, her sleep would be deep and dreamless.

She was wrong. There was no safety in her sleep. She stood trembling on his doorstep once again. It was so dark down there, so filthy. The rich, ripe smell of the garbage cans was overwhelming, and she thought she could hear things moving in the shadows. The door began to open. The Pear-shaped Man smiled at her and touched her with cold, soft fingers like a nest of grubs. He took hold of her by the arm and drew her inside, inside, inside, inside. . . .

Angela knocked on her door the next morning at ten. "Sunday brunch," she called out. "Don is making waffles. With chocolate chips and fresh strawberries. And bacon. And coffee. And O.J. Want some?"

Jessie sat up in bed. "Don? Is he here?"

"He stayed over," Angela said.

Jessie climbed out of bed and pulled on a paint-splattered pair of jeans. "You know I'd never turn down one of Don's brunches. I didn't even hear you guys come in."

"I snuck my head into your studio, but you were painting away, and you didn't even notice. You had that intent look you get sometimes, you know, with the tip of your tongue peeking out of one corner of your mouth. I figured it was better not to disturb the artist at work." She giggled. "How you avoided hearing the bed-springs, though, I'll never know."

Breakfast was a triumph. There were times when Jessie couldn't understand just what Angela saw in Donald the student shrink, but mealtimes were not among them. He was a splendid cook. Angela and Donald were still lingering over coffee, and Jessie over tea, at eleven, when they heard noises from the hall. Angela went to check. "Some guy's out there changing the lock," she said when she returned. "I wonder what that's all about."

"I'll be damned," Jessie said. "And on the weekend, too. That's time and a half. I never expected Selby to move so fast."

Angela looked at her curiously. "What do you know about this?"

So Jessie told them all about her meeting with the realtor and her encounters with the Pear-shaped Man. Angela giggled once or twice, and Donald slipped into his wise shrink face. "Tell me, Jessie," he said when she had finished, "don't you think you're overreacting a bit here?"

"No," Jessie said curtly.

"You're stonewalling," Donald said. "Really now, try and look at your actions objectively. What has this man done to you?"

"Nothing, and I intend to keep it that way," Jessie snapped. "I didn't ask for your opinion."

"You don't have to ask," Donald said. "We're friends, aren't we? I hate to see you getting upset over nothing. It sounds to me as though you're developing some kind of phobia about a harmless neighborhood character."

Angela giggled. "He's just got a crush on you, that's all. You're such a heartbreaker."

Jessie was getting annoyed. "You wouldn't think it was funny if he was leaving Cheez Doodles for you," she said angrily. "There's something . . . well, something *wrong* there. I can feel it."

Donald spread his hands. "Something wrong? Most definitely. The man is obviously very poorly socialized. He's unattractive, sloppy, he doesn't conform to normal standards of dress or personal hygiene, he has unusual eating habits and a great deal of difficulty relating to others. He's probably a very lonely person and no doubt deeply neurotic as well. But none of this makes him a killer or a rapist, does it? Why are you becoming so obsessed with him?"

"I am not becoming obsessed with him."

"Obviously you are," Donald said.

"She's in love," Angela teased.

Jessie stood up. "I am *not* becoming obsessed with him!" she shouted, "and this discussion has just ended."

That night, in her dream, Jessie saw inside for the first time. He drew her in, and she found she was too weak to resist. The lights were very bright inside, and it was warm and oh so humid, and the air seemed to move as if she had entered the mouth of some great beast, and the walls were orange and flaky and had a strange, sweet smell, and there were empty plastic Coke bottles everywhere and bowls of half-eaten Cheez Doodles, too, and the Pear-shaped Man said, "You can see my things, you can have my things," and he began to undress, unbuttoning his short-sleeved shirt, pulling it off, revealing dead, white, hairless flesh and two floppy breasts, and the right breast was stained with blue ink from his leaking pens, and he was smiling, smiling, and he undid his thin belt, and then pulled down the fly on his brown polyester pants, and Jessie woke screaming.

On Monday morning, Jessie packed up her cover painting, phoned a messenger service, and had them take it down to Pirouette for her. She wasn't up to another trip downtown. Adrian would want to chat, and Jessie wasn't in a very sociable mood. Angela kept needling her about the Pear-shaped Man, and it had left her in a foul temper. Nobody seemed to understand. There was something wrong with the Pear-shaped Man, something serious, something horrible. He was no joke. He was frightening. Somehow she had to prove it. She had to learn his name, had to find out what he was hiding.

She could hire a detective, except detectives were expensive. There had to be something she could do on her own. She could try his mailbox again. She'd be better off if she waited until the day the gas and electric bills came, though. He had lights in his apartment, so the electric company would know his name. The only problem was that the electric bill wasn't due for another couple of weeks.

The living room windows were wide open, Jessie noticed suddenly. Even the drapes had been drawn all the way back. Angela must have done it that morning before taking off for work. Jessie hesitated and then went to the window. She closed it, locked it, moved to the next, closed it, locked it. It made her feel safer. She told herself she wouldn't look out. It would be better if she didn't look out.

How could she not look out? She looked out. He was there, standing on the sidewalk below her, looking up. "You could see my things," he said in his high, thin voice. "I knew when I saw you that you'd want my things. You'd like them. We could have food." He reached into a bulgy pocket, brought out a single Cheez Doodle, held it up to her. His mouth moved silently.

"Get away from here, or I'll call the police!" Jessie shouted.

"I have something for you. Come to my house and you can have it. It's in my pocket. I'll give it to you."

"No you won't. Get away, I warn you. Leave me alone." She stepped back, closed the drapes. It was gloomy in here with the drapes pulled, but that was better than knowing that the Pear-shaped Man was looking in. Jessie turned on a light, picked up a paperback, and tried to read. She found herself turning pages rapidly and realized she didn't have the vaguest idea of what the words meant. She slammed down the book, marched into the kitchen, made a tuna salad sandwich on whole wheat toast. She wanted something with it, but she wasn't sure what. She took out a dill pickle and sliced it into quarters, arranged it neatly on her plate, searched through her cupboard for some potato chips. Then she poured a big fresh glass of milk and sat down to lunch.

She took one bite of the sandwich, made a face, and shoved it away. It tasted funny. Like the mayonnaise had gone bad or something. The pickle was too sour, and the chips seemed soggy and limp and much too salty. She didn't want chips anyway. She wanted something else. Some of those little orange cheese curls. She could picture them in her head, almost taste them. Her mouth watered.

Then she realized what she was thinking and almost gagged. She got up and scraped her lunch into the garbage. She had to get out of here, she thought wildly. She'd go see a movie or something, forget all about the Pear-shaped Man for a few hours. Maybe she could go to a singles' bar somewhere, pick someone up, get laid. At his place. Away from here. Away from the Pear-shaped Man. That was the ticket. A night away from the apartment would do her good.

She went to the window, pulled aside the drapes, peered out.

The Pear-shaped Man smiled, shifted from side to side. He had his misshapen briefcase under his arm. His pockets bulged. Jessie felt her skin crawl. He was *revolting*, she thought. But she wasn't going to let him keep her prisoner.

She gathered her things together, slipped a little steak knife into her purse just in case, and marched outside. "Would you like to see what I have in my case?" the Pear-shaped Man asked her when she emerged. Jessie had decided to ignore him. If she did not reply at all, just pretended he wasn't there, maybe he'd grow bored and leave her alone. She descended the steps briskly and set off down the street. The Pear-shaped Man followed close behind her. "They're all around us," he whispered. She could smell him hurrying a step or two behind her, puffing as he walked. "They are. They laugh at me. They don't understand, but they want my things. I can show you proof. I have it down in my house. I know you want to come see."

Jessie continued to ignore him. He followed her all the way to the bus stop.

The movie was a dud. Having skipped lunch, Jessie was hungry. She got a Coke and a tub of buttered popcorn from the candy counter. The Coke was three-quarters crushed ice, but it still tasted good. She couldn't eat the popcorn. The fake butter they used had a vaguely rancid smell that reminded her of the Pear-shaped Man. She tried two kernels and felt sick.

Afterward, though, she did a little better. His name was Jack, he said. He was a sound man on a local TV news show, and he had an interesting face: an easy smile, Clark Gable ears, nice gray eyes with friendly little crinkles in the corners. He bought her a drink and touched her hand; but the way he did it was a little clumsy, like he was a bit shy about this whole scene, and Jessie liked that. They had a few drinks together, and then he suggested dinner back at his place. Nothing fancy, he said. He had some cold cuts in the fridge; he could whip up some jumbo sandwiches and show her his stereo system, which was some kind of special super setup he'd rigged himself. That all sounded fine to her.

His apartment was on the twenty-third floor of a midtown high rise, and from his windows you could see sailboats tacking off on the horizon. Jack put the new Linda Ronstadt album on the stereo while he went to make the sandwiches. Jessie watched the sailboats. She was finally beginning to relax. "I have beer or ice tea," Jack called from the kitchen. "What'll it be?"

"Coke," she said absently.

"No Coke," he called back. "Beer or ice tea."

"Oh," she said, somehow annoyed. "Ice tea, then."

"You got it. Rye or wheat?"

"I don't care," she said. The boats were very graceful. She'd like to paint them someday. She could paint Jack, too. He looked like he had a nice body.

"Here we go," he said, emerging from the kitchen carrying a tray. "I hope you're hungry."

"Famished," Jessie said, turning away from the window. She went over to where he was setting the table and froze.

"What's wrong?" Jack said. He was holding out a white stoneware plate. On top of it was a truly gargantuan ham-and-Swiss sandwich on fresh deli rye, lavishly slathered with mustard, and next to it, filling up the rest of the plate, was a pile of puffy orange cheese curls. They seemed to writhe and move, to edge toward the sandwich, toward her. "Jessie?" Jack said.

She gave a choked, inarticulate cry and pushed the plate away wildly. Jack lost his grip; ham, Swiss cheese, bread, and Cheez Doodles scattered in all directions. A Cheez Doodle brushed against Jessie's leg. She whirled and ran from the apartment.

Jessie spent the night alone at a hotel and slept poorly. Even here, miles from the apartment, she could not escape the dream. It was the same as before, the same, but each night it seemed to grow longer, each night it went a little further. She was on the stoop, waiting, afraid. The door opened, and he drew her inside, the orange warm, the air like fetid breath, the Pear-shaped Man smiling. "You can see my things," he said, "you can have my things," and then he was undressing, his shirt first, his skin so white, dead flesh, heavy breasts with a blue ink stain, his belt, his pants falling, polyester puddling around his ankles, all the trash in his pockets scattering on the floor, and he really was pear-shaped, it wasn't just the way he dressed, and then the boxer shorts last of all, and Jessie looked down despite herself and there was no hair and it was small and wormy and kind of yellow, like a cheese curl, and it moved slightly and the Pear-shaped Man was saying, "I want your things now, give them to me, let me see your things," and why couldn't she run, her feet wouldn't move, but her hands did, her hands, and she began to undress.

The hotel detective woke her, pounding on her door, demanding to know what the problem was and why she was screaming.

\*    \*    \*

She timed her return home so that the Pear-shaped Man would be away on his morning run to Santino's Market when she arrived. The house was empty. Angela had already gone to work, leaving the living room windows open again. Jessie closed them, locked them, and pulled the drapes. With luck, the Pear-shaped Man would never know that she'd come home.

Already the day outside was swelteringly hot. It was going to be a real scorcher. Jessie felt sweaty and soiled. She stripped, dumped her clothing into the wicker hamper in her bedroom, and immersed herself in a long, cold shower. The icy water hurt, but it was a good clean kind of hurting, and it left her feeling invigorated. She dried her hair and wrapped herself in a huge, fluffy blue towel, then padded back to her bedroom, leaving wet footprints on the bare wood floors.

A halter top and a pair of cutoffs would be all she'd need in this heat, Jessie decided. She had a plan for the day firmly in mind. She'd get dressed, do a little work in her studio, and after that she could read or watch some soaps or something. She wouldn't go outside; she wouldn't even look out the window. If the Pear-shaped Man was at his vigil, it would be a long, hot, boring afternoon for him.

Jessie laid out her cutoffs and a white halter top on the bed, draped the wet towel over a bedpost, and went to her dresser for a fresh pair of panties. She ought to do a laundry soon, she thought absently as she snatched up a pair of pink bikini briefs.

A Cheez Doodle fell out.

Jessie recoiled, shuddering. It had been *inside*, she thought wildly, it had been inside the briefs. The powdery cheese had left a yellow stain on the fabric. The Cheez Doodle lay where it had fallen, in the open drawer on top of her underwear. Something like terror took hold of her. She balled the bikini briefs up in her fist and tossed them away with revulsion. She grabbed another pair of panties, shook them, and another Cheez Doodle leapt out. And then another. Another. She began to make a thin, hysterical sound, but she kept on. Five pairs, six, nine, that was all, but that was enough. Someone had opened her drawer and taken out every pair of panties and carefully wrapped a Cheez Doodle in each and put them all back.

*It was a ghastly joke*, she thought. Angela, it had to be Angela who'd done it, maybe she and Donald together. They thought this whole thing about the Pear-shaped Man was a big laugh, so they decided to see if they could really freak her out.

Except it hadn't been Angela. She knew it hadn't been Angela.

Jessie began to sob uncontrollably. She threw her balled-up panties to the floor and ran from the room, crushing Cheez Doodles into the carpet.

Out in the living room, she didn't know where to turn. She couldn't go back to her bedroom, *couldn't*, not just now, not until Angela got back, and she didn't want to go to the windows, even with the drapes closed. He was out there, Jessie could feel it, could feel him staring up at the windows. She grew suddenly aware of her nakedness and covered herself with her hands. She backed away from the windows, step by uncertain step, and retreated to her studio.

Inside she found a big square package leaning up against the door, with a note from Angela taped to it. "Jess, this came for you last evening," signed with Angie's big winged A. Jessie stared at the package, uncomprehending. It was from Pirouette. It was her painting, the cover she'd rushed to redo for them. Adrian had sent it back. Why?

She didn't want to know. She had to know.

Wildly, Jessie ripped at the brown paper wrappings, tore them away in long, ragged strips, baring the cover she'd painted. Adrian had written on the mat; she recognized his hand. "Not funny, kid," he'd scrawled. "Forget it."

"No," Jessie whimpered, backing off.

There it was, her painting, the familiar background, the trite embrace, the period costumes researched so carefully, but no, she hadn't done that, someone had changed it, it wasn't her work, the woman was her, her, her, slender and strong with sandy blond hair and green eyes full of rapture, and he was crushing her to him, to *him*, the wet lips and white skin, and he had a blue ink stain on his ruffled lace shirtfront and dandruff on his velvet jacket and his head was pointed and his hair was greasy and the fingers wrapped in her locks were stained yellow, and he was smiling thinly and pulling her to him and her mouth was open and her eyes half closed and it was him and it was her, and there was her own signature, there, down at the bottom.

"No," she said again. She backed away, tripped over an easel, and fell. She curled up into a little ball on the floor and lay there sobbing, and that was how Angela found her, hours later.

Angela laid her out on the couch and made a cold compress and pressed it to her forehead. Donald stood in the doorway between the living room and the studio, frowning, glancing first at Jessie and then in at the painting and then at Jessie again. Angela said soothing things and held Jessie's hand and got her a cup of tea; little by little her hysteria began to ebb. Donald crossed his arms and scowled. Finally, when Jessie had dried the last of her tears, he said, "This obsession of yours has gone too far."

"Don, don't," Angela said. "She's terrified."

"I can see that," Donald said. "That's why something has to be done. She's doing it to herself, honey."

Jessie had a hot cup of Morning Thunder halfway to her mouth. She stopped dead still. "I'm doing it to myself?" she repeated incredulously.

"Certainly," Donald said.

The complacency in his tone made Jessie suddenly, blazingly angry. "You stupid ignorant callous son of a bitch," she roared. "I'm doing it to myself, *I'm* doing it, *I'm* doing it, how *dare* you say that *I'm* doing it." She flung the teacup across the room, aiming for his fat head. Donald ducked; the cup shattered and the tea sent three long brown fingers running down the off-white wall. "Go on, let out your anger," he said. "I know you're upset. When you calm down, we can discuss this rationally, maybe get to the root of your problem."

Angela took her arm, but Jessie shook off the grip and stood, her hands balled into fists. "Go into my bedroom, you jerk, go in there right now and look around and come back and tell me what you see."

"If you'd like," Donald said. He walked over to the bedroom door, vanished, reemerged several moments later. "All right," he said patiently.

"Well?" Jessie demanded.

Donald shrugged. "It's a mess," he said. "Underpants all over the floor, lots of crushed cheese curls. Tell me what you think it means."

"He broke in here!" Jessie said.

"The Pear-shaped Man?" Donald queried pleasantly.

"*Of course* it was the Pear-shaped Man," Jessie screamed. "He snuck in here while we were all gone and he went into my bedroom and pawed through all my things and put Cheez Doodles in my underwear. He was *here*! He was touching my stuff."

Donald wore an expression of patient, compassionate wisdom. "Jessie, dear, I want you to think about what you just told us."

"There's nothing to think about!"

"Of course there is," he said. "Let's think it through together. The Pear-shaped Man was here, you think?"

"Yes."

"Why?"

"To do . . . to do what he did. It's disgusting. He's disgusting."

"Hmmm," Don said. "How, then? The locks were changed, remember? He can't even get in the building. He's never had a key to this apartment. There was no sign of forced entry. How did he get in with his bag of cheese curls?"

Jessie had him there. "Angela left the living room windows open," she said.

Angela looked stricken. "I did," she admitted. "Oh, Jessie, honey, I'm so sorry. It was hot. I just wanted to get a breeze, I didn't mean . . ."

"The windows are too high to reach from the sidewalk," Donald pointed out. "He'd have needed a ladder or something to stand on. He'd have needed to do it in broad daylight, from a busy street, with people coming and going all the time. He'd have had to have left the same way. There's the problem of the screens. He doesn't look like a very athletic sort, either."

"He did it," Jessie insisted. "He was here, wasn't he?"

"I know you think so, and I'm not trying to deny your feelings, just explore them. Has this Pear-shaped Man ever been invited into the apartment?"

"Of course not!" Jessie said. "What are you suggesting?"

"Nothing, Jess. Just consider. He climbs in through the windows with these cheese curls he intends to secrete in your drawers. Fine. How does he know which room is yours?"

Jessie frowned. "He . . . I don't know . . . he searched around, I guess."

"And found what clue? You've got three bedrooms here, one a studio, two full of women's clothing. How'd he pick the right one?"

"Maybe he did it in both."

"Angela, would you go check your bedroom, please?" Donald asked.

Angela rose hesitantly. "Well," she said, "okay." Jessie and Donald stared at each other until she returned a minute or so later. "All clean," she said.

"I don't know how he figured out which damned room was mine," Jessie said. "All I know is that he did. He had to. How else can you explain what happened, huh? Do you think I did it *myself*?"

Donald shrugged. "I don't know," he said calmly. He glanced over his shoulder into the studio. "Funny, though. That painting in there, him and you, he must have done that some other time, after you finished it but before you sent it to Pirouette. It's good work, too. Almost as good as yours."

Jessie had been trying very hard not to think about the painting. She opened her mouth to throw something back at him, but nothing flew out. She closed her mouth. Tears began to gather in the corners of her eyes. She suddenly felt weary, confused, and very alone. Angela had walked over to stand beside Donald. They were both looking at her. Jessie looked down at her hands helplessly and said, "What am I going to do? God. What am I going to *do*?"

God did not answer; Donald did. "Only one thing *to* do," he said briskly. "Face up to your fears. Exorcise them. Go down there and talk to the man, get to know him. By the time you come back up, you may pity him or have contempt for him or dislike him, but you won't fear him any longer; you'll see that he's only a human being and a rather sad one."

"Are you sure, Don?" Angela asked him.

"Completely. Confront this obsession of yours, Jessie. That's the only way you'll ever be free of it. Go down to the basement and visit with the Pear-shaped Man."

"There's nothing to be afraid of," Angela told her again.

"That's easy for you to say."

"Look, Jess, the minute you're inside, Don and I will come out and sit on the stoop. We'll be just an earshot away. All you'll have to do is let out the teeniest little yell and we'll come rushing right down. So you won't be alone, not really. And you've still got that knife in your purse, right?"

Jessie nodded.

"Come on, then, remember the time that purse snatcher tried to grab your shoulder bag? You decked him good. If this Pear-shaped Man tries anything, you're quick enough. Stab him. Run away. Yell for us. You'll be perfectly safe."

"I suppose you're right," Jessie said with a small sigh. They *were* right. She knew it. It didn't make any sense. He was a dirty, foul-smelling, unattractive man, maybe a little retarded, but nothing she couldn't handle, nothing she had to be afraid of, she didn't want to be crazy, she was letting this ridiculous obsession eat her alive and it had to end now, Donald was perfectly correct, she'd been doing it to herself all along and now she was going to take hold of it and stop it, certainly, it all made perfect sense and there was nothing to worry about, nothing to be afraid of, what could the Pear-shaped Man do to her, after all, what could he possibly *do* to her that was so terrifying? Nothing. Nothing.

Angela patted her on the back. Jessie took a deep breath, took the doorknob firmly in hand, and stepped out of the building into the hot, damp evening air. Everything was under control.

So why was she so scared?

Night was falling, but down under the stairs it had fallen already. Down under the stairs it was always night. The stoop cut off the morning sun, and the building itself blocked the afternoon light. It was dark, so dark. She stumbled over a crack in the cement, and her foot rang off the side of a metal garbage can. Jessie shuddered, imagining flies and maggots and other, worse things moving and breeding back there where the sun never shone. *No, mustn't think about that, it was only garbage, rotting and festering in the warm, humid dark, mustn't dwell on it.* She was at the door.

She raised her hand to knock, and then the fear took hold of her again. She could not move. *Nothing to be frightened of,* she told herself, *nothing at all.* What could he possibly *do* to her? Yet still she could not bring herself to knock. She stood before his door with her hand raised, her breath raw in her throat. It was so hot, so suffocatingly hot. She had to breathe. She had to get out from under the stoop, get back to where she could breathe.

A thin vertical crack of yellow light split the darkness. *No,* Jessie thought, *oh, please no.*

The door was opening.

Why did it have to open so slowly? Slowly, like in her dreams. Why did it have to open at all?

The light was so bright in there. As the door opened, Jessie found herself squinting.

The Pear-shaped Man stood smiling at her.

"I," Jessie began, "I, uh, I . . ."

"*There* she is," the Pear-shaped Man said in his tinny little squeak.

"What do you want from me?" Jessie blurted.

"I knew she'd come," he said, as though she wasn't there. "I knew she'd come for my things."

"No," Jessie said. She wanted to run away, but her feet would not move.

"You can come in," he said. He raised his hand, moved it toward her face. He touched her. Five fat white maggots crawled across her cheek and wriggled through her hair. His fingers smelled like cheese curls. His pinkie touched her ear and tried to burrow inside. She hadn't seen his other hand move until she felt it grip her upper arm, pulling, pulling. His flesh felt damp and cold. Jessie whimpered.

"Come in and see my things," he said. "You have to. You know you have to." And somehow she was inside then, and the door was closing behind her, and she was there, inside, alone with the Pear-shaped Man.

Jessie tried to get a grip on herself. *Nothing to be afraid of*, she repeated to herself, a litany, a charm, a chant, *nothing to be afraid of, what could he do to you, what could he do?* The room was L-shaped, low ceilinged, filthy. The sickly sweet smell was overwhelming. Four naked light bulbs burned in the fixture above, and along one wall was a row of old lamps without shades, bare bulbs blazing away. A three-legged card table stood against the opposite wall, its fourth corner propped up by a broken TV set with wires dangling through the shattered glass of its picture tube. On top of the card table was a big bowl of Cheez Doodles. Jessie looked away, feeling sick. She tried to step backward, and her foot hit an empty plastic Coke bottle. She almost fell. But the Pear-shaped Man caught her in his soft, damp grip and held her upright.

Jessie yanked herself free of him and backed away. Her hand went into her purse and closed around the knife. It made her feel better, stronger. She moved close to the boarded-up window. Outside she could make out Donald and Angela talking. The sound of their voices, so close at hand— that helped, too. She tried to summon up all of her strength. "How do you live like this?" she asked him. "Do you need help cleaning up the place? Are you sick?" It was so hard to force out the words.

"Sick," the Pear-shaped Man repeated. "Did they tell you I was sick? They lie about me. They lie about me all the time. Somebody should make them stop." If only he would stop smiling. His lips were so wet. But he never stopped smiling. "I knew you would come. Here. This is for you." He pulled it from a pocket, held it out.

"No," said Jessie. "I'm not hungry. Really." But she was hungry, she realized. She was famished. She found herself staring at the thick orange twist between his fingers, and suddenly she wanted it desperately. "No," she said again, but her voice was weaker now, barely more than a whisper, and the cheese curl was very close.

Her mouth sagged open. She felt it on her tongue, the roughness of the powdery cheese, the sweetness of it. It crunched softly between her teeth. She swallowed and licked the last orange flakes from her lower lip. She wanted more.

"I knew it was you," said the Pear-shaped Man. "Now your things are mine." Jessie stared at him. It was like in her nightmare. The Pear-shaped Man reached up and began to undo the little white plastic buttons on his shirt. She struggled to find her voice. He shrugged out of the shirt. His undershirt was yellow, with huge damp circles under his arms. He peeled it off, dropped it. He moved closer, and heavy white breasts flopped against his chest. The right one was covered by a wide blue smear. A dark little tongue slid between his lips. Fat white fingers worked at his belt like a team of dancing slugs. "These are for you," he said.

Jessie's knuckles were white around the hilt of the knife. "Stop," she said in a hoarse whisper.

His pants settled to the floor.

She couldn't take it. No more, no more. She pulled the knife free of her bag, raised it over her head. *"Stop!"*

"Ahh," said the Pear-shaped Man, "there it is."

She stabbed him.

The blade went in right to the hilt, plunged deep into his soft, white skin. She wrenched it down and out. The skin parted, a huge, meaty gash. The Pear-shaped Man was smiling his little smile. There was no blood, no blood at all. His flesh was soft and thick, all pale dead meat.

He moved closer, and Jessie stabbed him again. This time he reached up and knocked her hand away. The knife was embedded in his neck. The hilt wobbled back and forth as he padded toward her. His dead, white arms reached out and she pushed against him and her hand sank into his body like he was made of wet, rotten bread. "Oh," he said, "oh, oh, oh." Jessie opened her mouth to scream, and the Pear-shaped Man pressed those heavy wet lips to her own and swallowed at her sound. His pale eyes sucked at her. She felt his tongue darting forward, and it was round and black and oily, and then it was snaking down inside her, touching, tasting, feeling all her things. She was drowning in a sea of soft, damp flesh.

She woke to the sound of the door closing. It was only a small click, a latch sliding into place, but it was enough. Her eyes opened, and she pulled herself up. It was so hard to move. She felt heavy, tired. Outside they were laughing. They were laughing at her. It was dim and far-off, that laughter, but she knew it was meant for her.

Her hand was resting on her thigh. She stared at it and blinked. She wiggled her fingers, and they moved like five fat maggots. She had something soft and yellow under her nails and deep dirty yellow stains up near her fingertips.

She closed her eyes, ran her hand over her body, the soft heavy curves, the thicknesses, the strange hills and valleys. She pushed, and the flesh gave and gave and gave. She stood up weakly. There were her clothes, scattered on the floor. Piece by piece she pulled them on, and then she moved across the room. Her briefcase was down beside the door; she gathered it up, tucked it under her arm, she might need something, yes, it was good to have the briefcase. She pushed open the door and emerged into the warm night. She heard the voices above her: ". . . were right all along," a woman was saying, "I couldn't believe I'd been so silly. There's nothing sinister about him, really, he's just pathetic. Donald, I don't know how to thank you."

She came out from under the stoop and stood there. Her feet hurt so. She shifted her weight from one to the other and back again. They had stopped talking, and they were staring at her, Angela and Donald and a slender, pretty woman in blue jeans and work shirt. "Come back," she said, and her voice was thin and high. "Give them back. You took them, you took my things. You have to give them back."

The woman's laugh was like ice cubes tinkling in a glass of Coke.

"I think you've bothered Jessie quite enough," Donald said.

"She has my things," she said. "Please."

"I saw her come out, and she didn't have anything of yours," Donald said.

"She took all my things," she said.

Donald frowned. The woman with the sandy hair and the green eyes laughed again and put a hand on his arm. "Don't look so serious, Don. He's not all there."

They were all against her, she knew, looking at their faces. She clutched her briefcase to his chest. They'd taken her things, he couldn't remember exactly what, but they wouldn't get her case, he had stuff in there and they wouldn't get it. She turned away from them. He was hungry, she realized. She wanted something to eat. He had half a bag of Cheez Doodles left, she remembered. Downstairs. Down under the stoop.

As she descended, the Pear-shaped Man heard them talking about her. He opened the door and went inside to stay. The room smelled like home. He sat down, laid his case across his knees, and began to eat. He stuffed the cheese curls into his mouth in big handfuls and washed them down with sips from a glass of warm Coke straight from the bottle he'd opened that morning, or maybe yesterday. It was good. Nobody knew how good it was. They laughed at him, but they didn't know, they didn't know about all the nice things he had. No one knew. No one. Only someday he'd see somebody different, somebody to give his things to, somebody who would give him all their things. Yes. He'd like that. He'd know her when he saw her.

He'd know just what to say.

# LUCIUS SHEPARD

## Delta Sly Honey

Mr. Shepard has earned his living as a janitor, a musician, and has been getting published for four years. He was the John W. Campbell Award winner in 1985, and, in 1987, he won the Nebula for his novella *R&R*. His stories and novels have also been finalists for the Philip K. Dick Award, the World Fantasy Award, the British Science Fiction Award, the British Fantasy Award, and the Pushcart Prize. His latest novel is *Life During Wartime*, available from Bantam New Fiction. His 1987 short story "On the Border" is soon to be a major motion picture. He is currently living in Nantucket, Massachusetts, where he is finishing a novel set in the Pacific Northwest with the working title *The End of Life As We Know It*.

"Delta Sly Honey" is a Vietnam story. Originally published in the anthology, *In the Field of Fire*, edited by Jack Dann and Jeanne Van Buren Dann, it is a portrait of war as only a veteran of Vietnam could paint it.

—E.D.

# DELTA SLY HONEY

## Lucius Shepard

There was this guy I knew at Noc Linh, worked the corpse detail, guy name of Randall J. Willingham, a skinny red-haired Southern boy with a plague of freckles and eyes blue as poker chips, and sometimes when he got high, he'd wander up to the operations bunker and start spouting all kinds of shit over the radio, telling about his hometown and his dog, his opinion of the war (he was against it), and what it was like making love to his girlfriend, talking real pretty and wistful about her ways, the things she'd whisper and how she'd draw her knees up tight to her chest to let him go in deep. There was something pure and peaceful in his voice, his phrasing, and listening to him, you could feel the war draining out of you, and soon you'd be remembering your own girl, your own dog and hometown, not with heartsick longing but with joy in knowing you'd had at least that much sweetness of life. For many of us, his voice came to be the oracle of our luck, our survival, and even the brass who tried to stop his broadcasts finally realized he was doing a damn sight more good than any morale officer, and it got to where anytime the war was going slow and there was some free air, they'd call Randall up and ask if he felt in the mood to do a little talking.

The funny thing was that except for when he had a mike in his hand, you could hardly drag a word out of Randall. He had been a loner from day one of his tour, limiting his conversation to "Hey" and "How you?" and such, and his celebrity status caused him to become even less talkative. This was best explained by what he told us once over the air: "You meet ol' Randall J. on the street, and you gonna say, 'Why that can't be Randall J.! That dumb-lookin' hillbilly couldn't recite the swearin'-in oath, let alone be the hottest damn radio personality in South Vietnam!' And you'd be right on the money, 'cause Randall J. don't go more'n double figures for IQ, and he ain't got the imagination of a stump, and if you stopped him to say 'Howdy,' chances are he'd be stuck for a response. But lemme tell ya, when he puts his voice into a mike, ol' Randall J. becomes one with the airwaves, and the light that's been dark inside him goes bright, and his spirit streams out along Thunder Road and past the Napalm Coast,

270

mixin' with the ozone and changin' into Randall J. Willingham, the High Priest of the Soulful Truth and the Holy Ghost of the Sixty-Cycle Hum.''

The base was situated on a gently inclined hill set among other hills, all of which had once been part of the Michelin rubber plantation, but now were almost completely defoliated, transformed into dusty brown lumps. Nearly seven thousand men were stationed there, living in bunkers and tents dotting the slopes, and the only building with any degree of per-manence was an outsized Quonset hut that housed the PX; it stood just inside the wire at the base of the hill. I was part of the MP contingent, and I guess I was the closest thing Randall had to a friend. We weren't really tight, but being from a small Southern town myself, the son of gentry, I was familiar with his type—fey, quiet farmboys whose vulnerabilities run deep—and I felt both sympathy and responsibility for him. My sympathy wasn't misplaced: nobody could have had a worse job, especially when you took into account the fact that his top sergeant, a beady-eyed, brush-cut, tackle-sized Army lifer named Andrew Moon, had chosen him for his whip-ping boy. Every morning I'd pass the tin-roofed shed where the corpses were off-loaded (it, too, was just inside the wire, but on the opposite side of the hill from the PX), and there Randall would be, laboring among body bags that were piled around like huge black fruit, with Moon hovering in the background and scowling. I always made it a point to stop and talk to Randall in order to give him a break from Moon's tyranny, and though he never expressed his gratitude or said very much about anything, soon he began to call me by my Christian name, Curt, instead of by my rank. Each time I made to leave, I would see the strain come back into his face, and before I had gone beyond earshot, I would hear Moon reviling him. I believe it was those days of staring into stomach cavities, into charred hearts and brains, and Moon all the while screaming at him . . . I believe that was what had squeezed the poetry out of Randall and birthed his radio soul.

I tried to get Moon to lighten up. One afternoon I bearded him in his tent and asked why he was mistreating Randall. Of course I knew the answer. Men like Moon, men who have secured a little power and grown bloated from its use, they don't need an excuse for brutality; there's so much meanness inside them, it's bound to slop over onto somebody. But—think-ing I could handle him better than Randall—I planned to divert his mean-ness, set myself up as his target, and this seemed a good way to open.

He didn't bite, however; he just lay on his cot, squinting up at me and nodding sagely, as if he saw through my charade. His jowls were speckled with a few days' growth of stubble, hairs sparse and black as pig bristles. "Y'know," he said, "I couldn't figure why you were buddyin' up to that fool, so I had a look at your records." He grunted laughter. "Now I got it."

"Oh?" I said, maintaining my cool.

"You got quite a heritage, son! All that noble Southern blood, all them dead generals and senators. When I seen that, I said to myself, 'Don't get on this boy's case too heavy, Andy. He's just tryin' to be like his great-grandaddy, doin' a kindness now and then for the darkies and the poor white trash.' Ain't that right?"

I couldn't deny that a shadow of the truth attached to what he had said, but I refused to let him rankle me. "My motives aren't in question here," I told him.

"Well, neither are mine . . . 'least not by anyone who counts." He swung his legs off the cot and sat up, glowering at me. "You got some nice duty here, son. But you go fuckin' with me, I'll have your ass walkin' point in Quanh Tri 'fore you can blink. Understand?"

I felt as if I had been dipped in ice water. I knew he could do as he threatened—any man who's made top sergeant has also made some powerful friends—and I wanted no part of Quanh Tri.

He saw my fear and laughed. "Go on, get out!" he said, and as I stepped through the door, he added, "Come round the shed anytime, son. I ain't got nothin' against *noblesse oblige*. Fact is, I love to watch."

And I walked away, knowing that Randall was lost.

In retrospect, it's clear that Randall had broken under Moon's whip early on, that his drifty radio spiels were symptomatic of his dissolution. In another time and place, someone might have noticed his condition; but in Vietnam everything he did seemed a normal reaction to the craziness of the war, perhaps even a bit more restrained than normal, and we would have thought him really nuts if he hadn't acted weird. As it was, we considered him a flake, but not wrapped so tight that you couldn't poke fun at him, and I believe it was this misconception that brought matters to a head. . . .

Yet I'm not absolutely certain of that.

Several nights after my talk with Moon, I was on duty in the operations bunker when Randall did his broadcast. He always signed off in the same distinctive fashion, trying to contact the patrols of ghosts he claimed were haunting the free-fire zones. Instead of using ordinary call signs like Charlie Baker Able, he would invent others that suited the country lyricism of his style, names such as Lobo Angel Silver and Prairie Dawn Omega.

"Delta Sly Honey," he said that night. "Do you read? Over."

He sat a moment, listening to static filling in from nowhere.

"I know you're out there, Delta Sly Honey," he went on. "I can see you clear, walkin' the high country near Black Virgin Mountain, movin' through twists of fog like battle smoke and feelin' a little afraid, 'cause though you gone from the world, there's a world of fear 'tween here and the hereafter. Come back at me, Delta Sly Honey, and tell me how it's goin'." He stopped sending for a bit, and when he received no reply, he spoke again. "Maybe you don't think I'd understand your troubles, brothers. But I truly do. I know your hopes and fears, and how the spell of too much poison and fire and flyin' steel warped the chemistry of fate and made you wander off into the wars of the spirit 'stead of findin' rest beyond the grave. My soul's trackin' you as you move higher and higher toward the peace at the end of everything, passin' through mortar bursts throwin' up thick gouts of silence, with angels like tracers leadin' you on, listenin' to the cold white song of incoming stars. . . . Come on back at me, Delta Sly Honey. This here's your good buddy Randall J., earthbound at Noc Linh. Do you read?"

There was a wild burst of static, and then a voice answered, saying, "Randall J., Randall J.! This is Delta Sly Honey. Readin' you loud and clear."

I let out a laugh, and the officers sitting at the far end of the bunker turned their heads, grinning. But Randall stared in horror at the radio, as if it were leaking blood, not static. He thumbed the switch and said shakily, "What's your position, Delta Sly Honey? I repeat. What's your position?"

"Guess you might say our position's kinda relative," came the reply. "But far as you concerned, man, we just down the road. There's a place for you with us, Randall J. We waitin' for you."

Randall's Adam's apple worked, and he wet his lips. Under the hot bunker lights, his freckles stood out sharply.

"Y'know how it is when you're pinned down by fire?" the voice continued. "Lyin' flat with the flow of bullets passin' inches over your head? And you start thinkin' how easy it'd be just to raise up and get it over with. . . . You ever feel like that, Randall J.? Most times you keep flat, 'cause things ain't bad enough to make you go that route. But the way things been goin' for you, man, what with stickin' your hands into dead meat night and day—"

"Shut up," said Randall, his voice tight and small.

"—and that asshole Moon fuckin' with your mind, maybe it's time to consider your options."

"Shut up!" Randall screamed it, and I grabbed him by the shoulders. "Take it easy," I told him. "It's just some jerk-off puttin' you on." He shook me off; the vein in his temple was throbbing.

"I ain't tryin' to mess with you, man," said the voice. "I'm just layin' it out, showin' you there ain't no real options here. I know all them crazy thoughts that been flappin' round in your head, and I know how hard you been tryin' to control 'em. Ain't no point in controllin' 'em anymore, Randall J. You belong to us now. All you gotta do is to take a little walk down the road, and we be waitin'. We got some serious humpin' ahead of us, man. Out past the Napalm Coast, up beyond the high country . . ."

Randall bolted for the door, but I caught him and spun him around. He was breathing rapidly through his mouth, and his eyes seemed to be shining too brightly—like the way an old light bulb will flare up right before it goes dark for good. "Lemme go!" he said. "I gotta find 'em! I gotta tell 'em it ain't my time!"

"It's just someone playin' a goddamn joke," I said, and then it dawned on me. "It's Moon, Randall! You know it's him puttin' somebody up to this."

"I gotta find 'em!" he repeated, and with more strength than I would have given him credit for, he pushed me away and ran off into the dark.

He didn't return, not that night, not the next morning, and we reported him AWOL. We searched the base and the nearby villes to no avail, and since the countryside was rife with NLF patrols and VC, it was logical to assume he had been killed or captured. Over the next couple of days, Moon made frequent public denials of his complicity in the joke, but no one bought it. He took to walking around with his holster unlatched, a wary expression on his face. Though Randall hadn't had any real friends, many of us had been devoted to his broadcasts, and among those devotees were a number of men who . . . well, a civilian psychiatrist might have called them unstable, but in truth they were men who had chosen to exalt instability, to ritualize insanity as a means of maintaining their equilibrium in an unstable medium: it was likely some of them would attempt reprisals. Moon's best hope was that something would divert their attention, but three days after Randall's disappearance, a peculiar transmission came into operations; like all Randall's broadcasts, it was piped over the PA, and thus Moon's fate was sealed.

"Howdy, Noc Linh," said Randall or someone who sounded identical to him. "This here's Randall J. Willingham on patrol with Delta Sly Honey, speakin' to you from beyond the Napalm Coast. We been humpin' through rain and fog most of the day, with no sign of the enemy, just a few demons twistin' up from the gray and fadin' when we come near, and now we all hunkered down by the radio, restin' for tomorrow. Y'know, brothers, I used to be scared shitless of wakin' up here in the big nothin', but now it's gone and happened, I'm findin' it ain't so bad. 'Least I got the feelin' I'm headed someplace, whereas back at Noc Linh I was just spinnin' round and round, and close to losin' my mind. I hated ol' Sergeant Moon, and I hated him worse after he put someone up to hasslin' me on the radio. But now, though I reckon he's still pretty hateful, I can see he was actin' under the influence of a higher agency, one who was tryin' to help me get clear of Noc Linh . . . which was somethin' that had to be, no matter if I had to die to do it. Seems to me that's the nature of war, that all the violence has the effect of lettin' a little magic seep into the world by way of compensation. . . ."

To most of us, this broadcast signaled that Randall was alive, but we also knew what it portended for Moon. And therefore I wasn't terribly surprised when he summoned me to his tent the next morning. At first he tried to play sergeant, ordering me to ally myself with him; but seeing that this didn't work, he begged for my help. He was a mess: red-eyed, unshaven, an eyelid twitching.

"I can't do a thing," I told him.

"You're his friend!" he said. "If you tell 'em I didn't have nothin' to do with it, they'll believe you."

"The hell they will! They'll think I helped you." I studied him a second, enjoying his anxiety. "Who did help you?"

"I didn't do it, goddammit!" His voice had risen to a shout, and he had to struggle to keep calm. "I swear! It wasn't me!"

It was strange, my mental set at that moment. I found I believed him— I didn't think him capable of manufacturing sincerity—and yet I suddenly believed everything: that Randall was somehow both dead and alive, that Delta Sly Honey both did and did not exist, that whatever was happening was an event in which all possibility was manifest, in which truth and falsity had the same valence, in which the real and the illusory were undifferentiated. And at the center of this complex circumstance—a bulky, sweating monster—stood Moon. Innocent, perhaps. But guilty of a seminal crime.

"I can make it good for you," he said. "Hawaii . . . you want duty in Hawaii, I can arrange it. Hell, I can get you shipped Stateside."

He struck me then as a hideous genie offering three wishes, and the fact that he had the power to make his offer infuriated me. "If you can do all that," I said, "you ain't got a worry in the world." And I strode off, feeling righteous in my judgment.

Two nights later while returning to my hooch, I spotted a couple of men wearing tiger shorts dragging a large and apparently unconscious someone toward the barrier of concertina wire beside the PX—I knew it had to be Moon. I drew my pistol, sneaked along the back wall of the PX, and when they came abreast I stepped out and told them to put their burden down. They stopped but didn't turn loose of Moon. Both had blackened their faces with greasepaint, and to this had added fanciful designs in crimson, blue, and yellow that gave them the look of savages. They carried combat knives, and their eyes were pointed with the reflected brilliance of the perimeter lights. It was a hot night, but it seemed hotter there beside them, as if their craziness had a radiant value. "This ain't none of your affair, Curt," said the tallest of the two; despite his bad grammar, he had a soft, well-modulated voice, and I thought I heard a trace of amusement in it.

I peered at him, but was unable to recognize him beneath the paint. Again I told them to put Moon down.

"Sorry," said the tall guy. "Man's gotta pay for his crimes."

"He didn't do anything," I said. "You know damn well Randall's just AWOL."

The tall guy chuckled, and the other guy said, "Naw, we don't know that a-tall."

Moon groaned, tried to lift his head, then slumped back.

"No matter what he did or didn't do," said the tall guy, "the man deserves what's comin'."

"Yeah," said his pal. "And if it ain't us what does it, it'll be somebody else."

I knew he was right, and the idea of killing two men to save a third who was doomed in any event just didn't stack up. But though my sense of duty was weak where Moon was concerned, it hadn't entirely dissipated. "Let him go," I said.

The tall guy grinned, and the other one shook his head as if dismayed by my stubbornness. They appeared wholly untroubled by the pistol, possessed of an irrational confidence. "Be reasonable, Curt," said the tall guy. "This ain't gettin' you nowhere."

I couldn't believe his foolhardiness. "You see this?" I said, flourishing the pistol. "Gun, y'know? I'm gonna fuckin' shoot you with it, you don't let him go."

Moon let out another groan, and the tall guy rapped him hard on the back of the head with the hilt of his knife.

"Hey!" I said, training the pistol on his chest.

"Look here, Curt . . ." he began.

"Who the hell are you?" I stepped closer, but was still unable to identify him. "I don't know you."

"Randall told us 'bout you, Curt. He's a buddy of ours, ol' Randall is. We're with Delta Sly Honey."

I believed him for that first split second. My mouth grew cottony, and my hand trembled. But then I essayed a laugh. "Sure you are! Now put his ass down!"

"That's what you really want, huh?"

"Damn right!" I said. "Now!"

"Okay," he said. "You got it." And with a fluid stroke, he cut Moon's throat.

Moon's eyes popped open as the knife sliced through his tissues, and that—not the blood spilling onto the dust—was the thing that froze me: those bugged eyes in which an awful realization dawned and faded. They let him fall face downward. His legs spasmed, his right hand jittered. For a long moment, stunned, I stared at him, at the blood puddling beneath his head, and when I looked up I found that the two men were sprinting away, about to round the curve of the hill. I couldn't bring myself to fire. Mixed in my thoughts were the knowledge that killing them served no purpose and the fear that my bullets would have no effect. I glanced left and right, behind me, making sure that no one was watching, and then ran up the slope to my hooch.

Under my cot was a bottle of sour mash. I pulled it out and had a couple of drinks to steady myself; but steadiness was beyond me. I switched on a battery lamp and sat crosslegged, listening to the snores of my bunkmate. Lying on my duffel bag was an unfinished letter home, one I had begun nearly two weeks before; I doubted now I'd ever finish it. What would I tell my folks? That I had more or less sanctioned an execution? That I was losing my fucking mind? Usually I told them everything was fine, but after the scene I had just witnessed, I felt I was forever past that sort of blithe invention. I switched off the lamp and lay in the dark, the bottle resting on my chest. I had a third drink, a fourth, and gradually lost both count and consciousness.

I had a week's R & R coming and I took it, hoping debauch would shore me up. But I spent much of that week attempting to justify my inaction in terms of the inevitable and the supernatural, and failing in that attempt. You see, now as then, if pressed for an opinion, I would tell you that what happened at Noc Linh was the sad consequence of a joke gone sour, of a war twisted into a demonic exercise. Everything was explicable in that wise. And yet it's conceivable that the supernatural was involved, that—as Randall had suggested—a little magic had seeped into the world. In Vietnam, with all its horror and strangeness, it was difficult to distinguish between the magical and the mundane, and it's possible that thousands of supernatural events went unnoticed as such, obscured by the poignancies of death and fear, becoming quirky memories that years later might pass through your mind while you were washing the dishes or walking the dog, and give you a moment's pause, an eerie feeling that would almost instantly be ground away by the mills of the ordinary. But I'm certain that my qualification is due to the fact that I want there to have been some magic involved, anything to lessen my culpability, to shed a less damning light on the perversity and viciousness of my brothers-in-arms.

On returning to Noc Linh, I found that Randall had also returned. He claimed to be suffering from amnesia and would not admit to having made the broadcast that had triggered Moon's murder. The shrinks had decided that he was bucking for a Section Eight, had ordered him put back on the corpse detail, and as before, Randall could be seen laboring beneath the tin-roofed shed, transferring the contents of body bags into aluminum coffins. On the surface, little appeared to have changed. But Randall had become a pariah. He was insulted and whispered about and shunned. Whenever he came near, necks would stiffen and conversations die. If he had offed Moon himself, he would have been cheered; but the notion that he had used his influence to have his dirty work jobbed out didn't accord with the prevailing concept of honorable vengeance. Though I tried not to, I couldn't help feeling badly toward him myself. It was weird. I would approach with the best of intentions, but by the time I reached him, my hackles would have risen and I would walk on in hostile silence, as if he were exuding a chemical that had evoked my contempt. I did get close enough to him, however, to see that the mad brightness was missing from his eyes; I had the feeling that all his brightness was missing, that whatever quality had enabled him to do his broadcasts had been sucked dry.

One morning as I was passing the PX, whose shiny surfaces reflected a dynamited white glare of sun, I noticed a crowd of men pressing through the front door, apparently trying to catch sight of something inside. I pushed through them and found one of the canteen clerks—a lean kid with black hair and a wolfish face—engaged in beating Randall to a pulp. I pulled him off, threw him into a table, and kneeled beside Randall, who had collapsed to the floor. His cheekbones were lumped and discolored; blood poured from his nose, trickled from his mouth. His eyes met mine, and I felt nothing from him: he seemed muffled, vibeless, as if heavily sedated.

"They out to get me, Curt," he mumbled.

All my sympathy for him was suddenly resurrected. "It's okay, man," I said. "Sooner or later, it'll blow over." I handed him my bandanna, and he dabbed ineffectually at the flow from his nose. Watching him, I recalled Moon's categorization of my motives for befriending him, and I understood now that my true motives had less to do with our relative social status than with my belief that he could be saved, that—after months of standing by helplessly while the unsalvageable marched to their fates—I thought I might be able to effect some small good work. This may seem altruistic to the point of naïveté, and perhaps it was, perhaps the brimstone oppressiveness of the war had from the residue of old sermons heard and disregarded provoked some vain Christian reflex; but the need was strong in me, nonetheless, and I realized that I had fixed on it as a prerequisite to my own salvation.

Randall handed back the bandanna. "Ain't gonna blow over," he said. "Not with these guys."

I grabbed his elbow and hauled him to his feet. "What guys?"

He looked around as if afraid of eavesdroppers. "Delta Sly Honey!"

"Christ, Randall! Come on." I tried to guide him toward the door, but he wrenched free.

"They out to get me! They say I crossed over and they took care of Moon for me . . . and then I got away from 'em." He dug his fingers into my arm. "But I can't remember, Curt! I can't remember nothin'!"

My first impulse was to tell him to drop the amnesia act, but then I thought about the painted men who had scragged Moon: if they were after Randall, he was in big trouble. "Let's get you patched up," I said. "We'll talk about this later."

He gazed at me, dull and uncomprehending. "You gonna help me?" he asked in a tone of disbelief.

I doubted anyone could help him now, and maybe, I thought, that was also part of my motivation—the desire to know the good sin of honest failure. "Sure," I told him. "We'll figure out somethin'."

We started for the door, but on seeing the men gathered there, Randall balked. "What you want from me?" he shouted, giving a flailing, awkward wave with his left arm as if to make them vanish. "What the fuck you want?"

They stared coldly at him, and those stares were like bad answers. He hung his head and kept it hung all the way to the infirmary.

That night I set out to visit Randall, intending to advise him to confess, a tactic I perceived as his one hope of survival. I'd planned to see him early in the evening, but was called back on duty and didn't get clear until well after midnight. The base was quiet and deserted-feeling. Only a few lights picked out the darkened slopes, and had it not been for the heat and stench, it would have been easy to believe that the hill with its illuminated caves was a place of mild enchantment, inhabited by elves and not frightened men. The moon was almost full, and beneath it the PX shone like an immense silver lozenge. Though it had closed an hour before, its windows were lit, and—MP instincts engaged—I peered inside. Randall was backed against the bar, holding a knife to the neck of the wolfish clerk who had beaten him, and ranged in a loose circle around him, standing among the tables, were five men wearing tiger shorts, their faces painted with savage designs. I drew my pistol, eased around to the front and—wanting my entrance to have shock value—kicked the door open.

The five men turned their heads to me, but appeared not at all disconcerted. "How's she goin', Curt?" said one, and by his soft voice I recognized the tall guy who had slit Moon's throat.

"Tell 'em to leave me be!" Randall shrilled.

I fixed my gaze on the tall guy and with gunslinger menace said, "I'm not messin' with you tonight. Get out now or I'll take you down."

"You can't hurt me, Curt," he said.

"Don't gimme that ghost shit! Fuck with me, and you'll be humpin' with Delta Sly Honey for real."

"Even if you were right 'bout me, Curt, I wouldn't be scared of dyin'. I was dead where it counts halfway through my tour."

A scuffling at the bar, and I saw that Randall had wrestled the clerk to the floor. He wrapped his legs around the clerk's waist in a scissors and yanked his head back by the hair to expose his throat. "Leave me be," he said. Every nerve in his face was jumping.

"Let him go, Randall," said the tall guy. "We ain't after no innocent blood. We just want you to take a little walk . . . to cross back over."

"Get out!" I told him.

"You're workin' yourself in real deep, man," he said.

"This ain't no bullshit!" I said. "I *will* shoot."

"Look here, Curt," he said. "S'pose we're just plain ol' ordinary grunts. You gonna shoot us all? And if you do, don't you think we'd have friends who'd take it hard? Any way you slice it, you bookin' yourself a silver box and air freight home."

He came a step toward me, and I said, "Watch it, man!" He came another step, his devil mask split by a fierce grin. My heart felt hot and solid in my chest, no beats, and I thought, He's a ghost, his flesh is smoke, the paint a color in my eye. "Keep back!" I warned.

"Gonna kill me?" Again he grinned. "Go ahead." He lunged, a feint only, and I squeezed the trigger.

The gun jammed.

When I think now how this astounded me, I wonder at my idiocy. The gun jammed frequently. It was an absolute piece of shit, that weapon. But at the time its failure seemed a magical coincidence, a denial of the laws of chance. And adding to my astonishment was the reaction of the other men: they made no move toward Randall, as if no opportunity had been provided, no danger passed. Yet the tall guy looked somewhat shaken to me.

Randall let out a mewling noise, and that sound enlisted my competence. I edged between the tables and took a stand next to him. "Let me get the knife from him," I said. "No point in both of 'em dyin'."

The tall guy drew a deep breath as if to settle himself. "You reckon you can do that, Curt?"

"Maybe. If you guys wait outside, he won't be as scared and maybe I can get it."

They stared at me, unreadable.

"Gimme a chance."

"We ain't after no innocent blood." The tall guy's tone was firm, as if this were policy. "But . . ."

"Just a coupla minutes," I said. "That's all I'm askin'."

I could almost hear the tick of the tall guy's judgment. "Okay," he said at last. "But don't you go tryin' nothin' hinkey, Curt." Then, to Randall. "We be waitin', Randall J."

As soon as they were out the door, I kneeled beside Randall. Spittle flecked the clerk's lips, and when Randall shifted the knife a tad, his eyes rolled up into heaven. "Leave me be," said Randall. He might have been talking to the air, the walls, the world.

"Give it up," I said.

He just blinked.

"Let him go and I'll help you," I said. "But if you cut him, you on your own. That how you want it?"

"Un-unh."

"Well, turn him loose."

"I can't," he said, a catch in his voice. "I'm all froze up. If I move, I'll cut him." Sweat dripped into his eyes, and he blinked some more.

"How 'bout I take it from you? If you keep real still, if you lemme ease it outta your hand, maybe we can work it that way."

"I don't know. . . . I might mess up."

The clerk gave a long shuddery sigh and squeezed his eyes shut.

"You gonna be fine," I said to Randall. "Just keep your eyes on me, and you gonna be fine."

I stretched out my hand. The clerk was trembling, Randall was trembling, and when I touched the blade it was so full of vibration, it felt alive, as if all the energy in the room had been concentrated there. I tried pulling it away from the clerk's neck, but it wouldn't budge.

"You gotta loosen up, Randall," I said.

I tried again and, gripping the blade between my forefinger and thumb, managed to pry it an inch or so away from the line of blood it had drawn. My fingers were sweaty, the metal slick, and the blade felt like it was connected to a spring, that any second it would snap back and bite deep.

"My fingers are slippin'," I said, and the clerk whimpered.

"Ain't my fault if they do." Randall said this pleadingly, as if testing the waters, the potentials of his guilt and innocence, and I realized he was setting me up the way he had Moon's killers. It was a childlike attempt compared to the other, but I knew to his mind it would work out the same.

"The hell it ain't!" I said. "Don't do it, man!"

"It ain't my fault!" he insisted.

"Randall!"

I could feel his intent in the quiver of the blade. With my free hand, I grabbed the clerk's upper arm, and as the knife slipped, I jerked him to the side. The blade sliced his jaw, and he screeched; but the wound wasn't mortal.

I plucked the knife from Randall's hand, wanting to kill him myself. But I had invested too much in his salvation. I hauled him erect and over to the window; I smashed out the glass with a chair and pushed him through. Then I jumped after him. As I came to my feet, I saw the painted men closing in from the front of the PX and—still towing Randall along—I sprinted around the corner of the building and up the slope, calling for help. Lights flicked on, and heads popped from tent flaps. But when they spotted Randall, they ducked back inside.

I was afraid, but Randall's abject helplessness—his eyes rolling like a freaked calf's, his hands clawing at me for support—helped to steady me. The painted men seemed to be everywhere. They would materialize from behind tents, out of bunker mouths, grinning madly and waving moonstruck knives, and send us veering off in another direction, back and forth across the hill. Time and again, I thought they had us, and on several occasions, it was only by a hairsbreadth that I eluded the slash of a blade that looked to be bearing a charge of winking silver energy on its tip. I was wearing down, stumbling, gasping, and I was certain we couldn't last much longer. But we continued to evade them, and I began to sense that they were in no hurry to conclude the hunt; their pursuit had less an air of frenzy than of a ritual harassment, and eventually, as we staggered up to the mouth of the operations bunker and—I believed—safety, I realized that they had been herding us. I pushed Randall inside and glanced back from the sand-bagged entrance. The five men stood motionless a second, perhaps fifty feet away, then melted into the darkness.

I explained what had happened to the MP on duty in the bunker—a heavyset guy named Cousins—and though he had no love for Randall, he was a dutiful sort and gave us permission to wait out the night inside. Randall slumped down against the wall, resting his head on his knees, the picture of despair. But I believed that his survival was assured. With the testimony of the clerk, I thought the shrinks would have no choice but to send him elsewhere for examination and possible institutionalization. I felt good, accomplished, and passed the night chain-smoking, bullshitting with Cousins.

Then, toward dawn, a voice issued from the radio. It was greatly distorted, but it sounded very much like Randall's.

"Randall J.," it said. "This here's Delta Sly Honey. Do you read? Over."

Randall looked up, hearkening to the spit and fizzle of the static.

"I know you out there, Randall J.," the voice went on. "I can see you clear, sitting with the shadows of the bars upon your soul and blood on your hands. Ain't no virtuous blood, that's true. But it stains you alla same. Come back at me, Randall J. We gotta talk, you and me."

Randall let his head fall; with a finger, he traced a line in the dust.

"What's the point in keepin' this up, Randall J.?" said the voice. "You left the best part of you over here, the soulful part, and you can't go on much longer without it. Time to take that little walk for real, man. Time to get clear of what you done and pass on to what must be. We waitin' for you just north of base, Randall J. Don't make us come for you."

It was in my mind to say something to Randall, to break the disconsolate spell the voice appeared to be casting over him; but I found I had nothing left to give him, that I had spent my fund of altruism and was mostly weary of the whole business . . . as he must have been.

"Ain't nothin' to be 'fraid of out here," said the voice. "Only the wind and the gray whispers of phantom Charlie and the trail leadin' away from the world. There's good company for you, Randall J. Gotta man here used to be a poet, and he'll tell you stories 'bout the Wild North King and the Woman of Crystal. Got another fella, guy used to live in Indonesia, and he's fulla tales 'bout watchin' tigers come out on the highways to shit and cities of men dressed like women and islands where dragons still live. Then there's this kid from Opelika, claims to know some of your people down that way, and when he talks, you can just see that ol' farmboy moon heavin' up big and yellow over the barns, shinin' the blacktop so it looks like polished jet, and you can hear crazy music leakin' from the Dixieland café and smell the perfumed heat steamin' off the young girls' breasts. Don't make us wait no more, Randall J. We got work to do. Maybe it ain't much, just breakin' trail and walkin' point and keepin' a sharp eye out for demons . . . but it sure as hell beats shepherdin' the dead, now don't it?" A long pause. "You come on and take that walk, Randall J. We'll make you welcome, I promise. This here's Delta Sly Honey. Over and out."

Randall pulled himself to his feet and took a faltering few steps toward the mouth of the bunker. I blocked his path and he said, "Lemme go, Curt."

"Look here, Randall," I said. "I might can get you home if you just hang on."

"Home." The concept seemed to amuse him, as if it were something with the dubious reality of heaven or hell. "Lemme go."

In his eyes, then, I thought I could see all his broken parts, a disjointed shifting of lights and darks, and when I spoke I felt I was giving tongue to a vast consensus, one arrived at without either ballots or reasonable discourse. "If I let you go," I said, "be best you don't come back this time."

He stared at me, his face gone slack, and nodded.

Hardly anybody was outside, yet I had the idea everyone was watching us as we walked down the hill; under a leaden overcast, the base had a tense, muted atmosphere such as must have attended rainy dawns beneath the guillotine. The sentries at the main gate passed Randall through without question. He went a few paces along the road, then turned back, his face pale as a star in the half-light, and I wondered if he thought we were driving him off or if he believed he was being called to a better world. In my heart I knew which was the case. At last he set out again, quickly becoming a shadow, then the rumor of a shadow, then gone.

Walking back up the hill, I tried to sort out my thoughts, to determine what I was feeling, and it may be a testament to how crazy I was, how crazy we all were, that I felt less regret for a man lost than satisfaction in knowing that some perverted justice had been served, that the world of the war—tipped off-center by this unmilitary engagement and our focus upon it—could now go back to spinning true.

That night there was fried chicken in the mess, and vanilla ice cream, and afterward a movie about a more reasonable war, full of villainous Germans with Dracula accents and heroic grunts who took nothing but flesh wounds. When it was done, I walked back to my hooch and stood out front and had a smoke. In the northern sky was a flickering orange glow, one accompanied by the rumble of artillery. It was, I realized, just about this time of night that Randall had customarily begun his broadcasts. Somebody else must have realized this, because at that moment the PA was switched on. I half expected to hear Randall giving the news of Delta Sly Honey, but there was only static, sounding like the crackling of enormous flames. Listening to it, I felt disoriented, completely vulnerable, as if some huge black presence were on the verge of swallowing me up. And then a voice did speak. It wasn't Randall's, yet it had a similar countrified accent, and though the words weren't quite as fluent, they were redolent of his old raps, lending a folksy comprehensibility to the vastness of the cosmos, the strangeness of the war. I had no idea whether or not it was the voice that had summoned Randall to take his walk, no longer affecting an imitation, and I thought I recognized its soft well-modulated tones. But none of that mattered. I was so grateful, so relieved by this end to silence, that I went into my hooch and—armed with lies—sat down to finish my interrupted letter home.

# M. JOHN HARRISON

## Small Heirlooms

M. John Harrison's early novels include *The Pastel City*, *A Storm of Wings*, and *In Viriconium*, which introduced the mutable city of Viriconium, the setting for numerous short stories. His collection of stories, *The Ice Monkey*, was published to critical acclaim. He is currently completing *Climbers*, a novel arising from his passion for rock climbing, and working on *The Course of the Heart*, a metaphysical thriller.

Ostensibly a mainstream story, "Small Heirlooms," to me, is about hauntings and ghosts. The ghosts of the past, that—just by surviving our pain—are carried by us and incorporated into our futures.

—E.D.

Artist Paul Klee once defined fantasy not as that which is unreal, but as that which one can half-glimpse just beyond the borders of reality. This seems to me to be a good description for some of the work of British writer M. John Harrison. While in his best-known Viriconium tales Harrison paints a vivid, surreal, ever-shifting, fantasy landscape— another side of his work, represented by the following story, or by the brilliant "Egnaro," (published several years ago), portrays moments of everyday life shadowed by fantasy that lies, half-glimpsed, "just beyond the borders of reality."

Harrison makes his home in London.

—T.W.

# SMALL HEIRLOOMS

## M. John Harrison

In his thorough but ironic way, Kit discovered, her brother had named her his executor. This meant she would have to go through the mass of papers he had left. In a way she was pleased, although his books, with their mixture of autobiography and fiction, had always seemed to her hurtful and embarrassing. "You never know," she had often said to people, with a lightness she didn't feel, "when you might open the latest one and see yourself! And really: some of the things he invented are easily taken for fact." He had kept up writing until the day of his death.

It was a long journey from where she lived. All one December day she connected station to station like someone connecting up dots to make a picture. The different trains seemed to pass again and again through the same landscape; and although she would later say to someone, "I saw the most marvellous faces on Peterborough station—full of character!" she could hardly distinguish between the different travellers either.

She always tried to get a window seat, which she occupied in a slumped, awkward way, as if over the last decade she had become unused to herself. Her face, though still attractive, had also a kind of slumped heaviness; she had made it up carefully before she left home. The boy who sat across the table from her between Grantham and London found himself thinking: "She's older than you realise at first." Front face she had a perceptive thickening of the neck; her lips drooped at the corners. At the moment the breadth of her back was muscular, but in four or five years it would soften and thicken further. Rather than being fat she had a kind of mass, accentuated by her clumsy, often irritable gestures. "She's a powerful old thing," he thought. But the power of her body was beginning to be put solely into moving it around. He took out his cheque book and began to go through the stubs.

Kit ate a sweet, looking out at the unending procession of suburban golf courses and sodden recreation grounds; the lines of disused rolling stock in sidings; bits of woodland where ivy fattened the tree-trunk mysteriously in the dark winter air. She was bored and hot. A mile outside King's Cross people began putting their coats on. You could see them all along the carriage, all reaching up to the luggage rack at the same time, with a

286

movement they were unused to making, their sudden clumsiness compounded by the swaying of the train. She pushed her handbag away from her across the table.

"I'm sorry," she said absently to the boy.

Waiting for the train to stop, she heaved a sigh.

As she got to her feet her fur coat was thrown against his leg. Under the thick make-up, he saw, her skin was as coarsely textured as his mother's. "She *is* fat" he told himself, "after all. Her heaviness is only that, and two vodkas from the buffet in less than an hour." Even so he still saw it as a kind of repose, a kind of strength in repose; and surprised himself by thinking obscurely that it would get her through.

Dragging a battered canvas bag on a trolley behind her, she trudged slowly along the platform and vanished into the brightness of the Euston Road.

The last part of the journey turned out to be the quickest: nevertheless it was dark by the time she arrived in Reading. "Don't get on the train standing at Number Five, love," a guard warned her. "Unless you want to go straight to Portsmuff."

"Oh no," she explained, looking puzzledly at him. "I'm coming here. I'm definitely coming to Reading."

At John's small house in Darlington Gardens she found some washing-up in the sink and water in the electric kettle. The little bathroom next door to the kitchen had, in addition to its plastic containers of Flash and Fine Fare disinfectant, a fresh towel arranged neatly on the side of the bath, as if he had expected Kit, which in a way, she supposed, he had. The house was orderly, clean, but as dusty as it had been when he was alive. She made a cup of tea and took it into the lounge where she could drink it in front of the gas fire. Shelves of paperbacks, mostly detective stories arranged carefully by author, lined the two long sides of the room. The carpet and curtain fabrics were rough-textured, a comfortable mealy colour popular in contract furnishing. In the centre of the room on a low bamboo table was a pile of French and Spanish film magazines. Actresses had fascinated him.

Kit was tired. In the spare room the actresses stared at her levelly from the walls. He had favoured girls with a Slavic or Balkan look. She remembered him once saying to her sadly, "I suppose I shall soon have lived a whole life without ever having worn an ear ring." She couldn't find any blankets, and she was too fastidious to sleep on the mattress without a sheet, so she went downstairs again and spent the night on the sofa, under her coat.

In the morning she felt stronger and went straight into the room he had used as an office and began to empty out the two grey metal filing cabinets she found there.

Most of the material was in envelope wallets stuffed with undated sheets. There was an intermittent diary in spiral bound and loose-leaf notebooks: 1948 to 1960, with huge gaps where years had been removed or never written in. The oldest stuff, which went back to before the war, he had kept in four or five deteriorating *East Light* box files, their fastenings all broken, their marbled boards warped with damp and sunshine.

He had kept the curious, muddled, sporadic commentary on the world any novelist keeps. "This morning I saw from the top deck of a bus a woman sitting by a window using a magnifying glass to help her thread a needle." There were fragments he had never used, as in, " 'It's not my alcoholism he hates, it's my personality—' " dialogue evidently intended for Anais Tate in *Saint Govan's Head*, though she never spoke it; or which found their way into a book in modified form. Kit came across a title or two, like "The Empty Sign" (this had been written several times, over two or three journal entries, sometimes in capitals, sometimes in quote marks, sometimes in what appeared to be someone else's handwriting, as if John had been playing with a new pen; he had never to Kit's knowledge called any piece "The Empty Sign"); and some criticism—"*Once Upon a Time in America*, another film devoted to the proposition that human beings are cannibals with faces the colour of putty."

Every so often she would find something so disconcerting it hardly seemed to qualify as any of these things:

"The Expressionists chained to their mirrors—Rilke and Munch, Scheile and Kafka—never able to turn away for a moment. A column of doomed and disintegrating soldiers in the long war against the father and the society he has created to imprison them. The mirror is not a simple weapon. It is their only means of defence, their plan of attack. In it they are allowed to reassure themselves: their nightmare is always of an identity so subsumed under the father's that it becomes invisible to normal light, causing them to vanish as they watch."

Kit thought this unfair to their own father. She put it aside. Later it would have to be burned, in the waste bin or the grate according to how much more she had collected. She decided she could familiarise herself with the diaries, in a superficial way, in a morning. She found nothing that referred to her at all.

At half past ten she had to go out for shopping. It was one of those clear December mornings with pale but distinct shadows. After the small northern towns Kit was used to, the Reading streets seemed wide and endless, the red brick houses tall and elegant. Christmas trees were in all the shops, and bunches of holly which reminded her of something else John had written, in a letter to her while he was still up at Cambridge before the war: " 'The holly bears a berry as bright as any wound.' Every time you hear that carol you take the full weight of the medieval experience, which was just like a childhood. To them the words seemed mysterious and valuable in their own right, the berries so bright against the dark foliage of the tree. Rowan and yew berries are just as bright. So are hawthorn berries, especially when they are new. Hips and haws are as bright. All are instrumental and have their magical and symbolic associations, but none as dark and childlike as this myth of conscious sacrifice, organised, performed, *expressed*, as the matrix of a culture."

"John you put yourself in such a bad light with things like this," she had written back to him, unable to explain that it wasn't so much his atheism that dismayed her as his sudden articulacy, which had emptied Christmas for her as memory. She felt that she had lost all the holly they had collected as children together. Hadn't he even enjoyed singing the carols?

"You always used to love Christmas."

She bought sheets: bread: milk. She was away from Darlington Gardens for less than an hour. The moment she opened the front door again she knew someone was in the house. Along the narrow hall and on the stairs hung the smell of some unfashionably heavy perfume—thick, Byzantine, yet not at all unpleasant. The impression it gave of occupancy was so strong that Kit stood there on the doormat for a few seconds calling cheerfully, "Hello. Hello?" Had a neighbour come in while she was at the shops? "Hello?" But there was no answer. She went puzzledly in and out of the dusty rooms; looked from a window up and down the street. Later, in the bathroom, she discovered that one of the little round cakes of air-freshener had come unwrapped from its cellophane. At first she wasn't convinced that this powerful reek of violets, with its hard chemical edge, was what she had smelt. Then she was.

That afternoon, already bored with her brother's notebooks, she turned to the expensive black Twinlock binder which held the journal of his last three years, and almost immediately came upon this: "Concrete only yields more concrete. Since the war the cities of the Danube all look like Birmingham."

She bent her head over it.

When I was a boy (he went on) you could still see how they had once been the dark core of Europe. If you travelled south and east, the new Austria went behind you like a Bauhaus cakestand full of the same old stale Viennese Whirls, and you were lost in the steep cobbled streets which smelt of charcoal smoke and paprika, fresh leather from the saddler's. The children were throwing buttons against the walls as you passed, staring intently at them where they lay, as if trying to read the future from a stone. You could hear Magyar and Slovak spoken not just as languages but as incitements. There in the toe of Austria, at that three-way confluence of borders, you could see a dancing bear: and though the dance was rarely more than a kind of sore lumbering, with the feet turned in, to a few slaps on a tambourine, it was still impressive to see one of these big bemused animals appear among the gypsy girls on the pavement. They would take turns to dance in front of it; stare comically into its small eyes to make it notice them; then pirouette away. As performers themselves, they regarded it with grave affection and delight.

I loved sights like this and sought them out. I had some money. Being English gave me a sense of having escaped.

By day the girls often told fortunes with cards, favouring a discredited but popular Etteilla. (I don't know how old it was. Among its major arcana it included a symbol I have never seen in any traditional pack, but its *langue* was that of post-Napoleonic France: "Within a year your case will come up and you will acquire money"; "You will suffer an illness which will cost considerable money without efficacy. Finally a faith-healer will restore your health with a cheap remedy"; "Upside down, this card signifies payment of a debt you thought completely lost"; and so on. It was like having bits of Balzac, or Balzac's letters, read out to you.) They would stand curiously immobile in the street with its seventy-odd unwieldy cards displayed in a beautiful fan, while the crowds whirled round them head down into the cold wind of early spring. By night many of them were prostitutes. This other duty encouraged them to exchange their ear rings and astonishing tiered skirts for an overcoat and a poor satin slip, but they were in no way diminished by it.

To me, anyway, the two services seemed complementary, and I saw in the needs they fulfilled a symmetry the excitement of which, though it escapes me now, I could hardly contain. Huts and caravans amid the rubbish at the edge of a town or under the arches of some huge bleak railway viaduct, fires which made the night ambiguous, musical instruments which hardly belonged in Europe at all: increasingly I was drawn to the gypsy encampments.

Was I more than eighteen years old? It seems unlikely. Nevertheless I could tell, by the way the dim light pooled in the hollow of her collar bones, that the girl was less. She raised one arm in a quick ungainly motion to slide the curtain shut across the doorway; the satin lifted across her ribby sides. I thought her eyes vague, short-sighted. When she discovered I was English she showed me a newspaper clipping, a photograph of Thomas Maszaryk, pinned to the wall above the bed. "Good," she said sadly; she shook her head then nodded it immediately, as if she wasn't sure which gesture was appropriate. We laughed. It was February: you could hear the dogs barking in the night forty miles up and down the river, where the floodwater was frozen in mile-wide lakes. She lay down and opened her legs and they made the same shape as a fan of cards when it first begins to spread in the hand. I shivered and looked away.

"Tell our fortunes first."

Maszaryk had died not long before; the war was rehearsing itself with increasing confidence. Like many of the European gypsies, I suppose, she ended up in some camp or oven.

The afternoon was nearly over.

Kit sat on in her brother's cold front room, with its photomagazines and dust, unable somehow to reach over and switch on the lights or the gas fire, while the bright inks he had used, a fresh colour for every entry, fluoresced like a beacon in the last of the winter daylight.

"Years later," she read, "I could only think that Birkenau had been in the room with us even then. A burial kommando drunk on petrol and formalin was already waiting rowdily outside like the relatives at the door of the bridal suite, as she closed the curtain, spread the cards, then knelt over me thoughtfully to bring me off in the glum light with a quick, limping flick of the pelvis. However often I traced the line of her breastbone with my fingers, however much she smiled, the death camp was in there with us."

And then, almost wonderingly:

"Any child we might have had would have lived out its time not in the Theresienstadt, the family camp, but in Mengele's block."

She read and re-read this and then sat slumped in the chair, legs stuck out in front of her like an old woman until there was only time to get up, put on the light and the fire, make something to eat, and go to bed. She felt slow and exhausted, as if she had finally used up some great resource. Before she could go to sleep she had to hear a human voice. "Book at Bedtime" was *Le Grand Meaulnes*. She listened to a weather report. "Visibility nil."

In bed she decided over and over again, "He poisoned his own memories too."

Eventually she dropped off and after some time dreamed—if that was the right word for it—she was listening to a woman's footsteps tap-tapping on a polished wood-block floor. This took place in the lounge of some comfortable "country" hotel, with its low ceiling, panelled walls and red velvet sofa. It was full of great exotic indoor plants which had been planted in brass jugs, casseroles, bits of terra cotta balanced on tall awkward wooden stands, even a coal scuttle made of some orange-blonde wood, anything but proper pots. Kit heard herself say reasonably to the other woman, "Why don't you sit down?"

Cars were parked in the driveway outside. Through the open French windows—it was a warm night—she could see a Devon Rex cat moving thoughtfully from car to car, marking each bumper with a copious greenish spray. Suddenly it became bored and jumped in through the window. It was old, blind-looking. Brindled and slow, it weaved about in the open spaces of the wood-block as if it were pushing its way through a thicket of long entangled grass.

"Do you think he's in pain?" the other woman asked.

She had difficulty ordering her dinner.

"Mm . . . I think . . . yes, soup I think . . ."

Her voice became almost inaudible. She would like her steak spoiled, she admitted, "overdone. Sorry." She laughed apologetically.

Kit wanted to tell her: "The waiter doesn't care how you have your steak. You can see he is young and shy, but a little impatient too—he's used to people who know quite well what they want."

When the waiter had gone the heels began again, tap tap indecisively round the room. She rustled the newspapers and magazines in the wicker basket; went from picture to picture on the wall—a head in pencil, turned at an odd angle away from the artist; a still life with two lutes more real than the room; a bridge. In the end she flicked the ash off her cigarette and sat down with a copy of Vogue and a dry sherry. In a flash the old cat had jumped lightly on to her lap!

"He's not in pain," Kit said, "he only wants attention," and woke up as soon as she heard it, convinced again that there was someone in the house; that someone had been in the room with her.

She had no idea what the time was. When she switched the lamp on, white light sprayed off the door of the spare room; it was closed. She opened it and went out on to the landing and stood there helplessly, staring at the film posters, the cardboard boxes stuffed with old magazines, the lights in their dusty plastic globes. People say of someone, "She filled the house with her personality," without a clue of what they might mean. The perfume Kit had smelled that morning was like a sea around her—she thought that if she couldn't learn to swim in it she would drown—she was gripped by the panic of irreversible events. There was no likelihood, she saw, that it was the smell of an unwrapped air-freshener. It was Persian attar. She was in the heart of a rose.

Wherever she looked the sense of occupancy was appalling. Whoever was in the house with her was leaving each room just before Kit went in; or were they coming into it as soon as she had gone? John's desk with its broken IBM, his files and papers where Kit had strewn them over the floor, his bed under its threadbare candlewick cover, were folded into the heart of the rose. She opened the back door and looked out: the concrete path, netted over with suckers from some untended plant, the plumes of pampas grass at the end of the garden, even the rain falling steadily—all enfolded in the heart of a rose.

"Hello?" whispered Kit. No one answered. The house was full.

An hour later it was empty again. She got herself back upstairs, but she knew she wouldn't sleep, and inevitably her brother's papers were waiting there for her, the voice of his despair as his life began to seem more pointless, composed as a mystery—

"You can't cure people of their character," she read.

After this he had crossed something out then gone on, "You can't even change yourself. Experiments in that direction soon deteriorate into bitter, infuriated struggles. You haul yourself over the wall and glimpse new country. Good! You can never again be what you were! But even as you are congratulating yourself you discover tied to one leg the string of Christmas cards, gas bills, air letters and family snaps which will never allow you to be anyone else. A forty year old woman holds up a doll she has kept in a cardboard box under a bed since she was a child. She touches its clothes, which are falling to pieces; works tenderly its loose arm. The expression that trembles on the edge of realising itself in the slackening muscles of her lips and jaw is indescribably sad. How are you to explain to her that she has lost nothing by living the intervening years of her life? How is *she* to explain this to *you*?"

Kit thought about this until it got light. Who had he been trying to comfort, or separate himself from? Who had held up the doll? Some time after eight she remembered the dream that had woken her to the scent of attar, and saw clearly that both women were herself.

She wept.

"Perspective is unfair," she had written to him during the war. "We shouldn't have to live our lives unless we can live in them, thoughtlessly, like the animals."

By ten o'clock she was standing on the platform at Reading station, waiting for a train to Charing Cross. Towards London everything was a blue and grey haze. The rails made a curved perspective into it. The spaces suggested were immense. Kit knew without being told that if she were to go back to Darlington Gardens now, all the doors and windows of her brother's house would be wide open and every piece of paper in it gone, though in the end she had burned nothing. The smell of attar would be so strong it filled the street outside, as if the pavements had suddenly put forth great suffocating masses of flowers. Though she would not be able to see them she would hear the laughter of the children as they threw buttons against the wall; she would hear the tambourine keep time for the dancing bear.

"In the heart of the rose," she whispered to herself.

Sitting in the 12.15 a.m. King's Cross to Leeds the next day, she caught herself repeating this, like a line from a song. Unable to face the whole journey at once she had broken it with an old friend who lived in North London. Now she settled herself and got her luggage on to the rack. The train was crowded. While she was waiting for it to pull out she watched two girls on the platform kissing one another. One of them was wearing a man's thick grey overcoat much too large for her. "Those two imagine they've discovered something new."

So as to have eaten something before her vodka-and-tonic at half past eleven she brought back with it from the buffet two slices of toast. They lay thick and white under the BR napkin, in every way as much of a mistake as the book Judith had lent her to read on the way back: *Voyage in the Dark*. Every page or two she looked at her wrist watch. She gave up before the train had reached Slough, and instead tried to carry on with the letter she had already begun, "Dear Judith, I saw a boy with the face of your new painting. He was taking the money in the station cafe at King's Cross. His head was turned at the exact same angle; the exact same half-smile was on his face."

To this, before she could change her mind, she added quickly.

"Does Pentonville Road go to Pentonville? Who knows? (I expect you do, Judith!) If it does, Pentonville is some misty attractive distance where you can see a junction, trees, a white cupola. Everything goes away to there from the doors of King's Cross, through a foreground with choked buses in shadow, narrow-looking pavements." It was always difficult to write to people who had lived and worked all their lives in London. You tried to bring it alive for them, but how could you? Judith lived in Harrow, had said as they talked late into the night, "Don't think of getting up early in the morning." Kit looked out of the window. "For a moment," she wrote, "I was tempted not to go inside and catch the Leeds train, but to walk a little and see what happened to me."

After three quarters of an hour the train was halted (as the guard said) by a "lineside fire." The fire brigade was out, he reassured everyone, trying to find some means by which the train could pass. It was cold, and there was some weak sunshine. Out of the window Kit could see ploughed fields, trees, a stream; then in the distance lorries and cars on a motorway. When the train began to move again there was neither fire nor engine to be seen, only some factories and houses which looked like the outskirts of a town but weren't, and in the end the fire turned out to be a lot further ahead than anyone had expected. The landscape became very flat, although its sense of emptiness was relieved by birchwoods and spinneys. The sun went in again; a power station loomed up suddenly out of a thin local mist. "Ladies and gentlemen," the guard said without warning, "we are now approaching the scene of the fire. This will be visible on your right hand side in the direction of travel." A second or two later he came back on the loudspeaker and said, "It will be on your *left* hand side in the direction of travel." There was some laughter. Passengers began leaving their seats so they could poke their heads out of the windows in the doorways between the carriages. From half a mile away you could see dark grey smoke rising a hundred and fifty or two hundred feet in the air above the edge of some small town or village. The train slowed, jerked forward suddenly, slowed again. Old women walked up and down the gangway with vague, loose expectant smiles on their faces, like backward children at a pantomime. As the train rolled closer, at perhaps ten or fifteen miles an hour, you could see that the smoke cast a shadow across the empty fields: by now it looked much blacker and denser. The fire engines, two of them, were parked at the bottom of the railway embankment, on a bridge over a culverted stream. This made them look like toys with little flickering blue lights, arranged in a model of a landscape; all the values of the real landscape shifted suddenly to fit. The fire itself was disappointing—a small dump of discarded agricultural tyres in an old siding forty or fifty yards long, only a section of which had caught. It was a toy fire: but even though the deep red flames were twenty yards off, blown back on themselves by the wind, over the dump and away from the train, you could still feel the heat on the side of your face through the double glazed window. The firemen moved easily through the smoke, stepping in and out of the flames as they dragged the smouldering tyres apart, occasionally staring in at the passengers. Though the smoke had looked so black and thick, Kit has been protected from it to some extent by the air conditioning. Now, with the fire falling behind and the old ladies trooping back smiling to sit down, a movement of the air in the carriage seemed to bring it to her suddenly. She had expected the heavy acrid odour of burning rubber: but the smoke smelled first of attar of roses, and then after that of something utterly disgusting, and Kit thought, " 'At Birkenau the human fat is wasted; they do not manufacture soap,' " and had to get up and push her way down the carriage and into the lavatory, where she leaned over the washbasin in the corner and was copiously sick into it.

"The war ended," John had written. "The cold war began. Not long after the Communist seizure of power in Czechoslovakia, Thomas Maszaryk's son Jan, then Foreign Minister, was found dead in the courtyard beneath an open window in the ministry. This came home to me among all the other events, I think, not because I had any interest in Czech affairs but simply because I remembered the faith the girl had put in his father. We don't so much impose our concerns on others as bequeath them, like small heirlooms. They lose one significance then, discovered in a drawer years after, suddenly gain another."

Shivering defiantly, Kit wiped her mouth and looked round the lavatory.

"I know you're there" she said.

# PATRICIA C. WREDE

## The Improper Princess

Patricia C. Wrede started the Minneapolis Fantasy explosion with the publication of her first book, *Shadow Magic*. Since then she has published several works to increasing acclaim and a growing, loyal readership: *Daughter of Witches*, *The Seven Towers*, *The Harp of Imach Thysell*, and the recent *Caught in Crystal*, which made the *Washington Post* Bestsellers List, as well as the witty and wonderful *Talking to Dragons*, published as part of the MagicQuest Young Adult Fantasy series; short fiction published in the *Liavek* anthology series, which Wrede helped to create along with her fellow Minneapolis fantasy writers; and a regency fantasy written in the form of a correspondence between two young women, cowritten with yet another talented Minneapolis writer, Caroline Stevermer. Her work *The Seven Towers* has been turned into a play, and Wrede is currently at work on a retelling of the fairy tale "Snow White and Rose Red" to be published in the "Fairy Tales Series" of adult fairy-tale-based novels.

"The Improper Princess" is a charming tale that will particularly delight fans of *Talking to Dragons*, as it is set in the same world. This story points out Wrede's talent for taking the standard fare of fantasy and infusing it with new life, enthusiasm, and her own special brand of wit.

Wrede lives in the suburbs of Minneapolis with her husband, who is *not* a fantasy writer; she recently returned from a long Grand Tour of Europe and England.

—T.W.

# THE IMPROPER PRINCESS

## Patricia C. Wrede

Linderwall was a large kingdom, just east of the Mountains of Morning, where philosophers were highly respected and the number five was fashionable. The climate was unremarkable. The knights kept their armor brightly polished (mainly for show—it had been centuries since a dragon had come east). There were the usual periodic problems with royal children and uninvited fairy godmothers, but they were always the sort of thing that could be cleared up by finding the proper prince or princess to marry the unfortunate child a few years later. All in all, Linderwall was a very prosperous and pleasant place.

Cimorene hated it.

Cimorene was the youngest daughter of the king of Linderwall, and her parents found her rather trying. Their first six daughters were perfectly normal princesses, with long, golden hair and sweet dispositions, each more beautiful than the last. Cimorene was lovely enough, but her hair was jet black and she wore it in braids instead of curled and pinned like her sisters'.

And she wouldn't stop growing. Her parents were quite sure that no prince would want to marry a girl who could look him in the eye instead of gazing up at him becomingly through her lashes. As for the girl's disposition—well, when people were being polite, they said she was strong-minded. When they were angry or annoyed with her, they said she was as stubborn as a pig.

The king and queen did the best they could. They hired the most superior tutors and governesses to teach Cimorene all the things a princess ought to know—dancing, embroidery, drawing, and etiquette. There was a great deal of etiquette, from the proper way to curtsy before a visiting prince to how loudly it was permissible to scream when being carried off by a giant. (Linderwall still had an occasional problem with giants.)

Cimorene found it all very dull, but she pressed her lips together and learned it anyway. When she couldn't stand it any longer, she would go down to the castle armory and bully the armsmaster into giving her a fencing lesson. As she got older, she found her regular lessons more and more boring. Consequently, the fencing lessons became more and more frequent.

When she was twelve, her father found out.

"Fencing is not proper behavior for a princess," he told her in the gentle-but-firm tone recommended by the court philosopher.

Cimorene tilted her head to one side. "Why not?"

"It's . . . well, it's simply not done."

Cimorene considered. "Aren't I a princess?"

"Yes, of course you are, my dear," said her father with relief. He had been bracing himself for a storm of tears, which was the way his other daughters reacted to reprimands.

"Well, I fence," Cimorene said with the air of one delivering an unshakable argument. "So it is *too* done by a princess."

"That doesn't make it proper, dear," put in her mother gently.

"Why not?"

"It simply doesn't," the queen said firmly, and that was the end of Cimorene's fencing lessons.

When she was fourteen, her father discovered that she was making the court magician teach her magic.

"How long has this been going on?" he asked wearily, when she arrived in response to his summons.

"Since you stopped my fencing lessons," Cimorene said. "I suppose you're going to tell me it isn't proper behavior for a princess."

"Well, yes. I mean, it isn't proper."

"Nothing interesting seems to be proper," Cimorene said.

"You might find things more interesting if you applied yourself a little more, dear," Cimorene's mother said.

"I doubt it," Cimorene muttered, but she knew better than to argue when her mother used that tone of voice. And that was the end of the magic lessons.

The same thing happened over the Latin lessons from the court philosopher, the cooking lessons from the castle chef, the economics lessons from the court treasurer, and the juggling lessons from the court minstrel. Cimorene began to grow rather tired of it.

When she was sixteen, Cimorene summoned her fairy godmother.

"Cimorene, my dear, this sort of thing really isn't done," the fairy said, fanning away the scented blue smoke that had accompanied her appearance.

"People keep telling me that," Cimorene said.

"You should pay attention to them then," her godmother said irritably. "I'm not used to being hauled away from my tea without warning. And you aren't supposed to call me unless it is a matter of utmost importance to your life and future happiness."

"It *is* of utmost importance to my life and future happiness," Cimorene said.

"Oh, very well. You're a bit young to have fallen in love already; still, you always have been a precocious child. Tell me about him."

Cimorene sighed. "It isn't a him."

"Enchanted, is he?" the fairy said with a spark of interest. "A frog, perhaps? That used to be quite popular, but it seems to have gone out of fashion lately. Nowadays, all the princes are talking birds, or dogs, or hedgehogs."

"No, no, I'm not in love with anyone!"

"Then what, exactly, is your problem?" the fairy said in exasperation.

"This!" Cimorene gestured at the castle around her. "Embroidery lessons, and dancing, and—and being a princess!"

"My dear Cimorene!" the fairy said, shocked. "It's your heritage!"

"It's boring."

"Boring?" The fairy did not appear to believe what she was hearing.

"Boring. I want to do things, not sit around all day and listen to the court minstrel make up songs about how brave Daddy is and how lovely his wife and daughters are."

"Nonsense, my dear. This is just a stage you're going through. You'll outgrow it soon, and you'll be very glad you didn't do anything rash."

Cimorene looked at her godmother suspiciously. "You've been talking to my parents, haven't you?"

"Well, they do try to keep me up-to-date on what my godchildren are doing."

"I thought so," said Cimorene, and bade her fairy godmother a polite good-bye.

A few weeks later, Cimorene's parents took her to a tourney in Sathem-by-the-Mountains, the next kingdom over. Cimorene was quite sure that the only reason they were taking her was because her fairy godmother had told them that something had better be done about Cimorene, and soon. She kept this opinion to herself; anything was better than the endless rounds of dancing and embroidery lessons at home.

Cimorene realized her mistake almost as soon as they reached their destination. For the king of Sathem-by-the-Mountains had a son, a golden-haired, blue-eyed, and exceedingly handsome prince, whose duties appeared to consist entirely of dancing attendance on Cimorene.

"*Isn't* he handsome," sighed Cimorene's lady-in-waiting.

"Yes," Cimorene said without enthusiasm. "Unfortunately, he isn't anything else."

"Whatever do you mean?" the lady-in-waiting said in astonishment.

"He has no sense of humor, he isn't intelligent, he can't talk about anything except tourneys, and half of what he does say he gets wrong. I'm glad we're only staying three weeks; I don't think I could stand to be polite to him for much longer than that."

"But what about your engagement?" the lady-in-waiting cried, horrified.

"What engagement?" Cimorene said sharply.

The lady-in-waiting tried to mutter something about a mistake, but Cimorene put up her chin in her best princess fashion and insisted on an explanation. Finally, the lady-in-waiting broke down.

"I . . . I overheard Their Majesties discussing it yesterday," she sniffled into her handkerchief. "The stipulations and covenants and contracts and settlements have all been drawn up, and they're going to sign them the day after tomorrow and announce it on Th-Thursday."

"I see," said Cimorene. "Thank you for telling me. You may go."

The lady-in-waiting left, and Cimorene went to see her parents. They were annoyed and a little embarrassed to find that Cimorene had discovered their plans, but they were still very firm about it. "We were going to tell you tomorrow, when we signed the papers," her father said.

"We knew you'd be pleased, dear," her mother said, nodding. "He's such a good-looking boy."

"But I don't want to marry Prince Therandil," Cimorene said.

"Well, it's not exactly a brilliant match," Cimorene's father said, frowning. "But I didn't think you'd care how big his kingdom was."

"It's the prince I don't care for," Cimorene said.

"That's a great pity, dear, but it can't be helped," Cimorene's mother said placidly. "I'm afraid it isn't likely that you'll get another offer."

"Then I won't get married at all."

Both her parents looked slightly shocked. "My dear Cimorene!" said her father. "That's out of the question. You're a princess; it simply isn't *done*."

"I'm too young to get married!"

"Your great-aunt Rose was married at sixteen," her mother pointed out. "One really can't count all those years she spent asleep under that dreadful fairy's curse."

"I won't marry the prince of Sathem-by-the-Mountains!" Cimorene said desperately. "It isn't proper!"

"What?" said both her parents together.

"He hasn't rescued me from a giant or an ogre, or freed me from a magic spell," Cimorene said.

Both her parents looked uncomfortable. "Well, no," said Cimorene's father. "It's a bit late to start arranging it, but we might be able to manage something."

"I don't think it's necessary," Cimorene's mother said. She looked reprovingly at Cimorene. "You've never paid attention to what was or wasn't suitable before, dear; you can't start now. Proper or not, you will marry Prince Therandil three weeks from Thursday."

"But, Mother—"

"I'll send the wardrobe mistress to your room to start fitting your bride clothes," Cimorene's mother said firmly, and that was the end of the conversation.

Cimorene decided to try a more direct approach: She went to see Prince Therandil. He was in the castle armory, looking at swords. "Good morning, Princess," he said, when he finally noticed Cimorene. "Don't you think this is a lovely sword?"

Cimorene picked it up. "The balance is off," she said.

"I believe you're right," said Therandil after a moment's study. "Pity; now I'll have to find another. Is there something I can do for you?"

"Yes," said Cimorene. "You can *not* marry me."

"What?" Therandil looked confused.

"You don't really want to marry me, do you?" Cimorene said coaxingly.

"Well, no," Therandil replied, looking sheepish.

"Oh, good. Then you'll tell your father you don't want to marry me?"

"I couldn't do that!" Therandil said, shocked. "It wouldn't be right."

"Why not?" Cimorene demanded crossly.

"Because . . . because . . . well, because princes just don't do that!"

"Then how are you going to keep from marrying me?"

"I guess I won't be able to," Therandil said, after thinking hard for a moment. "What do you think of that sword over there with the silver hilt?"

Cimorene left in disgust and went out to the castle garden. She was very discouraged; it looked as if she were going to have to marry the prince of Sathem-by-the-Mountains whether she wanted to or not. "I'd rather be eaten by a dragon," she muttered.

"That can be arranged," said a voice from beside her left slipper.

Cimorene looked down and saw a small, green frog looking up at her. "I beg your pardon; did you speak?" she asked.

"You don't see anyone else around, do you?" said the frog.

"Oh!" said Cimorene. She had never met a talking frog before. "Are you an enchanted prince?" she asked a little doubtfully.

"No, but I've met a couple of them, and after a while you pick up a few things," said the frog. "Now, why is it that you want to be eaten by a dragon?"

"My parents want to marry me off to Prince Therandil," Cimorene explained.

"And you don't want to marry him? Sensible of you," said the frog. "I don't like Therandil; he used to skip rocks across the top of my pond. They always sank into my living room."

"I'm sorry," Cimorene said politely.

"Well," said the frog, "what are you going to do about it?"

"Marrying Therandil? I don't know. I've tried talking to my parents, but they won't listen, and neither will Therandil."

"I didn't ask what you'd said about it," the frog snapped. "I asked what you're going to do. Nine times out of ten, talking is a way of avoiding doing things."

"What kinds of things would you suggest?" Cimorene said, stung.

"You could challenge the prince to a duel," the frog said.

"He'd win," Cimorene said. "It's been four years since I've been allowed to do any fencing."

"You could turn him into a toad," the frog suggested.

"I never got past invisibility in my magic lessons," Cimorene said. "Transformations are advanced study."

The frog looked at her disapprovingly. "Can't you do anything?"

"I can curtsy," Cimorene said disgustedly. "I know seventeen different country dances, nine ways to agree with an ambassador from Cathay without actually promising him anything, and one hundred and forty-three embroidery stitches. And I can make cherries jubilee."

"Cherries jubilee?" asked the frog, and snapped at a passing fly.

"The castle chef taught me, before Father made him stop," Cimorene explained.

The frog munched briefly, then swallowed and said, "I suppose there's no help for it. You'll have to run away."

"Run away?" Cimorene said. "I don't like that idea; there are too many things that could go wrong."

"You don't like the idea of marrying Prince Therandil, either," the frog pointed out.

"Maybe I can think of some other way out of getting married."

The frog snorted. "Such as?" Cimorene didn't answer, and after a moment, the frog said, "I thought so. Do you want my advice or not?"

"Yes, please," said Cimorene. After all, she didn't have to follow it.

"Go to the main road outside the city and follow it away from the mountains," said the frog. "After a while, you will come to a small pavillion made of gold, surrounded by trees made of silver with emerald leaves. Go straight past it without stopping, and don't answer if anyone calls out to you from the pavillion. Keep on until you reach a hovel. Walk straight up to the door and knock three times; then snap your fingers and go inside. You'll find some personages there who can help you out of your difficulties, if you're polite about asking and they're in the right mood. And that's all."

The frog turned abruptly and dove into the pool. "Thank you very much," Cimorene called after it, thinking that the frog's advice sounded very odd indeed. She went back into the castle.

Cimorene spent the rest of the day being fitted and fussed over by the ladies-in-waiting until she was ready to scream. By the end of the formal banquet, at which she had to sit next to Prince Therandil and listen to endless stories of his prowess in battle, Cimorene was more than ready to take the frog's advice.

Late that night, when most of the castle was asleep, Cimorene bundled up five clean handkerchiefs and her best crown. Then she dug out the notes she had taken during her magic lessons and carefully cast a spell of invisibility. It seemed to work, but she was still very careful about sneaking out of the castle. After all, it had been a long time since she had practiced.

By morning, Cimorene was well outside the city, and visible again, walking down the main road that led away from the mountains. It was hot and dusty, and she began to wish she had brought a bottle of water instead of the handkerchiefs.

Just before noon, Cimorene spied a small grove of trees next to the road ahead of her. It looked like a cool, pleasant place to rest for a few minutes, and she hurried forward. When she reached the grove, however, she saw that the trees were made of the finest silver, and their shining green leaves were huge emeralds. In the center of the grove was a charming pavillion made of gold and hung with gold curtains.

Cimorene slowed down and looked longingly at the cool, green shade beneath the trees. Just then a woman's voice called out from the pavillion, "My dear, you look so tired and thirsty! Come and sit with me and share my luncheon."

The voice was so kind and coaxing that Cimorene took two steps toward the edge of the road before she remembered the frog's advice. "Oh, no," she thought to herself, "I'm not going to be caught this easily!" She turned without saying anything and hurried on down the road.

A little farther on, she came to a tiny, wretched-looking hovel made of cracked and weathered, grey boards. They door hung slantwise on a broken hinge, and the whole building looked as though it were going to topple over at any moment. Cimorene stopped and stared doubtfully at it, but she had followed the frog's advice this far and she thought it would be silly to stop now. So she shook the dust from her skirts and put on her crown (so as to make a good impression). She marched up to the door, knocked three times, and snapped her fingers just as the frog had told her. Then she pushed the door open and went inside.

The inside of the hovel was dark and cool and damp. Cimorene found it a pleasant relief after the hot, dusty road, but she wondered why no sunlight seemed to be coming through the cracks in the boards. She was still standing just inside the door, waiting for her eyes to adjust to the dark, when someone said crossly, "Is this that princess we've been waiting for?"

"Why don't you ask her?" said a deep, rumbly voice.

"I'm Cimorene, princess of Linderwall," Cimorene said, and tried to curtsy in the direction of the voices. "I was told you could help me."

"Help her?" said the first voice, and Cimorene heard a snort. "I think we should just eat her and be done with it."

Cimorene began to feel frightened. She felt behind her for the door, and started in surprise when her fingers touched damp stone instead of dry wood. Then a third voice said, "Not so fast, Woraug. Let's hear her story first."

So Cimorene took a deep breath and began to explain about the fencing lessons, and the magic lessons, and the Latin, and the juggling, and all the other things that weren't considered proper behavior for a princess, and she told the voices that she had run away from Sathem-by-the-Mountains to keep from having to marry Prince Therandil. "And what do you expect us to do about it?" one of the voices said curiously.

"I don't know," Cimorene said. "Except, of course, that I *would* rather not be eaten. I can't see who you are in this dark, you know."

"That can be fixed," said the voice. A moment later, a small ball of light appeared in the air above Cimorene's head. Cimorene stepped backward very quickly and ran into the wall. The voices belonged to dragons. Five of them lay on or sprawled over or curled around the various rocks and columns that filled the huge cave where Cimorene stood. She saw no sign of the hovel or the door through which she had entered.

Cimorene felt very frightened. The smallest of the dragons was easily three times as tall as she was, and they gave an overwhelming impression of shining, green scales and sharp, silver teeth. She swallowed very hard, wondering whether she really would rather be eaten by a dragon than marry Therandil.

"Well?" said the dragon just in front of her. "Just what are you asking us to do for you?"

"I—" Cimorene stopped short, as an idea occurred to her; then she asked cautiously, "Dragons are . . . are fond of princesses, aren't they?"

"Very," said the dragon, and smiled. The smile showed all of its teeth, which Cimorene did not find reassuring.

"That is, I've heard of dragons who have captive princesses to cook for them and . . . and so on," said Cimorene, who really had very little idea what captive princesses did all day.

The dragon in front of Cimorene nodded. One of the others, a yellowish-green in color, shifted restlessly and said, "Oh, let's just go ahead and eat her. It will save trouble."

Before any of the other dragons could answer, there was a loud booming noise and a sixth dragon slithered into the cave. Its scales were more grey than green, and the dragons by the door made way for it respectfully. "Kazul!" said the newcomer in a loud voice. "*Achoo!* Sorry I'm late, but a terrible thing happened on the way here, *achoo!*"

"What was it?" said the dragon to whom Cimorene had been talking.

"Ran into a wizard. *Achoo!* Had to eat him; no help for it. *Achoo, achoo.* And now look at me!" Every time the grey-green dragon sneezed, he emitted a small ball of fire that scorched the wall of the cave.

"Calm down, Roxim," said Kazul. "You're only making it worse."

"*Achoo!* Calm down? When I'm having an allergy attack? *Achoo*, oh, bother, *achoo!*" said the grey-green dragon. "Somebody give me a handkerchief. *Achoo!*"

"Here," said Cimorene, holding out one of the ones she had brought with her. "Use this." She was beginning to feel much less frightened, for the grey-green dragon reminded her of her great-uncle, who was old and rather hard of hearing, and of whom she was rather fond.

"What's that?" said Roxim. "*Achoo!* Oh, hurry up and give it here."

Kazul took the handkerchief from Cimorene, using two claws very delicately, and passed it to Roxim. The grey-green dragon mopped his streaming eyes and blew his nose. "That's better, I think. *Achoo!* Oh, drat!"

The ball of fire that accompanied the dragon's sneeze had reduced the handkerchief to a charred scrap. Cimorene hastily dug out another one and handed it to Kazul, feeling very glad that she had brought several spares.

Roxim went through two more handkerchiefs before his sneezing spasms finally stopped. "Much better," he said. "Now then, who's this that lent me the handkerchiefs? Somebody's new princess, eh?"

"We were just discussing that when you came in," Kazul said, and turned back to Cimorene. "You were saying? About cooking and so on."

"Couldn't I do that for one of you for a while?" Cimorene said.

The dragon smiled again, and Cimorene swallowed hard. "Possibly. Why would you want to do that?"

"Because then I wouldn't have to go home and marry Therandil," Cimorene said. "Being a dragon's princess is a perfectly respectable thing to do, so my parents couldn't complain. And it would be much more interesting than embroidery and dancing lessons."

Several of the dragons made snorting or choking noises. Cimorene jumped, then decided that they were laughing.

"This is ridiculous!" said a large, bright-green dragon on Cimorene's left.

"Why?" asked Kazul.

"A princess, volunteering? Out of the question!"

"That's easy for you to say," one of the other dragons grumbled. "You already have a princess. What about the rest of us?"

"Yes, don't be stuffy, Woraug," said another. "Besides, what else can we do with her?"

"Eat her," suggested the yellowish-green dragon in a bored tone.

"No proper princess would come out looking for dragons," Woraug objected.

"Well, I'm not a proper princess, then," Cimorene snapped. "I make cherries jubilee, and I volunteer for dragons, and I conjugate Latin verbs —or at least, I would if anyone would let me. So there!"

"Hear, hear," said the grey-green dragon.

"You see?" Woraug said. "Who would want an improper princess?"

"I would," said Kazul.

"Give her a trial run first," a purplish-green dragon advised.

"You can't be serious, Kazul," Woraug said irritably. "Why?"

"I like cherries jubilee," Kazul replied, still watching Cimorene. "And I like the look of her. Besides, the Latin scrolls in my library need cataloging, and if I can't find someone who knows a little of the language, I'll have to do it myself."

"And for that you'd take on a black-haired, snippy, little—"

"I'll thank you to be polite when you're discussing *my* princess," Kazul said, and smiled fiercely.

"Nice little gal," Roxim said, nodding approvingly and waving Cimorene's next-to-last handkerchief. "Got sense. Be good for you, Kazul."

"If that's settled, I'm going to go find a snack," said the yellowish-green dragon.

Woraug looked around, but the other dragons seemed to agree with Roxim. "Oh, very well," Woraug said grumpily. "It's your choice after all, Kazul."

"It certainly is. Now, Princess, if you'll come this way, I'll get you settled in."

Cimorene followed Kazul across the cave and down a tunnel. She was relieved to find that the ball of light came with her; she had the uncomfortable feeling that if she had tried to walk behind a dragon in the dark she would have stepped on its tail, which would not have been a good beginning.

Kazul led Cimorene through a long maze of tunnels and finally stopped in another chamber. "Here we are," the dragon said. "You can use the small room over on the right; I believe my last princess left most of the furnishings behind when she ran off with the knight."

"Thank you," Cimorene said. "When do I start my duties? And what are they, please?"

"You start right away," said Kazul. "I'll want dinner at seven. In the meantime you can start sorting the treasure." The dragon nodded toward a dark opening on the left. "I'm sure some of it needs repairing; there's at least one suit of armor with the leg off, and some of the cheaper magic swords are probably getting rusty. The rest of it really ought to be rearranged sensibly. I can never find anything when I want it."

"What about the library you mentioned?" Cimorene said.

"We'll see how well you do on the treasure room first," Kazul said. "The rest of your job I'll explain as we go along. You don't object to learning a little magic, do you?"

"Not at all," said Cimorene.

"Good. It'll make things much easier. Go and wash up a little, and I'll let you into the treasure room so you can get started."

Cimorene nodded and went to the room Kazul had told her to use. As she washed her face and hands, she felt happier than she had in a long time. She was not going to have to marry Therandil, and sorting a dragon's treasure sounded far more interesting than dancing or embroidery. She was even going to learn some magic! For the first time in her life, Cimorene was glad she was a princess. She dried her hands and turned to go back into the main chamber, wondering how best to persuade Kazul to help her brush up on her Latin. She didn't want the dragon to be disappointed in her skill. "*Draco, draconis, draconi,*" she muttered, and her lips curved into a smile. She had always been rather good at declining nouns. Still smiling, she started forward to begin her new duties.

# JOHN BRUNNER

## The Fable of the Farmer and Fox

John Brunner, the prominent and prolific author of such science fiction classics as *The Whole Man, Stand on Zanzibar*, and *The Sheep Look Up*, is not a name one expects to encounter in an anthology devoted to fantasy (nor is the following story what one expects to encounter from John Brunner), yet this neatly rendered fable, "The Fable of the Farmer and Fox," falls, like the ancient parables of Aesop, within the broad boundaries of the fantasy tale. We are delighted to be able to include it in this collection.

Brunner makes his home in England, and any readers unfamiliar with his work might try one of his excellent short story collections, the Hugo Award-winning novel *Stand on Zanzibar*, or his existential fantasy cycle, *The Compleat Traveller in Black*.

—T.W.

# THE FABLE OF THE FARMER AND FOX

## John Brunner

Once, so they say, a certain people received a teacher, no one knew whence. But he seemed kindly and wise, and because he brought knowledge of useful arts as well as voicing high and moral principles, they made him welcome, and he came to be considerably admired.

Some of the richer folk, however, jealous that anyone should exert more influence than they, resolved to pose a question to him that he could not answer. On a day, they waited for him in the road until he passed by with those who now were his disciples, and one whom they had appointed said to him, "If you believe, as you have often said, that the world was made by forces that are wholly good, how, then, account for sickness and deformity, for misery and death?"

The teacher said, "God loves the whole creation."

"So where is this God you talk about so freely?" they demanded.

"You may find God wheresoever you desire," the teacher said.

"We think little of that," they replied. "Are we to honor the creator of plague, the one who decreed that we must die and make our flesh a meal for worms?"

"Listen," the teacher said, "and I shall show you why."

There was (he said) a farmer, and he loved his land. He dug and sowed his fields, and from them fed his family. On days when gentlemen a-horseback passed, intent on hunting foxes, he waved his hat and cheered. For he kept chickens, too, and everybody knew that foxes ate them.

One evil year a murrain stole upon the winter mist. He spent that Yuletide alone; his wife had died, and his young children.

All that remained, save frosted vegetables, was a flock of hens chiefed by a weakly rooster.

Still, they did furnish eggs. From wood and straw he cobbled coops for broody hens. He raised clutch after clutch, named every chick and coaxed it through its growth, and learned to love them all.

One crisp, fresh day in autumn the hunt rushed by again, and when he checked his coops he found a baby vixen. She had sleek russet fur, bright eyes, and teeth of an amazing sharpness.

Seizing the farmer's finger as though it were her mother's nipple, she whimpered when it gave no milk.

It was his impulse to call back the hounds and toss her to them. Yet she was beautiful, and when he looked into her shining eyes he found his resolution waning. Out of loneliness he bore her to his fireside and gave her an egg he had been saving for his supper. She ate, and lay contentedly beside him. That night he slept well for the first time since his children died.

Time came when eggs would not suffice, and foxes can't make shift with leaves and roots. The vixen snarled from hunger keener than his and pawed at the chicken-coop bars. The farmer pondered long and thought of driving her back to the wild. Well, if he must, he must. . . .

Then came the sound of hunting horns again. He said at length, "If I turn you loose, the hounds will kill you. If I give you my chickens to eat, I'll likely starve. I love these silly birds I raise from eggs, but maybe that's because I depend on them to keep me alive, not because I've tended them since they were hatched and call them each by name. I cannot say. But do I not eat them when I have to—kill them in sorrow when they're old and pluck and boil them for my own sustentation? So the best I can say is this: I shall not love my chicks the less if you eat them. But if a huntsman sets his hounds to eating *you*, he will love neither you nor them. Come, little vixen! Choose your chicken!"

The vixen spoke. He heard her clearly, and her tone was one of vast surprise.

"Then you *are* God!"

She snatched her gift and ran. It was too heavy. The hounds caught up and tore her limb from limb. When the huntsmen came to boast how they had rid this and other farms of a dangerous fox, they found fifty chickens pecking round a farmer dead of long privation, but with a smile of bliss upon his face.

"We can make nothing of your foolish tale," said they, the rich, who were so jealous of the teacher's influence.

"But we can," said the common folk, and after that they paid no heed to what the rich sort ordered them to do, but ruled their lives after the teaching of him who had so lately been a stranger.

# JOYCE CAROL OATES

## Haunted

Joyce Carol Oates was brought up in the countryside around Lockport, New York. She is the author of eighteen novels and many volumes of short stories, poems, essays, and plays. In 1970 she won the National Book Award for her novel *Them*. She has twice been the recipient of the O'Henry Award for Continuing Achievement.

"Haunted" is a story of crime and punishment, imbued with Ms. Oates's unerring sense of character and place.

—E.D.

# HAUNTED

## Joyce Carol Oates

Haunted houses, forbidden houses. The old Medlock farm. The Erlich farm. The Minton farm on Elk Creek. *No Trespassing* the signs said, but we trespassed at will. *No Trespassing No Hunting No Fishing Under Penalty of Law* but we did what we pleased because who was there to stop us?

Our parents warned us against exploring these abandoned properties: the old houses and barns were dangerous, they said. We could get hurt, they said. I asked my mother if the houses were haunted and she said, Of course not, there aren't such things as ghosts, you know that. She was irritated with me; she guessed how I pretended to believe things I didn't believe, things I'd grown out of years before. It was a habit of childhood—pretending I was younger, more childish, than in fact I was. Opening my eyes wide and looking puzzled, worried. Girls are prone to such trickery; it's a form of camouflage when every other thought you think is a forbidden thought and with your eyes open staring sightless you can sink into dreams that leave your skin clammy and your heart pounding—dreams that don't seem to belong to you that must have come to you from somewhere else from someone you don't know who knows *you.*

There weren't such things as ghosts, they told us. That was just superstition. But we could injure ourselves tramping around where we weren't wanted—the floorboards and the staircases in old houses were likely to be rotted, the roofs ready to collapse, we could cut ourselves on nails and broken glass, we could fall into uncovered wells—and you never knew who you might meet up with, in an old house or barn that's supposed to be empty. "You mean a bum?—like somebody hitch-hiking along the road?" I asked. "It could be a bum, or it could be somebody you know," Mother told me evasively. "A man, or a boy—somebody you know—" Her voice trailed off in embarrassment and I knew enough not to ask another question.

There were things you didn't talk about, back then. I never talked about them with my own children; there weren't the words to say them.

We listened to what our parents said, we nearly always agreed with what they said, but we went off on the sly and did what we wanted to do. When we were little girls: my neighbor Mary Lou Siskin and me. And when we

were older, ten, eleven years old, tomboys, roughhouses our mothers called
us. We liked to hike in the woods and along the creek for miles; we'd cut
through farmers' fields, spy on their houses—on people we knew, kids we
knew from school—most of all we liked to explore abandoned houses,
boarded-up houses if we could break in; we'd scare ourselves thinking the
houses might be haunted though really we knew they weren't haunted,
there weren't such things as ghosts. Except—

I am writing in a dime-store notebook with lined pages and a speckled
cover, a notebook of the sort we used in grade school. *Once upon a time* as I
used to tell my children when they were tucked safely into bed and drifting
off to sleep. *Once upon a time* I'd begin, reading from a book because it was
safest so: the several times I told them my own stories they were frightened
by my voice and couldn't sleep and afterward I couldn't sleep either and
my husband would ask what was wrong and I'd say, Nothing, hiding my
face from him so he wouldn't see my look of contempt.

I write in pencil, so that I can erase easily, and I find that I am constantly
erasing, wearing holes in the paper. Mrs. Harding, our fifth grade teacher,
disciplined us for handing in messy notebooks: she was a heavy, toad-faced
woman, her voice was deep and husky and gleeful when she said, "You,
Melissa, what have you to say for yourself?" and I stood there mute, my
knees trembling. My friend Mary Lou laughed behind her hand, wriggled
in her seat she thought I was so funny. Tell the old witch to go to hell,
she'd say, she'll respect you then, but of course no one would ever say such
a thing to Mrs. Harding. Not even Mary Lou. "What have you to say for
yourself, Melissa? Handing in a notebook with a ripped page?" My grade
for the homework assignment was lowered from A to B, Mrs. Harding
grunted with satisfaction as she made the mark, a big swooping B in red
ink, creasing the page. "More is expected of you, Melissa, so you disappoint
me more," Mrs. Harding always said. So many years ago and I remember
those words more clearly than words I have heard the other day.

One morning there was a pretty substitute teacher in Mrs. Harding's
classroom. "Mrs. Harding is unwell, I'll be taking her place today," she
said, and we saw the nervousness in her face; we guessed there was a secret
she wouldn't tell and we waited and a few days later the principal himself
came to tell us that Mrs. Harding would not be back, she had died of a
stroke. He spoke carefully as if we were much younger children and might
be upset and Mary Lou caught my eye and winked and I sat there at my
desk feeling the strangest sensation, something flowing into the top of my
head, honey-rich and warm making its way down my spine. *Our Father Who
art in Heaven* I whispered in the prayer with the others my head bowed and
my hands clasped tight together but my thoughts were somewhere else
leaping wild and crazy somewhere else and I knew Mary Lou's were too.

On the school bus going home she whispered in my ear, "That was because of us, wasn't it!—what happened to that old bag Harding. But we won't tell anybody."

*Once upon a time there were two sisters, and one was very pretty and one was very ugly. . . .* Though Mary Lou Siskin wasn't my sister. And I wasn't ugly, really: just sallow-skinned, with a small pinched ferrety face. With dark almost lashless eyes that were set too close together and a nose that didn't look right. A look of yearning, and disappointment.

But Mary Lou *was* pretty, even rough and clumsy as she sometimes behaved. That long silky blond hair everybody remembered her for afterward, years afterward. . . . How, when she had to be identified, it was the long silky white-blond hair that was unmistakable. . . .

Sleepless nights, but I love them. I write during the nighttime hours and sleep during the day, I am of an age when you don't require more than a few hours sleep. My husband has been dead for nearly a year and my children are scattered and busily absorbed in their own selfish lives like all children and there is no one to interrupt me no one to pry into my business no one in the neighborhood who dares come knocking at my door to see if I am all right. Sometimes out of a mirror floats an unexpected face, a strange face, lined, ravaged, with deep-socketed eyes always damp, always blinking in shock or dismay or simple bewilderment—but I adroitly look away. I have no need to stare.

It's true, all you have heard of the vanity of the old. Believing ourselves young, still, behind our aged faces—mere children, and so very innocent!

Once when I was a young bride and almost pretty my color up when I was happy and my eyes shining we drove out into the country for a Sunday's excursion and he wanted to make love I knew, he was shy and fumbling as I but he wanted to make love and I ran into a cornfield in my stockings and high heels, I was playing at being a woman I never could be, Mary Lou Siskin maybe, Mary Lou whom my husband never knew, but I got out of breath and frightened, it was the wind in the cornstalks, that dry rustling sound, that dry terrible rustling sound like whispering like voices you can't quite identify and he caught me and tried to hold me and I pushed him away sobbing and he said, What's wrong? My God what's wrong? as if he really loved me as if his life was focused on me and I knew I could never be equal to it, that love, that importance, I knew I was only Melissa the ugly one the one the boys wouldn't give a second glance, and one day he'd understand and know how he'd been cheated. I pushed him away, I said, Leave me alone! don't touch me! You disgust me! I said.

He backed off and I hid my face, sobbing.

But later on I got pregnant just the same. Only a few weeks later.

\*        \*        \*

Always there were stories behind the abandoned houses and always the stories were sad. Because farmers went bankrupt and had to move away. Because somebody died and the farm couldn't be kept up and nobody wanted to buy it—like the Medlock farm across the creek. Mr. Medlock died aged seventy-nine and Mrs. Medlock refused to sell the farm and lived there alone until someone from the country health agency came to get her. Isn't it a shame, my parents said. The poor woman, they said. They told us never, never to poke around in the Medlocks' barns or house—the buildings were ready to cave in, they'd been in terrible repair even when the Medlocks were living.

It was said that Mrs. Medlock had gone off her head after she'd found her husband dead in one of the barns, lying flat on his back his eyes open and bulging, his mouth open, tongue protruding, she'd gone to look for him and found him like that and she'd never gotten over it they said, never got over the shock. They had to commit her to the state hospital for her own good (they said) and the house and the barns were boarded up, everywhere tall grass and thistles grew wild, dandelions in the spring, tiger lilies in the summer, and when we drove by I stared and stared narrowing my eyes so I wouldn't see someone looking out one of the windows—a face there, pale and quick— or a dark figure scrambling up the roof to hide behind the chimney— Mary Lou and I wondered was the house haunted, was the barn haunted where the old man had died, we crept around to spy, we couldn't stay away, coming closer and closer each time until something scared us and we ran away back through the woods clutching and pushing at each other until one day finally we went right up to the house to the back door and peeked in one of the windows. Mary Lou led the way, Mary Lou said not to be afraid, nobody lived there any more and nobody would catch us, it didn't matter that the land was posted, the police didn't arrest kids our ages.

We explored the barns, we dragged the wooden cover off the well and dropped stones inside. We called the cats but they wouldn't come close enough to be petted. They were barn cats, skinny and diseased-looking, they'd said at the country bureau that Mrs. Medlock had let a dozen cats live in the house with her so that the house was filthy from their messes. When the cats wouldn't come we got mad and threw stones at them and they ran away hissing—nasty dirty things, Mary Lou said. Once we crawled up on the tar-paper roof over the Medlocks' kitchen, just for fun, Mary Lou wanted to climb up the big roof too to the very top but I got frightened and said, No, no please don't, no Mary Lou please, and I sounded so strange Mary Lou looked at me and didn't tease or mock as she usually did. The roof was so steep, I'd known she would hurt herself. I could see her losing her footing and slipping, falling, I could see her astonished face and her flying hair as she fell, knowing nothing could save her. You're no fun, Mary Lou said, giving me a hard little pinch. But she didn't go climbing up the big roof.

Later we ran through the barns screaming at the top of our lungs just for fun for the hell of it as Mary Lou said, we tossed things in a heap, broken-off parts of farm implements, leather things from the horses' gear, handfuls of straw. The farm animals had been gone for years but their smell was still strong. Dried horse and cow droppings that looked like mud. Mary Lou said, "You know what—I'd like to burn this place down." And she looked at me and I said, "Okay—go on and do it, burn it down." And Mary Lou said, "You think I wouldn't? Just give me a match." And I said, "You know I don't have any match." And a look passed between us. And I felt something flooding at the top of my head, my throat tickled as if I didn't know would I laugh or cry and I said, "You're crazy—" and Mary Lou said with a sneering little laugh, "*You're* crazy, dumbbell. I was just testing you."

By the time Mary Lou was twelve years old Mother had got to hate her, was always trying to turn me against her so I'd make friends with other girls. Mary Lou had a fresh mouth, she said. Mary Lou didn't respect her elders—not even her own parents. Mother guessed that Mary Lou laughed at her behind her back, said things about all of us. She was mean and snippy and a smart-ass, rough sometimes as her brothers. Why didn't I make other friends? Why did I always go running when she stood out in the yard and called me? The Siskins weren't a whole lot better than white trash, the way Mr. Siskin worked that land of his.

In town, in school, Mary Lou sometimes ignored me when other girls were around, girls who lived in town, whose fathers weren't farmers like ours. But when it was time to ride home on the bus she'd sit with me as if nothing was wrong and I'd help her with her homework if she needed help, I hated her sometimes but then I'd forgive her as soon as she smiled at me, she'd say, "Hey 'Lissa are you mad at me?" and I'd make a face and say no as if it was an insult, being asked. Mary Lou was my sister I sometimes pretended, I told myself a story about us being sisters and looking alike, and Mary Lou said sometimes she'd like to leave her family her goddamned family and come live with me. Then the next day or the next hour she'd get moody and be nasty to me and get me almost crying. All the Siskins had mean streaks, bad tempers, she'd tell people. As if she was proud.

Her hair was a light blond, almost white in the sunshine, and when I first knew her she had to wear it braided tight around her head—her grandmother braided it for her, and she hated it. Like Gretel or Snow White in one of those damn dumb picture books for children, Mary Lou said. When she was older she wore it down and let it grow long so that it fell almost to her hips. It was very beautiful—silky and shimmering. I dreamt of Mary Lou's hair sometimes but the dreams were confused and I couldn't remember when I woke up whether I was the one with the long blond silky hair, or someone else. It took me a while to get my thoughts clear lying there in bed and then I'd remember Mary Lou, who was my best friend.

She was ten months older than I was, and an inch or so taller, a bit heavier, not fat but fleshy, solid and fleshy, with hard little muscles in her upper arms like a boy. Her eyes were blue like washed glass, her eyebrows and lashes were almost white, she had a snubbed nose and Slavic cheekbones and a mouth that could be sweet or twisty and smirky depending upon her mood. But she didn't like her face because it was round—a moon face she called it, staring at herself in the mirror though she knew damned well she was pretty—didn't older boys whistle at her, didn't the bus driver flirt with her?—calling her "Blondie" while he never called me anything at all.

Mother didn't like Mary Lou visiting with me when no one else was home in our house: she didn't trust her, she said. Thought she might steal something, or poke her nose into parts of the house where she wasn't welcome. That girl is a bad influence on you, she said. But it was all the same old crap I heard again and again so I didn't even listen. I'd have told her she was crazy except that would only make things worse.

Mary Lou said, "Don't you just hate them?—your mother, and mine? Sometimes I wish—"

I put my hands over my ears and didn't hear.

The Siskins lived two miles away from us, farther back the road where the road got narrower. Those days, it was unpaved, and never got plowed in the winter. I remember their barn with the yellow silo, I remember the muddy pond where the dairy cows came to drink, the muck they churned up in the spring. I remember Mary Lou saying she wished all the cows would die—they were always sick with something—so her father would give up and sell the farm and they could live in town in a nice house. I was hurt, her saying those things as if she'd forgotten about me and would leave me behind. Damn you to hell, I whispered under my breath.

I remember smoke rising from the Siskins' kitchen chimney, from their wood-burning stove, straight up into the winter sky like a breath you draw inside you deeper and deeper until you begin to feel faint.

Later on, that house was empty too. But boarded up only for a few months—the bank sold it at auction. (It turned out the bank owned most of the Siskin farm, even the dairy cows. So Mary Lou had been wrong about that all along and never knew.)

As I write I can hear the sound of glass breaking, I can feel glass underfoot. *Once upon a time there were two little princesses, two sisters, who did forbidden things.* That brittle terrible sensation under my shoes—slippery like water —"Anybody home? Hey—anybody home?" and there's an old calendar tacked to a kitchen wall, a faded picture of Jesus Christ in a long white gown stained with scarlet, thorns fitted to His bowed head. Mary Lou is going to scare me in another minute making me think that someone is in the house and the two of us will scream with laughter and run outside where it's safe. Wild frightened laughter and I never knew afterward what was funny or why we did these things. Smashing what remained of windows, wrenching at stairway railings to break them loose, running with our heads ducked so we wouldn't get cobwebs in our faces.

One of us found a dead bird, a starling, in what had been the parlor of the house. Turned it over with a foot—there's the open eye looking right up calm and matter-of-fact. *Melissa*, that eye tells me, silent and terrible, *I see you*.

That was the old Minton place, the stone house with the caved-in roof and the broken steps, like something in a picture book from long ago. From the road the house looked as if it might be big, but when we explored it we were disappointed to see that it wasn't much bigger than my own house, just four narrow rooms downstairs, another four upstairs, an attic with a steep ceiling, the roof partly caved in. The barns had collapsed in upon themselves; only their stone foundations remained solid. The land had been sold off over the years to other farmers, nobody had lived in the house for a long time. The old Minton house, people called it. On Elk Creek where Mary Lou's body was eventually found.

In seventh grade Mary Lou had a boyfriend she wasn't supposed to have and no one knew about it but me—an older boy who'd dropped out of school and worked as a farmhand. I thought he was a little slow—not in his speech which was fast enough, normal enough, but in his way of thinking. He was sixteen or seventeen years old. His name was Hans; he had crisp blond hair like the bristles of a brush, a coarse blemished face, derisive eyes. Mary Lou was crazy for him she said, aping the older girls in town who said they were "crazy for" certain boys or young men. Hans and Mary Lou kissed when they didn't think I was watching, in an old ruin of a cemetery behind the Minton house, on the creek bank, in the tall marsh grass by the end of the Siskins' driveway. Hans had a car borrowed from one of his brothers, a battered old Ford, the front bumper held up by wire, the running board scraping the ground. We'd be out walking on the road and Hans would come along tapping the horn and stop and Mary Lou would climb in but I'd hang back knowing they didn't want me and the hell with them: I preferred to be alone.

"You're just jealous of Hans and me," Mary Lou said, unforgivably, and I hadn't any reply. "Hans is sweet. Hans is nice. He isn't like people say," Mary Lou said in a quick bright false voice she'd picked up from one of the older, popular girls in town. "He's . . ." And she stared at me blinking and smiling not knowing what to say as if in fact she didn't know Hans at all. "He isn't *simple*," she said angrily, "he just doesn't like to talk a whole lot."

When I try to remember Hans Meunzer after so many decades I can see only a muscular boy with short-trimmed blond hair and protuberant ears, blemished skin, the shadow of a moustache on his upper lip—he's looking at me, eyes narrowed, crinkled, as if he understands how I fear him, how I wish him dead and gone, and he'd hate me too if he took me that seriously. But he doesn't take me that seriously, his gaze just slides right through me as if nobody's standing where I stand.

There were stories about all the abandoned houses but the worst story was about the Minton house over on the Elk Creek Road about three miles from where we lived. For no reason anybody ever discovered Mr. Minton had beaten his wife to death and afterward killed himself with a .12-gauge shotgun. He hadn't even been drinking, people said. And his farm hadn't been doing at all badly, considering how others were doing.

Looking at the ruin from the outside, overgrown with trumpet vine and wild rose, it seemed hard to believe that anything like that had happened. Things in the world even those things built by man are so quiet left to themselves . . .

The house had been deserted for years, as long as I could remember. Most of the land had been sold off but the heirs didn't want to deal with the house. They didn't want to sell it and they didn't want to raze it and they certainly didn't want to live in it so it stood empty. The property was posted with *No Trespassing* signs layered one atop another but nobody took them seriously. Vandals had broken into the house and caused damage, the McFarlane boys had tried to burn down the old hay barn one Halloween night. The summer Mary Lou started seeing Hans she and I climbed in the house through a rear window—the boards guarding it had long since been yanked away—and walked through the rooms slow as sleepwalkers our arms around each other's waists our eyes staring waiting to see Mr. Minton's ghost as we turned each corner. The inside smelled of mouse droppings, mildew, rot, old sorrow. Strips of wallpaper torn from the walls, plasterboard exposed, old furniture overturned and smashed, old yellowed sheets of newspaper underfoot, and broken glass, everywhere broken glass. Through the ravaged windows sunlight spilled in tremulous quivering bands. The air was afloat, alive: dancing dust atoms. "I'm afraid," Mary Lou whispered. She squeezed my waist and I felt my mouth go dry for hadn't I been hearing something upstairs, a low persistent murmuring like quarreling like one person trying to convince another going on and on and on but when I stood very still to listen the sound vanished and there were only the comforting summer sounds of birds, crickets, cicadas; birds, crickets, cicadas.

I knew how Mr. Minton had died: he'd placed the barrel of the shotgun beneath his chin and pulled the trigger with his big toe. They found him in the bedroom upstairs, most of his head blown off. They found his wife's body in the cistern in the cellar where he'd tried to hide her. "Do you think we should go upstairs?" Mary Lou asked, worried. Her fingers felt cold;

but I could see tiny sweat beads on her forehead. Her mother had braided her hair in one thick clumsy braid, the way she wore it most of the summer, but the bands of hair were loosening. "No," I said, frightened. "I don't know." We hesitated at the bottom of the stairs—just stood there for a long time. "Maybe not," Mary Lou said. "Damn stairs'd fall in on us."

In the parlor there were bloodstains on the floor and on the wall—I could see them. Mary Lou said in derision, "They're just waterstains, dummy."

I could hear the voices overhead, or was it a single droning persistent voice. I waited for Mary Lou to hear it but she never did.

Now we were safe, now we were retreating, Mary Lou said as if repentant, "Yeah—this house *is* special."

We looked through the debris in the kitchen hoping to find something of value but there wasn't anything—just smashed chinaware, old battered pots and pans, more old yellowed newspaper. But through the window we saw a garter snake sunning itself on a rusted water tank, stretched out to a length of two feet. It was a lovely coppery color, the scales gleaming like perspiration on a man's arm; it seemed to be asleep. Neither one of us screamed, or wanted to throw something—we just stood there watching it for the longest time.

Mary Lou didn't have a boyfriend any longer; Hans had stopped coming around. We saw him driving the old Ford now and then but he didn't seem to see us. Mr. Siskin had found out about him and Mary Lou and he'd been upset—acting like a damn crazy man Mary Lou said, asking her every kind of nasty question then interrupting her and not believing her anyway, then he'd put her to terrible shame by going over to see Hans and carrying on with him. "I hate them all," Mary Lou said, her face darkening with blood. "I wish—"

We rode our bicycles over to the Minton farm, or tramped through the fields to get there. It was the place we liked best. Sometimes we brought things to eat, cookies, bananas, candy bars; sitting on the broken stone steps out front, as if we lived in the house really, we were sisters who lived here having a picnic lunch out front. There were bees, flies, mosquitoes, but we brushed them away. We had to sit in the shade because the sun was so fierce and direct, a whitish heat pouring down from overhead.

"Would you ever like to run away from home?" Mary Lou said. "I don't know," I said uneasily. Mary Lou wiped at her mouth and gave me a mean narrow look. " 'I don't know,' " she said in a falsetto voice, mimicking me. At an upstairs window someone was watching us—was it a man or was it a woman—someone stood there listening hard and I couldn't move feeling so slow and dreamy in the heat like a fly caught on a sticky petal that's going to fold in on itself and swallow him up. Mary Lou crumpled up some wax paper and threw it into the weeds. She was dreamy too, slow and yawning. She said, "Shit—they'd just find me. Then everything would be worse."

I was covered in a thin film of sweat but I'd begun to shiver. Goose bumps were raised on my arms. I could see us sitting on the stone steps the way we'd look from the second floor of the house, Mary Lou sprawled with her legs apart, her braided hair slung over her shoulder, me sitting with my arms hugging my knees my backbone tight and straight knowing I was being watched. Mary Lou said, lowering her voice, "Did you ever touch yourself in a certain place, Melissa?" "No," I said, pretending I didn't know what she meant. "Hans wanted to do that," Mary Lou said. She sounded disgusted. Then she started to giggle. "I wouldn't let him, then he wanted to do something else—started unbuttoning his pants—wanted me to touch *him*. And . . ."

I wanted to hush her, to clap my hand over her mouth. But she just went on and I never said a word until we both started giggling together and couldn't stop. Afterward I didn't remember most of it or why I'd been so excited my face burning and my eyes seared as if I'd been staring into the sun.

On the way home Mary Lou said, "Some things are so sad you can't say them." But I pretended not to hear.

A few days later I came back to myself. Through the ravaged cornfield: the stalks dried and broken, the tassels burnt, that rustling whispering sound of the wind I can hear now if I listen closely. My head was aching with excitement. I was telling myself a story that we'd made plans to run away and live in the Minton house. I was carrying a willow switch I'd found on the ground, fallen from a tree but still green and springy, slapping at things with it as if it were a whip. Talking to myself. Laughing aloud. Wondering was I being watched.

I climbed in the house through the back window and brushed my hands on my jeans. My hair was sticking to the back of my neck.

At the foot of the stairs I called up, "Who's here?" in a voice meant to show it was all play; I knew I was alone.

My heart was beating hard and quick, like a bird caught in the hand. It was lonely without Mary Lou so I walked heavy to let them know I was there and wasn't afraid. I started singing, I started whistling. Talking to myself and slapping at things with the willow switch. Laughing aloud, a little angry. Why was I angry, well I didn't know, someone was whispering telling me to come upstairs, to walk on the inside of the stairs so the steps wouldn't collapse.

The house was beautiful inside if you had the right eyes to see it. If you didn't mind the smell. Glass underfoot, broken plaster, stained wallpaper hanging in shreds. Tall narrow windows looking out onto wild weedy patches of green. I heard something in one of the rooms but when I looked I saw nothing much more than an easy chair lying on its side. Vandals had ripped stuffing out of it and tried to set it afire. The material was filthy but I could see that it had been pretty once—a floral design—tiny yellow flowers and green ivy. A woman used to sit in the chair, a big woman with sly staring eyes. Knitting in her lap but she wasn't knitting just staring out the window watching to see who might be coming to visit.

Upstairs the rooms were airless and so hot I felt my skin prickle like shivering. I wasn't afraid!—I slapped at the walls with my springy willow switch. In one of the rooms high in a corner wasps buzzed around a fat wasp's nest. In another room I looked out the window leaning out the window to breathe thinking this was my window, I'd come to live here. She was telling me I had better lie down and rest because I was in danger of heatstroke and I pretended not to know what heatstroke was but she knew I knew because hadn't a cousin of mine collapsed haying just last summer, they said his face had gone blotched and red and he'd begun breathing faster and faster not getting enough oxygen until he collapsed. I was looking out at the overgrown apple orchard, I could smell the rot, a sweet winey smell, the sky was hazy like something you can't get clear in your vision, pressing in close and warm. A half mile away Elk Creek glittered through a screen of willow trees moving slow glittering with scales like winking.

Come away from that window, someone told me sternly.

But I took my time obeying.

In the biggest of the rooms was an old mattress pulled off rusty bedsprings and dumped on the floor. They'd torn some of the stuffing out of this too, there were scorch marks on it from cigarettes. The fabric was stained with something like rust and I didn't want to look at it but I had to. Once at Mary Lou's when I'd gone home with her after school there was a mattress lying out in the yard in the sun and Mary Lou told me in disgust that it was her youngest brother's mattress—he'd wet his bed again and the mattress had to be aired out. As if the stink would ever go away, Mary Lou said.

Something moved inside the mattress, a black glittering thing, it was a cockroach but I wasn't allowed to jump back. Suppose you have to lie down on that mattress and sleep, I was told. Suppose you can't go home until you do. My eyelids were heavy, my head was pounding with blood. A mosquito buzzed around me but I was too tired to brush it away. Lie down on that mattress, Melissa, she told me. You know you must be punished.

I knelt down, not on the mattress, but on the floor beside it. The smells in the room were close and rank but I didn't mind, my head was nodding with sleep. Rivulets of sweat ran down my face and sides, under my arms, but I didn't mind. I saw my hand move out slowly like a stranger's hand to touch the mattress and a shiny black cockroach scuttled away in fright, and a second cockroach, and a third—but I couldn't jump up and scream.

Lie down on that mattress and take your punishment.

I looked over my shoulder and there was a woman standing in the doorway—a woman I'd never seen before.

She was staring at me. Her eyes were shiny and dark. She licked her lips and said in a jeering voice, "What are you doing here in this house, miss?"

I was terrified. I tried to answer but I couldn't speak.

"Have you come to see me?" the woman asked.

She was no age I could guess. Older than my mother but not old-seeming. She wore men's clothes and she was tall as any man, with wide shoulders, and long legs, and big sagging breasts like cows' udders loose inside her shirt not harnessed in a brassiere like other women's. Her thick wiry gray hair was cut short as a man's and stuck up in tufts that looked greasy. Her eyes were small, and black, and set back deep in their sockets; the flesh around them looked bruised. I had never seen anyone like her before—her thighs were enormous, big as my body. There was a ring of loose soft flesh at the waistband of her trousers but she wasn't fat.

"I asked you a question, miss. Why are you here?"

I was so frightened I could feel my bladder contract. I stared at her, cowering by the mattress, and couldn't speak.

It seemed to please her that I was so frightened. She approached me, stooping a little to get through the doorway. She said, in a mock-kindly voice, "You've come to visit with me—is that it?"

"No," I said.

"No!" she said, laughing. "Why, of course you have."

"No. I don't know you."

She leaned over me, touched my forehead with her fingers. I shut my eyes waiting to be hurt but her touch was cool. She brushed my hair off my forehead where it was sticky with sweat. "I've seen you here before, you and that other one," she said. "What is her name? The blond one. The two of you, trespassing."

I couldn't move, my legs were paralyzed. Quick and darting and buzzing my thoughts bounded in every which direction but didn't take hold. "Melissa is *your* name, isn't it," the woman said. "And what is your sister's name?"

"She isn't my sister," I whispered.

"What is her name?"

"I don't know."

"You don't know!"

"—don't know," I said, cowering.

The woman drew back half sighing half grunting. She looked at me pityingly. "You'll have to be punished, then."

I could smell ashes about her, something cold. I started to whimper started to say I hadn't done anything wrong, hadn't hurt anything in the house, I had only been exploring—I wouldn't come back again . . .

She was smiling at me, uncovering her teeth. She could read my thoughts before I could think them.

The skin of her face was in layers like an onion, like she'd been sunburnt, or had a skin disease. There were patches that had begun to peel. Her look was wet and gloating. Don't hurt me, I wanted to say. Please don't hurt me.

I'd begun to cry. My nose was running like a baby's. I thought I would crawl past the woman I would get to my feet and run past her and escape but the woman stood in my way blocking my way leaning over me breathing damp and warm her breath like a cow's breath in my face. Don't hurt me, I said, and she said, "You know you have to be punished—you and your pretty blond sister."

"She isn't my sister," I said.

"And what is her name?"

The woman was bending over me, quivering with laughter.

"Speak up, miss. What is it?"

"I don't know—" I started to say. But my voice said, "Mary Lou."

The woman's big breasts spilled down into her belly, I could feel her shaking with laughter. But she spoke sternly saying that Mary Lou and I had been very bad girls and we knew it her house was forbidden territory and we knew it hadn't we known all along that others had come to grief beneath its roof?

"No," I started to say. But my voice said, "Yes."

The woman laughed, crouching above me. "Now, miss, 'Melissa' as they call you—your parents don't know where you are at this very moment, do they?"

"I don't know."

"Do they?"

"No."

"They don't know anything about you, do they?—what you do, and what you think? You and 'Mary Lou.' "

"No."

She regarded me for a long moment, smiling. Her smile was wide and friendly.

"You're a spunky little girl, aren't you, with a mind of your own, aren't you, you and your pretty little sister. I bet your bottoms have been warmed many a time," the woman said, showing her big tobacco-stained teeth in a grin, ". . . your tender little asses."

I began to giggle. My bladder tightened.

"Hand that here, miss," the woman said. She took the willow switch from my fingers—I had forgotten I was holding it. "I will now administer punishment: take down your jeans. Take down your panties. Lie down on that mattress. Hurry." She spoke briskly now, she was all business. "Hurry, Melissa! *And* your panties! Or do you want me to pull them down for you?"

She was slapping the switch impatiently against the palm of her left hand, making a wet scolding noise with her lips. Scolding and teasing. Her skin shone in patches, stretched tight over the big hard bones of her face. Her eyes were small, crinkling smaller, black and damp. She was so big she had to position herself carefully over me to give herself proper balance and leverage so that she wouldn't fall. I could hear her hoarse eager breathing as it came to me from all sides like the wind.

I had done as she told me. It wasn't me doing these things but they were done. Don't hurt me, I whispered, lying on my stomach on the mattress, my arms stretched above me and my fingernails digging into the floor. The coarse wood with splinters pricking my skin. Don't hurt me O please but the woman paid no heed her warm wet breath louder now and the floorboards creaking beneath her weight. "Now, miss, now 'Melissa' as they call you —this will be our secret won't it . . ."

When it was over she wiped at her mouth and said she would let me go today if I promised never to tell anybody if I sent my pretty little sister to her tomorrow.

She isn't my sister, I said, sobbing. When I could get my breath.

I had lost control of my bladder after all, I'd begun to pee even before the first swipe of the willow switch hit me on the buttocks, peeing in helpless spasms, and sobbing, and afterward the woman scolded me saying wasn't it a poor little baby wetting itself like that. But she sounded repentant too, stood well aside to let me pass, Off you go! Home you go! And don't forget!

And I ran out of the room hearing her laughter behind me and down the stairs running running as if I hadn't any weight my legs just blurry beneath me as if the air was water and I was swimming I ran out of the house and through the cornfield running in the cornfield sobbing as the corn stalks slapped at my face *Off you go! Home you go! And don't forget!*

I told Mary Lou about the Minton house and something that had happened to me there that was a secret and she didn't believe me at first saying with a jeer, "Was it a ghost? Was it Hans?" I said I couldn't tell. Couldn't tell what? she said. Couldn't tell, I said. Why not? she said.

"Because I promised."

"Promised who?" she said. She looked at me with her wide blue eyes like she was trying to hypnotize me. "You're a goddamned liar."

Later she started in again asking me what had happened what was the secret was it something to do with Hans? did he still like her? was he mad at her? and I said it didn't have anything to do with Hans not a thing to do with him. Twisting my mouth to show what I thought of him.

"Then who—?" Mary Lou asked.

"I told you it was a secret."

"Oh shit—what kind of a secret?"

"A secret."

"A secret *really?*"

I turned away from Mary Lou, trembling. My mouth kept twisting in a strange hurting smile. "Yes. A secret *really*," I said.

The last time I saw Mary Lou she wouldn't sit with me on the bus, walked past me holding her head high giving me a mean snippy look out of the corner of her eye. Then when she left for her stop she made sure she bumped me going by my seat, she leaned over to say, "I'll find out for myself, I hate you anyway," speaking loud enough for everybody on the bus to hear, "—I always have."

*Once upon a time* the fairy tales begin. But then they end and often you don't know really what has happened, what was meant to happen, you only know what you've been told, what the words suggest. Now that I have completed my story, filled up half my notebook with my handwriting that disappoints me, it is so shaky and childish—now the story is over I don't understand what it means. I know what happened in my life but I don't know what has happened in these pages.

Mary Lou was found murdered ten days after she said those words to me. Her body had been tossed into Elk Creek a quarter mile from the road and from the old Minton place. Where, it said in the paper, nobody had lived for fifteen years.

It said that Mary Lou had been thirteen years old at the time of her death. She'd been missing for seven days, had been the object of a countrywide search.

It said that nobody had lived in the Minton house for years but that derelicts sometimes sheltered there. It said that the body was unclothed and mutilated. There were no details.

This happened a long time ago.

The murderer (or murderers as the newspaper always said) was never found.

Hans Meunzer was arrested of course and kept in the county jail for three days while police questioned him but in the end they had to let him go, insufficient evidence to build a case it was explained in the newspaper though everybody knew he was the one wasn't he the one?—everybody knew. For years afterward they'd be saying that. Long after Hans was gone and the Siskins were gone, moved away nobody knew where.

Hans swore he hadn't done it, hadn't seen Mary Lou for weeks. There were people who testified in his behalf said he couldn't have done it for one thing he didn't have his brother's car any longer and he'd been working all that time. Working hard out in the fields—couldn't have slipped away long enough to do what police were saying he'd done. And Hans said over and over he was innocent. Sure he was innocent. Son of a bitch ought to be hanged my father said, everybody knew Hans was the one unless it was a derelict or a fisherman—fishermen often drove out to Elk Creek to fish for black bass, built fires on the creek bank and left messes behind—sometimes prowled around the Minton house too looking for things to steal. The police had records of automobile license plates belonging to some of these men, they questioned them but nothing came of it. Then there was that crazy man, that old hermit living in a tar-paper shanty near the Shaheen dump that everybody'd said ought to have been committed to the state hospital years ago. But everybody knew really it was Hans and Hans got out as quick as he could, just disappeared and not even his family knew where unless they were lying which probably they were though they claimed not.

Mother rocked me in her arms crying, the two of us crying, she told me that Mary Lou was happy now, Mary Lou was in Heaven now, Jesus Christ had taken her to live with Him and I knew that didn't I? I wanted to laugh but I didn't laugh. Mary Lou shouldn't have gone with boys, not a nasty boy like Hans, Mother said, she shouldn't have been sneaking around the way she did—I knew that didn't I? Mother's words filled my head flooding my head so there was no danger of laughing.

Jesus loves you too you know that don't you Melissa? Mother asked hugging me. I told her yes. I didn't laugh because I was crying.

They wouldn't let me go to the funeral, said it would scare me too much. Even though the casket was closed.

It's said that when you're older you remember things that happened a long time ago better than you remember things that have just happened and I have found that to be so.

For instance I can't remember when I bought this notebook at Woolworth's whether it was last week or last month or just a few days ago. I can't remember why I started writing in it, what purpose I told myself. But I remember Mary Lou stooping to say those words in my ear and I remember when Mary Lou's mother came over to ask us at suppertime a few days later if I had seen Mary Lou that day—I remember the very food on my plate, the mashed potatoes in a dry little mound. I remember hearing Mary Lou call my name standing out in the driveway cupping her hands to her mouth the way Mother hated her to do, it was white trash behavior.

" 'Lissa!" Mary Lou would call, and I'd call back, "Okay, I'm coming!" *Once upon a time.*

# KATHRYN PTACEK

## Dead Possums

Kathryn Ptacek, born in 1952, was raised in New Mexico. She received her B.A. in journalism, with a minor in history from the University of New Mexico in Albuquerque, where she was graduated with honors in 1974, and where she was a student of mystery writer Tony Hillerman. Afterward, she spent two years as an advertising-layout artist and then worked for the University of Mexico computing center as a technical writer and editor. After the sale of her first novel in 1979, she became a full-time novelist. Since then she's sold seventeen novels, including the bestselling historical romance *Satan's Angel*, an historical fantasy trilogy set in China, and five dark fantasies, among them *In Silence Sealed*, which was recently published. She's also edited two anthologies, *Women of Darkness* and *Women of the West*.

"Dead Possums" is about relationships and the spirits that invade the spaces that grow between sundered lives.

—E.D.

# DEAD POSSUMS

## Kathryn Ptacek

It was raining and nearly dark and already beginning to get foggy. Damn, how he hated the fog. Hank Strasak was dead-dog tired after a workday that began at five A.M., and now all he looked forward to was kicking off his shoes and lying back on the lumpy couch in the living room until Mary-Ann called him for dinner.

That was, if Mary-Ann was home.

They'd been having a few problems lately. Big problems. What an understatement. He tried to grin and caught a glimpse of himself in the rearview mirror. The grey light of dusk washed out his normally dark skin color, and he looked like he had rictus. He relaxed his facial muscles, and the frown that formed looked far more natural on his heavy features. A curl of untrimmed hair flopped into his eyes and he blew at it.

The car veered slightly, forcing his attention back to his driving. Damn, he'd better watch what he was doing. He'd nearly gone off the road back there.

Something grey flashed against the darker grey of the street, and without thinking he tapped the horn, then realized it wouldn't do any good. He applied the brakes, but the creature was already under the wheels. He felt the sickening thump, slammed on the brakes. The car fishtailed to a stop alongside a deserted orange traffic cone, and he sat there for a moment before getting out and walking back to the animal.

A possum. And it was about as dead as it could be. He stared down at the blood-flecked fur and felt a little sick. It was the first time he'd run over anything. The first time. He walked around to the front of the car and stared down at the splash of blood already beginning to wash away in the rain.

He got in the car and drove away. He would be home soon. Home.

"I'm home, hon!" he called as he walked into the house on Ashley Street. He was careful not to slam the door; Mary-Ann had told him many times before that she hated when he slammed the door, and since then he'd been very careful not to do it. Except, of course, when he was pissed at her and didn't care what got her angry.

Nothing. The house was silent.

328

No Mary-Ann. No Heather. Where was she? She should have been home from school by now. Christ, she should have been doing her homework. He knew she had a math test tomorrow, and they'd planned on him quizzing her the night before.

So where were they?

He walked through the hushed house, alien with its emptiness. He glanced in Heather's neat bedroom with its pictures of horses and cats salvaged from magazines and pinned on the walls, in their bedroom, in the kitchen. No one. Shrugging, he returned to the bedroom to get out of his damp clothing. As he changed, he realized how long it had been since he felt her presence there. Too long. Once in dry jeans and shirt, he returned to the kitchen to look out the window over the sink at the backyard. He could barely see it now in the early darkness, but that didn't matter. He knew each inch of that yard.

He was proud of it, that little space of greenery. He'd worked long hours on weekends to put in the lawn and the flower beds along the neat wooden fence, and almost every Sunday he was out there raking or trimming or just admiring his work.

At work they called him a farmer.

They also called him a Polack. Czech, he repeated he didn't know how many times, I'm Czech—Bohemian—and they just laughed and called him a Pole. And told him another insulting joke about a Polish couple on their wedding night.

God, how he hated them and that miserable job. The glass factory had been founded by his grandfather, who'd come to this country from Bohemia in the last decade of the previous century. He'd brought with him the fine technique of glassmaking that made Bohemia glass so famous.

Grandfather Heinrich Strasak had built the factory from the ground up, and it had become well known throughout the country, and then his father had inherited it. That's when the problems had begun. His father had no head for business, and by the time Hank was old enough to know what was going on, his father had lost the factory, and now the grandson of its founder was working in it, just like any other guy in town.

It wasn't fair, Hank thought, not for the first time; but that was the way it was, and there wasn't much he could do. Still, it galled him. Particularly as it remained the Strasak Glass Works, and each day when he drove under the wrought-iron arch proclaiming the name, he flinched.

He pushed away from the sink and sat down. Nearly six, and they weren't back. He made a sandwich of ham and cheese and drank a beer, and by the time the last crumb was wiped up, he was still alone. He hadn't bothered with the light, and sat in complete darkness watching the rain as it splattered down the windowpanes, and thought of the possum. Poor thing.

He sighed and rubbed a hand over his face, then got another beer and trailed into the living room. It was dark here, too, and he wondered what

Mary-Ann would do if she came home then and found him in a dark house. She'd know he was brooding again, and why had she married him when he was just a grumpy ol' Pole.

Czech, he would reply wearily, and wonder why she couldn't remember that after twelve years of marriage. He remembered that she was German and English. It wasn't hard.

But Mary-Ann, he knew, didn't have much time for him or for remembering such things as his birthday or their anniversary, or for sitting down in the evenings and just talking with him. Not since she discovered her new religion. When they were first married she'd worked in an office, but after Heather was born, she'd stayed home. He didn't mind, although it would have been nice to have two incomes. Still, he liked having her here for Heather. And she never complained, so he supposed she didn't mind, either.

But when Heather was four, Mary-Ann got interested in some really weird stuff. Restlessness, he thought. She bought those screaming-headline tabloids at the supermarket and read them to him at dinner. He laughed and said they were all made-up stories, and she got mad, and threw a plate at him. Luckily it missed. But it didn't stop there.

She took yoga lessons; that didn't last long before being replaced by est, and in turn by Gestalt, water therapy, Scientology, and nirvana-ism. A few years ago she announced she was "going" vegetarian and she refused thereafter to touch any meat—not only wouldn't she eat it, she wouldn't prepare dishes with meat in them. So he shopped after work and bought the hamburger and hot dogs and pork chops, and at Thanksgiving, when they weren't going to her folks' house, he fixed the turkey. Again, he didn't mind.

The beer can was empty, so he tossed it into the garbage and fetched another one. He sat down in the living room.

One day last year he got a phone call at work. He listened quietly, then went down to bail his wife out of jail. By the time he got back, everyone knew where he'd been and why, and they were laughing at him. Oh, not always outright, of course, but he could tell. As he went by his co-workers, they'd fall silent, as if they'd been talking about him, or a moment later someone would giggle. That's when he'd told them to stuff it, and Old Man Marsh's widow called him in and reamed him out on his attitude.

It was even harder on Heather, though. Her classmates laughed at her, called her names, and said her mother was a criminal and a nut and that she was just as nutty. She cried at night when he tucked her in and asked why her mother was different, and not knowing the answer, he said she was just being kind to animals. How could he say that her mother really was a nut?

The animal-rights group Mary-Ann had joined wasn't just any ordinary humane group, he had realized then. It was a militant organization not content in simply writing letters to senators and congressmen. It wanted action. Immediate action, and it didn't care how it got it. And it sure as hell didn't mind the headlines it got along the way. The group, Mary-Ann informed him, was prepared to take up arms in defense of the animals—and even to die in that defense.

Sure, he liked animals. He had a dog as a kid, but he wasn't about to treat it like a human. This group thought they were. Mary-Ann and her friends had gone to a medical laboratory just below North Hill to protest the use of animals in experiments. She was busted by the police for spray-painting "Thou shalt not kill" on the outside of the building, while her buddies were busy inside letting the rabbits and rats and cats and dogs out of the wire cages. Her friends got busted, too. "Liberating God's creatures," they'd claimed, and they chanted biblical verses from their cells. That's when he learned they were mixing religion with their politics.

He didn't talk to her on the drive home nor all of that night, and it was then he realized how far they'd grown apart. He thought once or twice about divorce, but wasn't sure he was ready for it. Most of the time everything seemed to go all right.

There was, of course, that time when they were at the Fletchers and their daughter Jill wanted to show the new trick she'd spent all week teaching her golden retriever. Before the little girl could start, Mary-Ann stood up and coldly announced that she didn't want to see the trick because it was cruel to force animals to do something they obviously didn't want to do. Jill's face darkened and she ran crying from the room, and that's when Hank stood and said they better be running along.

He yelled all the way home, and so had she, and Heather, crying, huddled in the back with her hands over her ears.

All that time he put up with the multitude of booklets strewn across the table at breakfast time and the stacks of photocopied fliers that the group put up in markets and utility poles and under windshield wipers of cars in parking lots, but which had to be stored someplace, and somehow his house got volunteered. He even put up with the occasional meeting held there, and when he knew the group was coming over, he'd take Heather out to a movie or to walk or to a special snack at one of the restaurants on the harbor.

They no longer made love. She lay on her side of the bed, and he on his, and whenever he rolled over and touched her, she flinched. Soon he stopped that. She didn't call him by name anymore, either, and strangely that bothered him more than the other. She called him "he" or "your father" when she talked to Heather. Never "Hank," and sometimes at night, when he couldn't sleep, he would think he had become a nonentity to her.

She stopped taking care of the house, and he would come home to find not only the breakfast dishes still in the sink, but those from the previous night, as well as an assortment of ants and roaches. He endured unmade beds, and mildewed towels and tiles, stacks of papers everywhere, a film of dust coating everything, and with Heather he made it an adventure on weekends to see what they could clean up next in the house. They managed to keep up with the housework most of the time, and if Mary-Ann was aware, she gave no indication. She continued making her phone calls and pounded away at their old Olympia typewriter by the hour, drafting one letter after another.

And he tried to understand. But he couldn't; not anymore. It was as if she'd crossed a line somewhere and was moving ahead, while he was standing still, watching her as she faded into the distance. The farther away she got, the less he understood. He didn't like the idea of experiments; no one did, but to actually destroy laboratory equipment worth thousands of dollars . . . to disrupt research . . . to get violent . . . that was incredible. And to upset a little girl because she taught her puppy a trick—he couldn't forgive her for that. Not ever. Nor had the Fletchers, apparently, because they were never invited back, even though he saw Jack at work almost every day.

And then there was the time the group started petitioning the City Council to outlaw the annual winter dogsled races because they were cruel to dogs. He'd blown up then, too, as he reminded her that dogs had always worked for humans—that's why they'd been domesticated, for God's sake, and one of their tasks had been to pull sleds across snow and ice. She'd countered that that activity was no longer necessary, and if a dog had a choice, it wouldn't pull a sled.

He argued; she countered. They got nowhere, and finally parted in silence. Silence kept them away from each other the next week, too, and that was when Heather began sucking her thumb again. Ten years old and she had a habit like that. Disgusted, he tried to stop her, but Mary-Ann told him to leave the girl alone. She was simply expressing herself.

He and his pillow and a ratty old afghan his mother had crocheted when he was nineteen moved out onto the couch that night and remained there.

Sometimes he thought he was living a nightmare. Sure, he knew he didn't have it as bad in some ways as other guys at work—like the guy who'd lost his family in the fire—but why had his life turned out this way? What had his marriage become?

He got another beer and clasped it lightly in his hands. Against his skin the cold metal tingled, awakening him, and he stood. He couldn't wait here all night; not when it looked like Mary-Ann wasn't coming home. She'd left him, then. But gone . . . where? He drained the can, then tossed it into the garbage and wondered with surprise where all those other cans had come from. The garbage can was completely full.

It didn't help, of course, that he suspected she was seeing some guy in the group. Suspected? Hell, he was pretty damned sure of his facts. And he bet right now she and Heather were over there.

And he was gonna get his family back.

It wasn't all that hard to locate them, after all. He just looked in her address book and when he found the name of the group's leader, he knew he had the right guy. He checked the address, then drove over there.

The rain sluiced over him as he got out of the car and went up the walk.

The doorbell was one of those with a tiny light in it, and it stared like an orange eye at him. Grimly he thumbed it. The door opened, and a man he'd seen several times at his house stood behind the screen door.

"Oh, hi, Hank. I didn't expect to see you here."

"I bet not."

"Want to come in?"

"Yeah." Hank jerked the screen open before the other man could make a move. "Richard, isn't it?" he asked as his eyes searched the living room. The other man nodded. Hank didn't see anything out of the ordinary there . . . no hint of them.

Almost as if Richard had read his mind, he grinned. "The others are downstairs."

"Downstairs?

"Basement," Richard called over his shoulder as he led the way. "Made it into a den a few years ago. Thought I'd need that for the kids to play in, but when my wife left me, she took the kids. So I just rattle around in this big house."

Yeah, until you rattle around with my wife.

He could hear the voices now, and knew that even now they wouldn't be socializing. Not these people. They were fanatics. They didn't have time for anything but their Cause. This was Business, after all.

They were there, both Heather and Mary-Ann. His wife looked up. Her blond hair was neatly pulled back, her face bereft of makeup. That was another thing he blamed on the group. She didn't style her hair now, or wear lipstick or eye shadow, and she wore dowdy clothes. She looked like she'd aged fifteen years.

The group members paused in their heated discussion as they recognized Hank. Heather, whose dark head had been bent studiously over a jigsaw puzzle, waved at him. He smiled at her.

"What are you doing here?" It was Mary-Ann.

No greeting. Hank repressed the belch he felt sprewing up from his stomach, even though he wanted to let it out so it would shock these people.

"I gotta talk with you."

"Can't it wait?"

"No."

She saw he meant it and excused herself and followed him back up the stairs. She glanced back once, and he knew Richard was watching them.

"What's this all about?" she demanded once they were in the living room. "How did you find me?"

"Why didn't you leave a note? I was getting worried. Something could have happened."

She folded her arms across her chest. "Well, nothing did, so what do you want? I don't have time to stand here. I've got to get back to work."

"I want you to come home with me."

"That's impossible."

"I want us to go home together and make love, and then talk afterward."
She stared at him coldly. "I can't."

"Hank." His voice was pleading. "Can't you even say my name?" She
didn't answer and he moved away.

"You've been drinking again."

She made it sound like he got drunk regularly. Sure, he enjoyed a few
beers after work, but he never drank the hard stuff. She knew that. But
with her conversion, she'd also given up alcohol and smoking. He wondered
when she would be nominated for sainthood.

"Just a few beers."

"You smell like an old wino."

"You on speaking terms with winos now?" The humor was lost on her;
on him, as well. Her foot tapped. A bad sign. "Come on, Annie, come
home now. We'll put on some good music, snuggle a little."

"Don't call me Annie. You know I hate that."

"What does he call you?"

"What?"

"I said what does he call you?" He jerked his chin toward the stairs. "I
bet he doesn't call you Mrs. Strasak. Are you having an affair with him?"
He held his breath.

Her gaze met his. "Yes."

He released the air. There, it was out in the open, and surely now he
would feel better. Why, though, did he feel a knot twisting inside his guts,
like the beer had gone sour or something. Why did he feel like he wanted
to explode and yell and scream?

Instead, he shifted his weight from one foot to the other, then said:
"How long has it been going on?"

"A year."

"That's all?"

"Yes."

"Yeah, you wouldn't lie. You might get struck down by a lightning bolt."

"I'm going back."

"No, you're not." He grabbed her arm before she could turn around.

"Let go."

"No." His fingers tightened.

"You're hurting me."

"You've hurt me for years now, Annie, and you didn't give a damn. I
wish I could hurt you, but I don't think there's any way." He released her
arm just as Richard walked into the room.

"Is everything all right here?"

The perfect host, Hank thought, and felt his head begin aching, as if a band
were tightening around it. She was probably right; he had drunk too much.

"Go on back," he said wearily. "I don't want to keep you away from your little fuzzy critters any longer."

She left. Without a backward look.

Hank let himself out quietly, and when he got in the car, he sat in the front seat, staring at the house. He didn't see the car door open or close, and was startled to hear Heather's voice.

"I'm lonely, Daddy."

"Oh, baby." He pulled her to his chest and stroked her rain-dampened hair. And knew what he could do to hurt his wife.

He kissed the top of his daughter's head, then started the car and drove home. He told her to sit in the car while he was in the house just a minute. Inside, he first packed a little suitcase with some of her clothing and favorite toys, then pulled a large case down and began tossing his things into it.

When he was done, he turned off the last light and left. The house stood black in the fog.

He took the curve wide, the car swinging over the solid yellow line into the left lane of what in the town one mile back was Port Boulevard, and Heather squealed with fright. The windshield wipers squeaked as they scraped an arc across the glass.

"Daddy, please," she pleaded, "slow down."

For answer, he pressed down on the accelerator, and the car leaped ahead in the wet darkness, its twin lights raking the dense forest that pressed closely on both sides. A wisp of fog curled around some of the tree trunks; leaves, plastered by the rain, slipped silently to the forest floor. Something thumped under the tires, and Heather twisted around on the seat to look back at the dead creature, painted a hellish red by the taillights.

"Daddy, you ran over an animal."

"It's just a possum," he said to the accusing tone, and tried not to feel guilty. "Sit down, and put your seat belt on like I told you."

Quietly she obeyed, and in the faint greenish light from the dashboard he saw the tears on her cheeks. She lifted one corner of her Sylvester and Tweety T-shirt and rubbed her eyes.

He shook his head, then jabbed at the cigarette lighter. She really liked animals; loved them, that is, and that was beginning to worry him. She cried over the horses getting killed in the westerns; didn't care if the good guy got it. Just the goddamn horses. And she'd leave the room if an animal on TV got hurt or killed. That was too much like her mother. He lit his cigarette. She was the only good thing that had come out of his marriage, and he wondered if it was too late for her. Had her mother already poisoned her?

Another thump under the tires jerked his attention back to the road. That had to be a pothole, didn't it? They would be reaching the interstate in a bit and when they did, he would—they would—be leaving Greystone Bay behind for good.

Rotten town, rotten job, rotten wife. Worse . . . a rotten life.

It would be different up north. He'd go to Boston, maybe, and look around. Boston would need good workers. He'd had a lot of different jobs in his lifetime, so he was qualified. God knows, he could learn quickly, too. Ash dribbled down his shirt front, and he coughed, then wiped the back of his hand across his mouth. His stomach was sour from all the beer he'd drunk earlier, and he was beginning to feel pressure in his bladder.

"Daddy, slow *down*."

That was the tenth or eleventh time, and he was getting tired of it. He knew she was right, but he wanted to get as far away from Mary-Ann tonight as possible. And the faster the better. He hunched over the wheel, shifting his weight from one buttock to the other. He was already stiff and they hadn't been on the road for ten minutes yet. It was gonna be a long night.

He tried not to think about what he'd done. He knew the fault wasn't all Mary-Ann's. Two made a marriage; two unmade it. He knew he'd said and done things that had only made the situation worse, and sometimes he'd just baited her so that she got angry, and yet . . . was that just the end of it after all this time? Not a farewell? Not even a handshake? And she still hadn't called him by name. He felt tears at the corners of his eyes.

He glanced at Heather, saw she had her favorite toy, the blue rabbit, tucked under one arm. He didn't remember her bringing that with her. She was looking out the window, her forehead pressed against the glass, but he knew she was sucking her thumb.

He glanced left and saw the small bloody carcass on the shoulder of the far side. Another possum. Jeez. It was about the fifth one they'd passed so far. What was with these damned animals? Why did they feel obligated to throw themselves under a car's wheels? Why didn't they just stay in the woods? Why were they running out in front of him tonight? God, the first one had been that afternoon and since then it hadn't stopped.

He looked back at the slick length of the road and decided he'd better slow down. The alcohol had slowed his reflexes, and it was hard to see now. The fog—that blinding sound-sucking fog wouldn't be missed, that was for sure—was creeping in from the sea, only a few miles to the east, and he didn't want to end back up at Bay Memorial Hospital and then have Mary-Ann come in and demand to know just what the hell was going on. Or even worse . . . what if she didn't come at all?

Silently Heather pointed to something up ahead, and too late he saw the tiny pinpoints of light that meant eyes of some animal that had just strayed out onto the road. He tried to brake, but once again the car ran quickly over the animal, and Heather screamed, as if it had been her own body he'd hurt.

The car slipped to one side and as he straightened, he saw the possum ahead on the wet tarmac, the animal sitting in the middle of the road just staring at him as if it had nothing better to do, and he jerked the wheel around to avoid the damned animal because he didn't like the way it was looking at him. The car went into a spin; he tried to bring it out, but the wheels locked on the slick surface, and the car skidded, then heaved itself off the road, crashing into the wide trunk of an oak with a sickening smack.

When he woke, he could feel the rain splashing on his face. And from nearby he heard the undulating wail of an ambulance or a patrol car, or maybe both. He grinned, tasting the saltiness of blood on his lips. He and Heather wouldn't be out here long, that was for sure. Someone was coming for them.

He saw the lights now strobing into the dark fog, and saw a stretcher being lifted into the back of the ambulance. Heather, then; God, he hoped she was all right. Kids generally were; they were young, healthy; she'd spring right back would his little Heather. There was nothing to worry about, was there?

He watched, though, in puzzled silence as the cop paused behind the ambulance to talk to one of the attendants. Why weren't they coming to get him? He wanted to go with Heather to the hospital. She was probably scared, probably crying, and he wanted to hold and comfort her.

"—not yet," the cop was saying as he tried to light a cigarette in the rain. Frustrated, he finally gave up, flicked the sodden mess to one side.

"—happened?"

"Looks like he might have gotten disoriented—maybe hit his head on the steering wheel—and crawled off into the woods. We're calling off the search tonight because of the fog. Can't see a thing. Hope it lifts by morning. See you back in town."

The cop slapped the attendant on the back, then they got back in their vehicles, and with sirens and lights flashing, they drove off. The only sound now was the drumming of the rain on the black pavement.

I'm here! Hank shouted, and only the wind soughing in the branches heard him. He struggled to move, but couldn't as pain like hot irons jabbed through his body. I'm here, he whimpered. Here. Alive.

The rain fell through the blinding fog, and it was only when the car was a few yards away that Hank saw the headlights glowing. He screamed for it to stop because he was lying stretched across the highway, but the driver didn't hear him, didn't see him.

Not in the fog.

The fog and blood wetly kissed his skin.

He screamed again when the second car came speeding down the highway, and the third only minutes later. He screamed long into the night, but no one heard. Not in the fog.

# LUCIUS SHEPARD

## Pictures Made of Stones

The prolific Lucius Shepard, author of science fiction, mainstream, and horror stories and novels, proved that he's no slouch when it comes to fantasy, either, with his World Fantasy Award—nominated story "The Painting of the Dragon Graule." In 1987 he produced two exemplary contemporary fantasy works, "The Glassblower's Dragon" (well worth seeking out in the October issue of *The Magazine of Fantasy and Science Fiction*) and the following piece, the exquisite and haunting "Pictures Made of Stones." Shepard, who has traveled all over the world and put these experiences to good use in his fiction, is currently living in a secluded cabin by the shore in Massachusetts.

This story originally appeared in *OMNI*.

—T.W.

# PICTURES MADE OF STONES

## Lucius Shepard

*This bunch of neckties drop into the bar for a boost
      before dinner
and start bullshitting about the war like it was the
      NFL or something,
tossing off casualty figures, arguing tactics, and I'm
      amused, right,
so I pull up a chair and say I'd be glad to fill them in
      about the war,
because I can't stand to let ignorance flourish . . .
      which sets them to muttering.
But before they can work up real hostility, I order a
      round of drinks
and get to talking about the time the patrol was on
      recon in Nicaragua,·
following the course of the Patuca through thick
      mountain jungle,
just after a flight of Russian choppers had laid down a
      cloud of gas.
I found myself alone, feeling relaxed, grinning like a
      saved Christian.
I'd never been at home in the jungle, but there I was,
      spacing on the scenery,
wondering why orchids had faces and monkeys were
      screaming my name,
and not a bit worried by the fact that the rest of the
      patrol had vanished.
All that mean green was looking beautiful, green like
      a perfect vice,
great sweeps and declensions of green, an entire
      vocabulary of green
scripted by the curves of leaves and vines . . . green
      tenses, green lives.*

*Even the air seemed to hold a wash of pale emerald*
*    throughout.*
*I'd heard about this gas the beaners had that turned*
*    you sideways to reality,*
*but as good as I was feeling, I didn't care what the*
*    hell was behind it.*
*It was as if I'd become more soldierly, more aligned*
*    with warring purpose,*
*and I understood that war was not an event bounded*
*    by time, defined by politics,*
*but was a principle underlying every life, the ground*
*    upon which our actions were deployed.*
*Maybe it was foolish to put so much stock in a delusion*
*    (I never thought it otherwise),*
*but I concluded that delusions were standard issue, and*
*    if you lucked onto a compelling one,*
*you didn't discard it just because it didn't accord with*
*    Army regs.*
*I walked higher and higher into the mountains,*
*    looking like death,*
*thin and feverish, my eyes gone black from seeing,*
*    fatigues rotting away.*
*But I was a miracle inside, ribbed with the silver of*
*    principle,*
*armored with the iron of a new intent, one I sensed but*
*    could not name.*
*The waitress, a brunet with trophy-sized balloons, she's*
*    been listening,*
*and now she asks, "What happened to the rest?" I just*
*    smile and shrug.*
*One of the neckties, a real Blow Dry in an Italian*
*    suit, onyx cuff links,*
*he says, "I've never heard of anything like that . . .*
*    that gas or whatever."*
*I laugh and tell him I could make a whole damn*
*    world out of the things he's never heard of,*
*and that half of everything sounds like fantasy,*
*    anyway . . . take the stock market, for example.*
*which gets a laugh from the others. But Mr. Blow*
*    Dry remains unconvinced*
*"I knew lots of guys like you in Nicaragua," I say.*
*    "They couldn't believe in what was killing them.*
*Thought because something wasn't real, it couldn't*

*do them any harm."*
The neckties struggle with this concept as I go on
  talking about war.
I came to a white village ringed by green mountains,
  with cane and corn
planted on the slopes, and mango trees shading the red
  tile roofs.
The inhabitants were women, children, and old men
  with wet black eyes as vacant as turtles' eyes,
who told me that their sons had been executed and
  buried in a mass grave.
Their voices were soft, unremorseful, their manner calm
  and resolute,
and I realized this was not evidence of resignation but
  that they were at peace.
The longer I stayed, the more I understood that this
  peace
was a by-product of war, filling the valley the way
  rainwater fills a shell crater,
creating of this violent form a placid surface and a
  tranquil depth,
and this inadvertent transformation was its only real
  incidence,
for all those modes of existence we label peace
  are nothing more than organisms that when
  irritated produce the pearls we officially sanction as
  conflicts.
I lived with a young widow, Serafina, in a house with
  dirt floors,
a charcoal stove, and a faded Madonna on the wall
  above a crude candlelit altar.
Days, I would put on the cotton shirt and trousers of a
  campesino and help her in the fields.
Nights, I would tell her stories of America and other
  dreams.
With us lived Ramon, her son, and her senile mother,
  Expectacion,
the only person in the village aside from me who was
  not at peace.
She loathed me and would haunt the doorway while
  her daughter and I made love,
cursing at me, muttering incoherencies such as "Your
  shadow is a demon, your hours broken glass,"

*and we would be forced to go into the hills to find some
  privacy.*
*Serafina was thick-waisted, heavy in the legs, her face
  written with cares,*
*but from her I learned that beauty was no measure,
  rather a kind of lucidity*
*that communicated perfectly its moods to whomever it
  permitted to see.*
*I wanted to be in love with her . . . more than
  wanted, I needed that solace*
*and I believed that love might someday override my
  other compulsions.*
*But though I knew passion with her, knew all the
  trappings of emotion,*
*I could not fall in love, though I suppose I might have,
  had I survived.*

*Mr. Blow Dry interrupts me, asking if I'm claiming
  to be a ghost*
*or if my statement has some symbolic relevance.
  "Neither," I tell him.*
*"Life and death are elusive in their meanings." He
  nods sagely, pretends to understand,*
*but the waitress leans close, touching my arm, and asks
  me to explain.*
*Her face, though beautiful by any standard, seems now
  to open,*
*to expose the revelatory beauty that I once perceived in
  Serafina's face,*
*and I see her failed years, her petty aspirations and
  self-absorption,*
*all this distilling into a consolation, a desire to provide
  me with remedies.*
*Though there may be no explanations, for the sake of
  her lucid mood,*
*I tell her of Ramon, eight years old, a slow-witted
  child with thin arms and dull eyes,*
*who would sit all day outside the house, making
  pictures of the stones*
*he gathered from the bed of a stream that carved a
  groove along the base of the eastern hill.*
*The stones were black and white, iron-colored and
  mossy green,*

*and the pictures had the simplicity of graphics, yet had
a certain power.*

*It was said that Ramon had been blessed with gifts of
prophecy and magic,*

*that he was the spiritual chargeman of the village and
of peace itself.*

*It made sense that peace—like war with its soldiers—
should operate*

*through an agency whose character is of a kind with its
essential idea.*

*But I can only testify that the picture he made on my
last night there*

*showed a shadowy man with a rifle, standing with a
hand outstretched,*

*and just beyond him, as if flung from his hand into
the air, a black bird was flying in a white sky.*

*And, too, there was that sense I had of his presence, of
being always in his scrutiny.*

*"Whether or not Ramon was as the villagers claimed,"
I tell the waitress,*

*"his truth is undeniable. Our lives are no more than
pictures made of stones,*

*and moment to moment we and the world are
transformed utterly.*

*Only war and the false dream of continuity are immune
to these little deaths.*

*Even peace can last for just so long as it's able to effect
a magical denial.*

*This is not philosophy, but signals a process too subtle
to wear a suit of words."*

*That last night Serafina and I went into a banana
grove to be alone,*

*and after making love, lying there, watching the
ragged shadows of the fronds*

*shifting across the thickets of stars and darkness
overhead,*

*she made a disconsolate noise, and when I asked what
was wrong,*

*she told me she was concerned about Expectacion, her
increasing irascibility and incoherence.*

*Then as if on cue, Expectacion appeared at the base of
the hill, staring at us,*

*looking like a huge black bird in her peaked shawl,*

*her voice a static of curses.*
*We ignored her, and eventually she moved off into the*
   *night toward home.*
*But when we returned to the house, a neighbor told us*
   *that Expectacion had run off into the hills,*
*heading west toward the great cliff that overlooked the*
   *Patuca.*
*Leaving Serafina to watch over Ramon, I went to bring*
   *back Expectacion.*
*As I climbed the western hill, I could feel my*
   *superficial peace dissolving,*
*my principle resurfacing, claiming me, and everything I*
   *saw took on an eerie valence,*
*and my thoughts became as black and deviant as the*
   *limbs of the trees,*
*which seemed like weird candelabras tipped with a*
   *thousand green flames,*
*illuminated by a golden full moon like an evil vowel*
   *howling silence.*
*Now and then I saw Expectacion moving above me, a*
   *shadow among shadows,*
*and I cursed her in my thoughts. . . . Old hag, mad*
   *ghost, gloom of a bitch.*
*A dozen times I nearly had her, but always she eluded*
   *me, and at last*
*I found her waiting on the cliff top. I almost caught*
   *her as she leaped,*
*appearing to vanish up and out into the dark, rather*
   *than falling.*
*I stood a moment, wondering how to tell Serafina what*
   *had happened,*
*and a voice called from the trail leading down to the*
   *left of the cliff,*
*commanding me to come toward it, to hold my hands*
   *high and not to run.*
*I did as ordered and soon confronted a patrol of men*
   *anonymous in their combat gear,*
*bulky olive-drab suits and helmets with smoked*
   *faceplates through which were visible*
*reflections of green numerals and diagrams from their*
   *computer readouts.*
*Rockets bristled from their backpacks, gas grenades for*
   *igniting the air in tunnels*

hung in clusters from their belts, and their computer-
  linked rifles hummed.
I was confused as to who they were, for their speech
  was an electric babble
that I translated into frequencies of pure meaning, but
  I believe now they were Cuban,
though had they been American, it would have made
  little difference.
They asked about the village, if there were women, if
  there were soldiers. . . .
I told them how it was, and they were delighted, they
  talked about the pleasures awaiting them.
They gave me food and drink, and asked me from
  which village I hailed,
for in my cotton trousers and embroidered shirt, they
  mistook me for a local.
I pretended to be grateful, but I hated them, I saw the
  inconstancy
with which they embodied the principle of war, and I
  knew what must be done.
That night I walked among them as they slept, perfect
  in my stealth,
a pure warrior, shadowless, free of the drugs of
  conscience and morality.
I slipped a rifle from a sleeping hand and swung it in
  a scything burst
that finished all but one, whose legs and arms were
  pierced by the rounds.
He tried to talk with me, and I think he understood
  why he was to die
but perhaps this was simply a conceit on my part,
  reflecting a need for understanding.
The moon was a drop of golden venom in his faceplate,
  his pleading hurt my head,
and his thoughts scurried like spiders for cover into the
  crevices of his brain.
I killed them all before they could hide and leave clues
  to my identity.
Then I stood, feeling more unified in purpose and place
  than ever.
Though Ramon may have enlisted me in the service of
  the village,
though in his picture I might be a protector, I saw that

*my act had been one of initiation,*
*a reentry into the war, an expression of its art and*
*governance.*
*I felt a shifting within me, I seemed to hear a click as*
*of stones being set in place.*
*The border between peace and war divided me, slicing*
*me in half,*
*but there was no doubt which of them was my ruler,*
*and I went down from the cliff,*
*away from the valley, dead to one world, already*
*reborn to the next.*


*The rush of traffic is braiding together with the ashen*
*twilight into dusk,*
*and the neckties are sitting with their heads down,*
*studying their hands*
*with the solemnity of men at a Rotary breakfast who*
*are contemplating*
*some preacherly truth that they hope will sustain them*
*through their business day.*
*"What happened then?" asks Mr. Blow Dry, and I*
*laugh long and hard*
*at the absolute ignorance of time and process that his*
*question reveals.*
*"You want to hear more?" I say. "Sure, I'll tell you*
*stories all night long.*
*I'll tell about The Volcano That Sang. The Fire That*
*Spoke My Name,*
*about the four-armed child I once saw during the*
*Battle of Bluefields.*
*Then you can go from here armed with sad expertise,*
*with a new pose of wisdom,*
*with a vital and seductive color to add to your cocktail*
*party opinions.*
*Sure, man! Buy another round! We'll talk, we'll*
*fucking communicate.*
*I'll make believe you're really here, and you can pretend*
*the world has never ended."*
*The neckties are alarmed, not wanting their*
*shallowness to be mistaken for what it is,*
*and they assure me that all I've said has made a*
*difference in their lives,*
*impressed by the hard-hitting glamour of pain with—*
*wow!—philosophy, too,*

and ignoring the possibility that I may be deluded or a
    liar or both.
But the waitress only looks at me, and as peace begins
    to spill from the bar into the warring street,
instead of her face, her beautiful lucid face that stuns
    me with its clarity of mood,
its intimations of something more than sympathy, of
    deeper interest,
I have a vision of a child's enormous grimy fingers
    reaching toward me. . . .

Listen, Ramon. What good is there in my continued
    service?
Is it that I am a counterweight, a potent pawn whose
    movements
help to maintain the delicate border between peace and
    war?
Even if so, sooner or later the border will erode and a
    harsh toll will be taken,
harsher for every moment that denies war's dominion.
I have died many times, always for the sake of
    principle, and I am not afraid.
I have lost the capacity for fear and for much else that
    makes a man.
But this woman is becoming real to me,
and though she is only an argument against an
    unendurable truth,
I need a death to consume me in light, to show me those
    things I might have learned in that valley where
    peace was the law and magic the rule.
Choose your stones with care, Ramon.
Give me back my world of random choices, of ordinary
    defeats.
Leave in place the green stone in my skull that is proof
    against the lie of time.
Stay your hand from the white stone in my groin that
    admits to heat and angels.
Pluck only the black stone from my heart, and tonight
    let me die for love.

# DOUGLAS E. WINTER

## Splatter: A Cautionary Tale

Douglas E. Winter has been hailed as "the conscience of horror and dark fantasy." His fiction, interviews, and criticism have appeared in magazines as diverse as *Gallery, Harper's Bazaar, Saturday Review*, and *Twilight Zone*, and in such major metropolitan newspapers as *The Washington Post,* the *Philadelphia Inquirer*, and the *Cleveland Plain-Dealer*. His books include *Stephen King: The Art of Darkness*, and a history of modern horror fiction, *Faces of Fear*. He is a practicing lawyer.

In "Splatter," he deals with pornography, which is a strong buzzword in today's society. What used to be defined solely as a sexual excess is now also used as a term that embraces excessive violence. But sometimes what lies within all of us is beyond acceptable standards of what we may express openly in society. Winter's "condensed novel" explores the contradictions in our treatment of such emotions . . . and the resultant chaos.

—E. D.

# SPLATTER: A Cautionary Tale

## Douglas E. Winter

**Apocalypse Domani.** In the hour before dawn, as night retreated into shadow, the dream chased Rehnquist awake. The gates of hell had opened, the cannibals had taken to the streets, and Rehnquist waited alone, betrayed by the light of the coming day. Soon, he knew, the zombies would find him, the windows would shatter, the doors burst inward, and the hands, stained with their endless feast, would beckon to him. They would eat of his flesh and drink of his blood, but spare his immortal soul; and at dawn, he would rise again, possessed of their hunger, their quenchless thirst, to view a grave new world through the vacant eyes of the dead next door.

**The Beyond.** "And you will face the sea of darkness, and all therein that may be explored." Tallis tipped his wine glass in empty salute. "So much for the poet." He glanced back along the east wing of the Corcoran Gallery, its chronology of Swiss impressionists dominated by Zweig's "L'Aldila," an oceanscape of burned sand littered with mummified remains. His attorney, Gavin Widmark, steered him from the bar and forced a smile: "Perhaps a bit more restraint." Tallis slipped a fresh glass of Chardonnay from the tray of a passing waiter. "Art," he said, his voice slurred and overloud, "is nothing but the absence of restraint." Across the room, a blonde woman faced them with a frown. "Ah, Thom," Widmark said, gesturing toward her. "Have you met Cameron Blake?"

**Cannibal Ferox.** Memory: the angry rain washing over Times Square, scattering the Women's March Against Pornography into the ironic embrace of ill-lit theater entrances. She stood beneath a lurid film poster: "Make Them Die Slowly!" it screamed, adding, as if an afterthought, "The Most Violent Film Ever!" And as she waited in the sudden shadows, clutching a placard whose red ink had smeared into a wound, she surveyed the faces emerging from the grindhouse lobby: the wisecracking black youths, shouting and shoving their way back onto the streets; the middleaged couple, moving warily through the unexpected phalanx of sternfaced women; and finally, the young man, alone, a hardcover novel by Thomas Tallis gripped to his chest. His fugitive eyes,

349

trapped behind thick wire-rimmed glasses, seemed to caution Cameron Blake as she stood with her sisters, hoping to take back the night.

**Dawn of the Dead.** At the shopping mall, the film posters taunted Rehnquist with the California dream of casual, sunbaked sex: for yet another summer, teen tedium reigned at the fourplex. He visited instead the video library, prowling the ever-thinning shelves of horror films—each battered box a brick in the wall of his defense—and wondering what he would do when they were gone. At the cashier's desk, he had seen the mimeographed petition: PROTECT YOUR RIGHTS—WHAT YOU NEED TO KNOW ABOUT H.R. 1762. But he didn't need to know what he could see even now, watching the shoppers outside, locked in the timestep of the suburban sleepwalk. "This was an important place in their lives," he said, although he knew that no one was listening.

**Eaten Alive.** "After all," said Cameron Blake as another slide jerked onto the screen, a pale captive writhing in bondage on a dusty motelroom bed, "what is important about a woman in these films is not how she feels, not what she does for a living, not what she thinks about the world around her . . . but simply how she bleeds." The slide projector clicked, and the audience fell silent. The next victim arched above a makeshift worktable, suspended by a meat hook that had been thrust into her vagina. Moist entrails spilled, coiling, onto the gore-stained floor below. From the back of the lecture hall, as the shocked whispers rose in protest, came the unmistakable sound of someone laughing.

**Friday the 13th.** He had decided to rent an eternal holiday favorite, and now, on his television screen, the bottle-blonde game-show maven staggered across the moonlit beach, her painted lips puckered in a knowing smile. "Kill her, Mommy, kill her," she mouthed, a sing-song soliloquy that he soon joined. The obligatory virgin fell before her, legs sprawled in an inviting wedge, and the axe poised, its shiny tip moistened expectantly with a shimmer of blood. Rehnquist closed his eyes; all too soon, he knew, we would visit the hospital room where the virgin lay safe abed, wondering what might still lurk at Camp Crystal Lake. But he imagined instead a different ending, one without sequel, one without blood, and he knew that he could not let it be.

**The Gates of Hell.** On the first morning of the hearings on H.R. 1762, Tallis mounted the steps to the Rayburn Building to observe the passionate parade: the war-film actor, pointing the finger of self-righteous accusation; the bearded psychiatrists, soft-spoken oracles of aggression models and impact studies; the schoolteachers and ministers, each with a story of shattered morality; and then the mothers, the fathers, the battered women, the rape victims, the abused children, lost in their tears and in search of a cause, pleading to the politicians who sat in solemn judgement above them. He saw, without surprise, that Cameron Blake stood with them in the hearing room, spokesman for the silent, the forgotten, the bruised, the violated, the sudden dead.

**Halloween.** That night, alone in his apartment, Rehnquist huddled with his videotapes, considering the minutes that would be lost to the censor's blade. Sometimes, when he closed his eyes, he envisioned stories and films that never were, and that now, perhaps, never would be. As his television flickered with the ultimate holiday of horror, he watched the starlet's daughter, pressed against the wall, another virgin prey to an unwelcome visitor; but as her mouth opened in a soundless scream, his eyes closed, and he saw her in her mother's place, heiress to that fateful room in the Bates Motel, a full-color nude trapped behind the shower curtain as the arm, wielding the long-handled knife, stiffened and thrust, stiffened and thrust again. And as her perfect body, spent, slipped to the blood-sprinkled tile, he opened his eyes and grinned: "It *was* the Boogeyman, wasn't it?"

**Inferno.** "No, my friends," pronounced the Reverend Wilson Macomber, scowling for the news cameras as he descended the steps of the Liberty Gospel Church in Clinton, Maryland. "I am speaking for our children. It is *their* future that is at stake. I hold in my hand a list . . ." The flashguns popped, and the minicams swept across the anxious gathering, then focused upon the waiting jumble of wooden blocks, doused with kerosene. Macomber suddenly smiled, and his flock, their arms laden with books and magazines, videotapes and record albums, smiled with him. He thrust a paperback into the eye of the nearest camera. "This one," he laughed, "shall truly be a firestarter." He tossed the book onto the waiting pyre, and proclaimed, with the clarity of unbending conviction, "Let there be light." And the flames burned long into the night.

**Just Before Dawn.** As she rubbed at her eyes, the headache seemed to flare, then pass; she motioned to the graduate student waiting at the door. Cameron Blake saw herself fifteen years before, comfortable in t-shirt and jeans, hair tossed wildly, full of herself and the knowledge that change lay just around the corner. She saw herself, and knew why she had left both a husband and a Wall Street law firm for the chance to teach the lessons of those fifteen years. Change did not lie in wait. Change was wrought, often painfully, and never without a fight. In the student's hands were the crumpled sheets of an awkward polemic: "Only Women Bleed: DePalma and the Politics of Voyeurism." In her eyes were the wet traces of self-doubt, but not tears; no, never tears. Cameron Blake smoothed the pages and unsheathed her red pen. "Why don't we start with *Body Double?*"

**The Keep.** Tallis silenced the stereo and stared into the blank screen of his computer. He had tried to write for hours, but his typing produced only indecipherable codes: words, sentences, paragraphs without life or logic.

Inside, he could feel only a mounting silence. He looked again to the newspaper clippings stacked neatly on his desk, a bloody testament to the power of words and images: Charles Manson's answer to the call of the Beatles' "Helter Skelter"; the obsession with *Taxi Driver* that had almost killed a president; the parents who had murdered countless infants in bedroom exorcisms. He drew his last novel, *Jeremiad*, from the bookshelf, and wondered what deaths had been rehearsed in its pages.

**The Last House on the Left.** Congressman James Stodder overturned the cardboard box, scattering its contents before the young attorney from the American Civil Liberties Union. He carefully catalogued each item for the subcommittee: black market photographs of the nude corpse of television actress Lauren Hayes, taken by her abductors moments after they had disemboweled her with a garden trowel; a videotape of Lucio Fulci's twice-banned *Apoteosi del Mistero*; an eight-millimeter film loop entitled *Little Boy Snuffed*, confiscated by the FBI in the back room of an adult bookstore in Pensacola, Florida; and a copy of the Clive Barker novel *Requiem*, its pages clipped at its most infamous scenes. "Now tell me," Stodder said, his voice shaking and rising to a shout, "which is fact and which is fiction?"

**Maniac.** Rehnquist keyed the volume control, drawn to the montage of violent film clips that preceded the C-SPAN highlights of the Stodder subcommittee. A film critic waved a tattered poster, savoring his moment before the cameras: "This is," he exclaimed, "the single most reprehensible film ever made. The question that should be asked is: are people so upset because the murderer is so heinous or because the murderer is being portrayed in such a positive and supportive light?" Rehnquist twisted the television dial, first to the top-rated police show, where fashionable vice cops pumped endless shotgun rounds into a drug dealer; then to the news reports of bodies stacked like cords of wood at a railhead in El Salvador; and finally to the solace of MTV, where Mick Jagger cavorted in the streets of a ruined city, singing of too much blood.

**Night of the Living Dead.** In the beginning, he remembered, there were no videotapes. There were no X ratings, no labels warning of sex or violence, no seizures of books on library shelves, no committees or investigations. In the beginning, there were dreams without color. There was peace, it was said, and prosperity; and he slept in that innocent belief until the night he had awakened in the back seat of his car, transfixed by the black-and-white nightmare, the apocalypse alive on the drive-in movie screen: "They're coming to get you, Barbara," the actor had warned. But Rehnquist knew that the zombies were coming for him, the windows shattering, the doors bursting inward. The dead, he had learned, were alive and hungry —hungry for him—and the dreams, ever after, were always the color red.

**Orgy of the Blood Parasites.** The gavel thundered again, and as the shouts subsided, Tallis returned to his prepared statement. "Under the proposed legislation," he read, without waiting for silence, "whether or not the depiction of violence constitutes pornography depends upon the perspective that the writer or the film director adopts. A story that is violent and that simply depicts women"—he winced at the renewed chorus of indignation—"that simply depicts women in positions of submission, or even display, is forbidden, regardless of the literary or political value of the work taken as a whole. On the other hand, a story that depicts women in positions of equality is lawful, no matter how graphic its violence. This . . ." He paused, looking first at James Stodder, than at each other member of the subcommittee. "This is thought control."

**Profondo Rosso.** Widmark led him through the gauntlet of reporters outside the Rayburn Building. Tallis looked to the west, but saw only row after row of white marble facades. "This is suicide," Widmark said. "You realize that, don't you? Take a look at this." He flourished an envelope stuffed with photocopies of news clippings and book reviews, then handed Tallis a letter detailing the lengthy cuts that Berkley had requested for the new novel. Tallis tore the letter in half, unread. "I need a drink," he said, and waved to the blonde woman who waited for him on the steps below. No one noticed the young man in wire-rimmed glasses who stood across the street, washed in the deep red of the setting sun.

**Quella Villa Accanto il Cimitero.** Rehnquist had found the answer on the front page of the *Washington Post*, while reading its reports of the latest testimony before Stodder's raging subcommittee. There, between boldfaced quotations from a midwestern police chief and a psychoanalyst with the unlikely name of Freudstein, was a clouded news photograph labeled GEORGETOWN PROFESSOR CAMERON BLAKE; its caption read, "Violence in fiction, film, may as well be real." His fingers had traced the outline of her face with nervous familiarity—the blonde hair, the thin lips parted in anxious warning, the wide dark eyes of Barbara Steele. When he raised his hand, he saw only the dark blur of newsprint along his fingertips. He knew then what he had to do.

**Reanimator.** They shared a booth at the Capitol Hilton coffee shop, trading Bloody Marys while searching for a common ground. The conversation veered from Lovecraft to the latest seafood restaurant in Old Town Alexandria; then Tallis, working his third cocktail, told of his year in Italy with Dario Argento, drawing honest laughter with an anecdote about the mistranslated script for *Lachrymae*. She countered with the story of the graduate student who had called him the most dangerous writer since Norman Mailer. "That's quite a compliment," he said. "But what do you think?" Cameron Blake shook her head: "I told her to try reading you first." As they left the hotel, he paused at the news-stand to buy a paperback copy of *Jeremiad*. "A gift for your student," he said, but when he reached to take her hand, she hesitated. In a moment, he was alone.

**Suspiria.** "Hello." It was his voice, hardly more than a sigh, that surprised Cameron Blake. The door slammed shut behind her, and he passed from the shadows into light, barring her way. She stepped back, taking the measure of the drab young man who had invaded her home; she thought, for a moment, that they had once met, strangers in a sudden rain. "I want to show you something," Rehnquist said; but as she pushed past him, intent on reaching the telephone, the videocassette that he had offered to her slipped away, shattering on the hardwood floor. In that moment, as the tape spooled lifelessly onto the floor, their destiny was sealed.

**The Texas Chainsaw Massacre.** Tallis hooked the telephone on the first ring. He had been waiting for her to call, but the voice at the other end, echoing in the hiss of long distance, was that of Gavin Widmark; it was his business voice, friendly but measured, and could herald only bad news. Berkley, despite three million copies of *Jeremiad* in print, had declined to publish the new novel. If only he would consider the proposed cuts . . . If only he would mediate the level of violence . . . If only . . . Without a word, Tallis placed the receiver gently back onto its cradle. He tipped another finger of gin into his glass and stared into the widening depths of the empty computer screen.

**The Undertaker and His Pals.** She knew, as Rehnquist unfolded the straight razor, that there would be no escape. A dark certainty inhabited his eyes as he advanced, the light shimmering on the blade, and she pressed against the wall, watching, waiting. "For you, Cameron," he said. The razor flashed, kissing his left wrist before licking evenly along the vein. She squeezed her eyes closed, but he called to her—"For you, Cameron"—and she looked again as the fingers of his left hand toppled to the carpet in a rain of blood. "For you, Cameron." The razor poised at his throat, slashing a sudden grin that vomited crimson across his chest, and as he staggered out into the street, blood trailing in his wake, she found that she could not stop watching.

**Videodrome.** Every picture tells a story, thought Detective Sergeant Richard Howe, stepping aside to clear the police photographer's field of vision. He knew that the prints on his desk tomorrow would seem to depict reality, their flattened images belying what he had sensed from the moment he arrived: the bloodstains splattering the floor of the Capitol Hill townhouse had been deeper and darker than any he had ever seen. He would not easily forget the woman's expression when he told her that the shorn fingertips were slabs of latex, the blood merely a concoction of corn syrup and food coloring. He looked again to the shattered videocassette, sealed in the plastic evidence bag: DIRECTED BY DAVID CRONENBERG read the label. He couldn't wait for the search warrant to issue; turning over this guy's apartment was going to be a scream.

**The Wizard of Gore.** When the first knock sounded at the door, Rehnquist set aside his worn copy of *Jeremiad*, marked at its most frightening passage: "and at dawn, he would rise again, possessed of their hunger, their quenchless thirst, to view a grave new world through the vacant eyes of the dead next door." At his feet curled the thin plastic tubing, stripped from his armpit and drained of stage blood. "It's not real," he said, and the knocking stopped. "It's *never* been real." The window to his left shattered, glass spraying in all directions; then the door burst inward, yawning on a single hinge, and the hands, the beckoning hands, thrust toward him. The long night had ended. The zombies had come for him at last.

**Xtro.** The Reverend Wilson Macomber rose to face the Stodder subcommittee, his deep voice echoing unamplified across the hearing room. "I don't know if anybody else has done this for you all, but I want to pray for you right now, and I want to ask everyone in this room who fears God to bow their head." He pressed a tiny New Testament to his heart. "Dear Father . . . I pray that you will destroy wickedness in this city and in every wicked city. I pray that you draw the line, as it is written here, and those that are righteous, let them be righteous still, and they that are filthy, let them be filthy still . . ." At the back of the hearing room, his face etched in the shadows, Tallis shifted uneasily. In Macomber's insectile stare, mirrored by the stony smile of James Stodder, the haunted eyes of Cameron Blake, he knew that it was over. As the vote began on H.R. 1762, he turned and walked away, into the sudden light of a silent day.

**Les Yeux Sans Visage.** Months later, in another kind of theater, green-shirted medical students witnessed the drama of stereotactic procedures, justice meted out in the final reel. "The target," announced the white-masked lecturer, gesturing with his scalpel, "is the cingulate gyrus." Here he paused for effect, glancing overhead to the video enlargement of the patient's exposed cerebral cortex. "Although some prefer to make lesions interrupting the fibers radiating to the frontal lobe." The blade moved with deceptive swiftness, neither in extreme closeup nor in slow motion; but the blood, which jetted for an instant across the neurosurgeon's steady right hand, was assuredly real.

**Zombie.** In an hour like many other hours, Rehnquist smiled as the warder rolled his wheelchair along the endless white corridors of St. Elizabeth's Hospital. He smiled at his newfound friends, with their funny number-names; he smiled at the darkened windows, crisscrossed with wire mesh to keep him safe; he smiled at the warmth of the urine puddling slowly beneath him. And as the wheelchair reached the end of another hallway, he smiled again and touched the angry scar along his forehead. He asked the warder—whose name, he thought, was Romero—if it was time to sleep again. He liked to sleep. In fact, he couldn't think of anything he would rather do than sleep. But sometimes, when he woke, smiling into the morning sun, he wondered why it was that he no longer dreamed.

# JOHN SKIPP AND CRAIG SPECTOR

## Gentlemen

John Skipp and Craig Spector have been collaborating on subversive horror for over five years now, having burst onto the scene with their first novels *The Light at the End* and *The Cleanup*, as well as the novelization of the Columbia Pictures film *Fright Night*. "Gentlemen" will appear in their current novel-in-progress.

Their latest novel *The Scream,* is a "heavy metal horror story about the good rockers, the bad rockers, and the moral majority." It was published by Bantam in February. Also planned are assaults on the film and record industries, more short stories, and perhaps even a dreamdate with Morton Downey, Jr.

"Gentlemen" is, quite simply, a terrifying story that has a most unlikely, if suitably tawdry, setting. It is a warning to all with tattered clothes.

—E.D.

# GENTLEMEN

## John Skipp and Craig Spector

TO BE A MAN.

The words are carved on the sweat-smeared oak of the bar's surface. They're the only four that never seem to change. Like the troll at the taps, the regulars that surround him, the TVs and the black velvet painting of the Hooter Girl that hangs in sad-eyed judgment over all.

TO BE A MAN.

As if that were all there is.

I always hated Bud. He loves it. We drink it. One after another, we pour them down, while Ralph Kramdon bellows about trips to the moon.

And the guys all laugh. You're goddamn right.

They know about being a man.

And now, at last, so do I.

I remember the night that my edification began. Every nuance. Every shade. The phone started ringing at 12:45, precisely. It was LeeAnn, of course. She'd just crashed and burned with another asshole relationship, and she needed to talk. And drink. Right now. I knew all this by the first ring. No one else ever called this late. No one.

"Damn," I muttered. "Not again."

There were a lot of good reasons for not answering. It was a shit-soaked night outside, cold rain falling in thick sheets. The steam head had finally kicked in, and I was down to my jeans. I was halfway into a lumpy joint of some absurdly good Jamaican. *Star Trek* would be on in fifteen minutes. Seeing LeeAnn would make me miserable, and I'd just wind up sourly wanking off when I got home. Yep, a lot of good reasons. I took another toke and settled back in my chair.

The phone rang again. I choked. The smoke exploded in my lungs. I began to cough violently, great red-meat wrenching hacks. The phone rang again. I roared back at it, defiant, my eyes tearing and my throat desperately lubing itself with bile.

The phone rang again, and I got out of the chair. What was the point? The phone would ring forever. The night was already completely ruined; LeeAnn's face had control of my mind. I snubbed the joint and placed the butt in my pocket, for later. The phone rang once more before I caught it. I coughed a little bit more at the receiver as I brought it to the side of my head. What did it matter? I already knew what the first words would be. First, my name. No *howdy, stranger, no long time no see.*

Just:

"David?"

Then:

"David, I need you . . ."

Like clockwork. I gave brief, fleeting audience to the idea of just hanging up, of pitching the receiver into the cradle without so much as a whimper. But then her voice, so characteristically vulnerable, spoke the final two words in the equation:

"David, *please* . . ."

I was slaughtered.

"Where are you?" I asked. Coughing had made me roughly twenty times more stoned in a matter of seconds; the air seemed thicker, my head felt muddier, and the crackle over the phone line raked like needles in my ears.

She let out a laugh I recognized: the resigned and barely-in-control one. I coughed. She laughed. I spoke.

"I still don't know where you are."

"I'm at this place called . . ." She paused; I could almost hear her neck craning, ". . . dammit, I can't tell. It's at Forty-eighth and Eighth. The beer is cheap. The guys are all jerks. It's my kind of place. Can you come?"

"Shouldn't the question be, 'How fast can you get here?' "

"Jesus, I really *am* predictable."

"You're not the only one," I assured her wearily. "Give me some time, okay? I don't have any clothes on."

"Hubba hubba."

"Don't tease me, LeeAnn. I'm not a well man."

"Aw, poor baby."

I closed my eyes, and LeeAnn was behind them: leaning against a bar with brass rails, china-doll lips pouting, green-eyed gaze languidly drifting as her T-shirt slowly hiked its way past her breasts and over her ash-blonde head. *Never happen,* my rational mind reminded me flatly. It sounded barely-in-control, too.

LeeAnn must have heard it. The teasing stopped. "Please hurry," she said. "I need you."

"I'm on my way. Stay there."

The phone went dead. LeeAnn never said good-bye anymore; it was too commital. I set down the receiver and caught a glimpse of myself in the bureau mirror. Gaunt, sensitive features. Aquiline nose. Deep-set eyes. Quietly receding hairline. An interesting face: not handsome, certainly not repulsive. I smiled. Loads of character. The face of a poet, even . . .

*Who was I kidding?* I thought. *It's the face of a fool.* The reflection nodded in sad affirmation. I looked at the piles of dirty clothes on the floor and grabbed up a dirty sweatshirt. Dress for success, I always say. Or *said*, rather.

Whatever.

At any rate, I was suited up and out the door before manly Captain Kirk had pronged the first of this evening's deep-space bimbos, way out where no man had gone before. The last three words from her lips echoed through me like a curse.

*I need you.*

Sure.

The cab ride was long and wet, cold rain pounding on the windows like a billion tiny fists. The whole way up, I brooded about LeeAnn. The whole way up, I hit alternately on the dwindling vial of blow in my jacket pocket and one of the two jumbo oilcans of Foster's lager that I'd scored just for the trip. The irony of getting wasted as a prelude to meeting a friend for drinks was not lost on me, but what could I say? LeeAnn made me crazy: the same kind of crazy that would inspire me to tromp out into a maelstrom on a moment's notice and woefully underdressed, from my army-surplus field jacket down to a pair of battered Reeboks with a dime-sized hole in the right sole. She unnerved me that thoroughly. I snorted and watched the passing streets slip by: each one, rain-slicked and on the verge of flooding; each one, dark and bleak and utterly depressing.

Any of them, an escape route: infinitely preferable to where I was going.

If I'd been stronger, maybe, I'd have taken one. Sure. Of course, the same line of inarguable reasoning could be applied to any other quarter of my world, from my unpublished short stories to my unfinished novel to my utterly unrequited love life, with exactly the same results. The gross total of which, combined with fifty cents, would buy me a packet of Gem safety blades.

The better to slit my miserable fucking throat with.

The thought deflated as quickly as it came. Of course I would never really do that. Neither, of course, would I tell the cabbie to turn around and take me home, or just grab LeeAnn by the hair and force her to my heap big masculine will, or do *anything* but what I always, always did. Which was to go to her: whenever, wherever her next whirlwind sortie ended. In tears, in disaster; in rain, sleet, or snow, good ol' Dave would be there, day or night, with the right words and the right drugs and a shoulder to cry on. Good ol' Dave was never more than a phone call away. I hated myself for being such a stooge to this endlessly cyclical farce, for being so hapless in the face of my own flaccid desire.

The cab sploshed indifferently onto Tenth Avenue, heading uptown. The beer sploshed in my roiling guts, heading south. And the memories came boiling up . . .

We went back a little ways, LeeAnn and I. Long enough to count. Worked for the same messenger service: humping the bullshit of the business world by day, pounding at the walls of our dreams at night. She was in the office, I was on the streets. She was sharp and funny and smarter than anyone else in the whole fleabag organization; I was the only one in the entire company who would talk to her without staring incessantly at her tits. No easy task, let me tell you. But I did it, because I valued her trust almost as much as I hungered for her touch.

So there we were, sharing in the adventure of being young and piss-poor in New York, trying desperately to make it in our respective careers: clone of Kerouac meets fledgling Bourke-White. Came to spend a lot of time together: scrutinizing my first drafts and her black-and-whites over a dinner of ravioli and Riunite; wandering the streets and parks in search of inspiration and free entertainment. We grew very tight. Very close.

With one rather glaring exemption.

You see, for all that deep meaningful contact, it never quite gelled for LeeAnn and me. It was ridiculous, yes. I mean, I'd heard the most heartfelt feelings she'd ever cared to offer without blushing or batting an eye; I would have taken a bullet or thrown myself gleefully into traffic to save the tiniest hair on her head.

Sure. I could do all that. But somehow I couldn't bridge the safe, comfy distance between friend and lover. I just couldn't bring myself to tell her how I felt, to grab her and give her the kind of kiss that would make her reciprocate my passion, my love.

In retrospect, I realize that I was waiting for *her* to do it. I cringe to think of it now, but it's true. Part of my heart sincerely believed that she would wake up one day with the realization that no one would ever love her like I did. No one else could be so tender, so compassionate, so understanding. No one else would bear with her through her tragedies and madnesses, devote themselves so selflessly and completely to her needs.

She would wake up one day, I told myself, kicking herself for her foolishness. And she would throw herself, weeping, into my arms. And I would tell her that it was okay, it was over now. And we would be swept away into a love that not even death could destroy.

One day, I knew, she would realize just how much she was saying when she said the words *Dave, I need you.*

That was the bullshit *I* believed. I preferred it to the cold hard truth.

As for LeeAnn, well . . .

LeeAnn preferred a different kind of guy.

A guy like Rodney, for example. I grimaced as his sneering pug loomed up like the answer in a magic eight-ball toy. Rod the bod, punk hunk *par excellence.* Took her on a three-month, nightmare tour of the Lower East Side, every nook and alley and rathole club that charged four bucks a beer. Rod, the artiste. Rod, the superintense. He was inspiring her, giving her photography a whole new edge. Sure. Asshole inspired her, all right: eventually o.d.'ed on crack and went nuts in her apartment, damned near inspiring her to death before heading off to be shot by the police.

I upended the first can, draining the dregs, and popped the second in a ceremonial toast. *Rot in hell, Rodney.*

*If they'll have you . . .*

After that it was Willis, the far side of the pendulum. I think she met him at a Soho gallery opening. Willis of the shining white mane, who was strong and stable and financially secure and about old enough to be her father. Willis wined and dined her like a princess; my god, he even proposed to her. And she actually accepted, to my unending shock and horror, though I think it was more political than emotional. He had connections. He could *help* her. That is, until she found that her Svengali absolutely forbade her to work after the wedding. Not a woman's place, you understand. LeeAnn shouldn't worry her pretty little head with thoughts of careers. LeeAnn should worry about tending to Willis's earthly needs.

Or how 'bout Roger, her latest disaster. Yeah, Roger was great. Handsome and fortyish and too hip to hurt; cut him and he'd probably bleed Ralph Lauren aftershave. Now *they* were an item, and *soooo* good for each other. He was doing a book on Central America, was going to take her along as his photographer. Maybe her big break. I remember her coming out of the office at checkout time, pulling me aside to tell me the great news . . .

The great news ended rather abruptly at the Midtown Women's Services clinic, at precisely the same microsecond that the urine test came back positive. That was six weeks ago, give or take a millenium.

Well, he did pay for exactly his half of the costs, which was awfully decent of him. But he wasn't there for her on the day it happened, with a smile or a hug or a hand to hold. I was. And he wasn't there in the guilt-wracked weeks after, or ever again.

I was.

Yeah, Roger was slime, and Roger went the way of the wind. But even he wasn't the worst. First, there was Martin.

There was *always* Martin. . . .

The cab cut up Tenth Avenue like a shark through dark waters. Forty-second Street floated by; I blinked back fractured patterns of garish light and color that winked like beacons to hungerlust and loneliness, previews of coming attractions that would never hit town. The moron-parade marched on in my brain: an onslaught of compelling, charismatic bastards who, for all their disparate differences, had held one thing in common. Which I had not.

LeeAnn.

Lithe, lissome bane of my existence. An otherwise intelligent woman who wouldn't take two ounces of the same shit on the job that she ate buckets of in her personal life. And who, for some equally unfathomable reason, liked her men either old and sensitive or young and macho. Old, macho men were chauvinistic pig-dog bastards.

Young, sensitive men were wimps . . .

I winced, biting back the thoughts, denying any possible truth. The cab turned onto Forty-eighth and crossed Ninth Avenue as the last of the Foster's slid down my throat. I felt bilious, and I needed to take a leak. My mind was burnt crispy. My nerves were live wires.

But as the cab slid up to the corner, I resolved that this time, *this* time it would be different. Tonight would mark the end of her love affair with the scum of the earth. I felt a queasy determination that I underscored with a toot of cocaine courage, an alkaloid surge of ersatz bravado. *It's my turn, dammit!* I told myself. If it could be done, it would be done.

It wasn't until I paid the cabbie and hit the pavement that I started to get nervous.

Maybe it was the way she sat, back framed in the grimy bay window, red and green neon backwashing her features like some DC comic damsel in distress. Maybe it was the window itself, which hung dripping like a plate-glass gullet. The way it displayed her.

Like bait . . .

I felt it, all right. As I hunkered over and puddle-dodged toward the door, it was there: a small, wormy gut-rush, synching with the Bud and Stroh's signs that blinked wanly behind the glass, vestige of some primal warning mechanism not entirely obliterated by the drugs. Saying: *No . . . No . . . No . . . No . . .*

It was enough to register. It was not enough to stop me. The place was a dump, all right, but I felt sure I'd seen worse. It was nestled in the middle of a block dominated by drug dealers, pimps, and pawnshops, with the occasional ratbag adult emporium tossed in for good measure. The sign above the awning read simply BAR, with a badly painted-over prefix that looked as though the name had changed hands so many times that they'd just given up. The grime on the big window was thick enough to carve my initials in. The street itself was mercifully void, thanks to the rain; a sole Chicano bum not too far from his teens sprawled by the doorway, oblivious to the pounding. He twitched and muttered sporadically.

I fingered the folding knife thrust deep into the right-hand pocket of my jacket, the one that I'd habitually carried since being mugged last summer. It was long and thin and very sharp; stainless-steel casing, stainless-steel blade. I had never pulled it, never even used it, and often wondered if I carried it as a kind of a talisman more than a weapon. I hoped that I wouldn't need it in either capacity tonight. The thought: *Oh shit,*

*LeeAnn, what are you into now?* loomed forth. The only possible answer was directly ahead.

The smell of bridges burning lay behind.

The first thing that hit me was the stink, a palpable presence that grew exponentially as the door shut behind. The usual stale smoke/stale beer bouquet, yes. But something else, underneath: a vague, foul underpinning. Familiar. Like . . .

*Sewage*, I realized. *Great.* My stomach rolled. I grimaced and took in the layout in an instant. The interior was long and low and dark, the furthest reaches of it enshrouded in greasy shadow some forty feet back. A pseudo-oldtime finger-sign pointed down some steps near the back, one word emblazoned in large gold script:

GENTLEMEN.

*The source, no doubt. This must be my night.* My bladder begged to differ. It wouldn't be long before I had to hit the hopper. It was no longer an idea I relished.

I noted that the rest of the decor was strictly Early K-mart: imitation-walnut paneling and formica as far as the eye could see. The bar itself was unique, hugging the wall to a point halfway down the far side. It was a large and graceless structure replete with tarnished brass hand and foot rails, and somehow managed to be constructed entirely of oak without being the tiniest bit attractive. Twin ceiling-mounted Zenith nineteen-inch TVs blasted cablevison mercilessly on either end.

The Hooter Girl adorned the center.

She looked like one of those paintings of the hydrocephalic sad-eyed children, pumped full of silicon and estrogen. The kind of black velvet sofa-sized monstrosities you see cranked out by the yard and offered up on abandoned gas-station aprons across America, right next to Elvis and Jesus and the moose on the mountain. Big moon eyes and tits like basketballs. Pure class. The neon color scheme had faded over the passage of smoke-filled time, leaving her once-electric tan lines merely jaundiced.

It might have been funny, under other circumstances. At the moment it was making me ill. That and every other sordid detail, from the fly-specked ceiling tiles to the screaming vids to the sodden regulars that lined the bar like crows on a barnyard fence. What the hell was I *doing* here, in this hole, at this hour?

The answer crossed the lateral distance of the room and wrapped herself around me before I could mutter a word. We stood there for what seemed a very long time. I probably would have remained in that position forever, but for the eyes that had followed her course to me. They were hungry, angry, gimlet eyes.

The hunger was for her.

The anger was all mine.

"Would you please tell me what the fuck is going on here?" I said under my breath. It came out a little more hysterical than I'd wished. *Good start, chump*, I thought. *Don't whine.*

"Thanks for coming," she whispered into my armpit. I waited for more. It did not seem to be forthcoming, but she added a squeeze for emphasis. The warm flesh of her back shuddered beneath my touch, but for all the wrong reasons.

"Hey, are you okay?" I asked, not entirely certain that I wanted to hear the answer.

She nodded and snuffled just the tiniest bit, but she didn't let go. It worried me. Very gently, I pried her arms from around my waist and started to say, "C'mon, Lee, what's going on h—"

I never finished. LeeAnn looked up.

She had a black eye. Slit-swollen. Nasty. A tiny crescent-shaped cut had congealed just under her left eyebrow. She smiled gamely, chagrined. Her right eye crinkled with little smile-lines; the left remained fixed and droopy, like a bad impression of the Amazing Melting Woman.

I don't know why I was so surprised. Maybe I wasn't. I'd seen it before. But I couldn't bear to see it again: not now, not ever. My gaze flitted spastically to my shoes, the tubes, the goons at the bar. Anywhere but her face. Her face was dangerous. Her face made *me* dangerous. I stared in red-eyed rage as twin Rambos dispensed endless all-beef lessons in how real men take care of business.

But the goons at the bar weren't watching that. They were watching us. They were watching me.

They were smiling.

It was too much. There was nowhere to turn with my anger but back to the source. The words that came were clipped and vicious, in a voice I barely recognized as my own. I didn't like it. I couldn't help it.

"*Who. Did. It.*"

LeeAnn shook her head. "Beer first," she said. It was not a suggestion. "And we'd better sit down." Then she pulled away, turned, and strode over to her place at the window end of the bar, next to the very payphone she'd probably used to call me, and gathered up her things. She gestured to the bartender, a withered old troll in a baggy white shirt who looked as if he'd spent all his younger days on some Lower West Side dock, trundling the very same kegs he now presided over. He grunted imperceptibly, ash falling from the Lucky pinched in one corner of his lips, and began refilling her emptied pitcher with deft, wordless efficiency. She was back in control that fast. However tenuous, she was in charge. Of herself. Of me.

I stood in stunned silence, the rage draining impotently out, as LeeAnn returned. She squeezed my arm lightly, imploringly, and then walked back toward the shadowed and empty booths. I was supposed to pay; it was understood. I watched her graceful trailing trek across the room. I watched her hips. I watched her ass.

I wasn't the only one watching.

Two of the clientele, a pair of drunken dimwits interchangeable as Heckel and Jeckel, leered at her in brief, neck-craning abandon. The third, a hairball with thick gold chains and too many teeth, managed a sidelong snickering appraisal before resuming his ogling of the washed-out and weary-looking blonde to his left.

The blonde, meanwhile, was oblivious to it all: staring off into her drink as if it were a gateway to another world entirely. She was the Hooter Girl made flesh and then stepped on. Not pleasant.

I stepped up to the bar, stoned and shell-shocked, drugs and wasted adrenaline making the seamy details painfully apparent. I fished out a crinkly ten-spot and stared blankly at the wooden expanse of the counter. It was scarred and pitted, with initials and epigraphs and other vital pearls of wisdom. Ritual scarification. One stuck out like a message in a bottle: four words, carved deeper than all the rest.

TO BE A MAN.

*To be a man.* A bitter sneer engraved itself across my face. *To be a man.* I'd heard enough of that shit to last me a lifetime. My old man had said it. My peer group had said it. The first caveman to bludgeon his object of desire and drag her home by the hair had grunted its equivalent.

*To be a man. You bet.* If my mind had lips, it would have spat out the words. *Somebody got nice and manly with LeeAnn tonight. It's written all over her face . . .*

I looked up. The blonde was glancing at me with weak and wounded eyes. I could see every crack and sag in her features. Ten years ago or so she must have been a real looker, but that was ancient history now. That kicked-around look spilled off of her in waves: the way she hugged her vitals, as if waiting for the next blow to fall; the way she'd sort of sunken into her own carcass, as if the extra padding might help; the way her eyes kept darting to the back of the room.

I stared, waiting for the pitcher to fill. And I wondered how the hell she could have let that happen to her.

Then the men's room door squealed open like a thing in pain.

And up stomped the Mighty Asshole.

The gnarled little man with the pitcher of beer was forgotten. So were the drunks and the hairball, the blonde, the dueling idiot boxes where Rambo played out his bloodless charade. Even LeeAnn slipped from my mind for one long, cold moment, as the entire spinning universe funneled down to the behemoth pounding up the cellar stairs.

Big as life and twice as ugly, he swaggered toward the bar, fumbling absently with his fly. Arms like girders. Eyes like meatballs. Feet pounding the floorboards like an overblown Bluto in a Max Fleisher cartoon, sending shock waves up my legs from halfway across the room.

The impulse to retreat must have come on a cellular level, because I had backed into a barstool before I even knew I was moving. Connecting with teetering solid matter jostled me back to the broader reality, and I cast a nervous glance over to LeeAnn. She was watching him, too.

We were *all* watching him.

It wasn't just that he was tanked, or that he was built like one. Or even that he was bearing down on us like some angry moron-god. Rather, it was his presence: the sheer force and volume of his rage. It was as vivid as the glow around a candle's flame, and black as the dead match that first fired it up.

The Mighty Asshole thundered over to his seat next to the blonde. The terror in her eyes answered my previous question quite nicely: they were an item. Like hammer and anvil, they were made for each other. I shuddered involuntarily.

Then the troll was back, pitcher and mugs clunking down onto the bar. He grinned at me, a toothless rictus, as I handed him the money. Looking into his eyes was like staring down an empty elevator shaft and never quite seeing the bottom. He smiled as he handed back my change, smiled as I hefted the goods, and kept right on smiling as I made my way back. The Asshole shot me a beady-eyed and territorial sneer as I hustled away.

I crossed the room like the guest of honor at a firing squad. The screaming of my nerves eased up only marginally, the farther away from the bar I drew. LeeAnn was already seated, tucked into one of the half-dozen claustrophobic, dimly-lit booths that ringed the desolate rear of the room. I joined her, setting down the pitcher and mugs, peeling off my wet jacket and tossing it into a heap on the bench. The beer sat untouched on the table. I sighed, grabbed the pitcher and filled both our mugs. LeeAnn watched. I handed her one, took a swig off my own, and waited.

Nothing.

"Well?" I said. It was meant to sound level and controlled, but it came out all wrong.

LeeAnn looked away. "Finish your beer," she said. She was serious. She was miserable.

"What?"

"Your beer." She was adamant. "Finish it."

I glared at her exasperatedly, then tipped back the mug, drained it in two gulps, and banged it on the table. "There," I said, "All gone. Happy?"

"Very," she said, refilling my mug. "Have another."

"What?! C'mon, LeeAnn, this is bullshit."

"Trust me, David. Drink up."

I stared at her for a moment longer, weighing the situation. I didn't want any more beer. I really didn't. In fact, the whole situation was beginning to grate on my nerves. My clothes were wet, the night was old, my bladder ached, and my patience was wearing thin. The words *don't play games with me, dammit* flickered through my mind on their way to my mouth. I caught them just in time.

But the anger remained. It was not lost on LeeAnn; she knew who it was for. Her whole body flinched back for a microsecond. The gesture was mostly surprise; but there was no getting around the fear, iris-black and widening, at its center. I'd seen fear in her eyes before, but I'd never been its cause.

I felt like a total shit.

"Jesus, kiddo," I whispered. "I'm sorry." Now it was her turn to avert the eyes. I looked at the mug of beer before me. It wasn't that much to ask. I wondered what the fuck was wrong with me.

I drained the goddamned mug.

"Okay," I said, deliberately, with as much aplomb as I could scrounge up. "The beer is drunk, and so am I. I'd sedated. I'm fine. I will not get angry.

"So tell me: was it someone you know?"

She nodded, still looking away. Her good eye glistened.

"One of your lovers?"

Another nod, with an accompanying tear; that one hurt. It wasn't phrased to hurt. It couldn't help itself.

"Who?"

No answer.

*"Who?"*

A small voice, barely there at all. "Martin."

For one terrible moment of silence, the world went cold and dead.

"Come again?" I said. Vacuum voice, through a throat constricted. I knew I'd heard it right, was terrified that I'd heard it right. My temples began to thud. The bile swilled in my guts.

"Martin," she said. Louder. Defiant.

*"The* Martin?" I pressed. She shrank back again; inside my skull, there was thunder. "Scum-sucking douchebag Martin? Originator-of-this-whole-downhill-slide Martin? *That* Martin? Is that what you're telling me?"

"Yes." Less a word than a squeak. She was still shrinking back, her spine flush with the booth. Retreating, now. Into herself.

"Are you serious?!"

"YES!" She screeched, the tears flowing freely.

*"JESUS!!"* I screamed, clapping my hands over my forehead. "You're sick!" She winced. "How could you *do* that?!"

But I already knew the answer. It was easy. She had help.

*Martin.*

The first, and the worst . . .

LeeAnn had broken up with him about two years ago, right around when we first met. I'd only seen the guy once or twice, when he came by the office to meet her after work. He seemed all right enough; tall and good-looking in a yuppified way. Real confident. Real smooth. They seemed like the perfect couple, and I was crushed.

But then I started hearing the horror stories: about how he constantly bullied and sniped at her; how the emotional abuse had begun to turn physical, and the physical act of love became brutal, supply-on-demand . . . until, when she finally grew sick of him and was no longer willing to offer herself, he went ahead and took her anyway . . .

Repeatedly.

No charges were ever filed. I hadn't really known her then, had only admired her from afar, and it wasn't my place to speak out. But I remembered seeing the bruises and hearing about the asshole ex-boyfriend following her around, making threatening phone calls and an ugly nuisance of himself.

And I remember, even then, wanting to tear his stupid throat out.

She'd been with him for almost two years: a very gradual descent into hell. She never talked about it much; I had to piece most of my knowledge together from the rumor mill and an outsider's perspective. But the bitch of it was, I think she really did love him. And that's what scarred her so badly: she cared, and she trusted him. She'd truly given him a piece of her heart. His betrayal was tantamount to a traumatic amputation; even after the shock she could still feel a twinge of the missing piece. The phantom pain, where it used to be.

And tonight she'd gone back, once again.

To find it.

I really didn't want to hear the gory details; I could fill them in well enough by rote. She was scared: of him, of herself. She had good reason to be. It was a twisted sort of *ourobouros*, the snake forever consuming its own tail, forever vomiting itself right back up; victim and victimizer, locked in an endlessly spiraling death dance.

And for the very first time I saw her, flung head-first off the pedestal and down into the slime. I saw her the way *they* must.

Flawed. Vulnerable.

Pathetic.

And for one bone-chilling moment, I thought that maybe Martin had a point . . .

*No.* The word was vehement, the voice very much my own. *No no no NO!* The vision ran completely counter to everything that I held dear, everything that I'd ever believed about the nature of love and the dignity of the human spirit. It made me crazy to think that such a thought had even entered my head . . .

. . . *but still I could see it, in psychotic Technicolor clarity: LeeAnn, cring-*

*ing before my swinging fist; the moment of glorious frisson, as flesh met surrendering flesh . . .*

*WHAT THE FUCK IS WRONG WITH ME?*, I silently screamed. My eyes snapped shut. The vision vanished. I whirled in my seat, away from LeeAnn and toward the bar, not wanting my face to betray the merest hint of what had just gone on inside my mind.

Then the bartender turned toward me. And nodded. And smiled.

And the pain in my bladder went nova.

It was remarkably like getting kicked in the balls: the same explosion of breath-stealing, strength-sapping anguish. It doubled me up in my seat, brought my face within inches of the table-top between LeeAnn and me. At that distance, with the dim light etching them in massive shadow, I couldn't help but see the four words crudely carved across its surface:

TO BE A MAN.

"What is it?" her voice said in quivering tones. Her tears were subsiding; she was regrouping in the rubble. I dragged my gaze up to hers with difficulty, still drowning in the pain.

"It's nothing, kiddo. Honest." I was trying to brush it aside, to hide it. It wasn't working. My voice was even more wobbly and wasted than hers.

"Don't bullshit me, Dave. You're in pain. Is it an ulcer?"

"I don't think so. I never had one before." But I had to briefly consider the possibility, because, *Jesus*, did it hurt!

"You look horrible."

"Thanks a lot."

"No, I'm seri—"

"LEEANN!" I thudded my fist against the table in pain and frustration and rage. "We didn't come here to talk about *my* goddamn pain! We came here to talk about yours! Now will you stop trying to change the fucking subject for a minute!"

She was stunned. In this, she was not alone. I could no more believe what I'd said than I could what I followed it up with.

"Baby, I'm not the one who got smacked around tonight! I'm not the one who went to Martin's and asked *him* to do it, either! I didn't even ask to come here! I only came because you begged me to, and I only did *that* because . . ."

I stopped, then. It was like slamming down the brakes at 120 m.p.h. The only sound in my head was the *screeeeeee* of rubber brain on asphalt bone. I blinked at the dust and smoke behind my eyes.

"Because why?" Her voice was soft as a whisper, warm as a beating heart. Her good eye was green and deep and inscrutable. It unnerved me, that eye, even more than its battered mate or the question that accompanied it. It scrutinized me with zoom-lens attention to every blackhead and ingrown hair on my soul.

*Because I love you*, my mind silently told her. *Because I'm a goddamn chump, that's why.*

I couldn't decide which conclusion was truer. I couldn't even sustain the internal debate. If I didn't get up and drag my ass down the stairs, I would let loose in my pants, and that was all there was to it. It was a matter of piss or die now, and there was no holding back.

"Excuse me a moment," I managed to mutter, rising up at half-mast and away from my seat.

But suddenly, LeeAnn didn't want to drop it. She grabbed my wrist just as I cleared the table. "David, please . . ." she said. It took everything I had to force the gentleness into my voice.

"I gotta pee, baby. Please. I'm gonna blow up if you don't let me go."

She actually smiled, then. In retrospect, were it not for the pain and embarrassment, that might have been the finest moment of my life. "I really do want to know," she said, soft as before. And her hand stayed right where it was.

I laid my free hand over it. The fingers meshed.

"Hold that thought," I whispered. Not entirely romantic; speech had gotten very difficult. Then I turned and beat a hasty retreat.

She watched me go. I could feel her eyes.

I knew what they were saying.

I will never forget.


Mark Twain once said that if God exists at all, he must surely be a malign thug. I wish it were true. It would be easier to blame God, or Fate, or the drugs, or the bar, or even LeeAnn.

But I know where the blame lays.

Right where it belongs.

I waddled away from the table with a smile on my face. The pain was still there . . . it kept me half doubled-over . . . but those last few moments had rendered it nearly insignificant. I was aglow with proximity to my heart's desire. I was aglow with impending triumph.

And that, of course, was when the Mighty Asshole chose to speak.

"Hey! Lookit the fuckin' *creampuff!*" he bellowed. "Guess you gotta go wee-wee, huh?"

There was a pause that crackled in my ears like static, dispersed by a ripple of harsh, raucous laughter. I turned to face a dozen mirthlessly-grinning eyes: the Asshole and his punching bag, the troll, and the hairball, and Heckel and Jeckel. All of them watching. Most of them laughing.

The Mighty Asshole, most of all.

Something clicked inside me. The words *I don't need this* took control of my brain. Under ordinary circumstances, I might have been scared. Not now.

I stared him down for a long defiant second.

Then I smiled. And curtsied. And blew him a kiss.

"Eat shit," I said.

Crude, but effective. I felt better almost instantly. The shock on his face was a joy to behold. I turned and scuttled down the stairs before he could rally; my mind raced in mad tandem with my feet. *Never mind them*, I told myself. *You've got to get your butt back there, tell her that you love her, give her the kiss that you've been dreaming about. The time has come. She WANTS you, man!*

Then the stairway ended, and my thoughts screeched to a halt.

I had reached my destination.

And the source.

The door itself was ill-hewn and splintery, lusterless and finger-smeared where the finish hadn't worn away entirely. The word GENTLEMEN was spelled out in eight-inch metal caps that glimmered flatly in the glare of the overhead bulb. I yanked on the handle; it was surprisingly heavy, beyond its mass. I pulled harder, and it reluctantly gave way.

I'd forgotten about the hinges, the terrible screeching sound they made. *Like a thing in pain*. The small hairs on the nape of my neck stood up like frightened sentries as the sound sawed through my eardrums and raked along my spine.

I stepped inside. The door creaked shut.

And the presence of the room assailed me.

There was the resonant *boom* that sent echoes bouncing off the filthy tiles. There was the overpoweringly ammoniacal sewage-stench, jolting up my nostrils like smelling salts. There was the dim insectoid buzz of the overhead fluorescents, spackling the interior with blotches of pulsing, spasming shadow.

And there was the *size* . . .

Mad, twirling Christ, it was huge. I stood in stunned amazement of what lay ahead. Now, the claustrophobic crapper of any midtown Manhattan working-class watering hole is just about big enough for the average-sized man to squeeze in and out of with an absolute maximum of discomfort. By comparison, this place was a fucking castle.

Twin rows of nonfunctional, moldy sinks: ten, in all. They lined a long tiled corridor on the way to the main room, from which I could make out a solitary stall.

*A solitary stall* . . .

Its door hung lopsidedly askew, as though wrenched violently off its hinges. An enormous pool of black, fetid water extended around it in a widening berth, apparently stemming from the blockage of gray, spongy effluvium that floated in the bowl like the lost continent of Atlantis. By craning my neck I could make out a pair of urinals just around the corner, clinging for dear life to the wall beyond.

*One stall. Two urinals. Ten sinks.*

Under any other circumstances it would've been weird enough to ponder. At the moment, my priorities were far more basic. I groaned, surveying the terrain. There was no way around it.

Only through it.

So I started in, holding my breath, gingerly skirting one of the main tributaries. Each of the sinks had its own mirror bolted to the wall above it. Nine of them had been smashed into glittering shards, held in place by inertia and thin metal frames. The buzzing light refracted off of them, making the streamlets of the pool appear to ripple with a malignant life of their own. The last mirror, the one nearest an adult novelty dispenser proffering big-ribbed condoms in tropical colors, was intact. My reflection fought its way back through the grit and haze; it looked pasty and haggard, forlorn.

"No wonder she's crazy about you," I muttered. "You gorgeous thing."

Something burbled, distinctly, from inside the stall.

"Huh?" I sputtered, startled, and turned to see a fresh ripple of foul water expanding outward in ever-increasing concentric rings. My thoughts turned to my quality footwear and nervously gauged the odds of making it over and back unscathed. It didn't look good.

The stall belched in agreement, sending out another wave.

I peeked around the corner, into the main body of the room. It was infinitely worse: the water actually deepened, and though it could only reasonably be a few inches, it looked bottomless. Some of the floor tiles were warped enough to form a series of little dry islands.

It was my only hope. Taking a last, desperate glance at my reflection, lips curled in disdain, I began to hippety-hop from dry spot to dry spot like a little kid crossing a creek. The beer made me clumsy, the drugs hypersensitized me, and the fumes burned like lye in my eyes and nose. But I made it, awkwardly straddling the sole oasis beneath the far urinal.

The stench was incredible. I momentarily regretted leaving my jacket upstairs, where a half-pack of Merits were serving no useful purpose. The joint was there, too, as were all of my matches. There was nothing I could do to abate the smell.

Those were the facts I had to face as I, at last, unzipped my fly.

And not a moment too soon; no sooner had I freed my screaming pecker than the pee blasted out and splished against the porcelain like a runaway firehose. I sighed, a deep and vastly relieved "Ahhhhhh. . . ." and leaned forward to brace myself against the wall, feeling slightly dizzy and a vague surge of pride at having made it.

I looked at the wall, while the bladder-pain receded. There was a profusion of graffiti there; the same sort of jerkoff witticisms that probably graced the pissoirs at the dawn of time. Crudely optimistic penises pounding into yawning pudenda. Tits like udders, hanging from faceless, howling female forms. Phone numbers advertising good times at someone else's expense. Initials. Dates. Dreams of seamy grandeur.

And the same four words:

TO BE A MAN.

In the stall, something big went *squish* and then sputtered. I could hear the tinkling of falling droplets, delicate as the tines of the tiniest music box as they sprinkled the surface of the pool.

My spine froze. My pissing and breathing cut off instinctively. I leaned back as far as I could and listened.

Nothing.

"This is stupid," I informed myself by way of the room at large. My paranoia burgeoned. "There's nobody in there."

Still nothing. Ripples, expanding quietly outward. I exhaled. My pissing resumed with great difficulty.

And the door to the men's room flew suddenly open.

I jerked, nearly spraying myself. From inside, the echoing screech of the hinges resounded like a billion bat shrieks in a cave. The door *screeeee*d and slammed shut like thunder. The walls boomed with the sound of amplified footsteps.

Every alarm in my nervous system went off. It was like pissing on the third rail of a subway track, a thousand volts of terror sizzling through me in the space of a second. The footsteps got closer, and I found myself wanting to get out of there very badly. *Relax*, I hissed silently, as internal organs tightened to pee faster. *You're stoned. This is stupid. Nothing's going to happen. Nothing's—*

"Well, well, well," he said, sneering. "Look it what we got here."

The footsteps came up behind me and paused. I didn't want to turn around and look.

I had to.

The Mighty Asshole stood at the edge of the swamp: arms crossed, legs spraddled, a hideous grin on his face. He said, "Looks like we got us a live one."

Something burbled and glooped in the toilet stall.

*What the fuck did he mean by that?* I wondered. The images it conjured up were not very pretty. The smile that flicked across my face was meant to look cool and unruffled. It failed. I flashed it anyway, trying to hide my desperation. He grinned back at me, flat-eyed and mean as a mouthful of snakes.

The Mighty Asshole sploshed, indifferent, through the pool of rancid liquid. He came up beside me, unzipped his fly, and finagled himself into trajectory with the urinal to my left. I took a deep, nasty breath and exhaled it at once, not looking at him. His pissing chorused with mine.

A moment passed.

"You're a faggot, you know it?" he said casually. "You're a little fucking faggot."

I looked at him then, peering straight into his idiot face.

"Yeah you," he continued. "A little fucking *faggot.*"

" 'Zat so?" I said. "Geez. This is sure news to me." My bladder was draining, like air from a flat, and with it, the pain and the fear.

"A faggot," he repeated, as loud as before, but his sense of utter mastery had dwindled a bit. Our eyes were locked, and I could see the sudden twitching of dim-witted uncertainty there.

"'Zat a fact," I said, marking time till I was done. I didn't want to fight him, that much was for sure. My knife was upstairs, with the Merits and the joint. He wasn't all that much bigger than me, but he was blitzed and stupid; even if I jawed him, he probably wouldn't know it, and we'd end up rolling around here in the slime of the ages.

"Thass a fact, alright." He slurred it, and it took a long time to get out. Good sign. My pissing was almost done; by the time he formulated another thought, I'd be gone.

"I know a woman who'd be interested to hear that," I said. "Yessiree. She'd find that pretty goddamned funny."

He laughed. I joined him.

He stopped. I didn't.

He hit me.

It was a short, straight-armed punch, with a lot of muscle behind it. It caught me square in the side of the head, sending hot black sparks pinging through my skull. I lurched to the side, off my little island, and straight into the sludge. Cold putrescence flooded up through the hole in my shoe.

"Shit!" I yelled, "Shit! Shit!" I splashed around to face him, waiting for my vision to clear. I could feel my ear starting to cauliflower, feel the hot trickle of blood seeping down. I thought about booting him right in the nuts, grinding his face into that same black water. I was furious. *"You stupid motherfu—"* I began.

And then stopped.

Suddenly.

Completely.

Stopped.

*In the pool. In the slime.*

It started with the sole of the right foot: a numbing sensation that I at first mistook for the cold. In the thin web of flesh between the first and second shafts of the metatarsus, seeping up through the sodden expanse of my gym sock, the horror took root and spread. Up along the flexor tendons, through their fibrous sheaths. Soaking into the flexor brevis digitorum. An impulse, shooting out at the speed of thought, socked into the motor nucleus at the fifth nerve of the brain.

I couldn't move.

The numbness spread.

*In the grume. Where He waits. Forever and ever.*

Up through fibula and tibia, dousing bone and soaking marrow. Up through muscle and sinew, tendrils snaking up arteries and conduits, putting frost in my ganglion, ice in my veins. Up through the femur and into the hip, the pelvis. Numbing my cock, my balls. Spreading down the other leg.

*Ancient. Eternally crawling.*

Blitzkreig in my bladder. In my spleen. Worming a finger up through my intestines. Oozing through the superficial fascia of the abdominal wall and then outward. Seeping through the pores. Bleeding through my sweat-shirt.

*Eternally struggling toward form.*

*And taking it.*

*For His own.*

My eyes riveted on the eyes of the man before me: moist and pulsing, the color of slugs. A spasm ran through us both, synchronized and uncon-trollable. Then I was pivoted and slammed facefirst into the filthy tiles above the urinal. I couldn't feel it.

I could feel nothing.

In the stall, the burbling became violently frantic. I managed to lift my head away from the wall. The magic-marker scrawlings hovered inches from my eyes.

Then they began to shift. To change.

And He began to speak.

YOU'RE JUST A LITTLE FUCKING FAGGOT, He said. OH YES YOU ARE.

My eyes were glued to the words as they synched with the voice booming inside my head.

JUST A LITTLE FUCKING CREAMPUFF FAGGOT WHO DOESN'T KNOW HOW TO TAKE CARE OF BUSINESS.

I thought about the blonde at the bar, her groveling eyes. I thought about LeeAnn. I wanted to scream.

He sensed it. It made Him happy.

LIKE HER, He said, immensely pleased. OH, YES. EXACTLY.

Something slithered out of the toilet bowl and landed on the floor with a thick, wet, splutting sound. LeeAnn appeared in grotesquely animated caricature on the wall before me, silently screaming as a monstrously bloated penis plunged in and out and in and

YOU DON'T KNOW HOW TO BE A MAN. YOU'RE *AFRAID* TO BE A MAN.

I tried to scream. I couldn't.

YOU'RE AFRAID TO GO OUT THERE AND *TAKE* WHAT YOU WANT.

Sliding up my larynx, out over my tongue. Pouring into the hollows behind my eyes. Oozing into the billion soft folds of my brain. Black static, eating inward from the periphery of my vision. Blocking out everything.

But the realization.

*Forever and ever.*

It was crawling toward me. I couldn't see it, couldn't turn my head, but I could hear the horror revisited in the breath of the man beside me.

And I could hear it, slithering. I could feel its hunger. I could taste its boundless greed. A tiny voice in my head shrieked *it's only the drugs,* but the voice was tiny, and hollow, and fading.

Something small and moist grabbed onto my pants leg.

NOW YOU'RE GOING TO KNOW WHAT IT IS . . .

Crawling up.

. . . TO BE A MAN . . .

Coming closer.

*Struggling toward form.*

TO BE A MAN

Tiny fingers clawed the base of my skull. My jaws were pried open. A caricature appeared on the wall, mocking me.

OH, YES.

And there was nothing I could do.

But let Him in.

When I came to, some ten minutes later, the Mighty Asshole was gone. I knew that I'd have no more trouble from him that night, or ever after. In fact, I could come back as much as I wished. Again. And again.

I belonged now. Completely.

He had not let us fall, cunning fuck that He was. When I came to, we were in front of the sole surviving mirror, and He was splashing freezing water in our face.

He cleaned us up: meticulously washing away the blood, smoothing back the disheveled hair. Tomorrow we'd get it cut, He informed me. Nice and short, maybe a flattop. And we'd start working out, put some meat on these bones.

*A real man,* He said, *always takes care of business.*

When we were nice and clean, He turned and bought us a big-ribbed condom. For later. He smiled at our face in the grimy mirror. It was a cruel smile, and infinitely calculated. His smile. The mirror grinned coldly back.

And He smashed it.

With my fist.

When we finally came up the stairs, twenty minutes had passed. LeeAnn was waiting anxiously at the table. "David!" she demanded. "What happened to you? I was really getting worried."

He lifted one finger, and told her to shush.

She obeyed.

"You're a sweetheart," He said, moving close.

Then He kissed her.

Passionately.

With my lips.


There is a book on the history of photojournalism on the endtable beside me. It was one of LeeAnn's favorites, but that's not why He keeps it around. He likes the pretty pictures.

And He likes to torture me.

Right now, it's open to the page on the liberation of the concentration camps, at the end of World War II. One photo in particular stands out, flickering in the dim light of the TV's hissing screen like footage from some long-forgotten newsreel. It's a black-and-white picture of the gate to Auschwitz. Perhaps it's even one of Margaret Bourke-White's; that would be nice, but I guess it doesn't really matter. So what if I can't make out the credit? I can make out the inscription clear enough: ARBEIT MACHT FREI, in huge iron letters. That's what's important.

ARBEIT MACHT FREI.

*Work Makes Freedom.*

I've thought about that a lot. One of the many thoughts that help me in the night, long after He's passed out in His favorite easychair, drunken and still dressed. Tonight, He didn't even get the damned field jacket off.

I'm so glad.

I'm sure that LeeAnn would be, too.

It took her over a year to tear away: thirteen months of steadily escalating madness. Oh, He was great, for the first month or so: strong and sensitive and very, very sincere. He made all the right moves, said all the right things. And she welcomed my newfound assertiveness, with an ardor that both amazed and destroyed me.

He waited with the patience of the ages, until the hooks were planted nice and deep. Until she fell for Him. Until she trusted Him. Until He could destroy her. It was amazing, how much groundwork I'd already lain. It made it infinitely easier for Him. And infinitely worse, for me.

And then, when the moment was right, He showed her His true self. Repeatedly.

I'll never forget the look of betrayal on her face.

It took her over six months to escape; we were living together by then. He tried to break her, and she fought Him. Escape cost her dearly: emotionally, mentally.

Physically.

But escape she did, and I love her for it. I've thought of her often, God knows. I've wondered how she's doing, wondered where she is.

But I don't really want to know.

And, besides, I never will.

Because every night after that, He dragged me downtown and back to the bar. The guys were all there, of course. The guys were always there. We got along famously, round after round, while the Hooter Girl sadly presided.

And every night after that, we went out in search of fresh meat. There were always women out there, waiting to be punished for something. He was always eager to oblige. He wanted me to watch. He needed me to forget. His failure. Her victory.

But I didn't, damn it.

I remembered.

Within the month, he'd found a suitable distraction: Lisa. She wasn't as sharp as LeeAnn, or as strong. But her blue eyes were bright, and her curvature dazzled, and her smile could have sold you the moon. We've been married now, the three of us, going on four years. We have kids, to my unending sorrow: Patricia, little David, Jr., and another damned soul on the way. Lisa's eyes no longer sparkle, and she hardly ever smiles. Thirty pounds of purpled padding grace the skeleton of her beauty like a shroud.

But tonight, that's all behind her.

It's taken four years. Four years of practice: at night, while He slept drunkenly on. Cell by cell. Inch by inch. Four very long years. LeeAnn would be proud.

I can move my right arm, you see.

Only when He sleeps, true, and not very much. It's not very strong, either. Yes, life is a bitch.

But it was strong enough to open the book tonight. And with a little strength to spare . . .

It'll be enough to reach the knife.

And so what if it takes me all night. ARBEIT MACHT FREI, right?

Sometimes, that's just what it takes.

To be a man.

# CRAIG SHAW GARDNER

## Demon Luck

One of the most popular forms of fantasy among the mass readership this year was humorous fantasy—the best known being Piers Anthony's *Xanth* series, which topped the nation's bestsellers lists. Other writers have turned to humorous fantasy as a result—and while some of these writers are simply jumping on a money-making bandwagon, no doubt, others are genuinely talented writers who have finally found an audience for their pun-ridden, satirical work. The best of the latter group, in my opinion, is Craig Shaw Gardner—already known to many readers for his excellent work in the horror field.

"Demon Luck" pokes gentle fun at some of the clichés and conventions of the modern fantasy genre. If this tale tickles you, seek out Gardner's intelligently humorous Ebenezum series—beginning with *A Malady of Magicks*—about a wizard who is allergic to his own magic. Then look up some of Gardner's horror stories, and you will be as impressed as I am by the scope of this writer's talents.

Gardner makes his home in Cambridge, Massachusetts, and has just completed a new Ebenezum novel.

—T.W.

# DEMON LUCK

## Craig Shaw Gardner

Gosha was truly the luckiest man in all the world. To be going to the Fair at Ithkar, ah, that was the sort of pleasure only found in dreams. And with what he had to sell, the finest fruits and vegetables in the entire Zoe Valley, could he leave the fair any less than a rich man?

The late summer sun beat down on his shoulders, warming them under his rough shirt. Small clouds of dust rose about the hooves of the horse that drew the wagon, and motes danced beneath Gosha's feet. The fields to either side of the road were full of butterflies, all yellow and orange, and every tree seemed to hold a bird that called to them as the merchant's wagon passed. Today the world smiled on Gosha, and Gosha smiled in return. What could be better?

"I agree entirely," said a voice close by Gosha's ear.

The merchant started and spun about. A small man, about four feet tall, sat next to him in the wagon. He was fairly well dressed, with quite a dazzling smile, made all the more so by the fact that both the man's clothing and skin were matching shades of blue.

"Close your mouth, please," the blue man said. "Gosha, this is your lucky day. And I am your good-luck demon."

Gosha turned away and looked at the road. The same gray mare still pulled the wagon. The same yellow fields lined either side, filled with the same brilliant butterflies.

He looked to his right again. The blue man smiled.

"Good-luck demon?" Gosha asked.

The blue man nodded.

Now Gosha considered himself a pragmatic man. One had to be able to assess a situation and act quickly upon it if one was to be successful in the mercantile arts. Therefore, should one find oneself engaged in conversation with a small blue man, whether one believed this was really happening or not, one should attempt to get all the information one could. Therefore, Gosha said: "I thought demons generally brought bad luck."

The demon nodded gravely. "A popularly held misconception."

Gosha persisted: "But wouldn't I have heard of good-luck demons? In

381

this hard world, a magical creature who brings good luck is almost too much to be believed."

"Exactly!" The demon grabbed Gosha's hand and pumped it vigorously. "Not only are you a lucky merchant, Gosha, but an extremely canny one as well. Lucky demons are one of the best-kept secrets in the realm. Let me phrase it thusly: If you were fortunate enough to have something like me to give you an edge over your fellow merchants, would you spread it around?"

Gosha shook his head slowly.

"But I'm being rude!" The demon grabbed Gosha's hand once again. "The name's Hotpoint. Pleased to make your acquaintance."

Hotpoint? Gosha supposed it was a fair name for a demon. That is, if he supposed anything at all. In a few short moments, he had gone from feeling one with the world into a state of total confusion. Gosha studied the short blue fellow at his side. What was the proper response to meeting a demon? The most proper one he could think of was to jump from the wagon and run screaming into the fields. But then what would happen to his fruit? And what about his son, fast asleep in the back of the wagon?

He hadn't given a thought to Lum since the demon's arrival. Nor had Lum taken any notice of what was happening. Not surprising; once the boy slept, it would take a hundred demons to rouse him. Perhaps, when the boy came round, he and Gosha could subdue Hotpoint. But what if the demon were truly what he said he was?

Hotpoint continued to talk as Gosha mulled over the problem. The demon commented on the beauty of the day, which he could appreciate despite the fact that, in his homeland, the standards were somewhat different. Hotpoint went on to praise Gosha's fruit at some length: the beautiful color, the absence of worms and bruises, the wonderful shapes, so round and succulent. Gosha began to worry about the size of the demon's appetite.

"Dear Gosha," the demon remarked, "instead of looking at me, you might do well to watch the road."

Gosha looked about to see a horse-drawn cart coming full gallop toward the wagon. The merchant reined in his own horse at once. "Whoa! Whoa!" cried the other driver. There was a substantial crash.

"Blight and war!" Gosha cursed as he jumped from his wagon. The collision had pushed the two right wheels into the ditch at the side of the road. The cart that had collided with the wagon sat next to it, minus both one wheel and its driver, who sat dazed in the ditch mud, surrounded by Gosha's fruit.

"What have you done?" Gosha cried. "Your carelessness has ruined half my goods! What will I sell in Ithkar?"

The other man groaned. He was short and stout, and, though he was dressed entirely in gray, Gosha could tell, from the cut of the clothes and the fine gold stitching, that the man's wardrobe had been produced by the finest tailors in Ithkar. The nerve of someone of his station being careless on the road!

The stout man looked up at Gosha. His eyes seemed to have gotten crossed in the fall. There was something in his gaze, though, that made the merchant hesitate.

"Are you all right, sir?" Gosha said in a somewhat softer voice.

"Hm?" The other man uncrossed his eyes. "Yes, yes, never felt better." He rubbed at the mud covering his face. He succeeded more in distributing it rather than removing it. "K'shew's the name. I was hoping to be at Ithkar Fair myself this year until . . ." He paused and coughed. "Until something came up."

Gosha reached out a hand and helped the other man to his feet. "Something came up?" he prompted.

"Yes." K'shew smiled, then grimaced as he tried to walk. "I found I must perform an errand"—he paused again and looked up the road in the direction he had come—"of the utmost urgency!"

"But you've hurt yourself and your wagon. Surely you can rest a bit."

"No, no!" The stout fellow shook his head so violently that his hat fell off. He grabbed it in midair and jammed it across his bald pate. "Most urgent! Most urgent!"

K'shew turned to survey the damage to his cart. He cleared his throat, made three quick passes in the air, and said an extremely long word so rapidly that Gosha couldn't quite catch it. There was a flash of golden light. When Gosha opened his eyes, he saw that K'shew's cart was whole again.

Gosha took a step back. A magician! He should have realized that anyone with an apostrophe in his name had to be important. Now this was an entirely different matter. It was one thing to feel sorry for an addled old man who'd fallen in the mud, but magicians who have accidents should be fully prepared to pay for their mistakes. Gosha pointed to the produce on the ground.

"The fruit," he intoned.

"Yes, a pity." K'shew frowned. "If I hadn't been in such a tizzy . . . well, let's see. I could magically make it whole again. No, no, they don't like that sort of thing in Ithkar, do they? Wouldn't want to get you in bad with the temple people. I guess there's no helping it."

Lum chose that moment to climb from the back of the wagon. He stretched his long legs and arms and jumped to the ground. With his skinny body and the yellow hair always in his eyes, he reminded his father of nothing so much as a rather untidy broom.

He yawned as he approached. "Has something happened?"

That was it. Gosha's wife might have badgered him into taking his youngest son along, but he would not suffer the adolescent gladly. "Something happen?" he screamed. "I've only been run into by a cart, spilling fruit all over the road! And that's besides gaining a so-called good-luck demon—" His voice died in his throat. Should he have even mentioned Hotpoint? The magician stared at the wagon seat where Hotpoint sat.

"I don't necessarily know if the 'good luck' part is true," Gosha added rapidly. "We only have the demon's word."

"I have no idea what you're talking about," the mage replied disdainfully. "Good-luck demons? The fall must have shaken you more severely than you realized."

"Demons?" Lum pulled his hair from his eyes so he could look around. "Where? What do they look like? I don't see anything."

"What do you mean?" Gosha sputtered. They had both looked right at Hotpoint. Unless—

Unless only he could see the demon!

The merchant groaned. "Oh, the fall was worse than I thought! My head is spinning! My produce is smashed to the ground, my livelihood destroyed."

K'shew frowned. "Oh, come, come. I was about to give you something." He laughed and slapped his knee. "I have the very thing." He ran to his cart, suddenly spry. "This will take but a second, merchant. Then I must hurry, hurry off!"

He rummaged through the things piled high above the cart for a moment, then gave a cry of discovery. "The very thing!" he repeated as he grunted and pulled and brought forth a bushel basket filled with apples. Nice-looking fruit, Gosha thought, good shape, good size, except that every apple was silver.

"I had intended to sell these at Ithkar Fair myself," K'shew said. "Now I don't know if I'll have the chance." He held the bushel out to Gosha. "A fair exchange, I think, for your damaged merchandise. I might also be able to arrange a prime location for you to set up your wagon, right next to the temple, for a small fee, of course." K'shew glanced back up the road. "Then again, I think it might be time I moved along."

Gosha was astonished. Before he could think of anything to say, the magician hopped back in his cart and spurred his horse to a gallop. Soon Gosha could see nothing but a dust cloud receding down the road.

He looked at the apples. They shone in the sunlight as if they had a light of their own. He inhaled their subtle fragrance, sweet yet tart. It made his mouth water. He wanted to hold one in his hand, to lift it to his mouth, to sink his teeth through that shining skin, to taste—

Gosha closed his eyes and turned away from the bushel. These apples weren't for eating, at least not by him. He was quite sure that, for every apple he consumed, an equal or greater amount of gold should never reach his pockets.

"Lum!" he called. "Salvage what you can from the ground, and find a place for these!"

He passed the bushel to his son. Lum struggled under the weight but finally managed to load the apples into the back of the wagon. Gosha smiled. Today even his misfortunes had happy conclusions. He may have exaggerated a bit when he had yelled at the magician; at most, perhaps, one-tenth of his produce was ruined. And how much more would he make by selling the silver apples? Truly, he was the luckiest man in all the world!

"Exactly as I predicted!" Hotpoint smiled at him. "With a good-luck demon at your side, how can you fail?"

Gosha frowned. Maybe the demon was right after all. It was hard to feel warmth for a creature whose clothes and skin were a matching blue, but Gosha at least climbed back into the seat next to him.

"Ah, those apples," Hotpoint said softly. "Each apple like a separate silver star. No one else in all Ithkar Fair will have their like. Now, friend Gosha, you have not only the finest produce from the Zoe Valley, but the most precious fruit in all the world. With goods like that, you hardly need luck at all."

Gosha allowed himself to smile at last. Maybe the demon was lucky after all. Perhaps he had entered a realm of good fortune so magnificent that it allowed the creature to appear. Perhaps he would be lucky from this day forward, the luckiest man in history.

It was then he saw the rider.

Hotpoint excused himself and hopped back into the wagon.

The horse and rider approached them from the direction the magician had come, moving twice as fast as the mage. The horse was jet black, a huge beast that, as fast as it was approaching, seemed to be moving more at a canter than a gallop. And if the beast was twice a horse, the man atop seemed double-sized as well. He wore robes as dark as the horse or darker, the color of a storm at night. But his face was the palest white, almost as if his skin were transparent and the color of the bone shone through. There seemed to be no noise but the horse's hooves, the sound of thunder rolling toward Gosha and his wagon.

The dark rider reined in his horse as he came abreast of the wagon, and then there was no noise at all. The rider stared at Gosha for a moment through the silence.

"Merchant!" the rider called, in a voice oddly slow and high, as if the large man seldom found a use for it. "Have you passed anyone else on this road?" The rider's eyes looked straight into Gosha's. The rider's eyes were the color of blood. Gosha's tongue felt dry in his mouth. He wanted to speak, but his lips would not part.

Lum jumped from the wagon's rear. "Yes, sir!" he cried. "A chubby gray fellow."

The rider smiled a death's-head grin. "Indeed. Did he say anything as he passed?"

Lum laughed. "He ran his cart right into our wagon."

"You must tell me more." The dark rider dismounted.

Gosha was horrified. He should have spoken up, insisted that no one had passed, and sent the rider on his way. But his idiot son had to feel talkative and prompt the rider to stay. Somehow, Gosha thought, the longer the rider stayed, the worse it would be for Lum and himself.

And where, perchance, was Hotpoint the good-luck demon? Gosha heard rustling noises from within the wagon at his back.

The dark rider approached. "Men call me N't'g'r'x."

Gosha's mouth dropped open again. Never had he heard a name with so many apostrophes. If K'shew, with only one apostrophe, had been a magician of some importance, what station must this dark rider hold? He shivered and cursed the day he learned spelling so that he might worry about such a thing.

"There is a demon here," N't'g'r'x whispered.

Gosha found his voice at last. He wasn't going to let anybody, even if he were to look like death itself, take his demon away. "Demons here?" He tried to laugh, but there was no conviction in it. "I am but a simple fruit merchant."

"So is the man who collided with your wagon," N't'g'r'x replied. "Or so he would like the fair-wards of Ithkar to believe."

K'shew a fruit merchant? Gosha shook his head in disbelief. Still, that would explain why he carried apples in his cart, even though the apples were silver. And he'd given the fruit to a competitor, with hardly any argument at all! Gosha wondered if all the merchants at Ithkar Fair were as just.

N't'g'r'x still watched him. Gosha marveled at just how much the dark rider did look like death itself. He cleared his throat. "K'shew said he was a magician."

N't'g'r'x waved the idea aside with one of his bony hands. "He brags about his demon line, but 'tis a minor piece of work. K'shew says many things. Did he give you anything?"

Gosha's heart sank. He would lose not only his good-luck demon, but his silver fruit as well. Perhaps he could deny receiving the apples from the mage, if only his son would stay quiet. Gosha shot a stern look in Lum's direction.

Lum saw Gosha's cautionary glare and nodded happily. "Yes, good sir," he said to N't'g'r'x. "For damaging our stock, the mage gave us a basket of silver apples."

"Silver apples?" The dark rider laughed, the sound of bones shaken in a coffin. "K'shew always was a rogue."

Gosha's heart fell lower still. Soon it should lodge in his foot. Why didn't his son just take the silver apples and give them to this rider?

"Wait a second," Lum said. "I'll get them for you."

Gosha cried out and fell back into the wagon. Perhaps his heart would pass from his body entirely, to fall among the apples and pears.

With his head atop the fruit, the merchant could hear the rustling sound again. Except, in the quiet of the wagon, it no longer sounded like rustling. It sounded like chewing.

"Hotpoint!" Gosha sat bolt upright. He dug furiously into the produce.

"Don't bother me when I've got my mouth full!" came the muffled reply from somewhere down at the end of the cart. A chill shook the length of Gosha's body. It was the end that held the silver apples.

And the apples drew the merchant's eye. They glowed, even here, away from the daylight. They shone so, he had to touch them and feel the smoothness of their skins. What would it be like to bite into one of them? Would the juice be warm and sweet, heated by the apple's glow?

Gosha could bear it no longer. A demon was destroying his goods, while outside a stranger who looked like death was engaged in animated conversation with his dullard son. What more did he have to live for? He would eat those silver apples, every one! Gosha hurled himself across the wagon, his mouth open to accept the fruit.

The fruit, however, seemed to be otherwise inclined. As Gosha skidded across the top of the produce mound, apples shifted, grapes squeezed, pears bounced, dates rolled. The wagon lurched as fruit pushed toward the rear with such force that Gosha heard the tearing of wood along the wagon's backboard. The board gave way, and he found himself lost in an avalanche.

He pushed himself free and found he was facing Hotpoint. The demon looked somewhat heavier than before. Hotpoint belched.

"I thought you were a good-luck demon!" Gosha cried.

"Ah," said Hotpoint happily. "But I did not mention good luck for whom!"

A dark shadow fell across both demon and merchant. Gosha turned to see N't'g'r'x. The dark man made four passes in the air, adding three noises that might have been words had they been spoken by anybody else.

Hotpoint disappeared.

Gosha yelped.

A skeletal hand appeared before his face.

"Let me help you up," N't'g'r'x intoned.

"Surely," replied Gosha. The man's grip was like ice.

"K'shew was a fruit merchant," N't'g'r'x answered the question in Gosha's eyes. "I am a wizard."

Gosha swallowed and instructed his son to pick up what fruit could be saved. He thought to ask another question. All he could manage was, "But why?"

"K'shew was not just a simple fruit-seller. For years, he has been the largest fruit merchant at Ithkar Fair, with twenty times the produce of other peddlers. Such a large discrepancy between businesses brought him to the attention of certain officials. We are very careful that everything remain honest at the fair. And K'shew's dealings seemed honest enough. But outside the fair"—the dark rider laughed—"you have seen a different story."

"So he tried to cheat me?" Gosha asked.

"More than that. When you crossed the sorcerous line K'shew had managed to draw over almost every road leading to Ithkar, a demon appeared in your wagon, intent upon destroying your goods. But could K'shew stop there? No, he had to give you magic apples, and those silver apples smell of sorcery even from this distance. If you had shown up at the gate with either demons or apples, they would have turned you away for illegal sorcery, and you would never have been allowed to participate in the fair again."

N't'g'r'x intertwined his bony fingers. "K'shew is a compulsive thief. His type often is. They don't know when to stop, and end up giving themselves away. I'm surprised he did not rent you a prime spot in the marketplace, right next to the temple. And you'd find the spot all right, under several feet of water, in the middle of the river Ith." N't'g'r'x laughed long and hard. It was not a pleasant sound.

An even more horrible noise erupted behind them. Lum stood, staring with horror at the silver apple in his hand. There was a bite out of it.

"This is vile!" he cried. "It tastes like a cross between vinegar and spoiled meat!"

"In an hour," the rider said as he remounted his horse, "your son shall have a stomachache as well." He reached within the folds of his dark cloak and threw something at Gosha's feet. When it hit the ground, the merchant heard the chink of metal.

"For your information on K'shew," N't'g'r'x called. "I go to catch the villain." And off he rode, like a dark leaf blown by the wind.

Lum got the remaining fruit loaded and climbed into the wagon front next to Gosha. The merchant took his son's complaints with a paternal stoicism. Horse and wagon climbed a hill, and at its summit they saw a great city in the distance, full of colored banners and gray-green spires.

"Ithkar," Gosha proclaimed.

Other roads joined theirs as they went down the hill to the city, and they soon fell into a procession of other carts and wagons, all on their way to the fair. The one behind them clanked with metal goods; cooking smells came from the one before. Gosha breathed them deeply, once again relaxed. He would have to send Lum back to the valley somewhat sooner than he had planned to bring more goods, but what he had should still sell quickly, and the money the dark rider had given him would surely more than make up the difference.

It had been a long and rather eventful day. Gosha sighed as the sun dipped below the horizon, and the towers of the city became dark silhouettes framed by violet clouds. Truly, he thought, I am the luckiest man in the world.

# JANE YOLEN

## Words of Power

"Words of Power," a moving tale of a young girl's coming of age, may be unfamiliar to Yolen's adult readers as it was published in a collection of young adult stories. Its original venue does not, however, diminish the clarity of vision or the validity of the story.

—T.W.

# WORDS OF POWER

## Jane Yolen

Late Blossoming Flower, the only child of her mother's old age, stared sulkily into the fire. A homely child, with a nose that threatened to turn into a beak and a mouth that seldom smiled, she was nonetheless cherished by her mother and the clan. Her loneness, the striking rise of her nose, the five strands of white hair that streaked through her shiny black hair, were all seen as the early signs of great power, the power her mother had given up when she had chosen to bear a child.

"I would never have made such a choice," Late Blossoming Flower told her mother. "I would never give up *my* power."

Her mother, who had the same fierce nose, the white streak of hair, and the bitter smile but was a striking beauty, replied gently, "You do not have that power yet. And if I had not given up mine, you would not be here now to make such a statement and to chide me for my choice." She shook her head. "Nor would you now be scolded for forgetting to do those things which are yours by duty."

Late Blossoming Flower bit back the reply that was no reply but merely angry words. She rose from the fireside and went out of the cliff house to feed the milk beast. As she climbed down the withy ladder to the valley below, she rehearsed that conversation with her mother as she had done so often before. Always her mother remained calm, her voice never rising into anger. It infuriated Flower, and she nursed that sore like all the others, counting them up as carefully as if she were toting them on a notch stick. The tally by now was long indeed.

But soon, she reminded herself, soon she would herself be a woman of power, though she was late coming to it. All the signs but one were on her. Under the chamois shirt her breasts had finally begun to bud. There was hair curling in the secret places of her body. Her waist and hips were changing to create a place for the Herb Belt to sit comfortably, instead of chafing her as it did now. And when at last the moon called to her and her first blood flowed, cleansing her body of man's sin, she would be allowed at last to go on her search for her own word of power and be free of her hated, ordinary chores. Boys could not go on such a search, for they were never able to rid themselves of the dirty blood-sin. But she took no great comfort in that, for not all girls who sought found. Still, Late Blossoming Flower knew she was the daughter of a woman of power, a woman so blessed that even though she had had a child and lost the use of the Shaping Hands she still retained the Word That Changes. Late Blossoming Flower never doubted that when she went on her journey she would find what it was she sought.

The unfed milk beast lowed longingly as her feet touched the ground. She bent and gathered up bits of earth, cupped the fragments in her hand, said the few phrases of the *Ke-waha*, the prayer to the land, then stood.

"I'm not *that* late," she said sharply to the agitated beast, and went to the wooden manger for maize.

It was the first day after the rising of the second moon, and the florets of the night-blooming panomom tree were open wide. The sickly sweet smell of the tiny clustered blossoms filled the valley, and all the women of the valley dreamed dreams.

The women of power dreamed in levels. Late Blossoming Flower's mother passed from one level to another with the ease of long practice, but her daughter's dream quester had difficulty going through. She wandered too long on the dreamscape paths, searching for a ladder or a rope or some other familiar token of passage.

When Late Blossoming Flower had awakened, her mother scolded her for her restless sleep.

"If you are to be a true woman of power, you must force yourself to lie down in the dream and fall asleep. Sleep within sleep, dream within dream. Only then will you wake at the next level." Her head had nodded gently every few words and she spoke softly, braiding her hair with quick and supple hands. "You must be like a gardener forcing an early bud to bring out the precious juices."

"Words. Just words," said Late Blossoming Flower. "And none of *those* words has power." She had risen from her pallet, shaking her own hair free of the loose night braiding, brushing it fiercely before plaiting it up again. She could not bear to listen to her mother's advice any longer and had let her thoughts drift instead to the reed hut on the edge of the valley, where old Sand Walker lived. A renegade healer, he lived apart from the others and, as a man, was little thought of. But Late Blossoming Flower liked to go and sit with him and listen to his stories of the time before time, when power had been so active in the world it could be plucked out of the air as easily as fruit from a tree. He said that dreams eventually explained themselves and that to discipline the dream figure was to bind its power. To Late Blossoming Flower that made more sense than all her mother's constant harping on the Forcing Way.

So intent was she on visiting the old man that day, she had raced through her chores, scanting the milk beast and the birds who squatted on hidden nests. She had collected only a few eggs and left them in the basket at the bottom of the cliff. Then, without a backward glance at the withy ladders spanning the levels or the people moving busily against the cliff face, she raced down the path toward Sand Walker's home.

As a girl child she had that freedom, given leave for part of each day to walk the many trails through the valley. On these walks she was supposed to learn the ways of the growing flowers, to watch the gentler creatures at their play, to come to a careful understanding of the way of predator and prey. It was time for her to know the outer landscape of her world as thoroughly as she would, one day, know the inner dream trails. But Late Blossoming Flower was a hurrying child. As if to make up for her late birth and the crushing burden of early power laid on her, she refused to take the time.

"My daughter," her mother often cautioned her, "a woman of true power must be in love with silence. You must learn all the outward sounds in order to approach the silence that lies within."

But Flower wanted no inner silence. She delighted in tuneless singing and loud sounds: the sharp hoarse cry of the night herons sailing across the marsh; the crisp howl of the jackals calling under the moon; even the scream of the rabbit in the teeth of the wolf. She sought to imitate *those* sounds, make them louder, sing them again in her own mouth. What was silence compared to sound?

And when she was with old Sand Walker in his hut, he sang with her. And told stories, joking stories, about the old women and their silences.

"Soon enough," Sand Walker said, "soon enough it will be silent and dark. In the grave. Those old *bawenahs*"—he used the word that meant the unclean female vulture—"those old *bawenahs* would make us rehearse for our coming deaths with their binding dreams. Laugh *now*, child. Sing out. Silence is for the dead ones, though they call themselves alive and walk the trails. But you and I, ho"—he poked her in the stomach lightly with his stick—"we know the value of noise. It blocks out thinking, and thinking means pain. Cry out for me, child. Loud. Louder."

And as if a trained dog, Late Blossoming Flower always dropped to her knees at this request and howled, scratching at the dirt and wagging her bottom. Then she would fall over on her back with laughter and the old man laughed with her.

All this was in her mind as she ran along the path toward Sand Walker's hut.

A rabbit darted into her way, then zagged back to escape her pounding feet. A few branches, emboldened by the coming summer, strayed across her path and whipped her arm, leaving red scratches. Impatient with the marks, she ignored them.

At the final turning the old man's hut loomed up. He was sitting, as always, in the doorway, humming, and eating a piece of yellowed fruit, the juices running down his chin. At the noise of her coming he looked up and grinned.

"Hai!" he said, more sound than greeting.

Flower skidded to a stop and squatted in the dirt beside him.

"You look tired," he said. "Did you dream?"

"I tried. But dreaming is so slow," Flower admitted.

"Dreaming is not living. You and I—we live. Have a bite?" He offered her what was left of the fruit, mostly core.

She took it so as not to offend him, holding the core near her mouth but not eating. The smell of the overripe, sickly sweet fruit made her close her eyes, and she was startled into a dream.

> The fruit was in her mouth and she could feel its sliding passage down her throat. It followed the twists of her inner pathways, dropping seeds as it went, until it landed heavily in her belly. There it began to burn, a small but significant fire in her gut.
>
> Bending over to ease the cramping, Flower turned her back on the old man's hut and crept along the trail toward the village. The trees along the trail and the muddle of gray-green wildflowers blurred into an indistinct mass as she went, as if she were seeing them through tears, though her cheeks were dry and her eyes clear.
>
> When she reached the cliffside she saw, to her surprise, that the withy ladders went down into a great hole in the earth instead of up toward the dwellings on the cliff face.
>
> It was deathly silent all around her. The usual chatter of children at their chores, the chant of women, the hum-buzz of men in the furrowed fields were gone. The cliff was as blank and as smooth as the shells of the eggs she had gathered that morning.
>
> And then she heard a low sound, compounded of moans and a strange hollow whistling, like an old man's laughter breathed out across a reed. Turning around, she followed the sound. It led her to the hole. She bent over it, and as she did, the sound resolved itself into a single word: *bawenah*. She saw a pale, shining face looking up at her from the hole, its mouth a smear of fruit. When the mouth opened, it was as round and as black as the hole. There were no teeth. There was no tongue. Yet still the mouth spoke: *bawenah*.

Flower awoke and stared at the old man. Pulpy fruit stained his scraggly beard. His eyes were filmy. Slowly his tongue emerged and licked his lips.

She turned and without another word to him walked home. Her hands cupped her stomach, pressing and releasing, all the way back, as if pressure alone could drive away the cramps.

Her mother was waiting for her at the top of the ladder, hands folded on her own belly. "So," she said, "it is your woman time."

Flower did not ask how she knew. Her mother was a woman of great power still and such knowledge was well within her grasp, though it annoyed Flower that it should be so.

"Yes," Flower answered, letting a small whine creep into her voice. "But you did not tell me it would hurt so."

"With some," her mother said, smiling and smoothing back the white stripe of hair with her hand, "with some, womanhood comes easy. With some it comes harder." Then, as they walked into their rooms, she added with a bitterness uncharacteristic of her, "Could your *healer* not do something for you?"

Flower was startled at her mother's tone. She knew that her association with the old man had annoyed her mother. But Flower had never realized it would hurt her so much. She began to answer her mother, then bit back her first angry reply. Instead, mastering her voice, she said. "I did not think to ask him for help. He is but a man. *I* am a woman."

"You are a woman today, truly," her mother said. She went over to the great chest she had carved before Flower's birth, a chest made of the wood of a lightning-struck panomom tree. The chest's sides were covered with carved signs of power: the florets of the tree with their three-foil flowers, the mouse and hare who were her mother's personal signs, the trailing arbet vine which was her father's, and the signs for the four moons: quarter, half, full, and closed faces.

When she opened the chest, it made a small creaking protest. Flower went over to look in. There, below her first cradle dress and leggings, nestled beside a tress of her first, fine baby hair, was the Herb Belt she had helped her mother make. It had fifteen pockets, one for each year she had been a girl.

They went outside, and her mother raised her voice in that wild ululation that could call all the women of power to her. It echoed around the clearing and across the fields to the gathering streams beyond, a high, fierce yodeling. And then she called out again, this time in a gentler voice that would bring the women who had borne and their girl children with them.

Flower knew it would be at least an hour before they all gathered; in the meantime she and her mother had much to do.

They went back into the rooms and turned around all the objects they owned, as a sign that Flower's life would now be turned around as well. Bowls, cups, pitchers were turned. Baskets of food and the drying racks were turned. Even the heavy chest was turned around. They left the bed pallets to the very last, and then, each holding an end, they walked the beds around until the ritual was complete.

Flower stripped in front of her mother, something she had not done completely in years. She resisted the impulse to cover her breasts. On her leggings were the blood sign. Carefully her mother packed those leggings into the panomom chest. Flower would not wear them again.

At the bottom of the chest, wrapped in a sweet-smelling woven-grass covering, was a white chamois dress and leggings. Flower's mother took them out and spread them on the bedding, her hand smoothing the nap. Then, with a pitcher of water freshened with violet flowers, she began to wash her daughter's body with a scrub made of the leaves of the sandarac tree. The nubby sandarac and the soothing rinse of the violet water were to remind Flower of the fierce and gentle sides of womanhood. All the while she scrubbed, Flower's mother chanted the songs of Woman: the seven-fold chant of Rising, the Way of Power, and the Praise to Earth and Moon.

The songs reminded Flower of something, and she tried to think of what it was as her mother's hands cleansed her of the sins of youth. It was while her mother was braiding her hair, plaiting in it reed ribbons that ended in a dangle of shells, that Flower remembered. The chants were like the cradle songs her mother had sung her when she was a child, with the same rise and fall, the same liquid sounds. She suddenly wanted to cry for the loss of those times and the pain she had given her mother, and she wondered why she felt so like weeping when anger was her usual way.

The white dress and leggings slipped on easily, indeed fit her perfectly, though she had never tried them on before, and that, too, was a sign of her mother's power.

And what of her own coming power, Flower wondered as she stood in the doorway watching the women assemble at the foot of the ladder. The women of power stood in the front, then the birth women, last of all the girls. She could name them all, her friends, her sisters in the tribe, who only lately had avoided her because of her association with the old man. She tried to smile at them, but her mouth would not obey her. In fact, her lower lip trembled and she willed it to stop, finally clamping it with her teeth.

"She is a woman," Flower's mother called down to them. The ritual words. They had known, even without her statement, had known from that first wild cry, what had happened. "Today she has come into her power, putting it on as a woman dons her white dress, but she does not yet know her own way. She goes now, as we all go at our time, to the far hills and beyond to seek the Word That Changes. She may find it or not, but she will tell of that when she has returned."

The women below began to sway and chant the words of the Searching Song, words which Flower had sung with them for fifteen years without really understanding their meaning. Fifteen years—far longer than any of the other girls—standing at the ladder's foot and watching another Girl-Become-Woman go off on her search. And that was why—she saw it now—she had fallen under Sand Walker's spell.

But now, standing above the singers, waiting for the Belt and the Blessing, she felt for the first time how strongly the power called to her. This was *her* moment, *her* time, and there would be no other. She pictured the old man in his hut and realized that if she did not find her word she would be bound to him forever.

"Mother," she began, wondering if it was too late to say all the things she should have said before, but her mother was coming toward her with the Belt and suddenly it was too late. Once the Belt was around her waist, she could not speak again until the Word formed in her mouth, with or without its accompanying power. Tears started in her eyes.

Her mother saw the tears, and perhaps she mistook them for something else. Tenderly she placed the Belt around Flower's waist, setting it on the hips, and tying it firmly behind her. Then she turned her daughter around, the way every object in the house had been turned, till she faced the valley again where all the assembled women could read the fear on her face.

> *Into the valley, in the fear we all face,*
> *Into the morning of your womanhood,*
> *Go with our blessing to guide you,*
> *Go with our blessing to guard you,*
> *Go with our blessing and bring back your word.*

The chant finished, Flower's mother pushed her toward the ladder and went back into the room and sat on the chest to do her own weeping.

Flower opened her eyes, surprised, for she had not realized that she had closed them. All the women had disappeared, back into the fields, into the woods; she did not know where, nor was she to wonder about them. Her journey had to be made alone. Talking to anyone on the road this day would spell doom to them both, to her quest for her power, to the questioner's very life.

As she walked out of the village, Flower noticed that everything along the way seemed different. Her power had, indeed, begun. The low bushes had a shadow self, like the moon's halo, standing behind. The trees were filled with eyes, peering out of the knotholes. The chattering of animals in the brush was a series of messages, though Flower knew that she was still unable to decipher them. And the path itself sparkled as if water rushed over it, tumbling the small stones.

She seemed to slip in and out of quick dreams that were familiar pieces of her old dreams stitched together in odd ways. Her childhood was sloughing off behind her with each step, a skin removed.

Further down the path, where the valley met the foothills leading to the far mountains, she could see Sand Walker's hut casting a long, dark, toothy shadow across the trail. Flower was not sure if the shadows lengthened because the sun was at the end of its day or because this was yet another dream. She closed her eyes, and when she opened them again, the long shadows were still there, though not nearly as dark or as menacing.

When she neared the hut, the old man was sitting silently out front. His shadow, unlike the hut's black shadow, was a strange shade of green.

She did not dare greet the old man, for fear of ruining her quest and because she did not want to hurt him. One part of her was still here with him, wild, casting green shadows, awake. He had no protection against her power. But surely she might give him one small sign of recognition. Composing her hands in front of her, she was prepared to signal him with a finger, when without warning he leaped up, grinning.

"*Ma-hane*, white girl," he cried, jumping into her path. "Do not forget to laugh, you in your white dress and leggings. If you do not laugh, you are one of the dead ones."

In great fear she reached out a hand toward him to silence him before he could harm them both, and power sprang unbidden from her fingertips. She had forgotten the Shaping Hands. And though they were as yet untrained and untried, still they were a great power. She watched in horror as five separate arrows of flame struck the old man's face, touching his eyes, his nostrils, his mouth, sealing them, melting his features like candle wax. He began to shrink under the fire, growing smaller and smaller, fading into a gray-green splotch that only slowly resolved itself into the form of a *sa-hawa*, a butterfly the color of leaf mold.

Flower did not dare speak, not even a word of comfort. She reached down and shook out the crumpled shirt, loosing the butterfly. It flapped its wings, tentatively at first, then with more strength, and finally managed to flutter up toward the top of the hut.

Folding the old man's tattered shirt and leggings with gentle hands, Flower laid them on the doorstep of his hut, still watching the fluttering *sa-hawa*. When she stood again, she had to shade her eyes with one hand to see it. It had flown away from the hut and was hovering between patches of wild onion in a small meadow on the flank of the nearest foothill.

Flower bit her lip. How could she follow the butterfly? It was going up the mountainside and her way lay straight down the road. Yet how could she not follow it? Sand Walker's transformation had been her doing. No one else might undo what she had so unwillingly, unthinkingly created.

To get to the meadow was easy. But if the butterfly went further up the mountainside, what could she do? There was only a goat track, and then the sheer cliff wall. As she hesitated, the *sa-hawa* rose into the air again, leaving the deep green spikes of onions to fly up toward the mountain itself.

Flower looked quickly down the trail, but the shadows of oncoming evening had closed that way. Ahead, the Path of Power—her Power—was still brightly lit.

"Oh, Mother," she thought. "Oh, my mothers, I need your blessing indeed." And so thinking, she plunged into the underbrush after the *sa-hawa*, heedless of the thorns tugging at her white leggings or the light on the Path of Power that suddenly and inexplicably went out.

The goat path had not been used for years, not by goats or by humans either. Briars tangled across it. Little rock slides blocked many turnings, and in others the pebbly surface slid away beneath her feet. Time and again she slipped and fell; her knees and palms bruised, and all the power in her Shaping Hands seemed to do no good. She could not call on it. Once when she fell she bit her underlip so hard it bled. And always, like some spirit guide, the little gray-green butterfly fluttered ahead, its wings glowing with five spots as round and marked as fingerprints.

Still Flower followed, unable to call out or cry out because a new woman on her quest for her Power must not speak until she has found her word. She still hoped, a doomed and forlorn hope, that once she had caught the *sa-hawa* she might also catch her Power or at least be allowed to continue on her quest. And she would take the butterfly with her and find at least enough of the Shaping Hands to turn him back into his own tattered, laughing, dismal self.

She went on. The only light now came from the five spots on the butterfly's wings and the pale moon rising over the jagged crest of First Mother, the leftmost mountain. The goat track had disappeared entirely. It was then the butterfly began to rise straight up, as if climbing the cliff face.

Out of breath, Flower stopped and listened, first to her own ragged breathing, then to the pounding of her heart. At last she was able to be quiet enough to hear the sounds of the night. The butterfly stopped, too, as if it was listening as well.

From far down the valley she heard the rise and fall of the running dogs, howling at the moon. Little chirrups of frogs, the pick-buzz of insect wings, and then the choughing of a nightbird's wings. She turned her head for a moment, fearful that it might be an eater-of-bugs. When she looked back, the *sa-hawa* was almost gone, edging up the great towering mountain that loomed over her.

Flower almost cried out then, in frustration and anger and fear, but she held her tongue and looked for a place to start the climb. She had to use hands and feet instead of eyes, for the moonlight made this a place of shadows—shadows within shadows—and only her hands and feet could see between the dark and dark.

She felt as if she had been climbing for hours, though the moon above her spoke of a shorter time, when the butterfly suddenly disappeared. Without the lure of its phosphorescent wings, Flower was too exhausted to continue. All the tears she had held back for so long suddenly rose to swamp her eyes. She snuffled loudly and crouched uncertainly on a ledge. Then, huddling against the rockface, she tried to stay awake, to draw warmth and courage from the mountain. But without wanting to, she fell asleep.

In the dream she spiraled up and up and up into the sky without ladder or rope to pull her, and she felt the words of a high scream fall from her lips, a yelping *kya*. She awoke terrified and shaking in the morning light, sitting on a thin ledge nearly a hundred feet up the mountainside. She had no memory of the climb and certainly no way to get down.

And then she saw the *sa-hawa* next to her and memory flooded back. She cupped her hand, ready to pounce on the butterfly, when it fluttered its wings in the sunlight and moved from its perch. Desperate to catch it, she leaned out, lost her balance, and began to fall.

"Oh, Mother," she screamed in her mind, and a single word came back to her. *Aki-la*. Eagle. She screamed it aloud.

As she fell, the bones of her arms lengthened and flattened, cracking sinew and marrow. Her small, sharp nose bone arched outward and she watched it slowly form into a black beak with a dull yellow membrane at the base. Her body, twisting, seemed to stretch, catching the wind, first beneath, then above; she could feel the swift air through her feathers and the high, sweet whistling of it rushing past her head. Spiraling up, she pumped her powerful wings once. Then, holding them flat, she soared.

*Aki-la*. Golden eagle, she thought. It was her Word of Power, the Word That Changes, hers and no one else's. And then all words left her and she knew only wind and sky and the land spread out far below.

How long she coursed the sky in her flat-winged glide she did not know. For her there was no time, no ticking off of moment after moment, only the long sweet soaring. But at last her stomach marked the time for her and, without realizing it, she was scanning the ground for prey. It was as if she had two sights now, one the sweeping farsight that showed her the land as a series of patterns and the other that closed up the space whenever she saw movement or heat in the grass that meant some small creature was moving below.

At the base of the mountain she spied a large mouse and her wings knew even before her mind, even before her stomach. They cleaved to her side and she dove down in one long, perilous swoop toward the brown creature that was suddenly still in the short grass.

The wind rushed by her as she dove, and a high singing filled her head, wordless visions of meat and blood.

*Kya*, she called, and followed it with a whistle. *Kya*, her hunting song.

Right before reaching the mouse, she threw out her wings and back-winged, extending her great claws as brakes. But her final sight of the mouse, larger than she had guessed, standing upright in the grass as if it had expected her, its black eyes meeting her own and the white stripe across its head gleaming in the early sun, stayed her. Some memory, some old human thought teased at her. Instead of striking the mouse, she landed gracefully by its side, her great claws gripping the earth, remembering ground, surrendering to it.

*Aki-la*. She thought the word again, opened her mouth, and spoke it to the quiet air. She could feel the change begin again. Marrow and sinew and muscle and bone responded, reversing themselves, growing and shrinking, molding and forming. It hurt, yet it did not hurt; the pain was delicious.

And still the mouse sat, its bright little eyes watching her until the transformation was complete. Then it squeaked a word, shook itself all over, as if trying to slough off its own skin and bones, and grew, filling earth and sky, resolving itself into a familiar figure with the fierce stare of an eagle and the soft voice of the mouse.

"Late Blossoming Flower," her mother said, and opened welcoming arms to her.

"I have found my word," Flower said as she ran into them. Then, unaccountably, she put her head on her mother's breast and began to sob.

"You have found much more," said her mother. "For see—I have tested you, tempted you to let your animal nature overcome your human nature. And see—you stopped before the hunger for meat, the thirst for blood, mastered you and left you forever in your eagle form."

"But I might have killed you," Flower gasped. "I might have eaten you. I was an eagle and you were my natural prey."

"But you did not," her mother said firmly. "Now I must go home."

"Wait," Flower said. "There is something . . . something I have to tell you."

Her mother turned and looked at Flower over her shoulder. "About the old man?"

Flower looked down.

"I know it already. There he is." She pointed to a gray-green butterfly hovering over a blossom. "He is the same undisciplined creature he always was."

"I must change him back. I must learn how, quickly, before he leaves."

"He will not leave," said her mother. "Not that one. Or he would have left our village long ago. No, he will wait until you learn your other powers and change him back so that he might sit on the edge of power and laugh at it as he has always done, as he did to me so long ago. And now, my little one who is my little one no longer, use your eagle wings to fly. I will be waiting at our home for your return."

Flower nodded, and then she moved away from her mother and held out her arms. She stretched them as far apart as she could. Even so—even farther—would her wings stretch. She looked up into the sky, now blue and cloudless and beckoning.

"*Aki-la!*" she cried, but her mouth was not as stern as her mother's or as any of the other women of power, for she knew how to laugh. She opened her laughing mouth again. "*Aki-la.*"

She felt the change come on her, more easily this time, and she threw herself into the air. The morning sun caught the wash of gold at her beak, like a necklace of power. *Kya*, she screamed into the waiting wind, *kya*, and, for the moment, forgot mother and butterfly and all the land below.

# LISA TUTTLE

## Jamie's Grave

Lisa Tuttle's short stories have appeared in numerous magazines and anthologies since the early 1970s. A native of Texas, she moved to England in 1980, and currently lives in London. Her most recent novel is *Gabriel*.

"Jamie's Grave" could be called fantasy or horror. Whichever you consider it, this contains one of the most intriguing notions in the genre.

—E.D.

# JAMIE'S GRAVE

## Lisa Tuttle

Mary sat at the kitchen table, a cup of tea gone cold by her left hand, and listened to the purring of the electric clock on the wall.

The house was clean and the larder well stocked. She had done the laundry and read her library books and it was too wet for gardening. She had baked a cake yesterday and this wasn't her day for making bread. She had already phoned Clive twice this week and could think of no excuse to phone again. Once she might have popped across the road to visit Jen, but she had been getting the feeling that her visits were no longer so welcome. There had been a time when Jen was grateful for Mary's company, a time when she had been lonely, too, but now Jen had her own baby to care for, and whenever Mary went over there—no matter what Jen said—Mary couldn't help feeling that she was intruding.

She looked at the clock again. In twenty minutes she could start her walk to the school.

Clive said she should get a job. He was right, and not just for the money. Mary knew she would be happier doing something useful. But what sort of job could she get? She had no experience, and in this Wiltshire village there was not much scope for employment. Other mothers already held the school jobs of crossing-guard and dinner-lady, and what other employer would allow her to fit her working hours to those when Jamie was in school? She wouldn't let someone else look after Jamie—no job was worth that. Her son was all she had in the world, all she cared about. If she could have kept him home with her and taught him herself, instead of having to send him to school, Mary knew she would have been perfectly content. She had been so happy when she had her baby, she hadn't even minded losing Clive. But babies grew up, and grew away. Jen was going to find that out in a few years.

Mary rose and walked to the sink, poured away the tea, rinsed and set the cup on the draining-board. She took her jacket from the hook beside the door and put it on, straightening her collar and fluffing her hair without a mirror. The clock gave a dim, clicking buzz, and it was time to leave.

The house where Mary lived with her son was one of six bungalows on the edge of a Wiltshire village, close enough to London, as well as to Reading, to be attractive to commuters. After the grimy, cramped house in Islington, the modern bungalow with its large garden and fresh country air had seemed the perfect place to settle down and raise a family. But while Mary had dreamed of being pregnant again, Clive had been dreaming of escape. The house for him was not a cosy nest, but a gift to Mary and a sop to his conscience as he left.

Five minutes' leisurely walk brought the village school in sight. Mary saw the children tumbling out the door like so many brightly colored toys, and she reached the gate at the same moment as Jamie from the other side.

Jamie was involved with his friends, laughing and leaping around. His eyes flickered over her, taking in her presence but not acknowledging it, and when she hugged him she could feel his reluctance to return to her and leave the exciting, still new world of school.

He pulled away quickly, and wouldn't let her hold his hand as they walked. But he talked to her, needing to share his day's experiences, giving them to her in excited, disconnected bursts of speech. She tried to make sense of what he said, but she couldn't always. He used strange words—sometimes in a different accent—picked up from the other children, and the events he described might have been imaginary, or related to schoolyard games rather than to reality. Once they had spent all their time together, in the same world. She had understood him better then, had understood him perfectly before he could even talk.

She looked at the little stranger walking beside her, and caught a sudden resemblance to Clive in one of his gestures. It struck her, unpleasantly, that he was well on his way to becoming a man.

"Would you like to help me make some biscuits this afternoon?" she asked.

He shook his head emphatically. "I got to dig," he said.

"Dig? In the garden? Oh, darling, it's so wet!"

He frowned and tilted back his head. "Isn't."

"I know it's stopped raining, but the ground . . ." Mary sighed, imagining the mess. "Why not wait until tomorrow? It might be nicer then, the sun might come out, it might be much nicer to dig in the garden tomorrow."

"I dig tomorrow, too," Jamie said. He began to chant, swinging his arms stiffly as he marched, "Dig! Dig! Dig!"

During the summer they had taken a trip to the seashore and Mary had bought him a plastic shovel. He had enjoyed digging in the soft sand, then, but had not mentioned it since. Mary wondered what had brought it back to mind—was it a chance word from his teacher, or an enthusiasm caught from one of the other children?—and realized she would probably never know.

He found his shovel in the toy chest, flinging other toys impatiently across the room. Not even the offer of a piece of cake could distract him. He suffered himself to be changed into other clothes, twitching impatiently all the while. When he had rushed out into the garden, Mary stood by the window and watched.

The plastic shovel, so useful for digging at the beach, was less efficient in the dense soil of the garden. As Jamie busily applied himself, the handle suddenly broke off in his hands. He looked for a moment almost comically shocked; then he began to howl.

Mary rushed out to comfort him, but he would not be distracted by her promises of other pleasures. All he wanted was to dig, and he would only be happy if she gave him a new shovel. Finally, she gave him one of her gardening spades, and left him to it.

She felt rejected, going into the house and closing the door, staying away from the windows. He didn't want her to hover, and she had no reason to fear for his safety in their own garden. Had she waited all day just for this?

The next day, Saturday, was worse. Mary looked forward to Saturdays now more fervently than she ever had as a child. On Saturdays she had Jamie to herself all day. They played games, she read him stories, they went for walks and had adventures. But that Saturday all Jamie wanted to do was dig.

She stood in the garden with him, staring at the vulnerable white bumps of his knees, and then at his stubborn, impatient face. "Why, darling? Why do you want to dig?"

He shrugged and looked at the ground, clutching the spade as if she might take it away from him.

"Jamie, please answer me. I asked you a question. Why are you digging?"

"I might find something," he said, after a reluctant pause. Then he looked at her, a slightly shifty, sideways look. "If I find something . . . can I keep it?"

"May I," she corrected automatically. Her spirits lifted as she imagined a treasure hunt, a game she might play with him. Already, her thoughts were going to her old costume jewelry, and coins . . . "Probably," she said. "Almost certainly, anything you find in our garden would be yours to keep. But there are exceptions. If it is something *very* valuable, like gold, it belongs to the Queen by right, so you would have to get her permission."

"Not gold," he said scornfully.

"No?"

"No. Not treasure." He shook his head and then he smiled and looked with obvious pride at his small excavation. "I'm digging a grave," he said. "You know what they do with graves? They put dead people inside. I might find one. I might find a skellington!"

"Skeleton," she said without thinking.

"Skeleton, yeah! Wicked, man! Skellyton!" He flopped down and resumed his digging.

Feeling stunned, Mary went inside.

"And that's what you phoned me about?" said Clive.

"He's your son, too, you know."

"I know he's my son. And I like to hear what he's doing. But you know I like to sleep in . . . you could have picked a better time than early on a Saturday morning to fill me in on his latest game."

"It's not a game."

"Well, what is it, then? A real grave? A real skeleton?"

"It's morbid!"

"It's natural. Look, he probably saw something on television, or heard something at school . . ."

"When I was little, I was afraid of dead things," Mary said.

"You think that's healthier? What do you want me to say, Mary? It'll pass, this craze. He'll forget about it and go on to something else. If you make a big deal about it, he'll keep on, to get a reaction. Don't make him think it's wrong. Want me to come over tomorrow and take him out somewhere? That's the quickest way to get his mind on to other things."

Mary thought of how empty the house was when her son was gone. At least now, although he was preoccupied, she was aware of his presence nearby. And, as usual, she reacted against her ex-husband. She was shaking her head before he had even finished speaking.

"No, not tomorrow. I had plans for tomorrow. I—"

"Next weekend. He could come here, spend the night—"

"Oh, Clive, he's so young!"

"Mary, you can't have it both ways. He's my son, too. You can't complain that I take no interest and leave it all to you, and then refuse to let me see him. I do miss him, you know."

"All right, next weekend. But just one day, not overnight. Please. He's all I have. When he's not here I miss him dreadfully."

Mary stood by the window watching Jamie dig his grave, and she missed him. She could see him, and she knew that if she rapped on the glass he would look up and see her, but that wasn't enough; it would never be enough. Once, she had been the whole world to him. Now, every day took him farther from her.

She thought of Heather, Jen's little baby. She thought of the solid weight of her in her arms, and that delicious, warm, milky smell of new babies. She remembered how it had felt to hold her, and how she had felt when she had to give her back. She remembered watching Jen nurse her child. The envy which had pierced her. The longing. It wasn't Jen's feelings which made Mary reluctant now to visit her but her own jealousy. She wanted a baby.

She went on standing by the window for nearly an hour, holding herself and grieving for the child she didn't have, while Jamie dug a grave.

For lunch Mary made cauliflower soup and toasted cheese sandwiches. Ignoring his protests that he could wash his own hands, she marched Jamie to the bathroom and scrubbed and scrubbed until all the soil beneath his fingernails was gone.

Twenty minutes later, a soup moustache above his upper lip, Jamie said, "I got to go back to my digging."

Inside, she cried a protest, but she remembered Clive's words. Maybe he did want a reaction from her. Maybe he would be less inclined to dig a grave if his mother seemed to favor it. So, with a false, bright smile she cheered him on, helped him back into his filthy pullover and wellies, and waved vigorously from the back door, as if seeing him off on an expedition.

"Come back in when you get cold," she said. "Or if you get hungry . . ."

She turned on Radio Four, got out her knitting and worked on the sweater which was to be a Christmas present for her sister in Scotland. She worked steadily for about an hour. Then the panic took her.

A falling-elevator sensation in her stomach, and then the cold. It was a purely visceral, wordless, objectless fear. Her shaking fingers dropped stitches and then dropped the knitting, and she lurched clumsily to her feet.

If anything happened to Jamie she would never forgive herself. If she was too late, if anything had happened to him—

She knew he was safe in the back garden, where there was nothing to hurt him. She knew she'd had this experience before, and there had never been anything threatening her son. Logic made no impact on the fear.

He was so fragile, he was so young, and the world was so dangerous. How could she have let him out of her sight for even a moment?

She ran to the back door and out, cursing herself.

She saw his bright yellow boots first. He was lying flat on the ground, on his stomach, and she couldn't see his head. It must have been hanging over the edge, into the hole he had dug.

"Jamie!" She didn't want to alarm him, but his name came out as a shriek of terror.

He didn't move.

Mary fell on the ground beside him and caught his body up in her arms. She was so frightened she couldn't breathe. But he was breathing; he was warm.

Jamie gave a little grunt and his eyelids fluttered. Then he was gazing up at her, dazed and sleepy-looking.

"Are you all right?" she demanded, although it was clear to her, now the panic had subsided, that he was fine.

"What?" he said groggily.

"Oh, you silly child! What do you mean by lying down out here, when the ground's so cold and wet . . . you'll catch your death . . . if you were tired, you should have come in. What a silly, to work so hard you had to lie down and take a nap!" She hugged him to her, and for once he seemed content to be held so, rubbing his dirty face against her sweater and clinging.

They rocked together in the moist grey air and country silence for a time, until Jamie gave a deep, shuddering sigh.

"What is it?"

"Hungry," he said. His voice was puzzled.

"Of course you are, poor darling, after so much hard work. It's not time for tea yet, but come inside and I'll give you a glass of milk and a biscuit. Would you like that?"

He seemed utterly exhausted, and she carried him inside. Although he had claimed to be hungry, he drank only a little milk and seemed without the energy even to nibble a biscuit. Mary settled him on the couch in front of the television, and when she came back a few minutes later she found him asleep.

After she had put Jamie to bed, Mary went back to the garden to look at his excavation.

It was a hole more round than square, no more than a foot across and probably not more than two foot deep. As Mary crouched down to look into it she saw another, smaller hole, within. She didn't think Jamie had made it; it seemed something quite different. She thought it looked like a tunnel, or the entrance to some small animal's burrow. She thought of blind, limbless creatures tunneling through the soft earth, driven by needs and guided by senses she couldn't know, and she shuddered. She thought of worms, but this tunnel was much too large. She had not been aware of moles in the garden, but possibly Jamie had accidentally uncovered evidence of one.

She picked up the spade which Jamie had abandoned, and used it to scoop earth back into the hole. Although she began casually, she soon began to work with a purpose, and her heart pounded as she pushed and shoveled furiously, under a pressure she could not explain to fill it in, cover up the evidence, make her garden whole again.

Finally she stood and tamped the earth down beneath her feet. With the grass gone, the marks of digging were obvious. She had done the best she could, but it wasn't good enough. It wasn't the same; it couldn't be.

As she walked back into the house, Mary heard a brief, faint scream, and immediately ran through to Jamie's room.

He was sitting up in bed, staring at her with wide-open yet unseeing eyes.

"Darling, what's wrong?"

She went to him, meaning to hug him, but her hands were covered with dirt from the hole; she couldn't touch him.

"What's that?" he asked, voice blurred with sleep, turning towards the window.

Mary looked and saw with a shock that the window was open, if only by a few inches. She didn't remember opening it, and she was sure it was too heavy for Jamie to lift by himself.

"I'll close it," she said, and went to do so. Her hands looked black against the white-painted sash, and she saw bits of earth crumble and fall away. She felt as disturbed by that as if it really had been grave-dirt, and felt she had to sweep it up immediately.

When she returned to the bed Jamie was lying down, apparently asleep. Careful not to touch him with her dirty hands, she bent down and kissed him, hovering close for a time to feel the warmth of his peaceful breathing against her face. She loved him so much she could not move or speak.

In the morning Jamie was subdued, so quiet that Mary worried he might be getting ill, and kept feeling his face for some evidence of a fever. His skin was cool, though, and he showed no other signs of disease. He said nothing more about wanting to dig, nothing about graves or skeletons—that craze appeared to have vanished as suddenly and inexplicably as it had arrived.

It was a wet and windy day, and Mary was glad Jamie didn't want to play in the garden. He seemed worried about something, though, following her around the house and demanding her attention. Mary didn't mind. In fact, she cherished this evidence that she was still needed.

When she asked what he wanted for his tea, the answer came promptly. "Two beefburgers. Please."

"Two!"

"Yes. Two, please."

"I think one will be enough, really, Jamie. You never have two. If you are very hungry, I could make extra chips."

He had that stubborn look on his face, the look that reminded her of his father. "Extra chips, too. But please may I have two beefburgers."

She was certain he wouldn't be able to eat them both. "Very well," she said. "After you've eaten your first beefburger, if you still want another one, I'll make it then."

"I want two—I know I want two! I want two now!"

"Calm down, Jamie," she said quietly. "You shall have two. But one at a time. That's the way we'll do it."

He sulked, and he played with his food when she served it, but he did manage to eat all the beefburger, and then immediately demanded a second, forgetting, this time, to say "please."

"You haven't eaten all your chips," she pointed out.

He glared. "You didn't *say* I had to eat all my chips first. You *said* if I ate one burger I could have another—you *said*."

"I know I said it, lovely, but the chips are part of your dinner, too, and if you're really hungry—"

"You *said!*"

His lower lip trembled, and there were tears in his eyes. How could she deny him? She couldn't bear his unhappiness, even though she was quite certain that he wasn't hungry and wouldn't be able to eat any more meat.

"All right, my darling," she said, and left her own unfinished meal to grow cold while she went back to the cooker. Clive would have been firm with him, she thought, and wondered if she had been wrong to give in. Maybe Jamie had wanted her to say no. The thought wearied her. It was too complicated. He had asked for food, and she would give it to him.

Jamie fidgeted in his chair when she put the food before him, and would not meet her eyes. He asked if he could watch TV while he ate. Curious, she agreed. "Just bring your plate in to me when you've finished."

A suspiciously few minutes later, Jamie returned with his plate. The second beefburger had vanished without a trace. There were only a few smashed peas and stray chips on the plate. Jamie went back to watch television while Mary did the washing-up. Almost immediately, above the noise of the television, she heard the back door open and close quietly. When she rejoined Jamie he seemed happier than he had all day, freed of some burden. They played together happily—if a little more rowdily than Mary liked—until his bedtime.

But after she had tucked him into bed, Mary went out into the dark garden. In the gloom the whiteness of a handkerchief gave off an almost phosphorescent glow, drawing her across the lawn to the site of Jamie's excavation.

Like some sort of offering, the beefburger had been placed on a clean white handkerchief and laid on the ground, on the bare patch. Mary stared at it for a moment, and then went back inside.

Mary usually woke to the sounds of Jamie moving about, but on Monday morning for once she had to wake him. He was pale and groggy, with greenish shadows beneath his eyes. But when she suggested he could stay home and spend the day resting in bed, he rallied and became almost frantic in his determination to go to school. He did seem better, out in the fresh air and away from the house, but she continued to worry about him after she had left him at school. Her thoughts led her to the doctor's. She didn't mind waiting until all the scheduled patients had been seen; she paged through old magazines, with nothing better to do.

Dr. Abden was a brisk, no-nonsense woman who had raised two children to safe and successful adulthood; Mary was able to trust her maternal wisdom enough to tell her the whole story of Jamie's grave.

"Perhaps he found his skeleton and didn't like it so much," said Dr. Abden. "There, don't look so alarmed, my dear! I didn't mean a human skeleton, of course. You mentioned seeing something like a tunnel . . . isn't it possible that your son came across a mole—a dead one? That first encounter with death can be a disturbing one. Perhaps he thought he killed it with his little shovel and so is guiltily trying to revive it . . . Perhaps he doesn't realize it is dead, and imagines he can make a pet of it. If you can get him to confide in you, I'm sure you'll be able to set his mind at rest. Of course, he may have forgotten the whole thing after a day at school."

Mary hoped that would be the case, but it was obvious as soon as she saw him that afternoon that his secret still worried him. He rejected all her coaxing offers of help, pushing her away, hugging his fear to himself, uneasy in her presence. So Mary waited, kept the distance he seemed to want, and watched.

He was sneaking food outside. Biscuits, bits of chocolate, an apple . . . she meant to let him continue, but at the thought of the mess eggs and baked beans would make in his pockets, she caught his hand before he could transfer food from his plate to his lap.

"Darling, you don't have to do that," she said. "I'll give you a plate, and you can put the food on that and take it out to your little friend. Just eat your own meal first."

His pale face went paler. "You know?"

Mary hesitated. "I know . . . you're upset about something. And I know you've been leaving food outside. Now, why don't you tell Mummy what's going on, and I'll help you."

Emotions battled on his face; then, surrender.

"He's hungry," Jamie said plaintively. "He's so hungry, so, so hungry. I keep giving him food, but it's not right . . . he won't eat it. I don't know what he . . . I don't want . . . I can't . . . I'm giving him everything and he won't eat. What does he eat, Mummy? What *else* does he eat?"

Mary imagined a mole's tiny corpse, Jamie thrusting food beneath its motionless snout. "Maybe he doesn't eat anything," she said.

"No, he has to! If you're alive, you have to eat."

"Well, Jamie, maybe he's dead."

She half expected some outburst, an excited protest against that idea, but Jamie shook his head, an oddly mature and thoughtful expression on his face. He had obviously considered this possibility before. "No, he's not dead. I thought, I thought when I found him in my grave, I thought he was dead, but then he wasn't. He isn't dead."

"Who isn't dead? What is this you're talking about, Jamie? Is it an animal?"

He looked puzzled. "You don't know?"

She shook her head. "Will you show him to me, darling?"

Jamie looked alarmed. He shook his head and began to tremble. Mary knelt beside his chair and put her arms around him, holding him close, safe and tight.

"It's all right," she said. "Mummy's here. It's all right . . ."

When he had calmed she thought to distract him, but he returned to the subject of feeding this unknown creature.

"Well," said Mary, "if he's not eating the food you give him, maybe he doesn't need to be fed. He might find his own food—animals usually do, you know, except for pets and babies."

"He's like a baby."

"How is he like a baby? What does he look like?"

"I don't know. I don't remember now—I can't. He doesn't look like anything—not like anything except himself."

It was only then that it occurred to Mary that there might be no animal at all, not even a dead mole. This creature Jamie had found was probably completely imaginary—that was why he couldn't show it to her.

"He can probably find his own food," Mary said.

But this idea obviously bothered Jamie, who began to fidget. "He needs me."

"How do you know that? Did he tell you? Can't he tell you what sort of food he wants, then?"

Jamie shrugged, nodded, then shook his head. "I have to get something for him."

"But he must have managed on his own before you found him—"

"He was all right before," Jamie agreed. "But he needs me now. I found him, so now I have to take care of him. But . . . he won't eat. I keep trying and trying, but he won't take the food. And he's hungry. What can I give him, Mummy? What can I give him to eat?"

Mary stopped trying to be reasonable, then, and let herself enter his fantasy.

"Don't worry, darling," she said. "We'll find something for your little friend—we'll try everything in the kitchen if we have to!"

With Jamie's help, Mary prepared a whole trayful of food: a saucer of milk and one of sweetened tea; water-biscuits spread with peanut butter; celery tops and chopped carrots; lettuce leaves; raisins; plain bread, buttered bread, and bread spread with honey. As she carried the tray outside, Mary wondered what sort of pests this would attract, then dismissed it as unimportant. She pretended to catch sight of Jamie's imaginary friend.

"Oh, we've got something he likes here," she said. "Just look at him smacking his lips!"

Jamie gave her a disapproving look. "You don't see him."

"How do you know? Isn't that him over there by the hedge?"

"If you saw him, you'd probably scream. And, anyway, he hasn't *got* lips."

"What does he look like? Is he so frightening?"

"It doesn't matter," Jamie said.

"Shall I put the tray down here?"

He nodded. The playfulness and interest he had shown in the kitchen had vanished, and he was worried again. He sighed. "If he doesn't eat this . . ."

"If he doesn't, there's plenty more in the kitchen we can try," said Mary.

"He's so hungry," Jamie murmured sadly.

He was concerned, when they went back inside, about locking the house. This was not a subject which had ever interested him before, but now he followed Mary around, and she demonstrated that both front and back doors were secure, and all the windows—particularly the window in his room— were shut and locked.

"There are other ways for things to get in, though," he said.

"No, of course not, darling."

"How do my dreams get in, then?"

"Your dreams?" She crouched beside him on the bedroom floor and stroked his hair. "Dreams don't come in from the outside, darling. Dreams are inside, in your head."

"They're already inside?"

"They aren't real, darling. They're imaginary. They aren't real and solid like I am, or like you are . . . they're just . . . like thoughts. Like make-believe. And they go away when you're awake."

"Oh," he said. She couldn't tell what he thought, or if her words had comforted him. She hugged him close until he wriggled to be free, and then she put him to bed.

She checked on him twice during the night, and both times he appeared to be sleeping soundly. Yet in the morning, again, he had the darkened eyes and grogginess of one who'd had a disturbed night.

She thought about taking him to the doctor instead of to school, but the memory of her conversation with Dr. Abden stopped her. This was something she had to cope with herself. There was nothing physically wrong with Jamie. His sleeplessness was obviously the result of worry, and the doctor had already reminded her that it was her duty, as his mother, to set his mind at rest. If only he would tell her what was wrong!

That afternoon Jamie was again subdued, quiet and good. Mary actually preferred him like this, but because such behavior wasn't normal for him, she worried even while she appreciated his nearness. They sat together playing games and looking through his books, taking turns reading to each other. Later, she left the dishes to soak in the sink and watched her son as he sat with his crayons and his coloring book, wondering what went on in his mind.

"Has your little friend gone away, to find food somewhere else?" she asked.

Jamie shook his head.

"We could put some more food out for him, you know. I don't mind. Anything you like."

Jamie was silent for a while, and then he said, "He doesn't need food."

"Doesn't he? That's very unusual. What does he live on?"

Jamie stopped coloring, the crayon frozen in his hand. Then he drew a deep, shuddering breath. "Love," he said, and began coloring again.

He was no longer worried about the doors and windows, and it was Mary, not Jamie, who prolonged the bedside chat and goodnight kisses, reluctant to leave him alone. He didn't seem afraid, but she was afraid for him, without knowing why.

"Goodnight, my darling," she said for the fifth or sixth last time, and made herself rise and move away from the bed. "Sleep well . . . call me if you need anything . . . I'll be awake . . ." Her voice trailed off. Already, it appeared, he was sleeping. She went out quietly and left his bedroom door ajar. If he made a sound, she would hear it.

She turned the television on low and slumped in a chair before it. She was too tired to think, too distracted to be entertained. She might as well go to bed herself, she thought.

So she turned off the television, tidied up, turned out the lights and checked the doors one last time. On her way to her own bedroom she decided to look in on Jamie, just to reassure herself that all was well.

Pushing the door open let in a swathe of light from the corridor. It fell across the bed, revealing Jamie lying uncovered, half curled on one side, and not alone.

There was something nestled close to him, in the crook of his arm; something grey and wet-looking, a featureless lump about the size of a loaf of bread; something like a gigantic slug pressed against his pyjama-covered chest and bare neck.

Horror might have frozen her—she couldn't have imagined coping with something like that in the garden or on the kitchen floor—but fear for her son propelled her forward. As she moved, the soft grey body rippled, turning, and it looked at Mary. For a face there was only a slightly flattened area with two round, black eyes and no mouth.

In her haste and terror Mary almost fell onto the bed. She caught hold of the thing and pulled it off her son, sobbing with revulsion.

She had expected it to be as cold and slimy as it looked, perhaps even insubstantial enough that the harsh touch of her hands could destroy it. In fact, it was warm and solid and surprisingly heavy. And it smelled like

Jamie. Not like Jamie now, but like Jamie as a baby—that sweet, milky scent which made her melt inside. Like Jen's baby. Like every helpless, harmless newborn. She closed her eyes, remembering.

Mary pressed her face against the soft flesh and inhaled. No skin had ever been so deliciously, silkenly smooth. Her lips moved against it. She could never have enough of touching and kissing it; she wished she was a cat and could lick her baby clean a hundred times a day.

Responding, it nuzzled back, head butting at her blindly, and she unbuttoned her blouse. Her breasts felt sore and heavy with milk, and she longed for the relief of nursing.

Somewhere nearby a child was crying, a sound that rasped at her nerves and distracted her. Someone was tugging at her clothes, at her arm, and crying, "Mummy," until she had, finally, to open her eyes.

A little boy with a pale, tear-stained face gazed up at her. "Don't," he said. "Don't, Mummy."

She knew who he was—he was her son. But he seemed somehow threatening, and she wrapped her arms more tightly around the creature that she held.

"Go to bed," she said firmly.

He began to weep, loudly and helplessly.

But that irritated her more, because he wasn't helpless; she knew he wasn't helpless.

"Stop crying," she said. "Go to bed. You're all right." She pushed him away from her with her hip, not daring to let go. But as she looked down she glimpsed something grey and formless lying pressed between her breasts. For just a moment she had a brief, distracting vision of a face without a mouth, always hungry, never satisfied. She thought of an open grave, and she closed her eyes.

"He needs me," she said.

At last she felt complete. She would never be alone again.

Within the protective circle of her arms, the creature had begun to feed.

# DELIA SHERMAN

## The Maid on the Shore

Delia Sherman is one of the most exciting new authors to appear in the fantasy field for quite some time. "The Maid on the Shore" is based on the old British ballad of the same name, a song many readers will be familiar with as recorded by contemporary celtic folk musicians such as John Renbourn, Martin Carthy, and Frankie Armstrong. Sherman's first novel, which will be published as part of the Ace Fantasy Specials series focusing on new authors, is also based on a folk ballad, "The Famous Flower of Serving Men"—in particular on the Martin Carthy reworking of that song; readers who enjoy this story will want to keep an eye out for Sherman's novel, currently titled *Witch's Maze*.

Sherman lives in a William Morris–like Victorian house in Boston, Massachusetts and teaches courses in, among other things, fantasy literature, at Boston University.

—T.W.

# THE MAID ON THE SHORE

## Delia Sherman

I live on a rocky coast at the easternmost tip of Newfoundland, in a stone cottage huddled under a cliff at the beach's edge. For caution's sake, my father had tumbled the stones that faced it to suggest poverty, a reeking seaweed fire and a dirt floor within. We did burn seaweed, but cleanly, in a well-vented hearth, and our floors were laid with polished stone flags softened here and there with wool rugs of my mother's weaving. The two bedrooms behind the kitchen were furnished with finely carved beds and chairs of walrus bone, and in the inmost room, rows of books lined the windowless walls.

I cannot remember a time when I did not read. Sheltered by my family's isolation, I learned of magic and of mankind from the volumes on my father's shelves. On winter nights, we would sit by the clean, salt-smelling fire—Mother, Father, me—each absorbed in a world that touched but did not invade the worlds of the others. Mother would card the wool from her sheep and spin the fluffy rolags into yarn, which she would wind, thread upon her handloom, and weave into fine cloth. Sometimes she sang as she worked, the cloth inspiring the song and the song the cloth, for her magic was wordless and deep and strange: the inhuman, shifting magic of the sea.

Father always sat at the other side of the hearth, a lap-desk of fine teak upon his knee, scratch-scratching with a gray goose quill on the thin pages of his notebook. His magic was all words. Spells, formulas, observations of the stars and moon, charms, cantrips, and incantations—he played with them through the winter evenings, muttering constantly under his breath as he blended spell with charm, formula with incantation to see what would come of it.

Sometimes I could coax Father out of his wizardly fog by begging him for a tale. He loved to speak of his life upon the Continent and in the fabled East, where magicians were still held in honor. But his favorite story, and mine, was of the one time when he had found himself without any words: the soft May night when he had seen my mother dancing naked on the shore. Under the moon she had danced and sung with her sisters, her body white and fluid as sea-foam, her hair black as a starless night.

Knowing that she was a seal-maiden, knowing that he should hide her sealskin if he wanted to possess her, knowing she would not return until next May Eve, my father cast aside both his knowledge and his clothing and walked naked down to the strand to meet her. As the sea takes a swimmer, the seal-maidens took him into their dance, and when the dawn-star rose and her sisters drew on their pelts to slide into the ocean, my mother held my father's hand and watched them go. Next morning she was with him still. Sometimes she would disappear for two weeks or three, but he neither asked where her sealskin was nor spied on her to find its hiding place. So she stayed with him, and within two years of that dancing, she bore him a maid-child: me.

My person and magic, because of my parentage, were strange, mixed things. Because I was a hybrid, I was barren as a mule. And my human and selkie blood mingled to give me a subtle, elusive magic that would seep away if I were to lose my virginity. Since such a fate seemed more distant than the ever-receding horizon, it troubled me not at all. On the winter evenings of my childhood, I would sit between Mother and Father on a sealskin rug, reading to myself and humming in counterpoint to Father's mutterings and Mother's singing. I understood and loved both their magics: Mother's songs and patterns spoke to me as though tongued; Father's words seeped into my bones like music. I was, I know now, content.

Although, as I have said, I had heard tales of mortal men in my father's books and rumor of them in my mother's songs, I never saw one until I was a woman grown. The autumn of my eighteenth year, an unlucky fisherman ran aground in a sudden squall on the rocks at the mouth of our bay. His boat splintered under the pounding of the waves, and my mother swam out and hauled him to shore, bruised, half frozen, terrified. Father insisted that she bring him into the cottage, and she dragged him through the door and dropped him beside the kitchen fire, where he lay panting and staring about him.

In that fisherman's wondering eyes, I saw my family anew. My father—small and spindle-shanked; a reader by the squint of his ice-blue eyes; a thinker by the animation of his dark, thin face. My mother—plump and white-skinned; strong, smooth muscles mounding her arms; hairs and white-less eyes black-brown and glowing like a healthy animal's. Me—plump and white-skinned like my mother, small like my father; black-haired, blue-eyed, seal-toothed; a child to look at but for my hips and heavy breasts. The fisherman drank our broth and reluctantly accepted Father's offer of a pallet beside our hearth. When dawn came, he was gone, and one of Father's books, left carelessly on a side table, went with him, and the finely woven cloth under it as well.

Mother roared her rage at the theft, and Father talked of moving. But as the days and weeks went by, our fear ebbed. The fisherman might have died making his way overland, or lost the book or the weaving; perhaps no one believed his story of a wizard and a selkie and their witch-daughter living alone in a distant bay. Winter came. We folded our sheep, stored the potatoes and dried the beans from Mother's garden, salted the last of the fish she had caught for us with her sharp seal's teeth, and settled in gratefully to our usual winter pursuits.

At midwinter, in the dark aftermath of a heavy snow, men came to hunt us out. Even now, I wake whimpering and bleating like a seal cub from dreams of the fishermen clubbing at my father until his blood pooled on the kitchen floor. Three of them came after Mother and me, their clubs uplifted and their eyes shiny with fear and lust. We roared and hurled ourselves at them. There was nothing in me of my father that night, but only a seal's fury and a seal's desire to rend and tear. We tore the throats from four of them, my mother and I, while the rest fled yammering from our cottage.

When all was quiet, we bundled their torn bodies out of the kitchen and down to the ocean, where the tide took them out to sea for the fish to eat. We scrubbed the blood from the polished flags with melted snow and fine sand. Then my mother stripped off her shawl and her linen bodice, her woolen skirt and her petticoats, and, taking the sealskin rug from the study floor, wrapped it around her naked shoulders.

I had always known that the rug upon which I sat and drowsed on winter days was Mother's sealskin, for the pelt smelled of her and never wore thin or lost its living gloss. From time to time, it and she would disappear together to lie upon the ice floes, and I would lie on ordinary sealskin before the study fire to support the fiction of my father's ignorance. But never before that day had I seen her go from woman to seal. One moment she was standing before the kitchen fire, a plump woman draped in a sealskin cloak. Then she seemed to flow, to melt into the floor like candle wax, and became a sad-eyed seal, sleek and whiskered. Urgently, she whistled to me, and I helped her drag my father's body across the rocky beach to the water, where she towed him out to sea under the solemn moon. I saw her from time to time thereafter, but only as a brown seal swimming out in the bay. At high tide she might come near and leave a fish on the rocky beach, but she never came ashore again. After a few years she stopped coming altogether. I think the sealers must have taken her.

After that midwinter's night I lived alone in the stone cottage. I suppose the fishermen reckoned me dead or swum out to sea with my selkie mother. In any case, they never returned. Suns rose and set, moons waxed and waned, snows fell and melted, and still I lived a maid on the shore, tending my mother's sheep and garden, reading my father's books, fishing for salmon and hunting for partridge and wild goose when I tired of shellfish and mutton.

Quiet as it was, it was life that suited me. Oh, sometimes I longed for some purpose for my magic, some reason to use my knowledge and power to an end other then charming fish to my hook or rabbits to my snare. When I raised a small offshore breeze to blow away a bank of clouds, I might be tempted to whistle up a tempest; when I squeezed a few drops of rain from a high cloud in a dry summer, I might be tempted to call down a flood. But there was no one near to be blown away or drowned, no one to display my powers for. Like the seasonal yearnings of my body, my ambition was a useless and unwanted legacy, which, for the most part, I did not brood over.

But I did brood over the fishermen. My father's daughter knew that they had acted from fear, from distrust, perhaps even from winter boredom. But my mother's daughter recognized an ancient enemy, and instinctively, unreasonably feared that they would return. Over the years, bitterness crept to high tide in my soul, tainting it like a well dug too close to the ocean. Time runs oddly for a wizard's child who does not age like a human woman or seal, so I do not know how long I lived alone on that rocky shore. But it was many and many a long year before men came again to break my solitude and my peace.

Again it was late autumn, the time of the worst storms, and a northeastern gale hunted early snow across the uplands. The gale blew for three days, whipping the ocean to a terrible frenzy of freezing water and stinging foam, scouring the gulls from the sky and driving both me and my sheep into shelter. On the third day the wind turned northwest, as it always does in these latitudes, bringing to my bay high tides, floating islands of kelp, and a trespasser.

I had been gathering a harvest of seaweed to cover and feed my garden, and near sundown was laboring back over the rocks, carrying a bundle of it on my back. Although I am almost as strong as a selkie, the sodden weight of the kelp dragged heavily at my shoulders, and I was forced to rest. As I stretched, my hands to the small of my back, I looked out across the bay. There floated a ship—a clipper by her proud sleekness—three-masted, many-sailed, and badly maimed by the storm. Her mainmast was down, her mizzenmast was splinted, and only a few rags of canvas flew from her foremast. Wearily, she rocked at anchor, and sailors swarmed over her like rats, cutting free the useless rigging and clearing the decks of the storm's debris.

As I gaped, my eye was caught by the one still figure in all the bustle, standing aft by the taffrail and holding a glass to his eye. I stood transfixed in its sights, arms akimbo, breasts thrust forward with unintended boldness. I could feel his eyes upon me, and their touch, even at that distance, was intimate and unwelcome. Shuddering, I bent to my bundle, hurried back to my cottage, and barred the door behind me.

By nightfall I had fretted myself into a rage. Was I not the daughter of a magician and a skin-changer, a sorceress in my own right, mistress of word and song and woven pattern? Why should I fear a crippled ship and her exhausted and battered crew? But memory mocked me with visions of a helpless fisherman and blood upon the kitchen floor, and I tossed between revenge and retreat, hatred and fear, until at last I fell asleep by my banked fire.

Early next morning a rapping came at my door. I started awake, the hair at my neck rising and prickling. Whoever it was knocked again, shy and soft, as though unsure of a welcome. Would a ravager, a pirate tap so mannerly at my front door? A third knock, weaker yet. Curious, I put on my shawl, drew the bolts, and opened. A young man stood before me.

"Aye?" I said coolly, folding my shaking hands under my apron.

"Ma'am," the young man said, and bowed awkwardly. He was a full head taller than I, with a sailor's blue eyes and a pale beard like a gosling's down blurring his cheeks. "Captain Pelican's compliments, ma'am, and may we please draw water from your stream? We've been a mortal long time at sea, and never a dipperful of clean water do we have aboard."

He was young and respectful, afraid only of frightening me, and my terror faded before his gaze. Mistress of myself once more, I made a shooing movement with my hand as though he were a gosling indeed. "Help 'eeself, boy. Water's free." I was careful to speak the common coast dialect, as though I were an ordinary fishwife with nothing strange or wonderful about me that must be feared or spoiled. But as they dipped the water from my stream into small barrels, I could feel the sailors' stares. The young man lingered by my door.

"I am Thomas Fletcher, ma'am, first mate of the clipper *Cape Town Maid*. We have sailed from China, around the Cape of Good Hope to Salem with a cargo of gold, porcelain, spices, and silks. Our captain is Elias Pelican." He faltered, reddened, continued. "He asks, ma'am, for grain if you can spare it, and news of forests with trees suitable for a jury mast, for we will never make Salem in this state." He smiled warmly down at me, and I found that I was smiling warmly in return.

"There do be fir above, and pine. It be up along the moor and not easy found. I'll lead 'ee," I said, wondering to hear my own voice betraying me.

The shadows were short by the time we had trekked over the moorland to a respectable stand of fir, and had lengthened almost to dusk before we returned, for the seamen bickered over the choice of a tree, then fought over the best way of felling and stripping it. My father had told me how seamen must work together, each individual becoming a part of a human mechanism called "crew," harmonious in action as canvas and wind, capstan and rope. As I listened to the sailors curse and pick at each other, I thought that this particular crew was no more harmonious, either in action or in voice, than a beach of bull seals in rut.

"Damn your eyes," shouted Mr. Fletcher at last when two of them had nearly come to blows over the angle and height of the cut they were to make. "Do you want the captain ashore?"

His words fell on the crew like a fog. Faces grayed; eyes dulled; voices fell utterly silent. Working quickly now, the men felled the tree, stripped it, and hauled it across the moor to the beach. Only their bodies and hands spoke to me, who knew from my mother how to understand the wordless speech of wind and fish and sheep, and told me that they were afraid.

Watching them stumble and fumble, I could not imagine how these men had survived the passage of the Horn without hanging themselves on the rigging or tumbling from the crosstrees. Indeed, some of them might have recently fallen from a lesser height, for they moved stiffly. One young man, with a bruised face and an angry eye, wore a shirt marked across the back with rusty stains that darkened and gleamed wetly as he worked.

Hating as I hated, fearing what I hate to fear, how could I lead these men so faithfully and so coolly watch them work? Now I can say that they gave me a new riddle to puzzle over, a new set of facts to mull, and that I had long been bored without being conscious of it. At the time I hardly knew how to account for my own actions. All day I watched the sailors labor over the fir tree; that night I dreamed of my mother standing by the shore, ankle-deep in the tide, changing. The strange thing was that she never became wholly seal or woman, but remained mutable: a woman's face and torso might end in a seal's hind flippers; a sleek, whiskered head might dart above a woman's full white breasts. I dreamed, too, of the bulls roaring on the beaches, of the remembered salt of human blood on my lips, the jar of human bones between my teeth. More than once, I woke sweating and trembling, only to slip again into uneasy dreaming. But when morning came, I opened the door to Mr. Fletcher's timid knock and asked him in most civilly to take a cup of chamomile tea.

He sat by the fire in my father's chair, nursing the thick brown mug between his hands and casting curious glances at the polished wooden furniture, the woven cloths, the pewter and china ranked on the heavy oak dresser.

"This puts me in mind of my mother's kitchen," he said at last. "You live here alone?"

"Aye." I considered not answering his implied question, but thought my silence might offend him. I did not want to offend him. He was a lovely man, strong and clean-limbed, and his sun-burnished face warmed my dark kitchen. "Our mam and dad drowned," I said. "It be two winters since, now."

His pity was quick and sweet to hear. "Poor girl, so young to be left alone," he said gently, not knowing that I was far older than he. "Why did you not leave this lonely place? There are fishing villages up and down this coast would welcome you, and men who would gladly marry you."

"Here I were born, and here 'tis fitty I stay," I said shortly. "Tell I, Mr. Fletcher, where be your mother's kitchen and what set 'ee to sailing?"

So he told me of the snug clapboard house in Gloucester, of his father who had followed the whales until his ship was lost, of his mother who had listened dry-eyed to her son's decision to serve the same harsh mistress. He had been a cabin boy on a whaler, an apprentice on a merchantman, a boatswain, and a mate. "I've turned my hand to most things, and know how a ship should be run. My last captain advanced me when his first mate was washed overboard, and it was as first mate I came aboard *The Cape Town Maid*, two years ago."

"Two years be a mortal long time afloat," I said. The animation faded from his face, and he shrugged heavily.

"Hast a sweetheart?"

More heavily still, he nodded, then fumbled in his waistcoat and brought out a tarnished locket, which he opened and held out to me. "Nancy Bride," he said, low and a little shaky. "The sweetest girl in Gloucester."

Being a black paper silhouette, the portrait could have been of any young girl with a straight nose and ringlets, but I read in the angle of his head and in the trembling of his broad hand that he saw his Nancy's loving face and no other smiling from that anonymous snippet. Suddenly, I was out of patience, even angry.

"Her be a clean-featured maid," I said. "Does 'ee think her'll have waited on 'ee all this long time?"

Mr. Fletcher flushed, snapped the locket shut, and restored it to his bosom. "She's as true as death, ma'am," he said stiffly. "I'd stake my soul on her."

I hastened to make up the ground I'd lost. "I'm thinking her be a lucky maid. So ye'll be a married man as soon as ever the banns can be called?"

"No," he said.

There was a long and uncomfortable pause. What ailed the man? I could make nothing of his sadness, except that it had nothing to do with me. He was stirring now in the chair as if preparing to leave. To keep him, I said, "'Tis an odd thing the captain's not come ashore."

Mr. Fletcher mumbled something into his waistcoat that I asked him to repeat. "I said, 'it's not the oddest thing about him,' ma'am." He hesitated; I waited. He had the air of a sheep at a gate—afraid to move, eager to be on the other side.

Slowly, he began to speak. "Although he's a merchant, he refuses to take paying passengers on board. He doesn't seem to care how many seasoned sailors there are among the crews he buys from the crimps, providing they come cheap enough. Why, there's hardly four men knew a belaying pin from a capstan spar when they shipped aboard, though they found out soon enough which falls the hardest on a man's back." He was fairly through the gate now and trotting.

"Two years is a long time at sea, as you've said, ma'am, and it's longer yet if you're sailing under a captain like Pelican. He's one who likes to put the cat among the pigeons just to see the feathers fly—never mind if the cat scratches or the pigeons peck. He'll order the scuppers cleaned by the dawn watch if the fancy takes him, or the deck holystoned at midnight, and it's twenty lashes for any sailor who might be a thought slow at leaping to obey. He's too free with the lash, and too free with his fists and his knife. Many's the time I've heard him say he'd rather flog sailors than eat a hot dinner, even though flogging has been against the law for thirty years or more. He's ordered ten strokes for a dirty shirt, though the men have no place to wash their linen except the scuppers, and he's filthy as bilge water himself."

Once Mr. Fletcher had begun, there was no more hope of stopping him than of turning a starving sheep from rich pasture. He was angry now, fairly flaming with it, and his sparkling eyes and flushed cheeks were a pleasure to watch.

"He tied Carbone high in the mainmast rigging once when a fever kept him from coming up with his watch. 'The sea air'll cure him,' he said, and left him there all night. Next morning, Carbone was all but dead, and two days later, he died. Round the Horn's a hard passage, and you expect to lose a dozen men or so to sickness and accident, but we've buried that many from dysentery and lash weals that have gone septic, and lost as many again overboard." Mr. Fletcher shook his head and fell silent.

"Could'ee not have cut down and bade Captain Bucko go whistle?" I asked curiously.

Mr. Fletcher stretched his eyes wide. "That would be mutiny, ma'am. It's no part of a first mate's job to countermand his captain's orders."

I doubted that it was part of a first mate's job to hang and flog his shipmates for no good reason but the captain's fancy, though I did not say so. But my scorn must have shown in my face, for as suddenly as it had broken out, his spate of words dried, and before I knew it, he was on his feet, thanking me for the tea and out the door.

My father had always said that confession was a relief to the soul, but telling me of the horrors aboard *The Cape Town Maid* had not relieved Mr. Fletcher. After that morning's confidences, he stayed well away from my door. He was certainly nowhere to be found when six of my sheep were stolen from the fold and slaughtered on the beach. "Captain's orders," one squint-eyed runt told me when I stormed out to confront the butchers. "Ye mun tak' it up wi' him."

I spun around to the bay and glared out at the *Maid*, rocking quietly in the swell. A familiar figure stood in the stern; the sun winked from the barrel of the glass he held. Outraged and terrified, I helplessly shook both my fists at that brazen eye and fled back to my cottage.

The next day they were finished at last, having taken four days to do a two-day job of work. The mast had been trimmed, banded with iron, floated out to *The Cape Town Maid*, stepped, and rigged. There was much going back and forth from shore with barrels and game and strings of fish. By sundown the strand was empty at last, and I ventured out of my cottage to care for my remaining sheep.

The clipper lay at anchor, her masts rerigged and proud against the rosy sky. Across the quiet bay came the boom of Captain Pelican's harsh voice as he harangued his men. I rejoiced that they'd be gone by morning so that I could sleep easy again. But I kept peering out my window at the *Maid's* moonlit shadow, restless and angry and sure that my anger would not simply sail with the clipper out of the bay.

Here, I told myself, was a use for my powers at last. Perhaps I should send lightning to strike the captain as he strutted on the poop; perhaps I should simply call up a storm and sink *The Cape Town Maid* with all hands aboard. I was still debating alternatives, when Mr. Fletcher knocked once more on my door.

He was cold, still, correct, as though his indiscretion and my scorn still rankled in his mind. "You're been so kind, ma'am, and so generous with the water and the sheep and all, that the captain asks you to come on board to view the cargo, take a glass of sherry wine, and be properly thanked. He will not take 'no' for an answer."

I looked past Mr. Fletcher at the faces of the men who accompanied him. All of them looked uneasy, but some looked eager as well, their eyes bright and flat like the eyes of those fishermen so many years ago.

"Nay, sir, no need for thanks," I said. "Water's free, I told 'ee, and help is, too. Though the captain could pay for they sheep, come 'pon that."

"The captain wishes to convey his thanks himself, ma'am," Mr. Fletcher repeated stubbornly. "He'll settle the matter of the sheep with you on the *Maid*." And he began to extoll the rareness and beauty of the cargo as if to dazzle me with the prospect of some rare and unnamed reward for my kindness.

I didn't listen to a word he said. Was the man daft, or did he think me so? A glass of sherry wine, indeed. If I went out to that ship, I would never return to the shore. A woman is not bad luck while a ship is at anchor, and no doubt the captain intended me to be dead and overboard long before the *Maid* sailed on the dawn tide.

As he spoke, Mr. Fletcher began to sweat and to avoid my eyes, and his voice took on a pleading note. He seemed to have settled with himself that he would not take me onto the ship by force. If he could persuade me, well, then, I would get what I deserved. But if he had to pick me up and carry me, protesting, his conscience might force him to defiance.

For a moment I considered pressing Mr. Fletcher into making a choice between the two sides of his sense of propriety. But I had a curiosity to meet this Captain Pelican.

So, "Thankee kindly, sir," I said as his eloquence began to run dry. "I'll be pleased to take sherry wine with your captain." And I set briskly off down the strand, trailed by Mr. Fletcher and the sailors.

They helped me into the stern of the longboat and rowed out to the ship. As we approached, I could see her figurehead clearly: a naked woman supporting her massive breasts in her hands and leering out at the innocent sea. We came alongside the ship, a ladder was lowered, and dozens of hard, eager hands pulled me onto the deck.

Captain Pelican was on the bridge, and Mr. Fletcher led me up to him ceremoniously. The captain was an imposing man, over six feet tall, fleshy in tight, dark trousers and frock coat. Above his high collar and frayed cravat, his face was dark, craggy, pitted like granite; his hair, iron-colored with dirt and grease, hung lank around his ears. He spat a brown stream of tobacco juice at my feet. "Please to meet you," he said.

I dropped a curtsy. My eyes were downcast as though with awe or fear, but I was trying very hard not to laugh. He was so ridiculous after all, whipping his sailors to show them that he was fearless and lawless as the ocean he sailed upon. But his swanking could not fool me, for under the reek of sweat and gin and old salt, I could smell fear upon him sharp as a knife.

Captain Pelican hitched up my chin with his finger and leered into my face. His pale eyes were rheumy. "Mr. Fletcher has pumped you some bilge about sherry wine and thanks," he said, "but I'll wager you know well I intend you no such courtesy. You'll spend a watch or two in my bunk, doing what a woman does best, then I've promised my crew they'll get what's left."

He stopped and showed me his tobacco-stained teeth, waiting, I suppose, for some sign of revulsion or terror. I imagined turning in his arms and tearing out his throat, or singing such a sea-spell that he would face the world with a walrus's head upon his shoulders, and I clapped my hands together like a child.

"O, thankee, sir, thankee," I cried. "Thee hast no notion what weary company a maidenhead be, and no proper man for to lighten me of un."

Captain Pelican looked taken aback by this speech, and not so happy as one might expect. "Well," he said, and cleared his throat. "Always glad to be of service to a lady. Some sherry wine?"

I clasped my hands over the greasy arm of his jacket and smiled. "Come, my dear, thee ben't shy." The top of my head fell short of his collarbone, and he was forced to crane over to look into my face.

"There's no hurry," he said hoarsely. Without taking his eyes from me, he shouted for Mr. Fletcher to bring the wine and two glasses, then led to the wooden bench that ran along the stern of the ship.

By this time I could all but taste the captain's blood on my lips. I sank onto the bench and into his arms; the sour odor of sweat, tobacco, and stale gin that hung around him made my head spin. He bent to kiss me, his massive head and shoulders black against the silver moonlight, his breath rank in the clean, salt air. Eagerly, I raised my mouth to him.

"Captain Pelican, sir," came Mr. Fletcher's prim voice. "Your sherry wine, sir."

The captain released me unkissed and damned Mr. Fletcher for a fish-buggering old woman. I sighed; the captain poured and handed me a glass of wine.

Sipping the sherry gave me time to reflect. The moonlight glittered at me from the watchful, rat-bright eyes of the crewmen. While they might stand by and cheer while I tore out their captain's throat, they were unlikely to set me safely ashore when I was done. Lust for my body or lust for my blood, both were alike to them. If I killed their captain, his crew was apt simply to skewer me where I sat, and throw his body and mine overboard, and good riddance to the pair of us. Unless, of course, I prevented them.

Captain Pelican finished his wine, laid aside his glass, and began to fumble at my bosom. I smiled, took a deep breath, and began to sing. Startled, he drew back his hands, lifted them to muzzle me, hesitated, and then, as the spell caught him, dropped them into his lap. I could feel him strain at the charm, testing his mortal will against my witch's power. But he could not break it.

My song was the lament that the heart of every seaport woman sings when her man sets sail. Its notes were love and longing and the dark night watches when a woman's spirit is at low tide and every breeze seems to sigh with the last prayers of drowning sailors. My seal's voice, low-pitched and resonant, carried its plaint to each crewman's bones. Not only the captain, sitting stiff and resistant by my side, but every man on that ship heard my song, and in my wordless melody, heard the ceaseless calling of his wife, sweetheart, sister, mother. From the foredeck came the sound of weeping.

Gradually, I wove into my song the slow, sleepy brush of waves over sand. Though he fought with all the strength of his will, the captain's lids drooped, and he began to slip sideways on the bench, the hilt of his sword poking into his ribs. Wind breathed in the rigging and sent small waves shushing gently against the hull. *The Cape Town Maid* slept.

Now, I thought, and turned to the silent figure slumped and wrinkled against the stern railing. I rolled his heavy body off the bench and tore open his coat and his shirt. Shadow caught in the folds of his untanned throat as if already it ran with blood. He's a monster, I thought as I crouched over him; I have wanted to kill him since I first saw his ship in my bay, and I *will* kill him. Now.

I lowered my mouth to his throat. His skin against my tongue was foul and slick, like rotting fish; I straightened and spat, and slowly my anger seeped from me. Words chased one another through my mind, cold and bright and quick: to murder will make me human; to flee will make me animal; there are more kinds of virginity than one.

The moon was slipping down the mainmast, barring the deck with black shadows. The webbed rigging cast intricate patterns on Captain Pelican's face, and moonlight silvered the hair on his bared chest. I brushed my fingers over the thatch, and it gave under my touch, springy as uncarded wool. Although his pelt was thick, there was not enough hair to weave a mat from. But it might be worked into a larger pattern. Humming thoughtfully, I gave the hair a little tug. It came easily free from his skin.

Singing as I worked, I opened and laid back the wings of his coat and linen shirt, then plucked all the hair from his chest. Under my busy hands, the naked skin shone almost luminous in the moonglow, its white expanse broken only by the faint shadows of his nipples. I cupped them in my palms; the flesh beneath them stretched, softened, swelled.

Song welled up within me, flowed from my lips and fingers, guiding and guided by the movement of my hands. I caressed the knot from his throat, stroked the stubble from his cheeks. Wherever my hands passed, the texture of his skin became finer, denser. When I had done with his face, my fingers wandered down across the heavy, round breasts to unclasp his belt. My palm rested on the captain's belly; my witch-song sank into his flesh. The world narrowed to the beating of my blood and his and the echo of the tide flowing in the notes of my song. Then Captain Pelican gave a great cry. It flew from his altered throat like a sea gull's plaintive scream, then died away to a whimper. So, too, died my song.

I knelt shivering on the deck until my limbs unknotted, then rose and found my way to the captain's cabin. From a small sea chest, I took six pieces of gold as payment for my slaughtered sheep, a brick of black tea, and a length of sea-green silk. When I came up again, I searched for Mr. Fletcher among the coiled ropes and the snoring sailors, and found him folded like a sleeping sheep at the foot of a companionway. From him I took the tarnished locket that held the silhouette of Nancy Bride, and his clasp knife.

The captain lay in the stern, a faint, pale glimmer against the dark wooden boards. I stove in five of the ship's longboats and, freighting the sixth with my booty, lowered it to the sea. The moon had long since sunk behind the cliffs and set. By the time I pushed off, dead night shrouded *The Cape Town Maid* and her slumbering crew. In a little while the tide would turn, the sky would lighten, and the crew would wake and sail the *Maid* out of my bay. They should be halfway to Salem before they found their captain. As I paddled the longboat back to the shore, I wondered what they would make of what they found.

# MICHAEL McDOWELL

## Halley's Passing

Michael McDowell is author of thirty books, published under his own name and four different pseudonymns. Under his own name he has published novels of the occult, historical novels, and romantic adventure novels. Under the pseudonyms (with various collaborators) he has written detective novels, thrillers, and male adventure novels. His most ambitious project to date has been *Blackwater*, which appeared as a series of six volumes, published monthly in 1983. He has written more than a dozen half-hour scripts for television, and his first film feature, *Beetlejuice*, was directed by Tim Burton (*Pee-Wee's Big Adventure*) for Geffen Pictures and Warner Brothers.

McDowell was born and raised in the deep South, which serves as a locale for *Blackwater* and several other of his novels. He was educated at Harvard and Brandeis, and has a Ph.D. in English literature. He divides his time between Boston and Los Angeles, and his hobbies are collecting American sheet music, 18th and 19th century death memorabilia, the documentation of American crime, and photographs of corpses, atrocities, and criminals.

"Halley's Passing," originally published in *The Twilight Zone*, is unquestionably the most distressingly violent story in this volume. I'll say no more.

—E.D.

# HALLEY'S PASSING

## Michael McDowell

"Would you like to keep that on your credit card?" asked the woman on the desk. Her name was Donna and she was dressed like Snow White because it was Halloween.

"No," said Mr. Farley, "I think I'll pay cash." Mr. Farley counted out twelve ten-dollar bills and laid them on the counter. Donna made sure there were twelve, then gave Mr. Farley change of three dollars and twenty-six cents. He watched to make certain she tore up the charge slips he had filled out two days before. She ripped them into thirds. Original copy, Customer's Receipt, Bank Copy, two intervening carbons—all bearing the impress of Mr. Farley's Visa card and his signature—they went into a trash basket that was invisible beneath the counter.

"Good-bye," said Mr. Farley. He took up his one small suitcase and walked out the front door of the hotel. His suitcase was light blue Samsonite with an X of tape underneath the handle to make it recognizable at an airport baggage claim.

It was seven o'clock. Mr. Farley took a taxi from the hotel to the airport. In the back of the taxi, he opened his case and took out a black loose-leaf notebook and wrote in it:

> 10385    *Double Tree Inn*
> *Dallas, Texas*
> *Checkout 1900/$116.74/*
> *Donna*

The taxi took Mr. Farley to the airport and cost him $12.50 with a tip that was generous but not too generous.

Mr. Farley went to the PSA counter and picked up an airline schedule and put it into the pocket of his jacket. Then he went to the Eastern counter and picked up another schedule. In a bar called the Range Room he sat at a small round table. He ordered a vodka martini from a waitress named Alyce. When she had brought it to him, and he had paid her and she had gone away, he opened his suitcase, pulled out his black loose-leaf notebook and added the notations:

*Taxi $10.20 + 2.30/#1718*
*Drink at Airport Bar*
*$2.75 + .75/Alyce*

He leafed backwards through the notebook and discovered that he had flown PSA three times in the past two months. Therefore he looked into the Eastern Schedule first. He looked on page 23 first because $2.30 had been the amount of the tip to the taxi driver. On page 23 of the Eastern airline schedule were flights from Dallas to Milwaukee, Wisconsin, and Mobile, Alabama. All of the flights to Milwaukee changed in Cincinnati or St. Louis. A direct flight to Mobile left at 9:10 p.m. arriving 10:50 p.m. Mr. Farley returned the black loose-leaf notebook to his case and got up from the table, spilling his drink in the process.

"I'm very sorry," he said to Alyce, and left another dollar bill for her inconvenience.

"That's all right," said Alyce.

Mr. Farley went to the Eastern ticket counter and bought a coach ticket to Mobile, Alabama. He asked for an aisle seat in the non-smoking section. He paid in cash and after taking out his black loose-leaf notebook, he checked his blue Samsonite bag. He went through security, momentarily surrendering a ringful of keys. The flight to Mobile departed Gate 15 but Mr. Farley sat in the seats allotted to Gate 13, directly across the way. He read through a copy of *USA Today* and he gave a Snickers bar to a child in a pumpkin costume who trick-or-treated him. He smiled at the child, not because he liked costumes or Halloween or children, but because he was pleased with himself for having been foresightful enough to buy three Snickers bars just in case he ran into trick-or-treating children on Halloween night. He opened his black loose-leaf notebook and amended the notation of his most recent bar tab:

*Drink at Airport Bar*
*$2.75 + 1.75/Alyce*

The flight for Mobile began boarding at 8:55 as the announcement was made for the early accommodation of those with young children or other difficulties, Mr. Farley went into the men's room.

A Latino man in his twenties with a blue shirt and a lock of hair dangling down his neck stood at a urinal, looking at the ceiling and softly farting. His urine splashed against the porcelain wall of the urinal. Mr. Farley went past the urinals and stood in front of the two stalls and peered under them.

He saw no legs or feet or shoes but he took the precaution of opening the doors. The stalls were empty, as he suspected, but Mr. Farley did not like to leave such matters to chance. The Latino man, looking downwards, flushed the urinal, zipping his trousers and backing away at the same time. Mr. Farley leaned down and took the Latino man by the waist. He swung the Latino man around so that he was facing the mirrors and the two sinks in the restroom and could see Mr. Farley's face.

"Man—" protested the Latino man.

Mr. Farley rolled his left arm around the Latino Man's belt and put his right hand on the Latino man's head. Mr. Farley pushed forward very swiftly with his right hand. The Latino man's head went straight down towards the sink in such a way that the cold-water faucet, shaped like a Maltese Cross, shattered the bone above the Latino man's right eye. Mr. Farley had gauged the strength of his attack so that the single blow served to press the Latino's head all the way down to the procelain. The chilled aluminum faucet was buried deeply in the Latino man's brain. Mr. Farley took the Latino man's wallet from his back pocket, removed the cash and his Social Security card. He gently dropped the wallet into the sink beneath the Latino man's head and turned on the hot water. Mr. Farley peered into the sink, and saw blood, blackish and brackish swirling into the rusting drain. Retrieving his black looseleaf notebook from the edge of the left hand sink where he'd left it, Mr. Farley walked out of the restroom. The Eastern flight to Mobile was boarding all seats and Mr. Farley walked on directly behind a young woman with brown hair and a green scarf and directly in front of a young woman with slightly darker brown hair in a yellow sweater-dress. Mr. Farley sat in Seat 4-C and next to him, in Seat 4-A, was a bearded man in a blue corduroy jacket who fell asleep before take-off. Mr. Farley reached into his pocket and pulled out the bills he'd taken from the Latino man's wallet. There were five five-dollar bills and nine one-dollar bills. Mr. Farley pulled out his own wallet and interleaved the Latino man's bills with his own, mixing them up. Mr. Farley reached into his shirt pocket and pulled out the Latino man's Social Security card, cupping it from sight and slipping it into the Eastern Airlines In-Flight Magazine. He turned on the reading light and opened the magazine. The Social Security card read:

IGNACIOS LAZO
424-70-4063

Mr. Farley slipped the Social Security card back into his shirt pocket. He exchanged the in-flight magazine for the black loose-leaf notebook in the seat back pocket. He held the notebook in his lap for several minutes while he watched the man in the blue corduroy jacket next to him, timing his breaths by the sweep second hand on his watch. The man seemed genuinely to be asleep. Mr. Farley declined a beverage from the stewardess, who did not wear a name tag, and put his finger to his lips with a smile to indicate that the man in the blue corduroy jacket was sleeping and probably wouldn't want to be disturbed. When the beverage cart was one row behind and conveniently blocking the aisle so that no one could look over his shoulder as he wrote, Mr. Farley opened the black loose-leaf notebook on his lap, and completed the entry for Halloween:

> *2155/Ignacios Lazo/c*
> *27/Dallas Texas/ Airport/*
> *RR/38/Head onto Faucet*

RR meant Rest Room, and Mr. Farley stared at the abbreviation for a few moments, wondering whether he shouldn't write out the words. There was a time when he had been a good deal given to abbreviations, but once, in looking over his book for a distant year, he had come across the notation CRB, and had had no idea what that stood for. Mr. Farley since that time had been careful about his notations. It didn't do to forget things. If you forgot things, you might repeat them. And if you inadvertently fell into a repetitious pattern—well then, you just might get into trouble.

Mr. Farley got up and went into the rest room at the forward end of the passenger cabin. He burned Ignacios Lazo's Social Security card, igniting it with a match torn from a book he had picked up at the casino at the MGM Grand Hotel in Las Vegas. He waited in the rest room till he could no longer smell the nitrate in the air from the burned match, then flushed the toilet, washed his hands, and returned to his seat.

The flight arrived in Mobile at three minutes past eleven. While waiting for his blue Samsonite bag, Mr. Farley went to a Yellow Pages telephone directory for Mobile. His flight from Dallas had been Eastern Flight No. 71, but Mr. Farley was not certain there would be that many hotels and motels in Mobile, Alabama, so he decided on number 36, which was half of 72 (the closest even number to 71). Mr. Farley turned to the pages advertising hotels and counted down thirty-six to the Oasis Hotel. He telephoned and found a room was available for fifty-six dollars. He asked what the cab fare from the airport would be and discovered it would be about twelve dollars, with tip. The reservations clerk asked for Mr. Farley's name, and Mr. Farley, looking down at the credit card in his hand, said, "Mr. T. L. Rachman." He spelled it for the clerk.

Mr. Rachman claimed his bag, and went outside for a taxi. He was first in line, and by 11:30 he had arrived at the Oasis Hotel, downtown in Mobile. In the hotel's Shore Room Lounge, a band was playing in Halloween costume. The clerk on the hotel desk was made up to look like a mummy.

"You go to a lot of trouble here for holidays, I guess," said Mr. Rachman pleasantly.

"Anything for a little change," said the clerk as he pressed Mr. Rachman's MasterCard against three copies of a voucher. Mr. Rachman signed his name on the topmost voucher and took back the card. Clerks never checked signatures at this point, and they never checked them later either, but Mr. Rachman's had a practiced hand, at least when it came to imitating a signature.

Mr. Rachman's room was on the fifth and topmost floor, and enjoyed a view down to the street. Mr. Rachman unpacked his small bag, carefully hanging his extra pair of trousers and his extra jacket. He set his extra pair of shoes, with trees inside, into the closet beneath the trousers and jacket. He placed his two laundered shirts inside the topmost bureau drawer, set his little carved box containing an extra watch and two pairs of cufflinks and a tie clip and extra pairs of brown and black shoelaces on top of the bureau, and set his toiletries case next to the sink in the bathroom. He opened his black loose-leaf notebook and though it was not yet midnight, he began the entry for 110185, beneath which he noted:

> *110185    Eastern 71 Dallas-Mobile*
> *Taxi $9.80 + 1.70*
> *Oasis Hotel/4th St*
> *T.L. Rachman*

In the bathroom, Mr. Rachman took scissors and cut up the Visa card bearing the name Thomas Farley, and flushed away the pieces. He went down to the lobby and went into the Shore Room Lounge and sat at the bar. He ordered a vodka martini and listened to the band. When the bartender went away to the rest room, Mr. Rachman poured his vodka martini into a basin of ice behind the bar. When the bartender returned, Mr. Rachman ordered another vodka martini.

The cocktail lounge—and every other bar in Mobile—closed at 1 a.m. Mr. Rachman returned to his room, and without ever turning on the light, he sat at his window and looked out into the street. After the laundry truck had arrived, unloaded, and driven off from the service entrance of the Hotel Oasis, Mr. Rachman retreated from the window. It was 4:37 on the morning of the first of November, 1985. Mr. Rachman pulled the shade and drew the curtains. Towards noon, when the maid came to make up the room, Mr. Rachman called out from the bathroom, "I'm taking a bath."

"I'll come back later," the maid called back.

"That's all right," Mr. Rachman said loudly. "Just leave a couple of fresh towels on the bed." He sat on the tile floor and ran his unsleeved arm up and down through the filled tub, making splashing noises.

\*   \*   \*

Mr. Rachman counted his money at sundown. He had four hundred fifty-eight dollars in cash. With all of it in his pocket, Mr. Rachman walked around the block to get his bearings. He had been in Mobile before, but he didn't remember exactly when. Mr. Rachman had his shoes shined in the lobby of a hotel that wasn't the one he was staying in. When he was done, he paid the shoe-shine boy seventy-five cents and a quarter tip, and got into the elevator behind a businessman who was carrying a briefcase. The businessman with the briefcase got off on the fourth floor, and just as the doors of the elevator were closing Mr. Rachman startled and said, "Oh this is my floor, too," and jumped off behind the businessman with the briefcase. Mr. Rachman put his hand into his pocket, and jingled his loose change as if he were looking for his room key. The businessman with the briefcase put down his briefcase beside Room 419 and fumbled in his pocket for his own room key. Mr. Rachman stopped and patted all the pockets of his jacket and trousers. "Did I leave it at the desk?" he murmured to himself. The businessman with the briefcase put the key into the lock of Room 419, and smiled a smile that said to Mr. Rachman, *It happens to me all the time, too.* Mr. Rachman smiled a small embarrassed smile, and said, "I sure hope I left it at the desk," and turned and started back down the hall past the businessman with the briefcase.

The businessman and his briefcase were already inside of Room 419 and the door was beginning to shut when Mr. Rachman suddenly changed direction in the hallway and pushed the door open.

"Hey," said the businessman. He held his briefcase up protectively before him. Mr. Rachman shut the door quietly behind him. Room 419 was a much nicer room than his own, though he didn't care for the painting above the bed. Mr. Rachman smiled, though, for the businessman was alone and that was always easier. Mr. Rachman pushed the businessman down on the bed and grabbed the briefcase away from him. The businessman reached for the telephone. The red light was blinking on the telephone telling the businessman he had a message at the desk. Mr. Rachman held the briefcase high above his head and then brought it down hard, giving a little twist to his wrist just at the last so that a corner of the rugged leather case smashed against the bridge of the businessman's nose, breaking it. The businessman gaped, and fell sideways on the bed. Mr. Rachman raised the case again and brought the side of it down against the businessman's cheek with such force that the handle of the case broke off in his hand and the businessman's cheekbones were splintered and shoved up into his right eye. Mr. Rachman took the case in both hands and swung it hard along the length of the businessman's body and caught him square beneath his chin in the midst of a choking scream so that the businessman's lower jaw was shattered, detached, and then embedded in the roof of his mouth. In the businessman's remaining eye was one second more of consciousness and then he was dead.

Mr. Rachman turned over the businessman's corpse and took out his wallet, discovering that his name was Edward P. Maguire, and that he was from Sudbury, Massachusetts. He had one hundred and thirty-three dollars in cash, which Mr. Rachman put into his pocket. Mr. Rachman glanced through the credit cards, but took only the New England Bell telephone credit card. Mr. Maguire's briefcase, though battered and bloody, had remained locked, secured by an unknown combination. Mr. Rachman would have taken the time to break it open and examine its contents but the telephone on the bedside table rang. The hotel desk might not have noticed Mr. Maguire's entrance into the hotel, but Mr. Rachman did not want to take a chance that Mr. Maguire's failure to answer the telephone would lead to an investigation. Mr. Rachman went quickly through the dead man's pockets, spilling his change onto the bedspread. He found the key of a Hertz rental car with the tag number indicated on a plastic ring. Mr. Rachman pocketed it. He turned the dead man over once more and pried open his shattered mouth. A thick broth of clotting blood and broken teeth spilled out over the knot of Mr. Maguire's tie. With the tips of two fingers, Mr. Rachman picked out a pointed fragment of incisor, and put it into his mouth, licking the blood from his fingers as he did so. As he peered out into the hallway, Mr. Rachman rolled the broken tooth around the roof of his mouth, and then pressed it there with his tongue till its jagged edge drew blood and he could taste it. No one was in the hall, and Mr. Rachman walked out of Room 419, drawing it closed behind him. He took the elevator down to the basement garage, and walked slowly about till he found Mr. Maguire's rented car. He drove out of the hotel garage and slowly circled several streets till he found a stationery store that was still open. Inside he bought a detailed street map of Mobile. He studied it by the interior roof light of the rented car. For two hours he drove through the outlying suburbs of the city, stopping now and then before a likely house, and noting its number on the map with a black felt-tip marker. At half-past eleven he returned to the Oasis Hotel and parked the rental car so that it would be visible from his window. He went up to his room, and noted in his diary, under 110185:

*1910/Edward P Maguire/c*
*43/Mobile Alabama/Hotel*
*Palafox 419/1133/Jaw and*
*Briefcase*

On a separate page in the back of the looseleaf notebook, he added:

*Edward P Maguire*
*(110185)/9 Farmer's*

*Road/Sudbury MA 01776/*
*617 392 3690*

That was just in case. Sometimes Mr. Rachman liked to visit widows. It added to the complexity of the pattern, and so far as Mr. Rachman was concerned, the one important thing was to maintain a pattern that couldn't be analyzed, that was arbitrary in every point. That was why he sometimes made use of the page of notations in the back of the book—because too much randomness was a pattern in itself. If he sometimes visited a widow after he had met her husband, he broke up the pattern of entirely unconnected deaths. Mr. Rachman, who was methodical to the very core of his being, spent a great percentage of his waking time in devising methods to make each night's work seem entirely apart from the last's. Mr. Rachman, when he was young, had lived in a great city and had simply thought that its very size would hide him. But even in a great city, his very pattern of randomness had become apparent, and he had very nearly been uncovered. Mr. Rachman judged that he would have to do better, and he began to travel. In the time since then, he had merely refined his technique. He varied the length of his stays, he varied his acquaintance. That's what he called them, and it wasn't a euphemism—he simply had no other word for them, and really, they were the people he got to know best, if only for a short time. He varied his methods, he varied the time of the evening, and he even varied his variety. Sometimes he would arrange to meet three old women in a row, three old women who lived in similar circumstances in a small geographical area, and then he would move on, and his next acquaintance would be a young man who exchanged his favors for cash. Mr. Rachman imagined a perfect pursuer, and expended a great deal of energy in evading and tricking this imaginary hound. Increasingly, over the years Mr. Rachman's greatest satisfaction lay in evading this nonexistent, dogged detective. His only fear was that there was a pattern in the carpet he wove which was invisible to him, but perfectly apparent to anyone who looked at it from a certain angle.

No one took notice of Mr. Maguire's rented car that night. Next morning Mr. Rachman told the chambermaid he wasn't feeling well and would spend the day in bed, so she needn't make it up. But he let her clean the bathroom as she hadn't been able to do the day before. He lay with his arm over his eyes. "I hope you feel better," said the chambermaid. "Do you have any aspirin?"

"I've already taken some," said Mr. Rachman, "but thank you. I think I'll just try to sleep."

That night, Mr. Rachman got up and watched the rented car. It had two parking tickets on the windshield. At 11:30 p.m. he went downstairs, got into the car, and drove around three blocks slowly, just in case he was being followed. He was not, so far as he could tell. He opened his map of Mobile, and picked the house he'd marked that was nearest a crease. It was 117 Shadyglade Lane in a suburb called Spring Hill. Mr. Rachman drove on, to the nearest of the other places he'd marked. He stopped in front of a house on Live Oak Street, about a mile away. No lights burned. He turned into the driveway and waited for fifteen minutes. He saw no movement in the house. He got out of his car, closing the door loudly, and walked around to the back door, not making any effort to be quiet.

There was no door bell so he pulled open the screen door and knocked loudly. He stood back and looked up at the back of the house. No lights came on that he could see. He knocked more loudly, then without waiting for a response he kicked at the base of the door, splintering it in its frame. He went into the kitchen, but did not turn on the light.

"Anybody home?" Mr. Rachman called out as he went from the kitchen into the dining room. He picked up a round glass bowl from the sideboard and hurled it at a picture. The bowl shattered noisily. No one came. Mr. Rachman looked in the other two rooms on the ground floor, then went upstairs, calling again, "It's Mr. Rachman!"

He went into the first bedroom, and saw that it belonged to a teenaged boy. He closed the door. He went into another bedroom and saw that it belonged to the parents of the teen-aged boy. He went through the bureau drawers, but found no cash. The father's shirts, however, were in Mr. Rachman size—16½ × 33—and he took two that still bore the paper bands from the laundry. Mr. Rachman checked the other rooms of the second floor just in case, but the house was empty. Mr. Rachman went out the back door again, crossed the back yard of the house, and pressed through the dense ligustrum thicket there. He found himself in the back yard of a ranch house with a patio and a brick barbeque. Mr. Rachman walked to the patio and picked up a pot of geraniums and hurled it through the sliding glass doors of the den. Then he walked quickly inside the house, searching for a light switch. A man in pajamas suddenly lurched through a doorway, and he too was reaching for the light switch. Mr. Rachman put one hand on the man's shoulder, and with his other he grabbed the man's wrist. Then Mr. Rachman gave a twist, and smashed the back of the man's elbow against the edge of a television set with such force that all the bones there shattered at once. Mr. Rachman then took the man by the waist, lifted him up and carried him over to the broken glass door. He turned him sideways and then pushed him against the long line of broken glass, only making sure that the shattered glass was embedded deep into his face and neck. When Mr. Rachman let the man go, he remained standing, so deep had the edge of broken door penetrated his head and chest. Just in case, Mr. Rachman pressed harder. Blood poured out over Mr. Rachman's hands. With a nod of satisfaction, Mr. Rachman released the man in pajamas and walked quickly back across the patio and disappeared into the shrubbery again. On the other side, he looked back, and could see the lights going on in the house. He heard a woman scream. He took out a handkerchief to cover his bloody hands and picked up the shirts which he'd left on the back porch of the first house. Then he got into his car and drove around till he came to a shopping mall. He parked near half a dozen other cars—probably belonging to night watchmen—and took off his blood-stained jacket. He tossed it out the window. He took off his shirt, and wiped off the blood that covered his hands. He threw that out of the window, too. He put on a fresh shirt and drove back to the Oasis Hotel. He parked the car around the block, threw the keys into an alleyway, and went back up to his room. In his black loose-leaf notebook he wrote, under 110285:

> *1205/unk./mc 35/Spring*
> *Hill (Mobile) Alabama/*
> *$0/Broken glass*

Mr. Rachman spent the rest of the night simply reading through his black loose-leaf notebook, not trying to remember what he could not easily bring to mind, but merely playing the part of the tireless investigator trying to discern a pattern. Mr. Rachman did not think he was fooling himself when he decided that he could not.

When the chambermaid came the next day, Mr. Rachman sat on a chair with the telephone cradled between his ear and his shoulder, now and then saying, "Yes" or "No, not at all" or "Once more and let me check those numbers," as he made notations on a pad of paper headed up with a silhouette cartouche of palm trees.

Mr. Rachman checked out of the Oasis Hotel a few minutes after sundown, and smiled a polite smile when the young woman on the desk apologized for having to charge him for an extra day. The bill came to $131.70 and Mr. Rachman paid in cash. As he watched the young woman on the desk tear up the credit card receipt, he remarked, "I don't like to get near my limit," and the young woman on the desk replied, "I won't even apply for one."

"But they sometimes come in handy, Marsha," said Mr. Rachman, employing her name aloud as a reminder to note it later in his diary. Nametags were a great help to Mr. Rachman in his travels, and he had been pleased to watch the rapid spread of their use. Before 1960 or thereabouts, hardly anyone had worn a nametag.

Mr. Rachman drove around downtown Mobile for an hour or so, just in case something turned up. Once, driving slowly down an alleyway that was scarcely wider than his car, a prostitute on yellow heels lurched at him out of a recessed doorway, plunging a painted hand through his rolled-down window. Mr. Rachman said, "Wrong sex," and drove on.

"Faggot!" the prostitute called after him.

Mr. Rachman didn't employ prostitutes except in emergencies, that is to say, when it was nearly dawn and he had not managed to make anyone's acquaintance for the night. Then he resorted to prostitutes, but not otherwise. Too easy to make that sort of thing a habit.

And habits were what Mr. Rachman had to avoid.

He drove to the airport, and took a ticket from a mechanized gate. He drove slowly around the parking lot, which was out of doors, and to one side of the airport buildings. He might have taken any of several spaces near the terminal, but Mr. Rachman drove slowly about the farther lanes. He could not drive very long, for fear of drawing the attention of a guard.

A blue Buick Skylark pulled into a space directly beneath a burning sodium lamp. Mr. Rachman made a sudden decision. He parked his car six vehicles down, and quickly climbed out with his blue Samsonite suitcase. He strode towards the terminal with purpose, coming abreast of the blue Buick Skylark. A woman, about thirty-five years old, was pulling a dark leather bag out of the backseat of the car. Mr. Rachman stopped suddenly, put down his case and patted the pockets of his trousers in alarm.

"My keys . . ." he said aloud.

Then he checked the pockets of his suit jacket. He often used the forgotten keys ploy. It didn't really constitute a habit, for it was an action that would never appear later as evidence.

The woman with the suitcase came between her car and the recreational vehicle that was parked next to it. She had a handbag over her shoulder. Mr. Rachman suddenly wanted very badly to make this one work for him. For one thing, this was a woman, and he hadn't made the acquaintance of a female since he'd been in Mobile. That would disrupt the pattern a bit. She had a purse, which might contain money. He liked the shape and size of her luggage, too.

"Excuse me," she said politely, trying to squeeze by him.

"I think I locked my keys in my car," said Mr. Rachman, moving aside for her.

She smiled a smile which suggested that she was sorry but that there was nothing she could do about it.

She had taken a single step towards the terminal when Mr. Rachman lifted his right leg and took a long stride forward. He caught the sole of his shoe against her right calf, and pushed her down to the pavement. The woman crashed to her knees on the pavement with such force that the bones of her knees shattered. She started to fall forward, but Mr. Rachman spryly caught one arm around her waist and placed his other hand on the back of her head. In his clutching fingers, he could feel the scream building in her mouth. He swiftly turned her head and smashed her face into the high-beam headlight of the blue Buick Skylark. He jerked her head out again, and even before the broken glass had spilled down the front of her suit jacket, Mr. Rachman plunged her head into the low-beam headlight. He jerked her head out, and awkwardly straddling her body, he pushed her between her Buick and the next car in the lane, a silver VW GTI. He pushed her head hard down against the pavement four times, though he was sure she was dead already. He let go her head, and peered at his fingers in the light of the sodium lamp. He smelled the splotches of blood on his third finger and his palm and his thumb. He tasted the blood, and then wiped it off on the back of the woman's bare leg. Another car turned down the lane, and Mr. Rachman threw himself onto the pavement, reaching for the woman's suitcase before the automobile lights played over it. He pulled it into the darkness between the cars. The automobile drove past. Mr. Rachman pulled the woman's handbag off her shoulder, and then rolled her beneath her car. Fishing inside the purse for her car keys, he opened the driver's door and unlocked the back door. He climbed into the car and pulled in her bag with him. He emptied its contents onto the floor, then crawled across the back seat and opened the opposite door. He retrieved his blue Samsonite suitcase from beneath the recreational vehicle where he'd kicked it as he struck up his acquaintance with the woman. The occupants of the car that had passed a few moments before walked in front of the Buick. Mr. Rachman ducked behind the back seat for a moment till he could no longer hear the voices—a man and a woman. He opened his Samsonite case and repacked all his belongings into the woman's black leather case. He reached into the woman's bag and pulled out her wallet. He took her Alabama driver's license and a Carte Blanche credit card that read A. B. Frost rather than Aileen Frost. He put the ticket in his pocket. Mr. Rachman was mostly indifferent to the matter of fingerprints, but he had a superstition against carbon paper of any sort.

Mr. Rachman surreptitiously checked the terminal display and found that a plane was leaving for Birmingham, Alabama in twenty minutes. It would probably begin to board in five minutes. Mr. Rachman rushed to the Delta ticket counter, and said breathlessly, "Am I too late to get on the plane to Birmingham? I haven't bought my ticket yet."

Mark, the airline employee said, "You're in plenty of time—the plane's been delayed."

This was not pleasant news. Mr. Rachman was anxious to leave Mobile. Aileen Frost was hidden beneath her car, it was true, and might not be found for a day or so—but there was always a chance that someone would find her quickly. Mr. Rachman didn't want to be around for any part of the investigation. Also, he couldn't now say, "Well, I think I'll go to Atlanta instead." That would draw dangerous attention to himself. Perhaps he should just return to Mr. Maguire's car and drive away. The evening was still early. He could find a house in the country, make the acquaintance of anyone who lived there, sit out quietly the daylight hours, and leave early the following evening.

"How long a delay?" Mr. Rachman asked Mark.

"Fifteen minutes," said Mark pleasantly, already making out the ticket. "What name?"

Not Frost, of course. And Rachman was already several days old.

"Como," he said, not knowing why.

"Perry?" asked Mark with a laugh.

"Peter," said Mr. Como.

Mr. Como sighed. He was already half enamoured of his alternative plan. But he couldn't leave now. Mark might remember a man who had rushed in, then rushed out again because he couldn't brook a fifteen-minute delay. The ticket from Mobile to Birmingham was $89, five dollars more than Mr. Como had predicted in his mind. Putting his ticket into the inside pocket of his jacket that did not contain Aileen Frost's ticket to Wilmington, Mr. Como went into the men's room and locked himself into a stall. Under the noise of the flushing toilet, he quickly tore up Aileen Frost's ticket, and stuffed the fragments into his jacket pocket. When he left the stall he washed his hands at the sink until the only other man in the rest room left. Then he wrapped the fragments in a paper towel and stuffed that deep into the waste paper basket. Aileen Frost's license and credit card he slipped into a knitting bag of a woman waiting for a plane to Houston.

Mr. Como had been given a window seat near the front of the plane. The seat beside him was empty. After figuring his expenses for the day, Mr. Como wrote in his black loose-leaf notebook:

*0745/Aileen Frost/fc*
*35/Mobile Airport Parking*
*Lot/$212/Car headlights*

Mr. Como was angry with himself. Two airport killings within a week. That was laziness. Mr. Como had fallen into the lazy, despicable habit of working as early in the evening as possible. This, even though Mr. Como had *never* failed, not a single night, not even when only minutes had remained till dawn. But he tended to fret, and he didn't rest easy till he had got the evening's business out of the way. That was the problem of course. He had no other business. So if he worked early, he was left with a long stretch of hours till he could sleep with the dawn. If he put off till late, he only spent the long hours fretting, wondering if he'd be put to trouble. *Trouble* to Mr. Como meant witnesses (whose acquaintance he had to make as well), or falling back on easy marks—prostitutes, nightwatchmen, hotel workers.

Or, worst of all, pursuit and flight, and then some sudden, uncomfortable place to wait out the daylight hours.

On every plane trip, Mr. Como made promises to himself: he'd use even more ingenuity, he'd rely on his expertise and work at late hours as well as early hours, he'd try to develop other interests. Yet he was at the extremity of his ingenuity, late hours fretted him beyond any pleasure he took in making a new acquaintance, and he had long since lost his interest in any pleasure but that moment he saw the blood of each night's new friend. And even that was only a febrile memory of what had once been a hot true necessity of desire.

Before the plane landed, Mr. Como invariably decided that he did too much thinking. For, finally, instinct had never failed him, though everything else—Mr. Como, the world Mr. Como inhabited, and Mr. Como's tastes—everything else changed.

"Ladies and gentlemen," said the captain's voice, "we have a special treat for you tonight. If you'll look out the left side of the plane, and up— towards the Pleiades—you'll see Halley's Comet. You'll see it better from up here than from down below. And I'd advise you to look now, because it won't be back in our lifetimes."

Mr. Como looked out of the window. Most of the other passengers didn't know which stars were the Pleiades, but Mr. Como did. Halley's Comet was a small blur to the right of the small constellation. Mr. Como gladly gave his seat to a young couple who wanted to see the comet. Mr. Como remembered the 1910 visitation quite clearly, and that time the comet had been spectacular. He'd been living in Canada, he thought, somewhere near Halifax. It was high in the sky then, brighter than Venus, with a real tail, and no one had to point it out to you. He tried to remember the time before—1834, he determined with a calculation of his fingernail on the glossy cover of the Delta In-flight magazine. But 1834 was beyond his power of recollection. The Comet was surely even brighter then, but where had he been at that time? Before airports, and hotels, and credit cards, and the convenience of nametags. He'd lived in one place then for long periods of time, and hadn't even kept proper records. There'd been a lust then, too, for the blood, and every night he'd done more than merely place an incrimsoned finger to his lips.

But everything had changed, evolved slowly and immeasurably, and he was not what once he'd been. Mr. Como knew he'd change again. The brightness of comets deteriorated with every pass. Perhaps on its next journey around the sun, Mr. Como wouldn't be able to see it at all.

# LUCIUS SHEPARD

## White Trains

Here is something different from Mr. Shepard. The following is a luminescent poem about the possibility of unexpected drama and danger in the ordinary world. Like much of Shepard's work, it is about transcendent experience; unlike most of his work, "White Trains" is lambent in its simple elegance.

—E.D.

# WHITE TRAINS

## Lucius Shepard

*White trains with no tracks*
*have been appearing on the outskirts*
*of small anonymous towns,*
*picket fence towns in Ohio, say,*
*or Iowa, places rife with solid American values,*
*populated by men with ruddy faces and weak hearts,*
*and women whose thoughts slide*
*like swaths of gingham through their minds.*
*They materialize from vapor or a cloud,*
*glide soundlessly to a halt in some proximate meadow,*
*old-fashioned white trains with pot-bellied smokestacks,*
*their coaches adorned with filigrees of palest ivory,*
*packed with men in ice cream suits and bowlers,*
*and lovely dark-haired women in lace gowns.*
*The passengers disembark, form into rows,*
*facing one another as if preparing for a cotillion,*
*and the men undo their trouser buttons,*
*their erections springing forth like lean white twigs,*
*and they enter the embrace of the women,*
*who lift their skirts to enfold them,*
*hiding them completely, making it appear*
*that strange lacy cocoons have dropped from the sky*
*to tremble and whisper on the bright green grass.*
*And when at last the women let fall their skirts,*
*each of them bears a single speck of blood*
*at the corner of their perfect mouths.*
*As for the men, they have vanished*
*like snow on a summer's day.*

*I myself was witness to one such apparition*
*on the outskirts of Parma, New York,*
*home to the Castle Monosodium Glutimate Works,*
*a town whose more prominent sophisticates*

*often drive to Buffalo for the weekend.*
*I had just completed a thirty-day sentence*
*for sullying the bail bondsman's beautiful daughter*
*(They all said she was a good girl*
*but you could find her name on every bathroom wall*
*between Nisack and Mitswego),*
*and having no wish to extend my stay*
*I headed for the city limits.*
*It was early morning, the eastern sky*
*still streaked with pink, mist threading*
*the hedgerows, and upon a meadow bordering*
*three convenience stores and a laundromat,*
*I found a number of worthies gathered,*
*watching the arrival of a white train.*
*There was Ernest Cardwell, the minister*
*of the Church of the Absolute Solstice,*
*whose congregation alone of all the Empire State*
*has written guarantee of salvation,*
*and there were a couple of cops big as bears*
*in blue suits, carrying standard issue golden guns,*
*and there was a group of scientists huddled*
*around the machines with which they were*
*attempting to measure the phenomenon,*
*and the mayor, too, was there, passing out*
*his card and declaring that he had no hand*
*in his unnatural business, and the scientists*
*were murmuring, and Cardwell was shouting*
*"Abomination," at the handsome men*
*and lovely women filing out of the coaches,*
*and as for me, well, thirty days and the memory*
*of the bail bondsman's beautiful daughter*
*had left me with a more pragmatic attitude,*
*and ignoring the scientists' cries of warning and*
*Cardwell's predictions of eternal hellfire,*
*the mayor's threats, and the cops' growling,*
*I went toward the nearest of the women*
*and gave her male partner a shove and was amazed*
*to see him vanish in a haze of sparkles*
*as if he had been made of something insubstantial*
*like Perrier or truth.*

*The woman's smile was cool and enigmatic*
*and as I unzipped, her gown enfolded me*
*in an aura of perfume and calm,*

*and through the lacework the sun acquired*
*a dim red value, and every sound was faraway,*
*and I could not feel the ground beneath my feet,*
*only the bright sensation of slipping inside her.*
*Her mouth was such a simple curve, so pure*
*a crimson, it looked to be a statement of principle,*
*and her dark brown eyes had no pupils.*
*Looking into them, I heard a sonorous music;*
*heavy German stuff, with lots of trumpet fanfares*
*and skirling crescendos, and the heaviness*
*of the music transfigured my thoughts,*
*so that it seemed what followed was a white act,*
*that I had become a magical beast with golden eyes,*
*coupling with an ephemera, a butterfly woman,*
*a creature of lace and heat and silky muscle . . .*
*though in retrospect I can say with assurance*
*that I've had better in my time.*

*I think I expected to vanish, to travel*
*on a white train through some egoless dimension,*
*taking the place of the poor soul I'd pushed aside,*
*(although it may be he never existed, that only*
*the women were real, or that from those blood drops*
*dark and solid as rubies at the corners of their mouths,*
*they bred new ranks of insubstantial partners),*
*but I only stood there jelly-kneed watching*
*the women board the train, still smiling.*
*The scientists surrounded me, asking questions,*
*offering great sums if I would allow them to do tests*
*and follow-ups to determine whether or not*
*I had contracted some sort of astral social disease,*
*and Cardwell was supplicating God to strike me down,*
*and the mayor was bawling at the cops to take me*
*in for questioning, but I was beyond the city limits*
*and they had no rights in the matter, and I walked*
*away from Parma, bearing signed contracts*
*from the scientists, and another presented me*
*by a publisher who, disguised as a tree stump,*
*had watched the entire proceeding, and now*
*owned the rights to the lie of my life story.*
*My future, it seemed, was assured.*

*White trains with no tracks*
*continue to appear on the outskirts*

*of small anonymous towns, places*
*whose reasons have dried up, towns*
*upon which dusk settles*
*like a statement of intrinsic greyness,*
*and some will tell you these trains*
*signal an Apocalyptic doom, and*
*others will say they are symptomatic*
*of mass hysteria, the reduction of culture*
*to a fearful and obscure whimsey, and*
*others yet will claim that the vanishing men*
*are emblematic of the realities of sexual politics*
*in this muddled, weak-muscled age.*
*But I believe they are expressions of a season*
*that occurs once every millennium or so,*
*a cosmic leap year, that they are merely*
*a kind of weather, as unimportant and unique*
*as a sun shower or a spell of warmth in mid-winter,*
*a brief white interruption of the ordinary*
*into which we may walk and emerge somewhat*
*refreshed, but nothing more.*
*I lecture frequently upon this subject*
*in towns such as Parma, towns whose lights*
*can be seen glittering in the dark folds of lost America*
*like formless scatters of stars, ruined constellations*
*whose mythic figure has abdicated to a better sky,*
*and my purpose is neither to illuminate nor confound,*
*but is rather to engage the interest of those women*
*whose touch is generally accompanied by*
*thirty days durance on cornbread and cold beans,*
*a sentence against which I have been immunized*
*by my elevated status, and perhaps my usage*
*of the experience is a measure of its truth,*
*or perhaps it is a measure of mine.*

*Whatever the case, white trains move silent as thought*
*through the empty fields, voyaging from nowhere*
*to nowhere, taking on no passengers, violating*
*no regulation other than the idea of order,*
*and once they have passed we shake our heads,*
*returning to the mild seasons of our lives,*
*and perhaps for a while we cling more avidly*
*to love and loves, realizing we inhabit a medium*
*of small magical transformations that like overcoats*
*can insulate us against the onset of heartbreak weather,*

*hoping at best to end in a thunder of agony
and prayer that will move us down through
archipelagoes of silver light to a morbid fairy tale
wherein we will labor like dwarves at the question
of forever, and listen to a grumbling static from above
that may or may not explain in some mystic tongue
the passage of white trains.*

# NATALIE BABBITT

## Simple Sentences

Natalie Babbitt's "Simple Sentences" comes from the author's collection *The Devil's Other Story Book*, the sequel to the very popular *The Devil's Story Book,* about the goings on Downunder. (No, we don't mean Australia.) Babbitt is an acclaimed children's book writer and artist, with several Newbury Honor books to her credit—best known, perhaps, for *Tuck Everlasting* and *The Eyes of the Amaryllis.*

This charming little tale is just one of many delightful pieces in the two Devil collections. I am sorry everyone can't hear it for the first time the way I did, in a dramatic reading performed by fantasy author and professional storyteller Jane Yolen as she sat crosslegged on the floor of her attic study, complete with Upper Crust British and Cockney accents . . .

—T.W.

# SIMPLE SENTENCES

## Natalie Babbitt

One afternoon in Hell, the Devil was napping in his throne room when a frightful hubbub in the hall outside brought him upright on the instant. "Now what?" he barked. "Can't I get a minute's peace?"

The door to the throne room opened and a minor demon stuck his head in. "Sorry," said the minor demon, "but we've got two new arrivals here and they're giving me fits with their entry forms."

"Show them in," said the Devil darkly. "I'll straighten them out."

So the minor demon brought in the two and stood them before the Devil, where the first one, a shabby, mean-looking rascal, dropped his jaw and said, "Well, I'll be sugared! If it ain't Old Scratch hisself!"

And the second, a long-nosed gentleman, opened his eyes wide and said, "Dear me—it's Lucifer!"

Now, the Devil isn't fond of fancy names like Lucifer, preferring simply to be called "the Devil" or, once in a while, "your Highness." And he certainly dislikes all disrespectful terms, of which Old Scratch is only one. So he scowled at the two who stood there, and said, "See here—I like things peaceful in Hell. We can't have all this rattle and disruption."

At which the two said, both at once, "But—"

"Hold on for half a second, can't you?" said the Devil testily. He turned to the minor demon. "What've you got on the pair of them so far?" he demanded.

The minor demon consulted the sheaf of papers he'd brought in with him. "This one," he said, pointing with his pencil to the rascal, "is in for picking pockets. And that one"—pointing to the long-nosed gentleman—"is down for the sin of pride and for writing books no one could understand."

"Well?" said the Devil. "That sounds all right. What's the matter with that?"

"But it's not a question of their sins," said the minor demon. "We've known about those for years. What it is is what happened up there that finished them off, don't you know. And I can't get their stories straight on that."

"Oh," said the Devil. "All right." And he turned to the two, who'd been waiting there, glaring at each other. "You," he said to the rascal. "What's *your* story?"

"All I know is," said the rascal in a whiny voice, "I was mindin' my own business, out on the public streets, when this lardy-dardy lamps me and commences screechin' fit to blast yer ears. Thinks I, 'This cove is off his chump,' so I do a bunk. But he shags me, and we both come a cropper in the gutter and sap our noodles, and—well—that pins the basket. Next thing I know, I'm standin' here ramfeezled and over at the knees, and he's comin' the ugly like I'm the party responsible."

"*What?*" said the Devil.

"If I may be permitted," sniffed the long-nosed gentleman. "What actually transpired is that this squalid and depraved illiterate was on the verge of appropriating my purse when I observed the action at the penultimate moment. And whilst I was attempting to apprehend him, we both seem to have stumbled on a curbstone, with resultant fractures and contusions, and I find I've been deprived of my life—and my hat—in a most abrupt and inconvenient fashion. Surely I can't be censured for reacting with extreme exasperation."

"*What?*" said the Devil.

"I think what they mean is—" began the minor demon.

"I know what they mean," said the Devil. "That one tried to pick this one's pocket. Just write it down like that."

"Chalk your pull, there," cried the rascal. "You've got it in the wrong box. Maybe I was on the filch, sure, that's my job. But I wasn't after this poor, mucked-out barebones, not for toffee. I know his type. More squeak than wool, you can stand on me for that. A barber's cat like him ain't never got a chinker to his name. Why, I'd go home by beggar's bush if I couldn't pick better than that!"

"*What?*" said the Devil.

"He means—" the minor demon tried again.

"I know what he means," said the Devil. "He means he *didn't* try to pick the other one's pocket. A misunderstanding. So just write it down like that."

"Oh, now, really," exclaimed the long-nosed gentleman. "I must protest. I tell you, I saw this felon's grubby hand reaching for my purse. I am not in the habit of misinterpreting evidence supplied by my own observations. Why, the meanest intelligence could easily discern that the fellow's a thoroughgoing prevaricator!"

"See what I mean?" said the minor demon to the Devil.

"I see," said the Devil.

The rascal stepped a little nearer to the Devil. "Look here, yer honor," he said. "I don't want to tread the shoe awry and chance yer gettin' magged. But it's above my bend how a chap with yer quick parts could hang in the hedge when it comes to separate between brass tacks and flimflam. I mean, this underdone swellhead could argue the leg off an iron pot, but it's still all flytrap. Take it from me."

The long-nosed gentleman stepped forward then, himself. "I'm cognizant of the fact," he said haughtily, "that I'm not by any stretch of the imagination in Paradise. And it may be that I'm naive to expect impartiality. All I can do is to iterate the unembellished fact that I observed what I observed, and what I observed was that this clumsy brigand tried to rob me."

The rascal narrowed his eyes. "Handsomely over the bricks there, puggy," he said in a threatening tone. "Clumsy, am I? Just because you've got yer head full of bees, that's no reason to draw the longbow. You never twigged me doin' *my* kind of work. Even if I was on the dip with a piker like you, you wouldn't twig me. When it comes to light fingers, I'm the top mahatma. No one ever twigs me. So play Tom Tell-Truth or else keep sloom."

The long-nosed gentleman's face turned very red. "Sir," he said in a strangled voice, "your impertinence is beyond all sufferance. I wouldn't dignify your statements with rebuttals if it weren't that I have such respect for veracity. And the plain, unvarnished truth is, you attempted to commit a felony."

The Devil clapped his hands with a sound like a pistol going off. "That's enough," he said. "I've heard enough. The plain, unvarnished truth is there's only one crime here: neither of you can speak a simple sentence."

And at this they both stopped short to gape at him, and both said, "*What?*"

The Devil turned to the minor demon. "Write down," he said, "that what happened was they both tripped over their tongues."

The minor demon nodded. "Very well. And what shall I put for their punishment?"

For the first time, the Devil smiled. "We'll put them in together, in a room designed for one," he said. "And there they'll stay till it all freezes over down here."

So the two were led away, both sputtering with shock, and the minor demon folded up his papers. "I do admire that punishment," he said to the Devil.

"Thank you," said the Devil, settling back to get on with his nap. "It was the simplest sentence I could think of."

# ALAN MOORE

## A Hypothetical Lizard

Readers of comic books will not be unfamiliar with the name Alan Moore, for his adult, sophisticated, dark, and haunting scripts for the British comic book series *The Watchmen* have created a cult sensation. American comic fans may know him best for his work on Marvel's Swamp Thing series.

Will Shetterly and Emma Bull, editors of the Liavek fantasy anthologies, commissioned this piece, Moore's first fantasy short story, three years ago, after admiring his work in the comic book field. "A Hypothetical Lizard," a disturbing and beautifully told Liavekan tale, has my vote for the best story of the year.

Moore makes his home in the north of England. A dark fantasy novel is in the works, squeezed between comic and film script deadlines. Shetterly and Bull, and Melissa Singer, who commissioned the dark fantasy novel, are to be commended for bringing this author to the attention of the wider fantasy audience.

—T.W.

# A HYPOTHETICAL LIZARD

## Alan Moore

Half her face was porcelain.

Seated upon her balcony, absently chewing the anemic blue flowers she had plucked from her window garden, Som-Som regarded the courtyard of the House Without Clocks. Unadorned and circular, it lay beneath her like a shadowy and stagnant well. The black flagstones, polished to an impassive luster by the passage of many feet, looked more like still water than stone when viewed from above. The cracks and fissures that might have spoiled the effect were visible only where veins of moss followed their winding seams through the otherwise featureless jet. It could as easily have been a delicate lattice of pond scum that would shatter and disperse with the first splash, the first ripple . . .

When Som-Som was five her mother had noticed the aching beauty prefigured in her infant face and had brought the uncomprehending child through the yammering maze of nighttime Liavek until they reached the pastel house with its round black courtyard. Yielding to the tug of her mother's hand, Som-Som dragged across the midnight slabs with the echo of her shuffling footsteps whispering back to her from the high, curved wall that bounded all but a quarter of the enclosure. The concave facade of the House Without Clocks itself completed the circle, and into its broad arc were set seven doors, each of a different color. It was at the central door, the white one, that her mother knocked.

There was the sound of small and careful footsteps, followed by the brief muttering of a latch as the door was unlocked from the other side. It glided noiselessly open. Dressed all in white against the whiteness of the chambers beyond, a fifteen-year-old girl stared out into the dark at them, her eyes remote and unquestioning. The garment she wore was shaped to her body and colored like snow, with faint blue shadows pooling in its folds and creases. It covered her from head to toe, save for the openings that had been cut away to reveal her right breast, her left hand, and her impenetrable masklike face.

Staring up at the slim figure framed in its icy rectangle of light, Som-Som had at first assumed that the girl's visible flesh was reddened by the application of paint or powder. Looking closer, she realized with a thrill of fascination and horror that the skin was entirely covered by small yet legible words, tattooed in vivid crimson upon the smooth white canvas beneath. Finely worded sentences, ambiguous and suggestive, spiraled out from the maroon bud of her nipple. Verses of elegant and cryptic passion followed the orbit of her left eye before resolving themselves into a perfect metaphor beneath the shadow of her cheekbone. Her fingers dripped with poetry.

She looked first at Som-Som and then at her mother, and there was no judgment in her eyes. As if something had been agreed upon, she turned and walked with tiny, precise steps into the arctic dazzle of the House Without Clocks. After an instant, Som-Som and her mother followed, closing the white door behind them.

The girl (whose name, Som-Som later learned, was Book) led the two of them through spectrally perfumed corridors to a room that was at once gigantic and blinding. White light, refracted through lenses and faceted glassware, seemed to hang in the air like a ghostly cobweb, so that the shapes and forms within the room were softened. At the center of this foggy phosphorescence, a tall woman reclined upon polar furs, the cushions strewn about her feet embossed with intricate frost patterns. The glimmering blur of her surroundings erased the wrinkles from her skin and made her ageless, but when she spoke her voice was old. Her name was Ouish, and she was the mistress and proprietor of the House Without Clocks.

The conversation that passed between the two women was low and obscure, and Som-Som caught little of it. At one point, Mistress Ouish rose from her bed of white pelts and hobbled across to inspect the child. The old woman had taken Som-Som's face lightly between thumb and forefinger, turning the head in order to study the profile. Her touch was like crepe, but surprisingly warm in a room that gleamed with such unearthly coldness. Evidently satisfied, she turned and nodded once to the girl called Book before returning to the embrace of her furs.

The tattooed servant left the room, returning some moments later bearing a small pouch of bleached leather. It jingled faintly as she walked. She handed it to Som-Som's mother, who looked frightened and uncertain. Its weight seemed to reassure her, and she did not resist or complain as Book took her lightly by the arm and guided her out of the white chamber. Long minutes passed before Som-Som realized that her mother was not coming back.

The first three years of her service at the House Without Clocks had been pleasant and undemanding. Nothing seemed to be expected of her save for the running of an occasional errand, or the proffering of some small assistance with the pinning of hair and the painting of faces. Those who served in the brothel were kind without patronage, and as the months passed, Som-Som had come to know all of them.

There was Khafi, a nineteen-year-old dislocationist who, lying upon his stomach, could curl his body backward until the buttocks were seated comfortably upon the top of his head while his face smiled out from between the ankles. There was Delice, a woman in middle age who used fourteen needles to provoke inconceivable pleasures and torments, all without leaving the faintest mark. Mopetel, suspending her own heartbeat and breath, could approximate a corpse-like state for more than two hours. Jazu had fine black hair growing all over his body and would walk upon all fours and only communicate in growls. And there was Rushushi, and Hata, and unblinking Loba Pak . . .

Living amidst this menagerie of exotics, where the singular was worn down by repeated contact until it became the commonplace, Som-Som was afforded a certain objectivity. Without discrimination or favor, she spent the best part of her days observing the animate rarities about her, wondering which of them provided a template for what she was to become. Eavesdropping upon Mistress Ouish and her closest associates, patiently decoding their under-language of pauses and accentuated syllables, Som-Som had determined that she was being preserved for something special. Special even amid the gallery of specialties that was the House Without Clocks. Would she be instructed in the art of driving men and women to ecstasy with the vibrations of her voice, like Hata? Would Mopetel's talent of impermanent death become hers? Smiling as she accepted the candied fruits and marzipans offered by her indulgent elders, she would study their faces and consider.

Upon her ninth birthday, Som-Som was escorted by Book to the dazzling sanctum of Mistress Ouish. Her parched smile disquieting with its uncharacteristic warmth, Mistress Ouish had dismissed Book and then patted the wintery hides beside her, gesturing for Som-Som to sit. With what looked like someone else's expression stitched across her face, the proprietor of the House Without Clocks informed Som-Som of what might be her unique position within that establishment.

If she wished, she would become a whore of sorcerers, exclusive to their use. Henceforth, only those cunning hands that sculpted fortune itself would have access to the warm slopes of her substance. She would come to understand the abstracted lusts of those that moved the secret levers of the world, and she would be happy in her service.

Kneeling at the very edge of the bed of silver fur, Som-Som had felt the world shudder to a standstill as the old woman's words rolled about inside her head, crashing together like huge glass planets.

Sorcerers?

Often, sent to fetch some minor philter or remedy for the older inhabitants of the House Without Clocks, Som-Som's errands had taken her to Wizard's Row. The street itself, shifting and inconstant, full of small movements at the periphery of the vision, presented no clear and consistent image that she could summon from her memory. Some of its denizens, however, were unforgetable. Their eyes. Their terrible, knowing eyes . . .

She pictured herself naked before a gaze that had known the depths of the oceans of chance in which people are but fishes, a gaze that saw the secret wave-patterns in those unfathomable tides of circumstance. In her stomach, something more ambiguous than either fear or exhilaration began to extend its tendrils. Somewhere far away, in a white room filled with obscuring brilliance, Mistress Ouish was detailing a list of those conditions that must be fulfilled before Som-Som could commence her new duties.

Firstly, it seemed that many who dealt in the manipulation of luck would themselves leave nothing to chance. Before such a sorcerer would enter fully into physical congress with another being, the inflexible observation of certain precautions was demanded. Foremost amongst these were those safe-guards pertaining to secrecy. The ecstasies of wizards were events of awesome and terrifying moment, during which their power was at its most capricious, its least contained.

It was not unknown for various phenomena to manifest spontaneously, or for the name of a luck-invested object to be murmured at the moment of release. In the world of the magicians, such indiscretions could be of lethal consequence. The most innocent of boudoir confidences, if relayed to an enemy of sufficient ruthlessness, might yield a dreadful harvest for the incautious thaumaturge. Perhaps he would be plucked from the night by cold hands with unblinking yellow eyes set into their palms, or perhaps a sore upon his neck would blossom into purple, babyish lips, whispering delirious obscenities into his ear until all reason was driven from him.

The intangible continent of fortune was a territory steeped in hazard, and she who would be the whore of sorcerers must also undertake to be the bride of Silence.

To this end, Som-Som would be taken to a specific residence in Wizard's Row, an address remarkable in that it could only be located upon the third and fifth days of the week. Here, the child would be given a small pickled worm, ocher in color, the chewing of which would render her unconscious and insensitive to pain. As she slept, her skull would be carefully opened, revealing the grayish pink mansion of her soul to the fingers of one who abided in that place, a physiomancer of great renown. At this juncture, the Silencing would commence.

Connecting the brain's hemispheres there existed a single gristly thread, the thoroughfare by which the urgent neural messages of the preverbal and intuitive right lobe might pass to its more rational and active counterpart upon the left. In Som-Som, this delicate bridge would be destroyed, severed by a sharp knife so as to permit no further communication between the two halves of the child's psyche.

Following her recovery from this surgery, the girl would be granted a year in which to adjust to her new perceptions. She would learn to balance and to pick up objects without the benefit of stereoscopic sight or depth of vision. After many bouts of tearful and frustrating paralysis, during which she would merely stand and tremble, making poignant half-completed gestures while her body remained torn between conflicting urges, she would finally achieve some measure of coordination and restored grace. Certainly, her movements would always possess a slow and slightly staggered quality, but if directed properly there was no reason why this dreamlike effect should not in itself be erotically enhancing. At the end of her year of readjustment, Som-Som would have a cast taken of her face, after which she would be fitted with the Broken Mask.

The Broken Mask was not so much broken as sliced cleanly in two. Made of porcelain and covering the entire head, it would be precisely bisected with a small, silver chisel, starting at the nape of the neck, traversing the cold and hairless cranium, descending the ridge of the nose to divide the expressionless lips forever. The left side of the mask would be taken away and crushed to a fine talcum before being thrown to the winds.

Prior to the fitting of the Broken Mask, Som-Som's head would be completely shaven, the scalp afterward rubbed with the foul-smelling mauve juices of a berry known to destroy the follicles of the hair so that there could be no regrowth. This would at least partially ensure her comfort during the next fifteen years, in which time the mask was not to be removed unless the slowly changing shape of the skull made it uncomfortable. In this eventuality, the mask would be taken from her and recast.

Covering the right side of her head, the flawless topography of the Broken Mask would be uninterrupted by any aperture for hearing or vision. The porcelain eye was opaque and white and blind. The porcelain ear heard nothing. Concealed beneath this shell, their organic counterparts would be similarly disadvantaged. Som-Som would see nothing with her right eye, and would be deaf in her right ear. Only in the uncovered half of her face would the perceptions be unimpaired.

By some paradoxical mirror-fluke of nature, those sensory impressions gleaned from the apparatus of the body's left side would be conveyed to the brain's right hemisphere. And there, due to the severing of the neural causeway that had connected both lobes, the information would remain. It would never reach those centers of cerebral activity that govern speech and communication, for they were situated in the left brain, a land now irretrievably lost beyond the surgically created chasm. Her eye would see, but her lips would know nothing of it. Conversation that her ear might gather would forever go unrepeated by a tongue ignorant of words it should shape.

She would not be blinded, not exactly. Her hearing would remain, after a fashion, and she would even be able to speak. But she would be Silenced.

Within the flattering opalescence of her white chamber, Mistress Ouish concluded her descriptions of the honors which awaited the stunned nine-year-old. She rang the tiny china bell that signaled Book to the room, terminating the audience. Stumbling over feet made suddenly too large by loss of circulation, Som-Som allowed the tattooed servant to lead her into the startling mundane daylight.

Poised upon the threshold, Book had turned to the blinking child beside her and smiled. It wrinkled the words written upon her cheeks, rendering them briefly illegible, and it was not a cruel smile.

"When you are Silenced and can reveal their conclusions to no one, I shall permit you to read all of my stories."

Her voice was uneven of pitch, as if she had long been unpracticed in its application. Raising her ungloved and crimsonspeckled hand she touched the calligraphy upon her forehead, and then, lowering it, lightly brushed the lyric spiral of her breast. Smiling once more, she turned and went inside the house, closing the white door behind her, an ambulatory pornography.

It was the first time that Som-Som had ever heard her speak.

The following day, Som-Som was escorted to an elusive residence where a man with a comb of white hair that had been varnished into a stiff dorsal fin running back across his skull gave her a tiny, brownish worm to chew. She noted that it was withered and ugly, but probably no more so than it had been in life. She placed it upon her tongue, because that was expected of her, and she began to chew.

She awoke as two separate people, unspeaking strangers who shared the same skin without collaboration or conference. She was conveyed back to the House Without Clocks in a small cart lined with cushions. She rattled through the arched entranceway and across the gargantuan inkblot of the courtyard, and all that had been promised eventually came to pass.

Twelve years ago.

Seated upon her balcony, her half-visible lips stained blue by the juices of the masticated blossoms, Som-Som regarded the courtyard of the House Without Clocks. Unrippled by the afternoon breeze, the black pond stared back at her. Here and there upon the impenetrably dark water, fallen leaves were floating, motionless scraps of sepia against the blackness.

Surely, if she were to topple forward with delicious slowness toward the midnight well beneath her, surely she would come to no harm? Dropping like a pebble, she would splash through the impassive jet of the surface, a tumbling commotion of silver in the cold, ebony waters surrounding her.

Up above, the ripples would race outward like pulses of agony throbbing from a wound. They would break in black, lapping wavelets against the courtyard walls of the House Without Clocks, and then the waters would once more become as still as stone.

Down below, kicking out with clean, unfaltering strokes, she would swim away beneath the ground, out below the curved walls of the House

Without Clocks, out under the City of Luck itself and into those uncharted, solid oceans that lay beyond. Diving deep, she would glide among the glittering veins of ore, through the buried and forgotten strata. Darting upward, she would flicker and twist through the warm shallows of the topsoil, surfacing occasionally to leap in a shimmering arc through the sunlight, droplets of soil beading in the air about her. Resubmerging, she would strike out for the cool solitude of the clay and sandstone, far, far beneath her . . .

Someone walked across the surface of the black water, wooden sandals scuffing audibly against its suddenly hardened substance, crunching through leaves that were quite dry. Unable to sustain itself before such contradictions, the illusion melted and was immediately beyond recall.

One side of Som-Som's face clouded in annoyance at this intrusion upon her reverie, half her brow clenching into a petulant frown while the other half remained uncreased and indifferent. Her single visible eye, one from a pair of gems made more exquisite by the loss of its twin, glared down at the visitor passing beneath her. Unnoticed upon her balcony, she studied the interloper, struck suddenly by some quirk of gait or posture that seemed familiar. Her left eye squinted slightly as she strained for a better view, deforming the symmetry of her bisected face into a mirthless wink.

The figure was slender and of medium height, swathed in gorgeous bandages of red silk from crown to ankle so that only the face, hands, and feet were left unwrapped. The delicate line of the shoulder and arm seemed unmistakably female, but there remained something masculine about the manner in which the torso joined with the narrow, angular hips. Walking unhurriedly across the courtyard, it paused before the pale yellow door that lay at the rightmost extremity of the House Without Clocks. There the figure hesitated, turning to survey the courtyard and giving Som-Som her first clear glimpse of a painted face at once strikingly alien and instantly recognizable.

The visitor's name was Rawra Chin, and She was a man.

During the years of her service within that drifting environment, her perceptions of the world limited both by her condition and by the virtual confinement that was its effective result, Som-Som had nonetheless contrived to reach a plateau of understanding, an internal vantage point overlooking the vast sphere of human activity from which the Broken Mask had excluded her. This perspective afforded her certain insights that were at once acute and peculiar.

She understood, for example, that quite apart from being a limitless ocean of fortune, the world was also a churning maelstrom of sex. Establishments such as the House Without Clocks were islands within that current, where people were washed ashore by the tides of need and loneliness. Some would remain there forever, lodged upon the high-tide line. Most would be sucked

ned by
uld not

f fourteen
nced when
the flatness
Rawra Chin
f personality,
Her a beauty

the remarkable
ced Rawra Chin's
he youth. So, too,
merous merchants,
avorite, asking after
shment.

this charisma within
dentify it. It remained
disparate components of
some imaginary point of
Her widely-spaced eyes,

who came to know Rawra
belief that Her charms orig-
s and hesitant lad Herself,
siognomy.

ed to inform everything from
hair, long and soft, so golden
ccasional icicle glitter of fear in
between them for prettiness but
threads of personality were woven
ng impression of vulnerability. As
y, Som-Som had no more idea than
in's adoring customers.

tea with Som-Som upon her balcony
its, a diversion popular with many of
out Clocks. Due to the singularity of
d reveal their longings or resentments
ed her often during the long, dull morn-
in floral infusions and the opportunity for

she had contributed little to these often

at she was able to share. Since
known nothing but darkness
ld offer conversationally was
agments, half-remembered
that Som-Som had known

half could not hear and was
ether the other person had
ld be engaged in a vivid
mployment at the House
artle Her by saying, "I
who rushed everywhere
qually obscure, followed
tely at Rawra Chin and
mouth.

nciations, Rawra Chin
had finished her non
of these bizarre ejacu-
of their conversational
on to these talks had

ions and anxieties of
enjoyed the exclu-
life was conducted.
t unvoiced even to
ture more true and
losophers.

took pride in her
ented themselves
oncealed beneath
had been Som-
to give a name
ingly attractive

ct a relatively
owever super-
fundamental

end to make
ilar avowals
Som sensed
ppraisal of
es of Her

intimate discussions, having no confidences th
the side of her brain that governed speech had
and silence for several years, the best that it cou
a string of inappropriate and disconnected f
impressions and anecdotes relating to the worl
before the Silencing.

Confusing matters further, Som-Som's verbal
forced to make interjections without knowing wh
finished speaking. Thus, while Rawra Chin wou
description of what She hoped to do once Her e
Without Clocks was ended, Som-Som would st
remember that my mother was an unlikable woma
to get her life over with the sooner," or something e
by a long silence during which she would stare pol
sip her floral infusion through the left corner of the

Though at first disoriented by these random pronu
grew accustomed to them, waiting until Som-Som
sequitur before resuming. The continuing presence
lations did not seem to lessen Rawra Chin's enjoyment
interludes. Som-Som supposed that her real contribut
been her simple presence.

Her function was that of a receptacle for the aspirat
others, although this fact never became oppressive. Sh
siveness of these glimpses into the way that ordinary
The fact that people would relate to her things that wer
their lovers gave Som-Som a perspective upon human na
comprehensive than that enjoyed by many sages and phi

This gave her a measure of personal power, and she
ability to unravel the many and varied personas that pres
to her, laying bare the essential characteristics that were c
their facades of affectation and self-deception. Rawra Chi
Som's only failure. Like everyone else, she had been unabl
to that rare and precious element upon which the bewilde
adolescent boy had founded Her identity.

On the other hand, Som-Som had been able to constr
complete picture of Rawra Chin's aversions and ambitions,
ficial these appeared without an understanding of Her mor
motivations.

Som-Som knew, for example, that Rawra Chin did not in
a lifetime's vocation of prostitution. While she had heard si
from most of the occupants of the House Without Clocks, So
a determination in Rawra Chin that was iron-hard, setting H
the future apart from the rather sad and much-thumbed fa
fellows.

Rawra Chin, She often assured Som-Som, would one day be a great performer who would travel the globe, transporting Her art to the masses by way of a celebrated company of dramaticians such as the Torn Stocking Troupe, or Dimuk Paparian's Mnemonic Players. The less aesthetically demanding acts of pantomime that She was called upon to perform each day behind the pale yellow door of the House Without Clocks were merely a clumsy rehearsal for the innumerable thespian triumphs waiting somewhere in Her future.

The pale yellow door gave access to that part of the house that was given over to romantic pursuits of a more theatrical nature, its four floors each housing a single specialist in the erotic arts, linked by a polished wooden staircase that zigzagged up outside the house from courtyard level toward the gray slate incline of the roof.

In the topmost chamber lived Mopetel, the corpse-mime. Beneath her lived Loba Pak, whose flesh had a freakish consistency that enabled her to adjust her features into the semblance of almost any woman between the ages of fourteen and seventy. Rawra Chin lived upon the second floor, acting out mundane and unimaginative roles for Her eager male clientele but compensating for this with Her charisma. On the first floor, immediately beyond the pale yellow door, there lived a brilliant and savagely passionate male actor named Foral Yatt whose talent had been subverted into a plaything by the many female customers who enjoyed his company, and with whom Rawra Chin had become amorously entangled.

Foral Yatt was the subject of a great number of those balcony conversations, conducted through the motionless fog of warm vapor that hung above their tea bowls, with Rawra Chin talking animatedly upon one side while Som-Som sat listening upon the other, breaking her silence intermittently to remark that she remembered the color of a quilt her grandmother had made for her when she was an infant, or that a brother whose name she could no longer call to mind had once knocked over the pot-boil and badly scalded his legs.

The heart of Rawra Chin's anguish concerning Foral Yatt seemed to lie in Her knowledge that if She were to achieve Her ambition, She must leave the intense and darkly attractive young actor while She progressed to greater things. She confessed to Som-Som that though in private She and Foral Yatt would make their plans as if they would quit the House Without Clocks together, pursuing parallel careers in the outside world, Rawra Chin knew that this was a fiction.

Despite the fact that Foral Yatt's raw talent dwarfed Her own to insignificance, he possessed neither the indefinable appeal of Rawra Chin or the remorseless drive that would propel him through the pale yellow door and into the pitch and swell of that better life that lay beyond. Adding masochistically to Her anguish, the wide-faced boy also felt troubled by the fact that She was using Her nearness to Foral Yatt to study the finer points of his superior craft, storing each nuance of characterization, each breath-takingly understated gesture, until that point in Her career-to-come when She might use them.

Having purged Herself for the moment of Her moral burden, Rawra Chin would sit and stare miserably at Som-Som, waiting for some acknowl-edgment of Her dilemma. Long moments would pass, measured in whatever units were appropriate within the House Without Clocks, until finally Som-Som would smile and say, "It was raining on the afternoon that I almost choked on a pebble," or "Her name was either Mur or Mar, and I think that she was my sister," after which Rawra Chin would finish Her tea and leave, feeling obscurely contented.

Despite Her tormented writhings, Rawra Chin had eventually summoned sufficient strength of character or sufficient callousness to inform Foral Yatt that She would be leaving him, having been offered a place in a small but critically acclaimed touring company by a customer who transpired to be the merchant without whose continuing financial support the company could not survive.

Som-Som could still remember the ugly playlet that the two estranged lovers had performed in the courtyard of the House on the morning that Rawra Chin was to leave. While the other inhabitants watched with boredom or amusement from their balconies, the players paced across the flat black stage, seemingly oblivious to the audience that watched from above as their angry accusals and sullen denials rang from the curving courtyard walls.

Foral Yatt pathetically followed Rawra Chin around the courtyard, almost staggering beneath the weight of that dreadful, unexpected betrayal. He was a tall, lean man with beautiful arms, his eyes dark and deep set, brimming with tears as he trailed behind Rawra Chin, an unwanted satellite still trapped within Her orbit by the irresistible gravity of Her mystique. The fact that he kept his skull shaven to a close stubble to facilitate the numerous changes of wig required by his customers only added to his air of desolation.

Rawra Chin remained a measured number of paces in front of him, occasionally directing some pained but dignified comment over Her shoulder while he ranted, incoherent with hurt, raging and confused. Som-Som suspected that She was in some oblique way enjoying this abuse from Her former lover, that She accepted his tirade as an inverted tribute to Her mesmeric influence over him.

Eventually, when desperation had driven Foral Yatt beyond all consid-erations of dignity, he threatened to kill himself. Pulling something from the small pouch that he wore at his belt, the distraught young actor held it aloft so that it glittered in the morning sunlight.

It was a miniature human skull, fashioned from green glass and holding no more than a mouthful of the clear, licorice-scented liquid that it had been designed to contain. No more than a mouthful was required. These suicidal trinkets could be purchased quite openly, and it was impossible to determine how many of Liavek's more pessimistically inclined citizens carried one of the death's-heads in anticipation of that day when life was no longer endurable.

His voice ragged with emotion, Foral Yatt swore that he would not be deserted in so casual a manner. He promised to end his life if Rawra Chin did not pick up Her baggage and carry it back through the pale yellow door to their chambers.

They stared at each other, and Som-Som had thought that she perceived a flicker of uncertainty dance across the widely-spaced eyes of the young boy as they moved from Foral Yatt's face to the skull-shaped bottle in his hand. The instant seemed to inflate into a massive balloon of silence, punctured by the sudden rattle of hooves and wheels from beyond the courtyard's arched entrance, signaling the arrival of the carriage that was to take Rawra Chin to join Her theater troupe. She darted one last glance at Foral Yatt and then, picking up Her baggage, turned and walked out through the archway.

Foral Yatt stood transfixed at the center of the huge black disc, still with one flawless arm raised, clutching its cold green fistful of oblivion. He stared blankly at the archway as if expecting Her to reappear and tell him it was all some ill-considered hoax. From beyond the encircling walls there came the jingle of reins followed by a slow clattering and the creaking of wood and leather as the carriage moved away down the winding streets of the City of Luck. After a pause during which it seemed that he would never move again, the actor slowly and falteringly lowered his arm.

Three floors above him, realizing the abandoned lover wouldn't kill himself, one of the denizens of the House Without Clocks pursed her shiny black lips discontentedly and made a clucking sound before retiring to her quarters. Hearing the sound, Foral Yatt tilted back his gray-stubbled skull and stared up at the watchers in surprise, as if previously unaware of their scrutiny. His eyes were full of miserable incomprehension, and it was a relief to Som-Som when he lowered them to the black tiles at his feet before walking slowly across the courtyard toward the pale yellow door, the glass skull now quite forgotten in his hand.

Scarcely a handful of months elapsed before news began to work its way back to the House Without Clocks of Rawra Chin's dizzying success. It seemed that Her elusive charisma was able to captivate audiences as easily as it had once enthralled Her individual customers. Her performance as the tragic and infertile Queen Gorda in Mossoc's *The Crib* was already the talk of Liavek's intelligentsia, and rumor had it that a special performance for His Scarlet Eminence was being considered.

Such talk was generally kept from the inconsolable Foral Yatt, but within the year Rawra Chin's fame had spread to the point where the embittered young actor was as aware of it as anyone. He seemed to take the news of Her stellar ascent with less resentment than might have been anticipated, once the initial despair of separation had lifted from him. Indeed, save for a coldness that would creep into his eyes at the mention of Her name, Foral Yatt made much of his indifference to his former lover's fortunes. He never spoke of Her, and those less insightful than Som-Som might have supposed that he had forgotten Her altogether.

Now, five years later, She had returned.

In the courtyard beneath Som-Som's balcony, Rawra Chin turned to face the pale yellow door, a resigned slump in Her shoulders. She lifted one hand to knock, and there was a sudden dazzling scintillation that seemed to play about Her fingers. It took Som-Som a moment to realize that the young man had chips of some reflective substance pasted to Her nails. The afternoon was hushed, as if holding its breath while it listened, and the sound of Rawra Chin's white knuckles upon the pale yellow wood was disproportionately loud.

Seated high above on her balcony, Som-Som found that she wanted desperately to call out, to warn Rawra Chin that it was a mistake to return to this place, that She should leave immediately. Silence, massive and absolute, surrounded her and would not permit her to make the smallest sound. She was embedded in silence, a tiny bubble of consciousness within an infinity of solid rock, mute and gray and endless. She struggled against it, willing her tongue to shape the vital words of warning, knowing as she did so that it was hopeless.

Below, someone unlocked the pale yellow door from inside and it creaked once, musically, as it opened. It was too late.

Som-Som's balcony was situated upon the third floor, the adjacent living area being one of four contained behind the violet door at the extreme left of the House Without Clocks' concave front. Thus, as she sat upon her balcony and gazed down at Rawra Chin she could not see who had opened the door. She supposed that it was Foral Yatt.

There was a surprisingly low exchange of words, following which the crimson-wrapped figure of the celebrated performer stepped inside the house and beyond Som-Som's vision. The pale yellow door closed with a sound like something sucking its teeth.

After that, there was only silence. Som-Som remained seated upon her balcony staring down at the pale yellow door with mute anguish in her one visible eye while the sky gradually darkened behind her. Finally, when the moment of her urgent need for a voice was long past, she spoke.

"I ran as fast as I could, but when I reached my mother's house the bird was already dead."

\*    \*    \*

Since the closing of the yellow door, no word had been spoken in the rooms that lay immediately behind it. Foral Yatt sat in a hard wooden chair beside the open fire, amber light flickering across one side of his lean face. Rawra Chin stood by the window, Her vivid crimson darkening to a dull, scablike burgundy against the failing light outside. Uncertain of how best to gauge the distance that had arisen between them, She watched the play of firelight upon the velvet of his shaven skull until the absence of conversation was more than She could endure.

"I brought you a gift."

Foral Yatt slowly turned his head toward Her, away from the fire, so that the shadow slid across his face, and his expression was no longer visible. Rawra Chin immersed one chalk-white hand in the black fur of the bag She carried, from whence it emerged holding a small copper ball between the mirror-tipped fingers. She held it out to him and, after a moment, he took it.

"What is it?"

She had forgotten how captivating his voice was, dry and deep and hungry, quite unlike Her own. Calm and evenly modulated, there remained a sense of something watchful and carnivorous lurking just beyond it, pacing quietly behind the accents and inflections. Rawra Chin licked Her lips.

"It's a toy . . . a toy of the intellect. I'm told that it's very relaxing. Many of the busiest merchants that I know find that it calms them immeasurably after the bustle of commerce."

Foral Yatt turned the smooth copper sphere between his fingers so that it gleamed red in the glow of the fire.

"What's special about it?"

Rawra Chin took a step away from the window, Her first tentative movement toward him since entering the House, and then paused. She let Her black fur bag drop with a soft thud, like the corpse of an enormous spider, onto the empty seat of the room's other chair. A certain establishing of territory accompanied the gesture, and Rawra Chin hoped She had not overstepped in Her eagerness. Foral Yatt's face was still in shadow, but he did not seem to react adversely to the wedge-end represented by the bag upon the chair, now less like a dead spider than a sleeping cat dozing before the hearth. Encouraged by this lack of obvious rebuke, Rawra Chin smiled, albeit nervously, as She replied to him.

"There might be a lizard asleep inside the ball, or there might not. That's the puzzle."

His silence seemed to invite elaboration.

"The story goes that there exists a lizard capable of hibernating for years or even centuries without food or air or moisture, slowing its vital processes so that a dozen winters might pass between each beat of its heart. I am told that it is a very small creature, no bigger than the top joint of my thumb when it is curled up.

"The people who make these ornaments allegedly place one of the sleeping reptiles inside each ball before sealing it. If you look closely, you can see that there's a seam around the middle."

Foral Yatt declined to do so, remaining seated, his back toward the fire, holding the ball in his right hand and turning it so that molten highlights rolled across its surface. Though an impenetrable shadow still concealed his expression, Rawra Chin sensed that the quality of his silence had changed. She felt whatever slight advantage She had gained begin to slip away. Why wouldn't he speak? Unable to keep the edge of unease from Her voice, She resumed Her monologue.

"You can't open it, and, and you have to think about whether there really is a lizard inside it or not. It's to do with how we perceive the world around us, and when you think about it you start to see that it doesn't matter if there's a lizard inside there or not, and then you can think about what's real and what isn't real, and . . ."

Her voice trailed off, as if suddenly aware of its own incoherence.

". . . and it's said to be very relaxing," She concluded lamely, after a flat, dismal pause.

"Why did you come back?"

"I don't know."

"You don't know."

It was as if Her words had hit a mirror, rebounding back at Her full of new meanings and implications, warped out of true by some fluke of the glass. Rawra Chin's fragile composure began to crumble before that flat, disinterested voice.

"I . . . I don't mean that I don't know. I just mean . . ."

She looked down at Her pale, well-kept hands to find that She was wringing them together. They looked like crabs mating after having been kept in the dark for too long.

"I mean that there was no real reason for me to come back here. My work, my career, it's all perfect. I have a lot of money. I have friends. I've just completed my role as Bromar's eldest daughter in *The Lucksmith* and everybody will talk about me for months. For a while, I do not have to work. I can do whatever I want.

"I didn't have to come back here."

Foral Yatt remained silent, the firelight behind his shaven head edging his skull with a trim of blurred phosphorescence as it shone through the stubble. The copper ball turned between his fingers, a miniature planet rolling from day into night.

"It's just that . . . this place, this house, it has something. There's something inside this house, and it's something true. It isn't a good thing.

It's just a true thing, and I don't know what the name of it is, and I don't even like it, but I know that it's true and I know that it's here and I felt, I don't know, I felt that I had to come back and look at it. It's like . . ."

Rawra Chin's hands seemed to pluck and squeeze the air before Her, as if the words She required were concealed beneath its skin, and that by probing She could guess at their shape. Separated now, the blanched crustacean lovers lay upon their backs, feebly waving their legs as they expired upon some unseen shoreline.

"It's like an accident I saw . . . a farmer, crushed beneath his cart. He was alive, but his ribs were broken and sticking through his side. I didn't know what they were at first, because it was all such a mess. There were a lot of people gathered 'round, but nobody could move the cart without hurting him even more than he was hurt already.

"It was summer, and there were a lot of flies. I remember him screaming and shouting for somebody to beat the flies away, and an old woman went out and did that for him, but until then nobody had moved, not until he screamed at them. It was horrible. I walked by as fast as I could because he was suffering and there was nothing anybody could do, except for the old woman who was beating the flies away with her apron.

"But I went back.

"I stopped just a little way down the road, and I went back. I couldn't help it. It was just that it was so real and so painful, that man, lying there under that terrible weight and screaming for his wife, his children, it was so real that it just cut through everything else in the world, all the things that my luck and my money have built up around me, and I knew that it meant something, and I went back there and I watched him drown on his own blood while the old woman told him not to worry, that his wife and children would be there soon.

"And that's why I came back to the House Without Clocks."

There was a long hyphen of silence. A copper world rotated between the fingers of a faceless and unanswering god.

"And I still love you."

Someone rapped twice upon the pale yellow door.

For a moment there was no movement within the room save for the illusion of motion engendered by the firelight. Then Foral Yatt rose from the hard wooden chair, still with the fire at his back and his face in eclipse. Crossing the room, ducking beneath the blackened beams that supported the low ceiling, he passed close enough for Her to raise Her hand and brush his arm, so that it would be thought an accident of passing. But She didn't.

Foral Yatt opened the door.

The figure on the other side of the threshold was perhaps forty years of age, a large and strong-boned woman with raw cheeks who wore a single garment like a tent of smoky gray fur. It covered the top of her head with a hole cut away to reveal the face, and then its striking, minimal lines dropped away to the floor. There was no opening in the fur through which she might extend her hands, which suggested to Rawra Chin that the woman must have servants to do everything for her, the feeding to her of meals not excluded. Even in the world that Rawra Chin had known over the previous five years, such arrogantly flaunted wealth was impressive.

As the inopportune visitor tilted back her head to speak, the flickering yellow light caught her face, and Rawra Chin noticed that the woman had an umber blemish, unpleasantly furry-looking, that almost entirely covered her left cheek. The woman had obviously attempted to conceal it beneath a thick coat of white powder with little success. The discoloration remained visible through the makeup as if it were a paper-thin flatfish that swam through her subcutaneous tissue, its dark shape discernible just below the clouded surface of her face.

When she spoke, her voice was distressingly loud, her tone strident and somehow abusive.

"Foral Yatt. Dear Foral Yatt, how long? How long has it been since I saw you last?"

Foral Yatt's reply was professionally polite, cooly inoffensive, and yet delivered at such volume that Rawra Chin winced involuntarily, even though She stood several paces behind him. It came to Her suddenly that the fur-draped woman must suffer from some defect of hearing.

"It has been two days since you were here, Donna Blerot. I have missed you."

A wave of hotness washed over Rawra Chin, cooling almost instantly to a leaden ingot in Her stomach. Foral Yatt had a customer, and She must leave him to his labors. Her disappointment was so big She could not admit that it was Hers. She resolved to leave immediately, hoping to keep it one step behind Her until She could reach Her own rooms in a lodging house on the far side of the City of Luck. Once She was safely behind closed doors She would let it have its way with Her, and then there would be tears. She was reaching for Her bag, sleeping there in its chair, when Foral Yatt spoke again.

"However, it is not convenient that I should see you tonight. A member of my family has come to visit"—here he gestured vaguely over his shoulder toward the stunned Rawra Chin—"and I regret that you and I must let our yearnings simmer untended for one more day. Please be patient, Donna Blerot. When finally we meet together, you know that our union will be the sweeter for this postponement."

Donna Blerot turned her head and gazed past Foral Yatt at the slim, crimson-swathed figure that stood in the flamelit room, almost like a flame Herself within the gaudy wrappings. The dame's eyes were frozen and merciless, boring into Rawra Chin for long instants before she turned them once more toward Foral Yatt, her expression softening.

"This is too bad, Foral Yatt. Simply too bad. But I shall forgive you. How could I ever do otherwise?"

She smiled, her teeth yellow and her lips too wide.

"Until tomorrow, then?"

"Until tomorrow, dearest Donna Blerot."

The woman turned from the door and Rawra Chin heard the slow, derisive clapping of her wooden sandals as she walked back across the black courtyard. Foral Yatt closed the door, sliding the bolt across. The sound of the bolt's passage, metal against metal, was electrifying in its implications, and Rawra Chin shuddered in resonance. The actor turned away from the closed portal and stared at Her, his face brazen in the fire glow.

His face seemed less chiseled and gaunt than She had remembered it. His eyes, conversely, were so riveting and intense that She knew Her recollection had not done them justice. Across a chamber so filled with swaying clots of darkness that it seemed like a ballroom for shadows, the two young men stared at each other. Neither spoke.

He walked toward Her, pausing only to set the small copper globe upon the polished white wood of his tabletop before continuing. His pace was so deliberate that Rawra Chin felt sure he must be aware of the tension that this deliciously prolonged approach kindled within Her. Unable to meet his gaze, She lowered Her lashes so that the quivering light of the room became streaks of incoherent brilliance. Her breathing grew shallow, and She trembled.

The warm, dry smell of his skin enveloped Her. She knew that he was standing just before Her, no more than a forearm's length away. Then he touched Her face. The shock of physical contact almost caused Her to jerk Her head back, but She controlled the impulse. Her heart rang like an anvil as his fingernail traced the line of Her jaw.

The ingenious arrangement of bandages that was Rawra Chin's costume had a single fastening, concealed behind a triangular black gem in a filigree surround that She wore upon the right side of Her throat. The pin pricked Her neck as Foral Yatt withdrew it from the blood-red windings, but even this seemed almost unbearably pleasant to Her in that aching, oversensitized state. She lifted Her gaze and his eyes swallowed Her whole. With his hands moving in languid, confident circles, he began to unwind the long band of brightly dyed gauze, starting from Her head and spiraling downward.

Free of the confining wrap, Her thick hair tumbled down upon Her white shoulders. She gasped and shook Her head from side to side, but it was not an indication of denial. A wave of thrilling coolness crept down Her body as progressively more of Her skin was exposed to the drafts of the room. It moved across Her belly and down to the angular and jutting hips, over the shaven pudenda and past the jumping, half-erect penis. It continued down Her thighs and on toward the rush carpeting, where the unraveled wrappings gathered in a widening red puddle about Her feet, as if Her naked flesh bled from a dozen imperceptible wounds.

He nodded his head to Her once, still without a sound, and She knelt upon the floor at his feet, Her knees pressed against the tangle of fallen bandages so that they would leave a faint lattice of impressions upon Her skin. Closing Her eyes, She allowed Her head to sink forward until it came to rest against the seat of the chair in which She had placed Her bag an eternity before. Its luscious dark fur and the hard wood were equally cool against Her burning cheek.

Behind Her, a single brief chime, Foral Yatt's buckle dropped unceremoniously to the rush matting. Upon an impulse, She allowed Her eyes to open, their gaze drifting across the chamber, drinking in the moment in all its infinitesimal detail. On the other side of the room, the copper ball rested upon the tabletop where Foral Yatt had placed it. It was like the freshly gouged eye of a brazen speaking-head, such as certain personages in Wizard's Row were reputed to possess.

It stared back at Rawra Chin, glittering suggestively, and all that came to pass behind the pale yellow door was reflected impartially, in perfect miniature, upon the convex surface of that lifeless and unblinking orb.

Later, lying flat upon Her stomach with their mingled sweat drying in the hollow of Her back, Rawra Chin allowed Her awareness to float tethered upon the margins of wakefulness while Foral Yatt squatted naked by the fire, adding fresh coals to sustain a fading redness that had burned low during the preceding hour. The air was heavy with the intoxicating bouquet of semen, and each of Her muscles slumped in blissful exhaustion.

Still, something nagged at Her, even in the sublime depths of Her sated torpor. There was yet something unresolved between the two of them, no matter how eloquent their lovemaking may have seemed. It was barely a real thing at all, more a disquieting absence than an intrusive presence, and She might have ignored it. This, however, proved more than She could bear. It was a cavity within Her that must be filled before She could be complete. Though reluctant to send ripples through the calm afterglow of their congress, eventually She found Her voice.

"Do you still love me?" This was followed, after a hesitant beat, by, "Despite what I did to you?"

She turned Her head so that the right side of Her face rested against the interwoven rushes. He crouched before the fire with his back toward Her as he carefully arranged cold black nuggets atop the bright embers. His skin glistened, a yellow smear of watercolor highlight running down the side toward the fire. She followed the line of his vertebrae with Her eyes to the plumbline-straight crease that bisected the hard buttocks, adoring him. He did not turn to Her as he replied.

"Is there a lizard asleep within the ball?"

Taking another piece of coal in a hand already blackened by dust, Foral Yatt placed a capstone atop the dark pyramid in the scaled-down hell of the fireplace. Nothing more was said behind the pale yellow door that night.

Upon the following morning, Rawra Chin visited Som-Som and took tea with her, as if the five-year hiatus in their ritual had never existed. She recounted a string of anecdotes from Her career, then paused to sip Her infusion while Som-Som informed Her that her mother had once closed a door, and that it had once been dark, and that once she had been unable to stop coughing. Rawra Chin's smooth reentry into the bizarre rhythms of their conversation did much to eradicate any distance between the two that might have flourished in their half decade of separation. Even so, it was not until the interlude approached its conclusion that the performer felt comfortable enough to broach the subject of Her resumed relationship with Foral Yatt.

"I won't be staying here forever, of course. In another month or so I must begin to consider my next role, and it would be impossible to do that here. But this time, when I leave, I believe I shall take him with me. I'm rich enough to keep him until he finds work of his own, and it seems ridiculous that someone with his talent should be wasting it upon . . ."

Her hands performed a curious movement that was part theatrical gesture and part genuine involuntary revulsion. It was as if they were retching with violent spasms that shuddered out from the slender throat of the wrist and on toward Her fingertips, where ten mirrors shivered in the cold morning sunlight.

". . . upon ugly, sick old women like that terrible Donna Blerot! He deserves so much better. I could look after him, I could find work for him, and then perhaps neither of us would need to come back to this place ever again, not even just to look at it. Don't you think that would be a good idea?"

Som-Som sipped her floral infusion through the corner of her mouth and said nothing.

"I think we can do it. I think that we can love each other and be together without anything going wrong between us. It was only my ambition that pushed us apart before, and I've fulfilled that now. Things can be just as they were, only somewhere else, in a better place than this."

Rawra Chin looked thoughtful, sucking the dazzling tip of Her right index finger so that it made a small and liquid popping sound when She pulled it from between Her lips. She did this twice. Behind Her, birds wheeled above the diverse skyline of Liavek. When She spoke again, Her voice had assumed a puzzled tone.

"Of course, he has changed. I suppose we've both changed. He's very quiet now, and very . . . very commanding. Yes, that's it exactly. Very commanding. It's wonderful, I'm not complaining at all. After all, those are his chambers and he's being kind enough to let me stay there for the next couple of months so that I don't need to keep up my rooms at the lodging house. I don't mind doing whatever he wants. I think, you know, I think it's good for me in a way, good for how I am as a person. Since my career broke out of the egg, nobody had told me what to do. I think that's spoiled me. It doesn't feel right, somehow. Not when people just defer to me all the time. I think I need someone to—"

"A sticky head looked out from between the cow's legs, and I screamed."

Som-Som's interjection was so startling that even Rawra Chin, accustomed to such utterances, was momentarily unnerved. Blinking, She waited to see if the half-masked woman intended to make any further comment before continuing.

"I'm having my clothes sent over from the lodging house. I have so many beautiful things it hardly seems fair. Foral Yatt says that he will store my wardrobe, but he does not want me to wear the more exotic creations while I am with him. He prefers plainer things."

Rawra Chin glanced down at the clothing She was dressed in. She wore a simple blouse of gray cotton and a skirt of similar material. Her white-gold hair swung about Her narrow shoulders and sparked life from the dusk-colored fabric with its contrast. It lay against Her blouse like wan torchlight reflected on wet, gray cobbles. Evidently satisfied with the novel restraint and subtlety of her costume, She raised Her lashes and smiled across the tea bowls at Som-Som.

"But enough of my affairs and vanities. Which side of luck have you yourself walked these five years gone?"

The divided face stared back at Her with its one live eye. No one spoke. Over the City of Luck, great scavenger birds dipped and shrieked, so that it sounded as if babies had been torn up from the earth and dragged wailing into the oppressive dome of the sky.

On the fifth day after Her arrival, Rawra Chin appeared upon Som-Som's balcony wearing breeches of leather with a stout length of rope looped about the waist as a belt. She did not refer to this reversal of Her sartorial tendencies, but after that Som-Som never again saw Her in a skirt and supposed that this was due to Foral Yatt's austere influence. The performer seemed also to forgo the application of face paint and the wearing of all jewelry save for a simple band of unadorned iron, which She wore upon the smallest finger of Her left hand. The ten slivers of mirror were long since vanished.

Two weeks after Her return, Foral Yatt persuaded Rawra Chin to shave off Her hair.

Sitting with Som-Som the following morning, She would break off from Her trail of conversation every few seconds and run one incredulous palm back from Her temple and across the stubble. Her talk had a forced gaiety, and there was something nervous and darting within Her eyes. Som-Som realized with some surprise that Rawra Chin no longer seemed attractive. It was as if Her charisma had leaked out of Her, or been sheared away as ruthlessly as the spun sunlight of Her hair.

"I think, I think I look better like this, don't you?"

Som-Som said nothing.

"I mean to say that it, well, it makes such a change. And I think it will do my hair a service, after it grows back. The colorings I use had made it so brittle, a new head of hair will be such a relief. And of course, Foral Yatt likes it this way."

The casual delivery of this last phrase was belied by an evasive glance and an air of restless self-consciousness.

"I mean, I understand how it must look, how it must look to people who don't know him, but . . ."

One hand rasped lightly across Her skull in a single, backward motion.

". . . but the way that I dress is important to him, the way I look, it's so important to him, the way that I look when we make love."

Som-Som cleared her throat and told the performer the name of the street where she had lived before the night when her mother had led her out by the hand, through the noise and toward the Silence. Rawra Chin continued Her monologue without acknowledging the interjection, Her eyes hollow and sleepless with their gaze still fixed on the grubby tiles.

"He's changed, you see. He wants different things now. And, and I don't mind. I love him. I don't mind what he wants me to do. I even like it, sometimes I like it for myself and not just for him. But the fact, the fact that I like it, that's something that frightens me. Not frightens me, really, but it's as if everything is changing and moving under my feet, and as if I'm changing too, and I feel as if I should be frightened, but I'm not. It's so easy, just slipping into it. It's so easy just to let it happen, and I don't mind. I love him and I don't mind."

From the dilated pupil of the courtyard, someone called Rawra Chin's name. Som-Som turned her gaze to the flagstones below, puzzling for a moment over the stranger that stood there before she was able to reconcile the familiar face with the unplaceable gait and manner, finally resolving these disparate impressions into Foral Yatt.

Rawra Chin had spoken the truth. Foral Yatt had changed.

Standing beneath them, looking up with one hand raised to shield his eyes from the sun, the bar of shadow cast across his features did not conceal the change that had come over them. The actor seemed less lean. Som-Som supposed that this was in part due to Rawra Chin's wealth supplementing his income and his diet.

His clothing, too, was noticeably different from the somber and functional raiment that he had appeared to favor. Foral Yatt wore a long tunic, its blue so deep and vibrant that it bordered upon iridescence. A wide orange sash was wound twice about his waist, and the billowing pants that he wore beneath were orange also, a fragile, mottled orange almost white in places. His feet were naked and exquisite, much smaller than Som-Som would have expected them to be. Something glittered, a sparkling fog about the toes.

"Rawra Chin? Our meal is almost prepared."

His voice had altered, too: lighter, a patina of melody imposed upon its assured tones. And there was something else, something which above all was responsible for the striking change in his aspect, something so obvious that it eluded her completely.

Rawra Chin murmured an apology as She made ready to leave, not bothering to tie up any loose ends remaining from Her conversation with Som-Som. As was Her custom, She reached out and squeezed Som-Som's wrist to let the half of her brain that was cut off from sight or sound know that her visitor was leaving. In response, the half-masked woman lifted her gaze until it met Rawra Chin's. When she spoke, her voice was filled with a sadness that seemed to have no bearing upon the content of her speech.

"I do not think that the food was so good, back then."

Rawra Chin's lips twitched once, a helpless little facial shrug, and then She turned and ran down the narrow wooden stairs that led to the courtyard below, where Foral Yatt awaited Her.

She joined him there and they exchanged a snatch of dialogue that was too low for Som-Som to hear before making their way toward the pale yellow door. Som-Som craned her neck to watch them go. Just before they passed from her sight, she identified the single glaring quirk that had so transformed the young actor.

Running along his brow in an uneven snow-line, curling around the topmost rim of his ears, Foral Yatt's hair was starting to grow out.

On the fifteenth night after Her arrival at the House Without Clocks, something occurred behind the pale yellow door that gave Rawra Chin Her first glimpse into the darkness that had been waiting for Her for five long years. She went indoors to share Her evening repast with Foral Yatt just as the sun was butchering the western horizon, and before morning She had seen the abyss. She was not to comprehend the immensity of the hungry void beneath Her for some three days further, but that first shattering look was the beginning. It was as if She dropped a pebble into the chasm that awaited Her and listened for the splash. When three days later the splash had still not come, She knew that the blackness was bottomless, and that there was no hope.

On the earlier evening, however, when She walked through the pale yellow door with the sunset at Her back and the rich aroma of the pot-boil hanging before Her, this shadow was yet to fall. It seemed to Her that all her anxieties were containable.

They ate their meal quickly, the two of them facing each other across the blanched wood of the table, and then Rawra Chin cleared away what debris there was while Foral Yatt retired to his bedchamber to prepare for the business of the evening ahead. Rawra Chin, scraping an obstinate scab of dried legume from the lip of his bowl, wondered idly what She would find to amuse Herself tonight during the hours when Her presence behind the pale yellow door was not required. On previous nights She had walked down to the harbor. Watching the moon's reflection in the iron-green water, She had tried to wring some cooling trickle of romance from Her situation.

With an abbreviated cry of pain and surprise She looked down to discover that She had split Her nail upon the nub of dried and hardened food. Her nails were a ruin, She thought, all of them bitten and uneven, many of them split or with raw pink about the quick. She wondered how long it would take for them to regain their former elegance, and as She did so She ran Her other hand back over Her razed scalp without being aware of the gesture.

Foral Yatt called to Her from the bedchamber and She went to see what he wanted, wiping Her hands upon the coarse gray fabric of Her shirt as She trudged across the rush matting.

Stepping through the door of the chamber, She was puzzled to discover that Foral Yatt had retired to bed, rather than preparing for the evening's duties. He lay upon the rough cotton of the sheets with his eyes half-closed and his hands resting limp upon the patches of dyed sackcloth that formed the counterpane.

"I cannot work this evening. I am ill."

Rawra Chin's brow knotted into a frown. He did not look discomforted, nor was his voice unsteady or less masterful, and yet he said that he was sick. It was as if he meant Her to understand that this was a lie but to respond as if it were irrefutable truth.

Searching within Herself She discovered, with only the briefest pang of surprise or disappointment, that She did not mind. She accommodated the fiction, because that was the easiest thing to do.

"But what of Mistress Ouish? There have been other nights lately when you have not worked. A room not in use is a drain on her resources. Others have been dismissed for as much."

Mistress Ouish, though now blind and close to death, was still the dominating presence at the House Without Clocks. Even Rawra Chin, who had not been employed at that establishment for five years, regarded the old woman with alloyed respect and fear. From his blatantly spurious sickbed, Foral Yatt spoke again.

"You are right. If no work is done here tonight, it will be the worse for me."

He raised his lowered lids and stared directly into Rawra Chin's eyes. He smiled, knowing that to smile altered nothing between them. The masquerade was accepted by mutual consent. His voice dry and measured, he continued.

"That is why you must do my work for me."

It was as if there were some sudden dysfunction within Rawra Chin's mind that rendered Her unable to glean any sense from Foral Yatt's words. "That," "must," "do," "work"—all of these sounded alien, so that She was almost convinced that the actor had coined them upon the spot. She ran the sentence through Her head again and again. "That is why you must do my work for me." "That is why you must do my work for me." What did it mean?

And then, recovering from the shock of the utterance, She knew.

She shook Her head and in Her horror still had room to be surprised by the absence of soft hair swinging against Her neck. Barely audibly, She said "No," but it didn't mean "I will not." It meant "Please don't."

But he did.

Donna Blerot took Her hand (His hand?) and pulled it up beneath the fur tent so that it came to rest upon the dampness between the disfigured woman's thick legs. Beneath her single outer garment the dame was naked, flesh damp and solid like dough.

Later, burying Herself in the woman's body as Donna Blerot sprawled back across the table, gasping noiselessly like a fish upon a slab, Rawra Chin looked down at her and saw the abyss. The bell of gray fur had ridden up to reveal the body beneath, so that it now covered Donna Blerot's face, birthmark and all. For a lurching instant the woman looked like a drowned thing washed up on the coastline of the Sea of Luck, a sheet already covering the puffy, fish-eaten face.

Fighting nausea, Rawra Chin shifted Her glance so that it came to rest upon Her own body, luminous with sweat, plunging mechanically forward, jerking back, thrusting and withdrawing like a gauntlet-manikin worked by the hand of another. She regarded the jutting hardness that grew from Her own loins and wondered how it was that She could be doing this thing. She felt no desire, no lust for the deaf woman and her bucking, heaving desperation. She felt nothing but shame and horror. How could Her body sustain such ardor in the face of that abomination?

Later still, Donna Blerot kissed Rawra Chin and left, closing the pale yellow door behind her. The performer sat naked in one of the wooden chairs, elbows resting upon the tabletop before Her, face concealed behind Her hands as if behind the slammed doors of a church. The memory of the matron's kiss was still thick about Her lips. It had seemed as if a fat and bitter mollusk were attempting to crawl into Her mouth, leaving its glistening saliva trail across Her chin. This imagery slithered out of Her mind and down Her throat, from whence it dropped into Her stomach. There was a faint, warning spasm, and Rawra Chin tortured Herself with an image of their hastily devoured meal from earlier that evening. The gelatinous, half-melted skirt of fat trailing from the gray-pink fingers of meat . . .

Struggling silently to keep from vomiting, She did not hear Foral Yatt leave his bedchamber until he was standing just beside Her.

"There. Was that so bad?"

Startled by his voice, Rawra Chin moved one hand so that only half of Her face remained concealed, and opened Her eyes. She was looking down at the floor, and She could see nothing of Foral Yatt above the knee without moving Her head, which seemed an unendurable prospect.

His feet were as white as the flesh of almonds.

Fixed to each of the toenails was a tiny mirror. Suspended beneath the surface of ten miniature, glittering pools, Rawra Chin's reflections stared back at Her, insects drowning in quicksilver.

Rising unsteadily from Her seat and pushing past Foral Yatt, Rawra Chin staggered to that chamber set aside for bathing and the performance of one's toilet. Lava rose in Her throat, flooding Her mouth, and She was sobbing as She emptied Herself noisily into a chipped and yellowed hand-basin. Drained, She gagged upon emptiness until the convulsions in Her gut subsided, and then raised Her head to look at the room about Her through a quivering lens of tears.

Something caught Her eye, a green blur twinkling from atop the chest where Foral Yatt kept his soaps and perfumes and oils. Rawra Chin wiped Her eyes with the blunt edge of one hand and tried to focus upon the distracting blot of emerald. It was a fixed point on which to anchor Her perceptions, still reeling in the wake of Her nausea. Gradually, the object swam into definition against the damp gloom of the washroom.

Tiny glass sockets stared at Her, unblinking. Behind them, within the translucent green brainpan, unguessable dreams marinated within cerebral juices that smelled of licorice.

Rawra Chin stared at the skull full of poison. It stared back at Her, its gaze concealing nothing.

Time passed in the House Without Clocks.

On the eighteenth night following Her arrival, Rawra Chin fell to the darkness. That which had only licked and tasted Her now distended its jaws and took Her at a bite.

She was drunk, although it would have happened had this not been the case. Miserable over the dinner table, She had taken an excess of wine in the hope of numbing the pangs of self-loathing. The alcohol served only to muddy Her anxieties, making them slippery, more difficult to apprehend.

She stood framed in the open doorway with one hand upon the pale yellow wood, looking out at the deserted courtyard, drinking great ragged lungfuls of autumn air. It did nothing to still the buzzing that droned inside Her head, a dismal hive somewhere between Her ears.

Gazing at the indifferent black flagstones, She understood that She must leave. Leave Foral Yatt. Leave at once and return to the soothing babble of Her wardrobe boys, the comforting dreariness of committing endless lines to Her memory. If She did not go immediately, She would be trapped forever, crushed beneath the hulking farm wagon of circumstance, screaming for someone to brush away the flies. If She did not go immediately . . .

From the chambers behind Her, Foral Yatt called Her name.

She looked up from the flagstones and there, on the opposite side of that wide obsidian pond, there reared the archway, with Liavek beyond it.

A note of mounting impatience discernible in his voice, Foral Yatt called again.

She turned and walked back into the house, closing the pale yellow door behind Her.


He was in the bedchamber, as had become customary since the evening when Rawra Chin had been called upon to service Donna Blerot, Her first knowledge of a woman. She supposed that Foral Yatt had summoned Her to order a repetition of that occasion, and for an instant She savored a fantasy of refusal, but for not longer than that.

"My love? Would you light the lantern for me? It is so dark in here."

Foral Yatt's voice, altering since Rawra Chin's arrival in that place, had moved into another stage of its metamorphosis. Softened to a deep velvet, it seduced rather than commanded.

Her fingers struggled with the flint for a second before the tinder caught, and then She lifted the flame to the wick of the lantern. A bubble of sulfurous yellow light expanded and contracted within the chamber, wavering until the flame grew still and its light clear. Rawra Chin turned from the lamp, white-hot maggots engraved upon Her retinas by the brilliance She had brought into being.

Foral Yatt lay upon his side on top of the patchwork counterpane, supporting himself upon one elbow, fingertips lost in the tight blond curls at his temples. A wide band of blue cosmetic color ran in a diagonal line across his face, overlaying the left side of his brow, sweeping down across the left eye, the bridge of the nose, the right cheek. A narrower band of red, little more than a single brushstroke, followed its upper edge over the ridges and hollows of his smooth, sculpted features, terminating beneath the right ear.

He was wearing one of Her costumes.

It was a gown, long and violet, gathered in extravagant ruffs at the shoulders so that the arms were bare. The collar was high, reaching to the point just above the bulge in Foral Yatt's throat, and below that the material was solid and opaque until it reached a demarcation line just beneath the breastbone. From there, the dress seemed to have been slashed into long strips that trailed down to the ankles, every second violet ribbon having been cut away and replaced by a panel of coral pink twine, knotted into snowflake patterns through which the skin beneath was visible. There were mirrors upon his toes and fingers.

Entering through a chink in the wall with a sound like a child blowing across the neck of a narrow jar, a breeze disturbed the perfumed air and caused the lantern flame to stutter. For a moment, armies of light and shadow rushed back and forth in quick-fire border disputes. The shadows gathered within Foral Yatt's eye sockets seemed to flow across his cheek like an overspill of tar before shrinking back to pool beneath the overhang of his brow. He smiled up at Her through lips fastidiously stained a rich indigo.

"I had to come back. I couldn't just leave you here."

The second word in each sentence was stressed in a lush and affected manner, so that even as Rawra Chin struggled to make sense of the actor's words, so too was She striving to identify that quirk of inflection, maddeningly familiar and yet beyond the grasp of her recall.

"But . . . what do you mean? You haven't been anywhere. You . . ."

Rawra Chin could feel something bearing down upon Her, coming toward Her with a hideous speed that froze the will and made evasion unthinkable. It was like stories She had heard concerning eclipses when men would see the giant moonshadow rushing toward them across the land, a vast planet of darkness rolling over the tiny fields and pastures with a speed that was only comparable to itself. Standing there in the scented chamber, She understood their terror. The shadow-world was almost upon Her. Another moment and She would be crushed beneath its endless, inescapable mass. From the bed, Foral Yatt spoke again. The pattern of emphasis within his speech continued to dance just beyond the fringes of recognition, mocking and unattainable.

"I left you. Don't you remember? I left you because it was so important to me that people should know my name. I know it must have seemed unfair to you, but you were only ordinary, and I am a special creature. I have something rare in me, a unique charm that men have not words to describe, and though I loved you deeply, deeply, it was my duty to expose the treasure that I am to the world and all its people. Surely this is not beyond your comprehension?"

Quite suddenly, Rawra Chin knew where She had heard the voice that Foral Yatt was using. The dark planet crashed upon Her, and She was lost.

"But all of that is done with now. Now, people everywhere know my name and are drawn like moths to the fire within me, whose nature only I can put a name to. Now I am complete, and I am free to love you once more. I adore you. I worship you. I love you, love you more than anything in the world save for celebrity. But . . ."

The parody was unspeakably vicious, undeniably accurate. Having identified the voice, Rawra Chin could do nothing more than accept the cruel mirror-image of the face that accompanied it. Nailed by the black weight of a phantom moon, She could only watch as Foral Yatt exposed all the conceits, the inanities, the small evasions that were the components of Her existence. The young man lounged upon the bed, touching a shimmering constellation of fingertips to the blue of his lower lip in a pantomime of anxiety and indecision. Looking up at Rawra Chin, his long lashes flashed an urgent semaphore pleading for sympathy while his jaw trembled beneath the burden of the words unspoken in the mouth above. Finally, when he had drawn out his melodramatic hesitation to the snapping-point of absurdity, the words spilled out in a breathless cascade.

". . . but do you still love me?"

He paused, blinking twice.

"Despite what I did to you?"

In one corner of the room the idiot child began to blow across the slender neck of its jar, and the patterns of light and shade within the chamber convulsed. Rawra Chin, adrift upon a lurching ocean of nightmare, heard a voice speak in the distance.

"Is there a lizard asleep within the ball?"

The voice was so deep and masculine that She assumed it must belong to Foral Yatt, except that Foral Yatt's voice wasn't like that anymore. Whose, then, could it be? When the answer came, Her senses were too brutalized to ring with more than the dullest peal of despair. It was Her voice. Of course it was Her voice.

On the bed, Foral Yatt smiled and flopped languidly onto his back. The smile he wore belonged to Foral Yatt rather than to his grotesque and pointed lampoon of Rawra Chin, but when he spoke it was with Her accents.

"Perhaps I am a ball. Perhaps the unfathomable quality that men perceive in me is a lizard, coiled within me, its material reality questionable, its effects upon the mind undisputed."

Their eyes were locked, their awareness of each other fixed in that moment of mutual understanding that has always existed between snakes and rabbits. Licking his indigo lips, Foral Yatt luxuriated in the taste of the long instant preceding the stroke of grace.

"Shall I tell you the name of my lizard? Shall I tell you the name of that thing that makes me vulnerable, makes me loved, worshipped, celebrated?"

Knowing the answer already, Rawra Chin shook Her head violently from side to side, but was unable to make the slightest sound.

"Guilt."

There. It had been said. He knew. The lantern flame quivered. The shadows charged and then fell back, regrouping for their next assault.

"You see, it is vital to what I am. It is the hurt that drives me, and without it I am nothing. Oh, my love, I feel so ashamed of all the misery that I have brought you."

Standing at the foot of the bed, swaying, the wine of their evening repast now bitter in Her belly, Rawra Chin became confused as the layers of meaning began to fold in upon each other, blossoming into new shapes like a toy of artfully creased paper. Was Foral Yatt describing feelings of his own or mimicking those agonies that he perceived in Her? Did he genuinely feel remorse for the venomous charade that he had perpetrated? At the center of the fear and confusion that tore through Rawra Chin like a hurricane, a nugget of resentment began to form, cold and bright in the still heart of the cyclone.

How dare he apologize? How dare he plead for understanding after this insufferable pageant of debasement? The anger grew within Rawra Chin as She gazed icily down at the figure upon the bed, the yielding and defenceless line of the body beneath the slatted violet gown gradually becoming as infuriating as the wheedling of that unbearable little-girl voice.

"Can you forgive me? Oh, my love, you seem so stern. How thoughtless I was to injure you in such a dreadful, careless fashion."

Foral Yatt sat up and reached toward Rawra Chin with imploring arms, pale as they emerged like swans' necks from the ruffs at the actor's shoulders. His eyes pleaded for release from the apparent agonies of self-flagellation that he was enduring, and his blue lips mouthed inaudible half-words of explanation and apology, puckering as if for a kiss of absolution.

With as much force as She could muster, Rawra Chin struck him across the mouth with the back of Her hand, smearing the blue lip dye over his cheek and Her knuckle.

The dry smack of the blow and the bark of pain from the actor rebounded back at them from the cold stone of the walls. Foral Yatt fell back, covering his face and rolling onto his side so that he lay curled upon the patchwork with his back to Rawra Chin.

Struck suddenly by the sight of his curving spine, visible through the disheveled violet fringes of his gown, Rawra Chin found that the anger in Her heart was matched by a sudden pressure at Her loins as a burgeoning erection reared against the restricting hide of Her ash-gray breeches. On the bed, Foral Yatt nursed his mouth and began to weep. Almost of their own volition, fingers that felt suddenly numb and overlarge moved toward the knot in Her rope belt, where it pressed in a hard fist of hemp against Rawra Chin's stomach.

She raped him twice, brutally, and there was no pleasure in it.

When it was done, She understood the damage that She had done to

Herself and began to sob noiselessly, in the way that men do, sitting there upon the edge of the counterpane with Her shoulders shuddering in silence. Foral Yatt lay on the bed behind her, staring at the far wall. Rawra Chin's seed had dried in a small, irregular oval on the plucked alabaster flesh above his right knee, a tight puckering of the skin beneath the thin, clear varnish. He picked at it absently with mirrored nails and said nothing.

The wick of the lantern grew shorter, until finally it guttered and died. Thus could the passage of hours be measured, there in the House Without Clocks.

"I had no right. No right to treat you like that . . "

"Please. It doesn't matter."

"Will you stay? Will you stay here with me?"

"I can't."

"But . . what am I to do if you go? There is no reason for you to leave."

"There's my work. My work and my career."

"But what about me? You're leaving me trapped here, don't you see? I'll never get away now. Please. I'll do anything you want, but don't leave me here."

"You should have thought of that before you took your revenge."

"Oh, please, I said that I was sorry. Can't you think of what we were to each other and forgive me?"

"It's too late, my love. It's far too late."

"I won't let you go. I won't let us be separated again."

"Please. I don't want a scene. What happened last time was so embarrassing."

"Oh, don't worry. Don't worry. I won't make any fuss at all."

"Good. Now, I must send one of the House-waifs to order my carriage for the morning and arrange to have my wardrobe moved back to the lodging house."

"Won't you leave me anything? Please. Let me keep the violet gown."

"No."

"Don't you see what you're doing to me? You're taking away everything! How has this happened?"

"Don't be naive. We are in the City of Luck."

"Here, you speak to me of luck? I am no longer sure that luck exists. Is there luck, or is there only circumstance without form or pattern, a senseless wave that obliterates all before it?"

"Is there a lizard asleep within the ball?"

Seated upon her balcony, absently chewing the anemic blue flowers she had plucked from her window garden, Som-Som regarded the courtyard of the House Without Clocks.

A carriage had arrived outside the curving walls with the first shafts of dawn, some short while ago. The half-masked woman had realized that Rawra Chin must be leaving the House to return to Her fabulous existence in the world beyond its seven variegated portals.

Since Rawra Chin had originally spoken of Her stay at the House in terms of months rather than weeks, Som-Som supposed that it was the dark undercurrents flowing between Her and Foral Yatt that had prompted this unannounced departure. She wondered if the performer would call upon her to say goodbye before She left, and felt a pang of sadness at the thought of their separation.

Countering this regret, there was a tremendous relief. Som-Som was glad that Rawra Chin had not allowed Herself to become a prisoner of the terrible gravity that the House possessed, and for this reason alone she hoped that luck would take the performer far beyond those walls that curved like gray, embracing arms.

The sound of the pale yellow door opening was jewel-sharp in the silent morning, and Som-Som leaned out from her balcony a little to watch the elegant, crimson-bandaged figure step out onto the cold black flagstones, where the chill of the night had left a faint dusting of frost.

To Som-Som, who had not enjoyed the perception of depth since her ninth year, it seemed that a self-propelling droplet of blood had leaked from a pale yellow gash in the skin of the House to roll across the frost-flecked black disk of the courtyard, trickling slowly toward the arch on the opposite side. Occasionally, a two-dimensional white hand would become visible, depending upon the perspective, a cream petal bobbing briefly to the surface of the red blot before vanishing again.

As the bead of crimson progressed across the yard, it became something that a person without her affliction would recognize as a human being. The figure paused at a point halfway across the courtyard and turned, tilting back its head to gaze directly at Som-Som, as if it had been aware of the half-masked woman's scrutiny since first setting foot outside the pale yellow door. From out of the redness, a face swam into view.

Foral Yatt stared up into Som-Som's eyes, both the one that blinked and the one that could not.

His expression seemed furtive for an instant, tinged with a guilt that Som-Som found disturbingly familiar, and then he smiled. Long seconds passed unrecorded while their eyes remained locked, and then he turned and continued across the wide circle of jet, passing out through the high stone archway.

After a moment there came the sound of reins snapping, followed by a rattle of hoof upon cobblestone as the carriage horses roused themselves and cantered off down the winding thoroughfares of Liavek, where the scent of a hundred simmering breakfasts hung reassuringly between the huddled buildings.

Som-Som sat motionless upon her balcony, her gaze still fixed upon the point where Foral Yatt had stood when he turned and looked at her. His smile remained there, an afterimage in her mind's eye. It was a smile of a type that Som-Som had seen before, and which she recognized instantly.

It was a wizard's smile. It was the expression of a luck-shaper who had finally achieved a satisfaction long postponed. For an unquantifiable time, Som-Som did not move. A blank expression was frozen onto her face so that those divided features regained a semblance of unity, the living half transformed to porcelain by her bewilderment.

Standing suddenly, she upset her chair so that it toppled to the balcony floor behind her. She moved rapidly, with an odd jerkiness. All of the training and discipline that had disguised her difficulties of locomotion were cast aside as she ran down the narrow wooden steps and across the rounded yard.

The pale yellow door was not locked.

Rawra Chin was seated at the table, rigid and upright in one of the straight-backed chairs. She seemed to be staring at two objects that rested on the white wood of the tabletop, barely distinct in the smoky dawn light. Approaching the table, Som-Som peered closer, squinting the eye that still possessed the ability to do so.

One of the objects was a plain copper ball that meant nothing to her. The other item seemed more like an egg with the top cleanly sliced off.

Except that it was green.

Except that it had empty, staring sockets and a lipless smile.

She noticed the odor of licorice at the same moment that she realized Rawra Chin had not breathed since her arrival in the chamber.

It was not a physical horror that propelled Som-Som backward through the pale yellow door, gasping and stumbling, shoved out into the courtyard by the immensity of what lay within. Neither was it an aversion to the presence of the dead. The whore of sorcerers is witness to worse things than simple mortality during the course of her service, and suicides at the House Without Clocks were frequent enough to be unremarkable. Certainly too frequent to engender so violent a reaction in one whose customers had, upon occasion, transformed into beings of a different species or entities of churning white vapor at the moment of their greatest pleasure.

Neither was it entirely a horror that preyed upon the mind, nor wholly a revulsion of the spirit. It had no shape, no dimension at all that she could grasp, and that was the fullest horror of it. A monstrous crime had been committed, an atrocity of appalling magnitude and scale that somehow remained both abstract and intangible. Having no perceivable edges, its monstrosity was thus infinite, and it was this that sent Som-Som reeling out backward into the cold, black courtyard.

She wanted to scream at the indifferent windows of the House Without Clocks, still shuttered against the morning light while those beyond enjoyed whatever sleep they had earned the previous evening. She wanted to cry out and wake the City of Luck itself, alerting it to this abomination, perpetrated while Liavek looked the other way, unsuspecting.

But of course, she could say nothing. The enormity of what had occurred remained locked within her, something scaly and cold and repugnant inside her mind, which could never be seen, never be touched or spoken of to another. Curled in the unreachable dark behind the porcelain mask it basked, beyond proof, beyond refute.

Hardly there at all.

# HONORABLE MENTIONS

# 1987

Joan Aiken, "The Lame King," *A Goose on Your Grave*.
——, "The Old Poet," *A Goose on Your Grave*.
Scott Baker, "Nesting Instinct," *The Architecture of Fear*.
Bob Booth, "The Play's the Thing," *Doom City*.
Jorge Luis Borges, "Paracelus and the Rose," translated by Norman Thomas di Giovanni, *Winter's Tales* (Robin Baird-Smith, ed.).
Poppy Z. Brite, "Angels (Goldengrove Unleaving)," *The Horror Show*, Fall.
——, "The Elder," *The Horror Show*, Jan.
——, "Love (Ash I)," *The Horror Show*, Fall.
R. L. Brockett, "Bristol Down," *Nightmares #1*.
John Brunner, "A Case of Painter's Ear," *Tales from the Forbidden Planet*.
Edward Bryant, "The Baku," *Night Visions IV*.
——, "Buggage," *Night Visions IV*.
——, "Frat Night," *Night Visions IV*.
Lois McMaster Bujold, "Garage Sale," *American Fantasy*, Spring.
Christopher Burns, "Among the Wounded," *Interzone #22*.
Ramsey Campbell, "Another World," *Tales from the Forbidden Planet*.
David Campton, "Repossession," *Whispers VI*.
Orson Scott Card, "Runaway," *IASFM*, June.
Susan Casper, "Covenant with a Dragon," *In the Field of Fire*.
——, "Under Her Skin," *Amazing*, March.
R. Chetwynd-Hayes, "Irma," *Dracula's Children*.
——, "Louis," *The House of Dracula*.
Mona A. Clee, "Just Like Their Masters," *Shadows 10*.
Lawrence C. Connolly, "Moon and the Devil," *The Horror Show*, Spring.
Fred Croft, "Mermaids," (poem) *Eldritch Tales #13*.
Kara Dalkey, "World in a Rock," *Wizards Row*.
Jack Dann, "Visitors," *IASFM*, Dec., *The Architecture of Fear*.
—— and Barry N. Malzberg, "Bringing it Home," *Twilight Zone*, Feb.
Pamela Dean, "Paint the Meadows with Delight," *Wizard's Row*.
Charles de Lint, *The Lark in the Morning*, (chapbook).
Thomas M. Disch, "Palindrome," *OMNI*, Sep.
Barbara W. Durbin, "Irene, Goodnight," *Whispers 23–24*.
*Patricia Eakins, "Forrago," Black Warrior Review 1987.*
George Alec Effinger, "Glimmer, Glimmer," *Playboy*, Nov.
Sam Eisenstein, "Straight Razor," *The Inner Garden*.

Carol Emshwiller, "Vilcabamba," *Twilight Zone*, August.

John M. Ford, "Green is the Color," *Wizard's Row*.

Sam Gafford, "The Horseman," *Eldritch Tales #4*.

Stephen Gallagher, "Like Clockwork," *F & SF*, Mar.

David Garnett, "Christmas Spirit," *Mayfair*, Dec.

Lisa Goldstein, "Cassandra's Photographs," *IASFM*, August.

Charles L. Grant, "Ellen, in Her Time," *The Architecture of Fear*.

———, "Everything to Live for," *Whispers VI*.

———, "Listen to the Music in my Hands," *Twilight Zone*, Feb.

———, "The Sheeted Dead," *In the Field of Fire*.

———, "This Old Man," *Night Cry*, Spring.

Melissa Mia Hall, "Moonflowers," *Shadows 10*.

Nancy Holder, "Shift," *Doom City*.

Robert Holdstock, "Scarrowfell," *Other Edens*.

Rachel Ingalls, "Third Time Lucky," *The Pearlkillers*.

Harvey Jacobs, "Stardust," *OMNI*, August.

Raymond Jean, "Bella B.'s Fantasy," translated by Juliette Dickstein, *Bella B.'s Fantasy & Other Stories*.

Roger Johnson, "The Dreaming City," *Deep Things out of Darkness*.

———, "The Taking," *Deep Things out of Darkness*.

A. J. Kerr, "The Ferryman," *Opus #1*.

John Kessel, "Credibility," *In the Field of Fire*.

Garry Kilworth, "Hogfoot Right and Bird-Hands," *Other Edens*.

Dean R. Koontz, "Miss Attila the Hun," *Night Visions IV*.

Ann K. Kotowicz, "Winter Gathering," *Twilight Zone*, April.

Rudy Kremberg, "Twenty-One Minutes," *Haunts*.

Nancy Kress, "Glass," *IASFM*, Sept.

Chris Lacher, "The Technique," *Eldritch Tales #14*.

Marc Laidlaw, "Snowblind," *Twilight Zone*, Feb.

Paul Lake, "Rat Boy," *F & SF*, May.

Joe R. Lansdale, "The Fat Man," *The Horror Show*, Jan.

———, "The God of the Razor," *Grue #5*.

———, "The Pit," *Black Lizard Anthology of Crime*.

Richard Lawson, "The Silver Leopards," *Spaceships & Spells*.

Alan W. Lear, "Call to Me, Call to Me," *Winter Chills 2*.

Thomas Ligotti, "Dr. Lacrian's Asylum," *Grue #5*.

———, "The Music of the Moon," *Fantasy Macabre #9*.

———, "Vastarien," *Crypt of Cthulhu #48*.

Bentley Little, "Projections," *The Horror Show*, Jan.

Brian Lumley, "The Thin People," *Whispers #23–24*.

Joseph Lyons, "Trust Me," *The Architecture of Fear*.

John Maclay, "New York Night," *Other Engagements*.

Sue Marra, "It Should Promise Something," *Ouroboros #7*.

Richard Christian Matheson, "Break-up," *Scars*.

———, "Hell," *Scars*.

———, "Timed Exposure," *Scars*.

Richard Matheson, "Buried Talents," *Masques II*.

Bruce McAllister, "Dream Baby," *In the Field of Fire*.

Robert McCammon, "Best Friends," *Night Visions IV*.
——, "The Deep End," *Night Visions IV*.
Mary Catherine McDaniel, "A Little of What You Fancy," *Writers of the Future Vol. 3*.
G. Wayne Miller, "Wiping the Slate Clean," *Masques II*.
A. R. Morlan, "What the Janitor Saw," (poem) *Night Cry*, Spring.
Andre Norton, "Moon Mirror," *13th World Fantasy Convention Program Book*.
Joyce Carol Oates, "The White Cat," *A Matter of Crime, Vol. 2*.
Paul Olson, "Homecoming," *The Horror Show*, Jan.
Barbara Owens, "The Greenhill Gang," *F & SF*, Feb.
Alexandros Papadiamantis, "The Haunted Bridge," translated by Elizabeth Constantinides, *Tales from a Greek Island*.
Claudia Peck, "The Gentle Art of Making Enemies," *Magic in Ithkar, Vol. 4*.
Richard Peck, "Shadows," *Visions*.
Janina Porazinska, "The Enchanted Book: A Tale of Krakow," picture book story, translated by Bozena Smith
Mark Rainey, "Threnody," *Deathrealm #3*.
Satyajit Ray, "Corvus," *The Unicorn Expedition & Other Fantastic Tales of India*.
Satyajit Ray, "Khagum," *The Unicorn Expedition & Other Fantastic Tales of India*.
Carol Reid, "A Feast of Ashes," *Fantasy Macabre 9*.
——, "Wondergirls," *The Horror Show*, Spring.
William Relling, Jr., "The Infinite Man," *New Blood*.
——, "Where Does Watson Road Go?" *Eldritch Tales #14*.
*Archie N. Roy, "Azrael's Atonement," Fantasy Macabre 9*.
Richard Paul Russo, "Dead Man on the Beach," *Twilight Zone*, June.
Jessica Amanda Salmonson, "The Bear and St. Peter," *Spaceships and Spells*.
——, "The Trilling Princess," *Devils and Demons*.
Elizabeth Scarborough, "Milk from a Maiden's Breast," *Tales from the Witch World, Vol. 1*.
Carol Severance, "Day of Strange Fortune," *Magic in Ithkar, Vol.4*.
——, "Isle of Illusion," *Tales from the Witch World, Volume 1*.
Lucius Shepard, "The Exercise of Faith," *Twilight Zone*, June.
——, "The Glassblower's Dragon," *F & SF*, Oct.
——, "Shades," *In the Field of Fire*.
Lewis Shiner, "Dancers," *Night Cry*, Summer.
David Smeds, "Goats," *In the Field of Fire*.
Melinda Snodgrass, "Requiem," *A Very Large Array*.
John Steptoe, "Mufaro's Beautiful Daughters: An African Tale," Illustrated Picture Book.
Bruce Sterling, "The Little Magic Shop," *IASFM*, Oct.
Julie Stevens, "Century Farm," *Whispers #23–24*.
Thomas Sullivan, "The Fence," *Shadows 10*.
Steve Rasnic Tem, "Dinosaur," *IASFM*, May.
——, "Ghost Signs," (poem) *Eldritch Tales #14*.
——, "Hidey Hole," *Masques II*.
——, "Leaks," *Whispers VI*.
Lisa Tuttle, "The Wound," *Other Edens*.
Robert E. Vardeman, "The Road of Dreams an Mirrors," *Tales from the Witch World, Volume 1*.
Karl Edward Wagner, "Endless Night," *The Architecture of Fear*.
——, "Lost Exits," *Why Not You and I?*
Paul Walter, "Grass Shark," *Twilight Zone*, June.
Ian Watson, "Salvage Rights," *F & SF*, Jan.
Connie Willis, "Winter's Tale," *IASFM*, Dec.

Douglas E. Winter, "Office Hours," *Shadows 10*.

Ken Wisman, "The Finder Keeper," *Shadows 10*.

Jane Yolen, "The Frog Prince," (poem) *F & SF*, Oct.

——, "The White Babe," *IASFM*, June.

——, "Wolf/Child," *Twilight Zone*, June.

George Zebrowski, "General Jaruzelski at the Zoo," *Twilight Zone*, April.

Roger Zelazny, "Quest's End," *OMNI*, June.

# ABOUT THE EDITORS

*Ellen Datlow* is the fiction editor of *OMNI* magazine, and has edited several anthologies, including *The Books of OMNI Science Fiction* and the forthcoming *Blood Is Not Enough*. She has published a number of award-winning stories by outstanding authors during her tenure at *OMNI*. She lives in Manhattan.

*Terri Windling* was for many years the fantasy editor at Ace Books. She was responsible for launching the careers of a number of the finest young fantasy writers, including Steven Brust, Charles de Lint, Patricia Wrede, and many others. She has also edited a number of anthologies, including *Elsewhere* (with Mark Arnold), and is responsible for packaging the *Borderland* series and (with Thomas Canty) the *Fairy Tales* series. She is currently an editor at Tor Books and a writer/visual artist at the Endicott Studio. She lives in Boston, Massachusetts.

# ABOUT THE ARTIST

*Thomas Canty* is one of the most distinguished young fantasy artists on the scene today. Winner of the World Fantasy Award for Best Artist, he has painted many jackets and covers for books, and is also a designer. He is also the packager of the *Night Lights* series of illustrated stories that glow in the dark. He lives in Braintree, Massachusetts.

# ABOUT THE PACKAGER

*James Frenkel* is the publisher of Bluejay Books, which was a major publisher of science fiction and fantasy from 1983 to 1986. Since then he has been a consulting editor for Tor Books and a packager. The editor of Dell's science fiction in the late 1970s, he has published some of the best new science fiction and fantasy writers, including Greg Bear, Orson Scott Card, Judith Tarr, John Varley, and Joan D. Vinge. He lives in Chappaqua, New York.